Praise for the novels

Looking for the Mahdi

"An impressive first novel."
—*New York Times Book Review*

"Fast-paced adventure." —*Publishers Weekly*

"A highly encouraging science fiction/thriller debut."
—*Kirkus Reviews*

"It's a great spy adventure with a serious point, and an extraordinary first novel." —*Locus*

"[T]hrilled me in a way I haven't been thrilled since I read William Gibson's *Sprawl* trilogy. It shares the near future setting, the compellingly believable political and technological extrapolation, and the murderously fast pace of Gibson's work." —*New York Review of Science Fiction*

Faraday's Orphans

"Wood's second novel examines the illusion of freedom in a controlling society." —*Library Journal*

"[An] endlessly imaginative look at the future, not least because of the simple, brutal, yet poetic language Wood has invented for her future Philadelphians." —*Booklist*

"For a truly dark worldview, nobody . . . holds a candle to N. Lee Wood's *Faraday's Orphans*." —*Locus*

Ace Books by N. Lee Wood

BLOODRIGHTS

N. Lee Wood

ACE BOOKS, NEW YORK

BLOODRIGHTS

An Ace Book / published by arrangement with
the author

PRINTING HISTORY
Ace hardcover edition / September 1999
Ace mass-market edition / September 2000

The Penguin Putnam Inc. World Wide Web site address is
http://www.penguinputnam.com

Check out the Ace Science Fiction & Fantasy newsletter
and much more on the Internet at Club PPI!

ISBN: 0-441-00763-5

ACE®
Ace Books are published
by The Berkley Publishing Group,
a division of Penguin Putnam Inc.,
375 Hudson Street, New York, New York 10014.
ACE and the "A" design are trademarks
belonging to Penguin Putnam Inc.

PRINTED IN THE UNITED STATES OF AMERICA

10 9 8 7 6 5 4 3 2 1

Blood is not thicker than love.
For the children of my heart:

Brent Alan Mahoney
Lynsey and Caroline Spruce

Book 1
Antonya

1

The lizard was restive, tiny nails prickling as it nestled in her shirt for warmth. She grimaced, her hand pressing its bony shape into the hollow between her breasts. "Settle down," she murmured. It protested, but stopped struggling. Its sticky tongue licked at the salt on her skin in forlorn hunger.

She perched in the snow-dusted branches of a puzzlebark tree, wood under her haunches creaking. Shivering with the cold, she pulled the hood of her heavy wool cloak around numbed cheeks. The sharp evergreen needles did little to shield her from the wind at her back. Her nose watered, even tucked into the scarf wrapped around her face, her breath warm and damp. Her jaws clenched to keep her teeth from chattering, but her eyes never left the small stone house in the shelter of the white hills.

The windows glowed in the twilight, wavering firelight punctuated by a passing shadow as the man walked around inside the warm building. His horse snorted, the haze of its breath giving away its position in the lean-to by the house. There was only one, she decided, and he was not waiting for company. She kept watch well into the night, until the buttery warmth of the window died away.

Luna Major had set, stars scattershot in stark relief against the black sky. She passed the time picking out constellations, recalling the names of stars. Counting the seconds between falling meteorites, she tried to estimate where the Belt would be in the heavens this time of year. She had no idea if the Belt was waning or waxing, but in the current scheme of things it didn't matter. Nor did she very much care, she realized. *Would you be disappointed in me, Father Andrae?* How far away was the comfort of his study now.

A little past midnight the temperature rose slightly as clouds blurred the night sky, and the icy glitter of stars was replaced by velvet snowflakes spiraling down in the stillness.

She slept, as she had learned from wolves, minutes snatched here and there and waking instantly alert. She woke as the sky turned pearl-gray, hesitant birdsong piping in the forest behind her. From her vantage in the tree, she spotted a white snow fox, only the tip of its tail rust-red, stalking its breakfast in the virgin snowbound fields. She watched its stealthy progress, paws held delicately out of the snow. It froze and pounced; then, as if it realized it had an audience, made a great show out of not caring that it had clearly missed its prey. She smiled ruefully, knowing exactly how it felt.

The lizard had eluded the lacings of her shirt to nestle at her shoulder, fast asleep with its snout burrowed into the warmth of her armpit. With gentle fingers she extricated the long tail anchored in a loop around her neck and nudged the animal back to its usual spot between her breasts, where it curled into an inert ball.

The man pounded the door open against the snowbank which had drifted up against the house during the night, the sound reaching her moments later. He was the biggest man she had ever seen, nearly twice as tall as she, and she had never been considered small. He wore a simple mantelet short enough not to interfere with the plain scabbarded sword at his side. The hilt, however, glittered with gold and jewels. Padded and laced breeches tucked into his boots were well made but without a nobleman's usual opulence. He had thrown back his furred hood, his curly black hair thick enough to serve as a cap. She noted the flash of gold in one ear, perhaps his only indulgence in personal adornment.

He led his horse out of the lean-to, a huge bay lowland Shire with a dirty white streak on its face matching the woolly fetlocks covering its hooves. Her own head wouldn't even come to its heavily muscled shoulder. He murmured to it, one arm draped over the horse's withers as he rubbed its muzzle affectionately.

It shook its head in irritation at the cold, shaggy mane whipping over its thick neck as the man lifted an immense saddle outweighing herself and tossed it over the beast's back with ease. His mount was better made for dragging a farmer's plow than for speed, but a normal palfrey would have found its back broken under the man's weight. The saddle he cinched onto the beast had obviously been custom-made, crafted from well-oiled leather. The saddle blanket underneath was simple but of good quality.

He buckled the straps around the animal's solid shoulders before throwing his rolled pack onto its rump, lashing it down securely. An unadorned riflebow was hung at the ready from the casing fastened to the saddle's pommel. The draught horse made only a token resistance to the bridle, placidly mouthing the bit.

He was a religious man, she was amused to see, but not overly zealous as he perfunctorily made his four bows to the wind and rain, fire and ice, then turned in the general direction of the Oracular City for a quick prayer. It was too chilly to stand around saying much more than the most abridged version of an Our Mother.

Her feet shifted, toes curled in her white furred boots as she balanced in the notch of the tree's branches. She drew the white woolskin hood over her face, knowing she would be hard to spot, a blob of snow in an evergreen tree not an unusual sight. He didn't discover her, but then he had no reason to be looking for her, either.

Heaving his bulk onto the animal's back, he settled himself into the saddle as the great beast grunted, its heavy legs braced to absorb his weight. Even on a horse that size, he reminded her of one of the Sisters on her small donkey. His stirrups hung to the beast's knees. He let the horse reconcile itself before he gently nudged it forward. It plodded ponderously through the snow, following the valley trail toward the distant seacoast mountains.

She waited for the jangle of the horse's harness to fade before she climbed down, dropping the last few feet to the ground on all fours like a cat. Retrieving her snow skis from where they had been buried during the night's snowfall, she laced them quickly to her boots. She shuffled up the rise of the hill before gliding down the gentle slope toward the stone house. The lizard tensed against her skin, holding fast with its tiny serrated claws. She ignored it.

The house, her home for most of the winter, held no surprises. Remnants of logs smoldered in the gray ash of the fireplace. He had left his Guild sign in charcoal in a bold angry scrawl on the thick plastered walls. Not legible graffiti, since most common Landsmen were illiterate; he had wanted to be sure his message was understood by any who saw it. This was a Guildhouse, he was warning the miserable thief and trespasser. Intruders had no business here, get out. She puzzled over the sign, his message clear enough, but she couldn't place the Guild. By his sheer size, plain dress and the crude design of a sword in the symbol, she guessed he might be an itinerant smith, traveling from city to city in search of work.

All else was gone. He had taken everything, her meager pack of extra provisions, the sheepskin bedding she'd kept by the fireplace, even the wineskin she'd hung on a peg hammered into a beam supporting the roof. She *tsk*ed to herself ruefully, wondering if she should try to steal it back from him.

Probably not, she decided. It was, after all, his right. And anything she left behind, even when hunting, deserved to be taken. What was vital she kept with her. All that had been lost were bulky luxuries which could be replaced later. The winter was nearly over anyway, she could resume her journey north into the Highlands, heading toward the only home she'd ever known.

She did regret the loss of the wineskin, then grinned fleetingly as she wondered what he'd make of it the first time he raised the skin to his mouth, expecting, oh, say, a sip of decent St. Nazaire? He'd most likely worry he'd been poisoned, and toss the wineskin away. Perhaps she had a chance to get it back after all.

A man on horseback was slower through snow than an agile woman on snow skis. Unaware she pursued him, he made no attempt to hide his tracks. It took little effort to keep up behind him without once catching sight. The snow began to fall again, but she didn't quicken her pace, judging the flurry was not yet severe enough to obscure the horse's hoofprints before he stopped to rest.

She paused once at a small mound, brushing the powdery snow away from the rounded horse droppings. Breaking one open, she held it in one bared hand, judging from its residual heat that she was coming up behind him too quickly. She brushed the dung off against her breeches before sheltering against a boulder. After a quick fifteen minute nap, she woke and set off again after her quarry.

She laughed silently when she spotted the flash of red in the snow off the trail. Tiny craters of frozen ice splattered around the hoofprints trampling out a circle, evidence of his frantic spitting. *Didn't care for the taste, good sir?* She retrieved the wineskin and found he had thrown it away still open. Most of the liquid had leaked away, only a cupful was left. She frowned, then took a judicious sip of the cold liquid. A shudder racked through her before she allowed herself a contented sigh, warmth splintering through her aching bones. In a few minutes she would feel enough energy pouring into her blood to last for hours. She endured another swallow, relishing the burst of heat following on its nauseating heels. Even the lizard woke, lapping at the sudden rash of sweat on her skin.

He was slowing by late afternoon, searching for shelter against the wind to spend the night. She heard him before she caught sight of him, less than a hundred meters in front of her, and glanced around for concealment. The forest had thinned out, the sturdy puzzlebark trees giving way to emaciated pines offering little cover. They would have to do, she decided, and crouched behind a trio of spindlepines leaning tiredly against each other for support. Her back to him, she pulled the white wool around herself and lay down on her side. With luck, his eyes were not as sharp as hers, and all he would see was just another lump of snow.

As it was, he didn't turn back on the trail to see her as he made considerable noise in setting up his camp for the night. Not more than necessary, she realized. He simply believed himself alone and in little danger, with no need to be discreet. She shrugged inside her cloak, and took advantage of the wait. Propping her skis against the spindlepines to use as a backrest, she dozed in the snow.

He had a nice fire going when she awoke, the smell of cooked meat making her mouth water. Peeking cautiously around her hood, she saw the smoke rising from a patch of tree and shrubs more hospitable than her own, the fire hidden by a swell in the road. A shift in the breeze, bad luck, and the big horse whickered as it caught her scent. All she could see was its swiveling ears as it tossed its head.

She smiled grimly, knowing she didn't smell quite like any humans the draft animal would be used to, but horses weren't terribly adept at describing to their owners exactly what it was they scented. Fear most often meant wolves, and interest meant human. Confusion generally erred on the side of fear. The horse whinnied nervously, stamping at the snow, and she heard the man mutter consolingly.

Of course, there was the other possibility, depending on how superstitious he might be. She considered a variety of eerie sounds, calls he might attribute to some malevolent spirit, a *loup-garou*, perhaps, or daemon cluricaune.

Not a good idea, she decided as she heard the rasp of steel pulled out of a scabbard. This close and he couldn't fail but to discover her.

She rolled onto her feet, hastily pushing the snow skis under the snow to hide them. She crouched in the snow as he tramped to the top of the rise, longdagger ready in his hand. Shaking her hood back just far enough to reveal her face, she grinned foolishly and spread empty hands. He stopped as he caught sight of her, eyes narrowed. In the shadow of her cloak and from a distance, she knew he would see a boy, not expecting a woman alone in the wilderness. As long as she kept her mouth shut and her body covered.

After a long moment, he rammed the dagger back into its sheath contemptuously. "Begone, little thief," he rasped out. "You'll have nothing here."

Chuckling to herself, she twisted her face into a mask of disappointment and alarm. *Who's calling who a thief, big man?* She pulled the cloak up around her shoulders, keeping hunched over to disguise her form as she bolted away, flailing in the snow like a witless forest brat. Her luck held, as he didn't uncover the skis. She retrieved them shortly before dawn, this time undetected.

He was more cautious as he traveled the next few days, and she was less circumspect at dogging him, letting him glimpse her once in a while through the trees. On the second day, the sharp crack of a riflebow and a squeal startled her. He had shot a snow hare. She watched impassively from the cover of the forest as he skinned and gutted it before spitting it to roast. He threw the head and entrails into the fire. While she understood his fastidiousness, the waste made her wince. Her fingers stroked the gaunt lizard underneath her cloak, sorry she couldn't offer it just a small piece of raw liver. The lizard didn't know, of course, and rumbled contentedly.

The next morning, he broke camp and set off, leaving behind half the roasted hare on a spit thrust into the ground. An offering left to appease her, in case she was a spirit after all. She still had half a loaf of coarse bread left, too hard and stale to turn moldy, but she had been eating from it sparingly to make it last in the meager winter.

Her stomach growled with hunger, but she took the time to lick the carcass carefully. On the other hand, perhaps he found her a nuisance and had left behind poisoned bait. But there was no smell, and no tingle on her tongue. That didn't necessarily mean it was safe.

The lizard stirred, smelling the meat, and poked its flat head out of the collar of her shirt. She fed it strips of flesh closest to the bone, knowing the lizard preferred it raw. Were it poisoned, the lizard would be the first as well as the last to know. She watched it closely as it held the meat in its claws, nibbling delicately with sharp little teeth. After half an hour, its belly had swollen enough to show the blue skin underneath the scales. It yawned contentedly, no effects of any poison. She laughed as it crawled into the hollow of her neck and began to clean the grease from its snout, long orange tongue sliding over its scales. Untangling it, she tucked it back into her shirt and ate the cold meat hurriedly, licking her fingers. The lizard washed, twisting around and bumping its small head against her rhythmically.

Like her, it could go days without food, and, like her, it was not overly fussy, making do with whatever became available. The winter hare was tough and stringy, the little fat it had dried out from being too long over the dying fire. Ripping the carcass apart, she shoved the remains into the pockets of her cloak, to chew on throughout the day as she tracked the big man already half a league in front of her.

Now he tried to conceal his tracks, hard for an armed man on a heavy horse to do in snow, but he was good. The constant snowfall drifting through the trees helped obscure the traces. He apparently knew this forest well enough to stray from the main road, brushing away hoofprints while dodging tree limbs to avoid knocking the snow from them. She nearly lost him once. By the time she had backtracked and picked up his faint trail again, it was already nightfall.

He had sheltered in the crook of tumbled boulders, building a small fire. He might want to avoid her, but he didn't fear her. This time she made no attempt to hide. His tethered horse nuzzled the little foliage sticking out of the snow. He lounged against the saddle and its packs, his arm resting on one raised knee and his other leg stretched out on her erstwhile sheepskin spread underneath him as he gazed absentmindedly into the fire. His sword lay sheathed and unbuckled, propped against the rock, but his riflebow lay beside him, a short bolt in the stock ready to fire, and his mantelet open far enough for her to spot the longdagger in his belt.

Careful to stay downwind of the horse, she crept toward the flames, until he started at the reflected gleam in her eyes just outside the firelight. He grunted in surprise, hand leaping to his dagger, then watched her.

He was older than she had first thought, late thirties, perhaps. His skin was far darker than a Northlander's, and his nose narrow and hooked. His ancestors were desert people, she decided, and wondered how he could tolerate the cold lands so well. Although not handsome, his face was even-featured, pleasant enough despite several days' growth of black beard that lent him a rough look. His mouth was thin, but distinctly shaped with the corners quirked up in the threat of a perpetual boyish smile.

"There can't be much heat at that distance, lad," he said finally, reluctant. He had a faint accent, the predominant Bashan vernacular no more his mother tongue than it was hers. "There's fire enough for two. Come warm yourself, as you like."

She grinned at him across the fire, keeping well out of arm's reach. The horse raised its head to stare at her, flicking its tail idly. She let the hood fall from her head as she shook back the cloak from her shoulders, then crouched with her hands held out toward the heat. Her hair glinted red-gold fire as it curled around her face.

He had his second shock of the night. "You're a woman!" he blurted.

She made her mouth an O of mock suprise, eyes widened with exaggerated wonder. "Am I?" she said, glancing down in feigned shock at the swelling in her blouse. "Yes, I see you're right, good sir, and thank you most sincerely for that astonishing information." Although as educated in Bashan as he was, she could hear the soft syllables of her own accent as she spoke.

He frowned, and leaned back disgustedly. "And a damned smart-mouthed outlander at that. What the hell is a foreign woman doing traveling alone in weather like this?"

"For the most part," she said serenely, "freezing my nipples off." She thought quickly as he appraised her, then added, "I'm neither thief nor whore, sir. I'm on a pilgrimage to the Oracular City." Why not? It was as good a destination as any.

His eyebrows rose, and in the light, she saw his eyes were not brown, but green. "On pilgrimage?" he asked doubtfully. "Are you then a cleric of the Faith?"

She laughed. "Do I appear to you a Priest?"

"Who looks at Priests?" he said, his tone flat.

He'd had an unpleasant history with the Faith, and didn't care who knew it, she realized. She cocked her head to study him, amused. "Then perhaps all Priests look as I do."

It took a moment, but he finally smiled. "Nay," he said, the humor coming back into his voice. "Were all Priests as pretty as you, surely I would have noticed before."

"You flatter me, sir, which is not only unnecessary but avails you naught."

"Naught was ventured, madam, merely an observation made."

She smiled, and nodded to acknowledge him, knowing exactly how to dimple her cheeks attractively, having practiced it in the mirror so often. Just enough to seem friendly without encouraging a sexual advance. Of course, there were men who would have considered her mere presence an invitation to rape. She kept her feet balanced under her, ready to leap away into the safety of the dark forest should he prove to be one of them. "And what is a man like you doing traveling the forest alone in the dead of winter?"

"I'm an armsman of the Guild of Defenders." Ah, that's right, she realized belatedly, remembering the Guild sign scrawled on the wall. *Sorry, Father Andrae. I know I should have paid better attention to my lessons.*

With the benefit of the obvious, she could see what she'd previously missed. The gold filigree and small gemstones in the hilt of his sword, the expensive if plain tack on his warhorse, the aristocratic education behind his foreign accent. Only the children of nobility were accepted into the Guild of Defenders, though a younger, indigent son of a minor baron, he might be. But what he was doing alone and so far from his own people, intrigued her.

"Of Myro, in the southern lands of Water Cross."

He blinked, surprised. "Yes."

"Your accent," she lied. She could have spoken Myronian, but that might be too much for him all at once. "You are far from Water Cross, and heading west. Are you likewise on pilgrimage?"

He snorted his derision. "In a sense." His face grew wary. "I'm on my way to Abadayho to offer my service to Lord Creskar. I have been without service for two years, my previous lord having died of the Fever."

"I see."

She did, too. He would have had a long time to learn to travel alone in a self-imposed quarantine, ruthlessly shunned by society. Now, proving himself free of the disease, he could return to his homelands. Which was more than she could do. He was watching her for any sign of revulsion or fright, and seemed relieved to find neither.

"I am Kerrick of Myro, the son of Kartic who was the son of Dormon," he said formally and paused. When she didn't respond, he added, "And you are, madam?"

"My name is Antonya."

There was an expectant silence. "Just . . . Antonya? No family, no Guild?"

She smiled but didn't answer.

He eyed her with no little skepticism. "Are there no Guilds in your Lands, madam?"

"But of course," she said cheerfully.

"Ah," he said finally. "I fear it would be rude to press you further, madam."

"Entirely," she agreed dryly. She winced as the lizard's claws hooked their way toward the top of her blouse. The fire had overheated it, and she knew it wanted a breath of fresh air. She stood quickly. "I am quite warmed now, Kerrick of Myro, and thank you for your hospitality."

"You leave?" Kerrick asked, startled. "It is pitch-black; these woods are full of wolves and other more dangerous creatures. It is not safe for a woman . . ."

"My sight has adjusted to the dark, and I have no fear of wolves. I have traveled the forest for some time, sir, as have you yourself, and found the forest beasts no more harmful for a woman alone than for a man alone."

At that moment, the wriggling lizard poked its snout up before its front paws to peer at Kerrick. Its eyes glowed iridescent green, night-vision retinas reflecting the gleam of the firelight. Kerrick's eyes widened, his breath hissed in, and he brought his hand up in a warding sign, a pagan gesture she knew predated the Faith by at least two thousand years. The lizard sniffed the air, disliking the smoke, and slithered backwards out of sight.

"I see now why you have no fear of the Weird, madam," he said, scowling at her suspiciously.

She laughed and drew the hood of her cloak up around her head. "Indeed, I have my fearsome fire-breathing dragon to protect me," she teased, watching Kerrick blush with embarrassment. "You also have a fine beast." Carefully, she walked to his tethered horse, and gently stroked its muzzle, making sure the animal got a full dose of her scent. If it caught wind of her again, it would be less likely to fear her. "Good night, sir. Perhaps we shall meet again."

"In the full light of day, I might hope," he added.

He still wasn't quite sure if she was human. Or actually alive. "In the full light of day," she agreed.

She didn't much care for the large northern cities, particularly those in the far High Plains. Northern cities tended to be dirty and polluted, crowded with far too many loutish men preoccupied with whoring and fighting and plotting new ways to wreak havoc against their neighbors. In the six years she'd spent traveling the Lands, she had learned the hard way to respect the cities and treat the inhabitants with the same cautious regard she showed the wolves of the forest, while trusting them far less.

Abadayho was a full week's walk, more in the snowbound mountain trails, but she knew she could travel it faster and leave less of a trace than Kerrick could on his plodding warhorse. The stars were out, the barest of light to see by as she kicked her snow skis quickly, gliding along the tree line.

Just before daybreak, she halted as the path through the forest split. The snow covered the forked road with a soft blanket, untrampled by man or beast. She rummaged for one of the gnawed legs of the hare, cracking the bone between her teeth to suck at the fat-rich marrow. The sky paled to rose, throwing blue shadows through the snow. Birds sang in the trees. She thought about the Oracular City, thought about Abadayho and Kerrick of Myro, weighing him carefully before she angled west and down from the northern mountains.

2

The village in the cleft of the mountain valley had once been prosperous, the substantial houses of quarried stone built for merchants and artisans, rather than crude peasant huts of wattle and daub, attesting to its former affluence. But the town had burned at least a decade before, the shells of tumbledown stone walls standing bleak in the snow. Those few houses not razed to the ground stood in skeletal silence with blank windows. Charred beams of roofs held up only sky now, not a single building left intact.

But it had yet to be abandoned; smoke rising thinly from a few rebuilt chimneys and bony sheep nibbling halfheartedly around the crude fences confirmed that human life still clung here, however tenuously.

The utter destruction had been systematic and impersonal. The village's tiny sajada had been the hardest hit, even the temple's outline obliterated to a pile of shattered stones in the village center. This had been more than a simple casualty of war between Lands. It had been a Purge, she decided, just as she spotted the woman and child threading their way through the ruins, heads down. The boy saw her first, his abrupt halt alerting his mother. They stood stock-still; not even the multiple layers of patched clothing were able to hide their emaciated bodies. Their eyes as wide as trapped deer, the two stared at her dumbly.

She shook her head to loosen the scarf from around her mouth, then smiled as she held up her hand, first two fingers together and raised in the sign of the Sisters of Beneficence. The woman didn't react for a long moment. Then she snatched the child and ran, the boy's legs beating a disjointed tempo against her hip as they vanished into the maze of rubble.

Well, hell, that wasn't the most promising of welcomes, she thought ruefully. She sucked cold air between her front teeth distractedly, the tiny sound disturbing the lizard curled against her chest. This Purge had been thorough, one of the worst she had ever seen, the remaining inhabitants still terrified years after. She wondered what heresy the town could possibly have committed to warrant this level of destruction and fear.

The last of her money had run out months ago. No stranger to this predicament, she knew well how to survive by scrounging, trapping, stealing and, when necessary, begging for charity. Ordinarily, her practice would have been to stay the evening, first sheltering by the sajada to do a few conjuring tricks, the sort of harmless sleight-of-hand that first drew out curious children, then their parents. Entertainment in these small villages was scarce, any diversion in their harsh, tedious life always a welcome relief. Then, while she went through the empty routine of devotions inside the sajada, the villagers would leave a few offerings of food on the stone porch for her dinner, and wine, if they had any. It was never much more than rough boiled grain porridge occasionally peppered with salt pork and wintered vegetables, but it kept her alive when hunting failed.

In the morning, she'd leave a small jumble of carved twigs and scavenged owl's feathers, artfully tied together with bright thread and a few glass beads, on the sajada's altar, the gift of a fake amulet in return for their hospitality. It never failed to amaze her how much stronger desperate faith was than common sense. The first time some woodcutter's ailing baby "miraculously" recovered from croup after its throat had been vigorously rubbed with the talisman, no one would remember all the times it had failed, and word of a mysterious white beguine would spread as her reputation grew.

But this village would be in no mood for a show of fool's magic, and she doubted they could spare the food. She had nothing of any real value for them. Regretfully, she turned away, leaving the devastated village behind.

Both trees and snow diminished as she came down from the mountain's flanks. Patches of forests still stood around areas logged clear for farmland and grazing. She passed a few more villages well inside the borders of Lord Creskar's Lands. While none had been as hard hit as the first, they all showed distinct signs of poverty. The fields seemed fertile enough, but the towns were shabby and unkempt, livestock and people thin. By the time she had studied the third village, she discerned the similarities: she saw few children, which she well knew meant one of two possibilities—either they were hidden or they were gone, neither of which spoke well for Lord Creskar.

When she reached the outskirts of Abadayho, she was surprised to find the outlands quite prosperous in contrast to the more remote parts of the Lord's holdings, to judge from the number of crofters' flats clustered in the fields radiating from the city walls. Cattle rambled through snow-dusted pastures, their hides well-fleshed, lowing contentedly as they filed home for the evening's milking.

The city itself had been built on the crest of a wide hill, surrounded by recently built defense walls, the stones still clean, fresh-cut from the quarry. The elegant masonry was mere icing over the real fortification, thick earthwork able to withstand the pounding of heavy artillery. Lord Creskar favored a profusion of bastions, and stocked them well, judging by the excess of cannon snouts bristling from the bastion faces. Between the high artillery wall and the second, classical curtain wall, a deep moat had been dug, and she chuckled, wondering if Lord Creskar had gone so far as to have it furnished with imported crocodiles as well.

In the distance, where the city walls curved around the hillside, a steady legion of troops marched while cavalry rode three abreast on the leeward road, bright colored pennants fluttering, the clash of horse harness faint in the wind. Arms and equipment glittered in the cold sunlight as soldiers streamed across a narrow bridge through the far barbican gate like a silver worm burrowing into its lair for the evening. His city well-stocked with soldiers, it did not appear Lord Creskar had much problem with idle men.

The walls were high, but not high enough to conceal the domes and spires of the city within. Towering over the slate-tiled rooftops of the tall houses favored by rich merchants, the superb gold dome and elegant bellspires of a great sajada gleamed.

The central gates of the city were open, and she spotted a small troop of falconers along the gentle slope of the glacis, heading home after a lazy day's hunt. The women's riding skirts fanned over the rumps of their horses, the cloth shining in the waning sunlight like jewels, ruby crimson, emerald green, lapis lazuli. Their gallants favored gold thread, and weaved their own way around the ladies like filigree in a brooch. Laughter drifted, the easy sound of well-fed people expecting little danger from the outside world.

The gates would close at sunset, but she had no intention of attempting to enter before morning. In the evening, the wealthy rode in on their fine horses while the few straggling crofters returning from late market drove their rough wagons out. She would shelter in a haybarn for the night and in the morning walk in with the honest merchants and fishmongers, harried couriers, the usual rabble of mendicants and mercenaries and moneychangers, the wide spectrum of wandering prostitutes, pickpockets and peddlers, the common rabble admitted daily when the gates opened for commerce. One more painted harlot would certainly be ignored as unimportant, or at worst waylaid with proffered business.

She disliked giving up her snow skis, and hated the long skirt even more, but she held no illusions that she could simply tuck her hair under a hat and pass herself off as a boy in leather breeches. She was no beauty, but still quite identifiably female. In the warmth of the haybarn, she unpacked the pockets of her cloak and turned it inside out, the white shorn wool making way for a patched and dirty burgundy velvet. By the little moonlight available, she applied the harlot's paint to her face, studying the effect critically in her tiny bronze mirror and smearing the paint to make herself as little attractive as possible. For good measure, she helped herself to a bit of the abundance of rank cow manure and rubbed it over her body thoroughly, being sure to apply it generously to her hair. The lizard liked the stink not at all, and protested by burrowing in her blouse and rubbing its rough snout resentfully against her skin.

While frequent bathing was not necessarily commonplace in the northern Lands, a man would have to be either dead drunk or desperate indeed to want to pay for her favors.

Before either the crofter or the sun rose, she left the barn, joining the few early travelers eager to get a jump on their neighbor's business. While attracting a few stares and wrinkled noses, she was left to herself as she plodded along the road toward the city.

A young courier cantered up beside her, pulling in his mount to look her over curiously. She glanced up, attempting a dispirited leer at him with charcoal-blackened teeth and gums. She lifted her breasts under her blouse with dirty hands and jiggled them suggestively.

"Itch for me, do ye, sir?" she said, attempting the broad accent of a lowland Monsants woman. Inwardly, she winced at the bad parody.

The boy sniffed, repelled by her strong smell. "Hardly." He was no more than fifteen, the best age for couriers competing with one another for speed and endurance, and he carried himself with the innocent arrogance of youth. "You should go home, girl," he said, not unkindly. *Girl?* she thought. He was younger than she by several years. "You'd be wasting your time in Abadayho. You'll find your competition is a bit more . . . ah . . . refined."

"Aye," she agreed cheerfully, "but I'm young and I'm cheap!"

He laughed, his horse dancing excitably under him. A fine beast, she saw, young and lean like the boy, bred to love running long distances without tiring.

"And I have big tits!" She laughed with him. "I'll show 'em to ye for a penny!" *Two to see my lizard.*

He touched his finger to his forehead in a mock salute. "Another time, perhaps, and best of luck to you, girl." He kicked the colt into a gallop, leaving her behind in a clatter of pebbles.

And that was as close as she got to having to practice her assumed trade. The watch at the gate looked her over with distaste, then admitted her without demanding either money or favors. Other merchants had to pay their tax to the city before they brought in their goods to sell, but it wouldn't be worth harassing her for a payment until she tried to leave. On leaving the city, all the harlots had to settle accounts with the watch on the money they'd earned while inside the walls. And mercy on those who hoped to evade the guards' fee then!

Once inside, she took to the back streets and within half an hour located the service door at the rear of a merchant's stables. The lock proved no problem, more ornamentation than security, the rust giving her slender pick more of a fight than the mechanism.

The merchant and his horses were not at home, the house above her silent. She stripped and washed herself in the trough, scrubbing the dung from her hair, scoured the charcoal from her mouth with a handful of straw, then re-dressed and was gone within minutes, careful to relock the port. When he finally returned, the merchant would never know his stables had served as her bath.

She bound her head with a scarf, both to protect her wet hair from the chill and to hide its color. Her face cleaned of whore's paint, she strolled to the city center and wandered the market. Someone had discarded an old basket with a broken handle behind one of the wagons, and she glanced around before casually picking it up. The bottom had rotted nearly through, but she worked the broken end back down into the cheap weavework and slung it over her arm. As long as she didn't put anything into it, it looked fine. Now she resembled any number of sleepy-eyed maids doing their early morning shopping. Except of course, she had not a single coin to her name.

Although she could manage a few tricks enough to amuse country villagers, she lacked a pickpocket's dexterity and daring. Nor did she have the street-performer skills to match those she would find in a city the size of Abadayho. Already, plenty had started up their acts; a fire-eater stripped to his barrel chest, a trio of scrawny adolescent jugglers, a singing dwarf in a fool's cap with his trained dog. There was always a hope that they could catch the interest of a company scout, join a regular Guild troupe that supplied a regular Guild wage. The rest of the unguilded musicians and mummers and marionette theaters worked hard for the tossed coins that provided little more than a roof and hot meal for the evening.

Her only other marketable skill was not one she cared to advertise. Public scribes were generally old men scribbling away in cramped stalls, their shops sometimes no more than a jealously guarded doorway next to a bakery. Between composing sickly love poems and legal notices dunning overdue debtors, the scribe could warm his arthritic hands on the wall behind the baking ovens. A young woman, and an outlander at that, fluent and literate in several Landstongues would certainly attract unwanted attention.

So, for the moment she was stone-cold broke. That didn't worry her. She still had a slice of old bread and the few scraps left of the hare. If worst came to worst, there was always rubbish left at the end of the market day, were she not too proud to jostle elbows with the beggars in search of edibles. And she wasn't.

She estimated Kerrick was a day behind her, and she would spend it exploring the city, memorizing the streets and alleys, learning what she could about Abadayho and its puissant Lord by listening to passing conversations. Gossip was always rife in inns and taverns where tongues were often loosened by too much drink, but that required money. For a woman without an escort, it was usually far more trouble for the small return. Her best chance was at the public wells, where useful information mixed with the women's vicious gossip of illicit romances all too often resulting in awkward pregnancies.

By the late afternoon's exodus, she had prowled the streets until her feet ached, learning little more than what she had already expected of Lord Creskar. It was time to find a mark.

The likeliest spot was wherever young bachelor Guildsmen from the middle trades gathered, not the soldiers who were generally too boisterous and aggressive, nor the lower workmen who knew their place too well to indulge in illusory courtesies. By Seventh Bell, she had targeted her quarry, a tall man near her own age wearing a quilted green jerkin with gold piping that matched his peaked hat. The iridescent plume of a pheasant's feather had been tucked into the cap at a jaunty angle, winking as he headed for the tavern at the end of the street.

Her hair had dried, and she pulled the loose curls roughly from under the scarf into disheveled tangles. She punched out what was left of the basket's rotted bottom before tugging the broken handle loose, letting it hang bent. With her clothes already unkempt, it didn't take much more to transform herself into the image of the victim of a hasty theft. She stood in the shadow of a doorway, tears already running down her cheeks and sniffed just loud enough for the rakish passerby to hear.

He turned, startled, one hand leaping to the hilt of his dagger. The blade was out of the sheath before he spotted her. Caution was a good survival trait for those living in large cities, but his instant alarm, eyes scanning suspiciously for her hidden accomplices, spoke ill for Lord Creskar's justice. It took no pretense at all for her to pull away in fright, her dark eyes wide. When no confederate jumped from the shadows onto him, he relaxed slightly and sheathed his dagger. Then he smiled at what he assumed to be a helpless young maid, but kept his hand on the hilt all the same.

"I won't hurt you," he said encouragingly and held out his hand. She shrank back, just enough for him to step forward. "What has happened to you?"

"I've been robbed," she said timidly, and held up the broken basket for him to see. "They took everything, and now I've no more money." She turned on the tears again, more forcefully, and wobbled her chin. "I can't go home with nothing, I don't know what I'll do . . ." Her voice went up a note, brushing hysteria.

The young man's wary eyes still darted left and right, and he made no suggestion that he might chase down the brigands. But by now he'd snaked one arm over her shoulder, prying her out of the doorway and holding her protectively while patting her shoulder. "Don't be afraid," he was saying in his most valiant manner. "I'll walk you home . . ."

"Oh, no!" She pulled away, but allowed him to keep hold

of her. "How can I face my good patroness like this when I've stupidly lost our meal and all our money? She'll turn me out, I know she will . . ." She choked back a wet snivel.

He hesitated; then the last of his mistrust vanished, and he steered her toward the tavern just as she expected he would. *You'd hate this, Father Andrae*, she thought, *a great deal*.

"You can't blame yourself," he was saying. "Calm yourself, my dear. You'll have a hot drink with me to recover your spirits, then we'll see if my mates and I can't help . . ."

He led her into the seedy tavern where he and his friends were busy proving to each other they were indubitably gentlemen of refined manners rather than merely the sons of humble tanners and tailors. They bought her a stiff drink of spiced hot wine while she spun out her tearful tale of being an orphan (common enough with the wars that periodically scorched the Lands) newly taken in by a distant cousin. Charmed by her foreign accent, which she thickened for their benefit, within the hour they had pooled their limited funds to purchase bread, meat and cheese from the unamused barkeep, enough for a comely maid and her ailing patroness.

At first she adamantly refused to take money from the boys, but finally allowed them to press a few small coins into her reluctant palm. Then her newfound protector insisted on walking her "home" in the growing dark. She led him toward the silkspinners' quarter, since she had claimed that Guild, and chose a suitably darkened house at random.

"My patroness is surely asleep," she whispered sotto voce, "I'll go round back. It's too dark for you but I know the way."

After a moment's protest, enough to prove his chivalry, he acquiesced, then seized her waist and kissed her, his mouth wet and clumsy. Apparently gallantry only went so far. As his hand fumbled with the fabric of her blouse, she hastily clutched his wrist with the semblance of feminine resistance while guiding his searching fingers to her breast to permit him a quick grope. God only knew how he would react to a handful of bony reptile.

Her hand pressed against his chest, his heartbeat rapid under her palm. She had no desire to be the object of the young man's passionate embrace; while merely inconvenient for her, it could be crushing for the lizard nestled in her blouse. Before he realized how, she had extracted herself from his grasp. "Good night," she said, smiled sweetly and vanished in the shadows behind the house before he could blurt out what she knew would come next: *Could I see you again?*

Maybe he would come looking for her, but probably not. With the toxins contained in her saliva from the lizard's constant presence, her young suitor would find himself feeling rather ill shortly, her kiss poisonous but not deadly. No doubt he would blame the quality of the innkeeper's wine, but vomiting would keep him too busy for the next day or so to search for her.

She hiked her skirt up, tucking the back hem between her thighs and into her belt. Clamping her arms and knees around an arcade pillar, she inched up to the second floor to scale the narrow roof ledge, running soundlessly along the shelf to reach the trellis of vines growing up along the crack between two windows. A quick rustle, a silent curse as her cloak snagged, a tug, and she was on the roof overlooking the small private plaza of a wealthy merchant.

The night was clear, a half-full Luna Major casting wan light over the snowcapped roofs. She smelled no change in the weather, and settled for the night against the rounded shaft of a series of chimney vents. The brickwork supporting the narrow pipes was warm, clear of snow, and the rain cap, if a bit smoky, provided her with shelter. The cheese was moldy, the meat overcooked but still hot and the bread good fresh maslin sweetened with honey. The lizard took its share of the meat, although clearly unhappy with the fare.

"We'll do better tomorrow, little one," she whispered to it, and smiled as she finished off the meal, gulping down both portions. City life didn't much agree with her, she decided, hooking a leg firmly around the chimney stack and drawing her cloak around her and over her head snugly.

Her stomach full, she slept soundly.

3

"Father Andrae, what makes it snow?"

Minutes before, she had lobbed a fat snowball at Brother Reule from behind her hiding place, a miniature fortress of stacked firewood. As the wet packed snow splattered across the apothecary's broad back, he had stopped dead in his tracks. Hands clawed, his shoulders hunched, he turned theatrically toward the girl, his eyes rolling in pretended fury under their bushy eyebrows.

"You . . . little . . ." he had growled at her, then dipped both hands down into the snow that came up halfway to his knees, flinging a flurry of snow in her direction. She squealed in delight and mock terror as he lumbered after her like an ox chasing a rabbit. As she rounded the apse of the dorter, Brother Reule huffing in pursuit, she had run straight into Father Andrae.

The abbot was still quick, despite his age. He caught her by the arms, lifting her up with her own momentum as he turned and set her solidly on her feet beside him. Brother Reule floundered around the corner and blindly pitched a huge handful of snow before he realized it was Father Andrae. Too late, the white blob spattered the front of the abbot's brown robe. Father Andrae gasped in surprise.

Brother Reule's hands covered his open mouth in dismay, his broad face nearly as white as the snow. Antonya laughed, falling backward into the soft snow, and flailed her small legs with glee. Brother Reule stared with a rictus grin of horrified embarrassment, his head bobbing in silent apology as Father Andrae recovered his poise and indignantly brushed the dripping mass of snow from his chest.

"Aren't you a bit old, Brother Apothecary, to be indulging in childish snowball fights? Surely you have more serious concerns needing your attention . . ." Father Andrae said dryly.

"Indeed, Father," Brother Reule agreed quickly, still murmuring apologies as he fled from the scene of the crime. Father Andrae rounded on Antonya, unable to keep the amused gleam out of his eye. She lay on her back in the snow, staring up at his stern face.

"And you, young lass, have better things to do than lead my weak-willed flock into temptation. Shame on you!"

Antonya quickly waved her arms and legs in the snow before she clambered to her feet. "Look, Father Andrae, I made an angel!" She didn't try to escape his grasp as he reached down and took her by the hand, but pointed emphatically to the blurry form in the snow.

"And you *are a little devil,*" he retorted, unimpressed. "*A negative and a positive cancel each other out, as you would know if you weren't sneaking off trying to avoid your mathematics lessons. To the study with you.*" His huge hand clamped securely around her tiny one, she had been dragged off toward the detested quills and ink and endless fragments of secondhand parchment to do her sums.

So she had asked the question about snow in a desperate attempt to distract him from the impending mathematics drills.

"*When the weather gets very cold, water freezes and becomes too heavy to be held up in the clouds. It becomes snowflakes and falls to the ground.*" He didn't even slow down as he explained.

"*Brother Alban says that snow is really dandruff from Luna Minor, and it falls to earth whenever she flies too close.*" Antonya was being dragged so fast, her words came breathlessly.

"*Brother Alban has a corrupt sense of humor that Brother Alban is going to wish he'd kept to himself,*" Father Andrae said darkly, still tramping through the snow.

"*What makes the weather so cold?*"

Father Andrae sighed, but didn't slow his pace. "It takes the sun an entire year to go around the earth, and sometimes it's closer to the earth than at others. When it's close, it's summer; when it's farther away, it's winter. When the sun is far enough away, it gets cold, like being too far from the hearth. Then the water that the sun has boiled away from the ocean into clouds during the summer freezes and falls back to the earth." The Abbot's breath made puffs of white steam, as if his words were attempting to take on tangible form.

"But if frozen water is too heavy for clouds to keep up, why does ice float?" Antonya demanded desperately, the study door in sight. Now she balked physically as well, wanting to stay out and play in the cold and the bright, sparkling snow. Father Andrae simply picked her up and carried her bodily into his study.

He set her down on the edge of his great desk, still holding her by the arms to prevent further escape, his amused eyes level with her own, hers glaring. "If you study your mathematics, perhaps one day you will grow up to be a famous scholar and God will reward you by yielding another of His mysteries to the force of human reason."

"But I don't want to be a famous scholar," she said hotly. "When I grow up, I'm going to be a famous warrior." She felt a small thrill of guilty pleasure as he winced, and pressed her advantage. "Then I won't have to study anymore. I'll leave then, and I'll do whatever I like, and nobody can make me do anything I don't want to. You won't make me do stupid mathematics ever again!"

He stood very still, his hands like iron bands fastened around her arms. "When you grow up," he said finally, his voice so quiet and level it frightened her, "then perhaps you will be a famous warrior. But you'll have to work very hard, and I think you'll find learning everything you can will make you a better warrior as much as it would a better scholar. There are very few warriors who ever lived to become famous by being stupid and ignorant. God does not smile upon fools."

"I'm not a fool," she said, calm now.

"Prove it, then," he demanded firmly, and plunked her down in the small chair in front of the table spread with scraps of parchment salvaged from the scriptorium. Faint blotches of ink still stained the scraped hides where the pigment had been etched in permanently. "If the Lord of the White Lands has four thousand soldiers and three hundred horses, and the Lord of the Black Lands has a thousand horses but only seven hundred soldiers, how many horses will Lord Black have to trade

*for how many soldiers of Lord White's so that each soldier
has a horse to ride as many days as every other soldier?"*

As Antonya struggled to even out horses to soldiers marching across the vellum page, the snow outside began to melt.

4

Water droplets splattered on the rooftop beside her head, the
minute spray icy against her face. She woke to bright sunshine
glistening off tiny melting icicles around the now-cold edge
of the chimney vent. Clear, measured drops spiraled down silently into the cacophony of peacocks strutting through the
atrium below. A fat, gray-haired maid spread seed for them
but didn't look up as Antonya stretched out her muscles, aching from the cold and awkward position. When the maid plodded back into the house, Antonya quickly scrambled down to
the street, searching for a deserted alley that would afford her
a few moments of privacy.

As a child, she had entertained herself with her body's
growing abilities. She'd delighted in the discovery that the
fingers of her left hand were double-jointed (oh, the time
wasted trying to make her right hand its equal!), and she had
spent hours in front of Father Andrae's bronze mirror sticking
her rolled tongue out at herself. Father Andrae had been
amused at her display of ear-wriggling, but far less so when
she demonstrated how she could make her eyes change from
deep brown to a pale yellow-white. The color of wolves' eyes.

But it certainly came in much handier than ear-wriggling,
she decided as she drained the pigment out of her irises.

She plaited her hair in a tight row against her scalp, dividing
what was left at the nape into two separate braids to clip the
ends into loops with massive gold pins above her ears. Three
strands of gold chain connected to the pins hung under her
chin.

Slipping the skirt from her narrow hips, she shook it out
and reversed it to its more elegant side, decorated with thick
tribal embroidery. Tied lengthwise around her waist, it now

reached only calf-high. She twisted her scarf into a belt to complete her outfit.

When she stepped out of the alley her cloak was again white and thrown back with careful boldness from her shoulders. Her boots had been brushed clean and relaced intricately. She wore the striking blue tattoos of a married woman from the Dark Plains on her cheeks and the space between her eyebrows. A heavy gold bracelet matching the hairpins weighted her left arm with her fictitious mate's rank.

That the "gold" was painted base metal she wasn't about to allow a goldsmith close enough to discover, and the first chance at a real bath would soon enough remove the marriage tattoos. While she was now more conspicuous, she had more freedom; Dark Plains women were the bankers and merchants of their tribes, often traveling independently of their quarrelsome warrior husbands, and were treated with cautious respect. By the time curiosity about her developed into an inconvenience, she would be gone.

Despite the sharp air, the sun was radiant, the late winter snow in the streets already thawing into slush. The lizard perched on her shoulder, half out of her blouse. Its black eyes glittered in the flat head, the serrated claws of its hind legs were hooked into her back, and its tail was anchored around her arm under her sleeve.

But it was more her arrogance and strange predatory eyes that maintained the pocket of deference around her. As she moved along with a haughtiness she didn't feel, neither the watchman who had allowed her to enter Abadayho nor the young gallant of the night before would have recognized her.

Expecting Kerrick to ride into the city in the morning, she had been mildly disappointed when the morning's rush did not include the big man. Shrugging, she headed toward the city's market square and was startled when his huge Shire was walked past her, led by a boy who smelled not much different than she had in her harlot's disguise, a clear indication of his level of apprenticeship. Its heavy hooves clopped against the rough pavement, the massive bay without Kerrick.

"Boy," she called out, pushing past the curious to reach him. He looked up with hostility, but didn't stop as she strode alongside him. "Where is this animal's rider?"

He sneered at her foreign accent. "How should I know?"

Holding up one of her precious coins, she asked, "Does this help your memory?"

The boy laughed. "You'll have to do better than that," he said, eying the gold in her plaited hair.

She pulled back her lips menacingly baring her teeth in a wide, wolfish smile. "It's this, greedy child, or I'll ask you again when I return with my husband. He's very adept at pulling the intestines of people who annoy him out through their asshole."

The boy squinted at her, not sure if the threat were genuine but deciding not to risk it anyway. He snatched the coin from her fingers and snapped, "Try Malselli's." At her narrow look of incomprehension, he added irritably, "Three streets west of the sajada. On the corner, you can't miss it." The boy had nerve, at least.

Malselli's was not much more than a literal hole in the wall, very easy to miss and she nearly did. But inside, it was larger than the unprepossessing exterior hinted at. The big man was indeed at the tavern, seated in a far corner with a half-empty tankard of beer. His head turned toward her as she opened the door. She knew the sunlight at her back made her a blank silhouette as she stepped into the tavern's dark interior. A few necks swiveled in interest. The big man watched her, his brow creased, puzzled as she approached.

She stood for a moment. "It's the full light of day, Kerrick of Myro," she said, this time in Myronian, and smiled as the shock of recognition spread across his face. He rose slightly, then fell back, staring open-mouthed at her.

"Madam," he finally managed to say.

"I've been waiting for you," she added.

By now, he had his amazement under control and only raised an eyebrow speculatively. "Indeed?" he said, and drained the last of his beer. She signaled the barkeep as she sat across from him.

"I should like to return your hospitality. May I buy you another?" Even seated, he towered over her.

He inspected her tattoos. "If your husband doesn't mind?" he asked ironically.

"He has no objection, nor any other, since he doesn't exist."

The barkeep set another tankard before Kerrick as well as a smaller cup for her, leery of the lizard as she paid. He didn't dare test the coins of a Dark Plains woman between his teeth before he turned away to leave the pair in relative privacy. Speaking Myronian would discourage most of those curious patrons trying to listen to their conversation.

"I see you've brought your familiar," he said wryly.

She scratched the small reptile under the chin with one finger, rewarded by its satisfied rumble. "It's called a lizard," she said reproachfully. "You find them under rocks and bushes. They're fairly common, even in Myro. I'm amazed you find it so mysterious."

He studied her for a moment. "Who are you, Antonya?" he demanded softly without touching the tankard. His hand rested on the table, but she saw his fingers twitch, the hilt of his longdagger visible at his waist. "What do you want with me?"

"You have no cause to fear me," she said seriously. "I'm no adept, if that's what you are thinking, nor sorceress nor woodfée. I am what I seem, a woman alone and in far more peril here in a city than you are in the forest." She glanced meaningfully at the biceps bigger around than her waist. "I mean you no harm, and could certainly do you none even if I did."

After a moment's consideration, he visibly relaxed, and sipped at his beer. "I have my doubts as to that."

"You flatter me again, sir."

"Not at all. So, Antonya of no place and no one, but of many surprises, you've sought me out. What is it I may do for you?"

"Tell me about Lord Creskar," she said promptly.

He chuckled. "Are you a spy, then?"

"Would you believe me if I said no?"

He scanned her disguise, studying the cheap jewelry and the counterfeit tattoos. "Would you believe *me* if I said yes?"

"No."

He smiled broadly. "Then first tell me who you spy for."

"Myself," she said casually. "I'm a very expensive spy, you see, my price so dear that I'm the only one who can afford me."

"That is the kind of humor that can get you tortured here

before you're drawn and quartered alive in the city square, madam," he chided her, glancing around the room. "Why Lord Creskar?"

"Because you plan to offer him your service." Kerrick said nothing. "I'm curious. Why him and not another?" she pressed. "You seem not to be enamored of Priests, and yet you must be aware that this Lord Creskar deals quite heavily with the Faith. You've eyes and you've seen the same villages as I." She let her eyes gesture for her, glancing toward the door. "And his city. So why Lord Creskar? Is he a good man despite appearances? Or is it only because he's rich?"

His eyes flashed in warning, and she heard him expel a long, low breath, an almost inaudible growl. "Both. And neither, nosy child. I would not offer my service to one I felt unworthy, but there haven't exactly been countless offers from eager lords all beating down my door contending for my right arm."

"You've a fine right arm," she pointed out. "And two years should be long enough. If you were going to get the Fever, you'd have had it by now." She kept her voice down, just in case there were any patrons who understood Myronian.

He snorted contemptuously, taking a deep drink of his beer and wiping the foam from his lip delicately with a fingertip like a gentleman rather than smearing it away with the back of his hand. "For many," he said, "two centuries would not be enough." He looked into the tankard grimly, speaking reluctantly to its contents, keeping his own voice low. "I wasn't just another armsman of my previous Lord, I was his First Chosen, closer to him than his own wife. We grew up as boys together; he was as dear to me as a brother. When the Fever took him, his friends and council abandoned him like so many rats from a sinking garbage scow. Were it not for me, he would have died alone, and he was a man who deserved better."

He glared up at her as he recounted the memory, daring her to show the slightest sign of repugnance. "His flesh melted away from his bones like butter in a fire, stinking pustules erupted on his skin. He shivered constantly and complained of cold although he sweated and burned. I bathed him, fed him, cleaned him when he vomited. I bandaged his sores and changed his soiled sheets. When he died in my arms, he was no more than a demented, pathetic skeleton. He didn't even know me." Kerrick stared at his hand on the table, as if surprised to find it had curled into a white-knuckled fist of its own accord. "After he died, I was rewarded for my loyalty by being banished. No one wanted to be too close to even the faintest breath of contamination. I fully expected the Fever to destroy me as well, how could it not when I breathed its stench, bathed in its corrupt humors, lived with it more closely than had I been its lover."

She kept her eyes steady, dispassionate. "But it didn't," she said casually when he stopped speaking.

For a long moment she thought he might not answer. Then he inhaled deeply, and looked at her, green eyes calm. "No," he agreed. "It didn't."

"Well," she said lightly, "that certainly must have put a crimp in your plans to ride valiantly off into the mountains and die a lonely hero's death, now didn't it?"

When he glowered at her she deliberately placed her hand on his huge forearm. Against the corded muscles under his dark skin, her fingers looked as delicate as porcelain. He glanced down at her hand in surprise, then looked questioningly at her. "This Lord Creskar is far luckier to have you than you are to have him," she said firmly.

He chuckled cynically. "If our good landlord there knew what you know, he would demand I leave immediately, then throw away the cup I drank from." Kerrick spoke softly, nearly whispering.

She grinned, feeling delightfully malicious. "Then let's tell him," she suggested brightly, "and I'll be happy to help you tear the place apart."

He studied her uneasily before deciding she joked. "Let's not," he said quietly. But he was smiling as he slipped his arm from under her touch.

She *tsk*ed as if disappointed to be thwarted from her fun.

"You've profited well for the price of a beer," he said, holding up the near empty tankard. "Anything else you'd like to know before I've finished it? No?" He drained the tankard and set it down on the table. "Care to buy me another, seeing as you're such a rich spy? Or are you a wealthy chieftain's woman now?"

"Ah." She raised her eyebrows apologetically. "That might present a small problem."

"You've no money," he guessed promptly, amused.

She pressed her hand to her throat with an expression of deep hurt. "No money?" she protested. "Of course I have money. Money is dirt, it's piss, I can get money from anywhere, even the air." She reached toward his head, pulling her only remaining coin from his ear.

"You'd best practice," he said, unimpressed. "I saw it behind your knuckles."

She shrugged and set the coin on the table before him. "Well, at least it's money, but I'm afraid it'll buy you only a very small beer."

He signaled the barkeep. "Then I'll buy this round while you entertain me with a story or two."

"Certainly," she agreed cheerfully.

She took a long, grateful drink from the large beer the proprietor brought her and when she set the tankard on the table, Kerrick held it there with one large finger pressed against the rim.

"Your turn," he said. "You're not a Priest, nor a spy, nor a Dark Plains woman, nor a *loup-garou*, no matter how much your yellow eyes say you are. Who are you, Antonya?"

She pursed her lips thoughtfully. "Well, would you believe I was born to poor but honest cheesemakers? Their only child, they affianced me at an early age to a vile and loutish man my senior by at least three decades, a high official of the Cheesemakers Guild. I couldn't stand the thought of his malodorous hands on my body, so rather than marry him I ran away to seek my fortune elsewhere."

He looked at her for a very long moment. "No," he said simply.

"Oh, dear," she said, undaunted. "Then how about the story where I was orphaned and sent away to live with two elderly sisters to learn laceweaving. The sisters were very attached to each other, and when one died the other collapsed from grief and followed her to the grave inside a week. Their niece, a greedy and most despicable woman, was afraid I would lay claim to the old ladies' inheritance, so she turned me out penniless, and here I've wandered to this very day."

Kerrick sat back, and crossed his arms over his massive chest, exhaling in one long, exasperated sigh, one eyebrow raised.

"No?"

"No."

"Well, perhaps you prefer—"

He cut her off sharply. "I *prefer* the truth."

"You wouldn't believe me," she said firmly, all pretense at humor gone.

"I'm capable of making my own decisions," he said, impassive. "I have been honest with you—surely I deserve the same courtesy."

"All right. I was born in the island countries far to the north. My mother was a lady of the noblest blood, and sole heir to her father's Lands." she said slowly, and stopped, waiting. When he didn't react, she added, "My father was a gallant warrior, driven from his own Lands by his usurping half brother. He sought refuge in my mother's domains, they fell in love. It was said their love was so powerful, it was as if they shared but one heart.

"My father left when I was a year old to try and reclaim his bloodrights. My mother sat day after day by a window in our palace, speaking to no one. One night, a bright star blazed across the sky. My mother cried out his name and fell down dead. The surgeons said her heart had literally cracked in two. Later, we were told that at the exact moment the star fell, my father had been murdered by an Assassin hired by his half brother. The knife had plunged straight into his chest, cutting his heart in half."

Not a muscle of Kerrick's face had moved. He picked up his beer and sipped thoughtfully, listening.

"A week later, his half brother landed his warships on our beaches and rode at the head of his troops, burning everything in his path. My mother's Lands and city were laid waste, our peoples enslaved, our palace razed to the ground. Once he had conquered our Lands, he began butchering every remaining child under the age of five, determined to ensure that his claim to my parents' Lands would go forever unchallenged. My nurse had me smuggled out, although it cost her her life. I was secretly carried by a fisherman's boat to the remote Isle of

Tembris where I was raised in a monastery by the Brothers of Blessed Reason. The abbot was my mother's distant cousin. Now I'm of age, I've come to reclaim my rightful Lands and place, both those of my mother and my father, to take back what belongs to me from my father's half brother."

"This half brother—" Kerrick said, his voice neutral, "has he a name?"

She rested her elbows on the table with her arms crossed. Finally, her voice colorless, she said, "His name is P'tre Terhune, Warrior-Priest and High Commander of the Oracular City's army. I am Antonya, daughter of R'bert Terhune of Laird's Ketch in Adalon, by the lady Latticea of Ashmael in the White Sea Islands."

He said nothing for a very long moment, expressionless. "That's quite a romantic tale," he said evenly.

"Yes," she agreed, without rancor, "isn't it?"

"You don't happen to have some proof of it, do you? Your father's signet ring, for example, or a birthmark over your heart shaped like a falling star?"

" 'Fraid not."

He smiled. "If you did, I'd be sure you were a liar. As it is, I almost believe you."

She laughed quietly. "But not quite. See? I knew we should have stayed with the cheesemaker story," she said ruefully.

The sajada's bells began to ring out the midday summons to the Faithful, and as if it were a signal, Kerrick threw back his head to finish his beer.

"At the very least," he said, "it was a story worth the price of a beer, madam, whether it be true or false." He set the empty tankard on the table and rose. "But I have business to attend to, so if you'll pardon me, I shall leave you now."

She looked up at the huge man towering above her. "Take me with you," she said. "I want to meet this Lord Creskar."

He looked surprised, then laughed. "Nay, madam, that I shall not. My business is my own, I have no need to complicate it further."

She smiled, nodding amiably, and sipped the last of her own beer. "Perhaps we'll meet again, Kerrick of Myro."

He touched his finger to his ear in a polite farewell. "Perhaps," he said. "Then again, perhaps not."

She watched him as he walked away, forced to stoop under the lintel of the tavern door with the graceful movement of a big man used to a world too small for him. The lizard by her ear yawned, jaws opening wide to expose its ridged blue orifice before its mouth snapped shut, sharp teeth clicking. She idly rubbed the scaly skin under its chin with one knuckle, pensive. The lizard grumbled contentedly. Smiling, she nodded to herself.

5

From the little she'd gleaned in passing conversations and the women's gossip around the fountains, Creskar was by all accounts a true and loyal disciple of the Faith. He had liberally furnished the sajada of Abadayho as well as its rambling priory with donations of gold plating for the dome and huge bronze bells for the four towers. Skilled workmen and artists decorated the elaborate interior, and plenty of laborers and menials were kept busy maintaining it. Judging from the condition of his outlying villages, they were an abundant source for the Citadel's Purges while ensuring that the population was kept submissive to both Lord Creskar's iron rule and the Word of the Faith.

In return, the Oracular City had given him license to fortify his city against his neighbors and retain a formidable army, which he used with more or less seasonal frequency to increase his power or expand the borders of his Land. He had been Lord of Abadayho for less than a decade, having inherited his estate from his less energetic father. His mother, much to Lord Creskar's shame, had been not only a commoner but an actress, finding her way into the late lord's affection through the glamour of the stage. When she died, the old man married a noblewoman younger than his own son to warm his declining years.

Popular rumor held that Creskar had persuaded his lovely young stepmother (and some said "lover") to poison the ailing old man, then rewarded her by tossing her out a window of the palace tower. Popular rumor was also discussed in very discreet voices.

Creskar's enthusiasm for battle often bordered on reckless, gaining him notoriety as a brave fighter. He also had a well-known dread of Assassins and spies sent by his disgruntled neighbors, and feared treason within his own ranks, as well, natural anxieties for a Lord who himself was not loath to use treason and spies for his own aspirations. The fact that three attempts had been made on his life in as many years did prove his fears to have some basis in fact.

Antonya didn't doubt that Creskar had ambitions to eventually take part in the Oracular City's affairs, but was equally sure his religious faith was genuine rather than a contrived bid for power. He spent every afternoon in the sajada, praying on his well-armored knees for the blessings of Priests he kept fat with the blood of his people.

Wanting to witness the ceremony when Kerrick swore service to Creskar, she likewise could be found each day among the crowds within the great dome. But nothing more exciting ever happened other than the pious chanting and interminable prayers Lord Creskar seemed to relish with as much enthusiasm as he did hawking, hunting and warfare.

Kerrick inevitably attended each of these observances, but obviously without the same fervor as his prospective Lord. Once he caught sight of Antonya in the crowd. She smiled brightly as he passed, he frowning irritably at her. By the fourth day, her interest in Creskar, and even in the big Defender, was waning. The longer she stayed, the more likely it was that people would notice the strange woman and begin asking questions. It was far too early for her own reputation as the White Beguine to have progressed to the point where she might hope to lead a popular uprising against the powerful High Commander for the Faith's military, nor would it ever if she were careless enough to be taken now as a heretic. Her plans, vague as they were, were to continue her circular route toward the Oracular City and investigate P'tre Terhune in his lair.

But every time she thought of Kerrick, something unsettled her, like a grain of sand caught between her skin and clothing. She had slipped into the stable where Kerrick boarded the bay, and was asleep in the hay set out the previous evening by the same surly boy she had accosted in the street. For all his size, the big man could move quietly. She woke to find him gazing down at her in bemusement.

"That fodder costs me a good three silver a day, madam," he said mildly. "My horse can't eat it with you lying atop his plate."

She stretched her arms as she sat up. "Then you're over-paying by at least two. I'm an expert dog in the manger and this is definitely second-rate fare. I'd complain, were I you."

He shook his head as she picked the loose stalks out of her cloak. "Antonya, why are you plaguing me?" He patted the bay's thick neck as the horse nibbled the compacted hay. "Do you need money? Is that it? I haven't much, but . . ."

"No, thank you, sir," she said, with a parody of insult. "I've gotten along quite well so far without your charity." She sat on the edge of the manger, allowing the bay to eat while she played with the coarse mane falling over its eyes.

He sighed. "Are you hoping for work, then? Once I am in the Lord Creskar's service, I promise I'll see what I can do for you. Perhaps a place could be found in the scullery of the palace kitchens . . ."

"I'd rather be devoured by a *loup-garou*," she said brightly. "However, you did raise an interesting question: why aren't you yet in his lordship's service?"

He glared at her for a long, annoyed moment. "His lordship wished me to undergo a period of religious cleansing to be sure the taint of the Fever has been totally excised," he said reluctantly.

She grinned. "It was my observation you don't hold much credence in either the Faith or its Priests."

"I observe the One Path," he said dryly.

"As do we all." She rubbed the soft muzzle of his bay as it pushed against her, blowing through its huge nostrils. Its rough tongue explored her hand in hope of finding something more tasty there than straw, massive yellow teeth nibbling at her fingers with surprising delicacy. "You will not be happy in his service, Kerrick."

He stared at her, incredulous. "My happiness is none of your concern, child."

"True enough. All the same, you were once a Lord's First Chosen. You deserve better than menial service as a common armsman. You're too good a man to waste your time on petty disputes between rival Lords over who owns what pigsty."

He reached down, picked her up under the arms like a small girl, and set her on her feet toward the door of the stable. "Your opinion of me is flattering, madam, but hardly of much use. I am a Defender in need of work. What would you expect me to do otherwise?"

"Come with me," she said, abruptly serious. "Help me to reclaim my Lands from my uncle."

Astonished, he laughed. "Such a magnificent offer, madam"—he mocked her with a sweeping bow—"even if I were to believe your story. But may I be so bold as to ask how you intend to pay my wages?"

"I can pay you nothing, Kerrick of Myro," she said, keeping her voice level. "Nothing but honor. Or is gold more important to you?"

His sardonic humor was gone. "Honor does not buy food, Antonya. Self-righteousness is a luxury only the rich can afford. I am neither mercenary nor monk, simply a Defender. Why don't you give up this ridiculous fantasy and go back to making cheese, or laceweaving, or whatever Guild you've absconded from before you're carried off and raped. Find a decent man and marry, give him sons as any normal woman should want instead of roaming the forests like a wild animal."

He picked up a currycomb to groom his horse, ignoring her as he angrily stroked the thick muscles along the bay's hide.

"I know you see the Lands as I do, sir," she said quietly to his back. "Petty fiefdoms seething under the boot of the Oracular City, wasted lives spent fighting over trifles while the Priests gamble on the outcome for their amusement. This clan prodded and lied to, whipped up into hatred and bloodshed against that clan. Great Lords fooling themselves that they create dynasties when they squabble with one another, then look the other way in shame as the Faith ride through to murder their brothers and steal their children, praying it doesn't happen to them. Dividing us one against the other. Keeping us submissive and weak."

She saw him trembling, his jaw clenched in anger. "And

you would change the world, madam?" he scoffed.

"Once the Faith served the Lands and all its people. Now we serve it. If I can take back my Lands from P'tre Terhune, is that not proof enough we need no longer be slaves to the Priests?"

He looked at her thoughtfully; then irked, his face hardened. "You are a madwoman if not a heretic as well. Perhaps you can find a convent willing to take you in. I swear my service this afternoon to Lord Creskar, and we will both go separate ways. Do not annoy me further, for your own sake. Good day, madam," he said firmly, and turned away.

He refused to face her again. "Good day, sir." She left.

She was at the sajada herself by afternoon, and as she slipped through the throng of worshippers and simply curious, she found a place to watch near the high altar. This time, if Kerrick was aware of her, he gave no hint of it. He was paying scrupulous attention to the methodical rituals, mouthing the proper formulas at the proper time, kneeling in unison with Lord Creskar and his men as the Priest in his gilt-embroidered robes chanted overhead.

Her eyes were sharp enough to notice when one of Creskar's armsmen studied her, puzzled, his head cocked to one side. He spoke briefly with an armsman on his right, who turned his head to look at her. She pretended a sudden great interest in the sajada's ceremonial trappings and the droning music of the rites.

Her heart leaped as she watched the first armsman step to Lord Creskar's side, whispering a few words in his ear. A young man standing next to him looked around at her, and she recognized the courier from the road outside the city walls.

Time to go, she thought as two of Creskar's armsmen began working their way toward her. She turned with what she hoped looked like disinterest, trapped in the crush of worshippers inside the sajada.

She had made it only halfway to the great doors when an armsman grabbed her firmly by the arm, jerking her none too gently around.

"Where are your tattoos, woman?" he said with a scowl. "Where are your yellow eyes?" He held his dagger point discreetly next to her ribs, jabbing her skin as he marched her back down the nave. In the hidden balcony above the vaulted dome, the choir had already begin the chant.

"Perhaps you have me confused with my sister, sir," she said desperately.

Heads swiveled at the unexpected altercation. The young courier had reached her by now. "You wouldn't by any chance be a whore, would you, madam?" he said wryly. "Or would that be another sister?"

She could see Kerrick frowning at her, standing well over the heads of the crowd. Beside him, Creskar scowled in annoyance at the disturbance. The Priest leaned out from the small podium on the high altar, looking irritable as he continued to chant doggedly.

"Shall we ask the Defender if he knows you?" the armsman said, dragging her forcefully toward the cluster of men standing before the high altar. The crowd jostled back to make room as she was pushed into the circle. Creskar glared at her hostilely. Above them, the Priest scowled and the choir came to a halting stop, bewildered faces peering down at them through the carvings of the parclose.

"Who are you?" Creskar demanded in the abrupt silence.

Before she could answer, the armsman standing with his knife pricking her side said, "I saw her in a tavern; she had tattoos and her eyes were not the same color. She sought out this Defender and I heard them speaking in Myronian. They were discussing spying, sir."

The armsman abruptly jerked her in front of him and thrust a hand down the neck of her blouse. Above her, someone tittered. She grimaced as the armsman grabbed the lizard roughly, its claws jerked from her skin as he pulled it out of her blouse. She watched him with a faint smile as he held up his wriggling prize, the lizard struggling futilely. Frightened, its scaly skin glistened with oil oozing from pores along its side, webbed little legs scrabbling in the air as its tail whipped back and forth.

"Behold her familiar," the armsman boasted.

In an hour, she knew, the man was going to feel very ill, the toxins in the oils seeping through his bare hand. *Serves him right*, she thought, and hoped he didn't kill the poor beast. Creskar studied her with narrowed eyes before his suspicious gaze slid up to the Defender standing beside him. The big man looked down at him calmly, one large hand resting on the hilt of his longdagger.

"I would not accuse me of being in league with spies, my Lord," he said quietly. "Despite all other blemishes on my past, my reputation is the one thing I have left which remains untarnished."

"No," Creskar finally said slowly, "not you," and turned back to Antonya, drawing his knife.

The Priest watched with alarm as Creskar's armsman pulled her toward the Lord, his dagger at her throat. "Do not spill blood in the Holy House of Faith!" the Priest cried out in alarm. Antonya knew his fear had nothing to do with any altruism on his part. "If you must, take her outside to kill her!" Creskar withdrew his dagger and nodded to his men. They began to drag her backwards.

"Wait." The armsman holding her prisoner hesitated as Kerrick turned to Creskar. "Sir, she's harmless," he said reluctantly.

Creskar stared up at him, spiteful eyes narrowed almost to slits. "Then you *do* know this woman?" he snarled. The Priest standing at the altar watched warily.

"She may be many things, including a lunatic, but not a spy." Unhurried, confident, Kerrick stepped next to the armsmen with the lizard, and took it gently from his grasp. Antonya winced.

Kerrick held the bony animal up. "It's only a lizard," he said scornfully. "Or do you fear small animals that live under rocks as well as unarmed madwomen, Lord Creskar?" Antonya suppressed a smile as he handed the beast back to her. It quickly hid itself behind her hair, its tail a necklace of blue scales around her throat. When Kerrick turned back to Creskar, he had his dagger in his hand, the blade held with deceptive ease. "Murdering an innocent madwoman would be the ignoble act of a coward, which I'm sure you are not, sir."

Creskar scowled, jammed his own dagger back into its sheath and turned away from the big man with arrogant disdain. He glared at Antonya with naked hatred and spat on the floor at her feet. Deliberately, he turned his back and stalked away as the others grumbled disapproval. The Priest bent his shaved head toward the Lord, leaning down from his lectern to converse in low tones.

Slowly, the big man turned, facing each of Creskar's men in turn, staring at them in silence. One by one, the others looked away nervously, glancing at her, or stared at the floor. Kerrick slammed the longdagger back into its sheath. One by one, the rest put up their arms and backed away. Although the spectators had fallen back a safe distance to give the dispute plenty of room, none were unconcerned enough to leave. The whispers behind them grew.

"Are you unharmed, madam?" Kerrick asked her in an undertone.

She thought it had been the lizard trembling, but discovered it was herself. She managed to smile. "Completely. I am indebted to you, Defender, but I think you've just ruined your chances of serving his Lordship on my account."

Kerrick shrugged casually, but she was sure he was unhappy.

The Priest straightened with a curious smile. Creskar stalked back toward Kerrick and Antonya, stopping just out of arm's reach of Kerrick. He spoke in a deliberately loud voice. "Evil often disguises itself in the cloak of innocence. This woman has appeared in different form to several in my city, and consorts with what may still be a familiar. That is reason enough to accuse her of being tainted with the Weird, possibly even of being a daemon shape-changer."

"Nay, Lord," Kerrick said quietly, his voice dangerously mild. "A bit of paint and rags do not make the woman a daemon. If that were so, every mummer and courtesan would be the Devil's own."

Creskar's sudden flush made it clear he had not missed Kerrick's innuendo about his own mother's past profession. "Would you call the Holy Priest a liar, then?" he said stubbornly, jabbing a thumb toward the smug cleric in gilt behind him. "Daemons are cunning and able to conjure enchantments to beguile mortal eyes. Could it be this woman has cast her spell to deceive you, Defender?"

Kerrick gazed up at the Priest with ill-disguised contempt. "I would never call a consecrated man of the Faith a liar. But surely daemons conjured from the Weird could not possibly stand within the dome of a holy sajada without bursting into flames. Is that not as you have preached?" The Priest frowned, but said nothing. "Are there else among you who fear I have been 'deceived'?" Kerrick turned his back on the Priest as he glared at Creskar's retinue.

The armsmen shuffled nervously as Antonya watched, her heart beating far too rapidly in her ears. The lizard stirred, still upset, and she stroked its scaly back to calm it.

The Priest called in his melodious voice from the pulpit, "But surely a trial would determine her innocence or guilt? We must allow the judgment of God to decide her fate."

Antonya's skin prickled in horror, knowing full well that those trials she could survive would serve to prove her guilt and those that proved her innocence would leave her mutilated, if not dead.

Creskar smiled at her expression, then said to Kerrick slyly, "Trials can exonerate only those of human blood. While I may accept your assurance she is no daemon, whether she is mad or a spy has yet to be settled. I challenge her. As you are not her Defender, step aside. Let her call her armsmen, or defend herself if she has none. If she is but an innocent madwoman, God will protect her."

Not that this was much better. God had an unfortunate tendency to favor the strong in such contests. If Kerrick stepped aside and she died, he would at best have been deceived by a spy. Chances were very slight she could survive. Yet to step aside was to admit he had his doubts, coming down thoroughly on Creskar's side and proving his loyalty to his Lord. All it would cost was the life of a stranger, and only a commoner at that.

Of course, there was always the faint possibility that by some miracle God might lend His hand to her favor. Then everyone would be happy, with the possible exception of Lord Creskar.

Kerrick stared at the Priest with a smoldering anger, then laughed harshly. "My lord," he said to Creskar, his manner almost friendly, "have I not yet satisfied you of my integrity that my word is not enough, you need God's own approval? Who is it you truly wish to test—this women, myself or God?

I caution you, my Lord, it is truly ill-advised to disparage the honor of a Defender."

Creskar paled slightly, but smiled in return, his face pinched tight with hatred. "You are not her Chosen, sir. I say again, stand aside. I have challenged her."

Kerrick stared down at him calculatingly. The smaller man seemed to hold his breath as he waited.

"Are you prepared to defend yourself, Antonya?" he asked her quietly, without taking his eyes of the Lord.

"It seems I have little choice in the matter," she said calmly, although she would not have wanted to admit how badly frightened she was. "However, I came a bit unprepared. I have no weapon. Your sword is a bit more than I could handle, but you wouldn't mind lending me your longdagger for a few minutes, would you?"

He blinked at her, amused and surprised. "You travel the forests alone, unarmed?"

"My lizard is company enough, and I was raised and educated in a monastery, sir. We used knives for spreading lard on bread. I hadn't much need or opportunity to learn self-defense there."

He muttered a coarse oath in his own language, shaking his head in disbelief before he turned toward the waiting assembly, Creskar in front with his hands on his hips. He was smiling.

"Hear me!" It was hard not to hear him, his booming voice resonating off the brightly painted stone walls. "I came to Abadayho to seek honorable service. I stand before the witness of God in His Faith and declare it is time for me to swear fealty again."

Kerrick's huge hand dropped onto Antonya's shoulder and he grinned maliciously as Creskar's jaw dropped in astonishment. Antonya breathed in silent thankful relief. Kerrick had called his bluff.

"I have found one I would serve. Are there any among you who would challenge me for the right to her patronage?"

A muttering of disapproval and amazement rustled behind Creskar as his expression turned from surprise to outrage. Above him, in his pulpit, the silent Priest glared with narrowed eyes.

"What lunacy is this?" Creskar finally sputtered furiously.

"Has she infected you as well with her madness?"

Kerrick gazed at him with mock bewilderment. "Madness, Lord Creskar? The woman has need of a Defender. I have need of service. What could be more reasonable?"

"She's not even of noble blood!" the Priest objected from his lectern. "Would you shame the Guild of your fathers to serve a low-born woman of no House or Family?"

Kerrick looked at Antonya, an eyebrow raised questioningly.

"Some call me the White Beguine, and although I have sworn no vows, I have indeed been sanctified by the order of the Sisters of Beneficence." She heard the murmurs spread through the sajada, the years she'd spent building up her reputation at least having had some effect. Even Kerrick looked surprised, her response not what he'd expected. "My name is Antonya Terhune," she said clearly, and was pleased to see the Priest's eyes widen, "daughter and rightful heir of R'bert Terhune, Lord of Adalon, by the lady Latticea of Ashmael."

"Lies!" the Priest shouted angrily. "Adalon is held by our Lord P'tre Terhune, Commander of the Army of the Oracular City."

"Exactly," she said dryly. "My uncle stole it from me."

"Your claim is a sham. R'bert Terhune did not have a living daughter as heir to his Lands."

"It appears P'tre must have missed one during his many Purges," Antonya shot back. The whispering behind her changed timbre slightly, the amazement dwindling as buried anger became audible. The Priest's mouth tightened as he glared.

"You aren't content to mock those of higher birth, Kerrick, you must mock the Faith?" Creskar reached for his dagger in the baldric slung across his chest. "Such insult is intolerable . . ."

Before Creskar's knife was halfway clear of its scabbard, steel sang in one clear note. In a blurred arch, Kerrick's sword came to a stop, and Creskar found himself looking cross-eyed down the blade of the big man's sword, point held against his throat. Kerrick's eyes were ringed red in his bloodless face. The light through the high clerestory windows winked from the exposed razor edge of the sword under Creskar's chin. No one moved. The sajada had become still.

"No blood!" the Priest suddenly shrilled. "Not in the sajada! I forbid it!" His mouth then clicked shut as he trembled with rage.

Kerrick smiled. "My Lord," he said to Creskar, his voice barely audible, "you do not stand so high nor I so low that you may dare to malign me or my Guild."

"Surely you can see she is no highborn child of any Lord," Creskar insisted, looking up at the big man steadily. He kept his hand on the hilt of his knife, sweating but unflinching. "Her claims are preposterous—why give her deceit your favor?"

"And if she speaks the truth?" Kerrick retorted mildly, and pressed the tip of his blade against Creskar's throat, making an indentation without breaking the man's skin. "I've had a bellyful of justifying myself to you, sir. I am free to offer my service as I will, for any reasons I like. Challenge me, if you wish . . . or stand aside."

The smaller man quivered with frustration. He glanced scornfully at the sharp blade at his throat before he stepped backward, away from the tip, and jammed his half-drawn knife back into its sheath.

Kerrick turned slowly, his sword held ready, facing each of the men in turn. Each of them, with varying expressions, stepped back and looked away. Then Kerrick faced Antonya. "Would you have my service, Lady Antonya Terhune?"

She smiled shakily. "Aye, sir, it would be a great honor."

"I forbid it! This mockery will not be sanctioned in the House of the Faith," the Priest declared firmly. "And you risk Holy Commination if you continue in your folly."

A rapt silence gripped the crowd. Kerrick peered at him, eyes narrowed. "Where is my crime? By what right can the Faith deny me my free will?" His tone was flat, respectful enough, but he was obviously not one who was fearful of Priests, much to the cleric's discomfort. If the Priest had hoped to cow him with the threat of ostracism, he had miscalculated.

"She is not the heir to R'bert Terhune. You may not swear to a false oath under the protection of the holy sajada."

Kerrick smiled slowly, and nodded. "Then surely you can have no objections if I swear an oath not to the heir of R'bert

Terhune, but to Antonya, the White Beguine, a lady of the Lands?"

The Priest's mouth opened, silently struggling with the words. "No," he said tersely.

"Then give us the Blessing of the Faith, Priest." Kerrick knelt before Antonya, his sword held by the blade in his right hand in front of her. Even on one knee, his eyes were level with her own.

"Accept, Lady Antonya, as your own this arm which I commit into your service. I vow as your champion to defend you from your enemies as if they were my own, for as long as either of us shall live."

She placed her hands on the guard of the sword's hilt, and looked up steadily at the Priest. "With the grace of God and the blessing of His Faith, I accept with respect and gratitude."

She remained gazing at the Priest; Creskar and his armsmen held their breaths. Not a whisper disturbed the expectant tension in the sajada as they waited to see if the Priest would stalk away without the blessing. The Priest's face contorted in sudden anger, but he raised his hand, three fingers held up in blessing, and gestured abruptly. "*Benedictus qui venit in nomine Oraculum sanctus*, I give you the Blessing of the Faith," he said sourly, the words rushed together, and dropped his hand as if it had been soiled.

Kerrick stood and sheathed his sword in a single, fluid motion, then turned to face Lord Creskar. "Do you still wish to accuse my Lady of being either spy or daemon, Lord Creskar? Call your best armsman, then. Or your worst if you can't afford the loss. She is innocent of your charges and more than God will defend her."

Antonya caught the look of consternation that passed between the silent men flanking Creskar. Disgusted, he crossed his arms over his chest and shook his head. "Nay," he said. "Throw your life away if you like, Kerrick. I had doubts if you could be truly free of the taint of your past. The Fever has obviously affected your sanity; your brain must be riddled with worms. I pray your caprice does not lead you to disaster."

Kerrick smiled, his eyes bland, but Antonya was not deceived by his apparent mildness. "Were this not a holy place, my Lord, I would answer you more vigorously. But your feeble attempts at trickery were at least amusing, and I hope you have learned not all are so slavishly eager to lick the dung from your boots as your hired men."

There were several sharply indrawn breaths as the two men glared at each other. Creskar returned Kerrick's wry smile, lips pulled taut across his teeth. "Enjoy your laughter, sir, at the expense of a powerful Lord with the backing of the Faith while you follow your false, mad whore."

Insults and threats exchanged, Creskar turned on his heel, walking swiftly with his shoulders hunched. He gestured at his armsmen with a chopped motion of his hand. Most of them followed him out of the vast sajada, trailed by a few reluctant stragglers.

Antonya placed her hand in Kerrick's proffered palm, feeling like a small child next to his huge bulk. They turned their backs to the Priest and walked through the murmuring crowd toward the doors of the sajada, past curious eyes watching them.

"I feel like I've just stolen the bride at the altar," Antonya said softly as she walked down the center aisle beside Kerrick, eyes forward, not glancing at the staring faces to either side. Kerrick chuckled quietly, but without humor.

"The jilted groom in this case is not likely to be any more pleased than if you had. I would strongly suggest, madam," Kerrick said lightly as they passed through the doors of the sajada, out of the gloom into the bright light of the late afternoon, "that it would be prudent for us to get the hell out of here."

"As quickly as possible," she agreed, smiling tightly.

6

Within the hour, Kerrick had been hit by sudden cramps, and had to dismount to vomit by the side of the road. He'd been very unhappy when she explained how he had accidentally poisoned himself handling her lizard with his bare hands.

"It's *poisonous*?" he demanded, appalled.

"Not fatally," she assured him. "As big as you are, it shouldn't affect you too badly. You'll feel better in a few hours."

He wiped his mouth with the back of his hand, glaring at her accusingly. "Small comfort, madam. Why doesn't it affect you?"

"Because I keep it next to my skin. It has little value in deterring unwanted lust being pressed upon me, but my purpose isn't so much delayed revenge as it is protection of another sort. I've built up a resistance to its venom which gives me a resistance to other poisons as well. The counteragents of my own humors are slightly poisonous." She tried to smile placatingly. "My kiss may not be deadly, sir, but you'll not likely want me twice."

"I didn't want you in the first place," he muttered, then turned hastily to heave again.

He recovered soon enough, or had the will to plow on despite his affliction. They spoke little during the first few days, intent on putting as much distance between themselves and Abadayho in as short a time as possible. The bay was built for strength, not speed, and reacted to Kerrick's urging with the barest flicker of placid ears.

She had ridden few horses in her life, none of them as large as Kerrick's. She perched on the roll over the bay's rump with her arms around Kerrick, trying to rock with the horse's shattering plod. The gentle behemoth slammed massive hooves down in its ponderous gait, each spine-numbing thud leaving her bruised and sore.

Kerrick slept as little as she did, watchful for Lord Creskar's men. She had no doubt they were followed, but the trade road south was heavily traveled, their safety in numbers. A week out of Abadayho, the road split and the crowd immediately diminished as most of their fellow journeyers headed west to the coast and the easier, if longer route to the Oracular City. Those few who remained on the road south were mostly messengers on lithe, fast horses who quickly left the bay far behind. Kerrick kept close to a small caravan of heavily laden mules led by a sour-faced merchant and his two silent sons. The merchant welcomed Kerrick's presence, no doubt worried about bandits on the road ahead.

A few hours later, the road through the rolling fields and orchards abruptly descended into a treacherous passage through the Luclaen Gorge. The slopes of worn mountains towered above them, rocky folds striated with black obsidian. Antonya breathed a silent sigh of relief, knowing they were no longer within Creskar's domains.

They were now well within the sprawling territory encompassing a hodgepodge of small fiefdoms stretching from the far foothills of the Shamris Steppes in the east to the Oracular City to the west. Known derisively as the Land of a Thousand Lords, these fragmentary provinces were ruled by minor noblemen, in actuality mere figureheads dominated by the Faith itself, answerable to their distant relatives within the Oracular City.

The Faith drew the bulk of its common soldiers from these sparse communities, leaving minor Lordlings meager resources for rebellion. Any Lord with the slightest inclination toward defiance was replaced by one more dependable, and any town that grew large or prosperous enough to threaten independence was quickly Purged. Only those Lands and those Lords at a far enough remove from the Oracular City could assert enough autonomy to maintain their limited freedom.

The road zigzagged down the desolate limestone canyons, the gouged walls of the chasms nearly as white as the snow still clinging to the rockface. It was slow and dangerous, and Antonya quickly realized the benefit of small, surefooted mules over horses as they deftly negotiated the winter-damaged trail to leave Kerrick and Antonya struggling to keep up. She and Kerrick dismounted, Kerrick leading the bay through the tiered canyon pass while Antonya walked behind.

She was surprised by how agile the beast was, setting his immense hooves delicately down on the narrow footpath barely wide enough for Antonya's own feet. In places, ice and snow had completely erased the footpath, leaving the road passable, it seemed, only for wild sheep. When the trail suddenly crumbled under the bay's weight, the seemingly clumsy animal simply locked his knees, lowered his head, and skidded calmly downhill in a cascade of broken rock, dragging Kerrick with him. Antonya gazed down in admiration from the edge of the road as horse and man regained their balance. Kerrick nonchalantly rubbed the bay's nose, murmuring as the horse twisted its great neck around to look back quizzically, as if wondering what was keeping her.

The road split as it bottomed out into the Yraz Massif, huge stands of oak and pine forests carpeting the plains. One fork turned west toward remote mountains, the quicker if more hazardous route toward the coast threading through the Tarax Valley. The mule caravan would follow the Xous River to the Priest-held mountain fortress of Kaesyn, the last refuge before the Oracular City.

Kerrick shook hands with the merchant before the man herded his mules west. They took the road leading south.

As the snow melted, the road rapidly turned to muddy slush. They passed only the occasional carriage and outriders slogging through deep rutted mud, or were passed by couriers, the hooves of their young lean horses hacking clots of mud behind them as they clipped by.

Two days later, Kerrick turned the bay off the worn road toward a thick burr of forest in the distance. The barely discernible path was washboarded from countless rainstorms. Dried puddles cracked like brown scabs, ice in the hollows splintered into faery lace.

By midafternoon, they were in the thick of the woodlands. Trees dripped with the melting snow, and by sundown they were both as wet as if they'd been caught in a downpour. Antonya was far more cold in the damp than she had been in snow. The lizard stirred slugglishly with cold lethargy, and she made no effort to shift the little reptile as it pushed its nose into the warmth of her armpit.

The sky had turned deep purple, the first stars visible, and she was grateful to see a small half-stone house in a clearing. Crudely constructed, the walls stood only shoulder-high, irregular stones shoved between crooked wood beams, cemented together with mud and straw. Smoke trickled from the open eaves under the roof, not even a chimney through the motley thatch to draw it off.

A short, dark man emerged from the house, bundled against the cold with a thick cloak of woven grasses, waiting patiently. When they were within earshot, he called out, "Greetings, Defender," and stepped off the planks serving as a porch to catch the bay's bridle.

Wordlessly, Kerrick dismounted, then picked Antonya off the back of the horse as easily as a child and set her on her feet. Her rump and back ached with the long ride.

"This is Y'qert," Kerrick said to Antonya. He didn't introduce her to Y'qert, but the small man simply smiled at her with a mouthful of blackened stumps of teeth before leading the bay around to an open stable by the side of the house. She followed Kerrick as Y'qert tied the reins to a post by a small farrier's forge. While the two men picked up the animal's massive hooves to discuss the condition of the horseshoes, Antonya looked around curiously.

Small mottled pigs wandered unmolested around the yard by the house. The ground, except where porcine snouts had plowed the slushed dirt into pocked clods, was compact and completely lifeless, the remains of a garden left fallow for the winter. A homely woman appeared in the doorway of the crude stone house. A gaunt chicken which might have originally sported whiter feathers in its youth strutted around the woman's feet. She kicked it back into the house before gesturing to Antonya.

The floor was simply a pit dug in the ground, covered with worn rushes compacted into mats. Posts haphazardly supported the sagging roof of the single long room. A squat stone hearth belched as much smoke as heat from its open maw, while a stew of questionable ingredients bubbled sullenly in a bronze pot hooked on a chain over the firepit. The remains of past meals were scattered everywhere, pecked at by chickens wandering around the room. Skinned hides had been tacked to wooden slats, and Antonya was grateful it was too cold for flies to have become much of a nuisance.

Outside, she heard the clanging of iron as Y'qert shaped a

new horseshoe. She seated herself on the top of a wooden chest to wait, out of the way. A large loom leaned against the wall with a half-finished rough woven cloth in the frame. Dirty-faced children peered around a tattered blanket stretched across one end of the house. One girl clutched a small piglet tightly in her arms, ignoring it as it peed and wriggled in protest. They didn't react when Antonya smiled.

Both men stooped through the doorway, Kerrick wiping soot from his sweating face. Just as dirty but less concerned about it, Y'qert squatted by the hearth. "Y'qert once served the Defenders Guild," Kerrick said, as if Antonya had asked a question, "but found that life as a forest woodcutter, while less comfortable, is more independent."

Y'qert nodded contentedly, not in the least subservient. "I still recognize my debts to the Guild," he said, his voice hoarse as if he spoke very little. "Those who wish are welcome here."

Life in the wild was more primitive, but she realized it was safer here from the ravages of Purges. In these subjugated lands children raised in the forests could vanish unseen into the trees before a rider even knew they were there. As if he could read her thoughts, Y'qert smiled, his eyes shrewd.

"We will sleep in the hayshed," Kerrick told her. "Y'qert has no room for guests." And it was no doubt cleaner.

Y'qert's wife gave them a stub of candle. Held cupped against the wind in Kerrick's hand, it emitted barely enough light to keep them from tripping in the dark as Y'qert led the way to a small wooden shed built against the back of the house. What warmth the shed might have absorbed from the house was negated by huge gaps between the wood slats of the walls. After the stench of the house, the hay smelled refreshingly clean.

Kerrick stuck the candle stub onto the lip of a post, then spread the sheepskin he'd stolen from Antonya over the animal fodder. He gestured graciously for her to use it.

"Since you're an expert on hay," Kerrick said cynically, "might I assume this doesn't meet with your usual standards?"

"I've slept in worse places, Kerrick," she said, dropping onto her erstwhile sheepskin, still as wonderfully soft and inviting as the day she'd stolen it herself. Kerrick packed the loose straw into a hollow before settling down with his cloak over his shoulder, shadows flickering in the yellow light. Mice squeaked unseen in the hay, protesting the invasion of their quarters.

She was asleep before Kerrick blew out the candle.

Too tired to wake and too unsettled for dreamless sleep, her thoughts shifted just under the surface of awareness. Her cloak didn't quite keep out the cold as she curled into a tight ball under it. Suddenly, she was awake, eyes startled open in the blackness. Kerrick's dim silhouette buckled on his armor in graceful, self-assured movement. Leather creaked softly. Faint light reflected points in his eyes as he glanced at her, his face blank in the shadows. She knew she had been asleep only a few hours.

"It's unlikely anyone would find us here, but we shouldn't linger too long within the reach of the Faith," he said, knowing she was awake although she hadn't moved.

She got to her feet, brushing off the damp hay. "Where to?"

"South to Myro. My sister Lirda lives in Lord C'ristan's House. It will be safer there."

Although his tone was casual, she noticed he didn't mention Myro was nearly seven hundred miles as the crow flies. It would take at least six or seven weeks to reach. She made no comment.

Moonlight cast fuzzy shadows from behind a thick haze of clouds, not enough light to make out more than vague shapes as she followed the Defender to where the bay had been tethered.

Y'qert came from the house but said nothing as Kerrick lifted her onto the back of the horse behind the saddle, then draped the sheepskin over her lap. He swung easily up into the saddle of the enormous horse, and leaned over to take the reins from the woodcutter. She heard the clink of coins as Kerrick dropped a small sack into Y'quert's hand. It disappeared into the layers of fur that he wore. As Kerrick clicked the bay into a walk, their host turned away without a backward glance.

A tiny sliver of moonlight filtering through the trees provided the only illumination. Antonya admired Kerrick's ability to follow in almost total darkness the nearly imperceptible trail that wound through the growing forest. Her arms as far around Kerrick's waist as she could reach, she pressed her cheek against his broad back and closed eyes gritty with weariness, trying to settle into the jarring roll of the horse's stride. She didn't feel Kerrick's hand settle lightly over her arm to keep her upright as, amazingly, she dozed off.

The sun broke over the tops of the trees before she woke, miles from Y'qert's forest.

7

When they reached the small village of Belludesta a few days later, Kerrick sent Antonya into town to purchase wool from a draper while he stayed in the cover of forest. If Priests or soldiers still searched for them, a peasant woman on foot would be less obvious than a giant on a warhorse. He waited impatiently until late in the day, picking burrs out of the bay's mane and tail, oiling his riflebow and refletching arrows. Near dusk, Antonya reappeared with a roll of undyed felted cloth balanced over one shoulder, more than he'd expected. Slightly wider than his outstretched arms' reach, it was twice as long as he was tall. Grinning, Antonya also produced an earthenware jug half filled with dark beer and a loaf of heavy brown bread. He didn't ask, she didn't enlighten him.

Kerrick ate a slice of the dark, nutty bread and washed it down with the beer before he got to work on the cloth. He carefully cut a small piece from one end to fashion into a rude hood, then slit the wool in the middle lengthwise down one half to make an oversized cape.

Antonya sat cross-legged on a rock, retrieved a small sewing kit from the pocket of her cloak, and sewed the end piece into a pointed, triangular hood. Kerrick merely grunted as she handed it to him although he was surprised at her flawless workmanship. Needlework of this quality was usually done only by professional Guildcrafters or leisured noblewomen.

She looked like neither. She was pretty, but not beautiful in the pale, delicate manner of a highborn lady. She was peasant-sturdy, but without the peasant's dull apathy, not yet broken by too much heavy labor, too many childbirths and too little food. Her clothes were plain, and he was certain she had fashioned them herself. But if the leather was the skins of forest animals, it been carefully tailored, the needlework delicate and even, sewn with the same precision as the hood.

The uncut portion of wool draped down from his shoulders over the Bay's rump, covering Antonya's head, while Kerrick wrapped the halves one against the other in front of himself over the horse's withers. With the hood over his head, the rain beaded off the wool and kept them both warm and dry with only Kerrick's thighs exposed to the rain. It would also serve to shelter them from the rain at night when they slept in the open forest.

They spoke little as they traveled, saving their strength for the journey. That she was not used to horseback was obvious from the way in which she rode. He could feel her tension as she clung to his back. Kerrick had expected her to complain, about the weather, about the pace, about the cold and discomfort, all the feminine protests he'd heard from other women unused to the hardship of horse and road. He was intrigued when she did not. He knew her backside must ache from the horse's broad croup, her back swaying at each punishing impact of its hooves.

His certainly did. Occasionally, she'd walk until negotiating the muddy ground became more of a problem than the back of the horse. He didn't mind. The bay was strong, but it wasn't fair to load the beast with the extra weight. Despite its size, the horse was not tireless, but it kept up a solid, steady pace day after day. When they stopped to rest, it was more for the animal's benefit than Antonya's.

Spring had came early to the southern lands, the air still chilled but the countryside rapidly turning green, flowers budding with the promise of an explosion of color to come. They passed into Water Cross through its narrow border with Asteria, skirting the hostile Sheruben Valleys and its powerful Lord. The lands of Asteria were sparsely populated, its seafaring citizens concentrated in the port capital of Donaq. Low drystone walls crisscrossed the rolling grasslands between forests, and what few tenant farmers or shepherds emerged from their stone huts to gather their flocks watched them pass with disinterest. But already Kerrick was feeling better, his head turned toward home.

A few days before they reached Myro, the gray clouds broke wide open, drizzle suddenly turning into torrential rain. Hail the size of large peas battered them as Kerrick wended his way through a patch of forest, hoping to find the shelter of a dense copse. The dull light behind the clouds had drained from the evening sky before he spotted the burnt-out ruins of some long dead nobleman's hunting lodge, barely large enough for three men and their dogs. No one had used the shelter for decades. Overgrown with ivy and weeds, the cavelike interior was dry, if cold. The downpour lessened momentarily, and in the brief lull, Kerrick was depressed when he didn't hear any hidden songbirds. Rain in a silent forest meant even birds had battened down for the duration.

As he tethered the bay in the shelter of trees overgrowing the entrance of the ruined lodge, Antonya prowled the forest through sheets of rain, searching. Kerrick draped the wool cape over the bay to keep off the worst of the rain and cold, unlashing the pack but leaving the saddle on, and rubbed the poor animal's muzzle consolingly. By the time he ducked into the hovel, Antonya had already managed to build a small fire in the lodge's old firepit.

He dumped the pack on the floor, which was covered more with dirt than mosaic tiles, the shattered faces of cherubs and satyrs filthy. Shaking water out of his eyes, he watched Antonya feed dead leaves and twigs into the flicker of yellow flames, amazed she had uncovered the dry kindling in the wet undergrowth. The kindling was damp enough to smoke, but she coaxed the tiny flames grudgingly to life.

"You'll need more than that to take the chill off our bones in this place," he said. He was tired, and the fatigue made him colder than normal. He sat on the pack, arms around his knees, shivering.

"True." Her hands rummaged in her cloak and withdrew a wineskin. "Take a sip of this. It tastes horrible, but it will help."

He frowned at it, puzzled, before he took a cautious taste. It was worse than horrible, and it was also very familiar. He gagged, choking the vile liquid down, then stared at the wineskin. She was watching him with mischievous eyes. "*You!*" he managed to gasp out.

"Me?" she said innocently.

She took the skin from him as his blood leaped with sudden heat. The weariness of the past several days lifted slightly, and he swallowed the bitter aftertaste left in his mouth. "What is that stuff?" he asked, choosing to ignore his sudden revelation.

"It's called *paynam tiktah* by the Parvathan Mountain peoples. It means 'bitter drink' in Daviak."

"So you've been to the Parvatha Mountains, then, have you?"

She smiled at his obvious dubiety. "Only as far as Haritath," she said. He wasn't sure he believed her. "But I learned to make it in Dothinia from a courtier there who fancies himself a wizard in the healing arts, among other things. He's also the one who gave me my lizard and taught me its uses."

"An alchemist?" Kerrick asked suspiciously.

She laughed wryly. "He'd like to think so, but he's not that good a wizard." She raised the wineskin in a mock toast. "It's brewed from wild berries and fermented in sheep dung to give it that unique musky flavor," she said and took a sip of her own.

He squeezed his eyes shut and shuddered, but the extra warmth was welcome, sweat popping out on his forehead. She glanced at the fading light through the open doorway and got to her feet. "Excuse me."

He assumed she was taking care of bodily urges with female modesty, and shook his head when she returned with three fat lengths of wood. "It's not easy to find in this season," she remarked, balancing two in the midst of the fire. The damp bark smoked briefly, and she squatted on hands and knees to blow on the flames before the dry wood underneath caught. She placed the third, wetter length next to the fire to dry out as much as possible. "But there's always something if you know where to look. Dead branches on trees, nests in hollow logs, windfalls in shelters of rocks."

Impressed, his opinion of her had changed, even against his better judgment, to one of cautious respect. He still didn't believe she could truly be the forgotten heir of R'bert Terhune, but if she wasn't, who the Hell *was* she?

"I've known forest witches," he said, his back resting against a large fragment of carved stone. "But they've all been half-savage pagans who rarely travel three miles from their lairs." Most of these unkempt, dirty hags were only poor demented women doing their best at living alone and keeping the superstitious at bay with faked garbled curses when they couldn't run away fast enough. Occasionally, a village would

gather courage enough to go on a witch hunt, like dogs snuffling after an elderly bear. Snaring some wretched crone,
they'd drag the helpless old woman to the stake, then have a
festival, feasting and laughing and drinking away their fears
as she roasted.

He watched her, the flickering fire shimmering in her eyes.
"How long have you lived in the forests?"

She pushed back her wet hair from her face. He could see
her calculating. "I've been on my own since I left the monastery, little more than six years. Although it wasn't all spent
living wild."

"I don't think I've ever met an educated woman who could
survive in the rough." *And with so little,* he didn't add.

She straightened, hands on her back as she popped out the
ache in her spine. "It's not easy, I'll admit. And brigands living
in the forests as well are far more a danger to me than wolves
or wildcats. It's a simple life. I've enjoyed most of it. But it's
not one I'd want to grow old living."

So she'd seen a few forest witches herself.

Warmer now, Kerrick stretched one leg toward the fire, his
arms looped loosely around the other, upraised knee. "Well,"
he teased, "now that you've given up this free and barbaric
life to become a refined lady, do you have any particular plans
in mind?" He grinned but Antonya was still watching the fire.

She took him seriously. "A few. Nothing concrete, however,
and they've altered as the circumstances merited. I've spent
the past few years just learning what normal life is like." She
smiled at his raised eyebrow, "And I do not mean sleeping in
caves and eating berries and roots. Growing up in a monastery
seemed a very natural existence, at least at the time. My
friends, companions and teachers were all monks living in isolation from the rest of the world. Who would look for a girl-
child in the midst of a bunch of chaste old men? I was safe
and well-loved there, but when I was sixteen, the prior decided
a full-grown woman was too much for the brotherhood."

She fell silent, watching the fire, and he waited. "He was
right, of course. He sent me to a convent in Managh run by
the Blessed Sisters of Beneficence, but a world inhabited only
by women is no less peculiar than one with only men. I didn't
care for it much, and didn't stay more than a couple of years,"

she said, a hard undercurrent of anger and sadness in her tone. "Having spent my life with books and celibates, I wanted to see the world.

"Had I taken vows, I could have lived out my life in perfect safety, protected from my uncle. It was not an ungenerous offer. But it takes money to ensure a comfortable place in the convent. I'm highborn, but penniless. I would have been a servant sister scrubbing floors rather than a leisured gentlewoman devoted to contemplation, and still consider myself lucky. If a poor peasant girl tries to escape a hateful life, like as not she'll be turned away from the doors of the convent, no matter how pious she is or how merciful the Sisters would like to be." She shrugged wryly. "If all women were accepted into the bosom of sisterly love, half the Lands would empty, husbands would be left without wives and the destitute and desperate would overwhelm the convents."

"But you were welcome despite your lack of a proper endowment?"

The reflections of orange flames danced in her eyes. "Oh, yes. The Sisters of Beneficence live well enough, high and low. No one goes too hungry, no one is beaten too harshly. Mother Clemence offered me a chance not given to many." Her tone was gentle, but the anger was still there. She paused, staring into the fire. "I suppose I was a fool to reject it." Her tone said otherwise. "It wasn't the sin of pride—I simply had no notion of what it was I was giving up. A woman like myself, alone? I would be extremely fortunate to find honest work in a rich man's house"—she grinned at Kerrick ironically— "or in the scullery of a Lord's kitchen."

He snorted but made no other comment.

The smile was gone. "More likely I might have found myself pressed into service as a whore, either driven to it by hunger or abducted against my will by a corrupt monger."

Outside, thunder rumbled through the darkened forest. "I don't believe you would have made a good whore," he said.

She laughed. "Or a bad one, either. And for the same reasons I would never have been a devout Sister. I have never been deft at pretending to be meek and obedient. I'll not gladly spread my legs to grovel before man nor God." Kerrick blinked, startled at her impiety, although her tone was matter-of-fact.

"Also it didn't take long to realize I would never become Abbess, regardless of my education or abilities. While I would be safe from my uncle's eye hiding behind the anonymity of a white veil, to rise too far in the hierarchy might catch his attention. It was not only to protect me, but to also protect those who sheltered me."

A streak of silent lightning outlined her face in silver a brief moment. They both waited for the thunder seconds later. "My uncle has never seen me," she continued, the rain slashing down harder outside their shelter. "He could come to a High Celebration of the Vernal Equinox, sit right next to me in the choir and never know the difference. But *not* if I were Mother Superior."

"And you aspired to that lofty seat?"

She glanced at him impishly. "At one time. If I were condemned to a life as a cenobite, I would be queen of the convent, if that was the only domain I could rule. I even briefly entertained a notion I might someday become the order's Episcopress. Mother Clemence and I had some rather candid discussions about why this was not possible, and why it would be to my benefit to respect duty and obedience while avoiding the sin of overreaching ambition."

Kerrick smiled. No doubt "candid discussions" meant fierce arguments and flying crockery. "I take it neither of you were successful in convincing the other."

"Oh, quite the contrary. She persuaded me beyond all shadow of doubt she was utterly correct, I would make a dreadful abbess," Antonya said lightly. "So I left."

A gust of wind blew in a spray of cold, wet air, momentarily threatening their fire. Antonya leaned on one elbow to coax the withering flames back to life. He watched as she held back her hair from her ash-smeared face and blew, her hands tough and blunt, muscles on her young arms hard. When she sat up and blinked away the smoke tears, she looked younger in the firelight than she had seemed in Abadayho. Then she smiled, and he saw the years in her ironic expression.

"I've spent the past four years exploring the Lands, avoiding only the Oracular City. I've walked more miles than a penitent pilgrim, and seen more domains in six years than most couriers in their lives. I've sailed on the Great Inland Sea, ridden a *qazaq* caravan from the Dark Plains to the Bay of Hunger. I've listened to the singing rocks of Peyra and danced at the Courts of Roixara. Father Andrae taught me my letters in half a dozen languages before I left the monastery"—she chuckled—"two of them unfortunately quite dead and totally useless outside a monastery, and I've learned half a dozen more since. I've lived with poor cotters and rich merchants, I've conversed with the princes of court and with the pariahs of the forest. I've listened to poets and prostitutes and peddlers. And I've created a name for myself as the White Beguine. I've wandered enough. Now it's time for me to fulfill my duty."

He wasn't sure if he believed her or not, but it made for an entertaining way to pass a cold stormy night. "Pray enlighten me, my noble Lady Antonya," he gently mocked her. "What would that be?"

"To take Adalon back from P'tre Terhune."

He shook his head ruefully. "How?"

"He's not well-loved, Kerrick. My uncle murdered his brother for secular gain but professes to be the humble champion of the Chalice of God, solemnly praying for the One who can Walk the Fire and lead all His people to the new Kingdom." Her voice trembled with scorn. "How many children has he abducted to serve the Priesthood? How many people has he killed, Kerrick? How many more will die?"

A sudden, painful memory he thought he'd long suppressed stabbed Kerrick through the heart: the sound of a woman's laugh, the sunlight gleaming on a baby's downy cheek. He was unable to speak as Antonya laughed bitterly. "How much damage has he done to the Faith itself? Do you suppose he *wants* the One to come and judge his sins?"

Kerrick's face grew cold and it had little to do with the chill rain outside. "Are you denying God?" he asked carefully.

She grinned, suddenly seeming as feral as a wolf. "Never God. Only my uncle. The Landsfolk have no interest in the internal politics of the Citadel over who's a heretic and who isn't. They are simple people with simple needs. They have children with bellies to fill, fields to plow and houses they'd just as soon keep the roof on. A blighted crop or a starving

flock of sheep is far more crucial than pretty rhetoric or eso-
teric philosophy. The time is ripe, peasants and Lords alike
from all over the Lands would rise up against Terhune, if they
had but one thing."

Her hair had dried now, the fire stirring the air in the shelter.
Strands of red-gold lifted from around her face.

"What would that be?" he asked quietly, his mouth gone
dry.

"Someone to lead them."

He didn't answer for a long time, and when he finally spoke,
he tried to keep the skepticism out of his voice. "A woman?"

Firelight glittered in her eyes—like madness, he thought.
"My sex is not by its very accident of birth completely feeble-
minded and useless. All things are born through woman. You,
me, God, the universe, life."

Kerrick shook his head wonderingly. "I thought you were
mad enough laying claim to Terhune Lands and bloodrights.
Now you warrant yourself to be a prophetess as well?"

" 'For I am but a single voice alone in the wilderness,' "
she said in a reasonable voice. " 'Crying out the Light shall
be revealed, and all flesh born of the blood of woman shall
see it together.' " She smiled, but it was a smile as hard as
flint. "One benefit of growing up in a monastery is that my
knowledge of the Book is as thorough as any Priest's, Kerrick.
I can quote it backward and forward and standing on my head,
but I'm not claiming any divine inspiration."

To his shock, her eyes had paled to the same yellow glow
of the flames, sending a shiver down his spine.

"Besides, who better than myself? Woman or no, I *am* my
father's only heir. My blood is as noble as any Lord's, but my
loyalty is firmly married to the Lands. I intend to unite the
Landsfolk, *all* the Landsfolk, reconcile those of noble blood
to the people they should rightly be protecting, because without that, I would be no better than the tyrant I seek to over-
throw. We need not live as groveling slaves with Terhune's
boot on our necks. To take back my bloodrights serves not
only myself, and not only the Landsfolk, but the Faith as well.
Should I succeed, then perhaps the One will come to lead an
honorable people worthy of His Light."

It was ridiculous, two dirty, hungry people sitting in a wet hovel, huddling over smoldering flames from a damp wood fire, to be speaking of defeating Terhune.

Yet as he stared at the light in her wolf-yellow eyes, if only for a moment, he *believed*.

8

P'tre Terhune strode through the arcaded halls of the Citadel, his fist clenching the hilt of his sword spasmodically. His red robes did little to hide the plain black leather attire underneath. The chains of his Office crossed his chest, holding the insignia of a Warrior of the One Path at their intersection. He ignored the murmuring and bowing clerks, pushing past them scornfully.

Two armed guards stood at attention before a door at the end of a passageway. Terhune's gray eyes narrowed with icy anger as the guards glanced at one another, then stood to one side. He flung open the door, striding inside with the guards nervously following on his heels. An elderly Priest turned in surprise. Terhune stood with legs apart and fists on his hips as he scowled up at the thin, white-haired man standing on the level above him where thousands of bound books towered on shelves.

The old man smiled. "You always did know how to make the best of an entrance, P'tre," he said mildly, then nodded at the two guards to dismiss them.

P'tre ignored the sarcasm. "Why was I not informed immediately?" he demanded.

"I didn't feel it important," the Priest said.

The younger man rocked back on his heels. "You felt! *You* felt! By the Mother of God, K'ferrin," he said, his voice grating with menace, "you would do well not to forget with whom you are dealing!"

The old man sighed, a book cradled in his arms half-hidden in his dark blue robes. "Dear boy," he said, feigning weariness, "I have lived through your predecessors and, although I am but a very old and tired man, I *may* even live through you."

Cold gray eyes locked with K'ferrin's, P'tre's naked hate

palpable. "Are you threatening me?" he demanded softly.

It was no secret that P'tre hadn't loved his father, but the son had never forgiven R'ldan Terhune's murderer. K'ferrin watched as P'tre touched the insignia of his Office on his chest with one hand while the other tightened around the hilt of his sword. The gesture not lost on him, he deliberately turned his back to the Warrior-Priest to return the book to its shelf. When he looked at P'tre again, he was smiling with malicious delight.

"You, P'tre?" he said casually. "I would hope never to be that . . . obvious. I am deeply flattered, however, you have not forgotten with whom *you* deal."

P'tre's hand tightened around the hilt, then dropped away. "I am the head of my Order. Word of heresy and impostors should not be kept from me."

K'ferrin slipped his hands, long and bony with blue veins showing through the papery skin, into the cuffs of his sleeves as he looked at P'tre speculatively. "Heresy?" he challenged quietly as he walked to one of the two curving staircases at either end of the room. "Impostors? I have heard only wild stories from a handful of ignorant rabble, mostly repeating the vaguest of rumors. Gossip tends to transmute hard facts into unbridled fancy. Geese become angels, and frogs become daemons."

P'tre pulled his lips into a grimace of a mean smile, walking stiff-legged toward the old man as K'ferrin reached the last step. He towered over K'ferrin, glaring down.

"Would a nobleman of the Houses who saw this woman with his own eyes and heard her claims with his own ears be respectable and reliable enough even for you?"

"Oh." K'ferrin nodded, indifferent. "That. I assume you're referring to Lord Creskar?"

P'tre's smile vanished as K'ferrin waved his hand contemptuously and brushed past him. "Lord Creskar may be of a great House, but he is still a fanatic, P'tre. Fanatics make very poor reporters; their information can seldom be counted on as accurate or objective."

"I serve the Oracle and the One Path," P'tre countered stiffly, "as has every Terhune for centuries. Not like you and your kind who serve only for your own ends. The Prophecy is being profaned!"

"Ach," K'ferrin said in disgust. Reaching his large chair, he lowered himself onto the embroidered pillows cushioning the carved oak. His hemorrhoids had flared again, and he tried to keep from wincing. "The Prophecy. You jump to the wildest conclusions on the flimsiest of evidence and invoke the Book as if that is enough to give your accusations legitimacy. The *Prophecy* my pimpled ass!"

P'tre gasped. "Speak not of the Book in that tone, old man," he warned.

"The *Book* may be interpreted any number of ways, P'tre," K'ferrin said firmly, bony hands laced over his stomach. "My version just happens to be a bit less bloodthirsty than yours. Protestations of piety aside, we both know your concerns have less to do with the affairs of the Faith than with your own private interests."

The Warrior-Priest paced the room, as if he couldn't stand the energy it took to stay still. "G'walch is nearly of age, K'ferrin. He's the One, I know it, I *feel* it. I will not tolerate any attempt that puts his Walk into jeopardy."

K'ferrin's smile thinned. He remembered well whose machinations had spoiled his own chance to have a candidate Walk the Fire. G'walch was kept under tighter guard than any previous hopeful. If P'tre noticed the acid in the old man's eyes, he ignored it.

"This . . . *madwoman*"—P'tre spat the word with utter contempt—"dares claim kinship with me, with *him* . . ."

"I doubt she's even aware of G'walch's existence," K'ferrin said, his tone pleasant. "All she's claiming is your Lands."

That stopped the Warrior-Priest. He stared at the old man incredulously. "*All?*" he repeated. "A threat against me is a threat against the Faith, K'ferrin. That's hardly trivial."

K'ferrin slipped his hands under the sleeves of his robe, rubbing his aching arthritic joints surreptitiously. "Do you speak for the Faith now, P'tre? I had believed I was still the Keeper. That should come as news to my fellow Reverences." The old man was satisfied by P'tre's sudden discomfort. "You are the commander of our armies, not an interpreter of the will of God. Leave the Oracle to those who have been *born* to be entrusted with its care."

After a reluctant moment, P'tre bowed stiffly, more a slight jerk from the waist than a proper obeisance. K'ferrin watched in fascination as the muscles of the Warrior-Priest's mouth trembled, the strain to keep from snarling making the expression even more apparent than the actual act. "That has always been the trouble with Landed Priests," K'ferrin said calmly, and enjoyed how P'tre's face paled. "How can you serve God's divine will with your whole being when your body and mind are still chained to dirt?"

"My *dirt* supplies this city and your coffers with a good deal of money, goods and men, K'ferrin. You may pretend to disdain it, but we both know you can't live without it. And who would you have me give it to? A petty clan of Lords who will carve it up between themselves like the carcass of a deer? Another kinsman? Which one? Or, perhaps I should hand it over to the Council. Tell me, Reverence, just what would it gain me to lose my Lands?"

The Warrior-Priest's gray eyes were too bright and hungry. The Terhune clan was not of pure Citadel blood, they were not descended from one of the Ancient Families. They had risen within the ranks of the Citadel over centuries by interbreeding with the Families, until the tarnish on their bloodline was certainly distant and faint but not enough to satisfy P'tre's ambitions. Yet while the Landsblood he hated prevented P'tre's rise to the highest echelons of the Faith that he craved, it also gave him a rich and powerful domain of significant strategic value to the Oracular City. Only by giving up that Land for the formal recognition by the Council of Reverences would he ever be accepted into the heart of power.

Or if his bloodline delivered the One.

K'ferrin didn't hesitate to trample whatever hopes P'tre harbored. As long as he lived, K'ferrin would never allow his deadliest rival powers equal to his own.

"I have absolutely no interest in your Lands, P'tre," he said lightly, the lie falling so easily from his lips he nearly believed it himself. "As far as this woman's claim is concerned, compared to what you stand to gain if, as you believe, G'walch *is* the One, I say Land is dirt and dirt is trivial." Before Terhune could explode further, he added, "Besides, she's hardly the first who's made that claim, although I have to admit she's been the most original thus far. You've managed in the past to stave off any who dared claim rights of kinship to your Lands without invoking the Army of the Faith to stamp out heresy. Your brother inherited your father's penchant for freely spreading his excellent seed, which did result in a host of bothersome bastards left in his wake."

"My *half*-brother," Terhune corrected furiously, then made a visible effort to calm himself. "My father was a great man and true Warrior of the Faith whose only lapse of judgment was to have been seduced by a filthy Landsbitch. Any corruption of R'bert's blood came from her, not the Terhunes. My father paid for that one mistake by raising a half-breed idiot who returned his charity with betrayal. All of R'bert's mongrel progeny have been like him, wretched fools unworthy to step foot on my Lands, never mind lay claim to them."

"And where your splendid father practiced generosity toward his lesser blooded kin, you've been terribly busy lately making sure you stamp them out, haven't you?" K'ferrin said gently, but didn't bother to mask the steely menace behind his voice. "Along with any other Landsfolk who inconvenience you. A certain amount of Purging is necessary to properly maintain the fear of God and the one true Faith. Discipline earns respect. But despotism earns only hatred and rebellion. You're creating an atmosphere of hostility that can become quite dangerous if you choose to push the Landsfolk too far."

"You can't be saying you *fear* such rabble?" Terhune snarled. "They exist solely to serve the Faith, and should learn proper respect for their betters or be wiped out like the cattle they are. Or are you becoming sentimental in your old age, K'ferrin?"

"Your faith is commendable," K'ferrin responded with an indifferent shrug. "But don't confuse sentimentality with common sense. Until the One is come to lead his True Blooded Sons into the Blessed Lands, we need our lesser brethren. Or will you be the drudge to pull the plow and chop the wood? Overzealous hornets protecting their hive can drive cattle mad, and stampeding cattle can kill the farmer. A good farmer rids his fields of hornets' nests." He smiled tenderly, as if P'tre were a cherished lover. "Need I be rid of you?"

"You do not frighten me, old man." P'tre began pacing the room again, his hands twitching with methodical restlessness. "Hornets and cattle, drivel for children," he snapped, a vicious glitter in his eye. "You're getting old, K'ferrin. You have no heir. Your seed has shriveled and degenerated. That spineless fat cretin your line spawned wasn't worthy of even becoming the Word. Your behavior is already suspect and it would not take much more to bring a charge of heresy against you. When G'walch Walks the Fire, you and all the rest of your ilk will pay dearly for your blasphemous arrogance."

"Truly, I should be quaking in terror, P'tre," K'ferrin said, his voice again flat. "But fortunately any charge of heresy you could raise against me would never hold. You haven't friends enough, within or without the Citadel. Were I vindictive, I might take offense at the mere suggestion, and you might find yourself condemned to burn before the day is out for your absurd accusations."

P'tre's eyes narrowed. "You wouldn't dare," he hissed.

"I am indeed an old man, but I'm not senile. You can neither goad me into conflict out of anger, nor menace me into supporting you out of fear. Until I am dead, I will remain Keeper of the Oracle, and my word is still law. If your Lands are under threat, P'tre, you will have to cope with it like every other common Lord, and make do with your resources in Adalon. Your real estate problems are not the concern of the Faithful and you are forbidden to use the Army of the Faith as your private militia."

Although K'ferrin's voice had thinned from age, it was still a voice experienced to command, a reminder of the true power the frail old man possessed. He still knew how to use it, and had the satisfaction of observing P'tre flinch. He languidly stretched one bony arm toward Terhune, hand hanging limp from the wrist.

Terhune visibly trembled with fury as returned K'ferrin's stare, then dropped his gaze in feigned defeat. "I beg your forgiveness, Your Reverence," he said haughtily and went to one knee, leather creaking. Touching K'ferrin's fingertips as if the hand were covered in poison, he bent over it, his kiss missing by several inches.

"Of course, *Priest*," K'ferrin replied, emphasizing their positions.

P'tre straightened with a sour look, whirled around and departed.

K'ferrin sat thoughtfully for several moments before he rose and went into the inner rooms. A middle-aged man was hunched over a large desk laboriously inscribing meticulous letters onto parchment. He did not look up from his work.

"You heard, B'nach?"

"Yes, Grandfather," the man responded, still concentrating on the parchment.

"What an irritating fool that man is. Did you record it?"

B'nach glanced up in mild surprise. "Of course, Grandfather."

"I'll want it by evening bell," K'ferrin ordered.

B'nach meekly lowered his eyes, looking at his parchment in regret before he pushed it to one side. Replacing it with another, he began transcribing his scrawled notation into neat, legible script as K'ferrin paced the room slowly, hands clasped behind his back.

"Where the Hell is *Ashrael* anyway?" he muttered to himself.

"Ashmael," B'nach corrected him. He spoke without looking up. "It's a small coastal city on a chain of rocky islands in the White Sea, off the Northwestern Highland." K'ferrin stopped pacing to squint speculatively at his grandson. "I looked it up."

"Could her claim have any merit?"

B'nach shrugged, and spoke to the tip of his scritching quill. "The White Sea Islands have changed hands rather violently over the past decades, along with Purges here and there, so the records are unclear. But apparently there was a Lord of Ashmael who did have a daughter named Latticea. R'bert traveled quite extensively throughout the Lands. Theoretically, it is possible."

K'ferrin had resumed his measured pace. "God preserve us from narrow-minded zealots. Sometimes I deeply regret having had old R'ldan assassinated," he said indifferently, "Now, there was a man who knew how to negotiate through difficulties, not put his head down and bull his way through."

And R'ldan been good at it as well, too good, which of course was why he'd had to be removed. B'nach made no comment, head down as he concentrated. K'ferrin ignored him, speaking to himself.

"Poor neglected R'bert, passionate like his dear brother, but for earthly delights rather than sacred aspirations. He did have an annoying habit of cooling his ardor by thrusting his over-heated prick into any available nook and cranny. But I would have thought his taste ran more to peasant girls and sheep than highborn ladies." He sighed. "Then, who can say what passes for 'ladies' that far north?"

B'nach showed no reaction at all as he critically examined first his scribbled notes and then the neat lettering taking shape under his Quill. Nor had K'ferrin expected him to.

"Terhune will soon discover my informant," K'ferrin said, now addressing his grandson while pacing the room. "What happened to that Silver River woman?"

"She's still there."

"Surprising that lecherous bastard didn't take to her."

"She was too obvious, Grandfather." If B'nach was aware at the searching look the old man shot him, he disregarded it. "P'tre probably only keeps her on because he knows she's a spy. Any information she can give us is tainted, and for him to remove her would create a vacancy for someone less . . . detectable."

K'ferrin studied his grandson with appreciation, and more than a little regret. He might have been the One, they had come so close. But although there was a disturbing bent to his morals which the old man found useless, B'nach also had a sharp eye for the foibles of others, which made his opinions valuable. Without the blood connection, B'nach's existence might have been terminated long ago. As it was, he was allowed to spend his time in quiet research, at the price of services rendered to his grandfather's less than pious schemes.

B'nach kept his head lowered and his tone colorless, but K'ferrin had lived too long with the younger man not to recognize resentment and unhappiness in the set of his shoulders or in the words he left unspoken. He smiled, pleased.

"Then give me your advice, my astute young kinsman. How best can we replace her?"

B'nach sighed in resignation and sat back to look up at the

old man. "P'tre sees women as toys, things to be played with and thrown away. I doubt he even sees them as living human beings worthy of love." He ignored his grandfather's grimace, the two enemies not so different from each other. "To catch his attention, she would have to be someone who knew how to walk the fine line between arousing Terhune while effectively resisting him."

K'ferrin's eyebrows rose in mild surprise. "*Resisting* him?"

B'nach's tongue darted momentarily between his teeth, wetting his lips before he spoke. He kept his attention focused on a point somewhere over K'ferrin's shoulder, unwilling to look him in the eye, an habitual mannerism that never failed to irritate the old man, as K'ferrin suspected B'nach well knew.

"Someone who attracts his interest while making it clear she has no reciprocal interest in him. Terhune is drawn to a challenge. He would see a strong-willed woman the same way he plays chess; his opponents know he hates to lose and fear his rages when he does, but they dare not simply play less than their best. Men have been executed for the mistake of allowing him to win. A woman who requires exertion on his part to seduce would thus be considered valuable, not a lifeless thing to be soiled and discarded. Terhune might then conceivably be inspired to 'turn' her against us, which would facilitate more accurate communication."

B'nach bit off his words and dropped his gaze back to his work, his unpleasant analysis discharged.

K'ferrin regarded him, thoughtfully eying the balding patch on his grandson's head with distracted reflection. "Such a woman as you propose might indeed be effective. But would she not most certainly become a rival for his affections which might make D'nyel jealous?"

B'nach became very still, the skin of his balding head flushing. But when he looked up, his eyes were empty. "D'nyel is not Terhune's lover, so there would be no reason for her to be jealous."

K'ferrin nodded, satisfied more by his grandson's reaction than his assurances. "On the off chance she is, you can control her . . . passion, can you not?"

The lifeless expression didn't change, but the old man could sense the fury seething below the surface. "Of course, Grand-father."

K'ferrin gazed at him almost affectionately. "You occasionally make me proud of my blood, B'nach. Can you find such a person as you describe?"

"I shall do my best, Your Reverence," B'nach said sullenly.

9

While barely half the size of Abadayho, Myro was a pleasant city, a bit more chaotic, its citizens a bit more contentious and indolent. But neither did the city have the stink of fear about it. The Faith had less domination in Water Cross, not due to any administrative skill of its Lord, but to its distance and relative unimportance to the Oracular City. The Faith maintained their sajadas in Water Cross, and Lord C'ristan provided a healthy export of money, goods and acolytes. Unhappy Priests often meant an unpleasant visit from Terhune's army and a sharp decrease in the Land's treasury. Purges here were infrequent, local Priests preferring to absorb any unorthodox customs into official doctrine rather than attempting to stamp out heresy by force, amusing Antonya with their blatant hypocrisy.

C'ristan had ruled Water Cross for over twenty years with a light hand and a light heart, making him both scorned and beloved in his subjects' eyes. Moreover, he was sensible enough to know exactly where he stood in their favor, and as long as the palace was well stocked and he had freedom to do much as he pleased, he allowed his domains to roll along of their own accord. The people of Water Cross, especially her Guildsmen, well knew they could have worse for a Lord, and endeavored to keep him happy, a willing bird in his gilded cage.

The only fly in Lord C'ristan's ointment was his total lack of sons. He had so far exhausted three wives and was currently hard at work on a fourth, but the end result was a baker's dozen of daughters, as well as numerous noble bastards littering the countryside, all healthy and strong. All female. He may have been the only person left in Water Cross who hadn't accepted the fact that there was something quite faulty with his root.

Without a male heir, Water Cross would be carved up as he married his daughters off to the scheming local aristocracy, or sons of more powerful neighboring Lords. Sons-in-law had a nasty habit of squabbling over property boundaries, and such disputes usually left the real estate in question in less than pristine condition. Neither C'ristan nor his Guildsmen were eager for his daughters to marry.

He especially feared his rich, northern neighbor, Lord Vodos of Hadzida. Vodos's Lands of the Sheruben Valleys were twice the size of C'ristan's and encompassed nearly all of C'ristan's northern border. His capital nestled at the foot of the Prasios Mountains. Huge, fertile fields spread out from Hadzida's city walls for hundreds of hectares, the forests rich with game, vineyards heavy with grapes, the waterways providing trade and transport as well as abundant fish. Vodos had endeavored to marry his only son and heir to C'ristan's eldest daughter, to be rebuffed more from fear than contempt. C'ristan had then watched with growing alarm as Vodos made measured, deliberate plans to take by force what he could not gain by negotiation.

C'ristan's own family was not comforting him with whole-hearted support, either. As his daughters grew older, the palace became more of a fortress prison than a home. His captive princesses languished in various towers and rebellious moods, under lock and key to prevent any embarrassing elopements with ambitious courtiers or disastrous kidnappings by equally ambitious neighbors.

Like her brother, Lirda of Myro was a Defender, guarding Lord C'ristan's harem of impatient daughters much as a jealous *bouteillier* keeps watch over the collection of precious vintages growing ever more venerable. Lord C'ristan welcomed Antonya with good cheer if not open arms, since having his watchdog's brother on hand to help safeguard his daughters' unsullied reputations (if not actual virginity) was advantageous in the face of their increasingly mutinous tempers.

Lord C'ristan's palace sprawled across the summit of a hillside overlooking Crontan Bay, light sea breezes perfuming the air with the tang of salt. Wild broom flowers covered the dunes in bright yellow every spring. The courtyard garden of the palace keep was large and square, if plain, well-worn flagstone edged with herbs and flowers. Arched columns shaded the covered walks along the stone building, punctuated at even intervals by heavy wooden doors. Wisteria grew up the columns and over the balconies of the upper floors. Behind their screen, Antonya watched Kerrick as he practiced below. She was amused to see she was not the only spectator, a soft giggle or a flash of jewelry betraying the curious women peeping through the white and purple flowers heavy along the ornate balustrades.

It was the highlight of the women's day, watching Kerrick's daily routine. He was naked to the waist, loose linen pants clinging to his sweating body revealing the hard muscles underneath. His feet stirred up the dust in the slight breeze. Seemingly oblivious to the watchers above him, he stood in impossible positions for minutes on end, muscles quivering with the effort to remain still. Then his dark skin gleamed as he exploded into an intricate whirling motion, blade flickering around him. The complex movement ended in another position held immobile for long minutes.

Antonya leaned over the balustrade, craning her neck for a better view without caring who saw her.

"Despite the problems he's had, my brother *is* the best." Lirda's voice startled her. Antonya glanced around at the tall, dark-haired woman looking over her shoulder at the man below. There was an odd absence of pride in the woman's voice. "No one could have a better right hand."

"Indeed," Antonya agreed sincerely.

The big woman turned to look down her nose at Antonya, its aquiline shape and her mocking green eyes matching her brother's. She crossed her bare arms, elegant bracelets jingling. Her court dress and feminine perfume did not hide the strong muscles of her body.

"Indeed," Lirda echoed. She made no attempt to mask her dislike. It was all too obvious she felt her brother had made an unworthy choice. "Lady." She tagged on the title as an afterthought, the sneer in her voice not quite concealed.

Antonya simply raised one eyebrow at the woman and

turned her attention back to the man below. Kerrick's blade glittered in the sunlight, and they could hear the shuffle of his feet against stone, the soft grunt of exertion. Sweat dripped from his chin, his dark hair was plastered into wet curls around his head, yet he never blinked, his concentration absolute.

"The Guild of Defenders is much like any other Guild. We have our own practices and philosophy," Lirda said. "But Kerrick keeps a stronger vigilance on maintaining his discipline than most."

"Why?"

Lirda smiled bitterly. "Perhaps you should ask him yourself."

As if he heard her, Kerrick suddenly paused, staring up into the shadows hidden in the wisteria, frowning. He looked briefly annoyed, then returned to his ritual.

Antonya heard the taunt in Lirda's voice, an angry challenge lurking below the surface of congeniality. *No sense being baited into something I'll regret*, she thought. And wondered if she already had.

"Perhaps you're right," she said serenely, and slipped past the tall woman. Emerging into the garden, she blinked at the sudden pain as her eyes adjusted to the bright sunlight. She sat on a stone bench at the edge of the columned walkway, watching Kerrick openly as he continued with his practice while ignoring her. He went from simple stance, heavy sword held lightly, to a slow, stylized parry and thrust, then to faster and more complex movements.

Soon, his blade was flashing at an incredible speed she couldn't have believed controllable, his body contorting, his face a grinning mask of strain as he *fused* with the sword in its wicked dance. It leaped from hand to hand as if of its own volition, flickering around him with such precision that the slightest misstep would have left him seriously cut. Dust whipped around in eddies, the only sounds in the courtyard now the blade whispering in the air, Kerrick's soft, grunting breath, the slap of metal against flesh. The women above had hushed.

Suddenly, he froze, the sword held unwavering in the same position and stance that he had started from. He took one, slow inhalation, exhaled and lowered the weapon. Panting, he leaned with his weight against his knees, sweat running in rivulets down his skin.

"Bravo," Antonya said quietly. "That was quite beautiful."

Kerrick glanced up at her seriously. "It's not meant as a performance, Lady." Although there was no criticism in his voice, she felt rebuked.

Above them, leaves rustled. A high titter and whispers revealed that the hidden female audience was still watching.

"Then perhaps you should practice in a place a bit less . . . exposed," she said with a grin.

He shrugged and picked up an oiled cloth from a bench, carefully wiping the traces of dust from the steel blade. "My attention is on the ritual, the goal is to attain perfection. Whether there are eyes to watch me or not is irrelevant."

She perched on the stone seat, arms around her updrawn knees. "Eyes or no, it looked damned perfect to me," she teased.

He shook his head, annoyed. "To you, perhaps. To me, self-knowledge will always prevent me from ever achieving perfection."

"You strain to reach what you can never grasp—is that not the philosophy of frustration?" she asked lightly.

Finished cleaning the blade, he bowed to it before he picked up the scabbard and slid the sword back into it firmly. "Don't mock me, madam," he said softly.

Her humor fled immediately. "My apologies, Kerrick. It was not my intent to mock you."

He nodded, accepting her apology. "It isn't very mysterious. Attaining a goal is not always as important as the attempt. By reaching a little further beyond your true grasp any achievement can be made. This is true for all things, as you should know, my would-be Lady of Adalon."

He set the scabbarded weapon on the bench beside her, and walked to the tiny fountain at the center of the garden. With cupped hands he splashed water over himself to cool his body and cleanse it of sweat. Antonya studied the scabbard, tracing her finger along the incised pattern on its leather surface.

Out of the corner of her eye, she could see him watching her as he pulled on his shirt, leaving his jerkin to one side. He tucked the shirt into his breeches, buckled the sword belt and chain cincture around his waist, then walked back and hooked the scabbard and sword to his belt. His damp shirt stuck to his skin.

She leaned her head to one side, squinting to look up at him through the bright light. "Can you teach me this, Kerrick? How to use a blade, how to fight?"

He grinned, putting one foot onto the bench beside her and leaning his arms against his thigh. "I've been wondering how long it would take before you asked. Aye, I can teach you to defend yourself, at least. If that's what you want."

"I want my bloodrights, Kerrick. What do *you* want?"

She was skeptical he would tell her, and she had never asked him directly before. It surprised her when he answered promptly.

"Revenge."

"Against who?"

He smiled. "The Faith."

"Ah." She waited.

"My wife and son were murdered," he said calmly. "I married Rayme a year before I became an armsman for Lord Clodin of Thylas in Qarthia, a distant kinsman of Lord C'ristan's. I was still an apprentice under my Guildmaster, so we were living with her parents in Dunn, a small village near the border of Qarthia and Water Cross. I had gone to Thylas with my Guildmaster when her village was Purged. Even the local Priest was shocked—no one knew of any heresy that could possibly have been committed. My son was too young to be taken to the Citadel to serve the Faith. He was only three months old. So he was shot in his mother's arms. The man was an excellent archer, my wife and son both died by the same arrow."

He gazed at her coolly, as if the simple recitation of facts was neatly dissected from any feelings he might once have had.

"I'm sorry, Kerrick," she said softly.

"It happened a long time ago." His voice was indifferent, but she didn't believe he had forgotten his grief.

She eyed him thoughtfully. "So you believed my pretty tale after all?" she asked. "Is that why you chose to become my armsman instead of Lord Creskar's?"

He grinned, teeth white in the morning light. There was no amusement behind the smile. "Nay, madam. *That*, I'm afraid, was an impetuous act of total folly I will no doubt come to regret the rest of my increasingly reduced life." He shrugged. "It seems I still have far to go before I attain perfection."

10

B'nach returned a few days later, guiding a young woman into K'ferrin's offices. When the girl caught sight of the old man, she gasped and quickly bowed. The rough-spun cloth of her gown and the pallor of her skin confirmed her as a low-caste troglodyte living in the squalid warrens that riddled the fabric of the Citadel. But the swift, wide-eyed glance she gave K'ferrin told him more about her. Young, innocent and very pretty. The perfect bait to snare Terhune on his own fleshy hook.

The old man sat in his high, carved seat, and beckoned imperiously to them with a bony hand. "Come closer, my child."

The girl obeyed tremblingly.

"Tell me your name," K'ferrin said gently.

The girl bobbed a quick curtsy before she answered. "Tannah, Your Reverence."

"Ah, Tannah. I have heard you are a devoted follower of the Word. Would you serve the Servants of the Oracle with all your heart and faith?"

He heard her quick indrawn breath before she replied, urgently sincere, "Indeed, Your Reverence." K'ferrin smiled at the simple ambition shining in her eyes. Service to one of the Great Reverences would mean a substantial step up in one's fortunes, especially someone with few other options.

He maintained his gentle smile although the girl kept her eyes down in deferential respect. "There is one I suspect of being a traitor, here within the sanctuary of the Citadel itself, but my suspicions are not enough to remove him. I must have proof he is a danger to the Faith, to the Oracle itself."

The girl gazed up at him, almost hypnotized, as wary as a

rabbit quivering beside its hollow, ready to bolt either way. "I need your help, but you must have the strength to abide this creature's unholy company, to watch him carefully for me where I cannot. This person is a most base man, and you may be asked to do things you wish not to do, yet present a face that says otherwise. Are you a virgin, child?"

Her eyes widened even further, and she swallowed. "Yes, Your Reverence," she whispered. "But I am betrothed—"

"Ah," K'ferrin cut her off, half turning from her. "Then I cannot ask you to forfeit your betrothed . . ."

"But, sir . . ." Close to tears, she reached one hand toward K'ferrin without touching him—that far he knew she dared not go. "My devotion to the Faith comes first . . ."

"To root out this evil, you must descend into its depths, wallow in its filth and pretend to enjoy it. You would have to submit to such vile wickedness that you would most certainly sacrifice your virginity, perhaps even risk your very life. It is too much to ask, and yet—" his voice faltered, and he placed one hand over his heart as if struggling with pain, "—and yet I fear the need of the Faith is so urgent . . ."

She creased her brow slightly, a charmingly naive look of concern. It was her holy duty; he had convinced her and now he waited for her to eventually come to that conclusion herself. *Hurry it up, you stupid little bitch, I haven't all day . . .*

"I would serve Your Reverence, and do whatever is necessary."

About time. He stood painfully, his age apparent in his stiff gait, and came quite close to her. She had the soft curves in her face and body of a girl still very young, and the sweet, almost cinnamon smell of a woman.

"You will be tested many times as you serve the Oracle," he said, looking down at her tenderly. "Are you sure you can hide your feelings for the sake of the Faith?"

She nodded, not understanding but eager to convince him she did. "Yes, Your Reverence."

His thin, bony hand slid up under her blouse until it held her young breast cupped in his palm. He rolled the nipple between his fingers, feeling it become hard. She stiffened under his touch.

From behind her, K'ferrin caught B'nach's look of disgust

as his grandson crossed his arms over his chest, his head held to one side to avoid watching the scene. The old man ignored him.

"Is this the way you will act when he who does not love you for your goodness and purity as I do touches you in this manner?" he rebuffed her as he fondled her other breast.

She shot him an intense, burning look he couldn't decipher. Then her body relaxed under his touch, although she was trembling, and she leaned slightly into his caress with her shoulders pulled back. He felt her hips move against his own thin groin in a tentative and charmingly naive fashion.

"No, Your Reverence," she murmured submissively.

He dropped his hands and resumed the guise of a kindly, grandfatherly figure once more. "Then B'nach will give you all you need to know, how you should conduct yourself to gain this evil man's confidence. We are depending on you, my child—do not fail us."

She bowed meekly and was led out of the room. While he waited for his kinsman to return, K'ferrin paced the room slowly, hands clasped behind his back. The look she had given him had disturbed him; a flash of malice he hadn't expected, not the look of a frightened, helpless girl. Perhaps it was only proof of the steel B'nach had told him the girl would need to hazard snagging Terhune's interest.

B'nach closed the door behind him and stood against it, waiting.

"She seems an excellent choice," K'ferrin said finally.

"Thank you, Your Reverence," B'nach said coldly.

He glanced sharply at the younger man, amused by his grandson's disgust. He enjoyed being able to control B'nach without completely destroying him. The fat cretin could still be useful, in so many ways. "I find I have been aroused by your young find," he said, although it was not the girl that aroused him. K'ferrin had never found female flesh tempting, even when it was young and as sexless as a boy's. "Summon my favorites. Even an old man must have his release, aye, my kinsman?"

The scribe could not conceal the revulsion in his eyes as he replied, "As you wish, Grandfather."

11

"Sweet Mother of God," Antonya groaned as she hefted the broadsword. Her arms and back ached. Her legs ached. She couldn't think of a part of her body which didn't ache. Three weeks into her lessons and she was already regretting the desire to learn the art of swordsmanship. She had always considered herself to be physically strong and athletic, but Kerrick had pushed her to limits she hadn't known she had. "This is *not* quite what I had in mind, Kerrick. Just how well do you really expect me to be able to fight with this thing if I tire after only a few minutes of waving it about?"

"Come now, Lady." Kerrick laughed. "These are very well-balanced blades, surely you cannot blame it on Lord C'ristan's fine steel. You are doing well enough, you need only to build up your endurance."

After two hours of practice, she was breathing heavily, and wiped the sweat from her forehead on her sleeve. For all his size, Kerrick stood lightly on his feet, spinning the heavy sword in his hand by the hilt like a toy, waiting.

"I'd rather we'd practiced with my knives again, quite frankly," she told him.

Kerrick shook his head to clear the sweat from his eyes, droplets spraying from the dark ends of the curls around his face. "If I didn't constantly growl at you to make you wear them, you'd as soon leave them behind as not."

"They're not very comfortable." Even now, they were heavy on her forearms, the sweat under the leather making her skin itch.

"Neither is death."

She grinned up at him, enjoying herself in a perverse way. It was much like Father Andrae's study, wanting the long tangle of equations or the wriggling lines of ancient script to yield up their secrets without the tedious work. Rebellious then, rebellious now. "At least I'm better at throwing knives, and I'm never going to be any good with this sword at all," she argued. "Doesn't it make more sense to practice with what I'm good at?"

Kerrick frowned. "An enemy is not always going to generously offer you a fight on your own terms. 'Oh, pardon me, I'll just wait here while you run and get your little knives, shall I?' You must learn to fight with what you have. Tomorrow, perhaps we'll try six-foot pigstickers, and the day after we'll graduate to knocking each other over the head with rocks. At the moment"—he gestured with his own blade, several feet long—"it's these lovely old-fashioned three-hundred-pound glaives. Do try to keep your guard up, madam."

She sighed, and held the sword up awkwardly with both hands, cringing as Kerrick swung at her. As his blade cut down, she caught it and, twisting with an effort, forced it to her left while stepping to the right. As the metal seared off her own, she sidestepped into his guard, trying to swing back at his middle. The shock of steel clashing against steel jarred her arms as his counterfeint slammed her own blow to one side, the blade nearly flying out of her hands.

Hurriedly, she stepped back, nearly falling.

Kerrick grimaced, disappointed. "The idea is not only to use the power of my attack to deflect itself, but to do so in a way you can make an opening without leaving yourself exposed."

Her arms hurt from the jarring blow, her anger flaring up against the pain. "Damn it, I'm *trying* to, Kerrick!" she snapped, rubbing at the leather sheaths on her forearms that held her throwing knives. "But just how the Hell do you expect me to defeat someone twice my size and four times my strength?"

His scowl hardened. "Do not be misled into believing my size is necessarily an advantage."

She looked at him, confused.

"The man who depends on his size and strength is more than a fool—he is often a dead fool. He defeats less skilled opponents easily by sloppy fighting, which amounts to little more than bludgeoning them to death with a club. But when he meets his real match, he forgets his size can handicap him as well as help."

"Of course. Being the biggest and meanest fellow around can be a real disability," she scoffed.

"I am indeed nearly twice your size and have three times your weight to hold me back. You've also an advantage you have already used, although you don't understand it, it seems."

"What?"

"You're a woman."

At that she burst out laughing. "And you had just finished explaining so well how chivalry is a misguided expectation."

He was unconcerned. "A woman is unexpected. There will always be a moment of hesitation which isn't chivalry, madam, merely surprise. In that moment, you have the advantage. Also your reflexes are faster than most men's, by simple virtue of your sex. Some men are as fast, and some women are as slow, but on the whole, you have a fine edge of speed that my size *and* my sex can't match. I've seen you, Lady. You're fast and quite agile, far more so than I."

She regarded him curiously. "Have you ever been beaten by a woman in a fight?"

"Aye," he said calmly. "Any number of times."

"That doesn't bother you?"

He grinned. "There is only one woman who has ever gotten the better of me in a fight, and that is my elder sister, Lirda. She regularly beat me black and blue as we were growing up, until the day I thrashed the blessed shit out of her. We called it even after that." He hefted the sword speculatively. "I was fortunate, madam. My sister taught me never to allow myself the luxury of considering my size an asset, or to disregard the abilities of a woman. It has held me in good stead on a few occasions."

"Fine, point taken." she scowled, still rubbing at her sore forearms. "Literally."

He paused. "Remember to use anything and everything you have, Lady. There is no such thing as a 'fair fight.' The only fair fight is the one you survive."

She was sore and bruised, tired of listening to Kerrick's endless lecturing, wishing for a good soak in the women's bath and a massage to ease the aches. "All right, all right. Are we finished yet with the lessons today?" she demanded.

His eyes narrowed; then the point of his weapon snapped

up at her. "Quite," he said tightly, and slashed at her.

Surprised, she jumped back, staring as the blade whipped with deadly force through the spot she had just vacated. She backed away from him as he swung again, jerking her face aside as the point snicked by a fraction of an inch from her eye.

"This is no game, girl," he hissed. He brought his blade arcing toward her just as she shifted her stance and desperately tried to parry. Kerrick caught her blade easily, whipping it around his own. As it slid to one side, drawing her along with it, the tip of his sword flicked a small cut on her cheek.

She gasped, stepping back and nearly dropping the sword as her free hand flew to her face. When she pulled it away there was blood on her palm. She stared at it in disbelief before looking up. He grinned at her humorlessly.

"Kerrick, what the Hell are you doing?"

"I am creating a Lady worthy of my service. Dead or alive, it makes no difference to me," he said. And lunged. She barely managed to strike the blade away, trying to sweep the edge of her sword back against Kerrick, but the blade never touched him. She stepped back, panting hard.

"You could have killed me by now, Kerrick," she gasped.

"And if you don't start fighting any better than you are now, I shall!" he roared. She caught a glimpse of clenched teeth as his blade hissed by her ear. Half ducking, half throwing her blade up to fend him off, she felt a slice of pain in her arm as the tip nicked her. From the corner of her eye she could see a spray of red.

Her fear was engulfed by a sudden icy anger as she counterattacked, lunging at him, her arms in agony. Her chest burned as she struggled to breathe. He slipped by her clumsy attack easily, and laughed at her. Then he hammered a series of blows at her, nearly driving her to her knees, forcing her to retreat. She nearly fell, tripping over her own feet, running backward to avoid him.

"Good! Come for me, brave child," he taunted.

She had no breath left to reply, feeling a strange, calm indignation settle over half of her while the other half was shrieking with pure terror.

His blade snapped at her, circling down on hers. She caught

it on the hilt, grunting as she threw him back with all the strength she had. It was as if she were attempting to move a mountain, but she managed to force him to step back before she jumped away, trying to keep her distance.

He stepped in with another parry, the tip flying again for her face. Instinctively, she threw up one arm as her sword dropped lower. His blade bit into the leather around her forearm that sheathed her small knives, only the flat of the dagger's blade preventing his edge from sinking into her flesh. His steel hissed against the small throwing knife, then snagged on the torn leather.

In a desperate effort, she staggered back, throwing him off balance as she dragged him down with his blade. She swung her own heavy sword futilely at his legs with the last of her strength, forcing him to hop away from her. As she felt his blade jerk free, she let her own go altogether. It spun off along the floor as she jumped in the opposite direction.

He lurched, seeking his balance. As she leapt, she could see Kerrick starting to turn to see behind him where she had gone, his blade swinging around with him. She kicked out as she hit the floor and rolled, hitting him squarely behind the knee with one foot. Then she squatted behind him as he staggered. Flipping one of the throwing knives into her palm, she threw it, hitting him obliquely behind the other knee. The aim was off, the hilt rather than the blade striking him, but there was enough force in the blow to kick his other leg out from under him. Immediately, her second knife replaced its twin in her hand.

As he crashed heavily to his knees, she jumped onto his back, wrapping her arms around his muscular neck, pressing the point of the small blade against the skin under his chin, forcing his head back on his neck.

He froze, waiting.

It took her several huge gasps of air before she could force the words out. "Drop it . . . damn you . . . or I swear . . . I'll cut your frigging throat!" She panted, sweating, every muscle trembling.

His sword clattered on the floor as he let it go. She could feel the stubble on his throat scratching against her arms as he chuckled. He spread his hands in mock defeat.

"I am at your mercy, madam," he said happily. "What is

your next move? Release me? I may pick up my weapon and come for you again, and I doubt you could stand much more. Frankly, I would advise you to kill me now while you still can."

She let her arm drop away from his throat, knife hanging limply from her hand as she sagged against his back, her head against his shoulder. "I'll take my chances," she said, and slid down his back to sit heavily on the floor, the fabric of her sweat-soaked shirt clinging to her skin.

He got to his feet slowly, bent to pick up his sword and turned, pressing the point against her chest. "*Never* take that kind of chance unless you have nothing to lose," he said seriously.

She looked down at the blade held gently against her heaving ribs. "While you're at it, would you mind retrieving my knife as well? I think it bounced off over in that direction."

He laughed, and slid the sword back into its sheath. Touching the spot under his chin where her knife had pricked him, he rubbed a spot of blood between his fingers pensively. As he went to recover her knife, she inspected her own wounds. The long scratch just below her shoulder was minimal. She pressed her palm against the open cut bleeding on her cheek. It was small, but painful.

"That hurt," she said, scowling as he handed her the knife.

"Hmm," Kerrick said, pursing his lips. He bent down to take her chin in one hand, turning her head to examine the cut. "It may have been a little deeper than I'd intended. You will live to fight another day, Lady. And I trust *now* you will consider these lessons in a more serious light. Failure on the field is permanent."

She glowered at him, then lay back on the floor, stretching out with her arms flopping weakly over her head. "You bastard," she murmured. "You could have bested me at any time. I didn't beat you."

"Nay, madam!" he protested. "You bested me, indeed. You found a weakness. You did the unexpected. You made an opportunity for yourself to fight me on your own terms, not mine, with your knives. You did quite well."

She touched her fingers to her cheek and inspected the tacky blood on her fingers. It was dark and already congealing. "Fine," she said. "Tomorrow, let's give the rocks a try instead."

He laughed.

12

B'nach heard the music of D'nyel's tenor piquoro, her favorite wind reed, through the door. Quietly as not to disturb her, he slipped inside, leaned against the door and closed his eyes, allowing himself to sink into the melody. She could produce double and sometimes triple harmonic notes coaxed lovingly from the simple carved wood, playing melodic runs in sweet tremolos that left echoes in the depths of his gut. When the song ended, she placed the wind reed down carefully in front of her.

"Did you like that one, B'nach?" she asked without looking at him. He smiled wryly and crossed the room to sit beside her.

"Very much," he said and waited for her to look up at him.

Tall and slender, with long fingers and limbs, her skin shone like rich dark sable, oiled smooth, her sheer white gown emphasizing the deepness of her color. He studied her profile: a broad forehead curving down to a nearly aquiline nose, which if a little more pronounced would have ruined the beauty of her features. Jet hair, pulled back sharply from her face, then billowed out and down her back in unconstrained abandon. Her full lips curved into a smile, revealing perfect teeth, the lashes of her eyes slowly rose, and he waited for the shock, the strange, tingling rush he had each time she looked at him. Almond-shaped eyes, lined lightly with kohl, were a startling sea-green, pure and clear.

She gazed at him seductively, then threw her head back, laughing.

"B'nach," she admonished, "you always have that same expression on your face when you come into my rooms. Why do you look like a little boy longing for candy, when you know that I am yours?"

The brief sweep of adrenaline passed, leaving his knees watery, and he sat down next to her, helping himself to her saturke fruit brandy.

"Mine?" he said, his voice free of any bitterness. "You belong to no one but yourself, D'nyel." He drank to hide his feelings. "Allow me the pleasure of admiring your physical beauty for the fleetest of moments before I need deal with the entire person, your convoluted mind and all your devious, amoral plots."

"Well," she remarked, unhurt by his assessment. " 'Amoral'? At least you didn't call me 'immoral.' "

"A split-hair's worth of difference, dearest heart."

She chuckled, unconcerned.

"What of your grandfather? And Tannah?"

He nodded, staring at his brandy. "All went as you said it would. He found her"—B'nach smiled bitterly—"an 'excellent choice.' But he's no fool. He'll see through her sooner than P'tre Terhune."

"I don't think so. Not immediately, and by then . . ." She smiled.

"D'nyel, has it ever occurred to you: P'tre thinks she spies on the old man, and he thinks she spies on Terhune for him. She, in turn, reports to us on both of them. Who else might have reason to use her, for information on us?"

D'nyel's eyes sparkled, and she leaned to kiss him lightly. "Even paranoia has its limits," she assured him. "And we have each other to watch our backs."

He snorted. "You depend on me for my inherited advantages. I depend on you for your ability to manipulate the Sectors against each other. Where does survival leave off and parasitism begin?"

She regarded him with amusement. "You are in a particularly glum mood tonight, sweet scribe. What *is* the matter?"

"Tannah," he snapped. "She's a child barely past puberty, still a virgin! What kind of person will she become after all this? Can't we at least spare the innocent?"

"Innocent?" To his discomfort, D'nyel began to laugh, an ungentle, derisive sound. "Sometimes I truly forget about you, B'nach. You still believe all that crap you were brought up with. Perhaps you *should* have Walked the Fire."

He turned away, his clenched jaw twitching. She had been his downfall, his descent into the Hell of her seductive embrace. She leaned over to kiss him and in spite of himself, he began to respond, hating himself for it. "Tannah is no innocent," she whispered, biting his ear delicately. "If she's a virgin, I'm an albino."

He pulled away to stare at her. "Then how is she to pass herself off as one with Terhune?"

D'nyel stroked his face lightly. "You naive, foolish man," she murmured. "Any woman with enough to lose or enough to gain can become a virgin again and again. Most men never know the difference."

"Terhune will," he said grimly.

"Yes, he would," she conceded. "But even that isn't impossible. A tuck of skin grafted here and there, a little wriggling and moaning, a spot of blood to mark his victory and Terhune will have his virgin."

He took her arms away from his shoulders, pushing her gently away. She subsided, a smug look on her face. "You did it?" he asked.

"Of course," she said proudly. "I gave her a good dose of poppy essence before I did my little needlepoint, treated the wound with a simple plaster of wild mallow root and it was healed in a week. I'm very good, B'nach. No one but Terhune would ever think to look, and he won't be checking for scars. The hardest part was keeping that little slut from ruining my hard work before its time."

By now, B'nach had his head in one hand, shielding his eyes. "I have trouble believing your handiwork was to spare another innocent child, D'nyel, much as I admire your skill. Wouldn't it have been easier just to find a real virgin?"

"Virgins are far more plentiful than a woman daring enough to take on P'tre Terhune. Tannah grew up in the warrens hard and fast, she has the experience and ruthlessness to know how to survive where your tender young virgins would never last an hour. She's as hard as your grandfather's heart, B'nach," D'nyel said, "which is exactly what we need. Oh, she's a talented enough actress to blubber like a child and weep copious tears when Terhune knocks her about, but I happen to know she has a lusty appetite for that sort of thing. I do so like to see people enjoy their work, don't you?"

He covered his face with both hands now, rubbing at his unshaven skin, feeling much older than he was.

"She's ideal for us, my love, a brilliant spy. She can sketch faces accurately; she's as talented as a First Rank Scribe, she can remember and describe the look of a place, the smell, the feel, so well you would think you lived there yourself."

He dropped his hands, smiling ironically. "But, D'nyel, I *do* live there," he said. "We *all* live there. What's the point?"

She *tsk*ed, as if to a slow child. "To kill your enemy is simple, but to control your enemy and make him serve your purposes takes more than a knife or poison. It requires information, as much as you can get. And isn't control what you and I both seek?"

"No," he said flatly. "That is what *you* seek. All I want is a little peace from these constant plots and conspiracies."

She examined his face, then presented him with what he knew full well was only a mask of childish hurt pride. "The only thing?"

He gazed at her, trying to keep his expression unreadable. "Not the only thing," he said. "I want you."

He held himself still while she surveyed him appraisingly. He held no illusions about himself. He was middle-aged and balding. His eyesight was fading, and his belly showed signs of increasing girth brought on by aging and lack of exercise. Worse, he knew he was a failure, in the eyes of the Citadel, in his grandfather's eyes, and most of all in his own. Finally, her gaze rose to his face.

"It might surprise you, B'nach," she said, her voice low and throaty. "My feelings for you are very intense. You are not the most attractive man nor the most skilled. But you have not lost that unique quality that attracted me to you all those years ago, made me stay long after I'd done what I'd been sent to do. Other lovers may be a necessary means to an end, but I desire no one but you, my love."

He smiled. "My current political connections notwithstanding."

She was unembarrassed. "Of course. Your position has much to do with it, B'nach. Power is a strong aphrodisiac."

"I have no power, D'nyel, I'm merely another of your tools," he said softly, the ache deepening in the pit of his stomach.

"Indeed, my darling." She kissed him lingeringly, her sinewy arms around his neck, sharp fingernails skimming gently over his back. "And I find the greatest pleasure in putting you to good use."

He took her gently down to the pillows. "Let us hope our partnership is a long and profitable one, then, D'nyel," he whispered against her cheek. "I very much dislike the thought of you ever becoming a liability rather than a confederate."

He felt her body stiffen momentarily, and he was gratified by her reaction to his unexpected, and quite uncharacteristic, threat. Inwardly, he sighed, pained. The vigilance could never be relaxed, not for even the briefest of moments.

Not with anyone.

13

"But *HOW?*"

Lord C'ristan couldn't hide the anxiety in his voice. He sprawled in his chair, the long, lean body beginning to turn soft. He was still handsome, despite the lines etched in his face from the troubles of the past few years. He fingered his worry beads, although Antonya doubted he used them to count prayers, as he stared at her with a mix of eagerness and doubt.

His wife sat apart from them, an exhausted lump of lace and silk as she breast-fed C'ristan's latest contribution to his growing harem of daughters. His eldest daughter, Verbena, attended her stepmother, a woman only slightly older than herself. Long past the age she could have expected to marry, Verbena eyed the infant with open envy and shot spiteful glances in her father's direction.

Two other daughters played draughts quietly under the watchful eye of the Defender Lirda. A fourth curled up with a vellum book in her skirts as she covertly sketched Kerrick's profile with a piece of oiled charcoal. The girl gazed at him longingly as he leaned against one wall with his arms crossed on his massive chest and studiously ignored her.

A gaunt, long-faced woman with iron-gray hair pulled back severely lounged at ease in another chair at a discreet distance, but listening carefully. Dressed in men's leathers, longdagger at her side, Jezral was a fellow Defender, one of the tall, pale-eyed warrior women of the frozen North, a rocky highland not too distant from the islands of the White Sea. She had hired on two years before as an ordinary armswoman to satisfy Lord C'ristan's ever growing urgency to keep his daughters safely unmarried. C'ristan had offered her a permanent position in his service several times, and while she had promised to give it serious consideration, she had yet to accept his proposal. Most likely, Antonya suspected, Jezral could not quite imagine herself locked into a lifetime of playing nursemaid.

Behind Jezral, a stocky man with a ragged shock of white in his dark hair from an old wound leaned against the back of her chair, watching silently. Sarnor was no Defender, nor of any Guild, his lack of aristocratic blood an inflexible barrier to loftier stations. As an unwanted child born into squalid poverty, he'd been sold by his parents to be hammered into a mercenary before he was even old enough to lift a blade. He'd earned his freedom decades ago, and now selectively bought his own recruits from the parents of other low-caste bastards littering the Lands. His was a cold, hard profession with no sentimental illusions of glory. No offers to swear noble service would be given or expected. Lord C'ristan loathed the necessity of bringing common mercenaries into his House, but paid Sarnor and his men well to keep watch on the northern borders.

"I haven't enough soldiers for a battle against Vodos, nor money enough to hire them," C'ristan was complaining. He sighed, the beads in his hands clacking. "Vodos has plenty of unmarried daughters. All I would need is a son, just *one*, to marry into his family and all my problems would be solved." He glanced reproachfully at the newborn infant. His wife ignored him, but Verbena stared back at him acidly.

"Don't blame the field if the corn you sow is bad, Father," she snapped.

Antonya watched as he flinched, his beads clicking faster. "I hold nothing against daughters, it's not their fault," he said rapidly, more to Verbena than to her. "But I can't change custom; my barons and Guildsmen could never accept a woman as heir to my Lands . . ." His voice trailed off as Antonya smiled.

"Really, Father?" Verbena said tightly.

"Not unless you could hold it, Verbena," he tried to mitigate. "Against *Vodos*? My barons would not support you in a war they had no hope of winning. Before my body was even cold, you'd find yourself packed off as a captive bride to that carbuncled son of his . . ."

"Rather than remaining a captive virgin here . . ." she said hotly.

"Which is why I'm proposing that you strike at him first before he strikes against you," Antonya cut in sharply, before the discussion could deteriorate into an all too familiar family squabble. "Now." The quarrel died abruptly, although the hostility remained thick.

"But *how* . . . ?" C'ristan repeated dejectedly.

"True, you haven't enough men, nor horse for that matter," Antonya said. "So the first thing to do is send an envoy to Lord Elotin in Medebah, offer him or one of his sons betrothal to one of your daughters in exchange for soldiers and horse."

C'ristan blanched, but before he could answer, Verbena retorted, "Not me!"

Any daughter of C'ristan's married into the tribes of the Nine Steppes would find life primitive, squalid and barbaric. Elotin was Lord of a hot, dusty and barren realm on the edge of desolate southern wastelands, and Medebah too small to call a city, just another isolated village built of shabby mud-brick like any other dotting the arid land of his domains. Barely more than a tribal chieftain, the only wealth or power the Lord of Medebah could boast of was the horde of unruly desert horsemen he used to occasionally raid along C'ristan's borders and the wealthier Lands of Dothinia in the east.

Lord C'ristan's brow wrinkled with anger; his daughters would marry whoever their father commanded them to. The four older daughters watched him in alarm, none of them harboring any desire to wed Lord Elotin or his sons. "No," Antonya agreed quickly. "Not you." She nodded at the suckling infant. "Affiance one of your babies. She will be too young to leave home for years, giving you time to work out other arrangements."

His anger abated. "I don't know why I agreed to even listen to this scheme of yours," C'ristan said gloomily. "Even with Elotin's great swarm of unwashed riffraff, we still wouldn't have enough men to stand against Vodos's troops. His men are professionals, organized and well equipped. Elotin would be more encumbrance than help. We'd never take Hadzida."

"Indeed," Antonya said. "That's why we are going to raise a big, noisy army and march it straight toward Kulteph on his northeastern border instead of Hadzida."

C'ristan said nothing, his mouth drawn down in deep lines of doubt. Kerrick stirred, and Antonya caught his puzzled frown. No doubt, Jezral and Sarnor wore similar expressions of skepticism.

"Why?" C'ristan asked finally. "It's true, Kulteph is small enough that we might raise enough men and horse to take her. But we'd never hold her. As soon as Vodos arrived to defend Kulteph, we'd be driven back. And an attack on Kulteph would certainly give Vodos enough justification to press his defense all the way to Myro."

"Exactly," Antonya said. "As soon as Vodos knew Kulteph was under attack, he *would* march his troops out of Hadzida. If he thought the threat against Kulteph was large enough, probably most of them. He knows you would have to have *all* your troops at Kulteph, leaving nothing in reserve to strike against Hadzida." Lord C'ristan stared at her, open-mouthed. "A suicidal attack against Kulteph would be too much of a challenge for Lord Vodos not to respond in force. Once he recovered Kulteph, he'd have the bulk of his army already in motion to sweep down into Myro and finish you off once and for all."

Lord C'ristan looked as if he were about to faint.

"Or so he would think," Sarnor said behind her, his raspy voice curious and amused. Antonya didn't glance away from C'ristan, but was pleased the mercenary had caught on.

"Or so he would think," she agreed.

"Well, he would think rightly," C'ristan protested. "I

haven't the men or horses to attack either Kulteph *or* Hadzida!"

"But you do have plenty of women and cattle," Antonya said calmly.

"Women and cattle? *What?*"

"We don't have to actually attack Kulteph. It just has to look like we are about to. Put women into armor, drape enough cows with harness, and from a distance it looks remarkably like a battalion. Surround them with enough real soldiers and horses on the outside, it'll pass even closer inspection. March the entire rowdy lot with banners waving and war cries and feet stamping up the dust, and by the time it gets within sight of Kulteph, I'd expect Lord Vodos to already be there to greet you.

"In the meantime, we will emplace your troops in every town and village from here to Hadzida, ready to strike while she's undefended. By the time Vodos realizes he's facing an army of maids and cowherds, your real army will take Hadzida hard and fast and cut off any escape into the Prasios Mountains. Then set Elotin's horde loose behind us. Let them burn crops and loot villages as they please, have a good time. Lord Vodos will find it difficult getting through that mayhem to Hadzida. By then, the city *and* the Sheruben Valleys will be ours."

"And all his Lands mine," C'ristan breathed, momentarily excited by the vision she had painted.

"No, your Lordship," Antonya said sharply. "His Lands will be *ours*. You will have secured the future and safety of your own domains, using my strategies. I need Lord Vodos and the Sheruben Valleys for my own designs."

C'ristan slumped back in his chair, his glum mood restored. "And if it doesn't work?"

"Then you lose," Antonya said calmly. "Instead of Lord Vodos invading Myro, taking your family hostage and executing you next year, he'll do it this year."

C'ristan glanced around at his family and armsmen helplessly before he scowled, worry beads clicking at a furious pace.

"Shit," he said sourly.

Antonya grinned, knowing he had just agreed.

C'ristan quickly found he had a few other surprises in store as well. While they waited for an answer from Lord Elotin, Jezral lost little time offering to lead the women's army of cattle against Kulteph. Sarnor, along with half a dozen of his bonded armsmen, offered Antonya his service and men, bored mercenaries eager for a fight. Kerrick had insisted both Jezral and Sarnor as well as his mercenaries swear their loyalties directly to the Lady Antonya Terhune of Adalon and Ashmael in a formal oath binding them to her as their sovereign Lady. As a woman of minor but noble blood, Jezral deliberated the requirement briefly, then shrugged and swore service as Antonya's Defender as a matter of routine.

Sarnor, on the other hand, had been amused and his younger armsmen astonished. Paid mercenaries were a necessary evil, guildless foreigners and outcasts tolerated only because they were useful. To swear them as armsmen of Adalon would not only make them full citizens of that Land, once Antonya had reclaimed it, but give them the prestige of full Guild rights. Yet Sarnor well understood that Antonya could not offer them money. Until they took Hadzida, their wages would still be paid by Lord C'ristan. Sarnor swore his oath with thick irony.

Although Landless and impoverished, Antonya had begun to accrete a small company of armsmen in her own name, important if she was to be accepted by the Landsfolk as a true blooded noblewoman. Nor were they the last of the defections, as Antonya found when she spoke with the Lady Verbena privately. Antonya had worried her proposals would shock the girl's gentler nature.

But Lady Verbena accepted with almost impatient irritation, feminine scruples more vicious than delicate. She was eager to join in the battle and whip up her sisters into a true fighting force of Amazons. She had several pragmatic ideas of her own which astonished Antonya as much for their brutality as their creativity.

When she finally managed to escape the young woman's ardent declarations of bloodthirsty support, Antonya sought out Kerrick. As she expected, she found him in the stable grooming the bay.

"Do you think me still a madwoman?" She perched on the edge of the stall, holding out bits of the apple she had stolen from the kitchens toward the bay's inquiring muzzle.

"Unquestionably," he said as he briskly rasped the curry-comb over the bay's hide, stripping away the last of the horse's winter coat in a flurry of shedding hair. Tufts of horsehair stuck to the sweat on his bare chest. "Your latest preposterous scheme is quite likely to get us all killed as well. Wherever did you learn your battle tactics, madam, is what I'd like to know."

"The Abbot's curriculum included more than merely pious theology. I have studied history, Kerrick, which abounds in object lessons on war and killing."

"Although I'd venture few that included such an imaginative use of cattle and maid servants."

"But you *will* support me in this campaign?" Antonya insisted, worried.

He turned to look at her, picking the fuzz out of the teeth of the currycomb. "Madam," he scolded, "I am your Defender and your First Chosen. I have vowed to follow you to the ends of the earth and into the depths of Hell, if that's where you should lead. However, I may curse you every step of the way, you understand."

She laughed, relieved. "No doubt yours will not be the only voice to turn the Devil's ears blue on my account." The lizard adjusted its claws tacked to her skin and she pushed the bay's nose away as it nibbled inquisitively at the movement under her shirt. "What's your opinion of Sarnor?"

"A good man," Kerrick said promptly, stroking the comb across the bay's neck on the other side of the big animal's withers. "He'll be as loyal as a paid mercenary is ever likely to be, noble oath or no. His armsmen respect him. Those who buy their freedom from him tend to stay on. He's quick to judge a situation, calculate a response and act without undue reliance on orders from his superiors."

"But not too . . . independent?"

"Give him a loose enough leash, he'll do well. Hem him in with a lot of meticulous details, he'll chafe."

"Hmmm." She frowned. "You know Jezral the best."

"A little before my time. But Lirda speaks well of her, although they're both fed up with baby-sitting Lord C'ristan's brood. Like as not, Jezral was thinking of leaving when you

appeared with your audacious designs, and the sheer reckless-
ness of it appeals to her. She's not as eager to do violence as
a man might be, but her reputation for ruthlessness once she
stirs to action is well-earned." He picked a burr out of the
horse's mane with gentle fingers. "Frankly, I consider her one
I'd least like to find myself confronting in a fight."

He lifted the horse's front hoof, grunting as he balanced the
hefty fetlock across his thigh. As he picked at the tough, horny
hoof, inspecting the shoe and hoof for stones and cracks, the
placid animal made no protest, still snuffling at Antonya in
search of sweets. She rubbed its forehead, brushing the fore-
lock out of its large, brown eyes. It blinked at her benignly,
short thick lashes blond against the dark irises.

"It's peaceful here, isn't it?" she said regretfully.

"It always is before a storm, Lady," he said, and dropped
the warhorse's massive hoof. It thudded solidly on the hay-
strewn floor.

14

By the time the couriers returned from Medebah with news
of Elotin's alliance, Jezral and Verbena had nearly finished
their preparations. Wagons and women set off on country
roads. But where humble maids and milk cows entered crofters' barns, mounted knights and cavalry came out, splendid in
their bright cloth, gleaming painted armor and wooden shields.
A good many of the "knights" swayed silently on their bovine
mounts, straw mannequins underneath the glitter of pot-metal
armor and paint. The cavalry grew quickly as it surged across
Water Cross toward Kulteph, expanding into a huge mounted
legion storming through the countryside.

Vodos would find it suspicious if C'ristan were not visibly
leading his own troops against Kulteph, and after some halfhearted protests, Lord C'ristan suited up in his best armor and
rode out at the head of the ersatz army, banners flying on either
side of his horse. For his part, C'ristan was happy enough to
avoid any real fighting while maintaining the veneer of honor.
Sarnor sent two of his senior captains, Ephraim and Tobias,

with Lord C'ristan to camouflage the herd of cattle with real troops, and to exert some control over the excitable ladies, who were enjoying themselves immensely. With headstrong Verbena in the vanguard, the two young officers and their men would have their hands full.

Antonya had less confidence in Elotin's motley bunch of horsemen. However, what they lacked in discipline, they made up for in number. Lord Elotin and his horsemen massed along the border, eager for plunder, and impatiently waited for the signal. Until it came, Elotin and his troops would do their best to give the impression that it was Water Cross they threatened, that C'ristan's assault on Kulteph was leaving him open to attack from Elotin's forces.

Kerrick had immediately seized the local sajada, much to the consternation of the Priests, a routine precaution the Defender carried out with relish. His men cleared the tiny carrels and passageways of the sajada's Great Tower of occupants, excited acolytes swarming around the High Priest, who like an arthritic sheepdog herding spring lambs, was attempting to maintain some semblance of order. The Priest sourly watched C'ristan's men lock the door to the sajada and hand the keys over to Kerrick. Armed guards were posted around the ports.

"The Ceremony of Oblation to the Holy Chalice is coming up, you know," the old man warned him acidly. "I expect the sajada to be open for blessed services at the very least."

"You will be able to go about your devotions as usual, Father," Kerrick said, not bothering to hide his amusement. "We are, after all, loyal servants of the True Faith and want only to protect you from the ravages of barbarian invaders and vandals."

The real reason, as they both knew, was the sajada's tower with its huge, polished signaling mirrors, the primary line of communication between the sajadas of the Faithful, interconnected all the way to the Oracular City. While communication was supposedly restricted to the affairs of the Faith, a Lord often surmised what was happening in neighboring Lands by the actions of his own Priests. No doubt Myro's sudden silence would alert the Citadel, and Vodos, too, through his own Priests, to some impending attack. But Antonya hoped Vodos would be convinced it was Myro's problem rather than his own.

The old Priest carried on as if he had not heard. "You are cutting us off from the Holy Word. Without the official astrological calculations from the Oracular City, how are we supposed to practice properly? Trying to rehearse our acolytes in a drafty Guildhall, the acoustics are dreadful. Absolutely dreadful."

Kerrick had no doubt that the Priest was far more worried about the bad influence the Alemasters Guild's stores of spirits might have on the impressionable lads than on the quality of their a cappella.

"And invaders and vandals, my eye," the Priest flared. "It's scarcely sensible for the peasants to go to all the bother of growing crops if you then tear it up before the harvest. If you people insist on brawling with one another, why can't you fight in the winter, when no cares if you rampage across their fields or not?"

Kerrick shrugged. "Winter is hard on the horses and no one enjoys a fight in the cold. Don't worry, Father, we'll leave enough in the fields for the tithes to keep you fat and happy." The skinny Priest glowered at him. "But complain if you would to Lord Elotin. It was he who chose to mass his troops against our borders." At least that was the official fiction being endorsed.

As the old man grumbled and went on his way, Kerrick jingled the keys to the sajada's Great Tower in one hand with ill-concealed glee.

Kerrick and Sarnor then sent out messengers, moving troops quietly into the hidden safety of Water Cross's forests close to the northern border, and into barns where no stand of trees could provide shelter. Of the Charcoal makers and woodcutters akin to Y'qert living deep within the wild stands, a good many of these taciturn guardians of the woods with ties to the Defenders guided C'ristan's troops across the trackless woodlands with silent, good-natured scorn.

While C'ristan's troops had kept their arms and horse, most of their armor was currently fastened to the back of a cow and on its way to Kulteph. The assault on Hadzida would have to be fast and hard; heavy armor would simply have slowed the soldiers down. Those who had light leather armor or chain mail wore it, but the army had a singularly scruffy look, no gleaming breastplates and feathered helmets among the plain worsted jerkins and rough breeches.

Kerrick and Antonya camped at Gath, a tiny village a few leagues from the border. Both Sarnor and Kerrick seemed at ease waiting, ceaselessly cleaning their weapons or grooming their horses as messengers came and went. Even Regine, the attendant C'ristan insisted Antonya retain to safeguard her dubious honor from gossips, placidly concentrated on her embroidery under the shade of an oak. But Antonya's nerves were strained. The longer they waited, the more chance Vodos had of detecting the ruse. By now, Antonya's counterfeit army were noisily approaching Kulteph, and Lord Vodos would have to make up his mind soon.

Word came a few hours after sunset. She had prepared for bed when Kerrick knocked lightly on the door of her chamber. She was up and dressing before Regine could open the door.

"He's taken the bait," Kerrick said. "Rode out of Hadzida a few hours ago, took a good six thousand troops with him, fifteen hundred on horse. He's left a garrison of less than two hundred men."

The lizard was safely tucked in Antonya's shirt, its movement restricted by the lacing around her torso. She wore no armor, only a leather jerkin, her coarse cloth breeches tucked into riding boots. Her hair had been plaited tightly back against her head, with neither hat nor helmet. She buckled the last strap of her throwing knives to her forearms and slung her cloak over her shoulders.

"Let's go," she said simply.

For all its bulk, Kerrick's bay kept good pace with the lithe horses from C'ristan's stables, thudding alongside Antonya's quicker mount. Kerrick had chosen an agile mare for her from Lord C'ristan's private stables. The four-year-old mottled white had a calm temper and a quick mouth, making her easy to ride, although Antonya was still awkward on horseback, her butt slapping the saddle as she did her best to post with the horse's gait. High in the shoulder and solid through the legs, the mare had both endurance and speed. Like her rider, she had yet to be tried in battle, although Kerrick had had the mare taken through her paces to be sure she was properly battle-trained.

Luna Minor was but a large speck among a billion others littering the night sky, its bigger twin a waning crescent shedding barely enough light to see by as the troop moved briskly north through the countryside. As they passed through silent villages, the column of infantry and horsemen grew. Word had already spread before them, every able-bodied man in Water Cross it seemed emerging from villages and towns with sword and crossbow, pikes and truncheon, even wood axes and pitchforks.

Antonya knew they cared little about their Lord's honor, nor would they be fighting for glory. The people of Water Cross were a contentious lot, quick to brawl over the price of a melon, but equally quick to unite in defense of their Land. This year or next, they knew they would eventually have to face Vodos. Striking first might be the only chance they had to protect their villages and families. Other than a few hushed orders rippling down the line, the only sounds were the heavy pounding of horses' hooves against the ground, the jingling of men and arms, the grunt of oxen pulling war wagons.

The stars had just begun to fade when they spearheaded deep into Lord Vodos's Lands. Behind Antonya, the column had swelled to a flood emptying out of Water Cross in a grim assault. The sky slowly lightened as they marched swiftly through the sleepy countryside, and by the time the sun broke over the low range of mountains on the horizon, Hadzida lay before them, the blue silhouettes of its spires visible in the distance. With their quarry in sight, the mood of the army rose to a feverish excitement, quickening their pace across the rolling fields. Frightened peasants abandoned plows and oxen, fleeing their thatched huts to scatter into the wooded hills and out of the path of the invaders. The bells of Hadzida's sajada rang out the alarm as the army thundered toward the city. Hadzida's garrison marched out onto the wide fields, the great gates closed firmly behind them as they waited confidently to meet their enemy head-on.

Kerrick reined in his mount beside Antonya on the crest of the hill. "Daen," he called out to a young armsman, his eyes examining the city before them. The young man kneed his own sturdy warhorse level with Kerrick's and still had to look up at the huge warrior. "You will stay here with the Lady Antonya. Keep her well back from the fighting."

"Aye, sir," Daen said promptly.

Antonya made no protest, understanding she was far too unskilled in combat, more likely to be a hindrance to her own troops trained for battle. Kerrick motioned the men to fall in behind him, and disappeared in a flood of armed men surging around Antonya and Daen like water flowing past an island. Rather than showing any indignation, Daen, a former mercenary, had taken his charge seriously to protect the Lady, quickly organizing a knot of guardsmen around her.

Even from a safe distance, she could see the dismay of the Hadzida garrison as they grasped the size of the army they had ridden out to meet, outnumbered more than ten to one. They had made the sortie in the belief C'ristan could not possibly have more than a few hundred soldiers to attack a vulnerable city. But as C'ristan's troops continued to pour over the horizon, they realized it was too late to call a retreat and fall back behind the safety of the walls.

Taking Hadzida should have been easy.

Unfortunately, things didn't quite go accordingly to plan. By the time the first shock wave reached the Hadzidan garrison making its suicide stand, Antonya heard rather than saw Lord Vodos's own army in the distance to their right, an ominous thunder rumbling through the ground. He'd ridden only halfway to Kulteph before suspicious scouts had realized the "army" massing against Kulteph was counterfeit. Ponderously turning his legions around, he was only a few leagues away by the time the outriders carrying the alarm from Hadzida reached him.

Battle had not been what Antonya expected, not at all like chess or anything akin to what she had read in the musty pages of Father Andrae's histories; no orderly charge against opposing forces, no neat and methodical offensive to breach the walls, calm officers barking orders and soldiers competently complying.

It was a mess. The screams of combat were indistinguishable from the screams of pain, the fighting more blind ferocity than reason. Horses and men clashed with furious brutality, metal blade ringing against metal. Through the brawling confusion, she could pick out the compact phalanxes of men stabbing through to the walls, scaling ladders behind them slowly arcing up against the stone.

Arrows rained down from the ramparts, some finding their way past protective shields. Antonya's cavalry swarmed over some grisly obstacle, an overturned war wagon, struggling oxen trapped in the harness trampled as men and horse hammered the huge, fortified gates. For a brief moment, she caught sight of Kerrick, yelling wordlessly over the clamor of battle. Then he was lost in the dust and noise.

She heard the sound of battle change as Lord Vodos's troops appeared, riding hard out of the rugged valley pass from the mouth of the shallow valley. A tightly wedged phalanx bore straight down on her army to cut deep into the center of the battle. She had the impression of a dam bursting, crushed in the torrent of horses breaking over them. Before she realized what had happened, the attack had reached her. A wave of foam-flecked horses rushed toward her, wild-eyed riders on their backs, bristling with steel.

Daen wheeled his horse, ramming the shoulder of his big mount against Antonya's white to put himself between her and the onslaught surging toward them. More of C'ristan's armsmen pressed around her to form a small pocket of protection as Daen bellowed, swinging a solid, studded mace around his head. It smashed into the face of an enemy horseman, the blow close enough to spray Antonya with a bright flash of red. Knocked out of his saddle, the man fell, his suddenly riderless horse milling bewildered in the swirling crush. The white suddenly slipped as another body was trampled, legs splayed, hooves skittering in the gore under it. Antonya was too busy to be frightened, preoccupied with trying to keep the tense mare under control.

Suddenly a stray arrow pierced the mare's shoulder. The horse screamed, rearing with front hooves pawing at the air. Antonya grabbed at the mane, the reins jerked loose from her hands as the white came down with stiff-locked front legs and threw down its head to punch back hooves viciously out behind it. The shock of impact as it hammered into another rider cost Antonya the last of her balance.

She hit the ground and rolled away desperately from the slashing hooves around her. Stumbling to her feet, she dragged her short falchion from its scabbard and pressed her back against the shield of the white's sweating hide. A Hadzidan foot soldier lurching through the press of horseflesh caught sight of her. He had lost his helmet, his stubbled face bare. A wound in his scalp had left stripes of blood down his skin. He grimaced, lips pulled back from his teeth in pain and fury, and swung his own blade at her head. She swung her arm up reflexively, steel cracked against her own sword in a jarring, savage blow, half driving her to her knees. Her arm went numb.

For a sickening moment, she watched him raise his sword again, knowing she couldn't deflect the next blow. She heard Daen shout as the blade arced up, saw the mare stumble as he rammed his own horse against the white. The mare whipped its back legs out in a wild, blind punch, barely missing both Antonya and the soldier. But it was enough to force the soldier off balance. In that moment, she had time to bring up her own sword, crudely ramming it with both hands into the man's gut. The impact traveled down her arms. She was close enough to him to smell the garlic on his breath as he stared open-mouthed at her. The blade snagged, pinned in his ribs as he pitched forward. She lost the falchion, unable to jerk it out before the white mare knocked her to the ground.

A nine-inch round warhorse hoof shod in heavy iron slammed against her side and sent her sprawling facedown into the dirt, breathless and groping on hands and knees. Then she was jerked upright, the brutal grip on her wrist so tight that the bones ground painfully together. Pulled into a run, her legs staggered helplessly under her, head spinning, unable to see.

Hands picked her up by the waist and threw her bodily onto the saddle of the white. One leg was shoved over as she floundered for the reins. Nauseous black sparkled at the corners of her vision, and she struggled to stay conscious and upright, her ribs seared in agony. Sawing none too gently at the bit in the mare's mouth, she let up only when the horse began to back up.

Daen leaned from his horse, holding the white's bridle by one mailed hand as they wheeled about, locked together. He stared at Antonya. "Well done, Lady," he yelled, barely audible over the din.

Gasping for breath, she couldn't manage a word, panting against dizzying pain as tears ran down her face. She turned the white around and fell back from the fighting closing in behind her. The body of the man she killed vanished under the feet and hooves of battle.

Daen retreated to a safe distance where Antonya could make out the chaotic battle more clearly. Lord Vodos's troops were breaking their way through C'ristan's men who were barely holding the ground between the city and its Lord. Antonya's soldiers scaling up the stone like incensed ants had taken the outer curtain wall, with fighting raging along the watchpaths. Another double phalanx of Vodos's troops slammed into C'ristan's men, pinching them off, forcing them back.

A thunderous rattle of huge chains and the creak of wood, the gates slowly began to swing down. As the drawbridge slammed against the opposite side of the muddy glacis, the last of Hadzida's defensive guard poured out, as well as a number of the townsmen, trapping C'ristan's men between them and Vodos's forces.

Antonya's breathing was laborious, every lungful of air painful. She wondered if she'd broken a rib, as another armsman handed her a shortsword to replace the one she'd lost. They stood silently on the hill, watching as C'ristan's men began losing ground. Her horse quivered under her, bright red blood from an arrow barb streaming down its left shoulder. Antonya's skin felt as if it were on fire, sweat running down her sides. She started as the lizard's tongue lapped at the sudden moisture, not even feeling its sharp claws digging into her skin. She allowed herself a moment of grateful surprise that the little reptile had survived, then glanced at Daen's grim face. If there was any hope of escape, she knew they would have to flee now.

"If we're going to lose anyway," she suggested quietly, her voice still breathy with pain, "let's do it in grand style."

He grinned at her, his young face pale under the dark hair, but his eyes bright. "Aye," he said fiercely. "Let's." He twisted on his saddle, his knees clamped against the horse's sides with competent ease Antonya could only envy. "Bring up the standards!" he called out to the small group of armsmen in her guard.

Two armsmen trotted up beside her, tall poles fastened to their harness holding aloft the silk oriflammes. C'ristan's blue and gold double-headed dragon snapped in the breeze to her left, and on her right, a shield of red on a plain white background, the Terhune family insignia. She hesitated, not from any sense of the theatrical, but because she had no idea where to lead her suicidal assault. Below her, C'ristan's men caught sight of the banners, and a ragged cheer floated up out of the clamor, the fight suddenly intensifying.

"Straight for the gate," she cried out as loudly as her painful ribs would allow, "*To me!*" and drummed her heels against the mare's sides. The excruciating jolt as the mare leapt forward made her scream in pain, the sound lost in the roar of the armsmen around her.

They bellowed their way down into the fray, urging their horses to a full gallop, punching into the fracas with exultant rage. Antonya kept her legs locked around the white as tightly as possible, swinging her blade blindly and, for the most part, ineffectually. She shouted unheard over the din, her throat ripped raw. Suddenly, the ground under the mare's hooves changed from the churned muck of the glacis to the solid thunk of heavy wood. The mare rattled across the drawbridge into the shadow of the walls.

Antonya realized, startled, she was through the gates and inside the ramparts, her armsmen pushing her before them in a surge of steel and flesh. Daen had lost his mace and was now laying about with his shortsword as he roared at the top of his lungs, leaning out to scythe at anyone not running in front of his horse fast enough.

The gates of the inner wall were already open, the townspeople taken by surprise sprinting into the safety of the streets beyond. C'ristan's army poured in behind them, on foot or horse, heading for the square to take both sajada and palace. The palace towered at the north end of the town on the rise of the hill, gray, bleak stone.

The battle subsided once inside the city, Vodo's soldiers either on the walls or outside. Antonya wheeled the white around to watch the army rushing in behind her. Fighting in the street was extremely one-sided, C'ristan's armed men against merchants and townsmen, old women throwing boiling water and crockery out of windows, the incongruous sound of annoyed roosters crowing and babies crying.

"Fire!" A townswoman's voice cut shrilly through the clamor. She hung out of a third-story balcony window gesturing frantically at the fighters below. *"The palace is on fire!"*

Heavy black smoke began to rise from the slit windows of the palace, flames shooting from under the wooden roofs and watchpaths. The conflict suddenly faltered, fire spreading out into the half-timbered houses of the walled city far more of an immediate threat than the hostile forces streaming into the narrow streets.

A Hadzidan officer charged out from the mouth of a street opposite Antonya, a half dozen foot soldiers behind him, all of them bloody and exhausted. He stumbled to a halt, staring at her, then at Daen and his men with their swords at the ready.

"Put down your arms," Antonya called to him, "and surrender." She glanced at the palace behind him, the fire now engulfing the entire west side of the roof. "Or die gallantly, if you prefer!"

He thought about it a moment before he threw his blade into the rough-cobbled street. The foot soldiers' swords clattered at their feet as they abandoned the battle.

"Take him," she said to Daen, nodding at the officer, then raised her voice to the defeated soldiers. "The rest of you should be fighting fire instead of us, before it spreads to the houses and you've nothing left to surrender." As Daen nudged his horse forward to separate the officer from his men, the soldiers glanced at one another briefly, then scattered, running toward the burning palace as they shouted for buckets and water.

Within minutes, the fight had gone out of the city like air from a punctured pig's bladder, attention focused on stopping the spread of flames. As Antonya trotted the mare up across the street toward the square, Vodos's men were giving up in droves, exchanging arms for buckets. The mare jittered under her, snorting nervously at the smoke. The armsman carrying C'ristan's banner had fallen. The gap-toothed boy clattering up beside her with her own colors badly soiled but waving proudly over his head had not been the same man she had ridden down the hill with. C'ristan's men caught sight of her standard before they saw her, cheering exuberantly as she edged her horse through the elated, dirty, triumphant men.

Her hands were raw; her arms, her side, her legs, ached from controlling her skittish mount. She kicked it forward, searching for Kerrick. His head appeared over the crowd as his huge warhorse pressed through. The bay merely flicked its ears in annoyance at arrows bobbing from its thick hide, bright red streaks of blood and the feathered shafts as colorful as festival decorations. Kerrick rode to her and extended his hand. Grasping each other's forearms tightly, they circled, grinning in childish delight.

"What happened?" she demanded, still not believing her luck.

"We were rescued, madam!" he shouted back, his voice hoarse. He laughed at her disbelief. "By an army of maids and milk cows!"

As soon as C'ristan had realized Vodos wasn't going to engage them at Kulteph, he led a small vanguard of troops and bore straight down on the undefended town, audaciously ordering its marshal to surrender or be burned to the ground. The frightened marshal, not yet realizing the true nature of the enormous army kicking up the dust behind them, immediately negotiated the terms of surrender with Lord C'ristan and gave up the city without a blow.

Sarnor left most of the real troops at Kulteph along with Ephraim and Tobias, then urged C'ristan and Verbena to drive the cattle toward Hadzida at a dead run through the night, hot on Vodos's heels. At least a quarter of the animals and no few of the ladies dropped in their tracks, but just as Antonya had reached the downed bridge into the city, forty thousand head of enraged cattle plowed into Vodos's force from behind. Verbena and her women shrieked and howled like daemon harpies. Foaming at the mouth much like the cattle, they stampeded the frenzied herd into the midst of the battle. Within minutes, one hundred and sixty thousand hooves had chewed everything in their path to bloody ribbons. Vodos's soldiers had broken and run, Antonya's own troops half fighting, half fleeing into the relative safety of the city walls.

The battle was already over by the time Elotin's band of marauders pelted into sight, the horizon behind them a curtain of black smoke as the fields burned in their wake. The vision of so much plump, juicy cattle free for the taking was irresistible. Hadzida's conquerors barely had time to close the gates before Elotin's tribesmen whooped and set off after runaway beef before it all scattered to the four winds.

"I can't believe it!" Antonya cried in the raucous din.

"Believe it!" Kerrick shouted, then threw his head back to laugh uproariously, his mouth stretched into a wide grin of amazed delight. She realized he hadn't expected to survive this encounter. "Believe it, Lady! Believe in a thousand impossible things and at least one of them may be true!"

Their sweating hands slid away and he pulled the bay around to ride beside her. Ignoring her painful ribs, Antonya breathed in the air as if it were perfume, savoring the thick smoke and the sweat of horses and men, leather and blood and dust.

Sarnor and C'ristan broke through the ranks, with Gesham, Daen's younger brother, riding behind them. Gesham was smiling broadly, while the dour-faced Sarnor managed to approximate a smile. C'ristan still looked dazed, as if he hadn't quite awakened from a particularly vivid dream. She nodded to them, and they fell in behind her.

Antonya's braid had come loose around her face, and she wiped the stray hair from her eyes with a grimy forearm streaked with blood. She gasped, and pressed a hand against an agonizing stab of pain in her bruised side, then caught Kerrick watching her.

"How do you feel?" he called. It was hard to hear him above the noise.

Wordlessly, she shook her head. "Drunk!" she mouthed.

Kerrick laughed.

Both wings of the palace were now in flames, the fire raging through the timbered rooftops and staining the stones black with smoke. Victors and vanquished alike raced along the streets, yelling for more water and buckets. Antonya, now sobered, reined in the white, to watch the palace burn. Fire was an enemy more feared than her conquering army. If it spread to the dry wood-timbered houses and crowded rooftops below, the city could become a trap, its populace burned alive. The fire along one colonnaded bay flickered and died to the sound of faint cheers.

"As long as the wind doesn't pick up, it should be confined to the palace grounds," Kerrick said casually. "Most likely."

Antonya eyed him silently, then turned the mare toward the sajada's square. Her jubilant troops managed to organize themselves into the semblance of an orderly retinue around her. Those townspeople not fighting the fire watched her from windows and the streets, fearful children wailing as they clung to their mothers' skirts, frail old men with stunned expressions, a woman burying her face in her apron and sobbing inconsolably. Sarnor and Daen ignored them, and as Antonya tore her gaze away, she caught Kerrick's raised eyebrow.

At the top of the wide steps of the sajada, Lord Vodos waited grimly for them, surrounded by those of his chief officers who had survived as well as terrified Guildmasters wringing their hands. His son, Bertil, stood beside him defiantly. Interestingly, Antonya noted, not a single Priest was in sight. No doubt they had received word of the ruse before Vodos had, and promptly abandoned their Lord to his fate.

She reined in the white, looking up at the Lord. He had been wounded, blood soaking through the rag tied around his left arm. Soot blackened his face, accentuating the angry lines as he stared at the victors in hatred. Sarnor dismounted, sword in hand, but Antonya waved him back, to Vodos's obvious surprise. She knew he saw her not as a warrior but as a half-grown woman.

"Lord Vodos," she called to him. "I am the Lady Antonya Terhune, daughter of R'bert, rightful heir to Adalon and Ashmael, and I do believe you have been defeated. Will you not surrender?"

He shot a disdainful glance at C'ristan and his waiting men before he looked at her. "I was given to understand I had been defeated by my Lord C'ristan of Myro."

C'ristan nudged his horse next to hers. "Nay . . ." he croaked, and cleared his throat nervously. "Nay, my Lord. I have placed my troops at the Lady's disposal; she commanded them and it is she to whom you would submit."

The officers and Guildsmen flanking Vodos murmured in

disbelief and alarm. He ignored them, turning to study Antonya narrowly.

"Then I would call on you, Lady, to treat my people honorably, with mercy and justice as befits one who would become their sovereign."

"Very prettily put, sir," she said dryly, hauling up on the reins of her restless horse. The arrow wound on its shoulder had stopped bleeding, but the animal went on dancing under her before an armsman grabbed the bridle to calm it.

Sarnor the mercenary stood with one foot on the bottom step of the sajada, not reacting as Lord Vodos glanced at him, unable to hide his angry humiliation. Kerrick dismounted and walked up the steps, stopping two down from the defeated man. "I am Kerrick of Myro, son of Kartic, son of Dormon, Master Ranked Defender and First Sworn of the Lady Antonya," he said. Lord Vodos nodded, understanding the courtesy. He would not be forced to suffer the indignity of surrendering to a commoner.

Vodos unbuckled his sword and scabbard and held it out to Kerrick, but kept his eyes on Antonya. "I yield, madam," he said, and went to one knee. "My Lands and city are yours." He bowed his head stiffly as Kerrick took his sword from his hands. Behind him, his officers and Guildmasters knelt in a haphazard wave with varying degrees of defiance and fear.

Bringing the man's sword down the steps, Kerrick handed it up to Antonya. She took it, and balanced it over her saddlebow. "It seems your palace no longer affords suitable accommodation, Lord Vodos." The man's jaw clenched, but he made no reply. "Have you a suggestion as to where I and my officers may find proper lodging?"

After an uncomfortable silence one of the Guildmasters glanced at Lord Vodos who nodded wearily. "I am Nerum of Hadzida, Guildmaster of his Lor . . ."—he coughed—"your Ladyship's Horse. Might I offer the Lady use of our Guildhall?" the man finished, his voice shaky.

"Thank you, sir, most kind of you," Antonya said, and turned to Sarnor. "Please take Lord Vodos and his men into custody. Be sure they are secure, but treat them well."

"And the Guildmasters?" Sarnor asked indifferently.

"Are free to go to their homes," Antonya said. Several of

them looked up at her in surprise. She raised her voice, the effort an agony, but she tried to keep the pain from showing. "None but my own men will be allowed to leave this city, and the citizens of Hadzida are advised to remain within their homes. Since the palace is burning, I expect the Guilds to find billets for my officers, be it Guildhalls or private houses, and to provide shelter for my troops outside the walls. However, no citizen is to be robbed or injured or treated in any way other than with courtesy. On my orders, sir."

She heard expressions of wonder ripple through the populace behind the barrier of cavalry. Sarnor nodded and signaled several of her armsmen, curtly issuing orders. As the guards moved in to seize Lord Vodos and his officers, Nerum and the other Guildmasters rose and scurried off the steps of the sajada.

"There's enough to worry about at the moment, Nerum," she said as he approached her mare, bobbing his courtesies nervously as he struggled to estimate Antonya's proper rank. The mare danced uneasily at the man's jerky motions. "Organize your Guilds to fight the fires, get the city calmed down. Then you may attend to the needs of our horse and soldiers. Those of my men who are free will aid you. Gesham?"

"Aye, madam," the young armsman said promptly, "I'll start rounding up a clean-up company." He led the worried Guildsman away from the sajada.

She glanced around for Kerrick, and saw he was occupied with C'ristan. "Sarnor," she said to the man still waiting quietly on her left, "Jezral?"

"Getting the women accounted for and settled down," the mercenary said. "A few of them are still out after the cattle, trying to chase off Elotin's pack. I've sent a party of armsmen to see none of the fair Water Cross maidens are rapt away along with their milk cows." Sarnor smiled faintly. "Although I'm placing my bets on the ladies against any of Elotin's grubby barbarians."

She chuckled, but not loudly against the stab of pain. The anesthetic euphoria of battle was wearing off, leaving her fatigued and hurting. "God, I do so hope Nerum's Guildhall has a decent bath."

15

Several days later the fires had finally been stamped out, leaving the palace a smoldering, charred ruin. An uneasy peace settled over Hadzida and the ravaged countryside as word of Lord Vodos's defeat spread through the Sheruben Valleys. Now the inhabitants waited to see what manner of ruler he would be replaced with.

Jezral had seen Lord Vodos's wife and daughters comfortably, if securely, confined, while Kerrick ensured that the Lord's remaining troops were disarmed and their commanding officers imprisoned. Hadzida's various Guildmasters quickly organized parties of civilians to clean up the debris and find accommodations for C'ristan's troops. Most would be housed in tents outside the walls, partly because of the lack of room within the city, and partly to keep looting to a minimum.

The majority of Elotin's band, still scattered over the countryside, continued pillaging defenseless villages with boyish delight. Those who had straggled to Hadzida had set up their own rude hide tents at a comfortable distance from C'ristan's troops. As Water Cross men and Hadzidans both carried off their dead for decent burial, the Nine Steppes warriors shouted bellicose comments in their own dialects, but were too busy gorging themselves into a stupor on roast beefsteaks and beer to make much trouble.

Three days after the collapse of Hadzida, Antonya ordered a victory feast. Nerum's Guildhall was as spacious as any of Lord C'ristan's own lodgings in Myro, the Guild of Horsemasters apparently thriving. By evening, she was seated in an ornate chair more impressive than comfortable at the far end of the hall, on a rounded dais two stone steps above the hall floor. She had bathed and dressed in fresh clothing, white shirt and jerkin hiding her bound ribs, black breeches tucked into leather boots. Loose sleeves hid the throwing knives strapped to her forearms. The red Terhune crest on her sleeveless silk tabard was her only adornment. Lord Vodos's own heavy broadsword in its opulent scabbard was buckled around the outside of her tabard. Her red-gold hair had been plaited back firmly on her bare head, and the lizard tucked discreetly away.

A broken horseshoe of tables curving down each end of the hall was occupied by a score of her officers. The Guild quickly organized its kitchens, nervous Guildsmen serving a continuous supply of roasted meats and plenty of good ale with almost frantic haste. On her left, the long table was separated by a fireplace large enough for four men to stand inside. At the moment, it contained the carcass of a huge boar roasting on a spit over a mountain of logs and coals. The flames picked out flickering highlights in the dark polished wood and gaily colored tapestries draped around the hall.

A small orchestra of mismatched jongleurs played as acrobats hastily pressed into service juggled and tumbled for the armsmen's entertainment. One poor female juggler utterly intimidated by the occupying troops broke so many plates that Antonya's men began to applaud as if it were part of the act, each crash bringing a cheer louder than the last. Finally, the girl retired, red-faced and quaking.

C'ristan sat at her right hand, his daughter Verbena one step below him. The young woman was still clad in the breeches and armor she'd worn on the campaign against Kulteph, and judging by her high spirits she wasn't likely to be returning to her skirts and needlepoint anytime soon. Several of her sisters sat among the victors, laughing as heartily as the men. Lord Elotin was among them, as loud and festive as the rest, but Antonya noticed him fidgeting, decidedly out of place in his rough furs and unkempt beard. He was doing his best to imitate the manners of the Water Cross men around him, however, while glancing covertly at the women to gauge the effect of his efforts.

On the other hand, C'ristan looked as glum as if he'd lost the battle, gloomily watching his harem enjoy themselves. He slumped even lower into his seat as Elotin saluted him from across the room, bellowing toasts to the health of his future father-in-law. C'ristan said little, preferring to finger his beads and drink steadily.

Jezral sat beside him, and Antonya, noticing the looks that the Guildsmen were giving the tall, gaunt woman, leaned past Lord C'ristan to remark, "It appears you shock our hosts, Captain. I believe they are unused to seeing women fighting in the ranks of soldiers." C'ristan winced.

Jezral smiled wryly and glanced up at Antonya, pale blue eyes guileless. "It does seem to be more a northern peculiarity, madam. But I suppose they might get used to it in time."

Antonya chuckled and sat back, sipping her ale carefully. She resisted the temptation to dull the pain in her ribs with drink, needing to keep her head clear. The Guildmaster Nerum sat between her and Kerrick, edgy and restless. He flinched whenever the big man made the slightest movement and his nervousness increased each time Antonya turned her head to speak with him. Like her, he barely touched his ale, and picked lethargically at the food placed in front of him.

But by the end of the evening, the anxious Hadzidan Guildsmen had begun to relax, a few uncertain smiles here and there as Antonya's men joked and sang and laughed without visible hostility.

The noise and the smiles died away as Sarnor led in Lord Vodos and four of his men, chains jangling as they walked up the center of the hall to face her. His son, Bertil, glared at her hatefully from behind his father. From the corner of her eye Antonya saw Verbena lean forward to examine the young man a decade or more her junior. Nerum froze as rigid as marble beside her and nearly as white.

Lord Vodos stopped ten paces away, his head held arrogantly high. None of the prisoners had been allowed to change or wash, still dusty and blood-spattered, although she was pleased to see Lord Vodos's injured arm had been attended to and carefully rebandaged.

"Kneel, sir," Sarnor said quietly behind him.

Awkward in the heavy shackles on his legs and wrists, Lord Vodos went to his knees, the clank of iron on the stone floor loud in the silence. He gazed up at Antonya, head unbowed as his son and officers followed.

"Captain Sarnor," Antonya said. "Why are these men in chains?"

The dour mercenary raised an eyebrow and said casually, "They are your prisoners, madam."

She had orchestrated this small act with him beforehand. "They know they are my prisoners. It is unnecessary to remind them of the fact. Please remove their irons." Lord Vodos's stoic expression didn't change.

Sarnor snapped his fingers and Antonya watched patiently as her armsmen helped Vodos and his men to their feet to release the shackles. Once his legs and hands had been freed, the defeated man bowed far more smoothly to her in a courtly gesture which allowed him to remain standing. "Our thanks, Lady," he said, without a trace of warmth in his tone.

"You gave me a good fight, Lord Vodos. You nearly prevailed against me."

"Unfortunately, I did not," he returned evenly.

"You're a very proud man. What should I do with you?" she asked him ruefully.

Had he suggested offering the Faith the chance to ransom his life, she would have been disappointed. But the Faith had little reason to want him alive, the defeat of strong Lords always in their interest in keeping the Lands unstable and weak and thus under their influence. To his credit, Lord Vodos knew it as well, not bothering to grasp at straws.

"I would expect you should execute me, which is the usual fate of fallen Lords, madam," he said, keeping his eyes level.

She smiled. "And your son as well, I suppose?"

Behind him, the younger man scowled, cursing her softly under his breath. His father, although he must have heard, didn't react. "I had hoped you might allow my wife and daughters, if not myself or my son, to go into exile, Lady Antonya, far away where they could no longer be a threat to you."

She exchanged an amused look with Kerrick. "I am an exile, Lord Vodos, as well as a daughter sent far away from the Lands of my birth. You see what an annoyance exiles can become." Lord Vodos kept his expression rigidly composed. "No, your family will not be exiled."

The Guildhall had become still, not even the sound of tankards against wooden tables or knives against platters could be heard. Every man, on either side of the conflict, listened with hushed attention.

Antonya sprawled in the huge chair, trying to look more relaxed than the uncomfortable seat would allow, especially with her tightly taped bruised ribs. "You're a remarkable man, Lord Vodos. You've been a good administrator of these Lands. Your roads are well maintained and policed, safe to travel even through the deepest of your forests. Your farms are fertile and well tended, the beasts of the meadows fat. Your crofters are hardy, your merchants content. Were it not for the fact our troops have burnt most of your grain in the fields, you would have had an excellent crop this year."

Elotin grinned hugely, pleased with this mention of his zealous handiwork. Vodos said nothing, watching Antonya.

"Hadzida is prosperous, your Guildmasters"—she waved a hand at the opulence of the hall—"do well," she finished dryly. "Your soldiers are properly armed, loyal and disciplined. You yourself are known to be a skilled diplomat as well as a just governor, neither too servile in dealing with the Faith nor giving them reason to Purge you. A rarity in these Lands."

He bowed his head slightly. "You honor me, Lady," he said in a lackluster monotone.

"Only by striking against you hard and fast, taking you by surprise and deception, had I any hope at all of defeating you, sir. You still damned near won. Even now, I doubt we could hold these Lands in the long run should your population decide to rebel against our occupation. These are not Lands and yours are not people I would gladly choose to fight again."

The Lord's face drained bloodless. He opened his mouth to speak, then closed it, swallowing hard. Beside her, the Guildmaster Nerus moaned aloud, looking as though he were about to faint.

They knew what she was saying. She could slaughter half the population and sell the rest into slavery, loot everything of any value before razing the city and every town in the countryside, salt the fields so that nothing could be harvested there for years to come. Total destruction was generally the best way to ensure that a neighbor could never again grow powerful enough to be a threat. It took Lord Vodos several more moments before he could speak.

"My Lands and my people are not without value, Lady." His voice was deliberately flat to keep it from shaking. "Surely you would find them more useful to you whole and alive rather than destroyed."

The silence was absolute, as if a collective breath had been inhaled and held, waiting. Antonya smiled thinly, elbow resting on the arm of her chair, her cheek cupped in one hand.

"Would it surprise you, sir, if I told you I intended to return your Lands to you? Intact?"

A brief murmur rippled through the hall like a breeze rustling the leaves of the forest. Vodos glanced at Lord C'ristan slouched morosely in his chair studying the dregs of his ale. C'ristan had been far from happy when informed of Antonya's plans for his perennial rival. Vodos scrutinized her with suspicion. Some of the color came back into his face. "Aye," he said slowly. "It would surprise me very much indeed."

"Nonetheless, that's exactly what I propose to do."

"Why?" he demanded bluntly.

"Because *you* are worth more to me whole and alive," she said calmly. "There is, of course, a price."

For the first time, the Lord smiled, a desolate, humorless tightening of his lips. "Of course."

"I will take the monies necessary out of your treasury to pay my soldiers and reimburse my own expenses for this campaign. No less, and no more. It will leave you somewhat the poorer, but not destitute."

He listened carefully, unmoved.

"I will leave behind a delegate as my personal representative along with a small company of armsmen to serve as his staff. He will observe but not interfere in any way with your authority. He is to be consulted and kept informed on all aspects of your activities and send regular reports to me. He will also be your liaison to the court of your neighbor and my ally, Lord C'ristan of Myro. You will publicly swear an oath of peace with Lord C'ristan, and he with you."

Lord Vodos remained impassive. Antonya crossed her legs, pushing the unfamiliar scabbard to one side. It clanked dully against the side of the carved chair.

"Your fields are in ruins, and the stores you have will be gone quickly as you are now feeding not only your own people but the troops which I have all over your Lands. Once I have extracted the monies from your treasury, and you have paid to repair the damage to your city and countryside, there will not be much left over to spend on importing food for your population, sir. You know as well as I that any of your less than friendly neighbors will take advantage of your difficulty and the price of corn will soon overreach your finances. You won't be able to afford to feed everyone. You will either have to choose who will starve, or impose a crippling tax on your people they might never recover from."

The muscles in Lord Vodos's jaw twitched, but he said nothing.

"However, in return for this oath of peace, Lord C'ristan will graciously supply you with what you need to feed your population this winter and enough grain to reseed your fields come spring. For this, you will pay no money. Now or ever."

Lord Vodos blinked, then nodded slowly.

"Further, to seal this compact between your two Lands, your son will marry Lord C'ristan's eldest daughter, Lady Verbena. However, it will be she who is her father's heir to his Lands, not your son. Water Cross is to remain intact and independent. The lady Verbena's Guildsmen will swear their alliance to her directly, and it will be on her sole authority to grant charters. Her husband will swear to protect her rights and those of her children by him to the honor of Water Cross, or those of her sisters should the couple have none. Your son, of course, will remain heir to Hadzida."

Lord Vodos's son, Bertil, was by all accounts a brooding young man, hot tempered and not overly graced in either physique or charm. Nevertheless, Antonya felt vaguely sorry for him. A marriage of convenience it would be, but she suspected it would likely be far less convenient for *him* than for Verbena. She inclined her head to one side to look at the young man standing behind his father's shoulder.

"That doesn't bother you, does it?" she asked.

"Not particularly," the younger man almost snarled. "If it means keeping our Lands in one piece and my family alive, I'd even stoop to marrying *you*." His voice carried clearly through the hall.

His father winced and a buzz of anger shot through the hall. The Guildsman Nerum shivered next to Antonya, then was visibly relieved as she laughed.

"Nothing quite that drastic will be necessary," she said to the sullen young man, then turned her attention back to his father. "Further, one tenth of your army is to serve in my forces under my command, Lord Vodos. Each man will serve no less than a year with four months of active battle duty. When one leaves, another will replace him. His wages will be paid out of your treasury. The other nine-tenths of your own army will remain under your control to protect your Lands and borders as well as those of your neighbor, Lord C'ristan. By this pact, Lord C'ristan's troops will also be required to come to your aid, should you need it."

She didn't miss the pensive look that passed over Lord Elotin's unshaven face as he digested this, realizing its implications. She could expect him to make a similar offer before too long.

"Is that all?" Lord Vodos asked, his tone bitter.

"Lord Vodos, I don't want your Lands," Antonya said softly. "I know what it is to lose one's bloodrights unjustly to another. Both my parents lost their heritage to one who took it from them by treachery, force and murder. I intend to take it back."

For a moment, Lord Vodos stood watching her silently, the only sound in the hall the crack of the wood burning in the huge fireplace. His eyes glittered in skeptical interest. "And how do you propose to do this, Lady?" he asked in a quiet voice, as if she and he were the only ones present. "Adalon is held by one far more powerful than either I or Lord C'ristan, even joined in this unholy alliance you suggest. Against the might of the Citadel? You haven't a chance, if you will pardon me for saying so."

"I mean to unite the south, my Lord. By diplomacy where I can, by the sword if necessary. You and Lord C'ristan will provide the first example. Not even P'tre Terhune can afford to strike against a united league. I get my rightful Lands back, and you and every other Lord in such a union will have the strength to resist the Purges. Surely a man such as yourself can envision the benefits in protecting interests outside your own borders?"

He shook his head dubiously. "Under your leadership?"

"Which Terhune would you rather serve, sir? P'tre or me? You *will* serve one or the other."

He didn't answer, gnawing on his lower lip thoughtfully. She stood and stepped around the edge of the table, down the steps toward him. The steel rasped as she drew out the long broadsword in a single motion. Firelight shimmered gold against the steel, matching her eyes now paled to wolf-yellow. Lord Vodos's own eyes widened, the bizarre effect not lost on him.

"Lastly, you will swear an oath of fealty to me to aid and protect my interests against any who might wish me harm." She balanced the tip of the sword against the floor, holding the hilt by both hands, between herself and Lord Vodos. "And you will do so *now*."

He remained unmoved. "An oath given under duress is hardly one I would expect you to trust," Lord Vodos said reluctantly. "And any oath given to a woman is even less likely to be regarded as binding upon me."

"True, my Lord. I respect your frankness in raising those points. However, you do have a choice," she said conversationally. "If your honor will not allow you to swear such an oath in good faith, then reject the terms I offer without disgrace. You will be admired by all for the strength of your convictions. I will execute you, of course, imprison your family, empty your treasury, disarm your troops, pillage and raze your cities, drive your people into either poverty or exile, and carve up your Lands into small pieces as rewards to my own men for their service." She shrugged. "That *is* how it's traditionally done."

Lord Vodos smiled tightly. "Aye, that's indeed how it's traditionally done," he agreed. But still he hesitated.

"You are an honest man, Lord Vodos," Antonya said calmly. "And I have pressing need of honest men. Could you really have hoped to negotiate terms any better than those I offer you?"

Wordlessly, he shook his head. He took the two steps to reach her and went to one knee. Grasping the blade of the upright sword tightly with his bare right hand, the edge bit into his flesh.

"Before these witnesses and under the eyes of God, I swear

my blood fealty to the Lady Antonya Terhune of Adalon and Ashmael—" Lord Vodos pitched his voice to carry through the hall while his eyes stared unblinkingly into hers, "to suffer her judgment loyally and true, to serve and protect her interests against all who bring her harm, on my honor as a Lord of these Lands and in good faith."

He kissed the flat of the blade, then pressed dry lips briefly to each of her hands resting on its hilt. He rose and stepped away, wrapping a cloth around the shallow cut in his palm as his son and officers mumbled their oaths quickly, watching stoically as they kissed the bloodied sword in turn and stepped back.

She sheathed the broadsword and said, "Guildsman Nerum, would you be so kind as to give up your place to my Lord Vodos and see that he and his men are provided with meat and ale?" She steered Vodos by the elbow up the steps between the two long tables.

The Guildsman slid from his seat, obviously grateful to get away. "My pleasure, madam," he murmured and bowed as he passed her, then gestured wildly at the Guildsmen standing paralyzed around the room. Immediately, the hall burst into motion and loud voices bordering on relieved hysteria. Lord Vodos stood by the Guildsman's chair waiting for Antonya while Sarnor, still carrying their shackles draped over one shoulder, cordially escorted the Lord's son and his men to vacant places at the table.

Before Antonya sat down, she said quietly, "Kerrick, would you mind handing me my own sword now, please?" As she unbuckled the belt of the Lord's broadsword, her Defender reached behind him to retrieve her sword belt from where it hung across the back of his chair. Lord Vodos took his own blade as Antonya handed it to him casually.

"I suppose I should make some sort of speech and ritual ceremony out of it," Antonya said with a smile, "but frankly, I think we've all had a bellyful of formalities tonight, don't you?"

Mutely, Lord Vodos buckled the sword belt around his waist, adjusting his sword on his hip by the chain with practiced ease. He said nothing, not meeting Antonya's gaze as she added lightly, "That's a fine blade, sir. Mind you clean the blood off before it pits the steel."

He waited politely for her to sit before he took his place and watched as a tankard was placed in front of him. An ashen Guildsman with shaking hands filled it with dark beer, foam rising and spilling over the top. Lord Vodos sipped it and set the tankard down carefully, staring into it for a long moment before he turned to look at Antonya.

"This is still somewhat of a shock," he said in a low voice. "I fully expected to lose my head tonight, madam."

"Mmm," she said and grinned. "Then we are both pleasantly surprised, my Lord. For a moment there, I feared you would force me to take it."

16

The world is round. It is very big and very round, and very difficult to understand why things don't simply slide off the top. She had paid dutiful attention as Father Andrae filled a bucket with water and tied a rope to the handle, and had less dutifully tried to stifle her laughter as he turned about in a circle, wooden bucket and water in an orbit around his whirling body.

"Now watch, Antonya," he had called out breathlessly, his brown cassock billowing around him. He lifted the rope, spinning the bucket in an elliptical circuit around his head. "See . . . how the water . . . stays inside the bucket? Even when . . . it's upside down?"

It was true, the water did stay inside the bucket. "But Father Andrae," she argued, watching with her chin tucked on her upraised knees, arms around her heavy skirts. "The world is not a bucket. Were it so, we would all be living at the bottom of a well and there would be a great handle stretched across the top of the sky."

The bucket slowed, water sloshing over the lip as he caught it and set it on the dusty ground. He glared at her, his face red and sweating over his beard. "You are . . . the most stubborn child . . . I have ever . . ." he started to say, then gave up the rest of it as he leaned with his hands on his knees to wheeze.

When he regained his breath, he took her to the hillside overlooking the bay of the monastery's island. The larger island of Malamor sprawled on the horizon in a long blue lump. Every morning dozens of fishing boats left Malamor's tiny harbor village of Sias, returning every night. Each month, Father Andrae and a few of the Brothers rowed across to perform the ceremonies for weddings and funerals, bless the naming of babies and officiate at coming-of-age festivities, act as impartial arbitrators to settle disputes, give advice to those who wanted it or simply listen patiently to those who only wanted an ear to complain to.

In return, the villagers gave the Brothers smoked herring and pickled sardines, salt cod and barrels of brined sprats, and, on occasion, fresh salmon. Two of the huge fish would fill a single barque, and Brother Sholto would light an extra candle at prayer if either were laden with the orange, jewellike roe. He would spread this salty goo on dark bread and eat it with such enthusiasm that Antonya thought it had to be the finest of God's own manna for which her own mortal taste buds were, alas, too unrefined to appreciate.

The day was clear and perfect, the light breeze chasing any clouds while the late summer sun warmed the air. The fishing boats of Sias had already gone out, a few still in sight scattered over the water to cast their nets.

"Now observe carefully, Antonya. When one of those boats touches the horizon, you will see the ship disappear before the sails do." Father Andrae demonstrated with a rock, mica flakes glittering in the granite. "Just as the tip of my finger is hidden as it goes by the curve."

So they watched, but none of the boats seemed in any hurry to demonstrate the laws of physics and geometry for them. She amused herself picking chamomile flowers, slitting the stems with a fingernail to insert the next one to make a long chain of the tiny white blossoms. She slipped the floral necklace over her head to take back to Brother Reule, who made medicines from the chamomile.

The stuttering bleat of goats heralded their approach before they emerged from the woods at the far end of the rocky beach.

They leaped from the shadows of trees into sunlight, ears flapping as they skipped across the beach toward scrubby saltbush. Behind them, Brother Alban whistled and waved his long crook at stragglers to herd them toward the path up the steep embankment leading back to the barn. He caught sight of his superior and Antonya, waving cheerfully.

Brother Alban puffed up the trail, the unusually warm weather bleaching the ground under his sandals to dusty white. Goats followed him, the younger kids cavorting and prancing while their mothers tore at the grass with blunt teeth.

"Blessed beautiful day, isn't it?" he said, and flopped down beside them, pushing off his sandals with his big toes.

"But not an idle one," Father Andrae said promptly.

"No, indeed," Brother Alban agreed, leaning back on his elbows, his face to the sun, and closing his eyes. "Working hard, are we?"

As if nettled by his younger subordinate's disbelief, Father Andrae said, "We are observing the evidence of natural phenomenon to support our postulation of the earth's spherical nature and so demonstrate the relationship of distant objects on geomorphic surfaces, to wit, those fishing vessels and the horizon."

Brother Alban cracked one eye open and glanced at Antonya. "Oh."

Antonya suppressed a grin. Annoyed, Father Andrae insisted, "We are simply taking advantage of an unusually clear day to increase our understanding of science."

"He is right, Antonya, the world is round," Brother Alban said. "Of course, it's easier for us because we're so close to the top, you see. But when I was a wee lad, my great-grandfather told us of the far southern lands where the earth is curved further down." The goatherd grinned at her. "There, goats have two legs shorter on one side than the other and can only go one direction, because if they turned around, naturally they would fall right over."

"But how do they ever get back to the barns, then?" she asked. Brother Alban had hundreds of tales of foreign lands filled with oddities she longed to travel and see for herself.

"Brother Alban," Father Andrae said irritably, "you do not help her comprehension by telling such specious tales, no mat-

ter how entertaining." Father Andrae wasn't much older than Brother Alban, and the two constantly engaged in good-natured bickering.

"My apologies, Father, but I did not say it was the truth, only that it was what I heard from my great-grandfather."

Father Andrae sighed. "Antonya, watch the ships, please."

She dutifully looked back out over the dark blue water laced with whitecaps, as Brother Alban chuckled. Suddenly, she spotted what the abbot had been hoping for.

"Look, Father Andrae, there's one with a big sail, see? Two sails, white and red!"

The abbot squinted into the distance, suddenly somber. "Brother, your eyes are better than mine," he said quietly. "What do you see there on the horizon?

Brother Alban shaded his eyes with one hand. "The girl's right," he said slowly. "A ship. A big one." The two men exchanged enigmatic looks.

"Antonya," Father Andrae said in his gentle voice. She looked at him sharply. Whenever he spoke in a tone that said there was nothing to be alarmed about, it was usually because something was very wrong indeed. "Your legs are faster then either mine or Brother Alban's. Run down to the kitchen and the forge. Tell the brothers to damp the fires at once, then go to my library and bring me my farglass. It's the little brass tube by the astrolabe. Run quickly now."

She was off like a rabbit, her thin legs pumping. By the time she reached the forge, her lungs were sour with acid and she held one hand against her side to quell the sharp pains.

"Father Andrae . . . says damp the fires," she wheezed to a startled Brother Hasuq, and was off as he began shouting out urgent orders.

Old Brother Lezar had fallen asleep outside with his back against the ovens for warmth. He jerked awake as she banged the kitchen door, his milky blind eyes wavering irritably. Inside, Brother Sholto looked up in surprise, leaning his elbows on the wide table as he bent over an open book. The smell of baking bread filled the kitchen.

"Damp the fires," she gasped. His chubby face drained as white as the flour on his hands. As she bolted back out the *door, she nearly ran down old Brother Lezar leaning on his stick in the doorway.*

"What is it? What's the matter?" he called after her in his thin, querulous voice.

"A ship!" she called back excitedly over her shoulder as she ran toward the library. "A big one! With red and white sails!"

"O Mater, libera nos a malo!" the old man cried out in fear.

She faltered just long enough to stare back in amazement, but the old monk had hobbled into the kitchen. She dashed into the library, grabbed the narrow tubular eyepiece and was pelting up the hill within seconds. Her excitement had given way to a thin uneasiness roiling in her stomach. Brother Alban knelt in the grass, his neck craned out, intensely studying the ship in the distance. The sails had grown larger, three square sails held aloft on masts and a larger square foresail scooping out the air before the ship. The vessel itself was still over the curve of the horizon, just as Father Andrae taught.

The abbot took the farglass and held it to one eye with shaking hands. The huge foresail fluttered on the wind, the red emblem undulating. Slowly, Father Andrae lowered the glass, Brother Alban watching his face anxiously.

"Miserere nobis," Brother Alban breathed, aghast at whatever it was he found in his superior's expression.

Antonya flopped to her belly beside the monks, still panting. "What is it?" she demanded. Father Andrae handed her the glass without a word. Bewildered, she held the end of the tube against one eye, squeezing the other shut and stared at the curved prow of the ship rising from the horizon like a dragonfish breaching the surface of a pond. The image wavered, unsteady in her hands, and she sat up to use her knees to brace the heavy brass instrument.

"What do you see, Antonya?" Father Andrae said quietly.

"A red shield with five points around it painted on a white sail with a wavy sun design in its center," she said promptly.

"Good, child. Not the sun, though. It is the Holy Oracle."

She glanced at him in astonishment. He sat serenely in the green grass, hands on his thighs as he watched the ship in the distance. The only sound was Brother Alban's murmured

*prayers and the hum of bees floating from one tiny white flower
to another.*

"What is it, Father?" she asked quietly.

"The flagship of P'tre Terhune of Adalon, High Lord Commander of the Faith." As the abbot spoke his name, Brother
Alban moaned softly and murmured prayers at an increased
pace, a frantic Our Mother breathlessly spilling over into
Blessed Martyrs. Father Andrae nodded toward the red and
white sails. "That is his seal, the red shield of Adalon with the
Womb of God emblazoned on its heart."

She had heard of P'tre Terhune. Whenever she found she
could not sleep, which was all too often, she would sneak out
of her tiny cell under the night stairs and creep up to put her
ear against the cracks in the door of the monks' dorter. Wrapping her blanket around her against the dark and chill, she
would shiver more with delight than cold at the bloodthirsty
stories the Brothers frightened each other with. But those had
been merely stories, ghost tales whispered in the dark. That
P'tre Terhune might be real had never occurred to her. Now
his red and white sails billowed ominously on the distant
breeze.

Father Andrae took the farglass from her hand, placing it
with exaggerated care on the grass beside him before he folded
his hands quietly in his lap. "If he lands his ship here, we will
all die," he said calmly.

"But why?" she asked, more amazed than afraid.

He smiled and turned his gaze away from the ship. "Because we are heretics, Antonya. It is heresy to preach that the
mysteries of the sacred universe can be pried apart with only
the human tools of profane logic and reason. It is heresy to
contend the Citadel of the Faith is not the final authority on
the will of God, that all men and women carry the altar of
God within their own breasts. It is heresy to have the courage
to think for yourself. And P'tre Terhune burns heretics. All he
can find." The abbot's eyes were cold, not calm, she suddenly
saw. She shivered as Brother Alban prayed faster, hands
clamped together, knocking his forehead rhythmically in the
grass.

"Should I be praying too, Father Andrae?"

"If it would make you feel better," he said indifferently,

looking out again at the ship in the distance. "God wills what He wills, and the bleating of lambs cannot stave off their slaughter."

"And you will let him kill you?" she demanded, appalled. "Not even fight to protect yourself?"

"Nothing I can do could stop him, child. I shall not compound his sin by adding to it with my own."

Her breath whistled in her nose as her anger grew. She felt the color drain from her eyes, almost a reflex, as a terrible energy trembled through her muscles, the tension unbearable. Not here. Not the Brothers. She would never allow it.

"Then I will not pray," she said slowly. "Rather I would curse him, curse him and his ship to founder on the rocks." She was standing up, her hands balled into fists as she screamed into the wind. "I curse you, P'tre Terhune, do you hear me? I curse you to drown and your flesh to be ripped from your bones by the teeth of all the daemons of the sea!"

She was dimly aware of Brother Alban's huge eyes staring at her, his mouth open, and Father Andrae's hands tugging at her dress to pull her away from the sheer face of the cliff. "Go to the bottom and die, then go to Hell and burn!" Her rage made her almost incoherent, but freed her spirit, a heady rush of passion.

A sudden yank pulled her off balance and she fell to her hands and knees, smelling the heavy scent of chamomile in the carpet of grass. Father Andrae stared at her as if he had never seen her before, while Brother Alban watched the ship anxiously.

"Sweet Mother of Heaven," Brother Alban breathed out. "It's working. Father, her curse is working. Look, the ship, it's disappearing! It's going down!"

With a sudden expression of anger and disgust, Father Andrae pushed away from her and snatched up the brass farglass. His hands were trembling as he put it to his eyes. "Don't be a daft fool," he snapped at the monk kneeling in the grass. "It's only turning away from us. It isn't sinking." He took the glass from his face. "We've been lucky, not blessed." Then he turned to Antonya, his wrinkled face pale with anger. "Antonya . . ."

"I will never let him hurt you, Father," she said fiercely,

cutting him off. "Not you nor any of the Brothers. Never."

His expression softened, confusion in the anger. "Child, superstitious curses are of no more use than your prayers. Who knows if the lambs pray for mercy or curse us to Hell when we butcher them?"

The sails had dwindled now, only white pennants fluttering on the tips of the masts visible. The wind blew strands of Antonya's hair back from her face, cooling the sudden rash of sweat on her brow.

"Then if God will not stop him, I will, Father," she said quietly. "I am no lamb to be led meekly to the slaughterhouse. Someday, I will kill him. I swear it."

The look of pain and disappointment in the old man's eyes hurt her, and she looked away, toward the ship as it vanished over the horizon, lost in the thin line between sky and sea.

17

"Salve regina coelorum!

"Salve domina astrum!

"Salve lunae et sol lumen, salve radix!

"Ex qua mundo lux est orta!"

B'nach closed his eyes against the sunlight pouring into the Crystal Sajada, amber gold burning through the capillaries in his eyelids. He tried to shut out everything but the music ringing through the vast domed temple. The vibration echoed in his gut, the harmonies filling him with emotion. His head bared, hands clasped together, he let his voice join with the thousands of others in praise of the Holy Mother of the stars and moon and sun. Beside him, he heard K'ferrin's reedy voice as a stale echo of his own.

"Lumen de Lumine,

"Dignare me, laudare te, Mater sacrata,

"Da mihi virtutem contra hostes tuos!"

Not a soul within the Citadel didn't send forth this invocation with the utmost sincerity. Every Priest, high or low, begged Our Mother, Goddess of Light, to protect him from his enemies. As if to reassure himself, B'nach touched the knife tucked in his belt.

Like all who entered the holiest of sajadas, he carried nothing of metal, but not all weapons were made of steel. Every Priest within the sajada was armed, from simple shivs carved of bone carried by the lowest acolyte to elaborate knives fashioned from layers of fine paper lacquered and pressed into thin blades as tough and deadly as steel. Carved from the tusk of an extinct leviathan sea-daemon, B'nach's knife was supposedly endowed with magical properties of the Weird. But he felt more secure in the keenness of its edge.

Young thurifers passed along the aisles separating the Orders, acrid sweet smoke drifting lazily from the porcelain censers swinging from their hands. B'nach inhaled the potent incense, and tilted his head so that when he opened his eyes again he would be looking up at the Crystal Dome just as the last notes of the song reverberated away. As the final harmonics echoed, he stared into blinding sunlight streaming through the glass. Dazzling color stabbed through his eyes.

Light through the curved dome stained all who stood within it in glorious splendor. Built by the same Ancient Masters who had created the Oracle to snare the starfire of Heaven, the seemingly fragile glass was indestructible, as old as the Chalice of God itself and just as mysterious. Harder than steel, the arcane crystal was impervious to storm or hammer or arrow, impenetrable to anything but light.

It bore no images of the Mother of God or Her Son, depiction of the divine in the imperfect clothing of humanity being too blasphemous, but the ancient artists had had no such scruples in portraying lesser celestial creatures. Blue and red, deep emerald green and delicate amethyst, translucent figures of winged seraphim and hallowed saints, all the angelic host of Heaven spiraled and writhed and contended with maleficent spirits as beautiful as themselves.

And they moved. By whatever magic the Ancients practiced, the lovely incubi and repulsive furies soaring above had altered over the years. B'nach could remember when *that* winged boy had held the hand of the flame-haired daemon over *there*, now slipped slowly but inexorably from his grasp. The brilliant figures glowed with an everchanging life of their own as the human mayflies below flickered briefly into being to stare and wonder and die.

"*Gloria,*" he whispered, letting the light wash over him with almost palpable warmth, wanting to *feel* it again as he had in childhood, his mind innocent of poison, body unsoiled with the corruption of shame. *All is goodness and mercy, all is love . . .*

Twelve thousand feet shuffled, murmured whispers dragging him out of his reverie. The moment fled, leaving him vaguely depressed. He winced, his neck aching from gazing up so long.

The reddish blotch of afterimages burned into his retinas. No doubt staring into the sunlight wouldn't help his fading eyesight, divine or no. The blurred figure of an elderly Priest resolved into His Reverence Philoniah, High Lord of the Sacred Sciences, heading on wobbly legs toward the spiral stairway of the *pulpitum*, a fat book under his stick-thin arm. His heels clicked across the marbled expanse surrounding the Oracle, the Chalice deceptively empty.

Carved steps led into the slight depression cupping the Oracle, but only the Saints had ever walked upon these stones, none ever returning. The *pulpitum* had been erected at a safe distance from the Light, yet even so, as the old man neared the tall lectern, the Oracle breathed to life.

Ornate silk embroidery trimmed the old Priest's light blue robes. As a Reverent High Lord, he was entitled to the precious gold adornment on his Order's robes, but gold was a metal the Oracle was particularly sensitive to. Being that close to the Chalice of Light would have made wearing it unbearable. As it was, just the nearness of life itself was enough to excite the Oracle. A faint golden glow shimmered behind the priest, cupped in the black stone Chalice. As his white hair stood on end, waving in the electric breeze, he eyed the huge globe of starfire with respect and fear.

The Great Sajada was silent but for the musical siren hum of the Oracle calling life to itself. The old Priest grasped the rail with one knobbed hand and climbed the twisting staircase, one ponderous step at a time. Behind the Priest, the Oracle sang softly to itself. His hair disheveled by the time he reached the top, the old man plopped the heavy book onto the lectern with a breathless grunt. Already he was sweating in the intense heat of the Light behind him.

He adjusted pinched spectacles on his nose, red-rimmed eyes squinting as he riffled through the pages of the Book. Looking up into the tiers of Priests, he waited irritably for complete silence.

"O Mother of Life, we praise and glorify Thy blessed Light which fills both Heaven and earth with Thy sacred Blood," the drone began, carrying clearly through the sajada. "Good Mother, as we are Thine, preserve us and defend us as Thy own property and possessions."

"*Gloria.*" B'nach responded automatically, his rejoinder lost in thousands of other voices. Beside him, K'ferrin groaned. Philoniah had chosen the longest ceremony in the Book. K'ferrin might be the Keeper of the Oracle, but tradition dictated that the heads of other Orders conducted the services on holy days, free to select the text as they pleased. Philoniah was not one to pass up indulging himself as the center of attention. The worship would go on for hours.

Although B'nach was careful not to smile, he was content to spend this celebration of summer solstice in the prayers and hymns of his lost youth.

"Mother of Life, we feed our souls on the milk of Your celestial Light as a child at its mother's breast, born anew in the innocence of a newborn babe. May it strengthen our Faith and deliver us from the evil we do ourselves."

"*Miserere nobis.*" The murmur echoed around the sajada and died away into quiet so complete that even in that huge dome B'nach could hear the flutter of pages as Philoniah thumbed through the Book. He waited patiently, although he knew the texts as well as, if not better than, any in the Citadel. The words of the Book had been scorched into him since childhood, like a brand on his soul. The old man removed his glasses to wipe the fogged lenses before painstakingly adjusting them on his sharp nose. He scanned the pages, dragging the silence out. B'nach ignored K'ferrin's sigh of exasperation.

"As it is written," Philoniah began, "Rejoice in the Light, for these are the Children which I have called to Me, blessed are they. P'arosh, the first of those who Walked the Fire to give the words of Prophecy, and he who was named M'veth who came after P'arosh, and he who was named Jeshu who came after M'veth, and she who was named Arhan who came after Jeshu, and he who was named J'orat who came after Arhan, and he who was named Sh'lam . . ."

As he listened to Philoniah reciting the names of failed Saints in a flat monotone, B'nach closed his eyes and prayed silently, knowing the progression by heart. He had always hated this part of the liturgy, while begging the Saints' forgiveness in his guilt. His heart thudded dully as the interminable list dragged on. The sajada seemed to hold its breath as Philoniah neared the end of the roster.

". . . and she who was named Sisava who came after G'beas . . ." The old man's voice faltered, but B'nach refused to open his eyes, breathing shallowly, feeling the prying stares around him like the touch of diseased fingers. ". . . and he who was the last before the One who will come, N'aldar who came after Sisava," Philoniah continued, "blessed are their names in testimony of the Light, forever and ever."

"*Gloria*," B'nach breathed in relief.

He had known N'aldar. Sisava was dead a year before he was born, one of T'ain Shan's breed. N'aldar had been only a few months younger than B'nach, fair-haired and shy, an aspirant from Philoniah's clan, although of distant blood to the old Priest. K'ferrin had forced his grandson to attend when the boy made his Walk.

B'nach had watched his friend being torn apart by the starfire. When N'aldar realized he had failed, his face shocked and distraught, he had bravely done his best to keep control of his mind and mouth as he described the sensations. His voice was faint but clear in the hush, the thousands who had attended the Walk silent. But the hatred and anger were visible in the eyes furtively glancing toward B'nach. After the fire had eaten away the boy's face, his voice became harder to understand, dissolving finally into gibberish when his mind broke.

Horrified, B'nach tried to run away as N'aldar began to scream. His grandfather's hand on his neck pinioning him, he squeezed his eyes shut, opening them only when K'ferrin shook him hard enough to rattle his teeth. He watched, shamed and sickened as the body trapped within the Light turned hazy, the golden luster of the Oracle changing to deepest red, like wine swirled in one of his grandfather's handblown glass decanters. The screams continued long after N'aldar's outline vanished.

B'nach had murdered him.

The Oracle gleamed for five days after the Walk. K'ferrin congratulated Philoniah; N'aldar's spirit had sustained the Light longer than most Saints. Surely, they had been very close.

But Philoniah knew, as did the rest of the Citadel, what lay behind K'ferrin's gracious words. N'aldar was dead because B'nach was still alive. And for as long as K'ferrin controlled his grandson, he also controlled the Oracle. Never had a Reverence been more powerful than K'ferrin, his triumph built on the failure of his blood. It was B'nach's punishment, and his disgrace. In the twenty years since N'aldar's Walk, the Oracle had starved for Saints.

Philoniah cleared his throat. "Holy Mother, from whom all life descends, we praise Thee and Thy children born of the union of darkness and light, cold and fire. Thou has given us the One Path on which to set our feet, and we follow the Way set before us . . ."

B'nach exhaled quietly. He had been through enough of these ceremonies to know no one would dare glance in his direction, no one even accidentally meeting his gaze. It gave him a perverse freedom to look around at the occupants inside the huge sajada.

The rows of Priests were divided into their five respective Sectors like different petals of a strange flower. As Keeper of the Holy Oracle, K'ferrin led his own burgundy-robed Priests, with B'nach at his side for reasons having nothing to do with honor.

Philoniah's Sacred Sciences were a wash of blue on his left, and mild mannered T'ain Shan, High Lord of the Profane Sciences stood with his yellow retinue at the far end. On B'nach's right, Terhune's black-clad Elite studded the red robes of the army like decay on the petal of a rose, Ameveth's green clad Engineers an uneasy leaf beside them.

Terhune stood in the midst of his Elite, his second in command, the *qazaq* D'arim, at his right hand. Where Terhune was tall and lean, the flat-faced man beside him was stocky and barrel-chested. If quite different physically, the two men were kindred spirits, as close as vipers entwined in the same nest. D'arim scanned the assembly with restless attention and B'nach shivered, looking away to avoid his eye.

"We have fallen away from the purity of Thy spirit," Philoniah droned on. "Cleanse us of the impurities of this world, that we may pass through Thy Blood anew and be reborn in perfection."

Only one white robe stood isolated in all that color, reflecting the kaleidoscope of light spattered on its virgin cloth. G'walch. B'nach stared in fascination at the boy standing modestly beside his uncle, P'tre Terhune. A sharp jab of his grandfather's elbow in B'nach's ribs jerked him back to attention. He dropped his gaze to the floor, more to avoid K'ferrin's glare than from any humility.

He couldn't have been caught off guard at a worse moment. "Many shall be called but only One is chosen," Philoniah was saying. "Weed out the unworthy from among us to find the One conceived of Thy Light and made Flesh, who will unite with Thee in the sanctity of Thy Womb and returned to us through Thy Blood, the Perfect One who will join all the Lands as One Land, bound in the one true Faith everlasting."

He didn't look at K'ferrin, although he knew the words hit at his grandfather like stones. But even with his head bowed meekly, B'nach had to fight his anger and resentment. A pureblooded son of the Blessed Families, he was born into the Faith and raised in the Citadel, with the same right to the sacraments as any. Others less innocent than himself, despite his disgrace, had no right to shame him into withdrawing from the holy liturgy. If he had failed, so had those who had shepherded him.

"Mother of Life, we Thy devout servants whose faith and devotion are known to Thee offer up ourselves to Thee in sacrifice."

"Orate, fratres et sororis ut meum ac vestrum sacrificium acceptable fiat apud Matre et Oraculum omnipotenem."

He heard the derision in his grandfather's voice even over the thousands of voices echoing in the sajada. Closing his eyes, he shut out the sounds around him by sheer will, listening only to the words, then only to the prayer in his own heart. He

thought about the sacrifices his grandfather had made, and who
had been the lamb and who the knife. How could God or the
Oracle still yearn for his blood, knowing it was tainted? Secretly, he frightened himself with heresy.

He wanted to live, even if it was a wretched existence of
guilt and cowardice, even with the scorn of the Faith heaped
on him. No one in the Citadel longed to see someone Crowned
in the Fire more than he; many would be all too happy to see
that day never arrive.

"Mother of Life, we humbly cast ourselves upon our knees
in Thy sight, look down in mercy upon all who trust in Thee,"
Philoniah read in his lackluster voice, and paused as the wor-
shipers knelt in a vast rustle of robes. B'nach reached out one
hand without looking up, supporting K'ferrin as the old man
levered himself to the floor. His grandfather fidgeted getting
the low bench hidden within his robes settled under him.
Barely high enough to support him so that he sat rather than
knelt, the stool alleviated the weight on his knees, but covered
by his robes it created the illusion of kneeling.

B'nach preferred to kneel, knowing he would almost relish
the pain after two hours on the cold stone. K'ferrin soon nodded off, his head jerking upright only when the long prayers
were punctuated with the occasional booming "*Gloria*" echoing through the sajada.

The sunlight streaming through the Crystal Dome had diminished by the time Philoniah reached the final pages of the
service. The old man's voice was hoarse, although he reso-
lutely lumbered toward the finish. "Seek among our hearts the
purity and goodness from which a new Light shall be born of
Thy Celestial Blood, and a new mankind shall walk Thy earth
in eternal rapture. *Gloria in excelsis.*" He looked up and slowly
closed the Book.

"*Sicut erat in principio, et nunc, et semper, et in saecula
saeculorum.*" Everyone in the huge assembly methodically
bowed their heads to the ground, not a sound in the domed
sajada except the breath of prayers and the subliminal melody
of the Oracle sighing for blood.

Mother of God, grant me courage . . . It had been the same
simple prayer he had repeated since his downfall, over and

over, until the repetition had become a worn rote, comforting if meaningless.

He was aware when others began to rise, mingled voices chatting as they filed out of the sajada. He stayed on his knees, forehead pressed to the back of his hands on the stone floor, still chanting his silent prayer. K'ferrin had already clambered up without his help, and B'nach ignored the slippered feet by his head as his grandfather shifted his weight impatiently. But not even the High Lord Keeper of the Oracle could prevent him from praying however long he wanted. Sometimes he imagined himself turned to stone, forever kneeling, immune to the needs of his own flesh, safe from the invasion of others. Finally, B'nach sat back on his haunches, weariness settling over him like a soothing blanket, and climbed to his feet.

"Your surfeit of piety fools no one, B'nach," K'ferrin hissed under his breath. "Will you next ape those cretins in Philoniah's Order who call themselves Flagellants, chanting as you whip yourself into a bloody froth, pierce your cheeks with needles, swallow burning stones?" B'nach didn't bother to look over at the group of emaciated men and women gathered around the High Lord of the Sacred Sciences. K'ferrin snorted his contempt. "Flatulents, they should be called. You make yourself look as ridiculous wallowing in your humiliation, if not merely hypocritical." K'ferrin sneered as he tucked his little wooden bench discreetly inside his overgown while expertly smiling and nodding graciously at passing acquaintances.

B'nach wished his longed-for courage could start by defying K'ferrin, but he was too tired for a quarrel. "Yes, Grandfather," he said submissively, then added, "Please forgive my hypocrisy." He kept his expression neutral as K'ferrin glanced at him sharply.

Whatever retort K'ferrin might have had was cut off by Terhune heading in their direction, D'arim by his side. The Warrior-Priest pushed through the crowd like the prow of a ship cleaving the water before it, monks jostling elbows in their haste to scramble out of his way. G'walch followed placidly in his wake.

"My dearest High Lord K'ferrin, walk with me, I beg you," Terhune said, without a hint of entreaty in his tone.

"It would be my greatest pleasure, my esteemed Priest," K'ferrin replied with the same level of insincerity.

"Perhaps my brother would be so kind as to walk with me?"

It took B'nach several heartbeats before he realized the soft voice belonged to G'walch and he was the brother the boy referred to. He stared speechless as G'walch slipped his hand into the crook of B'nach's arm. Terhune and K'ferrin studied them with wary mistrust.

"I would be honored," B'nach finally managed to say, with complete honesty. His head whirled, prickles of sweat breaking out on his skin, and he wondered if he'd inhaled too much of the narcotic incense during the ceremony.

After a moment, K'ferrin offered Terhune his arm, and the two pairs strolled together toward one of the five exits slowly disgorging the Faithful from the Great Sajada.

"I assume you know about Hadzida, Your Reverence?" Terhune said conversationally.

"Naturally," K'ferrin said, matching Terhune's bored tone. "I am aware of all the little squabbles that go on in the Lands, even those as distant as the Sheruben and Water Cross."

"Then it doesn't concern you that the woman gave the Sheruben *back* to Vodos?" Terhune said with deceptive calm. "Vodos has sworn a truce with C'ristan, and both of them as well as Elotin of the Nine Steppes have sworn an oath of fealty to her, an alliance which has tripled her forces overnight."

B'nach knew his grandfather well enough to sense the subtle change. K'ferrin hadn't known. His grandfather had expected Terhune to propose ransoming Lord Vodos, anticipating the pleasure of denying him. K'ferrin's own intelligence had assured him that with Lord Vodos executed as expected, his Lands would rebel within weeks against this new, if unusual, conqueror, costing the Faith nothing while eliminating both Vodos and the woman. A puppet replacement had already been groomed for the job, with K'ferrin, not Terhune, controlling the wealth of the Sheruben flowing into his coffers.

"Come now, P'tre," K'ferrin said scornfully, covering any surprise. "Do you really expect such oaths from minor Lords like C'ristan and, for God's sake, that grubby little savage *Elotin* to last longer than a few months? To a Landless *woman*?" He laughed, an elegant sound of contempt. "Lord

Vodos is a shrewd man; no doubt he promised what he had to until he can strike back. And what of it? While this is indeed an enjoyable little farce, it hardly concerns the affairs of the Faith."

"Better to prick a small pustule than allow it to grow into a fatal cancer, Your Reverence," P'tre said. "Allowing it to continue sets a bad example. It is an ill omen when Lords ally themselves for the first time against the Faith . . ."

"Against *Adalon*, P'tre . . ." K'ferrin interjected.

"Against the *Faith*, K'ferrin," P'tre shot back, all veneer of civility gone. He jerked his arm away. "Should she and her kind win against me because you failed to prevent it, how long will it take in their boldness to strike against *you*? Would you risk the Faith just to see my downfall? As you risk the Faith with that cowardly spat of yours preventing my nephew from Walking the Fire?"

K'ferrin and Terhune glared openly at one another in the wide corridor as B'nach stood with his head down, his face hot with shame. G'walch watched the confrontation with a faint smile. Other Priests retreated around them, leaving the four as an isolated island in the midst of the nervous crowd.

"You flatter yourself, Priest," K'ferrin hissed, his face mottled with anger. "No one is denying G'walch his Walk but you. Perhaps enough blood of the Blessed Families has washed away the imperfection of your line. If your *nephew* is indeed the One, he need have no fear of my worthless grandson."

Terhune's eyes narrowed. Few doubted that Terhune had had more to do with breeding G'walch than simply strategy. Only Terhune's luckless half sister knew the truth and she was conveniently dead.

B'nach trembled as D'arim moved between Terhune and K'ferrin, his hand resting casually on the hilt of his own ceremonial dagger. Feeling tainted, he fervently wished to flee back to the shadowed safety of his library.

"Uncle P'tre, I'm sure my High Lord K'ferrin is right," G'walch said, his young voice sweetly musical. "My brother is no risk to the Faith. He was like a man born blind. How can one appreciate the Light without first knowing the darkness? A man who has only known virtue and compassion has no defense against natural human corruption. What point is there in B'nach sacrificing his life now?"

Although there was no reproach in G'walch's voice, B'nach glanced up briefly at Terhune and his grandfather, uncertain how either of them were accepting this criticism. K'ferrin looked alarmed, but B'nach was amazed by Terhune's humble attention to the boy's words.

"How could I hope to aspire to the Walk if I carried any resentment or uncertainty within my heart?" G'walch turned his dazzling smile on K'ferrin. "Surely my Lord K'ferrin has the same hopes as you that I will succeed?"

"Of course, my child," K'ferrin said smoothly. "When the time is right." If G'walch heard the deceit in the old man's voice, he gave no sign.

"And you, my dearest brother?" B'nach started in surprise. The boy had turned to look up into his face, radiating tranquility. "Will you not pray for me?"

B'nach inhaled a deep, ragged breath, fighting the impulse to kneel before the boy and beg his blessing. "With all my heart," he said fervently. He prayed for G'walch to be crowned in the Chalice of Light. He prayed for G'walch to set him free.

He heard K'ferrin stifle an annoyed sigh. G'walch turned his face away, and B'nach felt as if a gentle breeze had suddenly died, leaving him sweating and uncomfortable.

"We are distracted from our true duty by a petty dispute over Lands," K'ferrin said reluctantly. "You have my permission, P'tre, to use the resources of the Faith against this annoying parvenu of yours." He cut short the smile of triumph that flickered over Terhune's lips. "Your Elite should be more than enough to bolster your own Land's regular armsmen. Break her and destroy this alliance, but no more Purges. You must humble these Lords, not destroy them."

"You do not give me enough men to make much difference, K'ferrin," Terhune protested.

K'ferrin snapped his fingers at B'nach. Reluctantly, he slipped his arm from under G'walch's hand to move obediently behind his grandfather. K'ferrin stared at Terhune with ill-disguised contempt.

"If you haven't enough men to crudely bludgeon her to her knees like a dull-witted bully, then take a lesson from your

enemy. Be creative, use your imagination." He snorted, a
sound too hostile to be a laugh. "You *do* have one, don't you?"

Terhune's face was stony as he bowed. "Of course, Your
Reverence," he said without a trace of irony. Enough imagination, B'nach was sure, to have invented any number of intriguing methods to take revenge on K'ferrin.

B'nach followed his grandfather's narrow back as they
strolled through the long corridor to their own Sector. He was
grateful to retreat to the Great Library, slip into the sanctuary
of his hidden nook buried behind his books and parchments.
There was work to be done, a pleasant distraction, but it took
time before his hand stopped shaking enough to trust taking
up the quill.

18

Lord Cristan's healer was an elderly man, lank white hair
drooping over a perpetual expression of befuddlement, which
did not lend him an air of medical prowess. He had boiled up
a thin gruel of willow bark before offering it with palsied
hands to Antonya.

Wearing only a light linen robe, she lay on a divan, her ribs
a solid mass of swollen blue flesh. She took the cup from the
old healer's hands, wincing at the persistent ache in her injured
wrist. As she forced down the bitter infusion, he examined the
bandages on her chest, groping not so much in distaste or
pleasure at fondling womanly flesh, she decided, but because
his eyesight was failing. She hastily shifted the lizard out of
the way of his bumbling fingers. The beast was unusually le-
thargic. It had escaped injury in the battle, but she wondered
if the medicine she was gagging down was affecting it.

Daen lounged on the window ledge overlooking the garden,
while Tobias carved a chess piece from a scrap of firewood,
his boot blade snicking idly. Woodchips littered the floor at
his feet. As Kerrick ducked through the doorway, the healer
squinted at the ceiling as if searching for answers in the arcane
cracks of plaster and smudges of candle soot. He muttered
vaguely before taking back the empty cup, then patted An-

tonya absently on the head as he might a small child before wandering in the general direction of the door, totally unaware of her scowl. Behind her, she heard Daen's muffled laughter.

Kerrick was trying to hide his grin as he took the elderly man by the elbow and steered him out of the room. After the man had gone, he turned toward Antonya, the door still open. "Lord Vodos wishes to meet with you. Are you up to it?"

"As much as I'm likely to be." She sighed, her voice strained from the bandages strapped tightly around her ribs.

The Lord must have been standing just outside the door. He nodded politely as he passed the Defender, striding confidently toward where Antonya lay supine. He stopped a few paces away, hesitating before bowing deeply to her with a bemused expression.

She chuckled. "Still not sure what the proper formalities are, my Lord? Or is it that you find the sight of your brash young conqueror trussed up like a midwinter's roast goose to be comical?"

"A bit of both, my Lady," he said easily. "However, I trust your health is improving rapidly."

"Not as rapidly as I'd like, to be honest," she said, a bit breathlessly. The bandages girdling her ribs left little room for air in her lungs. "But I'll be up and about before you start having second thoughts about insurrection."

His smile widened, although his eyes chilled. "You wound me, madam. I'm no oathbreaker, even to a woman."

She rested her weight on one elbow, wincing in pain. "I would never have had you swear your fealty to me if I thought you were, sir." She eyed him standing stiffly before her. "Thus, as my trusted ally, you are permitted to sit in my splendid presence," she added wryly. "Forgive me for not doing the honors myself. Daen, could you find a chair worthy of our illustrious guest?"

The Lord smiled and relaxed as the young armsman returned carrying a chair with short, ornately carved arms, its seat covered with a fine needlepoint cushion bearing Lord Vodos's own family crest. One leg had a faint char along the edge.

"We managed to save a few things from your palace, my Lord," Antonya said as he raised an eyebrow. "Would you care for a glass of wine?"

Lord Vodos settled onto his erstwhile furniture, adjusting his scabbarded sword around his outstretched legs. "Also rescued from my palace?" he asked without rancor.

"Unfortunately, no," she said as Kerrick poured the red wine into pewter cups. "As you will no doubt know from the taste. I'm afraid the best I have to offer you is meager soldier's fare, generous on spirits but rather lacking in quality. We've likewise depleted our good Guildmaster Nerum's cellar as well as his larder. Until your Lands are again up to producing your outstanding wines, we'll have to settle for this."

Kerrick handed a mug to Vodos. "My Lands will be productive again faster than you might think, Lady Antonya," he said with pride in his voice. "Our people are as excellent as our wines."

Antonya lifted her pewter mug toward him. "Then to the speedy recovery of your domains, my Lord, and the quick return of something better than this dreadful muck."

Vodos smiled and drank deeply without a grimace, then dabbed the corners of his mouth genteelly with his knuckles. "Lord C'ristan's first supply of grain has arrived," he said, his demeanor abruptly businesslike. "I've charged my own men with the distribution as they know my Land best and where the need is greatest. But we've had a few complaints from C'ristan's officials suspecting my people of skimming grain to sell on the black market."

"And is there truth to this charge?"

He shrugged one shoulder. "No matter how many cats, one may only limit the number of mice in a granary but never eliminate them completely. In the past, I've found it wiser to tolerate a small amount of graft rather than waste time and effort trying to eradicate it." He smiled grimly. "However, I suspect the complaint is less concerned with the crime than with resentment that it is *my* people who are profiting rather than C'ristan's."

He sat with deceptive ease, but too motionless as he watched her.

"Is this creating a problem with supply?" she asked.

"Not yet," he said obliquely.

She frowned. "I see. I will speak with my Lord C'ristan. I need cooperation, not antagonism. However, I meant what I promised. These are your Lands, Lord Vodos. Govern them as you will."

He nodded, satisfied. "Then there is another problem I'd like to broach, if I may, Lady. After years of dragging his cold feet, my dear Lord C'ristan is now exceedingly anxious to see my son married off to his charming daughter. However, there are no Priests in Hadzida. Not one returned after the city surrendered."

The situation might have appeared trivial, but Antonya knew Lord Vodos was far more interested in the strange desertion of Priests from Hadzida than with the details of a proper wedding for his son. She noticed Kerrick stiffening. "Have you searched for a parish Priest in any of the outlying villages?"

He nodded. "Indeed. My troops found sajadas locked and deserted, the signaling fires damped. I've sent messengers to Asteria where a few of our Priests have taken refuge. The rest are nowhere to be found, and I assume they are on their way to the Oracular City. Those few of the Faith we could find are most reluctant to return, and my Lord Mufrid of Donaq adamantly declined to join in your coalition. Nor has Lord C'ristan found any Priests within his own borders available to conduct spiritual ceremonies. Lord Elotin is less sure, as his communications are not as organized as ours, but it seems Medebah is experiencing a sudden ecclesiastical lack as well."

Tobias had stopped carving; the room was quiet.

"Terhune has pulled them out," Antonya said finally.

"So it appears," Lord Vodos agreed flatly. "Lady Antonya, forgive me if I sound like an old tutor lecturing an impudent young student. You do not lack for courage or cleverness, but you are still quite inexperienced. You have a few hundred armsmen loyal to you. Lord C'ristan's tenth to you is fifteen hundred armed men and four hundred horse. My tenth is near double that. Elotin may or may not supply you with more than his tenth, depending on whether his greed outweighs his caution. You now have monies available to pay additional mercenaries, but no more, I would guess, than a few thousand. That gives you an army of fewer than ten thousand men and considerably less horse, and most of the men have been lifelong enemies of the very soldiers they suddenly find themselves companions-in-arms with. This makes for a volatile situation."

She glanced up behind Vodos to meet Kerrick's eyes.

"Madam," Vodos continued steadily, "Terhune commands an Oracular Army half of a million strong, all seasoned soldiers, well trained and well equipped with arms and horse. You haven't a bloody prayer."

"You've sworn an oath to defend my Lady from her enemies," Kerrick said quietly behind him.

Lord Vodos chuckled humorlessly. "And so I shall. But I no longer have the brashness of youth as do your young armsman. You don't live to be my age by rushing into battle eager to die for a glorious cause."

He drained the rest of his wine and looked back at Antonya. "Nay, the wise thing would be for me to supply you with my tribute of armsmen and not a single soldier more. Those of my men and C'ristan's not too stupid to realize they were committing suicide would soon desert, as would most of the hired mercenaries. You would be crushed. Terhune would march into the Sheruben, Purge a few villages here and there and impose a penalty on those Lands who supported you, just to make his point. He might execute me and C'ristan." Vodos shrugged. "Then again he might not. A Lord cowed is easier to control than an ambitious newcomer. It is an acceptable risk."

The silence in the room was heavy. "You've impressed me as being a wise man, my Lord," Antonya said softly, "as well as honest."

"On the other hand," Vodos continued, as indifferently as if discussing the weather, "were I and my Lord C'ristan as well as whatever semblance of an army Elotin can scrape together to support you with everything we've got, you could raise a force of slightly more than"—he calculated for a moment, more for effect, she suspected—"sixty thousand men and half as many horse. I doubt Terhune will use his entire army against us, half to put down a simple rebellion with half in reserve in the Citadel. Given the slightest chance at winning, your army would be fighting for its life, and fighting hard. The odds then would be a mere three to one against us."

Behind him, Kerrick scowled.

"We would still most likely lose, my Lord, and Terhune would never spare you then," Antonya said. The willow bark potion was wearing off; there was a dull throb in her chest.

"I've already lost, madam. Perhaps being beaten by a girl-child has bruised my pride and made me rash. Perhaps I'm getting old and would rather die in a good fight than live as a whipped dog. Maybe I'll risk everything now because if I do what is 'wise,' the Land my son inherits will be nothing more than a pauperized mound of sod."

"Perhaps and maybe, my Lord," Antonya said wryly. "And perhaps and maybe you'd want something in return for this call above and beyond your sworn pledge?"

"Aye," he said candidly. "Once you reclaim your father's Land, it would be in my interest to continue this alliance, and maintain a unified south to hold back the Faith's aggressions." His eyes hardened. "But as *equals*. If we should survive this venture, release me from my vow of servitude to you."

She smiled. "Agreed." She ignored the rustle and murmur of surprised armsmen behind her.

If Lord Vodos was amazed at the speed at which she accepted, he hid it by rising to his feet and bowing smoothly. "You haven't much time, madam. I beg leave to begin organizing my men."

She leaned back against the divan, unable to hide the pain any longer. "By all means, Lord Vodos," she said, closing her eyes.

When she didn't hear him depart, she opened her eyes to find him studying her. "Lady Antonya, you will need to be ready soon to ride, if not fight as well."

She chuckled painfully. "I'm working on it, sir."

"With all due respect for my esteemed friend Lord C'ristan," Vodos said cynically, his lack of respect evident, "his healer is more suited for pulling splinters from the fingers of small children, if his elderly eyes could even see well enough to find a splinter. Personally, I wouldn't trust the man to trim my beard." He hesitated. "I would send to you my own man, Guyus. He's a soldier's man and has treated me before for injured ribs, among more serious wounds. It is his opinion that binding the chest does more harm than good. Restricting breathing may ease the pain, but concentrates the baleful humors in the lungs."

She regarded Vodos carefully.

"I know of no one better able to get you back on a horse."

She didn't bother to admit she hated the backs of horses. "I am most grateful, sir," she said.

19

The two Elite standing guard outside the massive doors of Terhune's apartments were as inert and blank-faced as statues, as if unaware of the *qazaq* leaning with one foot propped against the opposite wall waiting patiently. They remained immobile as a woman shrieked, her cry muffled behind the carved doors.

D'arim paused in trimming his nails with his boot knife, cocking his head to listen with remote curiosity. The wail subsided to a barely audible sob, broken into a carnal rhythm as regular as a heartbeat. He returned his attention to his hands.

An hour ticked by. D'arim sighed, finished his manicure and slipped the knife back into its sheath. He rubbed a forefinger and thumb against his eyelids, massaging the tiredness threatening to blossom into a full-blown headache. He changed position, propped his other foot against the wall, crossed his arms over his barrel chest and rolled his head on his thick neck to ease the small cramp between his shoulders.

And waited.

Yawning, he leaned his head back to examine the dulled frescoes on the vaulted ceiling above his head, trying to pick out the figures of ancient heroes and saints in the flaking paint. The angle made his neck kink even worse, so he contemplated the geometric pattern of mosaic tiles on the floor under his feet.

A maidservant shuffled nervously down the hall with a stack of laundry in her arms, the steamy fragrance of freshly pressed linen pleasant in the chill air. D'arim grinned as she jumped at another piercing scream, the linens threatening to tumble from her jittery arms before she hurried past, her eyes downcast. His smile faded quickly.

Another hour passed before a pair of Elites marched down the wide hall from where the maidservant had disappeared, replacements escorted by Briston, a captain D'arim knew well. The captain ignored him as the guardsmen came to a halt before the two standing outside the doors. The four saluted sharply and exchanged places with quick military precision. Then Briston turned, the four guardsmen at attention behind him. The five men saluted D'arim, backs stiff, faces expressionless, arms locked into place, and waited.

D'arim hadn't moved, his posture still loose and relaxed as he regarded the younger captain. A head taller than the *qazaq*, Briston was handsome almost to the point of pretty; gold where D'arim was charcoal, blue eyes deceptively mild where D'arim's black irises were hidden by the epicanthic fold of his eyelids, an aquiline nose to D'arim's squashed nose set between equally flattened cheekbones. He had been handpicked for his loyalty, his fighting skills, and, most important to D'arim, his quick intelligence. It was both his best quality and his potential downfall, were that intelligence ever to become infected with any personal ambition.

D'arim trusted him, up to an uneasy point, and even admitted to himself to liking the man, within reason, which was as high in his affections as anyone, male or female, could ever hope to reach. But Briston was not a friend. With the exception of P'tre Terhune, D'arim had no friends in the Citadel, nor did he encourage any notion of familiarity among his men. He had no lover, no children, no vices nor weakness which could be exploited by his enemies. His ruthlessness made him feared, but he played no favorites, having no favorites, and his impersonal discipline made him respected. The closest he'd venture from his self-imposed hermetic isolation was the occasional chess game played with Briston. D'arim enjoyed the man's lively competitive spirit and his cynical wit. In return, the young captain knew his place, never assumed familiarity with his superior, never attempted to intrude past the barriers D'arim erected.

Finally, D'arim returned the salute with an easiness bordering on lazy. The guardsmen snapped into an inflexible pose only remotely resembling relaxed. But Briston's glacial expression warmed to D'arim's faint smile.

"Still here, sir?" he said, unable to keep the irony out of his voice.

D'arim shrugged. "I've been ordered to attend on my High Lord Commander's pleasure. If it's his pleasure I should wait outside his doors and hold up this wall for hours on end, then I do so gladly."

The woman's bleak wail quavered behind the doors, making both replacements jerk in surprise. D'arim shot them an acid glare, all pretense of languor gone. It was sufficient. Nothing less than a full-scale attack would cause either to so much as blink.

Briston had not been startled by the cry; his lips thinned with contempt. The glance he exchanged with D'arim left the *qazaq* mildly disturbed, seeing in it a reflection of his own feelings: fear, disgust, frustration and, most troubling, a deep sadness. The expression vanished instantly, replaced by the blank mask all Terhune's Elite habitually wore.

D'arim nodded stiffly at Briston. "That's all, Captain."

Briston turned on his heel smartly, marching the two guardsmen down the corridor in the same direction the servant had gone, their bootsteps resonating against the walls.

The screams eventually stopped, although the doors remained shut. This wasn't the first time P'tre had kept D'arim lingering in the hallway, but it was happening more frequently and for longer periods of time. That P'tre treated him with as little courtesy as he might the lowest of menials didn't bother the *qazaq*. D'arim was a patient man; it was the wasted time that annoyed him.

His bladder began to ache uncomfortably as the light faded from the hallway, long shadows creeping along the floor. He was wondering if he dared leave for the few minutes necessary, when the faint sounds of normal movement alerted the guards. Their swords clanged as they snapped rigidly to attention seconds before the doors were opened from the inside. D'arim's casual demeanor instantly disappeared, his own bearing as hardened as his men's at Terhune's approach.

Terhune didn't bother with returning his second-in-command's salute. "Inside, D'arim," he ordered brusquely.

He turned away without waiting for the *qazaq*'s response. D'arim saluted his back, more for the benefit of the guards, and strode into Terhune's private tower apartments. The servants shut the doors behind him.

Like Briston, D'arim also knew his position and respected its limitations. But Terhune's blatant lack of respect in front of subordinates angered him. He had never pretended to be anything more than what he was, a low-caste peasant's son from a destitute Land humbled under the Purge, and his pride was not easily wounded. It was Terhune's increasingly discourteous manner toward his closest companion that adversely influenced his status in the eyes of the Elite. If his men began to doubt D'arim had less than the full support of their High Lord, it would diminish his effectiveness as Terhune's right-hand man as well as Terhune's own power.

He kept his expression carefully neutral as he followed Terhune into his apartments, attentive to the man's mood and ready to adopt whatever attitude was required.

Terhune led him to the tower's open balcony, the tapestries pulled back to let in the cool evening air. To D'arim's relief, when Terhune turned he was smiling, relaxed and calm. His dark hair was tousled and instead of his usual armor he had on a well-worn overgown fastened loosely around his lean body with the embroidered sash D'arim had presented to him several years previously.

Terhune settled onto one of the floor cushions in the balcony alcove, pushed a gaming board on the top of a small table out of the way and extended a hand toward D'arim. "Sit, my brother. Wine?"

D'arim reached out to clasp Terhune's hand, the grasp warm and firm, and allowed his commander to pull him down to the pillows beside him. "Aye, with pleasure." His full bladder told him otherwise.

Terhune glanced at one of the young servants, his look order enough, and the boy scurried to obey. As D'arim settled himself on the floor, he noted that neither the twilight breeze nor the spice of Terhune's perfume could quite cover up the faint musk of sex. He scanned Terhune's face, noting the puffiness around his gray eyes, the slight tension behind the smile. The rage always lurking below P'tre's skin was still there, his lust unsatisfied.

The servant returned and D'arim looked away, uneasy. He waited for the boy to kneel and take a sip from the wine. Both men watched the servant for signs of poison, knowing from tedious habit exactly how long to wait before accepting the cup. Finally, D'arim took his own and drank first as a courtesy to Terhune.

Another servant settled himself just behind the wooden latticework separating the balcony alcove from the main room, cradling a pillar-harp between his legs. The harpist strummed the instrument lightly, his fingers barely touching the strings to keep the music quiet, unobtrusive.

As D'arim placed his cup on the table, he winced, his neck stiff. Immediately, Terhune settled his hand on his shoulder, kneading the tight muscles under the leather. "Turn around," he said, and D'arim set his back to him, loosening his jerkin and the collar of his shirt to allow Terhune's strong fingers to massage his shoulders and neck.

"God's hairy teeth, you're tense," Terhune said, his voice gentle. D'arim let his head hang forward on his chest, eyes shut. "My fault, I'm afraid, leaving you to cool your heels in a drafty hall for half a day." D'arim grunted, uncommunicative. It felt good, not so much having the kinks kneaded out of aching muscles, but the familiar comfort of long companionship. "Forgive me for keeping you so long."

"I can't forgive you, since I haven't blamed you," D'arim said. "It would, however, make my life easier if you would choose to behave toward me less as your friend and more as your military adjunct, at least in front of my men." The hands against his neck paused, fingers pressing hard against his skin. D'arim's heart skipped a beat. "I can't serve you as well as I wish if you undermine my authority by openly displaying our personal intimacy." He kept his voice casual.

Terhune's hands fell away. D'arim twisted to look at his old companion, dismayed by the naked anger on Terhune's face.

"I'll do as I please without need of your whining."

D'arim let none of the anxiety he felt show in his face or voice. "Treat me how you like in private, P'tre," he said firmly, "friend or slave, but unless you want to relieve me of my command, treat me in public as the agent your own authority deserves."

Terhune's face was distorted with warring emotions before settling into an expression of brooding regret. "Not a slave, D'arim, never that," he said quietly. "I hate it when I'm forced to admit you're right, mostly because I detest being wrong."

The harpist played on in the tightened silence.

"I assume there was some reason you sent for me, other than to satisfy your curiosity as to how long my legs could hold up standing around on your doorstep," D'arim said lightly. He had known Terhune long enough to calculate the exact tone necessary to appease his anger. He was relieved to see Terhune slowly smile, then chuckle, the tension diminished if not gone.

"Or your bladder," Terhune replied, teasing.

D'arim didn't want to think about his bladder at the moment.

"This woman, Antonya—" As Terhune paused to drink, D'arim tucked one leg under himself and waited. "I want her."

"Dead, I assume," D'arim said indifferently and was surprised when Terhune didn't respond.

Terhune gazed into the fading sunset, red clouds darkening to violet. Slowly, he shook his head. "No. I want her alive."

D'arim snorted in astonishment. "What in God's love for?"

Terhune rubbed his knuckles thoughtfully, as if soothing an ache. "She's not the first to claim my half brother as her sire."

Puzzled, D'arim shrugged. "So what?"

"Perhaps it's true."

"And perhaps it's not. What does it matter? Even if she *is* R'bert's spat, she's only a bastard girl-child anyway."

Terhune grinned fleetingly. "Aye. But what do you suppose K'ferrin would do if I acknowledged her as my half-brother's true daughter? And since I have no children of my own, not only declared her my heir to Adalon but abdicated in her favor?"

"Probably have you both assassinated," D'arim said promptly.

Terhune laughed. D'arim did not.

D'arim had known Terhune from boyhood, the two learning to fight together, gambling, hawking, drinking, and scheming since before puberty. They had shared secrets and horses and even women, and no one knew Terhune better than the squat, grim *qazaq* Terhune called "brother." But the man D'arim watched drain the wine from his cup was a stranger, his gray eyes cold and distant.

"And where does G'walch stand?" D'arim pressed softly.

Terhune glanced away, his expression enigmatic. "Once G'walch Walks the Fire, we'll have an end to all this petty maneuvering."

D'arim had no doubts Terhune believed in his nephew's destiny. But it was the present which concerned the *qazaq*. In a sudden flash of intuition, he suspected G'walch had had a good deal to do with Terhune's reluctance to simply eliminate his enemy.

"Ah," he said, instantly regretting it as Terhune frowned. "Meantime, we need to deal with problems at hand," he added hastily. "It will be more difficult to take the woman alive, you know. She has considerable troops of her own now."

"A Fever-addled Defender and a motley bunch of mercenary rabble. Hardly a crushing force one quails before." Terhune signaled the servant to replenish his wine. Although his eyes had reddened, his hands were steady and his voice clear. "No, Vodos is the only one I need worry about," he said. To D'arim's relief, now that Terhune could deal with the actual plotting, he was more animated, the dark mood lifting. "He's the only fox running in that bunch of hares. Battle bred and trained, brains as well as heart. Good soldier."

D'arim listened attentively. Terhune's praise for Vodos was only that of a hunter relishing a worthy quarry. His admiration would not prevent him from having Vodos flayed and burnt alive on the altar of his own sajada while his city was Purged.

"What of Lord C'ristan? He's also pledged his men to her . . ."

Terhune scowled and shook his head as he drained his cup and gestured for more wine. "C'ristan uses mercenaries, far too many to make his armies reliable."

"Elotin has horses enough to make up for any lack of cavalry . . ."

"Elotin I needn't waste words on," Terhune cut him off. "Don't presume to lecture me on ignorant peasant scum."

Stung, D'arim hid his reaction by raising his cup to his mouth. Although he let the sweetened wine brush his lips, he didn't drink, his bladder becoming too painful. "So how do we go about snaring the fox and cropping our young doe's ears?" he asked when he could trust his voice again.

"I'll take twenty thousand of the Elite from the Citadel and drive them south into the Sheruben." D'arim felt his mouth pinch with disapproval. If Terhune planned to employ nearly the full force of the Elite, he would be depleting the number of standing troops in the Citadel. And the common soldiers, whom the Elite kept under tight control.

As if he read the concern in D'arim's eyes, Terhune smiled, his good humor restored. "Don't worry, my friend. We'll leave enough behind to keep K'ferrin's hounds at bay. Fifty thousand of my troops are ready to move from Adalon. Split those into two divisions, one will march directly from Sholika, the other down to Ghalaz, commandeer whatever ships we need to sail down the coast into Donaq. While the Elite march in overland, my armsmen from Sholika will cut off any escape to the northeast. Trap her in the Xos Valley, cut her off from the Sheruben, then pinch toward the middle and squeeze." Terhune drew out the last word with relish, illustrating with his fist.

"Why not simply sail from here to Thylas and march into the Sheruben through Qarthia?" D'arim asked.

"All ships sailing from the Citadel are for the business of the Faith only," P'tre said, his mood souring. "It's possible I could confiscate enough stinking fishing barges . . ."

He let the idea drift, his fury with K'ferrin spiraling into the black whirlpool of malevolent violence D'arim increasingly feared. P'tre downed the wine in his cup, slamming the empty cup onto the table as a signal for it to be refilled.

"You're not drinking," P'tre observed irritably. "Is there something wrong with my wine?"

Immediately, D'arim drained his cup and watched glumly as it was refilled. "Not at all. I'm only thinking a sea approach wouldn't be that great an advantage, in any event." D'arim said, his voice even. "The currents this late in the year are wrong along the west coast, anyway; we'd as likely lose time as gain."

"Is that your expert opinion, Admiral?" P'tre teased, although his bloodshot eyes were grim.

"Of course," D'arim said firmly. "You didn't throw me out to sea for two years just for the pleasure of making me seasick, P'tre. Wait a few months, and both the wind and the currents will shift. Or we could march overland in the same amount of time." D'arim would be just as glad to have solid reliable horseflesh under him than the constant threat of a horrible, watery death just a sliver of wood away from under his feet. "Possibly even a bit faster," he added.

P'tre's anger subsided. He grunted his acceptance after a moment's consideration, to D'arim's relief. Then, "Six weeks. I want everything in place ready to strike in six weeks."

D'arim's heart sank. Outside, stars had begun to pop through the rents in clouds invisible in the gloom. D'arim remained silent, already calculating the logistics of P'tre's strategy.

Marching twenty thousand troops overland into the Sheruben would take every bit of his six weeks, pushing them as hard as he could. D'arim silently cursed both P'tre for his obstinate ambitions as well as this wretched woman. P'tre's armsmen in Laird's Ketch could be ready to sail and march within the week, a quick few days' march down to the harbor city of Sholika, and reach Ghalaz in a fortnight. Although Sholika had nothing on the scale of the Citadel's warships, a dozen good-sized corvettes could ferry men and horses along the coastline into Donaq, secure Asteria and press south. With two waves of forces against her from Adalon, the woman's ragtag troops would be near exhaustion by the time the Elite arrived to hit them from behind . . .

But while D'arim deliberated more tedious details—inventories of food and supplies, the best places to stop to reshoe horses, the quickest if more difficult routes overland versus longer routes more favorable to restocking provisions, P'tre's eyes glittered with enthusiasm of a different sort.

"I want her taken alive. Consider it a hunt, D'arim, a fine, grand hunt." D'arim said nothing, having never considered war as anything more than what it was: organized killing, not a sport. This late in the year, the mild autumn weather wouldn't outlast a long march. The *qazaq* preferred a short, hard campaign before the winter rains bogged them down into a less glorious Hell of cold mud.

"Send out the hounds," P'tre enthused, "let fly the falcons, a fine reward for the man who bags her, and woe to those who fail."

"When do you want us to start?"

"Is instantly too soon for you?"

D'arim sighed. "I'd best be going, then."

Terhune laughed and drained his cup. He was now quite obviously drunk, and D'arim watched him warily as he got to his feet, only a slight waver in his posture giving him away. He allowed Terhune to pull him roughly to his feet, returning his bearish hug with stubble-rasping kisses and backslapping hard enough to knock the wind from each other. He made himself smile as Terhune drew back, holding him by the shoulders and gazing at him fondly.

"My old friend," Terhune said, "my dearest brother, no man could have better than you." For a disturbing moment, D'arim was sure the man would weep, his emotions lugubrious with wine. Then Terhune's smile widened, his eyes glittering coldly, and he led D'arim out of the private alcove into the wide central room.

The manservants had lit the oil lamps, flames casting shadows against the high walls. Figures in the tapestries moved with the mock life of sputtering light. The harpist bowed to no one as he dragged his pillar-harp and himself away from Terhune's attention.

Terhune's huge canopied bed, which took up most of one end of the tower room, could easily have slept ten. And all their horses, so they had once joked. As D'arim passed, the curtains drawn around the bed twitched. He stopped, staring at the girl huddled in the tangle of bedclothes. The girl quickly withdrew.

He turned toward Terhune with barely restrained anger. "Who is that?" he demanded, far more sharply than he'd intended. "God damn it, P'tre, how much has she heard?"

Terhune seemed too drunk to notice his impudence. Instead, he averted his gaze like a chagrined child caught at some mischief, attempting to think of a quick excuse. Then his guilty attitude shifted abruptly to one of false good humor. He grinned as he ripped back the embroidered curtains.

The girl crouched as far away as she could, holding the edge of a sheet up to shield her naked pubescent body. This, D'arim knew, had been the source of the screams he'd listened to for hours. His face prickled as large green eyes regarded him steadily, dark lashes wet.

"This?" Terhune said too brightly, the laughter in his voice brittle. "This is Tannah. Say hello, Tannah."

In spite of her bruised face, she was pretty, the beauty of a child on the verge of womanhood. Dark lines of scraped raw skin marked her wrists and neck. D'arim felt his stomach turn over, sickened, knowing the poor girl would now have to die.

"What is she doing here?" he asked, the calm in his own voice dimly surprising. "You should have sent her away before we spoke."

Terhune turned to him, the flat expression in his face alien, unreadable. "She's nobody, D'arim, only a worthless little warren brat. One of thousands of scruffy mushroom lickers breeding like rats in the muck under our floors. Why? Do you have a problem?"

D'arim swallowed and forced himself to shake his head. "No, P'tre. Of course not. No problem."

"Good night, then."

Terhune's drunken embarrassment and feigned mirth were both replaced by something more familiar and far more deadly; casual malice. Not trusting himself to speak, D'arim bowed and walked to the doors, not seeing the servants as they opened them, nor the men saluting him as he walked through. He wanted to believe P'tre hadn't meant for him to see the girl, that it had been an honest mistake. But he knew that when P'tre had finished with her, he could kill her himself without a scruple, but would derive more pleasure in ordering his second-in-command to do the deed.

D'arim was a soldier, not a common murderer. Not the cold-blooded killer of children.

Another test, P'tre? Why? How many will it take . . . ?

He walked blindly up the corridor until it emptied out into a busy main passageway cutting through the Citadel. Suddenly disoriented, he stopped, not knowing where he was. He leaned against a wall, forehead pressed to the back of his hand, fingers digging at the stone. The pain stabbing his heart was irrationally confused with the urgent need pressing his bladder. The senselessness of it made him want to laugh, if only to fight down his own black anger.

"Commander?"

He saw the Elite uniform from the corner of his eye, suddenly horrified any of his men should witness his weakness. He straightened, struggling for self-control and turned to focus on the Elite officer watching him cautiously.

"Sir?"

It was Briston, he was relieved and absurdly grateful to see. The man stood courteously at an angle to shield D'arim from inquisitive stares.

"What?" It came out as a croak. He cleared his throat.

"Is there anything I can do for you, sir?"

The pressure in his groin was unbearable. "Yes," D'arim whispered hoarsely. "Get me to the nearest lavatory before I piss my goddamned pants."

20

It takes time to organize sixty thousand men and half as many horse. All the men were suspicious of those they now would have to trust their backs to. The Sherubens considered the Myronians lazy and capricious, more concerned with filling their bellies and their women than fighting. For their part, the Myronians despised the Sherubans as being impossibly dull, pompous cattle.

Both, however, readily agreed that the Medebans were completely hopeless rustics, lower than the meanest of felons regularly found dangling from the gallows. Antonya felt rather sorry for poor Lord Elotin; his beard had been stylishly trimmed by a Water Cross surgeon and he'd even gone to the trouble of having his hair washed and the lice combed out. A tiny hint of pleated lace at the neck and sleeves peeked out of his rough leathers. Gem-studded rings had sprouted on both hands, and he'd developed the habit of nervously twisting them around his fingers, particularly the largest one signifying his betrothal to the infant Myronian princess. He'd also taken to bowing so deeply and formally to any woman who so much as glanced in his direction, making no distinction in his courtesy between washerwomen and the most noble of ladies, that Antonya feared his back would give out before long. His jaw set, he ignored the amused sniggers of the Sherubens and Myronians as well as jeers of his own unkempt warriors.

But while the Sherubans and Myronians might laugh at the scruffy Nine Steppe warriors, they did not sneer at their horses. Most knights had but one horse while the rich could boast as many as three, a warhorse doubling as baggage transport, a palfrey for the journey, and a spare ridden by an attending squire.

The poorest of Elotin's warriors couldn't hold his head up with dignity if he owned anything less than a dozen of the wiry, tenacious animals. A Medeban tribal chieftain's wealth was measured in the number of stallions he possessed, bridal dowries in terms of brood mares and sturdy-legged colts, distances between towns measured not by miles or leagues but by how far in a day a Medeban horse could carry a fully armed man. Myronians and the Sherubens bargained hard with the Medebans, eager to acquire a few desert-bred horses of their own.

The number of foot soldiers who became mounted squires, and squires who became their own knights, doubled, while Elotin's men began sporting strange bits of finery of their own. Dirty braided hair tucked into a peaked and feathered velvet hat, the front half of an elaborately inlaid and polished bronze Hadzidan corselet tied over a proud tribal chest with plain rope.

Antonya watched a young Water Cross musician sitting cross-legged on the ground, doing his best to bridge the language gap to explain to a darkly suspicious Medeban warrior how to play a beautiful mandolin with two strings missing, while the object of the young bard's ardent desire nibbled the grass beside them. When next she saw the mandolin, it hung from the Medeban's saddle, bouncing against his horse's ribs happily being used, it seemed, as a fancy portable larder.

Between them, Antonya, C'ristan and Vodos had done what they could to mitigate the ingrained bigotry. Carefully ar-

ranged wagers were placed on which army would meet the
Army of the Faith first, who would break and run and who
would stand and fight, whose names would win immortal fame
in song and whose would be reviled for the sniveling cowards
they undoubtedly were. The speculations grew more fanciful
as money was laid down to laughter and good-natured taunts.
More serious quarrels were dealt with promptly, the first few
drunken brawls and knifings ending with the offenders dangling by their necks, a reminder for the men to reserve their
bloodthirst for the battlefield.

By the time Antonya rode out of Hadzida, everything possible had been done to bond the three diverse groups into a
single fighting force. Vodos led his troops out of Kulteph
through the narrow valleys on the eastern range of the Sherubens, Bertil by his side and Verbena, still in breeches and
armor, sticking close to Bertil. They would come out near the
coast on the border of Asteria and drive their battalions up
hard on Donaq's seaward flank. C'ristan, Kerrick and Antonya
would skirt the northwestern edge of the Sheruban, turning
east through the narrow Xous Pass, coming out a day's ride
from Donaq on her northern side. It made little difference,
really, if Mufrid surrendered his capital or not; what mattered
was scissoring off the city from her nearest ally, Lord Braethe
of Tursak, that tiny slice of Land being all that stood between
Antonya and the borders of Adalon.

Meanwhile, Sarnor's mercenaries led a combined company
of Elotin's warriors and soldiers from Myro and Hedzida
northwest to construct battle fortifications along the Sheruben
border against the troops of the Faith they knew would be
coming.

At the first sight of Vodos's troops, Donaq had unexpectedly
thrown open the gates without a fight. Three days later, Antonya rode at the head of her small vanguard, astonished by
the crowd pouring out into the streets, chanting her name:
AnTONya! AnTONya! AnTONya! like some magical incan-
tation to ward off disaster. Thousands of outstretched hands
surged toward her like a sea of anemones, waves of Asterians
welcoming the invaders with distraught haste and pained
smiles pulled back too far to be sincere.

Kerrick had leaned toward her, towering over her from his

bay. "Don't read too much into this, my Lady. Fear has never been a good substitute for loyalty and they'd be cheering P'tre with equal fervor within the hour should he suddenly materialize on the border."

" 'Thou art but mortal dust,' is it?" she joked.

"Better believe it," he said without a smile.

As it turned out, Mufrid had resolved his dilemma by fleeing along with most of his barons. He'd hastily packed up his best clothes and plate, favorite hunting dogs, falcons, sons and mistresses, along with as much of his treasury he could cart away and, under cover of night, sailed southeast toward the relative safety of Dothinia, leaving behind his wife to fend for herself as best she could.

Lady Thylma greeted Antonya on the palace steps, her dazed ten-year-old daughter and Donaq's Guildsmasters beside her. But beneath the Lady's gracious smiles and flattering praise, it was all too easy to see her fury and hope that either Antonya or P'tre Terhune, she didn't give a tinker's damn which, would catch the miserable bastard she'd married, and cut off various parts of his anatomy with dull and rusty instruments.

While Mufrid had saved his own skin, he had strategically left his wife and Lands in a position where any oaths of fealty were impossible. With both husband and sons as deserters, Lady Thylma's authority was uncertain, an abandoned wife neither widow nor regent.

"Frankly, madam, it doesn't make a goddamned bit of difference to me," Antonya had finally managed to interject into the woman's hysterical defense. "It's Adalon I want, not Asteria."

Antonya had been in Donaq just long enough to rest the horse and troops, restock supplies and assure the abandoned wife she could look forward to an early widowhood, when word arrived that P'tre Terhune was on the move.

21

Fighting a war over great distances, D'arim knew, was a bit like a snail race. A single courier on a fast horse could cover twice the distance in a day than could a division of armed and mounted men burdened with military equipment and all the provisions necessary for a long march. Tired couriers could stop at roadside inns for a hot meal and a clean bed, or simply throw down a blanket under a tree if weather permitted. Were the rider in a hurry, his tired horse could be exchanged for a fresh mount along the way for a reasonable sum. A snowstorm was a mere nuisance to a single rider; to an army, winter snows could be a catastrophe.

Several thousand heavy warhorse and formidably armed men riding through a small village would send townsfolk snatching anything not nailed down, fleeing into their houses to lock their doors and windows behind them. They wouldn't reappear until the army had plodded through the center of their hapless town, cursing in its wake as they began repairing the inevitable damage.

Infantry always marched before cavalry. The slightest morning rainfall, and heavy hooves and wagon wheels would quickly churn the roads to impassable mud. Hungry horses and foot soldiers alike stripped fields and orchards like locusts. A march had to be precisely timed to get the maximum distance out of men and horse before stopping for the night. Camps were established in the last waning hours of sunlight, tents thrown up, horses cooled down, fed, watered, camp kitchens built and food dispensed before arms were checked and cleaned and men rolled into their heavy cloaks to sleep scant hours until sunrise. Any minor breakdown along the chain of command, any unforeseen accident, an adverse change in the weather, and a march could become a tactical nightmare. Even when all went well, waging war was still a considerable pain in the ass.

On the other hand, there was always some comfort in knowing the other poor bastard you were fighting had to deal with the same logistical headaches as you.

Daybreak came cold and gray as D'arim rode out of the Citadel at the head of his troops. On the horizon, a thin band of wet sand slit the sea from the tarnished sky with wicked sharpness. Mud flats and estuaries stretched three hundred miles on either side of the Oracular City, seawater washing low isthmuses of limestone rock that dotted the wasteland. Any army foolish enough to drag heavy cannon or horse couldn't withstand the sucking mud and quicksand for long.

Arched wooden bridges on tar-soaked pilings spanned the breaks in the flats. Daily traffic streamed in and out of the city along these narrow bridges, the only safe passage through the salt marshes to reach the road leading east toward the mountains. Heavily armed watchtowers clung to the cliffs along the Xous River, dominated by the great mountain fortress of Kaesyn overlooking both land route and river to keep the Citadel in contact with its Priests in the outlying Lands beyond the mountains and secure from attack from the east. The Oracular City was invulnerable from land.

On the rocky shoreline facing the sea, a long harbor curved around a semicircular cove as neat as if a Promethean sea creature had risen from the depths of the ocean to take an immense bite out of the sheer rock. Light cruisers prowled the waters to guard the Citadel's back, deadly shepherds for the fat fishing boats bobbing through rough waters. In addition to shrimp and sea fish, the Priests were well supplied with mussels and oysters and blue rock crabs gathered from tide pools on the shore. Heavy warships packed the harbor, ready to sail in vigorous pursuit of heretics. The city was impregnable by sea.

In the midst of these sea flats, the Oracular City crowned a huge mountain of granite, a rough oval of rock two miles in diameter and rising twenty-five hundred feet. Tall houses squeezed into narrow streets up the mountain, steps zigzagging toward the high walls of the Citadel. On the lee side of the city, protected from the harsh sea wind, farmers tended terraced fields and orchards with fanatical care. The Oracular City imported most of its luxuries, but the Priests made sure the city could supply enough of its own food to sustain its occupants and withstand any attack or siege.

D'arim's mood was foul and he was secretly pleased the weather reflected it. The tide was still going out, the towering city's upside-down reflection in the wet marsh broken by long expanses of salt grass. A bitter wind blew steadily, dark clouds gliding across the flat roof of sky. D'arim glanced back at the long lines of soldiers winding sinuously across the marsh. Underneath the silt, clusters of grizzled saltbush and tidal pools lay deep ridges of hidden bedrock, an intricate spine of steppingstones flared like the twisted spokes of a woman's broken fan under the silk of mud. Very few were trusted with the secret charts of the Oracular City's surrounding marshlands. A hundred steps to the left or right and the horses would sink into quicksand, heavily armored men sucked down pitilessly into the cold depths of Hell.

The only route used by merchants and pilgrims and couriers for everyday traffic was easily defended. The vital wooden bridges connecting the limestone islands dotting the mud flats had been built to be destroyed on a moment's notice. The majority of D'arim's wagons and baggage horse plodded along the safety of the bridges, pushing gaping spectators aside. D'arim would have preferred to lead the entire company of men and equipment out of the Citadel via the safety of the pilgrims' road before turning south once the solid plainlands had been reached. P'tre, however, favored the grand gesture, deciding the infantry and lighter cavalry would negotiate the marshes.

To the civilians watching from the safety of the bridges, the lines of troops winding their way through the estuaries seemed to be, miraculously, walking on water, the fine muck under the soldiers' boots glimmering under a thin sheet of salt water. D'arim felt the pressure of time, a full twenty leagues to cross before the tide turned back relentlessly on their heels. He cantered back along the line of infantry marching three abreast, their eyes intent on the feet of those in front for any misstep. He pretended not to see the occasional clandestine probe with the shaft of a lance at the mud, making sure there really was something secure on which to place one's boots. Not a man, nor horse, nor wagon would be rescued if caught by the sucking mud, left to drown as his companions raced the tide.

His shaggy chestnut gelding was smaller than the usual charger, its blunt head and barrel chest making it appear clumsy, but D'arim appreciated the animal's endurance, bred on the High Steppes and accustomed to long, arduous treks over rough terrain. It bore the *qazaq*'s weight without complaint, even increased as it was by a heavy-plated corset and gauntlets over his chain-mail shirt and breeches, arbalest and longax slung to one side of the high pommeled saddle and his round strap iron shield on the other.

He rode with one hand braced casually on the hilt of his sword to keep the long blade from slapping his leg as he trotted back along the line. Constantly scanning the Elite troops, he was alert to any signs of limping in the horse, any faltering among his men. His helmet visor up, he was aware of Terhune's approach but looked up only when Terhune reined in beside him from a canter. His expression was neutral as he gave his High Lord a rigidly correct salute.

Terhune returned it with proper respect, then tugged his own horse's muzzle to one side as it nipped at D'arim's unkempt pony. The gelding merely shook its head in reproach, coarse mane veiling its face. The white stallion that Terhune favored was the best of his stables, high-strung warhorses specially bred to combine the swiftness of a charger with the endurance and brawn of a battle-trained Percheron.

Terhune had presented several to D'arim as gifts, and D'arim knew his stubborn choice of the shaggy Steppe pony irked his commander. Inarguably Terhune's cream-and-silver warhorse was far more handsome than the dusty little chestnut. But it wasn't nostalgia for D'arim's lost youth on the dry plains. Like him, the gelding was patient and simple and, like him, it had the stamina to run any of the Elite's more refined mounts dead into the ground and still go for miles more, including the regal stallion cantering beside him with its opulent harness jingling and silks aflutter, immaculate braided tail bound in a tasseled leather queue.

They rode together without speaking, the crow and the falcon, Terhune silent as D'arim barked out the occasional command or rebuke to the column of Elite troops winding its way out of the Citadel and across the long expanse of marshland.

"D'arim . . ." Terhune said finally.

"Sir!" D'arim responded promptly, uncompromisingly military.

Terhune scowled. "Don't."

D'arim didn't pretend he didn't understand. "As you command, my Lord." He met Terhune's eyes evenly, impersonal.

"Goddamn you, D'arim." Terhune looked away in frustration.

D'arim immediately chided himself for his small moment of mean satisfaction. It was beneath him to indulge in such pettiness. He rode erect in the saddle, eyes in front and lowered his voice.

"This is neither the time nor the place, my Lord Commander . . ."

Terhune cut him off. "Then when would that time or place be?" He wheeled his horse around, blocking the gelding to force them both to a standstill. D'arim watched the Elite ride by as if on inspection, knowing none would dare even glance at the two with open curiosity. "You have been avoiding me."

"Not at all. I've been busy on your own orders. Sir."

Terhune's snort of disgust said he didn't believe him. His white pawed one hoof at the mud in agitation, blowing air noisily from delicately flared nostrils. The gelding braced its splay legs placidly, only the muscles of its rump twitching away biting flies. A cold wind blew the decaying salt smell of the marsh as gulls shrilled, wheeling overhead through the mist. Their clean white sleekness didn't camouflage the malevolence in their yellow eyes. D'arim had never liked gulls, never enjoyed sailing, was never comfortable with the vast expanse of water stretching away forever. He was even less comfortable in the midst of the killing muck all around him.

"Do you want the girl?" Terhune finally asked him quietly.

"Have you finished with her, then?" D'arim didn't bother to soften his contempt. He'd been grateful for other second-hand gifts once Terhune had tired of them: horses, jewelry, even whores. It wasn't false vanity which wounded him. "No, I don't want her."

"Then what *do* you want?" Terhune demanded.

D'arim looked up at the glaring man as if seeing him for the first time. He had given up what little he had for a man who owned more than most men dream of in a lifetime. A man with a hunger that couldn't be satisfied with anything less than everything. He'd sacrificed his freedom and even his dignity for Terhune, willingly, and been made to love him for it.

Taken in the Purge, D'arim had been old enough to remember chopping at the parched, barren soil, hauling well water for miles to coax the few stunted crops to survive long enough to get them through the winter and start the futile cycle again. The perpetual hunger grinding in his stomach like a stone, their grain seized by the overlords and Priests. The squalid hut he shared with his parents and five starveling siblings, the reek of sweat and dung and despair. The constant weeping of his mother, either birthing yet another stillborn child or being beaten by his father, a toothless, shriveled, bitter old man of thirty.

Then, on a clear, hot day, his gods had descended like a whirlwind from Heaven, thundering out of myth in a solid mass of bright steel and taken him off to a magical realm he could never have imagined. Plucked up in mid-run and flung across a saddle, he'd buried his face in his captor's chest in terror as, amid the screams of women, squealing pigs and squawking chickens, his little insignificant village was wiped from existence.

Penned in a courtyard with other stolen children, he had been too awed to be afraid. He'd been dazzled by the gleaming weapons of the soldiers, the quick laughter and odd-sounding language. When the tall, black-haired man with the blaze of red on his tunic strode through, kicking soldiers and stableboys out of his way with equal disregard, D'arim had gawked at him brazenly. He barely reached the man's waist, fascinated by the jeweled golden hilt of the sword hanging from the man's belt. Something had made the large man stop and look down on the little *qazaq* child and laugh.

"You want it, boy?" he said, his voice deep and gruff.

Although he had yet to understand the words, D'arim grasped their meaning. He nodded and eagerly reached for the glittering treasure.

The man knocked him down with a casual swipe of his hand. D'arim had seen it coming, too accustomed to his now-dead father's battering to be taken by surprise. He let himself

roll with the slap and landed crouched on his feet, watching
the man cautiously. He didn't weep, nor did he cringe as the
big man stepped toward him, simply ready to dodge the next
blow.

A boy his own age appeared by the man's side, the same
gray eyes and black hair. The boy scowled. The man laughed
again, then tossed a few coins to a Priest. Sold to R'ldan Terhune, D'arim became his son P'tre's constant companion.

To a hungry peasant child suddenly transported into a world
of powerful men and fantastic wealth, the parched mountains
of Laird's Ketch had been a fantasy come true. He dressed in
clothes with no holes or lice, his hunger eased with decent
food for the first time in his short life, although the malnutri-
tion of his childhood permanently stunted his height. He was
grateful to be allowed to crouch silently at P'tre's feet as the
clerk attempted to instill grammar and mathematics and as-
trology and poetry and philosophy into his noble student.
Where P'tre had slumped in his chair, wistfully gazing out the
window, impatient to ride and hawk, D'arim drank in the lessons like honeyed wine to a man half-dead of thirst.

A year later, R'ldan had inherited his office as High Lord
Commander of the Army of the Faith. The white starburst of
the Oracle blossomed in the center of the red Terhune crest,
and D'arim rode in splendor beside P'tre amidst two thousand
men escorting their new High Lord Commander to the Holy
Citadel of the Oracle.

P'tre had been happier there, just another mischievous boy
pleased to play the master to his awed apprentice. D'arim had
been a quick student, becoming as skilled with horse and
sword as P'tre, loving to ride and wrestle and fight. He'd discovered his own talent for intrigue and subversion, with his
ingenuity used always and only for the benefit of the Terhune
family.

P'tre Terhune was his hero, his god, the physical embodiment of this wonderful dream. D'arim worshipped his youthful
Lord as much as any of the hunting hounds that shared their
apartments. They became inseparable, rode together, lived together, ate from the same plate and slept in the same bed
together.

It became a source of secret pride that only *he* knew how

to manage the dark moods that had plagued P'tre all his life. *That damned Terhune boy is in a rage again. Somebody fetch D'arim.* No one else knew how to make P'tre laugh when he was sullen, or scold him when he had gone too far, or when to allow himself to be beaten to drain off the worst of P'tre's black temper. He had never doubted his love was returned. P'tre had recklessly risked his own life in battle more than once to save his friend.

But with R'ldan murdered, without his father's restraining hand, P'tre's violent moods became more frequent and harder to appease. Terhune tested D'arim's blind devotion time and again with D'arim always eager to prove himself.

While he would have followed P'tre into Hell, if that was his young Lord's desire, D'arim felt that sailing came passably close to duplicating the terrors of the underworld. P'tre loved the sea, loved the thrill of water rushing against the prow, the snap of wind in the sails. Realizing his *qazaq*'s dread of the water, P'tre had ordered D'arim to take command of a fleet of warships and set him off to sail the rough northern seas in a fat, wallowing three-masted barque.

For two years, D'arim had lain awake, sweating in his bunk in the captain's quarters, terrorized by the creaking of wood planks as they were constantly battered by waves, the ominous moaning and popping of wooden masts in the storm winds, the eerie lament of sea daemons echoing through the seemingly flimsy hull.

But he'd also learned how to swim and how to sight the sun and stars with an astrolabe to navigate his way through uncharted waters. He learned to keep down his meals of salt fish and hardtack, forced himself to climb the shrouds, shaking and palms sweating, up into the fore-topcastle crowning the dizzyingly high mast and scan the horizon for land and storms. He learned to mask his fear and how to delegate authority to men of more experience; learned when to listen to the advice of mariners born on the sea and when to forcefully assert his own authority. He learned how to command respect.

He returned with bronzed skin and hardened muscles, bursting with self-confidence, and had warmly thanked P'tre for his wisdom, grateful for the maturing adventure. From then on, he viewed each of P'tre's "tests" as a clever system to make him stronger, smarter, a more worthy warrior to serve the Terhune Family.

He wasn't sure exactly when his idol's glow began to fade and he started to see the man. Troubled, D'arim tried to deny the growing resentment making him feeling traitorous. Once the Faith and the Terhunes had been inextricably one and the same. When had it happened that he could no longer ignore P'tre's deceit and cruelty, with D'arim's devotion shifting slowly but inexorably to the Faith?

Life, D'arim had decided, was continual proof of God's cruel joke on humanity. Old men gained enough experience to teach them wisdom, but by the time they had grown sufficiently enlightened to do the world any good, their bodies were too frail and worn. Chained by arthritis and palsy and senility, they cackled away their hard-earned wisdom, unheard, impatiently ignored. The young would be forever condemned to muddle through on their own, hating and loving and killing and wondering when it would all make sense.

He was beginning to feel like an old, old man. What *did* he want from Terhune?

"Your respect, P'tre," he said quietly. "Nothing more."

Terhune looked hurt, his mouth drawn down. Leaning from his saddle, he seized D'arim's arm to draw him close. Their legs brushed against each other, armored greaves rasping. "You have it," P'tre said earnestly. "You've always had that and more, my brother. I love you, I'd do anything for you. I swear by everything I hold sacred, it's the truth."

Tears rimming P'tre's eyes threatened to spill over. D'arim stared at him, his chest suddenly aching, longing to believe him, needing to have his boyhood trust restored.

"I can't bear your doubt, D'arim," P'tre said urgently. "Test me, I beg it of you—ask anything of me so I can prove it to you."

Stop the terror.

He almost said it, his mouth open with the words forming on his tongue. *Stop this senseless execution of your best men, give them back your confidence before you damage your own cause beyond repair. For the love of God, give me back my faith in you.*

And as these words formed in his mind, he saw the twinge

in P'tre's cheek, the steel behind the wet gaze and knew he'd nearly been trapped again. Any demand for proof would be proof itself of distrust, and for P'tre Terhune distrust was the same as treason.

Something D'arim couldn't name cracked within him like tiny fractures spreading throughout his entire being. He forced himself to counterfeit a smile. "Your offer is proof enough for me, P'tre. I am satisfied."

The momentary disappointment on P'tre's face distressed but didn't surprise D'arim. The harder he tried to serve him, the more P'tre wanted to hurt him, break him. D'arim knew the man really did love him like a brother, with the depth of familial jealousy and greed and hatred only one brother could feel for another.

Terhune unbuckled his mailed gauntlet from his left hand with exaggerated force and yanked off the underlying deerskin glove. He removed a heavy gold ring from his index finger, the inset carnelian stone carved with the Terhune insignia, and held it out to D'arim. "Let no man doubt my respect and trust in you," he said loudly. "Let this signify to all the enduring bond between us."

It meant nothing. No more than the thousands of other gifts Terhune had given him out of remorse or bribery or settling a calculated burden of obligation onto D'arim's shoulders. The ring looked new and he suspected P'tre had readied his props ahead of time to orchestrate this little ceremony.

Methodically, D'arim stripped off his own gauntlet. Despite his greater height, Terhune's hands were narrower than his own, his fingers slimmer. D'arim pushed the ring past the knuckle of his little finger, coarse black hairs curling around elegant gold.

They clasped hands in a firm grip, Terhune's bright smile of triumph vicious. The white shied nervously as their hands slid away, its mouth working at the bit. It half reared, slipping in the mud. The gelding took a cautious step back, wary of the spikes embedded in the wrapping around the white's hocks. D'arim patted the gelding's neck and murmured un-necessarily to calm it as Terhune spurred his horse into a gallop toward the front of his troops, careful not to stray more than a few feet from the narrow winding column.

D'arim waited until Terhune had ridden out of sight before he pulled out the small purse he kept under his quilted surcoat, stripped the ring from his finger and dropped it into the leather bag, drawing the string tight before he tucked it away. He never wore jewelry, especially rings, which interfered with his sword grip, as P'tre well knew. It would eventually be stored with all the other trinkets P'tre had given him, unwanted but impossible to give away or sell. The air was damp and cold, his fingers numb as he wriggled his hand back into the glove and replaced his gauntlet.

When he straightened, he spotted Briston on the opposite side of the moving column, watching him with one eyebrow raised speculatively. For some reason, the captain's boldness did not irritate him. He merely nodded in response to the man's silent salute.

22

The message arrived early in the morning, the stars still visible in the sallow night sky. The courier was barely out of his teens, his horse near dead under him when he rode into Antonya's camp. Now, he shivered under a thick wool horse blanket and sipped warmed sweetened wine. Terhune's army had been reported on the northern border of the Sheruben. Details were sketchy, and the figures more than likely exaggerated, but it was clear that the enemy was considerably less than the half a million Lord Vodos had feared.

"No more than twenty thousand Elite among them," Kerrick said phlegmatically. "Rather a lot for a Purge on a village as small as Adil. Not that they had much pleasure of it."

The sun had yet to rise, night air dank with the smell of a storm brewing. Antonya shoved her legs into fur-lined boots as Regine waited with her quilted jerkin.

"No?"

"Hardly a soul left by the time they arrived. The local Priest must have warned the villagers. Everyone packed up what they could carry away with them and fled into the woodlands. Of course, Terhune kept it by the book, all the houses fired and the sajada destroyed."

"Where is he now?"

"Camped on the road just outside Roupen. A shepherds' village, two hundred souls at the most. Likewise a ghost town."

"But Terhune hasn't Purged it yet?"

"No. He hasn't been able to provoke Vodos into retaliation. Terhune is likely to proceed into the Sheruben with more caution, wondering where our good Lord does plan to strike at him."

"How disappointing for him." She smiled.

Kerrick didn't. "That's not the least of the news, Lady. A price has been set on your head."

This time, she laughed aloud. "Really." It wasn't a question. "Just to satisfy my pride, how much is my death worth to my uncle?"

"Nothing." His eyes were level as she looked up, puzzled. "He wants you alive. His horse's weight in gold to the man who takes you alive, execution for the man who slays you."

The implications sank in, her face prickling with disbelief. "I'm flattered."

"I don't think the intent is to flatter you, madam," Kerrick said unnecessarily. She glared at him, until he added, "And I would advise being particularly alert to any overly fervent pledges of loyalty, guilty consciences usually feeling the need to cover their pangs."

"Clever. Greed oiling the wheels of betrayal, while suspicion sows the seeds of mutiny."

Kerrick finally smiled, gently. "Did you really expect one Terhune to be any less cunning than another, Lady?"

She frowned. "Send word to Vodos. He may begin his attack on my uncle at his leisure."

And the rain began to fall.

23

After four days of nonstop rain, whatever good mood he'd begun this campaign on, Terhune had swiftly lost in the cold and the muck and the thousand petty irritations grinding his army down to a crawl. Not even the Purge of Adil had lightened his disposition, the whole task perfunctory as his Elite strolled through grubby streets and set alight empty houses. His armsmen loitered idly as the town burned, all that was needed, Terhune seethed, was a few boar carcasses and a hogshead of ale to turn it into a cheap country festival.

He didn't find D'arim's sullen silence to his liking, either. It was only a bit of sport. He'd enjoyed keeping D'arim waiting while he amused himself with her, then the delicious tension as the girl sniveled under the bedclothes while he discussed the campaign with his commander, anticipating D'arim's agitation when he discovered her.

But he'd miscalculated, hadn't expected the *qazaq* bastard to have taken it so hard. He wished he'd never seen the wretched girl, angry with D'arim for spoiling the game. Now he'd have to kill her himself, though not immediately; killing her now might make the strain between him and D'arim even worse. Someday, he thought sourly, the grubby little peasant would push him too far.

He watched the rain from the open flap of his tent, water pounding the ground with a wrath reflecting his own. Not even campfires could survive, and Terhune's jaw clenched as the wind blew over yet another tent. To add insult to injury, the sky opened even further and launched a barrage of hailstones the size of grapes. Horses whinnied as the ice bullets ricocheted off their exposed hides.

Holding a cape over his head for protection, D'arim trotted toward Terhune, short bandy legs splashing through ankle-high water. He stopped when he reached Terhune's tent, simply eying him without a word. After a moment, Terhune frowned and turned to allow the man into the shelter of the tent. D'arim shook his cape, although he was obviously soaked through to the skin.

"Whose idea was it to go overland in the first place?" Terhune said, trying for a jest to lighten the air. D'arim didn't smile.

"Mine. A storm on land is a major inconvenience. A storm at sea is a major disaster."

His attempt at levity rejected, Terhune's black mood returned. A fleeting wave of remorse swept through him with the realization that he'd pushed too far, damaged beyond repair the only friendship he had ever known. He turned his face away brusquely. "What do you want?"

"Lord Creskar of Abadayho has arrived, with four thousand troops at your disposal."

"Marvelous," Terhune said bitterly. "Another four thousand and one mouths to feed while we sit around in the mud doing nothing."

"Four thousand and two."

Terhune glanced at him, unsure if the man joked. D'arim's expression gave away nothing.

"Lord Creskar brings a guest who very much desires to speak with you. A member of Antonya's inner circle, who is remarkably curious to know how much your horse weighs."

Slowly, a smile twitched Terhune's mouth, and as if in response to the change of fortune, the rain dwindled to a stop.

24

It was over with appalling speed.

Lord Vodos had sent a messenger who rode into the camp before dawn with good news and bad news. His scouts reported that while Terhune's army was still encamped on the outskirts of an abandoned village, setting up battle trenches and drilling along the wide fields where the two armies would meet, it wasn't nearly as formidable as expected, the bulk of his forces armsmen from Adalon. What this meant, he wasn't sure, and the possibility of a second wave of reinforcements from the Oracular Army had to be considered. The bad news was that Terhune's forces had increased with the arrival of Lord Creskar of Abadayho, the exact number uncertain. Vodos's scouts had estimated near to ten thousand, but given his Lordship's familiarity with the exaggeration that large numbers of troops always seemed to induce, he would suppose it half that figure. In either case, he urgently requested Antonya to meet with his son before any further action was taken. Bertil would meet her at Bretch, a small town far outside Terhune's reach, safely within the Sheruben.

In the early hours of the morning, Antonya rode in the vanguard of a small company along the road toward the Sheruben, mists brushing through forest pines along the hilltops. Bretch appeared in the distance, a peaceful blue silhouette beyond the yellowed cornfields. With Kerrick and Daen beside her in the fore, Sarnor's mercenaries brought up the rear to sandwich the twenty or so of Elotin's unruly horsemen between them. Confident they were well away from any danger from Terhune, the armsmen rode without helmets or chain mail.

Bretch was a village of barely more than several dozen houses surrounding the small sajada, the defensive wall built of timber and brick seemingly more decorative than functional. Bertil waited for them by the open gates with a similar escort. The young man's sullen temperament had diminished since she'd last seen him, but somehow she doubted it was due to the joys of married life.

"My father sends his greetings, Lady," he said once they were within earshot. She couldn't help smiling; a neat way to satisfy courtesy without committing hypocrisy. The boy might end up a diplomat yet.

She opened her mouth to respond, when a sudden shout went up from behind her. Like a dog alerted to sudden danger, Bertil straightened on his horse, his startled gaze over her shoulder. She turned as several hundred Elite horsemen materialized from the edge of the woods, bearing down the short distance from the trees to the road along their right flank with terrible speed. Their hoarse shouts reverberated in the still morning air, temporarily stupefying the soldiers and horsemen gaping at them from the road.

"Retreat!" She heard Bertil's command to his own small escort. "Fall back!"

Antonya's own armsmen had little time to react before the Elite horsemen slammed into the center of her company, footmen with pikes and riflebows in tight wedged formations behind them. It was as easy as slicing through butter with a heated knife. Elotin's Medeban tribesmen simply took one look at the oncoming enemy, whirled their wiry desert horses about and took off at full speed across the empty fields, leaving the vanguard cut off from the rear.

As Bertil's men fell back behind the walls, they attempted to close the gates while Antonya's armsmen pushed against them in a desperate scrimmage. She heard Kerrick's cursing, every second somehow crystal clear if uncontrollable. The arrow that felled her horse slid into its neck with barely a whisper. The ground rushed up at her as the animal pitched forward on its knees and collapsed onto one side. She flung her arms out, pitched headlong into a large puddle in the muddy road. She sprawled facedown, then scrambled out of the way as her horse rolled over on her, legs kicking in its death throes.

"Alive, you bastards!" She heard the harsh scream. Spitting mud from her mouth, she wiped away the muck from her eyes to focus on P'tre Terhune. She couldn't make out more than a malevolent silhouette, the rising sun behind him casting him in a dazzling nimbus of light. "I want the bloody bitch *alive*!"

He vanished in the melee as her own armsmen swarmed

around her, those in front of her hacking ferociously at the
Elite troops while those behind desperate to rush her to a safer
distance. Suddenly, the Elite line wavered, hesitated as a cry
of alarm went up. It didn't quite mask the warbling howls of
Medeban warriors.

"Get down!" Daen shouted, falling half over her as he
pushed them both back into the muck. She caught barely a
glimpse before flinging her arms over her head, bellies of rugged desert horses above them as they leaped into the battle,
wild-eyed Medeban warriors whirling swords and whooping
with bloodlust.

The shock wave worked, splitting the Elite troops. Confused, their ranks broken, Terhune's horsemen fled at a near
rout for the safety of the trees, leaving the more unfortunate
footmen behind to fend off the Medeban attack the best they
could. With the taste of victory seducing them, the Medebans
scythed through the thicket of footmen in their haste to pursue
the Elite cavalry.

"*No!*" Kerrick bellowed. Blood dripped from his nose creating a red beard on his face. "It's a trap, come back!"

Somehow, Sarnor had made his way from the rear to reach
Antonya. Bertil's men had abandoned their effort to close the
gates, trapping Antonya outside. The remaining armsmen hurriedly pushed their way into the town, bolting the gates shut
behind them, cutting off refuge for whatever Medeban warriors
still survived.

The village appeared deserted, other than for Antonya's
armsmen, not so much as a stray dog emerged from the stone-
and-thatch houses inside the walls. Bertil and his men had
vanished, abandoning her to her fate.

Kerrick wiped at his face, smearing blood. "Dull-witted
clods of horseshit!" he swore at the Medebans, still incensed.
"There'll be one for every ten come back out of that wood in
one piece!"

"But exceedingly brave clods of horseshit." Trembling, Antonya shook off Daen's protective hand around her arm. "They
bought us enough time to get inside the walls. And I didn't so
much as unsheathe my sword!" she spat in disgust.

Sarnor chuckled. "It would be a miracle if you could even
find it under all that mud, Lady."

"Bertil," Kerrick growled, the name issuing in a hiss of fury.

"That traitorous little bastard set us up for an ambush. I'll kill him, with my bare hands . . ."

"You'll have to do it later," Daen called down, having climbed up to what passed for battlements along the top of the wall. "They're back, and this isn't going to hold them for long."

Antonya quickly scaled the ladder to survey their surroundings. Several of her armsmen lay dead. Terhune's cavalry rode out of the woods in a leisurely wave. At their head, P'tre Terhune in elegant armor rode a splendid white horse. Antonya and her armsmen lined the battlements in silence, watching the fields between the wood and the village fill with cavalry and foot soldiers. Terhune reined in his horse as he neared the village walls, out of arrowshot. He unbuckled his plumed helmet and removed it, peering up at her curiously.

From the corner of her eye, she caught Daen and Gesham squatting on the battlement's stone floor, surreptitiously loading an elongated arrow into Daen's large riflebow. With a grunt, Gesham used his feet as a brace as he cranked the last notch in his brother's bowstring. Daen was an excellent shot, but it was doubtful he had the range to shoot Terhune, a gesture of futile defiance.

"If Bertil did arrange this ambush, he must have had an escape route set up beforehand," Sarnor said quietly. He wasn't speaking to Antonya; it was Kerrick who nodded fractionally.

"We meet at last," Terhune called to her, amusement in his voice. "You're not quite what I expected, I'm afraid."

She wiped back grime-spattered hair from her forehead. "What did you expect? Someone cleaner?"

Terhune laughed. "My apologies, it was most unsporting to have killed your horse."

"Then perhaps you won't mind if I return the favor," Antonya called down, as Daen rose smoothly, aimed, and pulled the trigger, the loud *thwock* of the bowstring as it fired reverberating along the battlement walls.

Startled, Terhune sawed on his horse's reins, pulling its head severely to one side. It half reared in protest. The arrow traveled farther than Antonya had expected, punching into the ground a bare six inches from his horse's hooves. If Terhune had remained where he'd been, the arrow would have struck his unprotected face. The exposed shaft quivered, buried halfway up its length.

Terhune's amiable humor vanished, fury mottling his cheeks. "I had thought to offer you more lenient terms of surrender," he shouted, his horse prancing nervously under him. "I'm grateful you have reminded me of the futility of dealing with common scum."

He wheeled his horse around, shouting orders to his men as he lunged through their ranks. Kerrick had already climbed down to the small courtyard below, gesturing violently as he issued orders to Antonya's armsmen. Sarnor remained beside her as they watched Terhune's retreat.

"It'll be a Purge," Sarnor said simply, with sour satisfaction, Antonya suspected. "Gesham." The young armsman looked up at his captain inquiringly. "You and Daen, see if you can unearth any villagers who haven't fled. Tobias, Ephraim, take three men, search for Bertil and his men, check the perimeter walls for hidden escape holes. We haven't much time."

Sarnor's mercenaries nodded curtly, then hurried off. He helped Antonya descend from the battlement wall, catching her by the waist to lift her down the last few feet. They stood uneasily together, before Antonya spoke.

"Unless Lord C'ristan appears over the horizon to rescue us at the last minute, I'd say our chances are minimal. It doesn't seem likely, with Bertil's defection, that we can depend on Lord Vodos."

"What's important now," Kerrick advised her, "is to secure your person from capture for as long as possible while we either try to discover another way out, or organize a defense here at the gates to hold this position long enough to allow you to escape."

She caught Sarnor's fleeting smile. He obviously held out no such hopes. This tiny village hadn't been built to withstand a concentrated attack. As if to underscore their weakness, one of Sarnor's men called down, "Ram!" seconds before the gates shuddered under a heavy blow.

"The safest place would be the sajada," Sarnor suggested. For a brief moment, Antonya felt like a piece of baggage as the two men lifted her up almost bodily, each taking one arm as they sprinted for the protection of the sajada. "Who stays with her?" Sarnor demanded.

"Only me. You'll need every man we've got for the fight."

"Good luck," was Sarnor's only reply as Kerrick shoved her inside the temple, followed her in and slammed the stout wooden doors, shutting out both sound and light. Antonya blinked in the sudden quiet gloom, dust swirling hazily along the stone floor. Kerrick dropped the two solid bars into place, and bolted them securely to the iron fastenings. She heard a muffled shout outside, the booming of the ram against the gates.

"Signaling tower," Kerrick said calmly, gesturing for her to follow him up the stairs. "Only one man can climb the steps at a time, easier to defend."

And the view was better from a height as well, she discovered. Once the gates had cracked, it took Terhune's men scant minutes to smash their way into the village. As the Elite poured into the courtyard, they were met by silence; not a soul was to be seen. Antonya and Kerrick were screened from sight, hidden behind the slit apertures in the stone tower.

Once inside, Terhune's men advanced warily, searching for the hidden enemy, armored shields forming a protective shell. They didn't have to wait long; a barrage of arrows whistled, felling five of Terhune's men despite their shields. The dead and the wounded were quickly pulled back, the holes in the defense sealed seamlessly.

"They're good," Kerrick admitted grimly.

Then the Purge began. Terhune's men set fire to the houses, one by one. If the intent was to drive Sarnor and his men from their hiding places, it netted only moderate success. Her armsmen were fighting for their lives, desperately courageous, expecting no quarter.

As more of the village burned, the air filled with dark smoke, obscuring the fighting below. Heat shimmered in the air, black flakes of ash and cinders floating on the waves. Even from the relative safety of the sajada, both Kerrick and Antonya were sweating.

A break in the smoke, and Antonya flinched as two of Terhune's Elite dragged Gesham, forehead gushing blood, through the street below. She heard but did not see Terhune as he bellowed. A surge of black smoke obscured the men below.

"Where is she!"

Whatever answer the young armsman made, the reaction it inspired made her turn away from the window, the scream prickling the hair on the nape of her neck. She pressed her back against the cool of the stone wall, closing her eyes.

"He wouldn't spare anyone in return for your surrender," Kerrick said in answer to her unspoken question. She nodded mutely, feeling sick.

A heavy boom from below echoed up the tower. A few tense seconds later, it was repeated. "They're breaking in the doors to the sajada," Kerrick said tersely. He unsheathed his sword, rolling his head around on his shoulders to limber the muscles for the inevitable fight.

"We've found it!" They both turned at the shout from below. His face covered in a bizarre mask of soot and blood, Sarnor gestured wildly at the sajada windows above him to catch their attention, obviously blind to their position. "Bertil's bolthole!" He twisted toward an unseen struggle, then glanced back a final time in frustration before racing out of sight. Terhune's Elite were apparently finding Purging the village more difficult than they'd expected.

The sajada doors below splintered, a shout of triumph drifting up the tower. Kerrick muttered curses under his breath, knowing that while the tower would be easier to defend, it would also become their trap. "Our only hope is to go back down, into the gallery."

Antonya sniffed the air, watching Kerrick catch the scent a moment after she had. Terhune's men didn't know she was in the sajada. They weren't searching for her; they were busy burning it down.

"We'd better hurry," she said.

They descended from the tower without trouble, using the cover of roiling smoke to creep along the gallery above the altar. Below them, Terhune's soldiers strolled through the aisles of the small building, expertly torching the brocade tapestries and wooden stalls, brushing the thin layer of rushes on the floor into corners to feed the flames. The yellow firelight glittered off their armor. Above them, a panicked sparrow frantically searched for a way out, fluttering through the smoke.

Behind the altar, they found the stairs leading to the Priest's chambers but the heavy wood door securely locked. The fire spread with fearful speed, Antonya and Kerrick both coughing in the thick haze. The door had been solidly built, withstanding even Kerrick's shoulder slammed against it. There was no need to worry that the soldiers would hear the noise; the crackle of flames had ripened into a monstrous roar, the heat becoming intolerable. The door at last yielded, the bolts of the iron hinges ripped from the wood. Terhune's men had retreated, the entire floor below engulfed in the flames.

The Priest had obviously expected trouble, the room was nearly barren, clean spots in the dust evidence of where any valuable objects had been recently removed. She noticed with an odd detachment how smoke drifting up from below through the cracks in the floorboards formed a ghostly rectangular pattern where a thick carpet had once covered the planks, less dust blocking the gaps. Yellow fingers of flame explored the cracks, the paint along the base of the walls blistering.

Light through leaded glass in the only window cast odd colors through the clouded room. Below them, the tiled roof slanted toward a low brick wall enveloped with clinging honeysuckle vines. Clematis and roses closer to the sajada shriveled in the heat. The roofs of houses crowding up to the little garden wall had already disappeared as the thatch burned briskly.

"Stand back, Lady," Kerrick warned. He smashed his mailed fist through the glass.

The air suddenly rushing in acted like lamp oil poured onto a burning hearth, the room exploded into flames around them. The force of the blast knocked them both off their feet. She beat at her clothing as it caught fire, blinded and choking as her lungs were seared, unable to inhale enough air even to scream. The lizard scrambled frantically between the lacings of her shirt, fell to the floor and sprinted away. Dropping to her hands and knees, she grabbed for it and missed as it vanished in the smoke.

As she groped her way along the floor, she could hear nothing except the roar of the blaze, wood snapping and popping. Suddenly, she felt herself being lifted bodily into the air, her sight blurry through the tears. Kerrick's hair was on fire, turning him a hellish blond. They swayed as the floor buckled underneath them.

"Sarnor!" Kerrick bellowed, and pitched Antonya out the window.

She hit the tiled roof, felt the bones in her shoulder crack, and rolled off the edge to the garden below. The withering flora did little to cushion her fall. Blackness pressed in around her vision as she struggled to her knees. She desperately scraped the tears from her eyes with the palm of her good hand, staring up at the window above. For a frozen moment, Kerrick stood poised, one foot on the sill ready to jump. He glanced up as burning roof timbers collapsed on him, and disappeared in a tremendous crash.

Too stunned to scream, Antonya gazed at the blaze pouring from the window like volcanic Hell. She wasn't aware of falling, not even able to feel relief for being already unconscious when her face hit the ground.

Book 2
The Oracular City

25

Antonya gazed out the tower window, open book in her lap
unread. Beyond the inner walls of the Citadel, the rain-
dampened slate of square roofs shone darkly in the sunlight.
The primary road into the city, the Avenue of Saints, mean-
dered down toward twin towers on either side of the Great
Gate, the only entrance through the outer fortifications encircling the Oracular City.

She could hear the shrill cries of merchants hawking their
goods in crowded streets, children laughing, women scolding,
the constant clang of ironmongers and the tattoo of carpenters,
the clop of horses' hooves against cobbled stones, sheep bleating, all the normal sounds of the city remote just beyond the
solid bulwark of the Citadel walls.

Inside the Citadel, the fortress was considerably quieter.
Jealously guarded territories of the Orders divided the maze
of halls and stairs like a psychotic spider's web, with the great
Crystal Sajada in its center, the holiest shrine in the world. At
night, the gleam of the Oracle within could be seen for miles.
She stared at the rooftops below as if from on a cloud in
Heaven, and as remote.

She had seen very little else in the past few weeks of her
imprisonment, nor had she much cared. She had been defeated,
Kerrick was dead, the fate of the rest unknown. Her shoulder
still pained her, which she was glad of. She almost resented
her body's healing, regretting she hadn't joined those she'd
led to ruin and death.

The clash of armed guards coming to attention outside the
ironbound door signaled the arrival of Terhune's armsmen.
She braced herself as she heard bolts pulled back into stone
walls, the whine of metal on metal as the door was pushed
open. A young Elite officer smiled at her pleasantly, his light
blue eyes benign.

"The High Lord Commander requests your presence, madam."

As if she had a choice. He led the armed escort accompanying her to Terhune's private quarters, ushering her inside before shutting the door. P'tre Terhune was sprawled on large floor cushions playing a solitary game on an inlaid wood dicing tray. He rose to greet her, ivory cubes rattling where he abandoned them. He had traded his soldier's attire for a soft gray overgown, the hem of his underrobe showing the red of his Order. An intricately embroidered sash cinched his robes loosely at the waist.

On the open balcony, young men set two places for dinner with their eyes carefully lowered, moving about their duties silently.

"Welcome, my dear Antonya . . ."

She glared at him, her eyes blazing yellow. "To you, sir, I am *Lady* Antonya."

Startled, the servants glanced up at her covertly, but Terhune ignored them. "Forgive my error, madam. One might be forgiven in assuming that you are merely my prisoner, as you've no weapons, no armsmen here, and no Lands."

"Prisoner or not, Uncle," she said quietly, "you cannot change what is. I *am* the Lady Antonya Terhune."

He feigned a mock bow. "Lady," he said. When he straightened, he was smiling tightly. "I fear we've gotten off to a bad start." He spread his hands, beckoning her to sit. "I beg you to accept my humble apology as well as my hospitality." His voice was gentle, but she heard the steel behind it that he couldn't quite rid it of.

"Come now, Uncle. Must you insist we posture like actors in a farce? Why not drop this feeble attempt at courtesy and get to whatever it is you want of me."

Terhune lost his smile. "Surely courtesy is warranted even among enemies, madam, when one is host and the other his guest."

Antonya met his gray eyes levelly. "My apologies. How rude of me to prejudge your hospitality by the fact that I was brought here against my will under armed escort."

He indicated the open balcony with a sweep of his hand. "Too lovely an evening to waste a splendid sunset inside.

Would you care to join me? Don't be afraid; I give you my solemn word I have no intention of tossing you over the edge."

He held out his hand to her. After a moment, she allowed him to grasp her by the fingertips and lead her out onto the balcony. Brocade pillows had been scattered around a low carved table. He seated her before he lowered himself opposite. A young man settled onto his heels behind her, his counterpart behind Terhune. Another, even younger man, served the food. His face was impassive but his hand trembled as he set the platters before them. Clear sauce over the baked fish cleverly resembled ripples on the surface of a stream.

Terhune opened a carved box to offer her a delicate set of matching silver, and, as if he could read the look on her face, laughed softly. She picked the larger of a pair of forks, examining the thin shaft with two straight tines on one end. The knob on the other end had been cast to resemble a pomegranate, matching the slender knife still in the box.

"I assume that as a Lady you are familiar with court etiquette," Terhune said ironically. "Or had you expected me to be an ignorant barbarian slurping raw meat from the end of my dagger?"

She smiled at the challenge, then held the delicate implement properly to impale a portion of fish. Her hand stopped halfway to her mouth as the servant behind her inhaled sharply. Glancing at Terhune, she saw nothing but amusement, placed the fish in her mouth and ate. It was delicious. The two servants exchanged worried looks.

"You honor me, madam." Terhune nodded to the man on his left. The taster took the second fork from the box and speared a small portion of fish from Terhune's dish. He chewed it rapidly, and swallowed. Terhune watched him for a moment, then grunted. The man scuttled back as Terhune began to eat. "I hope you will not think ill of me if I don't return your most gracious gesture. Caution within the Citadel is indispensable, even in one's own household." He grinned. "*Especially* in one's own household."

She stared at the fish in front of her, her appetite gone, but continued to eat without tasting it. "What have I to fear, Terhune? If you wanted me dead, you could have killed me by now."

Terhune swallowed before he answered. "Oh, not I, madam. But who knows where an arrow comes from when it is shot in the dark?"

The servant poured the wine and Terhune's taster took an obligatory sip. The man beside Antonya reached for her cup, but she placed her hand over it. He looked at Terhune for instructions, anxious.

"If my food or drink is poisoned, then no one will die in my place for it," Antonya said firmly.

Terhune savored his own wine, regarding her over the rim as he leaned back on the pillows. "Admirable sentiment, Lady, if misguided. I can see why you have a certain popularity with the Landsfolk."

The servant continued to bring dishes to the table, Terhune's taster continuing to test each one while the young man beside Antonya sat awkwardly idle. Finally he took a flagon of wine from the servant and kept her cup full to make himself useful.

Terhune remained unperturbed, conversing on light subjects: the origin of the fish, its method of preparation, the subtle seasonings used, alternate ways of presenting it. Antonya ate in silence.

As the servant set a bowl of snow flavored with almonds in front of her, honey drizzled artfully over the top, she saw the shadow of a woman move behind the latticework separating the balcony and the main room. Soon the first plaintive notes of a piquoro wind reed could be heard.

Terhune cleared his throat before singing softly against the music in Dothinian, his voice rough but clear. It was a love song, one Antonya had heard in Roixara. For a moment, her eyes misted with the memory of a wizened old man with hunched back, lively eyes and a voice like a castrated frog serenading her by the edge of the sea. The absurd juxtaposition of the deadly High Lord Commander of the Oracular Army and a harmless little wizard in his misshapen green robes who had befriended her and introduced her to the Dothinian court not so long ago made her want to laugh, in spite of her grief.

"Do you understand the words?" he broke off to ask her, bringing her back to the present.

"Aye," she said, intrigued. "Pretty lies to pretty women are a Dothinian specialty. Your accent is admirable. It appears you truly haven't spent your entire life slaughtering innocent people."

His eyes flashed in irritation, but he finished the song.

"Court etiquette, choice fare, genteel poetry." Antonya shook her head. "You are going to a lot of trouble to demonstrate how refined and cultured you are to someone you obviously consider a lowborn impostor. Really, *Uncle*, I can't say it's worth the effort."

He flushed slightly, then snapped his fingers. The musician behind the screen bowed and walked away. Terhune remained silent for several moments, obviously struggling with his temper. "I trust your health is improved?" he tried again, his voice strained.

"Terhunes have always been a sturdy lot, have we not?"

He shook his head. "Whoever or . . . *whatever* you are, you are not my half brother's child. Admit your deception and renounce your claims to my Lands, *Lady*."

"In return for my life?"

"But of course."

She laughed without humor. "No, Uncle. I will never renounce my heritage or my claims."

"Do you wish so badly to die?"

She shrugged. "I don't believe that's what you have in mind. Not even you would pay so much gold to take me alive just for the pleasure of killing me yourself."

"There is another alternative." She raised an eyebrow at his thin smile, as toothy and cold-blooded as a crocodile's. "I will acknowledge your dubious claim of kinship, declare you my true niece and heir, and legitimize your rather empty titles. I will relinquish all claim to Adalon and turn it over to you."

She watched him, wary.

"Then you will marry me. As your legal husband, there will be no further dispute as to the rightful possession of my Lands. It will be yours in name but mine to rule."

Stunned, her mouth dropped open. He laughed. "Are you insane?" she said hotly. "Incest as well as theft?"

"Oh, come now," he said reasonably. "I am not such a beast as you make me. If you truly harbor some fantasy you are of my blood, it need not be a consummated marriage. I have no intention of making myself ridiculous professing undying love for you, madam, and I hold no illusions you feel anything but aversion for me. It doesn't offend me if I am not pleasing to you. Be my wife in name only, take as many lovers as you can bed, and I wouldn't care."

"I see. And all this, of course, is to demonstrate what I would forfeit should I reject your most generous offer."

He glared at her, and gulped a large mouthful of wine before slamming the cup down onto the table. He ignored the servant as the man nervously refilled his cup.

"Do you require witnesses or signed contracts? You may have that as well. I'll even write it in my own blood, should you find that necessary. There are worse things than being my wife, madam. I can be a generous man. Ask of me as you desire. You would gain far more than Adalon. You would have my wealth, power, protection."

"Indeed," she said dryly. "And who would protect me from you, Uncle?"

"Obey me, as a good wife and woman should, and you needn't fear me. Defy me, and I will find ways far less agreeable to convince you to give me what I want."

She looked at him steadily. "No doubt you are more versed in such ways than you are in empty courtship rituals. But why give up Adalon at all? You must need me more than I thought, Terhune, else you would have already used those means to persuade me."

"Look around you, *Lady* Antonya. Is what I offer you so hateful and paltry?"

His servants had become so motionless they seemed like statues. She felt her cheeks burn with reckless anger, and drained the pigment from her irises, although her head ached from the effort. A muscle in Terhune's jaw twitched. He did not like the Weird, but his dread of it had its limits.

"I look around me, Terhune, and all I see is terrified people. Is that the nature of your power and wealth? You offer to share that power with me, but it is only the power to enslave others as I must in turn grovel before you. Then it is hateful and paltry indeed."

"Think very carefully before you refuse," he said quietly. "You've laid claim to my Lands, and now it's within your

grasp. You would have everything you could hope to bargain
for . . ."

She laughed harshly. "You don't know how to bargain, Terhune. You only know how to steal. You take what you want
with threats and tyranny. The humblest fishmonger has more
integrity than you; you're no more than a rutting wild boar
snorting to widen his mudhole . . ."

He slapped her. The force snapped her head to one side,
knocking her to the floor. She looked up at him, her face burning where his hand had struck her. She smiled.

"Why do you provoke me, Antonya?" he asked softly, fists
curled with white-knuckled anger. "What does it gain you?"

"You wouldn't understand. It's not what I hope to gain,
Uncle," she said calmly. "It's what I choose not to lose. My
honor."

He stared at her a long moment before he stood. "As you
wish. Keep your *honor*, madam. For all the good it will do
you."

Although she'd known it was inevitable, she was not by
nature a martyr. Suddenly, she was very, very afraid.

26

*She enjoyed helping Brother Alban milk the goats. They
were friendly beasts, funny-faced with their long, flopping ears
and strange brown slit-irised eyes. She liked how their teats
were warm and soft in her hands and the sound of the milk
squirting into the bucket. She didn't like hauling the full buckets to the kitchen quite as much.*

*Her favorites, twins she had named Mee Mee and Yoo Yoo,
butted against her playfully as she carried the heavy bucket of
milk outside. Their mother, Pok, was as round as the rainbar-
rel outside Father Andrae's study, ready to drop her kids any
day. Brother Alban hoped she would have more females, since
he hated having to kill newborns. If she had twin bucks, he'd
fatten one for a few months, but they simply couldn't afford to
fatten two.*

It seemed unfair to her that baby goats should be doomed

*at birth simply because they were males. But Father Andrae
had explained to her at great length that God wasn't interested
in fairness. Only survival.*

*Life on the island was hard enough. Windswept and rocky,
the monastery found it difficult to cultivate much more than
what it needed to survive. Goats could eat nearly anything,
even the salt grass that grew in tough clumps along the gravel
beaches, pine nuts littering the small forest at the sheltered
end of the island. Female goats were prized for milk and
cheese. Males simply ate too much for their meat to be a sufficient return. Still, Antonya couldn't rid herself of resentment
against an unjust God.*

*She escaped the twins to climb through the slats in the wood
fence without spilling the milk. It was a fine day, thin wisps of
clouds moving fast across the cold blue sky, the breeze fluttering the laundry hanging outside the wash shed. She smelled
fresh bread and roasting hops from the round kitchen built
like the head of a giant thistle against the far end of the re-
fectory, the chimneys around its domed top trickling fragrant
smoke into the air.*

*She ran across the rocky ground toward the kitchen on
toughened bare feet, red-gold hair tumbling behind her in the
breeze. Old Brother Lezar scowled under his bushy eyebrows
as she thumped down the steps into the warm kitchen. His eyes
white as the milk, it was pathetic but funny the way he pretended he could still see perfectly well, thank you very much,
and everyone else had to pretend he could, too.*

*"Don't you spill any of that, Antonya!" he scolded, swing-
ing his thick wooden spoon in her general direction.*

*She ducked under the spoon, tapping it easily out of her
way as she passed, and crying out, "Ouch! Ow! Oh, please,
Brother Lezar, don't beat me anymore! I'm black and blue!"*

*Brother Lezar hmphed with satisfaction, a staunch advocate
of the spare-the-rod-spoil-the-child discipline, while fat
Brother Sholto shook his finger silently at her in amused disapproval as he took the bucket. She had to clamp both hands
over her mouth to stifle the giggles that threatened to give the
game away.*

*Antonya sat on the huge wooden table dominating the
center of the kitchen, its battered, scarred surface dark with*

decades of grease. Most of the goat's milk would be used to make cheese, but Brother Sholto had come from the southern countries of Cabestan, bringing with him his talent for rich cuisine the cold northern Lands lacked, his specialty flaky pastries with layers of savory spiced meats and honey glazing. Today, he was simmering a huge copper pan of milk over the low embers in one oven while he baked bread in another. His sleeves rolled up and pinned above his dimpled elbows, he kneaded the dough out on the long wooden table, the muscles of his arms strong underneath the layers of fat. Once in a while he dusted the flour off his hands to stir the bubbling milk.

After hours of cooking, the milk would turn a rich, caramelized brown, as thick as custard and twice as sweet. Antonya could almost taste it now, her mouth watering as she wriggled. Her bare heels banged against the table in childish restlessness until Brother Lezar, exasperated, shooed her out of the kitchen, waving his spoon like a goatherd's crook.

Her back ached and she thought it was from carrying the heavy milk buckets. Thankfully, the milking was done for the day. Halfway to the forges, where she knew she could quite easily get into some kind of interesting trouble, she felt a warm trickle down the inside of her thighs. Puzzled, she stopped, gathering up her skirts to look underneath. It was blood.

She stared at it in horror, a thin, meandering dribble of bright red and dark clots streaking down her legs. I'm going to die, *she thought. The concept was so remote, so unimaginable, she couldn't quite come up with the emotion she thought was proper for someone who knew they were about to die. Dazed, she dropped her skirts, forgetting all about the forge.*

Father Andrae didn't like to be disturbed when he was in his study, and she rarely bothered him during his hours of private research. She stood in the open door behind him, watching his hunched back as he scribbled over his massive writing desk. She wondered how she was going to tell him, when he finally straightened, paused, and turned around to look at her questioningly.

"I'm going to die," she said calmly. That seemed to put it succinctly enough.

He regarded her over the top of his spectacles for a long moment, his creased face puzzled. "We're all going to die," he said finally. *"Is this a theological question, Antonya?"*

She took a step into the big room, the smell of musty books and tallow candles warm and comforting. "No, I'm mean I'm going to die now. Right away."

He blinked, then carefully removed the spectacles from his nose, cradling them in his large, gnarled hands. "Is there some particular reason you believe this?" he said gently, without alarm.

He didn't seem too upset by the news. She lifted her skirts, nearly dragging them over her head to expose her naked legs. She wore nothing underneath. Holding one leg out at a twisted angle, like a dancer, to show him the blood, she said, "All my guts are coming out and I'm going to bleed to death." She wondered if God would make her study half as much once she was in Heaven, as Father Andrae did now.

At least his jaw dropped, she was gratified to see. Dying people should be taken seriously. Amazingly, Father Andrae's face went a strange white color, then flushed a deep red. He looked shocked and embarrassed and about to laugh all at the same time, which confused her. Turning away, he said in a strangled voice, "Drop your skirts, child," and his shoulders shook.

She thought he might be grieving, which was what people were supposed to do when loved ones died, and he was wiping tears from his eyes when he finally turned back to her. But he was smiling, which didn't fit in at all with her notions of proper mourning behavior.

He held his arms out to her. "Come here, Antonya," he said, his voice rich with affection. And that broke through whatever was blocking her feelings. Her chin instantly wobbled, and she threw herself sobbing into his arms, hugging him tightly. He smelled like old-man sweat and woolen robes, onions and chimney soot and bitter ink, and for all the rest of her life this would smell like love.

"You're not going to die," he murmured softly, stroking her hair gently and brushing away tears from her cheeks.

She pulled away just enough to look up into his face. "I'm not?" she said suspiciously, a bit disappointed because dying *was at least a momentous occasion. There weren't many momentous occasions in this little monastery on an isolated island.*

He laughed and, after several faltering attempts, tried to explain it to her. Before, she was a little girl. But when girls get their blood, then it means they become women. Their bodies change, and the pains she felt and the blood were completely normal.

"Am I a woman now?" she asked, the excitement of dying forgotten.

Father Andrae had that look on his face again that said he was trying to explain something without using the right words. "Not exactly a woman, no. But soon you will be. And now you will have to be more careful, because being a woman has responsibilities that little girls shouldn't have to think about."

"Like what?"

"Like . . . what to do when . . . men . . . or boys . . . that is . . ."

"Are you trying to tell me about sex, Father Andrae?" she offered helpfully.

He looked shocked for a second time in as many minutes. "What could you know about sex, child?"

She recited proudly, "I know when a man and a woman do sex together, the man has a penis but Brother Alban calls it lots of funny names and when it gets longer and hard, then the man puts it inside the woman and makes it go back and forth until . . ." Until what she couldn't quite imagine. "Until he's finished, and then the woman gets very fat and has six or seven babies."

She waited expectantly for him to praise her cleverness, but instead Father Andrae stared at her in a way that made her think he might be ill. "Has anyone . . . any of the Brothers . . . ?" He choked, unable to go on.

"Of course not," she said, bewildered. "I watch Brother Alban breed the goats and the rabbits, and I figured how different can it be? Anyway, it doesn't look like it would be all that much fun."

Father Andrae took a long breath in, and held it so long she thought he might have forgotten about it before he exhaled. "I think I shall send for one of the Sisters to pay us a visit *next month. I don't believe an old monk is quite the expert you need on this particular subject."*

Now she remembered why she had come in the first place. "But now that I'm a woman, am I going to bleed all the time?"

"No, it'll go away in a few days, Antonya."

She nodded firmly. "Good," she declared. "It's not very comfortable, and I'm glad I won't have to go through that again."

Father Andrae looked startled. "Oh, dear."

27

Antonya woke slowly, aware of the pain before she remembered where she was. She opened her eyes to the gloom. "Father Andrae . . ." she whispered, reluctant to let him go even if it was only a dream.

She lay on her back, the stones cold through the thin cotton shift. It hurt to breathe, although she was fairly sure he hadn't broken any ribs. Terhune seemed too much an expert on inflicting pain without actually crippling his victims.

She wondered how much time had gone by, having no way to judge the day from night. Someone had removed the woman's body, the darkened stain still on the floor. Shuddering, she tried to shut out the image and failed. The woman had been no more than a child, at first sly, whining piteously, then truly terrified as Terhune tortured her.

"You can stop her pain, Antonya," he called to her. "All you have to do is say the word . . ."

Eventually, she did, promising Terhune anything he wanted. On her knees, chained, pleading for the life of a stranger. He turned, his face drawn into a terrible smile. "As you wish, *Lady*."

The girl's expression turned from one of hope to horror as he drew the point of his knife up her belly, slitting open her abdomen. She screamed in agony, as Antonya screamed, straining at the chains. The girl's intestines oozed out of the wound, a bright rush of blood mixed with the green sludge of her wastes.

He grabbed the girl by her hair, twisting her face to his. "A fitting end for a spy to spill her guts, isn't it, Tannah?" he said, and laughed at his own joke. The girl died with her hands scrabbling futilely at the uncoiling gore.

Then he turned his attention to Antonya. "Her pain is over, my dear niece, as you wished. Yours is about to begin. But beg me to be merciful, and I shall be."

She did not. Through it all, she kept her mouth clamped shut, grunting with pain, but biting back the screams. He beat her harder, trying to force the words from her. She would not give in, could not. He meant to break her. Her silence was all she had left to fight him.

When he stopped, she lay half-conscious curled on her side, her forehead pressed against the damp stone floor next to his boots. Never in her life had she even imagined she could hurt so much. She listened with detached awareness to the jingle of metal and whisper of leather as he undid his breeches.

"If you are really a Terhune, you are under my authority, girl," he said above her, his voice thick. "And as a woman, it is your duty to submit to my will as the head of your family. But if you are not, then the niceties of law need not concern the lot of menial peasants." She felt his weight on her back, rough hands on her hips as he breathed into her ear. "Either way, it is my God-given right to do with you as I please."

Her wrists tightly clamped in iron manacles, the chain between them warmed where it had stretched across her stomach. Her shoulder throbbed where broken bones had not yet healed properly, and Terhune's less than gentle treatment hadn't helped any. She groaned softly as she rolled onto her side, sitting up slowly, her head pounding. The inside of her thighs ached clear to her spine.

"Scream, girl," he'd grunted in her ear. "I want to hear you scream . . ." The plunge into unconsciousness came as a welcome relief.

Blood pooled between her legs, thick and tacky as it congealed. *All my guts are coming out and I'm going to bleed to death.* She smiled bitterly. Terhune had hurt her badly, but she'd live. Unfortunately.

As she stood, she caught sight of the guard standing watching her in the dim shadows, the candlelight through the open grid of the cell door forming a halo around his head, his face a blank mask.

She paused, gauging him, then walked gingerly to the bucket of water in the corner, the only furnishing in the cell. The cold water smelled faintly of rot, but it helped wash the crusted blood from her face, her manacles jingling. Water dripped from her hair as she sat down gingerly, her back to the wall. She closed her eyes and leaned her head back against the stone. The shift came only to her knees, wet where she had lain in her own blood. But the blood was cold and it seemed she'd stopped bleeding.

She heard the guard shift nervously, but didn't bother to open her eyes. He coughed, clearing his throat. When she still didn't respond, he asked quietly, "Why didn't you scream?"

With her eyes still closed, she said tiredly, "I'm sorry, I didn't realize it was a public performance. I'll try to be more entertaining next time."

He didn't answer, and she dozed after that, dreamlessly. When she woke again, stiff and nauseated, the faint light remained the same; the faceless guard against the door could have been anyone. But someone had thrown a blanket over her . . . no, it was a soldier's wool cloak. She hurt too much to puzzle over it, gratefully drew the cloak up to her chin and dove back into the black stupor.

The smell of food woke her again, the guard gone. Men talked in low murmurs, too faint to distinguish words over the clink of knives and cups in the anteroom. The aroma of fresh baked bread made her mouth water. She tried to escape back into sleep, and failed.

The cell door creaked open as the guard returned, the sliver of light painful to her eyes although she knew it was not that bright. Furtively, he set a wooden plank of food in front of her. All she could make out in the gloom was a reflection of light in his eyes. Like a wary animal, she waited until he backed up to the open door before she picked up the bread. She could chew on one side of her mouth only; her jaw hurt where Terhune had kicked her. One tooth was loose; her tongue ruefully wiggled a molar.

It was decent bread, the coarse, nutty rations that provided soldier's fare, and covered with a strong melted cheese. She chided herself for wishing for some good dark beer to wash it down.

"You shouldn't refuse to scream," the guard said in the darkness, his voice hushed as if afraid someone might over-hear. "Defiance only makes him more violent."

She swallowed carefully before she said, "We've already had this conversation," then realized it could well have been with someone else. "What difference would it make? Had I pleaded for help, would you have valiantly come rushing to my rescue?"

When he didn't reply, she chuckled, a forced, painful sound, then chewed methodically in silence, trying not to think, trying not to imagine Terhune's return. Next time, she was quite sure, it wouldn't be possible to keep it inside. She would break before she could goad him into killing her. She hoped the darkness hid her trembling.

As soon as she'd finished eating, the guard quickly removed the wooden plank. She suspected her guards did not have per-mission to feed their prisoner, and there might be trouble if they were caught. She sucked the last of the grease from her fingers before she drew her knees up to her chest to keep warm, and gripped the cloak tightly around her, hoping no one would return for that.

Nothing happened for days. The guards cycled through, feeding her on occasion. She drank out of the scummy water bucket and found it oddly touching when the guard turned his back as she raised her shift and squatted to piss over the nar-row sewer hole. They said nothing more to her, nor she to them.

Everyone waited for Terhune.

28

B'nach woke in a sweat-pooled bed and stared at the ceiling of his bedchamber, his gut aching from the dreams. *D'nyel.* Tonight she was with someone else, he knew it. Sometimes his jealousy was so intense he wanted to howl and never stop. He envisioned those long legs wrapped around someone else's hips, the black roses of her nipples in someone else's mouth, ebony hair in someone else's hands. His erection throbbed painfully with every heartbeat.

Abruptly, he kicked the tangled bedclothes from around his legs and sat up, his mind churning. He might have been the One if it hadn't been for her. He was suddenly furious. She had seduced him, that sweet wonderful corruption ruining him forever. K'ferrin had been heartbroken, the only time B'nach had ever seen the old man weep. But once the egg had been cracked, his grandfather had no further reason to disguise his true nature. B'nach soon learned the depths of the real corruption riddling the Citadel.

Then as quickly as the anger came, the fear and shame flooded in behind. She had saved him from certain death in the Oracle, he knew it so well. How could he ever hate her for that?

Sitting on the edge of the narrow bed, he leaned his elbows on his knees and scratched his thinning scalp. Depressed, he thought of trying to go back to sleep, knowing it was futile. Instead, he went through his ritual morning mental exercises, the same exercises he'd done since he could first remember. Even if it was pointless now, he liked the routine of clearing his mind, letting himself believe all was right with the world, that it was possible to love and be loved without price, without conditions.

He padded to the washstand to splash cold water on his face, gasped, then took his underrobe off the iron peg hammered into the wall. He pulled it on over his head before choosing an overgown from his grand selection of three, all in patched and shabby condition.

He shoved his feet into worn shoes and opened the door to the outer room. A child of six rubbed sleepy eyes as her mother, B'nach's servant-of-the-week, exited the tiny kitchen to set a tray of smoked fish and cheese and a pot of tea in front of B'nach without bothering to look at him. He watched her with a twinge of guilt as she whisked the child from its makeshift bed of floor cushions before disappearing bleary-eyed back into the kitchen. True morning was an hour or so away, the Citadel just beginning to stir, and he tried to ignore the soft murmur of voices as she scolded the cranky child.

K'ferrin didn't allow his grandson to retain servants of his own in order to keep B'nach isolated, always dependent on the old man's household. In a way, he didn't mind. Although it prevented him from fostering any allies of his own, it also meant he had no responsibilities other than to himself. He sipped the hastily warmed tea, bitter, twice-heated, and ate the fish without appetite. Wrapping the cheese with a piece of hard bread in a cloth, he shoved it into his pocket before he left his own rooms without a word to the serving woman.

It was still cold along the passageway leading into the round gallery, not many people other than the usual house guards and insomniacs like himself were awake. B'nach pulled the hood of his overgown up to keep his ears warm, chafing his hands tucked inside his sleeves to keep the blood circulating. As another man stepped from a doorway, he glanced at him warily out of force of habit. Even well inside K'ferrin's own protected domain within the Citadel, nothing was ever completely safe.

Like B'nach, the man had cowled his face. He wore K'ferrin's colors, and when he smiled, B'nach smiled back, oddly pleased with this rare display of cordiality. The man fell into step beside him quietly and they walked together in silent companionship.

"B'nach . . ." the man whispered.

As B'nach looked up, he realized several things all at once and knew he would have seen it sooner had he not been so tired and preoccupied. The man wore the familiar burgundy of B'nach's own Order, even to the plain manteau splotched with ink marking him as a fellow scribe, but B'nach had never seen him before. His robe didn't fit properly, the big man straining it at the seams. B'nach scuttled away nervously, stopped by the man's grip on his arm and the point of a knife pricking his side. His first reaction, he noted with detached surprise, was disappointment, not fright; he was about to be murdered and he would never know by who or for what reason.

"Easy there, easy," the stranger whispered as if gentling a skittish horse. "I don't want to hurt you. Just walk with me."

Then B'nach was afraid, angry at himself for having had his hands poked up uselessly inside his sleeves instead of near his own knife.

"What do you want?" he whispered back, glad his voice didn't shake. They passed another cowled Priest in the passageway, a harried scribe like himself hugging his inkbox against his chest and hurrying along on his own activities. He didn't look up, too distracted to catch the look of desperate pleading in B'nach's eyes.

"Would K'ferrin want the woman who calls herself Lady Antonya, Terhune's niece?"

B'nach glanced at the man by his side, startled. Light blue eyes flashed a warning reinforced by a sharp jab in B'nach's ribs.

"Possibly," B'nach said cautiously. "Depending on what you require in return."

"Nothing," the man murmured. "Be in the corridor connecting the west end to the third-level gallery at mid-bell exactly. Bring armed men; you'll need them." The man stopped and looked at B'nach directly. "If you're not there, I'll assume you don't want her. You won't be offered the chance twice."

B'nach started as the stranger removed the tip of his knife and calmly walked away, his back confidently to the scribe.

At midday, the four bellspires around the Crystal Sajada tolled Sext while B'nach and three of K'ferrin's personal armsmen strolled toward the west end of the gallery. Although most people were at their midday meal, a few hastened about their own business along the wide corridor while others lingered by the double rows of columns, chatting with companions. Footsteps clicked like metronomes across the tiles in time with the music of buzzing conversation. Sunlight streaming in arched windows on the mezzanine balconies above cast dancing silhouettes across the mosaic floor.

Four of Terhune's armsmen escorted a woman, carving a respectful path before them. They gave no indication they were aware of B'nach or his own escort as they approached.

As the two parties met, B'nach recognized one of the guards in Elite black behind the woman by his light blue eyes. His heart beat rapidly in his ears as the men stopped, facing each other. K'ferrin's house guards already had their daggers out.

Her hands chained in front of her, the woman stared apathetically at B'nach with exhausted eyes, dark bruises on her face. She wore a full-length soldier's cloak hiding whatever further injuries she might have. Her feet were bare and filthy.

"What foolishness is this?" the senior of Terhune's guards demanded, frowning at the drawn knives more in irritation than alarm. "Get out of our way . . ." His eyes widened as he felt the blue-eyed man's knife at his back.

"Give us the woman," the tallest of K'ferrin's men said in a low voice. B'nach quickly glanced around; no one in the spacious gallery seemed aware that anything was wrong.

Like chess pieces moving into position, the two groups reshuffled, knives at the ready, one against the other. Then one of Terhune's men grabbed the woman, his arm around her neck to hold a knife to her throat. "Leave now," the man said reasonably, "or I'll kill her."

B'nach caught the frustrated alarm on the blue-eyed man's face as K'ferrin's men faltered, lowering their knives. Those loitering in the gallery had finally become mindful that something was amiss, clearing a wide circle to leave the adversaries in isolation.

The woman moaned, but the look crossing her face was anger, not fear. She sagged as if overcome with dismay. The man holding her jerked on her roughly. Then he staggered as she drove her elbow into his stomach, and kicked back hard against his shin. The knife wavered away from her neck. His grip loosened just enough for her to straighten and crack her head under his chin in a savage punch. He dropped like a stone. She whipped around, snarling as she looked for another attacker.

B'nach took a prudent step away as the two groups struggled, a sudden disorderly scramble of knives and fists. Another
of Terhune's guards whipped his knife at the woman. She
danced away nimbly, both her chained hands grabbing the
guard by his wrist, somehow leading him by the knife-hand
past her. He stumbled, off balance, before she kicked one small
foot neatly and precisely between his legs. B'nach winced at
the impact. Stunned, the man tottered backward, then sat down
on the floor with a blank look in his eyes, his mouth gaping
like a fish sucking air. He tucked his hands into his groin, his
knife clattering uselessly beside him. The woman swung her
fettered hands in a swift arc, smashing him viciously in the
head with her chains for good measure. The man went down.

Within seconds, three of Terhune's men lay on the floor,
two of them quite dead with blood pooling rapidly underneath
them. The third moaned, half-conscious. The fourth guard, the
blue-eyed man, held the woman by one arm, his other hand
still clenching a bloody knife. As K'ferrin's men circled him
uneasily, the man shoved the woman spinning into B'nach's
arms, her manacles jangling. He dropped the knife and held
out empty hands away from his sides, then looked at B'nach
with a strange smile.

"He's with us," B'nach said, although he wondered. The
house guards muttered but didn't stop the blue-eyed man from
following as they turned and trotted quickly toward the safety
of K'ferrin's Sector, frightened spectators scattering out of
their way. No one would have seen a thing when questions
were asked, B'nach well knew; everyone would have been
busy somewhere else at the time.

In minutes, they had reached K'ferrin's demesne, and a
small phalanx of armed men accreted around them. When they
came to the massive internal siege doors of K'ferrin's offices,
the guards peeled away to take up defensive posts behind
them. B'nach, the woman and the four men were nearly
pushed inside K'ferrin's chambers as the door slammed locked
behind them.

For a moment, B'nach was unable to do more than try to
catch his breath. Two of K'ferrin's guards had already
searched the blue-eyed man while the third held the woman

by one arm in the center of the room. She stared up at the old man, who stood at the top of the staircase.

Panting, B'nach sat down wearily and dabbed at his sweating forehead with the hem of his sleeve. K'ferrin negotiated his way down the curved stairs looking very pleased, B'nach noticed distantly. The old man stopped in front of the woman, keeping his eyes on her as he said, "Well done, my kinsman."

Still too winded to speak, B'nach simply nodded.

"Welcome, Lady Antonya," K'ferrin said amiably. "I am the Reverence K'ferrin, High Lord Keeper of the Holy Oracle. You're safe with us now."

The woman looked at him impassively.

K'ferrin snapped his fingers, and the guard at her elbow drew his dagger. B'nach tensed, then almost giggled with nerves when the man began working the narrow blade into the lock of the woman's manacles. After a few minutes, the irons snapped open.

K'ferrin looked over her shoulder to where his guards held the blue-eyed man between them. "And you are?" he asked benignly, although B'nach knew the man stood a good chance of being summarily executed within the next few minutes. Perhaps he knew it as well.

"My name is Briston, Your Reverence," he said diffidently, bowing his head formally to the old man.

"One of Terhune's Elite, I believe?"

The man straightened with a smile. "And captain of his Guard, up until about ten minutes ago."

"You've betrayed your High Lord Commander, oathbreaker," K'ferrin said casually, and B'nach braced himself.

"Aye," Briston said. "There is a limit to how much loyalty fear can command." He looked at the old man boldly, unafraid. B'nach admired him, ashamed he hadn't had the courage to face death with as much dignity.

K'ferrin studied him, then nodded brusquely at his men. "Escort him downstairs, please." The guards shoved their prisoner in front of them, conveying him down the internal passages to the small private prison cells underneath K'ferrin's chambers.

B'nach expelled a sigh of relief. If K'ferrin was going to have the man murdered, it would be done later and in secret.

At least he wouldn't have to watch. He found he was trembling.

K'ferrin gently steered the woman by one elbow toward one of the elegant chairs in his office. "Poor child, such a dreadful experience. B'nach, would you be so kind as to get the Lady Antonya some wine?"

B'nach got to his feet heavily and poured a cup of wine. As he brought it toward her, he raised it to his mouth to take the customary sip.

"Don't do that," she said hoarsely, stopping him.

B'nach exchanged glances with his grandfather. "It's to prove it's not poisoned," he explained apologetically.

"I know what it's for. Don't do it." She held out her hand for the wine, and drank deeply when he'd given it to her. She lowered the cup with a tired sigh. "And what do *you* want of me, K'ferrin?"

The old man bristled, unused to such directness especially from women, but quickly smoothed over it. She had her eyes cast down and B'nach wasn't sure if she'd even noticed. "Only to see you safe, dear Lady. You're our guest, rest assured we'll treat you kindly. You have nothing to fear from us . . . or from P'tre Terhune any further."

She smiled bitterly. "I see."

No doubt she did. Quite clearly.

"You must be weary," K'ferrin said. "Perhaps you would like a hot bath before you rest?" She didn't respond. "B'nach, please see our guest is made comfortable." The old man was still as smug as a cat in cream as he bowed extravagantly to the woman. He would no doubt lock himself away in his bedchamber to celebrate with his favorites for the next hour or so, B'nach was sure.

She allowed B'nach to lead her out the same internal doorway Briston had gone, but instead of following the stairway down to the locked dungeons below, he led her up into the tower's private rooms. She glanced around at the comfortable furnishings. A cool breeze stirred wind chimes in a sunny balcony window covered with a wrought-iron grille.

"A gilded cage, then, is it?" she said stoically.

"You will be safe here, Lady," B'nach promised her. "No one will harm you."

She crossed to the window and sat down on the pillows on the small ledge. The window overlooked the high-walled garden, but no matter how ornate the wrought iron, the bars that enclosed the balcony were as secure as any prison's.

"I will send up a woman to help you bathe. Do you require anything else? Food? Wine?"

She stared unblinkingly out the window without responding. After a moment's hesitation, he bowed, more sincerely than had his grandfather, and left her alone and silent.

29

K'ferrin sent B'nach to interview Terhune's erstwhile captain. The catacombs riddling the ground under the Citadel were carved out of living rock, a massive network of vaulted cells and crypts echoing human voices and the drip of hidden water. It was bitterly cold and stank of mildew, urine and burnt tallow.

He arrived with one of his grandfather's guards, both of them following the jailer's young assistant as he sullenly led them down into the maze. Only a candle lantern lighted their way, throwing eerie shadows against the rough walls. The boy stopped in front of a heavy wooden door studded with thick iron rivets. It looked like any of hundreds lining the passageways. He stood on tiptoe, pushing back the circular eyehole cover to check the prisoner, then fiddled with a large ring of keys to find the correct one. The lock mechanism thudded back, and with a grunt the boy tugged open the heavy iron fortified door. B'nach entered alone while the jailer's assistant shut it behind him before escorting the guard further down the passageway out of earshot to give the scribe and the prisoner privacy. When B'nach was finished, he would call out.

The cell wasn't as bad as it might have been. Although the air was damp, the cell itself was dry. A small table supported a candle held upright in its own wax and there were several additional tapers stacked in a small niche carved into the rock. Remains of a meal as well as a wine jug proved at least that the jailer was feeding his prisoner reasonably well. Briston sat on a rough cot as B'nach entered, still dressed in the black of Terhune's Elite, his cloak wrapped closely around him against the chill. An iron fetter had been clamped around the man's neck, the thick chain bolted to the wall long enough to afford him room to walk around.

Terhune's former guard smiled pleasantly, the same cordial expression B'nach had first seen before the man had shoved a knife against his side. There was no place for B'nach to sit, so he slipped his cold hands inside his sleeves and leaned back against the iron door well out of the reach of the man's chains.

After a moment's silence, Briston said, prompting him, "I'm still alive, so I must assume you want something of me."

"His Reverence has sent me to ask you a few questions," B'nach said as sternly as he could manage, uncomfortable.

Briston nodded, waiting. When B'nach faltered, unsure where to begin, his smile grew. "You haven't much experience at conducting interrogations, have you?"

For some reason, B'nach was more relieved than irritated. "No," he admitted. "It's not a customary part of my work. But my grandfather thought you might be more forthcoming with me, having sought me out for this incident."

An echo of a scream quavered through the passageways, and B'nach and Briston exchanged a silent look before they both ignored it. Torture was an everyday part of life in the Citadel, both men too inured to the sounds to bother commenting on it.

"Why?" B'nach asked vaguely. Fortunately, Briston understood.

"It's rather a long story," he warned.

"We have the time."

Briston folded his hands neatly in his lap. "Our High Lord Commander Terhune has begun to confuse the army's loyalty to the Faith with absolute obedience to him and his family personally. His nephew is not yet ready for his Walk, but other events are happening too quickly for Terhune to delay it much longer. The Lady Antonya presents a possible obstacle to his aspirations."

"Why then hasn't he removed her as he's done other 'obstacles' in his path?" B'nach asked, his tone more bitter than he'd intended.

"It's whispered G'walch himself asked for her life to be spared." While B'nach suspected that G'walch held considerable influence over Terhune, it nonetheless surprised him that the boy cared enough about such earthly matters to interfere in his uncle's secular activities.

"If she is his niece," Briston said, "that makes her of G'walch's blood as well. Terhune resolved to recognize her as kin before forcing her into marrying him despite their degree of consanguinity." His blue eyes crinkled with amusement at B'nach's incredulity. "After which, Terhune would give up all claim to Adalon, transfer his Lands as dower to his bride while freeing himself from any further obstacles K'ferrin could raise against his being formally recognized by the Council of Reverences."

"While still controlling his Lands through his wife."

"Of course. Once he'd properly broken her to his will."

"But surely," B'nach protested, "he must realize the Council would never be fooled by such a blatant scheme?"

Briston chuckled softly. "It wouldn't matter. He would have fulfilled the letter of the law and have sufficient might behind him to possibly sway majority opinion to his favor. And if he couldn't, he still has G'walch. The problem remains that in either case incest and torture of a blooded Terhune is making not a few of the Faithful nervous, including members of his Elite." Briston paused. "*If* she is a Terhune," he said emphatically.

"And does Terhune believe the woman is of his blood?" B'nach knew as well as the prisoner that family ties had never before been an obstacle to P'tre's ambitions.

Briston shrugged. "Possibly. There are others in the Citadel who are kin to P'tre, but he and G'walch are the last of his father's line . . . except *perhaps* the Lady Antonya. It is possible he thinks of ensuring his chances of begetting another aspirant should his . . . nephew fail." The hesitation was slight, but B'nach heard it well enough. "Regardless of whether or not she is of his blood, the belief that she is the rightful heir to Adalon is already widespread. Including in Adalon. Terhune has started Purges of his own people to put down insurrection."

If he noticed B'nach's shudder, he pretended not to.

"As our High Lord Commander, he has the right to enforce

his authority among his own men, within reason." Briston raised an eyebrow ironically. "The judicious use of scourges, the rack and the stocks are all an acceptable part of military discipline. Soldiers can usually expect to survive those."

B'nach was shivering, hoping it didn't show on his face. Briston shifted slightly on the cot, chains rattling softly.

"But now Terhune is starting to Purge inside the Citadel as well. Those who displease him disappear in the night. When they reappear, they've been slowly tortured to death, their mutiliated corpses left in the guards' quarters as a warning to others."

"Then why risk giving us the Lady Antonya?"

"Terhune isn't being selective lately who he sentences to death. Treason can be anything from plotting to assassinate him to being a few minutes late with a report. He sees betrayal behind every tree." The prisoner smiled ruefully. "And what loyal guardsman would want to disappoint his commander?"

"He's going mad?" B'nach asked dubiously.

Briston shrugged, setting the chain jingling again. "Mad? I don't know. He believes when his nephew is Crowned in the Fire, he himself will reign over the secular concerns of the new world as the boy's Protector. His will be the sword to scythe away all those deemed unworthy of the Faith reborn"— Briston's smile was twisted—"which includes just about everyone, it seems. Perhaps that's madness enough. But he's not yet the right arm of God and suspicion breeds suspicion. He's losing the respect of his own troops. Without that . . ." He shook his head eloquently.

"Are there others, others like you . . . in Terhune's Elite . . . ?" B'nach asked hesitantly.

The man's light blue eyes flickered to him, hard and narrowed. "If there are, I'm afraid you'd be forced to try and torture that out of me. I'll not tell you willingly."

"You couldn't have arranged this alone," B'nach pressed.

Briston laughed. "You really aren't very good at this," he said kindly. "Go back to your calligraphy, B'nach, and tell K'ferrin to send professionals next time."

B'nach felt the burn of humiliation on his face. "If that's what you prefer," he said stiffly, trying to keep as much dignity in his voice as he could. He turned, ready to shout for the guard.

"My apologies, scribe," Briston said quickly, stopping him. "Of course I would not prefer that." When B'nach turned back, the man was regarding him curiously with his head cocked to one side. "I meant no insult." He seemed sincere.

B'nach said stiffly, "I have no more questions."

His tone carefully respectful, Briston said, "Might I be permitted to ask a few of my own before you go, then?"

B'nach searched for hints of ridicule and found none. He nodded, not trusting his own voice.

"Where is the Lady Antonya Terhune?"

That surprised him. "Safe enough," he said. "Not here, if that is your concern. Why do you care?"

The man could make his frown look like a smile. "Soldiers admire courage."

B'nach waited, and when it was obvious it was all the man would tell him, he said, "Any other questions?"

"Why didn't you Walk the Fire?"

A hard stone dropped into the pit of his stomach. Briston looked back at him benignly. "I preferred to live," B'nach said finally, his voice strangled.

After deliberating the answer, Briston nodded. "Sensible."

B'nach found he was trembling. "Anything else?"

Smiling, Briston shook his head and B'nach immediately called out for the guard, impatient to leave. As he walked up the narrow stone stairway, the faint shriek of a prisoner being tortured somewhere in the underground catacombs followed behind him. Only then did B'nach realize the blue-eyed man hadn't inquired after his own fate.

30

"**You told me nothing,**" D'nyel chided him as they lay with sweat-slicked limbs twisted together, white on black on white. His pitiful gratitude to be back in her favor disgusted her, his lovemaking too frantic and joyless to be gratifying for her. At least her tediously boring scribe had gotten it over with quickly.

"I've been so busy, there hasn't been time." He blushed, and looked away. She heard the deception in his voice as well as the stubbornness. B'nach knew he was an inept liar, but she decided not to press him on it, and let her anger subside.

Terhune had been enraged when he discovered the woman had been spirited out of his private jail and snatched away by B'nach and his grandfather's guards. Frankly, B'nach's daring in reaching for such a dangerous prize astonished D'nyel. Terhune was baying for his blood and she felt a twinge of sympathy for the hapless scribe.

She knew most of the story anyway, having heard all about it firsthand from the man who had survived the trap. Terhune did not tolerate failure. When she'd returned to her own rooms, the door to her hidden tower was marked. Only Terhune knew what she kept in her tower and where she kept the key. It was a small part of Terhune's sadistic humor to hide the key whenever he had left her a present upstairs. Excited and furious, she spent an hour before finding the key under the lip of a saturke wine jug, held in place with a bit of wax.

Terhune had left the man strapped firmly on the table with his mouth gagged. As she opened the door to the room, his wild eyes filled with relief to find it was only a woman. He urged her to release him, his words muffled behind the cloth, *hurry, please hurry,* before the executioner arrived.

She had smiled, running her palms against her body with almost carnal delight as she walked around the table. "Lovely, lovely . . ." she breathed. He was young and very strong. It took quite a bit of poppy extract to calm him enough to drag out all the intriguing details. Her mind was on the man in the tower as she murmured against B'nach's ear, more sound than words.

"I may look the fool," B'nach said, startling her. "I may even play the part, but *you* should know me better."

His rebuke confused her, and for a brief moment alarmed her, thinking he had discovered her hostage. "What do you mean?"

"I play the woman with you, D'nyel. But do you think me so blinded by your beauty or made mindless out of desire for you? I know why you're here, and it isn't out of any great passion for me. Just please tell me you don't love *him*."

She pulled away from him and drew her discarded robe around her shoulders, baffled by his peculiar behavior. "Love who?"

"Terhune." She nearly laughed with relief. "The entire Citadel knows he is your lover," B'nach continued bitterly. "Why else would you be with him so often? Convince me you don't whisper secrets in his ear when you lie with him."

"I see your grandfather has been at it again." She turned over several possible reactions before deciding that the most obvious wouldn't work. There would be times when he was weak and wanted to see her in tears. Not now. "It's no secret Terhune was once my lover. But we haven't shared a bed for many years, whatever you choose to believe." She added derisively, "We do not suit each other's tastes."

She stood, pacing the room in feigned indignation while her mind ticked over the prospects of how best to handle B'nach's strange mood. "Now I see why you didn't keep me informed. You feared that had I known of your plans, I would have run straight to P'tre and thwarted them, is that it?" She might have, had she seen any advantage in doing so for herself. "You don't trust me," she said, laying wounded pride in her voice.

He lay with his head propped on one hand, watching her resentfully, his eyes hard, an unpliant expression she was not used to seeing in him. "You know he killed your spy, the girl Tannah." She read his unspoken question easily, B'nach never having learned how to keep his thoughts off his face. Had she betrayed the girl?

"A shame to lose such talent," she said warily, answering his suspicions obliquely. "I would have liked to have saved her had I been able to. But Tannah understood the risks." All the same, D'nyel didn't add, they had obtained as much from her as they were likely to; the girl had already outlived her usefulness.

"How old was she? Fourteen? Fifteen?" B'nach insisted. His other hand clawed into the fabric of the pillows. "About my age when I first met you?"

"So what? What difference does it make?" she snapped.

He rolled onto his stomach, his back to her to avoid her eyes. "What kind of man can take this much shame and treachery and abuse and still be fool enough to call it love?" His jaw clenched, the muscles under the skin spasming. "I should send you from me, finish it for good and tell you to leave."

"Have you really changed so much, B'nach?" she asked quietly.

She watched in fascination as he struggled with the challenge. After a moment, the light died and he bent his head. She had to stifle her smile of triumph.

"Not enough, D'nyel," he said bleakly. "Not nearly enough." Resigned, he sank down on the floor cushions to lie on his back, as vulnerable as the man bound to the table in her tower. "Just tell me what my punishment will be and get it over with."

She dressed quickly, her anger now quite real. As she cinched her underrobe around her waist and pulled on the soft overgown, she was aware of B'nach watching her.

"Perhaps you're right, B'nach," she said, annoyed. He didn't respond. "We should finish it, I *should* leave you."

At that, she was pleased to see the spark of fear in his eyes. "Please, D'nyel, I didn't mean it . . ."

She cut him off abruptly. "I need time to reconsider the nature of our relationship."

His face was ashen. "How much time?" he asked thickly.

"I'll let you know." She left without looking back. As she strode quickly down the long corridor, long legs eating up distance and anger, she began to smile. It worked out far more conveniently this way. Now she wouldn't have to worry about being disturbed at an inopportune moment or having to hide her work from the irritating little librarian.

31

Antonya submitted indifferently to being bathed and bandaged and fed as if she were a child. She felt nothing: no pain, no grief, no hope, no fear. This emptiness was almost pleasant, her mind clearer with her emotions drained. She knew the lull was only temporary, feeling the pressure of the future like a cloud blowing at her back.

Her guardian, a matronly woman with iron-gray hair, wasn't unkind, but all her attempts to draw Antonya into conversation failed. Not that she ignored the woman; that took too much effort. She simply listened politely without responding. Eventually her guardian gave up, sat alone by the fire and turned her attention to her needlework.

Well after dusk, the old man appeared like a grinning scarecrow, his pudgy kinsman hovering behind him. B'nach examined her politely but thoroughly, removing the gold earrings and necklace her guardian insisted on decorating her with, like a child with a doll.

Nothing of metal, B'nach apologized, which was when she learned they were taking her to the great Crystal Sajada and the Holy Oracle. A tingle of interest awakened along her nerves, the rekindling of curiosity intruding into her fragile apathy almost annoying.

She saw little during the quick walk to the sajada, wedged firmly into the center of armed guards on every side. The Keeper kept her pinned between him and B'nach, his hard fingers cold even through the fabric of her robe, the librarian holding her arm with an awkward gentleness.

Tall doors swung open to admit them, giving her barely enough time to notice intricate carved figures before she was swept into the sajada. Cold air brushed her cheeks as her eyes adjusted to the gloom. Moonlight lent everything a silver gleam within the huge interior of the temple. Row upon row of monks filed into the cold dome, silent except for the shuffle of their feet, robes rustling, the chatter of teeth against the chill. Isolated in the center of the sajada, an immense stone bowl hummed with a low vibration just below audibility. The hair on her neck prickled in animal alarm.

Her sight adjusted to the dark, colors oddly distorted in the moonlight. In the midst of burgundy-turned-to-darkest-violet and greens-turned-to-brown, a flash of pure white caught her eye.

A boy watched her placidly, his fine blond hair glowing in the pale light. Dressed in white, he stood out in the forest of tall, hard men in black, their ranks spotted here and there with Terhune red moonlight-faded to the color of dried blood. Beside him, a stocky, flat-faced man kept watch, dark eyes alert, obviously the boy's bodyguard. The boy spoke quietly to the cowled Priest on his other side. Immediately, the Priest whirled to glare at Antonya, his hatred and anger palpable even at a distance.

P'tre Terhune. She felt her heart kick, the thrill of fear remote, as if it were someone else whose muscles trembled, wanting to flee. K'ferrin's hand tightened its grip on her arm possessively.

"O sanctissima, Mater amata, ora pro nobis!"

The sudden burst of song startled her, and she looked away, grateful to be released from Terhune's stare. Small choirs of boys stood at the foot of every section, tiny boxes in each hand. Their voices echoed in the cavern of the sajada, high and clear.

"Exaudi nos, Mater aeterne, omnes habitantes in hoc sajadum!"

The reply rejoinder rolled like thunder inside the Sajada. The choir of boys raised their small boxes over their heads.

"Suscipe hanc oblationem, quam tibi offerimus ob memorium Lumen de Lumune verum."

She suddenly knew what the boxes held, having once held one herself years before. She recognized the song; this was the celebration of the lunar conjunction, when Luna Minor swallowed her larger brother, Luna Major, the union into one before rebirth and renewal. At the moment of eclipse, white doves would be released. Confused, she studied the sealed interior of the huge Sajada, wondering how the birds would get out, free to fly away.

"Introibo ad altare lumine, emitte lucem tuam et veritatum tuem."

Where the Keeper's voice was thin and reedy, not bothering to hide his utter boredom, the librarian's singing was surprisingly rich, thick with emotion. For a disorienting moment, she was back in the tiny sajada of Tembris, surrounded by Father Andrae's soft baritone, Brother Reule's robust off-key tenor, Brother Sholto's lisping southern accent tripping over the sacred verse he barely understood.

"In spiritu humiliatis, fiat sacrificium nostram in conspectu tuo hodie ut placent tibi."

The memory was overpowering. Her mouth opened and the words came out all on their own, astonishing her as much as the two men beside her. She could almost feel the heartbeat of a frightened bird in her hands, feathers sticking to her palms. The old leper, Brother Migius, bred them to produce the whitest flock possible for the ritual signifying the purity of the twin moons. The Brothers had chosen their doves, but Antonya wanted the only mottled gray despite Father Andrae's urging. She wanted a unique bird to stand out from the rest as it flew away.

The sajada grew subtly darker as the moons drew together. In the sudden gloom she heard rather than saw the birds extracted from their cages, heard the flutter of wings as they were released.

"May this offering which we have blest ascend to Heaven, carried by the hands of Thy Light and kindle within us purity with the flame of everlasting grace." The single voice was that of a child, quavering with stage fright, invisible in the shadows.

A tense silence settled over the crowd, the only sound that of thousands of wings rushing frantically in the lightless sajada. A spark of light flashed, just long enough to see the outline of a bird, then another, and another. A huge flare blossomed in the darkness as the Oracle raged to life. Antonya gasped, stunned. Immediately, the birds wheeled and plunged into the light. The sajada erupted in a blaze of cold fire, blinding in its intensity. The Priests burst into cheers.

She shielded her eyes, bewildered as the huge flock of doves swooped into the globe of light. None coming out. They flew in ever tighter circles, trapped inside the Oracle, crowded by more and more birds diving into the Light. Within minutes, every bird had flown into the trap, tumbling as they slammed into one another.

"Gloria! Gloria in excelsis!"

She felt the librarian's hand shake, still gripping her arm, and glanced up at him. The man's face was deathly pale, sweat shining on his forehead as he watched the birds. His breathing whistled, fast and ragged. He seemed totally unaware of her presence. The sound in the sajada changed and she realized it came from the trapped birds. When she looked back, many of them had fallen into the curve of black stone cradling the Light, twitching like still-living insects burning at the bottom of a lantern. Feathers were stripped off the bodies, swirling on their own in the reddening sphere, a huge goosedown pillow savagely ripped apart. Appalled, she clamped her hands over her ears, not able to shut out the tortured cries of thousands of dying birds.

K'ferrin jerked her arms down from her ears, glaring at her. She didn't notice him, her attention focused on the horror in the Light. A dozen young monks were hunched over tiny portable desks, scribbling on parchment as quickly as they could. What they could possibly be recording from the screams of suffering animals, she couldn't imagine.

"Sweet Mother of God," she breathed. This was nothing like the ceremony on Tembris she remembered from childhood. Each brother released his bird, cheering as it fluttered out the high arched windows of the sajada into the moonlight. Luna Major bulged from the side of his sister, elongating, before the two moons separated once again. The birds flew out the stone windows toward the moons, or more likely simply used the light to escape to the cover of the forest.

By morning, most of the doves would have returned to the brick dovecote, and all the monks would pretend not to notice. It didn't matter that they couldn't really fly to the moon, any more than Luna Minor really ate Luna Major and gave birth to him again. It was the metaphorical symbolism which was important, Father Andrae explained patiently, never meant to be taken literally. She didn't care about ontology or epistemology, barely old enough to be able to pronounce the words, never mind understand them. But even as a child, she knew this was supposed to be a time of joy, a celebration of birth from darkness, the two divided made whole, the celestial male and female rejoined and from the whole reborn anew.

This was death. Senseless, futile, grotesque death. Squeezing her eyes shut, Antonya turned her face away and prayed it would stop.

"They're trained to go toward the light," K'ferrin's amused voice said. She didn't answer, fighting a wave of nausea welling up in her throat. "They're raised in total darkness and only fed when a light is shined. That way none of them evade proper sacrifice."

"Similar to the way Aspirants are trained," B'nach said quietly.

K'ferrin's grip tightened painfully, forcing her eyes open. But his attention was not on her. "Careful, my kinsman. You are not yet so tainted by worldly sin that you may abstain from marrying the Light should it become necessary."

Obviously frightened, the librarian bowed his head and murmured barely audible apologies. Neither spoke again as they watched the remainder of the hapless birds slowly drop into a pile of corpses within the Oracle. The last dove fell, wings twitching feebly in the cloud of blood, as the choir sang the final verses of the lunar conjunction. A fine haze of blood swirled through the Light, the bodies disintegrating. The monks sang until the moons had separated, until the Oracle cleared, the corpses gone. The Light glowed a soft gold, empty and lifeless.

Antonya remained silent, the oppressiveness deadening her mind. With the phalanx of armed guards crowded around her, she allowed herself to be led out of the sajada, into the Great Hall.

Standing quietly beside K'ferrin, securely enclosed within his Guard, she watched as the Keeper spoke with an old man he called his dearly beloved brother Philoniah. Neither man showed the slightest affection for the other. The old Priest's indifferent eyes flickered toward her as K'ferrin commented more loudly than necessary about her suffering, a vile insult to the noble Terhune blood, that same august blood running in G'walch's veins. That was why she was here, she realized. As they milled around her, Priests eyed her bruised face with malicious interest, if without sympathy.

She ignored them all, doing her best to shut out the world. She thought instead of Father Andrae laughing as she excitedly insisted the gray dove had reached the moon before all the others. She felt Brother Hasuq's arms as strong as the iron he smithed picking her up by the waist, lifting her toward the windows.

"Where is it now, Antonya? Can you see clear to the moon?"

Her gray never returned and she wanted to believe it had truly flown all the way to the heavens, symbolism or no. Whatever the Ancients had built the Oracle for, it wasn't for this. She had never been more sure of anything in her life. Her eyes ached as she fought the tears welling under her lashes, mourning the innocent and dead birds that would never reach the safety of the moons.

B'nach touched her arm gently, concerned. Startled, she looked up and realized her eyes smarted for another reason. For a fleeting moment her irises had been a pale gold, the color of the Oracle.

The librarian drew back, surprised, then glanced around to see if anyone else had seen the change. When he looked back, she made certain her eyes were again dark, indifferent. K'ferrin had finished his harangue, Terhune and his nephew vanished in the crowd. B'nach opened his mouth as if to speak, stared at her hard and shut it.

That night she dreamed, dreamed of Kerrick trapped in the Oracle, his hair on fire as he struggled, bathed in the deadly golden glow of her own eyes. She screamed, waking herself, and lay in the dark, drenched in sweat and shaking.

32

The high arched windows of the Great Library were set with plain glass squares, old and purpled; light filtered through thick dust on their surface. Researchers strolled through the tiers of parchment and leather, scribes silent but for their pens as they copied works at the long scriptorium tables. It should have been a peaceful place, but while the archives lay within the security of K'ferrin's authority, it was still vulnerable to noises from the outside world.

At the moment, the clangor of stone being hacked, men shouting orders, the sawing of wood and hammering of nails, invaded the sanctuary of the library. Most of the researchers had fled. The only scribes remaining grumbled bitterly while scribbling as fast as they could, under strict orders from their superiors.

Finally even B'nach was driven out of his private refuge. But he could hardly complain to K'ferrin about the nuisance; his grandfather was its cause. Irritated, he wandered out to the open terrace overlooking the construction site and glared at the disorder.

K'ferrin's private garden encompassed nearly half an acre. The stately fountain which had formed the centerpiece of the garden was four hundred years old, now crumbling and defunct. Its plumbing had broken, leaving only a stagnant pond of scummy water. Ameveth had sent an Engineer to see if it could be repaired, but he advised knocking out the entire thing and building another from scratch.

Whether or not that was true, it pleased K'ferrin. He'd combed the archives for ideas, sketching ever more complex and grandiose designs. The new fountain would be far larger than the old, dominating the garden with nubile naiads and muscular centaurs cavorting, water spraying from the marble mouths of fantastic fish, a riot of hermaphroditic cupids clinging to the wet backs of winged horses.

B'nach hated it. Not only because it was so flamboyantly tasteless, but because its sheer size would overpower the garden. As a boy, B'nach had often sat on the lip of the venerable fountain, splashing bare feet at gold- and scarlet-scaled fish darting through speckled sunlight to hide under the shadows of pond lilies. The garden had been large enough for a small stand of fruit trees to play under, bright flowers to attract birds and butterflies. Sunlight sifted through the leaves of a gnarled horse chestnut where B'nach had left bread for the squirrels nesting in the boles far beyond his reach. The old gardener had clipped ancient shrubs into fantastic animals to delight the privileged golden child B'nach had once been.

No doubt the roots of the dignified old tree were a main culprit in breaking the pipes of the ancient fountain. Now its massive trunk and limbs lay butchered into pieces to dry into next winter's firewood. The squirrels were gone, as was the old gardener. The topiary had been pulled out of the ground, roots naked, withered branches glinting here and there with bits of forgotten copper wire.

B'nach watched morosely as a dozen workmen hacked the old fountain to pieces. A few Engineers supervised the work as they stood to one side bickering over their charts. Another strode vigilantly amongst the manual laborers, his thin birch whip ready to descend on the backs of any caught slow or clumsy.

The skilled artisans were already at work carving sections for the new fountain, the rough shapes of horse heads and nude satyrs chiseled out of white stone. The rest were either low-level Engineer acolytes or city menials being used as no more than draft animals, their muscles strained in sharp relief as they carried rubble to dump into a huge oxcart. Most were naked to the waist, their grimacing features obscured between arms steadying the loads slung on their backs.

The oxen nibbled at the wreckage of flowerbeds, placidly chewing bright pink asters and sunny yellow calendulas, tiny violas and delicate blue cupflowers into a mash of cud. B'nach made no attempt to divert the animals from the ruined plants.

One menial staggered toward the cart, wearing only torn breeches to the knees, the dust on his bare feet and chest sweat-streaked. Bent nearly double by his load, he lurched up the plank of the oxcart as it sagged under his weight. He pushed the sling from his forehead, swaying to maintain his balance, as the load of broken stone clattered into the cart. He braced his hands on his thighs, then looked up directly at B'nach. Panting open-mouthed for breath, he grinned as B'nach recognized him with a thrill of shock.

Although the workman seemed neither slow nor clumsy, his back displayed a copious amount of red weals left by the foreman's caning, far more than his companions bore. He shook out his empty sling before walking back down the plank. The foreman caught sight of him standing by the cart and strode toward the man, birch raised, then faltered as B'nach stepped into the sunlight to wave him off brusquely.

Briston waited with his sling hanging limply at his side as B'nach approached. He bowed politely when B'nach stopped. "Greetings . . . my Lord . . . scribe," he said calmly, still breathless.

"K'ferrin should never have let you out," B'nach blurted.

The man straightened, and raked back the hair sticking to his sweating brow, his nails ragged and dirty, knuckles skinned raw. "Your mercy and compassion are overwhelming," he said dryly.

B'nach's face flushed. "I meant you are too dangerous a man to be set free."

Briston smiled, although his blue eyes were cold. " 'Free'? I hardly think my current condition merits that description, sir. I've been divested of my chains only because they get in the way of the work. Rest assured, when the day is done I am again liberally festooned with iron and discreetly tucked away in your cellars."

"I can't understand why he's let you out," B'nach said doggedly.

"Perhaps he enjoys watching one of Terhune's fallen Elite humbled with servile labor. Perhaps he enjoys watching me punished for betraying my overlord, a warning to those who might think of defying *him*." He glanced to one side, a gesture to indicate he was aware of the unseen presence. It took all of B'nach's effort to keep from looking up at the arched windows across the garden, to ignore the twitch of heavy curtains shielding the dim rooms beyond. "Perhaps he just enjoys watching," Briston said with a mocking smile.

While Briston was indeed a handsome man, despite the dirt and welts, B'nach doubted the covert eyes belonged to K'ferrin. His grandfather's tastes were more idiosyncratic. More likely, it was the Keeper's unpleasant little cossets who were observing the young prisoner's downfall, no doubt with a certain wistful relish.

"In any case," Briston continued when B'nach didn't reply, "I'm grateful enough for the work. Fresh air, sunlight, a bit of healthy exercise." He grinned broadly. "My cup runneth over."

"I know who you are, *what* you are. You're no cowed un- skilled laborer; these people can't keep you here," B'nach in- sisted, keeping his voice low. He gestured nervously at the garden, at the Engineers scowling at them from a distance. "You could escape."

The derisive expression had vanished, Briston studying him calmly. "But I haven't," he said, not denying he was capable of it.

"Why not?"

After a long moment the man idly scratched his neck that was pale with stone powder. "Where would I go?" he asked indifferently. "At the moment, it amuses me to stay. I'm con- tent enough to take the days as they come, one at a time." The faint, mocking smile returned. "Just as you do, B'nach. But when your days run out, what will *you* do? Will you run? Will you fight? Or will you allow yourself to be led meekly to the slaughter, gentle lamb that you've been bred to be?"

B'nach opened his mouth, then closed it, his throat too tight to speak. Aware he looked the gaping fool, he stepped away from the prisoner, back into the safety of the shadowed col- onnade. He turned away abruptly as Briston made a cynical bow, the man's low laughter almost inaudible.

Walking swiftly away, he heard the sharp sound of a whip against naked flesh and winced as if it had fallen on his own back.

33

Immediately after his grandfather had dragged her into the Great Sajada to taunt Terhune, the woman had been deposited back in her secured cage. Several weeks passed, and K'ferrin seemed to have forgotten her existence, uninterested in her other than as a prize to hold over Terhune's head. B'nach visited her, concerned.

Although the bruises on her face had faded, her injuries healing, it was as if something deep within her soul had been damaged. She spoke little, barely ate, sitting day after day at the window, staring unblinkingly through her ornate prison bars. Sometimes, she would touch them, as if repeatedly surprised to find they were still real.

The guardian reported she slept poorly, often crying out in her sleep. But whatever terrors haunted her dreams they did not seem to affect her waking hours. He watched her, uncertain how to approach this silent woman. She was not like others he had seen broken in spirit or mind, rocking and weeping inconsolably. She had simply withdrawn, like an ascetic monk, aware but with no further interest in the world.

Agnes, her guardian, sat by the room's small hearth, embroidering delicate flowers on silk which matched neither her blunt fingers nor her surly expression. Her silver needle caught the light of the dying fire. B'nach ignored her as easily as he'd learned to ignore all his grandfather's servants and dragged a chair to sit closer to the woman by the window. She gave no indication she was even aware of him.

"Lady Antonya?" he said softly.

She didn't react, as still as statuary.

"Lady?" When she didn't answer, he leaned closer to her, and placed his fingertips gently on her knee.

"Don't touch me, please," she said softly, without looking at him.

He retreated, baffled. The guardian smirked briefly before

returning to her embroidery. Antonya didn't acknowledge B'nach's presence for several minutes, then turned slowly toward him, as if it were physically painful to move. Perhaps it was, he thought.

"What do you want?" she asked without animosity.

He tried to smile reassuringly. "Conversation."

She stared at him distantly. "About what?"

"Anything you like. The nature of the universe. Are the stars made of fire or ice? When angels dance on the heads of pins, do they prefer galliards or pavanes?"

He thought he saw a hint of a smile. "I'm not much of a dazzling conversationalist."

"You've already made a start," he said.

She looked away, indifferent. After several minutes, he sighed. "Lady Antonya, I don't want anything from you. If you need anything, please tell me. If you'd prefer to be left alone, I'll respect that as well. You are safe here, no one will disturb you."

"I'm only another chess piece," she said in a voice almost too low for him to hear. "A pawn shuffled from player to player. Terhune, K'ferrin, it doesn't matter." She flashed him a definitely wry look. "But whose chess pieces are they? God's? Nobody's? And you, B'nach? Are you a rook or a bishop in this little game?"

He chuckled. "I don't think I rate even as high as a baron, actually." It gave him an idea. "Do you play?"

He felt almost victorious as she turned to face him directly. "I was taught to play in Dothinia," she said. "Do you know their court rules?"

"You could teach me," he said.

Her smile widened enough to reveal a sliver of teeth, but this time genuine. For some reason, it made him happy.

34

As he did whenever he was unable to sleep, B'nach went to pray alone in the Great Sajada, on his knees with his forehead pressed to the cool stone. The Oracle glowed ghostly faint, the air lifeless. Sometimes he prayed with feverish desperation, sometimes he simply knelt and let his mind wander. Tonight he hoped for nothing more than a few moments of peace in the quiet solitude. Close to dawn, he jerked out of a muddled fog too troubled to be sleep, suddenly aware of another person kneeling by his side, watching him.

G'walch.

B'nach nearly fell over scuttling away from the boy as if he were a scorpion. Then he froze, sitting on the stone floor with his mouth hanging open. G'walch smiled as B'nach frantically scanned the sajada.

"My uncle is not here," the boy said. He gestured delicately toward the shadowed arch behind them where a squat silhouette stood in the gloom. "Although I am well guarded. Do not be afraid."

B'nach took several more breaths before he could calm his heartbeat. G'walch turned toward the Oracle, his palms against his knees. Closing his eyes, he raised his face toward the faint glow as if he could feel the energy there caressing his skin.

"Would you pray with me, my brother?" he asked softly. *"In principio erat Luminum, et Luminum erat apud Oraculum, et Oraculum erat Luminum . . ."* In the beginning was Light, and the Light was within the Oracle, and the Oracle was the Light . . .

Too stunned to resist, B'nach whispered the chant. . . . *"In Oraculum vita erat, et vita erat lux veritum, et lux in tenebris lucet, et tenebrae eam non comprehenderunt . . ."* In the Oracle was life and the life was the light of truth, and the light shineth in darkness and the darkness did not comprehend . . . He faltered, unable to go on. The boy broke off, studying him curiously. "G'walch . . ." B'nach finally was able to choke out, close to weeping.

"Your grandfather was very clever to have brought the woman to services," G'walch said calmly. B'nach stared determinedly at the patterns in the marble floor. "My uncle confessed what he'd done to my poor cousin." It took an effort, but B'nach forced himself to look up at the boy. "Every detail of it."

"How can you . . . ?" B'nach couldn't finish.

"Bear it?" G'walch asked. When B'nach silently nodded, he smiled. "Easily. I love my uncle, B'nach. But I know exactly what he is and what he's capable of. I don't need to understand him, nor even forgive him. All I need ever do is love him. As I love you."

B'nach stared at the boy, the prepubescent softness in his face framed with baby-fine hair, limbs still dimpled as a child's. But the pale gray eyes watching him were not a child's, nor was his voice either callow or arrogant. The boy leaned forward and kissed B'nach gently on the lips, a delicate touch completely devoid of sexuality.

"If you asked it of me," B'nach whispered, trembling, "you know I would Walk the Fire." For a perverse moment, he hoped the boy would ask him to, anything to release him from this shame.

"I ask nothing of anyone," G'walch said. "I am like the Light which has no will of its own but changes all it touches. The Light does not need life, but there is no life without the Light. The Light gives and asks for nothing, because it is everything."

B'nach looked away, watching the faint glimmer of the Oracle sleeping restlessly in its black Chalice. "The Light asks for nothing except the lives and bodies of Saints," B'nach said bitterly.

The boy said nothing for a long moment. "No, my brother, you are wrong." He rose gracefully, and walked toward the Oracle. B'nach watched in open-mouthed surprise as G'walch passed the empty *pulpitum*.

Sensing life, the Oracle ignited in a sudden burst of light. Reflexively, B'nach threw up one arm to shield his eyes, blinking against the blaze.

"The Light asks for *nothing*." The boy's voice carried clearly despite the high-pitched whine ringing through the Crystal Sajada. B'nach jumped as G'walch's vigilant guard darted past him. He recognized the man with a thrill of fear. D'arim.

But the *qazaq* paid no attention to him, all his awareness locked on the boy. G'walch shrugged off his simple white robe. Naked, he held his hands out from his side and placed one foot on the bottom step of the Chalice. Even at this distance, B'nach could feel the strange cold fire of the Light rasping against his skin, and wondered how the boy could bear to be so close.

B'nach was aware of several others now within the sajada, the alarmed murmurs of people drawn to the sudden noise and light.

"The Light only *is*," G'walch said. "It exists and nothing more. It is we who ask of it, we who want wisdom given to us, not to be transcended into wisdom itself." B'nach could not see the child's face but he could hear the unmistakable triumph in his laughter bordering on madness. "Receive, not *become* . . ."

The Oracle pulsated, straining against the limits of the Chalice. An eerie melody echoed from the glass designs above. In the brilliant Light, B'nach thought he could see ancient figures writhing with an unearthly life of their own, beckoning.

"They did not *love* . . ." As the boy took a second step up to the Chalice, B'nach cried out, reaching his arms toward him futilely. D'arim ran a few steps before he stopped, his fists held quivering down by his side with visible effort.

"G'walch . . ." D'arim called out, his harsh voice pleading. "G'walch, please come back . . ."

The boy turned away sluggishly from the Oracle, looking over his shoulder. The *qazaq* slowly knelt. "For the mercy of God, don't!"

B'nach's skin began to itch, the Light pressing against his face abrasive. His eyes burned as if they might melt like candle wax. B'nach heard the boy's sigh resonating through the Oracle.

"You are right. I am not yet ready," G'walch said sadly. B'nach's limbs went rubbery with relief as the boy stepped down from the Chalice. Behind him, the Light flickered woe-fully. "I cannot be deterred by the pleas of others," he said to D'arim, lethargically. "It is not enough to ignore them, I must not hear them. I must hear nothing . . ." His voice slurred. "Hear only the Light . . ." As he staggered, D'arim rose and caught him easily as the boy collapsed.

The *quazaq* lifted the unconscious boy in his arms, striding swiftly away from the Oracle. He hesitated as he passed B'nach still sitting on the stone floor.

The boy's limbs hung as disjointedly as an abandoned doll's. The whites of his eyes showed in thin slivers. The baby-fine hair had burned away, leaving him completely bald. His skin was flushed, inflamed under a dusting of ashy flakes. He was breathing shallowly; his chest fluttered with quiet con-vulsions.

"I blame you," the *qazaq* snarled. "You've tempted him to try before he is ready, to prove he can transcend the obstacle you've become." B'nach stared up at the stocky man, unable to protest his innocence. "You should be dead."

They both turned, startled, as the robe G'walch had aban-doned at the base of the Chalice burst into flame. It slithered along the floor, lifted up on a current of its own immolation and the wind of the Light. Like a boneless thing, it fluttered helplessly up the step. One limp sleeve stretched toward the Oracle, the very edge touching the outer periphery of the Light.

An explosion burst through the sajada in a brilliant flash of white, the Light shrieking. B'nach cowered on the floor, his hands over his head. He trembled violently as the sound died away, lifting his head to see the blurred form of D'arim still standing, hunched over the boy protectively with his back to the Oracle.

The robe had vanished, the Light glowing contentedly.

D'arim straightened, glancing around the sajada at the wit-nesses gathering at the far edges of the dome. "Don't let me catch you alone here again," he growled softly in the sudden silence.

The *qazaq* carried the boy out of the sajada. Those who had been drawn to the commotion watched B'nach from a distance, none making any effort to help him. He cringed at a soft sound, barely glimpsing the flutter of white before he realized it was a bird.

He gazed up at the unblinking red eye of a dove, its iris a tiny dot of black at its center, staring down at him stupidly. Head bobbing, it shuffled out from the corner of a pillar just below the foot of the stained-glass dome, then turned, white tail feathers spread, brushing droppings from the stone. It cooed faintly and pecked at something at its feet before it turned again, disappearing with a flash of ivory wings into the shadows of the Great Sajada.

Unable to stand, B'nach huddled isolated on the floor and wept quietly.

35

"If it is to be done, it must be done soon."

The urgent voice of the taller man was soft, near a whisper. He and his companion stood in the shadows, the silence in the corridors cold. Thick cowls drawn up over both men's faces hid their features.

"I understand," the second man replied bitterly. "But it is a hard thing for me, you know this."

The first remained silent for a long moment. Then, "Aye. I understand," he said. His voice was gentle. "But what else can you do?"

They scanned the dark, empty corridor, alert and anxious.

"Can your man be trusted?" the tall man asked.

Both knew who the person in question was, no names necessary. The second man considered the question carefully, then sighed. "I don't know. He is still alive, which is curious enough. I can only say I believe so. But if he's been broken . . . a mended pot is never as good as it was when whole."

The tall man snorted in mild derision. "What of the other?"

This time his companion did not hesitate. "No. He is not quite the coward we've thought him, but his honesty makes him a risk. He is too close as it is. He must know nothing."

A solitary monk plodded down the corridor, the slap of sandals announcing his presence before he shuffled tiredly into view. The two men drew farther back into the shadows, motionless until the intruder had passed.

"And the boy?"

The second man shrugged. "God alone knows." The first waited patiently, but it was all the other would say.

The first man sighed, annoyed. "It needn't have come to this. You should have taken *his* place, years ago." Again, names were unnecessary. "You could still. Many would gladly follow you even now."

The second man laughed, a hushed exhalation. "And you know exactly why that would be impossible." He did nothing to hide either his scorn or his accent, obviously not Citadel-born. "Nor would I want his place if I can only have it by treachery and murder. That I am forced to betray him makes me sick enough without adding the sin of false ambition to it. What kind of men would follow me then? None I would want. Nor you."

They stood in silence together, listening to the sajada bells' hollow echoes. Only those luckless monks sentenced to penance would be awake at this hour.

And traitors.

"There will be a terrible price to pay," the first man said finally. He glanced at his companion, dark blue eyes violet in the gloom. "Many of them your friends and brothers."

The second man shrugged, the movement barely visible under the shapeless overgown. "Many are dying now, for no better reason."

"If you succeed with this, it may trigger a war you may not live to regret."

"Aye." The word was sad. "I never dreamed I would live to say how sick of war I've become."

"Then why not simply kill him—?"

"No." The second man cut him off sharply. "There are limits, even for treason."

"Peace, sir." The voice was placating, almost amused. "Whether he lives or dies is no concern of mine, unless you've paid for the pleasure. All will be as you've instructed, once you are outside the city. You must make your own arrangements inside. Agreed?"

"Agreed," the second man said reluctantly.

The pause was longer this time. "Then, do we do it?"

The second man cursed softly under his breath in a language the other didn't understand, although the anger and sorrow were readily apparent. Finally: "Yes."

The first man breathed in relief. "I'll send word out tonight. At midmonth exactly, you must be ready."

"We'll be ready."

The first man walked away silently and vanished into the shadows. The second watched after him for a long time, then headed for the shelter of the Faith's barracks.

36

D'nyel hadn't responded to any of B'nach's tentative efforts at reconciliation, the messages and small gifts he sent ignored. Nor had he really expected her to. She often punished him with rejection, leaving him to wallow in lonely self-pity. When she became bored, she would return. He, of course, would be so thankful that he would make no complaint. And would hate himself for it. Now even the comfort of the sajada was being denied to him.

He spent much of his free time in prison, playing chess with the Lady Antonya. As odd as their situation was, he found it a reprieve from the constant conspiracies of the Citadel, illusory though he knew it to be. But he felt a need to safeguard this tiny peaceful refuge for himself, and a growing desire to protect her. Unfortunately, he knew it would take exactly the same subterfuge his grandfather or D'nyel or Terhune employed to bend their world to their liking. He also knew he had precious little talent for deceit.

"A shame to let such an opportunity go to waste," he nonetheless murmured to his grandfather a few days later. "She could be a valuable resource, of course."

"Who?" The old man, preoccupied, shuffled through the papers covering every surface of his huge desk.

"The Lady Antonya."

"Mmm."

B'nach knew K'ferrin wasn't listening. The old man pursed

his lips as he ran a finger down long columns of script in a leather-bound book, cross-checking one page against another which he held in his other hand. K'ferrin might outwardly despise the worldly wealth of the Lands, but he was relentless in managing his share of it.

B'nach should have let it drop. K'ferrin's lack of interest was as final a comment as any he could make. As his grandfather discarded another paper onto a growing pile, B'nach picked up the rejected pages, meticulously lining the edges up. He cleared his throat.

"What do you intend to do about her?"

"About who?" K'ferrin scowled over the rims of his spectacles.

"Lady Antonya." B'nach swallowed. "Terhune's niece."

K'ferrin's annoyance gave way to a crafty amusement. "Are your passions changing, my kinsman?" he taunted. B'nach started, and felt his face redden. "Don't tell me you plan to throw over the dusky maiden for the torrid embrace of an ersatz Terhune?"

"I have no carnal attraction to the lady," B'nach said stiffly. "My interest in her is purely one of intellectual curiosity." His skin grew hotter as K'ferrin snickered. "In any case, the question is still reasonable. She is a valuable source of information about the Lands and the people. Certainly it would be wasteful for her to remain idle . . ."

K'ferrin raised his hand. "Stop, stop," he said cheerfully. "Your unexpected assertiveness has overpowered me." He closed the book and locked it. "Do what you wish with the 'Lady Antonya,' so long as she remains safe and secure. She is nothing to me but a bit of insurance against Terhune."

"I wish to take her into the library," B'nach said, trying to keep his voice steady.

K'ferrin shrugged. "Take her wherever you like, as long as you stay within my authority. Take her on the tables in the library, let the sweaty lust of your intellectual curiosity smear the ink of the ancient tomes. Take her on the rooftop in broad daylight, if you choose." The old man grinned, teeth spaced between receding gray gums. "Of course, I'll know each moan she makes wherever you 'take' her, as I have always enjoyed the reports of every piggy grunt and fart you've ever made with that whore D'nyel."

B'nach fought to keep his anger from showing, bowing with as much dignity as he could in the wake of K'ferrin's spiteful laughter.

That evening, the Lady was ushered into his small office in the library. Agnes held one arm possessively while Rudel kept a close eye on her escort. B'nach had noted the armsman in charge of his grandfather's bodyguard had arranged to attend more than a routine number of the Lady's Guard, in order to spend time with the Lady's guardian. As, no doubt, K'ferrin well knew and encouraged the chatter between the guardian and her ardent suitor.

B'nach stood as Antonya was led into his office, suddenly shy. Her guardian followed and raised an eyebrow when he politely, but firmly, dismissed her. Agnes silently regarded him with a contemptuous smile, but B'nach held his ground, trying to keep his expression haughty, until the woman bowed and left. She would complain to her balding lover, Rudel, who no doubt would report back to K'ferrin. But for now the two of them would have to be content with leaning their ears against the door. Secretly, B'nach breathed a sigh of relief.

"My Lady," he said, showing her to cushions laid out on the floor before the low table in one corner of his office, which he had actually cleared himself, books and papers stacked in untidy piles. He was pleased to see her eyeing the overflowing shelves and piles of books with interest. "I'm grateful that you accepted my invitation."

She laughed, a low, soft sound. "The Citadel appears to be renowned for its gracious invitations enforced by armed escort."

Flustered, he rang for Vamal.

The library's chief clerk habitually worked alone at night, his own tiny desk tucked into a discreet alcove of the library. His grandfather's underling was nearly as old as K'ferrin, but B'nach knew Vamal's love of books transcended any sense of loyalty he might have had toward the Keeper. The slender clerk stepped inside B'nach's office, bowing with perfunctory courtesy.

"The Lady Antonya," B'nach introduced her. The scribe

turned dark eyes toward her. "My assistant, Vamal."

The clerk's eyebrows rose at this somewhat imprecise description. B'nach had no assistants, despite being the Chief Librarian.

"A pleasure, sir," she said graciously.

"Mine," Vamal replied in his rusty voice. "I've heard you have a fondness for books and are well educated."

"For a woman?" she asked cynically.

"For anyone."

"I had very good teachers."

She glanced from B'nach to the clerk and back again, curiously. "I am the Chief Librarian as well as personal scribe to His Reverence," B'nach said. "It is no false vanity to tell you no one knows the archives of the Citadel better than I. I can offer you access to the largest and finest library in the world."

Unimpressed, she asked, "At what price?"

Caught off guard, Vamal couldn't quite muffle his snicker. But as B'nach glared at him, Antonya returned the clerk's smile, hers chilling. "I'll even save you time. Terhune knows my weakness. Tell me what you want, then torture and kill your clerk if I do not oblige you."

The clerk's humor vanished, his jaw dropping in astonishment.

"Oh, don't worry," Antonya assured him. "I'll do it. Not because I'm such a noble person, but I know I couldn't sleep with the guilt at night if I didn't."

B'nach made a sharp gesture and Vamal bowed politely and retreated. "That was uncalled for. Surely I've given you no reason to suspect me of that sort of conduct."

"Neither did Terhune. At first."

"I am hardly his equal." He tried to smile and failed. "Even my servants have more authority than I; torture and murder aren't one of my prerogatives. But I don't believe that that is truly your price. It will buy you, for a day, a week, maybe more. But there would come a time when you became insensitive to the pain caused in your name, and then it's no longer effective."

"You speak from personal experience?" she asked mockingly.

"Unfortunately, yes." B'nach stood, offering her his hand. After a moment, she allowed him to raise her to her feet. "But before you refuse my offer, madam, allow me to show you its value."

The old clerk had regained his composure, standing up from his post by the door as they entered the library to follow at a respectful distance. Not that Antonya took the slightest notice of either of them. Her attention was riveted on the books, shelves packed with books, stacks upon stacks of rolled parchments and bound folios, tiny coverless volumes to huge leather-bound tomes so heavy two men were needed to lift them. B'nach walked behind her, watching her trail her fingers along their spines, enjoying the look of wonder in her eyes.

"How many . . . ?" she breathed.

"Thousands," B'nach said.

"Hundreds of thousands," Vamal corrected from behind him, but showed no penitence when B'nach glared at him. He shrugged and went back to his alcove at B'nach's curt signal.

"Some are over nine centuries old, collected from all over the world," B'nach continued, following her around the corner of a stack. She disappeared, and after a moment's flutter of alarm, he backed up to find her down another long aisle, still entranced. Then she stopped, her eyes hardening as she turned to him.

"*Stolen* from all over the world," she said.

B'nach shrugged. "Some may have been, surely. Others were written by Priests within the Citadel, some brought in with converts from other Lands. Some were donations from Lords. However they came to be here, there is no finer or complete library in existence."

"I'm tempted, B'nach. Let's get down to the bargaining now."

He gestured at the books. "This is my world, Lady. I have never been outside the Citadel, the Lands exist for me only as words on paper. You, on the other hand, have traveled to many places I can only dream of. In what spare time I have, I write." He couldn't help the self-effacing blush creeping back into his cheeks. "I'd like to fancy myself an historian. I want to record your journeys, the places you've seen, what different peoples and their customs are like. In return, I offer you what little power I hold in the Citadel, access to the library." He smiled. "Not so sinister a proposal, is it?

She watched him closely. "And what does our Lord Keeper want?"

"From you? Nothing but your continued value as his prisoner."

"And when I am no longer of value as a pawn in his game?"

B'nach tried to reassure her. "Perhaps then he'll free you," he said with an effort to keep a straight face.

Antonya laughed outright. "You're a poor liar, Librarian. Did you know that? It's why I always beat you at chess."

He shrugged ruefully. "I had very bad teachers." He examined the ragged edge of his thumbnail to avoid her eyes. "In any case, probably nothing will happen. My grandfather collects prisoners the way some people collect wine, the rarer and more risky, the better." He thought of the man Briston, kept alive for no reason he could see. But B'nach also knew the old man would not hesitate to decant the blood of any prisoner, should the necessity arise.

"How long have you been a prisoner, B'nach?"

He laughed hollowly. "I was born a prisoner. Everyone in the Citadel was born a prisoner. After a while, you get used to it."

"No," she said softly. "I don't think so."

"No, perhaps not."

"But K'ferrin is your grandfather, your blood kin," Antonya said quietly. "Surely that must mean something . . ."

"Blood means nothing," he said bitterly. "My grandfather holds about as much warm familial affection for me as your uncle P'tre has for you." He noted she didn't flinch. "Like you, I survive only because I'm a useful pawn in someone else's game."

He watched her as she ran her fingertips thoughtfully along one shelf of books. "And like you, I welcome escape in whatever guise it takes." She turned and smiled. "I would accept your offer, B'nach, gratefully."

Although her expression was innocent, her tone made him uneasy.

37

The days passed more quickly now as Antonya felt her spirit reawaken. She explored the library's resources, probing for anything to support her remote hope of eventually regaining her freedom. The wealth of knowledge was staggering. And although either Vamal or B'nach accompanied her at every step, they appeared unconcerned with her search, more worried, she suspected, about her inadvertently tearing the parchment or dripping candle wax on the precious tomes than anything she might have discovered from their contents.

They knew she hadn't a prayer of escape—what did it matter if she discovered every secret of the Citadel now? Nor did B'nach seem to mind the large holes in her narrative of her adventures through the Lands, names of friends omitted, key strategies skipped over. He seemed fascinated with her childhood with the Brothers of Blessed Reason, and while she indulged his curiosity, she found herself reluctant to tell him much more than the bare facts, not willing to even mention Father Andrae.

The nights were growing colder, trees relinquishing their leaves to the cold sea winds. She had healed, physically, although her arm ached with the coming winter. Agnes had tucked her into bed with motherly attention before she left for the night, locking the door securely behind her. Antonya lay curled like a cat under a thick goosedown coverlet when a sudden scuffle woke her from her light sleep. She turned over, heart pounding, as she heard the distinct sound of a grunt and a body thudding against the door.

The heavy door scraped open, and she saw the outline of two men dragging the limp body of a third into the dark room. They shut the door and dropped the body onto the floor. One man quickly lashed the fallen guard's hands behind his back and hogtied them to his feet before jamming a gag into his mouth. The second slipped the fallen man's knife out of his scabbard. She recognized Rudel as he moaned softly through the gag.

The two intruders crept toward her through the shadows. One, carrying a bundle, wore the distinctive robes of Terhune's Elite guard. The other was in K'ferrin's armored uniform. She looked around wildly, then slipped naked out of the bed searching for cover.

"Lady Antonya?" the man in K'ferrin's gear whispered, and stepped into the moonlight enough for her to see his face.

It was Briston, the man who had helped spirit her out of Terhune's prison and into K'ferrin's. The second man seemed familiar, but she couldn't place him. She watched him from her hiding place behind a chest as he flipped aside the empty bedclothes and cursed softly. He turned, still holding the bundle in his arms.

"Lady, we're not here to hurt you," Briston urged. "Please, we haven't much time. We've come to get you out of the city."

She stepped cautiously out from behind the chest, crouching naked in the moonlight. All three froze. Then Briston smiled, and deftly flipped Rudel's knife to hold it by the blade, the hilt toward her. "Is this enough to prove us?" he whispered.

Keeping her eyes on him, she crept forward slowly and snatched the knife from his hand. Briston gestured abruptly to his companion, and the man stepped back. Deliberately, Briston withdrew his own long dagger from his belt, blade hissing. He set it on the floor, watching her as he stood with his hands away from his body.

The tip of her knife darted up as he took one step toward her over his own dagger. "Either kill me now or trust me. We haven't time for any other argument."

She straightened, lowering the knife. "I assume I have enough time at least to dress?" she asked quietly. She made no attempt to cover her nakedness, and he made no pretense of polite manners.

"We've brought what you need." The second man tossed her the bundle. It was a robe, its red color black in the moonlight, edged with the moon-silvered glint of gold thread. She looked at it speculatively before she handed it back to him.

"I'll want to go to the library first," she said, keeping her voice low as she glanced at the bound guard.

The two men exchanged worried glances. "Madam, we haven't . . ."

"There are papers there I need. I'm not leaving without them," she said firmly as she hurriedly pulled on her own overgown, not bothering with an underrobe, and cinched the belt around her waist. She thrust the knife into the pocket. "You're wasting time, gentlemen."

"This is madness . . ." the second man murmured angrily. Beneath their epicanthic fold his eyes were tense in the flat planes of his face. Then, with a jolt, she realized where she had seen him before, standing next to P'tre Terhune and the boy G'walch in the Great Sajada.

Briston regarded her with a measured look. "If you need them, you shall have them," he said finally.

"Damnation take you, Briston," the other man hissed between his teeth. "There's no *time* . . ."

"D'arim, it won't take long," Briston said. "We'll meet you in half an hour, yes?" he pressed Antonya, his eyes flashing.

"Yes."

D'arim exhaled, furious. "Half an hour," he repeated. "No more." He hesitated, then gripped Briston's hand fiercely before he slipped to the door, glanced out and vanished.

Rudel lay curled up on the floor, blood trickling from his head, but his eyes were open, watching as they stepped over him. He would live, and Antonya was somehow oddly grateful, if only for Agnes's sake. Briston turned his hood up over his head, then took Antonya by the arm as they stepped into the corridor. At this time of night there were few walking the halls of the Sector, and those would see only one of K'ferrin's guards escorting the Reverence's prisoner.

B'nach was still working in the library, as she expected he would be. Keeping his face concealed, Briston thrust her into the room and turned to stand guard outside. B'nach looked up in mild surprise.

"Antonya?" he asked questioningly.

"I couldn't sleep," she said, trying to appear calm and weary, although her nerves sang with tension. "I thought I'd read a bit, if you don't mind." While she was only allowed into the library after the final bell, when it was empty of scholars, she had never come this late before.

He glanced down regretfully at his manuscript. "I'm very busy, and Vamal isn't here," he said, then paused thoughtfully while she held her breath. She had yet to be permitted into the inner rooms unescorted, and prayed he trusted her enough now to lift the stricture.

"My apologies for disturbing you, perhaps tomorrow . . ."

"No, no," he assured her, as she knew he would. He stood, lighting another lantern for her. "If you need any help, call out." He smiled, and for a moment, she felt regret for deceiving him, mingled with relief. She nodded her thanks and passed by him into the large Library Hall, eerily quiet in the deserted emptiness.

The moonlight was strong enough to make out the titles even without the lantern, although she already knew exactly which books she wanted and where they were. She set the lantern on the long scholar's table and half-raced to the manuscripts, quickly opening the large volumes to the charts she wanted. Slipping the dagger out of her pocket, she cut the vellum pages from the bindings of one volume and rolled them quickly before stuffing them up her overgown, under the belt. Cursing softly to herself, she darted to another volume, and a third, opening and slicing pages out of the precious archives.

She had a fourth volume open on the scholar's table, golden light winking on the pages she flipped through desperately, when B'nach called out, "Finding everything?" She looked up in alarm at his figure silhouetted in the doorway, forcing herself to smile casually.

"Yes, thank you," she said, heart hammering. A trickle of sweat ran down her ribs.

"Right, then." She couldn't make out his shadowed face. After a pause that seemed to stretch out centuries, he turned and disappeared, going back to his writing desk. As she heard the faint scritch of his quill, she rested her forehead on the open book for a moment in relief, then carefully slit two more pages from its spine.

She had no more time. Forcing her dry throat to swallow, she wiped the sweat from her face. She affected an audible yawn as she walked out of the library into the little antechamber, and rubbed at her eyes sleepily.

"I suppose I was really more tired than I thought," she said, placing the lantern on his desk. "My concentration isn't good as it is, and it's too hard to keep my eyes focused in this light. Thank you, anyway."

He opened the small glass and blew out the candle before he looked up at her with an odd, puzzled expression. "My pleasure."

She had to force herself to turn her back to him and walk slowly, nonchalantly, out the door. The cowled man in K'ferrin's uniform took her by one arm as it closed, cutting her off from B'nach's sight.

"A few very dead Priests are going to be found within the hour, madam," Briston whispered as they hurried along the corridor. She clamped her arms tightly around her waist to keep the rolled parchment from falling out of her robe. "If you have no more pressing delays?"

"None," she said, breathlessly.

They said nothing further, taking a sudden turn away from her own cell and down a flight of steps into the desolate gallery, their footsteps echoing too loudly in the quiet. D'arim stepped out from behind one massive pillar, eyes darting anxiously as he silently handed Briston and Antonya crimson robes. She pulled hers on over her gown. D'arim eyed her angrily as he spoke to Briston.

"We've got less than ten minutes before the Guard changes. After that, I suggest we all save P'tre the trouble and graciously slit our own throats. Can we please go now?"

Briston chuckled harshly. "Aye."

She knew that they were close to Terhune's Sector of the Citadel by all the twists and turns, passageways connected between the spokes leading to the Great Sajada like snarled threads of a spider's web. Her heart leapt when they turned a corner onto a wide, deserted corridor she recognized as the one K'ferrin had conducted her to, leading directly into the Crystal Sajada. At the far end, the great doors were closed and sealed, K'ferrin's burgundy-robed Guards of the Oracle standing hostile watch, the black-armored Elite watching them. The Elite recognized D'arim, stiffening into a salute.

Then they were past, turning away from the sajada and slowing to a stroll as five Priests wearing Terhune's red crossed the corridor fifty yards in front of them. A couple nodded in their direction, and D'arim returned the gesture gravely before the group passed the pillared aisle and vanished.

D'arim and Briston both grabbed her by the arms as they turned into yet another passageway, hurrying her along columned corridors. She heard D'arim curse and caught the movement from the corner of her eye a split second after the two men had already reacted.

"Briston, no!" she cried out, her voice echoing in the silence.

Briston had B'nach shoved against the wall, his arm across the librarian's neck and the point of his dagger pressed into the curve of the frightened man's jaw. The second man had already fallen; D'arim bent over him as Vamal whimpered, eyes rolling in his head. His hands groped at the spreading blotch of blood on his belly, staining the fabric of his burgundy robe deep violet.

"B'nach . . ." She was suddenly terrified that they would have to kill the librarian to prevent him from betraying them. As Briston glanced at her, his teeth bared, she realized he waited for her word. "Don't kill him," she said, trying not to make it sound like pleading.

His breath nearly cut off by Briston's arm, B'nach eyed the man curled up on the floor, and slowly reached into his own robes.

"Careful, little man," Briston warned.

B'nach slipped a small book from the folds of his robe, holding it out toward Antonya. She took it out of his shaking hand.

"Let him go," she said quietly, and ignored the look Briston traded with D'arim. Briston stepped back from the scribe, his hands clenching into fists in spasmodic tension. "Why, B'nach?"

The scribe held his hand to his throat, swallowing and said hoarsely, "It's my own work, a history of the Saints. You may find this of use as well what you've stolen from the library."

"We should kill him now," D'arim muttered angrily to Briston.

B'nach glanced at the men anxiously, licking dry lips. "For God's sake, don't tell me where you're taking her. I don't want to know," he said rapidly. She stared at him uncomprehendingly. "Not preventing you from escaping may be treason, but I know what will happen if I stop you."

D'arim grabbed her roughly. "We stay or go, kill him or not, but we do it *now*, Lady!" he said urgently, his face so close to hers she felt the warmth of his breath.

"We go," she said quickly, and as quickly squeezed B'nach's hand firmly. "How could anyone think you a coward?"

She had time only once to look back, seeing B'nach bending over the wounded man on the floor, too intent on trying to help his companion to watch her go.

Minutes later, Briston yanked her around, drawing her cowl more firmly around her face and pressing his hand on her head to lower it as they approached the massive siege gate. Four of Terhune's Elite defended the doors. Antonya grasped how deep they had to be into Terhune's own Sector as D'arim swaggered up to the guards, one thumb hooked into his belt, the other on the hilt of his knife. His entire attitude radiated pure arrogance.

The guards saluted D'arim sharply and opened the gates without challenge, the immense doors slowly grinding back far enough to let the three of them through. Only after the gates had been closed behind them did she stare at D'arim curiously. His mouth quirked up in a bitter smile as he spared her a quick, ironic glance.

As they stepped out into the night air, the darkness pressed down on them with almost physical force, stars scattershot across the black of heaven. Antonya breathed in sharply, feeling the cold air burn her lungs, the first time she had been outside the walls of the Citadel since P'tre Terhune had taken her captive.

Outside, soldiers in Terhune's military armor and their horses were milling about in organized confusion. No one challenged them as they marched across the courtyard, the stones shining wetly in the damp night air.

Antonya caught a glimpse of the Crystal Sajada glistening above the towering gray stone around them before they passed under an archway wide enough to allow ten armed men on horseback to ride through it side by side. Torches set in iron brackets against the walls threw off flickering light and shadows.

For a moment, she knew something was not right, then realized: For all the men in the courtyard, all the echoes of boots tramping as they came and went, the clopping of shod horses on cobblestone, it was oddly quiet, no murmur of affable greetings between Priests, no muted laughter. The silence hung in the air like a malignant shroud.

They reached the large stables, the captain's office no more than one of the stalls fitted with a rough desk and a brazier behind him for warmth. D'arim strode confidently to the Captain of the Horse and handed him a rolled parchment.

The balding captain regarded the man wearing Terhune's red with a petty bureaucrat's inborn air of disdain underneath the thin mask of respect. He wore no Priest's robes, only a sleeveless quilted jaquette against the night chill, the striped cloth of the padded armholes having seen better days. His shirtsleeves were rolled back, the hair on his tanned arms as gray as his short beard.

He frowned with exaggerated annoyance, carving even deeper furrows in his worn face as he unrolled the parchment, his lips moving slightly as he read the neat lines of calligraphy.

"Sir, I regret I can't accept this," the captain said, obviously taking a good deal of pleasure in his ability to frustrate his superiors, "as it doesn't have the High Lord Commander's seal." He glowered as he thrust the rolled parchment back toward D'arim. His expression changed to one of surprise as D'arim indifferently slid the point of his dagger through the man's eye. Bones crunched as he jabbed the blade sharply into the skull, killing the captain instantly. Antonya gasped, then clamped her mouth shut. Her eyes darted around her, but no one seemed to have noticed. As yet.

While Briston kept watch, D'arim walked behind the corpse and pushed it off the stool. He wiped the blade on the man's jaquette before rolling the body under the desk and rummaging through the documents littering its top. Using the same dagger with which he'd just murdered the captain, he cut loose the wax seal on one of the papers he plucked off the desk. He passed the blade of the knife through the flames of the brazier a few times and pressed it briefly against the back of the hardened seal and peeled away the paper loosened from the wax. Antonya smelled seared wax as he fused the back of the seal onto the parchment he'd presented to the captain.

"Now it does," D'arim muttered, and rolled it up.

They left the captain's office, the empty stall deceptively peaceful, as if the man had stepped out for a moment to relieve himself behind the stables. Marching at a brisk pace, but not so fast as to bring attention to themselves, they reached an officer leading two horses out of the stalls, already saddled and ready to ride. At the far end of the stables, two Priests conferred in muted voices. As they saw the saddled horses, they started toward the trio.

"What is this?" D'arim snapped in annoyance. He handed the officer the rolled document with Terhune's seal plainly visible. "Where are *my* horses? It says here quite clearly *three* mounts. Where is the third?"

The horses, lean, fast couriers, tossed their heads nervously at D'arim's angry tone. The officer recognized him, paling instantly as he apologized and clutched the document in one hand unread. "Sir, I didn't know it was you. I was told only two." He glanced bewildered toward the two Priests who had stopped a short distance away.

"I don't care what you were *told*, the orders are for *three*, I want *three* and I want them *now*," D'arim roared in fury. "I haven't time for this incompetence. We'll take these two miserable flea-bitten nags. Saddle the roan from my personal stable. *Get moving!*"

"Yes, sir!" The officer scrambled away to saddle a third horse as Briston boosted Antonya onto one of the horses already fitted. It snorted, stamping hind legs with impatience. The two Priests had recognized D'arim and backed away deferentially. Whatever the problem was, they wanted no part of it. The officer was leading out the third horse as Briston swung up onto his own.

"I'll not tolerate this sort of laggardly negligence again," D'arim growled. "Perhaps you might see the main gates are opened for us without further delay?" He jammed his foot into one stirrup, grabbed the pommel of the saddlebow and heaved himself up onto the horse.

"Certainly, sir!" The officer trotted in front of them as they clattered toward the main gates.

"Keep your head down, madam," D'arim cautioned softly as he came alongside her, then nudged his horse to the front. The officer shouted out orders to open the gates, waving the counterfeit orders at the guards. After a moment's wavering, the orders were passed on and the huge chains began to rattle. Formidable pulleys and tackle rumbled as the Great Gates opened on the vista of a broad boulevard stretching away from the heart of the Oracular City.

Not sure whether her heart pounded more from excitement or terror, Antonya clung to the saddlebow as the nervous horses bolted thorugh the gateway, clattering over the access bridge and out into the night.

Briston pulled up beside her as they followed D'arim at a brisk pace, iron-shod hooves striking occasional sparks against cobblestone. "I would guess we have about five minutes before someone finds our late captain," he said over the sound of hooves. "We have to be out the City Gate by then, and ride for Hell."

Speechless, she nodded, fighting to hang on to the high-spirited horse cantering under her. The streets of the city were eerily empty, as if all the inhabitants were awake and watching safely behind their barred windows. Low tombs lined both sides of the broad Boulevard of Saints, empty memorials for the victims of the Oracle's voracious hunger. Shrouded with withered garlands, the smell of decaying flowers perfumed the night air.

The huge City Gate loomed in the mists in front of them, scarred by time and weather, broodingly pale. D'arim rode with his cowl thrown back on his shoulders, head high and recognizable. They had less trouble than Antonya expected, the soldier at the postern shouting orders and the gate thrown open before they reached it.

They clattered down the cobbled promenade across the glacis and cantered across the long Pilgrim's Bridge, hooves booming against the wooden planking. The tide was still rising, tiny fish popping the surface of the black waters under the bridge. Once past the last of the defense rings around the city, D'arim kicked his horse into a flat-out run. Briston and Antonya crouched low in their saddles, following the chalky rump of his horse.

They turned out onto the southern road that stretched across the edge of the marshy plains, the Oracular City towering behind them like a vast mountain of rock against the sky, the shimmer of the ocean gleaming phosphorescent lines in distant breakers, when the bells of the Crystal Sajada began to ring out the alarm.

"*HayyYAHHhhaahh!*" D'arim bellowed in glee and exhilaration into his horse's ears, his heels drumming into the animal's sides. The roan pulled his ears back against his head, neck stretched out as he raced through the darkness, legs thundering against the clayish ground under iron-shod hooves. As D'arim's animal began to pull away from them, Briston laughed, whooping and pounding at his own mount, the two men bellowing against the wind.

Antonya could not relish the thrill of the chase as the two Priests obviously did, but there was no less determination as she whipped the reins across the horse's neck, urging him on faster. She didn't dare look back. The whip of cold wind and mane teared her eyes as they streaked across the marshlands.

Faster. Please run faster.

38

D'nyel paced the small tower room restlessly, gnawing her bottom lip. Terhune should have sent for her by now. The captive strapped to her table had struggled violently, wrenching against the leather until his wrists and ankles bled. Now he lay inert, watching her with terrified eyes.

She sat down on the stool, arranging her clothing around her with graceful indifference, then cupped her chin in one hand, gazing at the man without really seeing him. He began to weep helplessly. "Please . . ." Severed vocal cords had turned his voice to a hoarse whisper. "Please don't do this . . ."

"Hush," she said distractedly. "Don't bother me now."

A forceful knock on the door in her outer room made her jump, stifling a small scream. "Healer?" a man's voice called out. "You are summoned by my Lord Commander Terhune."

"I'll be with you in a moment," she replied, trying to keep her voice casual. She opened her medicinal chest to grab a small bottle. Her captive tried to resist as she poured the liquid into his mouth, deftly stroking his throat to force it down. His eyes rolled with wild terror. "Relax," she said quietly. "It's only a sedative, not poison. You've done enough damage to yourself already."

The polite knock rapidly became an insistent pounding. After a few tense moments, the man's eyes fluttered and closed. D'nyel locked the door to her inner rooms behind her, pulling the tapestry over it. Crossing to the door, she fumbled with the latch before she could open it, one of Terhune's black Elite pacing the hall impatiently.

"About time, Healer," he growled.

"I was with a patient," she said calmly. "May I help you?"

"My Lord Commander Terhune requests your presence. Now."

She had to trot quickly to keep up as they crossed the wide gallery and turned off into the heart of Terhune's Sector. Although she had made this visit often enough, she still found Terhune's Sector of the Citadel nerve-racking. Her own offices lay well within the maze of galleries of the Profane Sciences Sector. The head of her Medical Arts Order was an unassuming old man who had garnered enough blackmail during his years as a Lord Healer to be left alone and content, uninterested in politics outside his own circle. Students mingled with deference toward their teachers tempered with fraternal loyalty to the Profane Sciences. A constant hum of conversation filled the galleries, Healers and Alchemists and Astrologers clustered along the narrow stone benches in the open plazas around the gardens.

Even the atmosphere in K'ferrin's Sector, the rarefied discussions of philosophical and theological Sacred Arts, the heated debates on the Book of Prophecy, were far more congenial than P'tre Terhune's own corner of the Citadel.

On the face of it, the wide corridors leading away from the Oracle into the Citadel's Military Sector were as light and spacious, the gardens along the porticos as pleasant and colorful. But a brooding darkness settled within P'tre's dominion, a malevolent silence nearly palpable in the cold marble corridors.

The guard stopped outside Terhune's quarters, and D'nyel smiled sweetly at the two Elite standing watch. Although neither of them smiled back, their eyes softened. She knew her slender charm and beautiful face made it more difficult to believe her capable of harm, and she did all she could to encourage that fallacy. Their own stupid chauvinism did half the work for her.

P'tre didn't keep her waiting long. She was shocked at his haggardness but kept it to herself, aware of the heightened alarm in his servants. He waved her brusquely into his inner chamber, where an Elite officer knelt stiffly in the middle of the floor, hands on his thighs, his Order's knife laid ceremonially in front of him. The armsman stared at it fixedly as Terhune paced the room, seemingly unaware of his existence. A livid bruise had swollen shut the armsman's right eye.

"Antonya has escaped," P'tre Terhune said without preamble.

"I know," she said softly. The entire Citadel knew.

"Treason in my own Elite!" he spit out bitterly, his eyes bloodshot, ringed with red in a pale, unshaven face.

She glanced around quickly. The kneeling officer remained as still as stone, unblinking, while those servants luckless enough to be trapped inside Terhune's quarters cowered as far away as they could manage. She was sure there would be blood for them to clean up before the day was out, their own or his guard's, she wasn't sure.

"Several of my men including my Captain of the Horse were murdered, documents falsified—they stole three horses, got on them and simply rode away and *nobody stopped them*!" He swung around to scream the last at the Elite guard still kneeling on the floor, spittle flying from his mouth. The man didn't even blink.

She watched P'tre with fascination, suddenly terrified he was about to hand over this hapless guard openly to her. The servants would be mopping up plenty of her own blood if Terhune were not more careful.

Terhune stood with clenched fists, trembling as he fought to get himself back under control. "Nobody stopped them," he repeated, more softly. He turned, his eyes feverishly bright, and took several steps away from the kneeling guard as if knowing that if he got too close he'd kill the man himself. "I have very polite soldiers, don't you think?" he hissed at her.

Keeping silent, she studied Terhune cautiously as he stalked the room. "It was D'arim. That oath-breaking bastard D'arim who betrayed me." She struggled to keep the dismay off her own face. That she hadn't known. If D'arim had finally mutinied against him, then who knew how deep the rot ran in Terhune's own Guard?

He suddenly stopped, his head thrown back, tendons standing out in stark relief as he fought to keep in the strangled cry: *"D'arim!"* He punched himself hard in the chest with one fist, and again, tears leaking from his eyes, squeezed shut as he grunted under the self-inflicted blows. Again. She winced at each blow.

After several more, his hand dropped and he stood still, shuddering breaths racking him. He opened his eyes and stared at her, calmer. "Half of those who allowed them to escape committed suicide rather than face me," he said, his voice almost subdued.

Involuntarily, her eyes darted toward the kneeling man. Terhune chuckled, a dry, harsh sound. "No, the lieutenant wasn't even there. He's only the messenger boy."

He strode to the large chair by the window and threw himself into it. Staring moodily out over the gray, cold skies, he rested his chin on one fist while his other hand methodically squeezed the carved knob of the arm.

"All of my men are traitors," he said quietly. "*All* of them."

She stole one more glance at the white-faced guard before she approached Terhune cautiously, as if she were walking naked into the lair of an enraged tiger. "P'tre, you know that can't be true," she said, keeping her voice level and reasonable. He looked up at her, all the madness and fury gone from his face.

Suddenly she understood the role she was there to play: Terhune would rage, threatening to Purge his Guard. Without D'arim as his buffer, she was needed to talk him out of it. The Guard had already suffered severe bloodletting and he couldn't afford to execute many more, but a betrayal this critical could not be allowed to go unpunished.

She placed her hand lightly on his arm, stroking it as gently as if they were lovers alone together. "Not all your Guard could possibly be traitors. They serve the Faith, P'tre, just as you do, as we *all* do," she said appeasingly. She was sweating with both fear and excitement as she leaned over toward him, an overtly sexual posture assumed solely for the benefit of an audience. He watched her shrewdly as she gestured to the kneeling guard, "He wasn't even there, you said so yourself, and yet he knew his duty. He came to you with the news, knowing your wrath. Surely *he* can't be a traitor."

Terhune turned to stare at the man. "No," he said, seemingly reluctant. "You . . ."

"Sir," the man barely breathed.

"Get out."

The guard smoothly retrieved his knife, stood and bowed before striding quickly for the door, unable to keep the look of relief off his bruised face. D'nyel didn't doubt that if she ran into him again, the armsman would thank her lavishly for "saving" his life. She might even offer her services as Healer, the distended bruise to his eye a possible risk to his sight. Gratitude could be a useful tool as well. Even under the circumstances, her mind turned over the possibilities and how best she might exploit them.

"Yes," Terhune growled. "Everybody out. *Get out!*" He stood up from the chair, screaming. Instantly, his servants scurried for the door, colliding with one another in their near hysteria. It might have been comical if D'nyel hadn't been so badly frightened herself.

Then she was alone with Terhune. When the door clicked shut behind the last of them, she knew no one would be daring enough to press an ear to the door. "Now that you've managed to scare them all away, what is it you really want from me, P'tre?" she said boldly.

His fury vanished. In its place was an ice-cold expression that unnerved her even more than the display of temper had.

"You and B'nach have had another falling out, the rumor is."

"The rumor is correct."

"Then you will have to arrange a falling back in, and soon."

She slid the tip of her tongue over her lips nervously. "P'tre, I manipulate B'nach and, through him K'ferrin, very carefully. If I 'arrange' this reconciliation too soon, it not only diminishes the amount of control I have, but will look remarkably suspect . . ."

Terhune swung on her, eyes hard. "I don't care, D'nyel. B'nach and Antonya spent a lot time together, especially since he had little else to do while pining for your luscious charms. He might even have been involved in her escape. If anyone would know where Antonya would go and who her allies are within the Citadel, that fat dunce would." His fingers bit painfully into her arm as he marched her toward the door. "Worm it out of him. Fast."

"P'tre . . ."

He ignored her protest. "Antonya could not have escaped so easily without substantial help. B'nach is an idiot, he could do nothing without K'ferrin. It must be K'ferrin behind this plot. The old bastard knows he can't get rid of me as easily as he did my father, so he's using her out of petty spite to discredit me, keep me confined, turn the face of the Faith against me."

He pulled D'nyel along relentlessly, his voice eerily calm, breathless, his mad eyes focused on a distant vision. "But K'ferrin is afraid. He can't risk allowing G'walch to Walk the Fire because he knows he's the One. He knows his Family will sink into the muck when mine ascends to its rightful glory. So he must attack me like a jackal in the dark, laughing at me behind my back, turning the Orders against me. But he's over-stepped himself this time."

He lowered his intense gaze on her. "I need to bring a charge of heresy against him. Convince those senile fools on the Council that the woman is a danger to the Faith, that he knew her to be, yet conspired in her escape. Remove him, and I can turn the tide back before it's too late. But I need proof. You can do this . . ."

"But P'tre," she protested, alarmed. "What if there isn't anything, if he didn't . . . ?"

He jerked her around, his hands wrenching her close to his face with bruising strength. His breath was warm and sour. She knew at that moment how close he was to killing her.

"He did. I know he did. Now *do it*, D'nyel. I don't care how, I don't care what it takes, just get it done."

He had her thrust out of the room and the door closed before she could utter another word.

39

D'arim's aim had been too true. Vamal was only a clerk, not even Citadel-bred, but he'd been one of the few of his grand-father's menials B'nach had ever liked. He knelt on the floor, cradling the man's head in his lap. He didn't bother to call for help, as they both knew he was doomed.

"I had to follow you, but I would never have said anything," the clerk whispered hoarsely. "I swear it." It seemed important to him.

"I know," B'nach assured him. It was easy to say, such a simple lie. Had Vamal lived, K'ferrin had the means to force the old man to say anything he wished him to. The truth didn't matter now. "I know you wouldn't have." He smiled at the grateful relief in Vamal's eyes, amazed at how much difference such a small lie could make.

The blood had flowed into a bright pool between Vamal's splayed legs. They watched it grow, the glitter of wetness pulsing faintly between the woven threads of Vamal's gown.

"It hurts," Vamal murmured. "I'm so cold . . ."

It took B'nach a few seconds before he realized Vamal was staring at nothing, already dead. He closed the man's eyes with gentle fingers but didn't leave the lifeless clerk, waiting patiently until a passerby spotted them and raised the alarm.

Thinking.

If the clerk had been found dead alone, there would have been questions. But no one would doubt the librarian's word that his clerk had been trying to protect his master from an unknown assailant and simply gotten in the way of the knife meant for B'nach. It would be trickier explaining why the two were so far outside K'ferrin's territory. Could he do it? Could he fabricate a complete fiction and be believed?

The entire Citadel knew he was incapable of lying convincingly. He could easily put on his abject servility, humiliation fitting around his shoulders like an old, comfortable cloak. B'nach the Coward sat on the floor doing nothing while the clerk bled to death in his arms. It was all in character.

Mother of God, grant me courage . . .

Startled out of his thoughts by the alarm, he allowed himself to be raised to his feet by K'ferrin's armed guards, as much blood on his own robes by now as on the dead man, and bustled quickly away. B'nach went to his own rooms and changed his clothes, washing the blood off his body, and threw the robes into the fire. As thick smoke belched from the hearth, his woman servant stood silently in the doorway of the kitchen, the child at her side half buried in her skirt sucking his thumb with his forefinger up his nose, watching him.

Then he waited to be summomed. The servant padded nervously around him, placing food in front of him at the appropriate times, taking it away untouched. The silence of his room was broken only by the drip of a water clock placidly counting out the minutes and hours. The morning sky had reddened, the woman snuffing out the stubs of candles, when the knock finally came.

He answered it himself, opening it to three of K'ferrin's personal bodyguards. He simply nodded to their murmured apologies before he followed them down the interior corridor past the locked doors of his beloved library and into K'ferrin's chambers. He made no protest, if mildly surprised, as the men searched him and confiscated his small ceremonial bone knife. He was only aware he had not been listening when the guard coughed again, saying softly, "Sir . . ."

"Excuse me?"

"His Reverence's orders. You're to go in. Privately."

A flutter of fear twisted his stomach, wrenching him out of his distraction. "I see. Thank you."

Mother of God, grant me courage . . .

He had rarely ventured into the Reverence's private sanctum, where no one lived but the old man and his two favorites. The metal banister on the curving stairway was ice cold in his palm as he climbed. He stopped before the closed doors, sweating as he knocked.

They opened without a squeak, the sweet smell of incense and saturke wine heavy in the air, but not quite covering the musky odor of sex. For a moment, B'nach saw no one, then recognized the small figure peering up at him. Hunchbacked and deformed, it smiled, baby teeth glinting in the dark. Its eyes, however, were tired and old.

"Welcome, cousin. Please come in," the thing said in its raspy child's voice. B'nach had never been able to see the family resemblance in the little freaks, but then he had hardly been able to see it in K'ferrin, either.

He stumbled into the darkened room, half-blind in the gloom. Heavy velvet curtains had been drawn across the arched windows overlooking the garden, light that filtered in around the edges casting blood-red shadows. A tiny hand slipped into his own, warm and soft in his clammy palm, to lead him deeper into the room. B'nach shuddered, but made no attempt to pull away.

As his eyes adjusted, he spotted a huge bed behind an arched doorway, almost a room in itself. Constructed like a miniature theater, it was enclosed on three sides by ornate wood paneling, with a carved canopy over the open side. Thick posts rose from floor to ceiling, carved with gilt grapevines twining up the wood. Gauze drapes obscured the occupants within like thick fog.

A hand appeared around one edge, its spatulate fingertips reminding B'nach of a frog's, but there was nothing reptilian about the face. Luminescent eyes watched him alertly, bowed red lips pursed into a smile. Suddenly, its mouth opened into a gaping grin, red tongue wriggling as it dribbled a viscous white fluid down its chin. B'nach shut his eyes, feeling sick. The twins giggled, the two voices joined in snickering harmony.

"Stop it," the old man's voice snapped.

The giggles were cut off as if with a knife.

"Greetings, my cherished kinsman," K'ferrin said. His voice was slightly slurred and B'nach realized the old man was drunk.

He forced his eyes open. The gauze fabric had been drawn back completely from the open side of the bed, and B'nach stood rigid, staring down at his grandfather. K'ferrin lay sprawled languidly across the feather mattress, his thin arms and legs loose-jointed in the mounds and valleys of bedclothes. His skin hung in loose folds over his skeleton, blue veins tracing knobby threads through his pale skin. He was naked but for some kind of metal-and-leather device strapped on his hips, ugly with short blunt spikes along the groin and, B'nach could see from his vantage, a curved shaft inserted into the old man's anus. Whatever sexual play he had been indulging in now finished, K'ferrin's thickened penis lay limp against the device trapping it, a trail of slime glistening on metal.

K'ferrin lifted a long clay pipe to his mouth, his movements sluggish. The bowl glowed briefly before the smoke curled from the old man's nostrils. B'nach caught the bitter odor of the narcotic, fighting the impulse to cough. The twin holding B'nach's hand dropped it and crawled onto the bed, pulling itself up laboriously hand over hand. Small dark bruises dappled its crooked back and buttocks, neatly matching the pattern of spikes on the old man's girdle.

Its deformed sibling slid up on the opposite side, identical miniature gargoyles nestling themselves against the old man's skinny chest. Four hands stroked his body while two others twitched in sympathetic response, the vestiges of Siamese twins.

"Your Reverence," B'nach managed to force out, his voice no more than a whisper.

The man in the bed smiled and shuddered with silent laughter. "Oh, isn't he lovely, my pets?" his grandfather asked the two monsters beside him. Still watching B'nach with heavy-lidded eyes, the twins made no response. " 'Your Reverence.' How it pleases me to see it possible such virtue and devotion could arise from my crooked root."

B'nach began to tremble. *Mother of God, grant me courage* . . . His head reeled from the smoke, his stomach pushing acid up into his throat. His grandfather studied him with narrowed, bloodshot eyes, ignoring the twin's fondling. The monsters watched as well, faces impassive as their hands moved by long habit.

"The woman has absconded," K'ferrin said finally.

Unable to concentrate, B'nach blinked stupidly. "Your Reverence?"

"The Lady Antonya. P'tre Terhune's precious niece. She's gone. Escaped." K'ferrin enunciated each word clearly, obviously annoyed with B'nach's thick wits. He was not nearly as inebriated with wine and drugs as he pretended to be. And suddenly B'nach knew why he had been summoned to the old man's obscene playpen.

If K'ferrin decided B'nach had had anything to do with Antonya's flight, he would never leave this room alive. The twins stared at him, waiting.

He was a dead man.

The insight hit him like a light in the back of his brain. He was already a dead man. Dead, dead, dead. He had nothing to lose. He was free. Something within him stirred, like a long forgotten creature wakened from a torpid sleep. He felt as if he were being split into two people, the one suddenly aware and exuberantly alive inside the dumb marionette façade he wore like a costume of skin. The creature within peered out of the holes in his skull, amazed at his body's ability to react in just the proper manner without thought.

The puppet gaped in surprise and fear, and he heard himself

say, "But how?"—knowing these were exactly the right words, the right tone. B'nach watched his grandfather in fascination as the old man weighed his reaction.

"That man Briston. He's escaped as well. With D'arim." His grandfather smiled without humor. "D'arim has deserted Terhune."

B'nach didn't answer.

"Didn't you know?" K'ferrin demanded, his voice lethally soft. The twins' hands froze, immobile against the old man's chest.

"*Me?* My God, no! How could I?" The creature within used B'nach's mouth with the precise amount of surprise, and stopped. He admired the puppet's ability to know when not to protest further.

K'ferrin examined him for a long, tense moment, then relaxed, satisfied. "Did you see her last night?"

Someone had seen her in the library, B'nach thought, panic rising in his throat. There were spies everywhere. He would be caught . . .

"No, Grandfather, I swear it."

K'ferrin's eyes narrowed. "The guard they left alive heard her say she needed something from the library."

B'nach swallowed against the dryness in his mouth. "I never saw her. I was working alone all evening."

Again, he stood quaking as the old man sucked another lungful of smoke from his pipe, squinting through the haze dubiously. "Until you left the library unattended so you could slink off sniffing around D'nyel's skirts like a whipped dog."

B'nach's shoulders slumped, an uncomfortable flush crawling on his cheeks, but he couldn't believe his luck: Of course! His grandfather had supplied the lie for him. He didn't even need D'nyel to back up the alibi. All the Citadel sniggered at his hopeless obsession with her, and no doubt the juicy details of their latest quarrel had been thoroughly gossiped over.

He squirmed, whining imploringly, "Grandfather . . ." and stopped when he heard the old man's viscous laugh.

How easy this is, he rejoiced while his body trembled and sweated and wrung its hands with a skill born of decades of shame.

"What could the woman have wanted from the library?"

"I don't know, but I'll begin a complete inventory immediately, now, this night," he said in a desperate rush as if trying
to make amends, avoid the old man's wrath by making plans.
"If anything is missing, I'll soon find out . . ."

He observed the old man observing him, the creature within
amused. B'nach knew exactly what he would do, thinking rapidly as his puppet body jerked its way through the motions of
groveling.

He had seen her remove the pages, and done nothing to stop
her. His memory was excellent; he could study what had been
taken and satisfy his grandfather with unrelated pages from
substitute books, clouding the evidence. The books she'd mutilated need not even be removed from the library. They could
be hidden simply by moving them from one stack to another.
Any scholar applying to see any of those particular volumes
could be told they were being used by others or in the bindery
being re-covered. Missing pages could be faked from memory,
the leaves pasted in expertly enough to cover the loss. Only
he would ever know which pages had been counterfeited.

No one would have reason to suspect him of such uncharacteristic deceit and betrayal.

How incredibly easy this is.

Finally satisfied, K'ferrin cut off B'nach's deluge of whining.

"What will you do, Grandfather?" he finally made himself
say, his voice shaking. "She could be dangerous . . ."

K'ferrin lounged on the feather pillows, his mood amicable.
"She's only a woman, for God's sake," he snorted. "Any man
who puts either his faith or his fear in women is an idiot." He
eyed B'nach, bloodshot eyes contemptuous. "I will never
fathom why men waste so much time and bother over such
repulsive creatures. Fat blobs of flesh all over their sickly bodies, constantly noisy with weeping and empty chatter."

He sighed, addressing the ceiling as he absently fondled one
of the twins. "Man is an imperfect species, still enslaved by
the need to procreate." He shuddered. "The necessity of placing one's clean and elegant parts inside such stinking decay is
bad enough, but to enjoy it is true perversion."

He refocused his attention on B'nach standing tensely. "You
are weak," he said dismissively. "It's forgivable. But to see a

man like P'tre Terhune frightened? Simply disgusting. Frankly, the world would be better off if all women were locked away from the rest of the human race to spend their lives doing what they were designed for, kept perpetually pregnant and bearing children. Men can find more refined pleasures elsewhere."

He gazed down at the twins fondly, pinching one by the nipple. It smiled, but its breath hissed in pain. As soon as K'ferrin looked back up at B'nach, the smile vanished, the little gargoyle exchanging a sullen glance with its twin as it furtively rubbed bruised skin.

"However, annoyed as I am to have my property abducted, I think she may be more use left running free around the countryside."

"But why?" Widen the eyes, make the jaw just a bit slack. *Yes.*

"I'm tiring of Terhune's constant intrigues against me."

"Sir?" *No, a misstep.* But the body knew what to do as K'ferrin shot a sharp glance at him. Not even B'nach was that dense, even when terrified. "You don't mean to assassinate him? But he's the Commander of the Oracular Army!"

The old man smiled thinly. "I've done it before. But no, I don't intend to assassinate him. His Elite grow weary of defending the worthless Terhune honor and real estate. Even D'arim has turned on him and what's left of the army is already demoralized. *I* am still the Keeper of the Oracle. Mine is the will, his is the means, the body obeys the mind. He must be reminded of that fact."

B'nach licked his dry lips. Whatever his grandfather planned to do, if not have Terhune assassinated, B'nach knew not to inquire. But he couldn't help asking, "What about G'walch?"

The old man's bloodless lips twisted around the long stem of his pipe. "Mmmm," he said indolently. His flaccid penis squirmed to life, its purple head rising like a blind slug, pulsating. He opened his legs wider as the twins cooed, slithering down to stroke the inside of the old man's thighs. There was something desperately contrived about their behavior. "What *about* G'walch?"

At that, the odd disjoined sensation vanished, the creature

within suddenly silent. B'nach stood trembling with disgust and fear, and no idea what to do next.

The old man suddenly sucked in his breath, his hips rocking slightly as the twin's efforts finally began to have their desired effect. "You may go now." K'ferrin let his head loll back on the pillows, his eyes closed.

Against the odds, he had succeeded. But as much as he wanted to bolt from the room, B'nach stood rooted, staring down at his grandfather. He wanted to strangle the old man, longed to feel his scrawny neck crushed between his hands.

The twins looked up curiously. Slowly, a knowing smile spread across K'ferrin's face, although he did not open his eyes. "Despise me as you will, B'nach. But bear in mind my blood also runs in your veins. Blood calls to blood. Do you really think your desires are so different from my own? If the tree is tainted, so is the fruit. Remember that."

"I should like to kill you," B'nach said quietly.

K'ferrin's smile widened. "But you won't," he said, finally opening his eyes. "Pray for me. Pray I live a long time, my dearest kinsman," he said softly. "You will not have much time to savor my death once I'm gone." His breath caught in his throat and he grabbed one of the twins by its Siamesed, useless arm. It squealed in alarm as he dragged it up on its belly, protests muffled as he squashed its cherub face into the pillows. He rolled over on top of the tiny body, pinning it underneath him.

"Now, unless you would care to join us, leave," K'ferrin said, his voice husky. The other twin escaped, slithering quickly out of the bed as K'ferrin thrust his steelclad hips against its sibling with brutal strength. It took B'nach by the hand and tugged on him gently, drawing him away through the darkened room toward the outer door. B'nach tried to block his ears to the old man's grunts and the little monster's pained whimpers. He thought he would be sick.

The gargoyle unlatched the door, the sudden sliver of light too bright against B'nach's retinas.

"Please go now, cousin," the thing said softly as it pushed him out into the anteroom. Its third arm quivered in agitation, unable to control its spastic movement. Its large, dark eyes blinked, and B'nach was astonished to see a sudden tear on its cheek.

It hesitated, fearfully. "Pray for us, too," it said almost inaudibly, then firmly shut the door.

40

The drug had nearly worn off by the time D'nyel returned. As she unlocked the door to the tower and climbed up the long stairway, she heard the table above creaking. He stopped struggling as soon as she entered the little room, and wept quietly, defeated. She shook her head in amused annoyance, but her humor was short-lived.

Terhune had been a useful benefactor over the years. She was the best healer the Citadel had known for centuries, having only done what was necessary in her pursuit of knowledge. Each human body she explored gave her more insight to the healing arts. For every victim who died under her hand, she had healed twenty who had given up all hope of surviving. And after all, they had been condemned men. Why shouldn't she have used them if they were to die anyway? Why waste the knowledge they could give her?

Terhune might or might not be as deranged as his performance would have her believe. But his Sector was near a state of mutiny. If he fell, she would fall with him. She couldn't allow that.

Not now. Not when she'd reached so high and nearly grasped the prize. The head of the Medical Arts Order was in ailing health, his gnarled hands too crippled with arthritis to teach, his stamina flagging. Soon, a successor would have to be named from those who had reached the First Ranks of Healers. Young as she was, even female, she hadn't been deaf to the rumors whispered behind knowing hands.

She focused on her latest project, realizing she had been looking straight at the man without even seeing him. She smiled. He trembled, but was unable to tear his gaze away. When she came close to the table, he flinched violently, his chest rising and falling with shuddering breaths. She unwrapped the bandages, studying the work she'd done so far, running her finger lightly beside the incisions. She'd been studying blood circulation, and although she'd made several incisions, nothing had gone too deep, nothing festered with infection. He had one patch of deadened flesh where the vein grafting hadn't taken, but nothing fatal. She could repair him easily enough.

"What's your name?" she asked gently.

His eyes widened. "Catrus."

"Catrus . . ." She caressed his name in the same low, throaty voice she used when she made love with B'nach. Her fingers trailed up his arm as she strolled along the table, then stroked the hair back from his forehead as if they were two lovers sharing a bed. She felt no pity for victims, nor had she any now. She had learned how to keep them alive longer and longer to study how the living body functioned, but eventually, they all died and she threw away the carcasses with as little concern as she would gnawed chicken bones.

"Such a fine body," she purred. This time only his mouth worked, his voice strangled. "But I think I have another use for you . . ."

From the cabinets she pulled down a small stoneware bottle, needles and a rolled spool of suturing thread. She uncorked the bottle and poured the thick liquid onto his wounds. While he watched in horrified fascination, it frothed into pink foam. He moaned as she scrubbed the dried blood and fat away until the wound bled freely.

Dipping the thread into the liquid, she passed the wet strand through the eye of a curved needle. "Try not to move around so much," she said as he cringed from her. Quickly and expertly, she began to sew the incision closed.

"You're . . . letting me live?" he said in desperate hope.

She paused, as if the idea surprised even her. "It does look that way, doesn't it?"

His eyes suddenly rolled up in his head as he fainted, which at least made her work easier.

41

The land rose as they rode south. A serrated edge of black in the distance became trees, marshlands abruptly giving way to forest. Within minutes, they were in the thick of the woods, following a path through the towering firs only D'arim seemed to know.

The horses had slowed to a trot, foam flecking their mouths. Nothing more than vague shapes could be made out in the dark of the forest. Her horse, near exhaustion, slid on a patch of dewy grass, and stumbled as Antonya hauled its head up by the reins. It recovered, but stood trembling under her. Briston swore quietly, wheeling his horse around to press his mount against hers and get it moving again.

The forest opened into a tiny meadow, starlight cold in the small patch of sky overhead. She heard D'arim speak, and another, unfamiliar voice answered him from the shadows. Large shapes moved in the dimness, a horse snorted, twin puffs of white breath blown from its nostrils ghostly in the early morning cold. D'arim dismounted as the man appeared out of the tree line with three fresh horses stamping restively. D'arim and the stranger grasped each other's wrists in a tight wordless handshake.

Briston dismounted, clasped her by the waist and swung her down off the spent horse, its head hanging in exhaustion. She had her feet barely on the ground before he heaved her as easily up into the saddle of a skittish mare, murmuring to it softly as he gathered the reins and gave them to her.

For a brief moment, he held her hands between his own, his fingers hard under his leather gloves. He looked up, his mouth half-opened as if about to say something. Then he smiled and let her go.

Briston exchanged a few short words she couldn't make out with D'arim and the stranger, then looped the reins over the head of a piebald horse and swung up into the saddle. The animal sidled nervously and he leaned over to pat its neck. D'arim mounted the third horse, an oddly stocky animal with a shaggy coat, as the stranger, leading the three spent horses, melted into the forest shadow, even the sound fading away within moments as if he'd never been there.

With only starlight filtering through the thick clouds, they had to follow a nearly imperceptible trail through the trees in near total darkness. D'arim stopped several times to listen to the night sounds, small insects rustling, night birds singing, frogs croaking.

The air lightened to vaporous gray, stars dying in the morning mist. Just before sunrise, D'arim reined in his horse, exchanging a quick glance with Briston. Briston abruptly seized Antonya's mare by the bridle, turning both horses off the trail and driving them into the surrounding bush. Branches whipped at her face as she swore softly. When she looked around, D'arim had vanished.

Briston pulled to a halt, and frantically gestured to her to be silent. The horses pawed the ground nervously as he held them both tightly in check, patting their necks with his free hand to calm them.

Both animals' ears swiveled forward, heads jerking up expectantly. Then Antonya heard it as well.

The sky had lightened enough to see the pale shapes of riders in the low mist covering the forest floor. Twenty horsemen cantered by on the trail she and Briston had just left, heading in the direction they had just come. Arms and harness jangled, low voices and muffled laughter mixed with the pounding of hooves, branches snapping. Birds startled from their roosts fluttered overhead. Briston tugged on the reins of his mount gently to urge both horses deeper into the bush, rigidly silent.

The two animals were alert, but well trained. They remained quiet, not responding to the horses riding past, only their ears flickering. Briston sat waiting for several minutes after she could no longer hear the cavalry. When she looked at him questioningly, he shook his head, still waiting.

Then she heard the call of a bird she knew had never nested in this forest. Briston grinned, tapped his horse on the flanks with his heels and picked their way out of the bush more carefully than they had entered.

It was midmorning before they broke cover of the forest, and they stopped beside a stream to water the horses and rest. D'arim allowed scant time before they were once again on the move.

By nightfall of the third day, they had put enough distance between their pursuers and themselves to satisfy the wary *qa-zaq*, and stopped for the night. The horses cropped at what forage there was under the shelter of trees, while Briston bus-ied himself with setting up camp, unsaddling and rubbing down their tired mounts, building a small fire to heat water and boil soldiers' rations of jerked meat into edibility.

Only once did Antonya attempt to help him, removing the bridle from her own horse. He moved hastily to relieve her of even that nominal chore and she didn't question his deference any further. Nor did D'arim, she noted. Briston quickly and efficiently saw to what few needs his superior had before at-tending to his own.

Sitting on the fallen log and staring into the light of the tiny fire, the *qazaq* seemed somehow smaller, huddled bleakly with his hands tucked between his knees for warmth. He must have been aware of her, but didn't bother to glance up as she studied him before moving around the fire to sit beside him. Neither spoke, watching the flames dance, sparks like tiny fireflies spi-raling up on the heat. It was not a companionable silence, neither was it awkward. A log sagged as the smaller ones beneath it burned through, and rolled from the fire. D'arim picked up a long branch to poke the vagrant log back into the coals.

"D'arim," she said softly. He was listening, although he didn't respond, still watching the fire remotely. "May I ask who you are next to turn me over to?"

At that, she saw a hint of a smile, his impassive face soft-ening. "No, madam." After such a long pause that she'd thought that was all he intended to say, he turned his head to examine her intently. She returned the look calmly. "It would be best you should remain innocent of any knowledge that might harm others were we to fail. If we succeed, you'll know soon enough. Be content to know you are among friends and are no longer anyone's hostage."

"If I am not a pawn in someone else's game, then you know I will fight P'tre for Adalon." He didn't respond, as if he wasn't really listening. "You would be welcome, D'arim," she insisted softly. "There is a place for you with me, if you choose."

At that, he laughed, a low, harsh sound like a cry of pain. "I'll swear no oaths to you, madam," he said. "Any I would give you would be as worthless as the one I swore to P'tre Terhune."

"Then swear no oaths. I've no interest in binding men to me with either chains or vows. Stay as long as you like and leave when you please. Fight because it is what your heart tells you is right."

" 'Right'? How can a heretic ever be right?"

"I was raised by the Brothers of Blessed Reason," she said shortly. "What is heretical and what is not is a matter of politics, not truth. It also doesn't change the fact that I am the lawful heir to Adalon."

Then he slowly shook his head, in disbelief rather than denial. "Forgive me, but I can see nothing of P'tre's blood in you, in either your manner or appearance."

She smiled, unoffended. "And how much of P'tre can you see in G'walch?" He didn't answer, and after a moment looked away, back into whatever visions or memories he saw in the flames. "My mother's people are quite fair, and R'bert shared only half his blood with P'tre, my father's mother a Landswoman, not Citadel-bred. Is it so surprising, then, the differences between my uncle and myself?"

He remained silent. Whatever his thoughts might be, he was unwilling to share them with her. She sighed in frustration.

"With you by my side, D'arim, half of P'tre's Elite would desert, and probably all of his armsmen in Adalon. You have an obligation to the people of these Lands to repair the damage you and P'tre have done in the name of the Faith. How much bloodshed of innocents might we be spared? Without you, how many more will die . . . ?"

He had closed his eyes tightly. "Stop," he said simply. It took him several deep breaths before he placed his palms against his thighs and leaned back to stare at her. "*Now* I can see his serpent-tongued blood in you, woman," he said, his accent soft. "I've been scourged with guilt and burdened with duty long enough. I've betrayed a friend and brother. If God wills it, then you'll prevail without me. But I'll do no more than I have done."

They both glanced up briefly as Briston appeared, illuminated in the firelight, listening.

"Forgive me, D'arim," she said. "My need has made me ungracious and my ambition selfish." He didn't answer. "What will you do now?"

The *qazaq*'s mouth smiled bitterly as he glanced past her to where Briston stood at a respectful distance. "I don't know. Perhaps return to the Steppes where I was born."

"And you?" She looked up at Briston through the fire.

Briston stared pleadingly at D'arim. "As I have always done. Once we have delivered you safely, I'll do as he commands."

D'arim shook his head. "No, no more. I have no right to your loyalty, far less your obedience. Nor do I think I could bear it now. I shall return home alone, knowing I'll likely find there is no longer any place for me. There would be even less for you."

"I'll make you the same proposal, then," Antonya offered to Briston. "You would be welcome to come with me, if you choose."

Briston was still regarding the *qazaq*. "I shall consider it, madam," he said, his hoarse voice stricken, and turned away.

Nothing more was said, each bedding down with their own thoughts. They rose at the first hint of light and rode without further conversation. Only once during the long day's ride did she catch Briston's eye on her, pensive. She returned the look evenly, but said nothing nor made any gesture, not even a smile.

They met no one on the thin, meandering track through the woods, heard nothing in the trees but birdsong, saw nothing but the white flash of a deer's tail as it fled. By the time the sky visible through the canopy of leaves turned to red, they reached a low stone hut built at the edge of a tiny woodcutter's clearing, dense thatch roof in good repair. Her heart quickened, recognizing this as a Guildhouse, knowing they had reached their destination.

As they reined in their tired horses, a man stepped from the doorway of the house, his dark beard curving around his mouth to a sharp point on his chin. His head was bare, a ragged line of white hair bright against the dark curls of his scalp. He smiled as he saw her, eyes crinkled in his tanned face.

Antonya slid from the saddle, her muscles quivering with exhaustion.

"Welcome back, madam," Sarnor said wryly as she strode toward him, then flushed with open-mouthed astonishment as she threw herself into his arms and hugged the mercenary tightly. Awkwardly he patted her on her back, then held her out at arm's length as two men chuckled behind him. She looked past his shoulder, her eyes wet, to see Daen and Gesham grinning shyly. Gesham, she noted with heartache, had lost a hand, his left arm ending several inches below the elbow.

"I never believed I'd see you again," she said hoarsely, her chest tight, holding her hand out to both of them. Sarnor willingly let her go and the two armsmen were embarrassed and pleased as she embraced each of them in turn.

Sarnor surveyed the two Priests still seated on their mounts with ill-disguised dislike. "You'd be D'arim, I assume?" the mercenary said shortly. Briston exchanged a glance with D'arim before the *qazaq* nodded noncommittally.

The mercenary pulled a small leather bag from his jerkin, hefting in his hand to make it clink before he tossed it toward D'arim. He caught it easily.

"I regret it's not quite what you paid for her, but it should be sufficient compensation for your trouble," Sarnor said. "It's fair enough, I assure you—the current rate for betrayal."

Briston scowled, but the *qazaq* gazed back expressionlessly. Antonya pulled away from the two young armsmen, quickly brushing away her tears as she glared at the mercenary. "Sarnor, these men risked their lives and more to get me out."

He glanced at her dubiously. "And have you asked yourself why, madam?" He looked back at them, his expression hard. "Or them? Do you even know who he *is*? Priests do not as a rule break their oaths, and certainly not those within the Elite."

D'arim remained stolid, but Briston flushed with anger. "My

own reason is quite simple, sir. My oath to the Faith comes before all others," he said hotly, then more calmly to Antonya, "And my vow to the Terhunes was to the rightful heir of Adalon."

She smiled at him.

"And you?" Sarnor asked D'arim, unimpressed.

"Sarnor . . ." Antonya protested.

"I had no illusions that you would welcome us with open arms, sir," D'arim said stoically to Sarnor. "I am exactly what you think of me, an oathbreaker and a traitor." He dropped the pouch onto the ground. The coins spilled out at the horse's feet, glinting gold in the dirt. "But not for money."

Sarnor gazed down at the discarded coins, his mouth pursed reflectively. When he looked back at the *qazaq*, his contempt was tempered with a respectful curiosity.

D'arim looked down at Antonya from his horse. "I wish you well, madam," he said quietly, but made no move to offer his hand.

"And I you, sir. Go with my gratitude and God's mercy."

His eyes narrowed, all that showed of a smile, before he tugged his gelding around. He paused for a moment, only long enough to grasp Briston's forearm in a tight embrace, which the younger man returned, his own emotion naked on his face before their hands parted. The *qazaq* kicked his mount into a weary trot and vanished into the trees.

"Well, then," Sarnor said to Briston cynically. He stooped to retrieve the gold D'arim had rejected. "Our good Lady has always found her most faithful allies in the unlikeliest of men. Far be it for me to pass further judgment on you." He stood and dropped the last of the money into its pouch before tucking it away in his jerkin. "Be welcome among us, sir."

Briston dismounted, and held his horse by the bridle with one hand while he warily accepted Sarnor's perfunctory handshake.

"I'll show you where to quarter your beast, if you like," Daen offered. Then, like a child bursting with a secret, he grinned at Antonya. "Why not go inside and make yourself comfortable, Lady?" He merely laughed as Sarnor suddenly smacked an open palm hard against the back of his head.

Puzzled, Antonya followed the mercenary into the house,

ducking her head under the low lintel. Inside, the Guildhouse was shadowed in gloom, but there was enough light to make out the huge bearish form slowly rising at the opposite end of the single room. She inhaled in alarm, her heart thumping as she stared at the beast materializing in front of her.

Where a nose should have been, two holes showed in skin horribly webbed and laced with raw vermilion scars. Eyes stared from a menacing mask of tissue and bone. The skull was nearly hairless; what patches there were grew in thin straggles. A crack appeared under the ragged nostrils exposing teeth in what at one time might have been a smile. The exposed skin of the muscular arms was similarly webbed with red scars. A soft chuckle emanated from the huge, disfigured shape. Antonya remained very still.

"I knew you would not cry out," the hideous creature said, the rough voice oddly trembling with emotion.

She hurled herself at the monster, flinging her arms around the thick neck to hug him tightly. "You're alive!" she sobbed. "Oh, Kerrick, you're alive!"

Awkwardly, his arms went around her slender form and embraced her like a small child, tears on the ravaged face before he set her back on her feet. She tilted her head to study him, reaching up to touch his ruined face sorrowfully.

"I survived the fire," he said, then hesitated. "Am I . . . is it terrible for you to look on me?" His voice was forlorn, full of dread and need.

She kissed him gently on his ruined mouth, a chaste and gentle kiss. "Yes, it's terrible," she said. "I love you, and it's terrible." She smiled as her own tears slid hotly down her cheek, then kissed his hands and held them firmly. "How could it not be?"

Daen had reappeared with Briston, the former Elite regarding the huge disfigured man with suspicion. Kerrick ignored him, his eyes on Antonya as if afraid she would disappear. After a moment, the edges of the slit that formed his mouth turned upward in a ghost of his old smile and he nodded, the stiffness in his body relaxing.

"Well," he said, dismissing his moment of weakness. "You might be happy I managed to save this for you after you lost it. You always were careless." He reached inside his shirt to extract the lizard, new tail growing out from the stump. "Only a little worse for wear. I've become rather attached to the little beast."

"Then keep it, Kerrick. It looks quite happy where it is."

Kerrick opened the pouch at his side and pulled out a pair of leather arm sheaths with twinned knives. "I suspect you've lost your knives as well. You'll be needing these. Try to remember to wear them, Antonya."

She smiled at the sight of them, grabbed them eagerly. Sliding one of the throwing knives out of its sheath, she admired the cold steel blades balanced with a black hilt trimmed with a spiraled band of flat gold. "They're beautiful," she said softly.

The weight in her throat made it hard for her to say anything further, and she busied herself with strapping them to her forearms.

When she looked up, Kerrick and Briston were both watching her strangely. "Lord Vodos is waiting for you at Kulteph, my Lady," Kerrick said. "Once word is out that you are alive and safe, you can be sure the rest will follow within days. Are you still intent on moving against P'tre Terhune for Adalon?"

"Aye," she said very quietly. "And more. Much, much more."

42

His wounds healed well enough, although he was left with several long scarlet scars down his chest which D'nyel found interesting. She hadn't really paid that much attention to the challenges of scarification before, none of her subjects having lived long enough to worry about it.

She kept him bound for a time while she fed him soft bread and poured tea laced with a strong narcotic down his throat. It kept him asleep, for the most part at least. The little time he was awake he babbled wild promises in his whispery voice, he'd behave, do anything she wanted, of course he wouldn't try to escape . . .

She ignored him, waiting for the narcotic to take effect. In a few weeks, once she was sure he had become thoroughly addicted, she brought up a bucket of water, soap and clean clothes, and unshackled him. His ribs and pelvis jutted out in sharp relief from the weight he'd lost. He was so weak, he posed no threat at all to her as she helped him to sit up. His back had festered with urine-soaked bedsores and he stank of shit and sweat.

"You are a mess," she said sternly. "Clean yourself up." Although he had a thick growth of long stubble on his face, she didn't trust him with a razor. He was shaking so badly in any case, he couldn't have used it had he been given one. She locked him in the room and left him alone, unchained.

When she returned in the evening with a cup of drugged tea, Catrus had washed and dressed himself. He sat on his heels, arms wrapped around his knees, shivering in one corner. He stared avidly at the cup in her hands. It wasn't really necessary to disguise the drugs any longer; he knew what it was he craved.

She held out the laced tea. He shuffled forward and snatched the cup from her, squatting on the floor to guzzle it down. He nearly sobbed in relief when he lowered the empty cup, the drug's respite giving him enough energy to glare at her with hatred in his eyes.

"What are you going to do with me?" he said, his speech already starting to slur from the blend of narcotics.

"Anything I want."

The drug dulled his wits to a strange level of acceptance. "I'll escape," he said calmly, then looked faintly alarmed, as if he had given away his plans by mistake.

She smiled, amused, and perched on top of the stool. "You could try. May I ask where you would go?"

She could see him fighting through the lethargy, trying to think. "Leave the city . . ." he said thickly.

"Oho," she laughed. "That's good. You're Citadel-born, aren't you?" His worried expression verified it. "I'm sure the Landsfolk on whose faces you've been wiping the shit off your boots for the past few centuries will welcome you with open arms, *Priest*."

She slid off the stool, and walked to stand over him. "Don't forget I'm the only one who can give you more of this," she said, leaning down to take the empty cup from his unresisting hand. "You think it's unbearable to go three days without it?" She chuckled, a low, nasty sound. "Pray you'll never have to know how it feels to go four. And on the fifth day, you *will* die. Very, very painfully."

Reaching down to grab him by the hair, she dug hard fingers into his greasy scalp. He winced as she jerked his head back on his neck to face her, but didn't fight her. He stared dully, the narcotic in full effect. "Look at me well, Catrus. I'm all that stands between you and Hell, and you'll do exactly as I tell you. Do you understand?"

His eyes flickered, and it took him several slack-jawed moments before he slowly nodded.

43

This time, when P'tre Terhune entered K'ferrin's offices, his manner was subdued, although B'nach shivered with fright. Terhune's upper lip barely twitched as the old man graciously offered him a seat. He remained standing with legs braced, one fist spasmodically clenching and unclenching the hilt of his sheathed dagger.

"You sent for me?"

"Aye, P'tre," K'ferrin replied in an amiable tone. "This unexpected turn of events has given us much to discuss . . ."

"Shall we cut directly to the heart of the matter? How many troops will you allow me to use against her this time, and what price must I pay for the Keeper's approval?"

K'ferrin smiled. "Ah. Candid as usual. But I'm afraid, P'tre, that you've seriously miscalculated. You should have killed the Landsbitch when you had the chance. As it stands now"—the old man waved a cavalier hand—"things are quite different."

P'tre's eyes narrowed, and B'nach made a quick, surreptitious gesture to the guards at the door behind the commander. This time, the sneer P'tre shot at the librarian was unmistakable.

" 'Different'? Different in what sense?"

"Different in the sense that you've lost D'arim, you've lost the woman, and you're likely to lose your Order if you don't stop charging about long enough to *think*," K'ferrin snapped, the affable façade gone. "Your personal dispute over who is the rightful heir to Adalon has severely damaged the stability of the Oracular City and those whose lives are devoted to serving her. I have said it before, P'tre: you cannot serve God's divine will while you are chained to dirt."

B'nach clenched his hands, hidden inside his sleeves, to stop their uncontrollable shaking. The blood drained from P'tre's face as he realized what K'ferrin meant to do.

"You will give up Adalon," K'ferrin said gently.

"Never . . ." It was barely a whisper.

"You were willing to renounce your bloodrights and name the woman as your heir, or are my spies misinformed?" K'ferrin didn't wait for an answer. "Give up your Lands, or G'walch will never Walk the Fire."

"You can't prevent his Walk!" P'tre flared, his face turning from white to an angry red. "You have no right—!"

K'ferrin laughed. "I have every right. As Keeper of the Oracle, if it is my verdict that G'walch's bloodlines are too close to one who has proven tainted, he will be judged unworthy of the attempt."

"And if I renounce my Lands, you will allow G'walch his Walk?"

"Eventually."

Although he had been prepared for Terhune's outburst, B'nach jumped at the ferocity of the explosion. "*Eventually!* You would have me give up my Lands in return for *nothing*!" Terhune took a menacing step toward the Keeper. "I will have your sworn word that the moment I renounce Adalon, G'walch Walks the Fire, or else . . ."

K'ferrin had remained icily calm. He smiled as P'tre, realizing his mistake, faltered. "Or else what, P'tre?" Although the muscles in Terhune's jaw twitched, he remained silent. "You have nothing left with which to bargain. Renounce your Lands, or before this night is over, you will be stripped of your command of the Oracular Army, and imprisoned on a charge of heresy. You might have a small problem finding anyone willing to be an advocate in your defense, as well."

"And who shall you have rule Adalon in my stead?" P'tre was barely able to keep his voice steady, even at a whisper.

Recognizing capitulation, K'ferrin's smile widened. "I thought your lovely niece was an inspired choice myself. Also, this way there's no need to bind yourself to an unsavory marriage. She is remarkably popular in the Lands, and Adalon will still be governed by a Terhune. A nice, clean, peaceful transfer of power. Naturally, we shall endeavor to make her welcome without overtaxing her domains. For the time being. Once she has settled firmly enough into her place, I'm sure she will become more compliant with the rule of the Faith."

For a shocked moment, B'nach was certain Terhune was about to leap on the old man and tear him limb from limb, regardless of the consequences. K'ferrin must have sensed it as well, for he took a cautious step back, his hand half raised to gesture to his guards. "You have no choice," he said softly. "Do it."

Although P'tre made an obvious effort to hide it, the anguish and fury leaked through. Then he bowed stiffly. "As you wish."

As Terhune turned to go, K'ferrin added, "*Tonight*, P'tre." Terhune stopped but didn't face the old man, his entire body quivering like a hunting dog left out in the rain. "Have the formal abdication of your Lands before the Council by sunset."

Terhune made no reply, merely jerking his head in a nod, and left. B'nach felt nearly ill as the trembling in his legs subsided, his gut still knotted. After the guards had closed the doors behind them, K'ferrin rubbed his hands together in glee, turning to B'nach with boyish exultation. "God, I do so love this game!"

"*Game*?" B'nach exhaled in disbelief. "P'tre Terhune has lost his right-hand man, his enemy is offered his bloodrights, and his nephew's future remains in doubt. He has little to lose by striking at you. This time, he might just succeed. It's no game!"

K'ferrin sobered, but his elation was undimmed. "There you are quite wrong, my kinsman. It is all and nothing but a game. The higher the stakes, the better the enjoyment."

"Even if it kills you?" B'nach couldn't help asking.

"Kind of you, B'nach, to worry about my well-being," he

said dryly. "But once my eyes have closed for the final time, I don't give a tinker's damn if the entire Citadel is swallowed whole into the bowels of the earth."

His grandfather's attitude didn't surprise B'nach, only his forthright admission. "Don't you even fear God's wrath?" B'nach asked with more calm than he'd expected.

K'ferrin chuckled, a rheumy wheeze in his chest sounding more like a cry of pain. "I gave up my belief in God the day you were corrupted, B'nach. I'd placed all my dreams and hopes in you, so who better to know what is in P'tre's heart than one who has also lost everything he ever held more precious than life itself?" B'nach blinked in astonishment, his grandfather's honesty taking his breath away. "All that is left for me now is the game, and I shall play it as best I can until I die.

"Then you and all the others may rot."

44

Several miles before Kulteph, Lord Vodos and his troop rode out to meet Antonya. The tall Lord seemed to have aged a decade in less than a year, the lines in his face deeper, his hair grayer. The day was cool, clear skies and a crisp breeze fluttering their cloaks. To Antonya's amazement, Bertil followed Vodos, Verbena, now heavily pregnant, beside her husband.

"Greetings, madam," Lord Vodos called out once they were within earshot. "It is an unexpected pleasure to see you have survived and are in good health."

"Unexpected, I'm sure," Antonya retorted, her gaze aimed at Bertil. "A pleasure for your son, I'm not quite so certain. You betrayed us at Bretch."

"Not true!" Verbena blurted. "He's innocent . . ."

Bertil frowned. "Be quiet," he told his wife brusquely. "I'm quite capable of defending myself, thank you." Verbena bridled, but was silent. "You were betrayed at Bretch, Lady," Bertil said. "But not by me. It's no secret that I despise you for what you've done to my family and our Lands, but I am my father's son. I would never dishonor him by plotting such treachery behind his back."

"If not you, who then?"

"Lord C'ristan," Kerrick said softly from beside her. She turned to stare up at him, unable to read his expression in the ruined face. The bay shook its head, ears twitching at gnats, and he patted the thick neck absently.

"You knew? Why didn't you tell me?"

"I thought it better that you hear it for yourself, firsthand."

Verbena wept, her head bowed over her swollen belly. Pregnancy and sorrow had not been kind to her, her eyes puffy and red, her skin blotched. "It's true, Lady. My father hated you and Lord Vodos for disrupting his rule in Water Cross. Once he learned I was pregnant, he became like a madman, accusing me of treason by fornicating with the enemy. He beat me, trying to kill the baby. Bertil and my stepmother helped me to escape. My father offered to betray you to Terhune in return for help in breaking his truce. He wanted Lord Vodos and my husband murdered, and my return as his hostage to Myro." The young woman's voice choked; she was unable to go on.

"He sent false messages," Vodos continued impassively. "And while you and my son were ambushed at Bretch, I found myself under sudden attack by Terhune's forces in one direction and C'ristan's men from the other. Half my army was destroyed, I barely managed to escape with my life."

Bertil had sidled his horse closer to his wife's, his arm solicitously around her shoulder as she sobbed quietly.

"I take it Lord C'ristan didn't live long enough to enjoy the fruits of his crimes?" Antonya said dryly, understanding the girl's misery.

"An accident." Vodos's tone said otherwise. "He fell from his horse while out hunting stags. Meanwhile, every minor baron in Water Cross is competing for the vacancy. My son has survived three assassination attempts and my daughter-in-law two foiled kidnappings. The Sheruben is in chaos, fighting Terhune from one direction and Water Cross from the other. Your conflict with me weakened my Lands sufficiently that so far we have been able to defend ourselves only by tossing chivalrous warfare to the winds and employing guerrilla tactics. The Sheruben, Water Cross, Silver River, Qarthia, Asteria, it's all the same story, everyone fighting each other while trying to fend off Terhune."

"Which is why we're here, Lady," one of Vodos's party said as three men prodded their horses forward. They threw back the hoods of their cloaks to reveal two of them wearing Terhune's Elite livery, and the third a Priest in K'ferrin's burgundy.

She inhaled sharply, jerking on her horse's bridle in alarm. When Kerrick reached to grab her reins, she stared at him in disbelief, then shot an accusing look at Vodos. Without thinking, she shook her arm, dropping a throwing knife into one palm. Kerrick yanked his hands away as she swept the blade at him warningly.

"I'll not go back to the Citadel, not alive."

"Peace, madam," the Priest said. His ironic smile irritated her. "His Reverence sends you his fondest regards, only sorry you felt it necessary to spurn his hospitality in such an unceremonious manner. We come with only peace in hand, if you care to accept it."

The older of Terhune's armsmen spoke. "My name is Hezron, marshal of Adalon . . ." His gaze flickered past her toward Briston. ". . . as that man should no doubt be able to verify. This is my lieutenant, G'froi, chatelain of Laird's Ketch. P'tre Terhune has formally abdicated his titles, and declared you his successor. We have come to acknowledge the Lady Antonya Terhune as his only niece, the daughter of his elder brother, R'bert, rightful heir of Adalon." His tone was decidedly unenthusiastic.

While she was absorbing that shock, the Priest added, "There is, of course, only the minor question of heresy to be remedied. Profess your devotion to the one true Faith, and all should be in order."

"I have never been anything but a true believer in the one Faith," Antonya said dryly.

"And naturally you will recognize His Reverence K'ferrin, Keeper of the Oracle, as your supreme spiritual master?"

When she didn't answer, the Priest smirked, exchanging glances with Terhune's marshal.

"Do it, Antonya," Kerrick said softly, bending down from

the bay to whisper in her ear. "There's no choice. Your followers are scattered, C'ristan is dead, Verbena exiled, Vodos weakened. Refuse, and the South will slide into civil war. So move your mouth if not your heart."

She sighed, knowing he was right. "I recognize His Reverence K'ferrin, Keeper of the Oracle, as my supreme spiritual master," she said with as much enthusiasm as Hezron had exhibited.

"Well, that should cover everything, then," the Priest said, smiling broadly.

"That's it?" Antonya watched him closely, still wary.

"That's it."

The chatelain spoke up for the first time. "Long live the Lady of Adalon."

Book 3
The Lady of Adalon

45

"These Lands belong to *me,* madam. I rule them as I like, and no amount of your ludicrous blather to my peasants is going to change that fact." Lord Manauf of Geis was red-faced with anger, the dark flush of his skin an amazing scarlet hue.

The Lord verged on obesity, his jowls overlapping the sweat-stained lace around his throat, velvet quilted jaquette barely closing around his gut. He stood with his legs braced apart, hands on his hips with his thick pelvis thrust forward, the picture of every arrogant, ignorant nobleman Antonya had ever met.

K'ferrin's gift of Adalon had been well-barbed with poison, and Antonya knew she had little hope of holding on to it for long if she couldn't forge mutual defense pacts between her neighbors. At the very least, she needed a promise of neutrality from Lord Manauf. His Lands were not large, but she needed this minor, narrow tract which had as its main and nearly only consequential feature a navigable part of the river Fleche, a perfect defensible area which would seal her hold on Adalon like the cork in the bottle.

Lord Manauf's manner of government was glaringly apparent during her ride through these Lands. Villages were in shabby condition, wattle-and-daub shacks barely standing. Fields showed signs of scorching, and at the single meager fair she and her party passed, the sheep and geese were as thin as their hawkers. At one crossroad in the forest, three corpses in an advanced stage of decay hung from branches, all poorly dressed peasants. The equally decayed head of a buck deer they had poached rotted on a stake.

She had been riding nonstop for seven weeks with a company of only twenty men, needing speed over protection. Determined to win over obstinate Lords balking at supporting a woman, she had used every technique she knew and invented ones where she didn't, appealing to honor, or greed, or fear, or any other motive to convince a Lord his best interests lay in her security. Verging on exhaustion when she had arrived midmorning in his capital city of Herylium, she found Lord Manauf had gone off to his hunting villa in the Linomenne Forest some fifty kilometers away. He left word he would meet with her on his return, the precise date vague.

Lord Manauf obviously hoped to bypass the meeting altogether, and avoid committing himself one way or the other. If they had waited to ride out the next day, no doubt Lord Manauf would have disappeared into the shady green lanes of the oaks after boar, not to emerge until his irksome guests had given up and gone home. When their party arrived in the late afternoon, Lord Manauf was in the villa's compound overseeing the next day's hunt. He hadn't expected her to arrive so quickly and made little effort to hide his annoyance. He adamantly rejected any notion of cooperation with the Lady Antonya, and was now doing his best to intimidate this tired, haggard woman with his aristocratic demeanor.

His wife cowered in the background, doing her best to be invisible. That she was with him rather than in Herylium's palace was a good indication of Lord Manauf's low opinion of women. He was one of those Lords who preferred to leave his affairs with his chancellors rather than his wife, keeping her constantly under his watchful, jealous eye. It seemed inconceivable to Antonya that this pathetic creature had the slightest shred of courage left to indulge in even the most innocent flirtation; the woman's spirit seemed utterly crushed.

Manauf's four long-nosed sons hovered behind their father, black, unblinking eyes watching him with ill-concealed hatred and avarice. The eldest, as lanky as his father was fat, mimicked his father's stance, haughty disdain twisting his thin lips in a credible likeness.

"Sir," Antonya pressed, "I only say that a true Lord is a servant of his people and his Lands. One cannot govern effectively unless . . ."

"*I am no servant!*" Lord Manauf bellowed. "My family has held these Lands for generations, my blood is as pure as any nobleman's anywhere. I grovel before no one, I *rule*."

His hunting dogs put back their ears and whined, nervously slinking around men's legs at the angry tone of their master's voice. No doubt he had expected a similar reaction from Antonya.

She sighed impatiently. "But you do not *govern*, sir. To govern is to put the interests of your people first. Surely you can see it is a matter of self-interest, for if they prosper, then so do you . . ."

The audience was small enough, the Lord's family and retainers in his forester's house, her armsmen, Briston and Lord Vodos in her entourage barely fitting into the manor hall.

"You may rule Adalon as you see fit, madam, but my people prosper only when they have my strong hand gripped around their stiff necks. Peasants are like women and children, sneaky malingerers constantly shirking their duties to their rightful Lord. If I didn't keep the rod handy and liberally applied, they'd all be off stealing right and left from my granaries and poaching from my forests instead of working the Land *which I own!*"

Antonya's nerves were fraying. Her back and rump ached from too long on horseback, her shoulder from too long sleeping on the ground. A week before, and she could have danced verbal rings around Lord Manauf. He was a bully and a blustering coward. She would have appealed to his own puffed up self-image as a brilliant warrior, praised him as a protector of fair ladies and righteous honor, letting him preen while she pretended admiration, and subtly implanted fear, glossing it all over with his appetite for money.

She was sick and tired of bullies.

"These Lands, sir, provide you with the goods to support your palace and the fine clothes your family wears and weapons for your armsmen. And where does it come from? From the backs and sweat of your peasants, that's where." Her voice shook with anger. "And what do they get in return from you? Starvation, contempt, and brutality. I would say, *sir*, you need them far more than they need *you*."

She ignored Lord Vodos's frown. Lord Manauf's face darkened to a beet-red, eyes popping. "You are inciting rebellion and sedition on my Lands, madam, and that I will not tolerate!"

She rose from her seat, her hands clenched, only remotely

aware of Manauf's men fingering their weapons uneasily. Briston moved closer to her side protectively.

"The simplest peasant could do a better job of ruling than you have, my Lord. And, yes, even a woman. While you're out with your men behaving like children squabbling over toys, women make sure your house is in order, food on your table, clean linen on your bed. Women haggle with shopkeepers, just as you should be doing with your Guildsmen; women keep the household accounts, just as you should be doing with your stewards; women raise their sons to be trustworthy and loyal to their family, just as you should be doing with your barons."

She was breathless, but spoke rapidly to stem any retort from the dumbfounded Lord. Behind him, his nobles muttered with growing hostility. Lord Vodos watched her, his lips pursed disapprovingly.

"*Women*, sir, manage their servants with a firm but just hand to keep order, just as you should be doing with your peasants, and *women*, sir, work hard to oblige their overbearing, stupid pigs of husbands to avoid being beaten, as you should be doing with those Lords around you with stronger armies than your own. Your *wife* knows more about how to run these Lands than you."

Lord Manauf gaped, his face now nearly purple, and fumbled for his longdagger. He had not seen active battle in years, his reflexes slowed from too much food and indolence. Before his dagger was halfway out of its scabbard, Antonya had effortlessly flicked a knife into one hand, her fingers holding the blade lightly, poised to throw. The Lord froze, trembling with impotent rage.

"Perhaps your widow might give it a try?" Antonya said softly.

The woman in question sank to her knees, hands outstretched. "For the love of God . . ." she pleaded, terrified.

"Shut up, Mother," the eldest son snapped, his grin feral. It was all too obvious he would welcome his father's removal, impatient to take the old man's place. The three boys behind him echoed his smirk, and Antonya belatedly realized she had pressed too hard. Killing Manauf was no solution, his odious sons would be the same problem, their mother would only have exchanged one tyrant for four more.

"Far enough, madam," Vodos said quietly. He turned to the furious Lord. "I humbly beg your pardon, my Lord. My Lady Antonya suffers from the frailty of her sex, we have overtaxed her delicate nature with our arduous journey. She is not herself."

Antonya stared at Vodos in outrage. He met her eyes, his expression tight. "Perhaps my Lady would care to rest while I discuss our concerns with Lord Manauf, between *men*?" He didn't wait for an answer. "Briston?"

"My Lord," the ex-Priest said promptly. He lifted the knife from her hand before offering it back hilt-first meaningfully.

Barely managing to suppress her anger, she slid her knife into its sheath, then allowed Briston to steer her up the stairway leading to the upper halls and into her room. Lord Manauf and his family had taken over his steward's rooms, leaving only a tiny chamber vacated by the forester's clerk to make way for Antonya. Her men, like Manauf's, would find their own accommodations among the dogs in the wilted rushes on the floor of the hall, or in the stables and courtyard.

The chamber was austere, the only furniture the narrow poster bed and a plain commode beside it. The door at least closed securely. She kicked it viciously shut, blocking out the sudden babble of voices below to a dull blur. She needed only three long strides to reach the window overlooking the enclosed court of the villa. Beyond the walls, a team of oxen pulled a wheeled plow through a field cleared in the woods. One man urged the animals on with a long flail as another struggled to guide the colter and moldboard over the ground. In the darkened furrows of fresh plowed earth, ragged cotters broke up clods with heavy mallets, all women with children.

"Bastard. How dare he . . ." Antonya said through gritted teeth.

Behind her, she heard Briston sigh. "Which bastard would that be, madam?"

She turned, still shaking with anger. "All of them."

Briston hooked his thumbs casually into his belt and leaned against the bedpost, causing the framework to creak ominously. He regarded her with uneasy skepticism.

"Frankly, if one of the bastards you're referring to at the moment is Lord Vodos, you should thank him profusely the next opportunity you get." She scowled at his mild rebuke. "You strike enough discomfort into manly hearts as it is, but to openly suggest to nobles that they can be easily replaced by peasants or even their wives only worsens your endeavors. You'll win no arguments that way. Our good Lord Vodos rescued you from a rather ticklish situation."

Her indignation crumbled. "I know. It doesn't make me like it. *Bastards*. Why does it always have to *be* this way?"

He shrugged. "Because that's the way the world is. You'll just have to accept it."

"I'll *never* accept it!" Her voice rose, anguished. "You serve me, Briston, and I'm a woman."

His expression remained bland. "I serve the Lady Antonya Terhune of Adalon," he said quietly. "There's a difference."

She glared at him. "Then you're a bastard, too." She seized the water pitcher from the commode and heaved it at him. Startled, he ducked as the pitcher sailed over his head and smashed against the door, pottery shards and water spraying the room.

"*You're all bloody bastards, every fucking one of you!*" she screamed, and sent the chamber pot after the water pitcher. This one smacked him in the chest, cracking in two. The wind knocked from him, he staggered back onto his rump, more off-balance than hurt. As she kicked over the commode and picked it up by the legs, he drew his knees up and covered his head with his arms. "You rape and you steal and you murder and you have the temerity to blame *us* for your sins? You lying, treacherous, selfish *bastards!*"

He flung himself to one side as she hurled the commode at him, the wood shattering against the wall, then gaped at the broken pieces. "Sweet Mother of God," he breathed, thankful there was nothing left for her to throw. Half crawling, half lurching to his feet, he stumbled toward her with one hand outstretched.

"Antonya . . ."

He stopped, staring incredulously down at the point of her dagger held to his ribs.

"Don't touch me," she whispered, white-faced. He had not a single doubt she would kill him if he tried.

He backed off, hands held palm up. She crouched breathlessly with the knife in one hand, her eyes glittering. In the sudden lull, he heard the silence in the house, listening.

She threw her head back and screamed, a long incoherent wail of fury and pain, and drove the blade into the bedpost. It stuck, the gold band of the hilt winking. She turned her back to him, clamping her arms around her shoulders to hold herself tightly as she sobbed.

Briston let his arms drop, gulping in several lungfuls of air in sheer relief. Rubbing the stubble on his face, he waited until her weeping had subsided.

"For God's sake, Lady, I'd never harm you," he said reproachfully.

She laughed, a wet, suffocating sound without humor. "Sometimes I don't believe I'm going to feel anything but anger and hatred ever again in my life," she choked out, her words like hiccups.

He stepped closer to peer around the veil of hair over her face, trying to catch her eye. She refused to look at him.

"You scare the piss out of me, girl," he said.

At that, she did look up, her eyes puffy and bloodshot. "I?" she said scornfully. "I didn't hurt you."

He laughed, the sound strained. "No, you didn't," he agreed. "I've seen you in a fight, and I can recognize a childish tantrum when I see one." He avoided glancing at the knife, the blade still shivering in the wood, fully aware how close she had come to stabbing him. "But you don't need a knife to hurt me easily enough."

She wiped her cheeks fiercely in speechless disbelief.

"I love you, Antonya. I want to make love to you." He winced as she recoiled from him in unmasked alarm. "See how easy that was? Right to the heart."

She stood wide-eyed and trembling as he smiled sadly. "I'll confess it, I'm a bastard. We're *all* bastards. But if you say 'stop,' I'll stop." Keeping his eyes on hers, he deliberately raised one hand, his fingers touching her under the chin. He held her that way for several moments, then slowly bent his face to hers. Pausing with his lips just brushing hers, he waited.

When she said nothing, he kissed her.

Half an hour later, she gasped, a sound of panic. "Stop."

Briston groaned softly. "Truly?"

When she didn't answer, he rolled away, bedclothes rustling as he sat up on the narrow bed and hitched his breeches back up over his hips. He groped for his shirt in the tangle of sheets, mopping his sweating face with it. "Our good clerk should get the housemaids to hang out his mattress and give it a thorough beating," he said, his voice shaky as he fumbled with the undone lace of his breeches. "The straw's gone far too lumpy and hard on a poor man's back . . ."

He stopped as she clutched his arm, her eyes frightened. Wordlessly, he let her pull him down against her bare flesh.

When she cried out next, it was in pleasure.

The sun had set when she fell asleep, the waning light through the window painting the walls russet and blue. Briston carefully extricated his limbs from hers. Conversation and the laughter of drinking men floated up from the manor hall below, the quarrel apparently forestalled. She murmured in her sleep but didn't awake as he slid from the bed, dressing quietly as he watched her.

The skin around her eyes was dark against the exhausted pallor of her face. Her cheek nestled into the pillow, tousled hair gold against white. The bedclothes had slipped from her shoulder, one arm outflung, revealing the swell of her breast. Briston felt a small ache of desire ripple through his gut, then smiled as he picked up his boots with one hand and used his thick jerkin to lift his sword belt from the post, muffling the clink of the chain.

Grimacing, he juggled boots and sword to lift the iron latch on the door with studied care. He scowled as the door creaked open to reveal Daen standing outside, his expression innocent. Briston stepped barefoot onto the landing and closed the door before he spoke.

"Voyeurism now, is it?" he said quietly.

"Only ensuring you were left undisturbed," the young armsman whispered back with a grin.

Briston glowered, without noticeable effect on the armsman, as he pulled on his boots and buckled the sword around his hips. He leaned over the landing to gauge the mood below, then nodded to Daen. The armsman gripped the hilt of his sword meaningfully. He would remain on guard outside the Lady's door until he was relieved.

The cheers and laughter were bolstered by the amount of ale being consumed. Any animosity between Antonya's party and Lord Manauf had been smoothed over, the fat Lord bellowing cheerfully, his sons less exuberant but just as drunk. Vodos spotted Briston mid-toast and turned the salute slyly toward him. A dog stood to bark, hairs bristling along its skinny shoulders. It yelped as it was roughly cuffed to silence by one of the nobles. Manauf turned to look.

"What ho!" Manauf bawled out. "Our conquering Lord has returned from the war!" He twisted on the wooden bench to yell at his wife, knocking over his own tankard and nearly falling off himself. "Woman! A drink for our gallant hero!"

As the woman scurried to obey, Briston noted her lip was cut, swollen and blue. She handed him the tankard timidly, not daring to look at him, then backed away. Briston shrugged to himself; no man had the right to interfere with another's domestic affairs, no matter how contemptible the behavior might be considered.

Manauf caught him eying his wife's bruised face and laughed harder. "I take it our virile champion has managed to tame the sulky vixen by taking a firm stave of his own to her, eh?" His words were slurred with drink.

Briston paused with his ale halfway to his mouth, regarding the fat Lord stolidly. Vodos raised an eyebrow at Briston.

Manauf turned to address his sons, gesturing broadly. "That's the way to do it, boys! Quench a bitch's fire with a good hosing where it'll do the most good! That's what they all want."

Vodos exchanged a startled glance with Briston as Lord Manauf's men laughed uproariously with him. Slowly, Briston smiled, then laughed himself, gulping at his drink before banging the tankard down hard against the table, ale sloshing.

"Good one, my Lord Manauf!" he shouted, and moved to straddle the bench next to the man, throwing an arm around his shoulder.

The Lord's drunken eyes crinkled in the layers of fat, small and red. "Your virago has a sharp mouth on her as well, my lad. Perhaps you filled it with more than curses, a bit of your cream to sweeten her tart?"

The Lord pounded both fists on the trestle table, overcome with his own wit. Briston threw his head back, laughing heartily, then leaned over with exaggerated care to speak into the man's ear, as if confessing a vulgar secret in confidence. His sons and nobles elbowed one another, grinning slyly.

"If you ever again utter another insult to my Lady within my hearing, my Lord, I shall personally rip off your stunted prick and stuff it down your foul throat," Briston whispered amicably.

The fat Lord jerked away, gaping in shock. Briston winked with exaggerated parody as Manauf's armsmen guffawed at their Lord's reaction to whatever scandalous revelation he had been privy to.

Grinning broadly at the man's uncertain bewilderment, Briston shouted with laughter, his eyes hard. Lord Manauf's lips twitched into a strained smile.

Briston smacked him on the back with good cheer, so hard that Manauf's meaty rump slid half off the bench, nearly driving him under the trestle table. It took him several moments to wrestle his bulk upright, his feet scrabbling for purchase in the loose rushes, hands clutching at the table slippery with spilled ale.

The boisterous drinking and crude jokes went on for several hours, but none of them were directed at either Briston or Antonya. Well past midnight, several of Manauf's armsmen had to help heave their Lord's bulk up the stairs to his rooms, and the rest of the men on either side began settling into the straw on the floor, their cloaks wrapped around themselves. Lord Vodos yawned, arms stretching, before he left for the comfort of the hayloft in the stables. Nicoli relieved Daen of his watch in front of the Lady's door, and Daen joined the others for the night, scratching his ginger hair sleepily.

The rush candles had burned down, several guttering their last in the holders along the wall, shadows trembling. Briston sat upright in the rushes, listening to the night sounds of men and dogs snoring, crickets and the squeaking of mice, the wind whistling along the chimneys. Something was not right, although he couldn't figure out what was making him uneasy.

After a while, he stood, slapping the bits of straw off his cloak and breeches before stepping inside the small privy to relieve himself. He dipped his hands into the lavatorium, splashing the icy water against his face. Then, unable to sleep, he strode outside.

The air was crisp, stars bright in the night sky, the waning light from Luna Major casting everything in shades of silver. He descended the stone steps, then looked briefly into the doorway of the cellar. Among the stacked firewood and barrels of salt fish and grain, uneven stacks of building timber, cartwheels and axles, the Lord's servants slept. Briston spotted the unlucky clerk turned out of his own sparse room curled up against a large bag of chestnuts, his mouth turned down with disgruntled annoyance, even in sleep.

Across the courtyard, Tobias shared the duty with one of Manauf's armsmen, the two suspicious of each other but cordial enough. Briston acknowledged his man's nod with one of his own, then strode to the fortified gateway of the compound, looking out into the dark.

He leaned back with his hands braced against his spine to crack the stiffness from it. Behind him in the distance, he heard a faint rustle and a stifled giggle, almost inaudible, camouflaged as it was by ordinary night sounds. His hand on the hilt of his shortsword, he tilted his head, listening carefully, unsure from what direction the noise had come. He heard nothing.

Silently, he slipped past the side of the house, glancing around the corner at the back, and scowled. There, directly under Lady Antonya's window, two of the Lord's long-nosed sons were attempting to climb the trestle of ivy against the wall. A small length of cord was looped around one boy's belt, not long enough for climbing but well suited for trussing up reluctant maids. Not quite sober enough to negotiate the tangle of leaves, the elder hung halfway up the wall with his feet and hands snared while his brother pushed against his rear end from below.

"Stop pushing, goddamn it," the older one snarled.

The younger brother sniggered. "Stop falling, then."

Briston stepped out into the open, his shortsword drawn and held casually by his side. "Good evening, my Lords," he said in a friendly tone. The two boys froze, looking down at him.

"Would you be needing some help in climbing down from there?"

The younger one toppled out of the ivy with a small squeal of fear, landing in a painful jumble of arms and legs. He clambered to his feet as his brother scrambled down with less awkwardness. They stood side by side for a moment, panting and confused. The older boy reached for his dagger.

Briston grimaced with distaste. The moonlight glinted evilly off his bare blade. "Don't be stupid, lad," he said scornfully. The two exchanged looks, backing up a few steps before they turned and ran, knocking into each other in their haste to be gone. Briston watched them go before he rammed his short-sword back into its sheath.

He muttered angrily under his breath as he walked to the stables. Gesham was the closest to the door, sleeping soundly with his good arm flung around the shoulders of a large wolf-hound. The dog nestled its narrow head against the man's chest as affectionately as a lover. Briston nudged the young arms-man awake with his toe.

"Wha . . . ?" Gesham's eyes blinked in the dark.

"Posting an extra guard," Briston said quietly.

"Oh." Not quite awake, Gesham disentangled himself from his companion, the dog whining unhappily. He sleepily followed Briston out into the night to take up his guard under Antonya's window.

"Keep a watch out for rats," Briston said.

It took a moment for Gesham to absorb. "Rats?"

"The big, blue-blooded kind with too much ale in their bellies and not enough brains in their heads."

"Oh." Gesham's grumpy expression changed to a grin. "What should I do if I catch one?"

Briston snorted. "Cut off his tail."

The armsman chuckled, fully awake now. "My pleasure."

Briston had Daen relieve him just before dawn, taking half a loaf of dark bread and a pot of ale for the tired armsman before Gesham snatched an hour or two of sleep himself. The rest of the men were stirring in the early morning cool, mists still in the trees of the forest a short distance behind the manor house. The servants had already fired the chimneys in the kitchen beside the manor to cook breakfast when Briston knocked on Antonya's door.

She answered it, already dressed, her hair plaited smoothly. Her eyes had lost their fatigued hollowness, her face was flushed. They stood awkwardly silent for a moment, then she smiled shyly.

"I trust you slept well, madam?" Briston said.

"Very well, sir. My thanks."

Lord Vodos was up, conversing amiably with a few of Manauf's barons, the fat Lord not in evidence. Vodos turned as they walked down the stairway. Antonya's back stiffened uneasily.

"My Lord Vodos . . ." she began, her voice strained.

The Lord bowed, a graceful courtly gesture out of place in this rough setting. "My dearest Lady Antonya," he said smoothly, cutting her off. "You look much recovered of your sweet nature, I'm pleased to see. Shall we breakfast before we ride?"

She blinked in surprise. *Ride*?

Vodos tucked her hand firmly around his arm, leading her to the table. As she sat, one of Manauf's servants handed her a pot of beer and a slab of cold salted lard on a chunk of coarse bread, hot and fresh from the kitchen. Like Manauf's wife, the boy had been long brutalized into submission, scurrying timidly around the room with downcast eyes too frightened to have dared looking at anyone.

"What of our gracious host, Lord Manauf?" Antonya asked, realizing men were eating without waiting for their overlord's appearance.

"It seems my Lord Manauf overindulged in spirits last night and is not feeling well this morning," Vodos said phlegmatically.

She glanced at Briston, shrugged, and ate without another word. As she drained the last of her beer, Vodos stood pointedly. Their horses had been saddled and readied as she walked out of the manor house. As she swung her leg over the saddle, gathering the reins from the armsman holding her bridle, the rest of her company mounted their horses. The jingle of harness and friendly banter of men was a cheerful sound in the crisp morning air.

"I take it you came to a suitable agreement with my Lord Manauf during my . . . incapacitation?" Antonya said to Lord Vodos.

Vodos pulled his horse around, prompting it even with hers as it snorted, stamping a leg in its eagerness. Briston kneed his own horse to bring him up on Antonya's opposite side, eying the Lord curiously.

"Aye," Vodos said blandly. "Our good Lord has pledged his support, agreeing to supply as many horse and armed men as we might need of him, as well as free access across his Land. Moreover, we have his consent to erect a war fortress on the Islet of Jasnor with which to control access along the Fleche."

Antonya stared at him in open-mouthed astonishment. "And what did we have to agree to in return for this most generous concession?"

"Not a thing, Lady. It was simply an agreement reached between two like-minded gentlemen of noble blood."

She sat back in the saddle, dumbfounded. "I see."

Vodos's lips quirked almost mischievously. "Of course, his change of heart did come shortly after I gave him my solemn word that should he be unable to come to an agreement with the Lady of Adalon, I would take it as a personal affront, return with my own troops to his pissant little county to stomp him and his four flea-ridden kittens into the dirt so hard there wouldn't be a spot of grease left to show where they had ever existed."

Behind Antonya, Gesham burst into laughter, overhearing. Briston chuckled quietly.

"I trust you put that to him in slightly more diplomatic terms?" she said, a slow grin spreading across her face.

Vodos affected an appearance of hurt pride. "No doubt, madam, my dearest wife, a most capable and intelligent woman for whom I have the utmost respect, could have found a more elegant turn of phrase than I, but I did try my poor best."

Antonya laughed aloud. "You bastard," she said fondly.

Vodos touched his fingertips to his hat. "Your servant," he said, and spurred his horse into a trot.

They rode out of the courtyard of Lord Manauf's hunting manor, his pack of hunting dogs barking joyfully at their horses' heels in a raucous farewell.

46

Kerrick found himself in a continuously sullen mood, disgruntled by Antonya's forays about the Lands, as reckless as ever, with only Vodos and Briston and a small escort for protection. Once G'froi and Hezron had been sent packing, he and Sarnor were left behind at the fortress of Laird's Ketch to run the more tedious affairs in Adalon: the reorganization of Adalon's army, enforcing Antonya's arrangement with distant Lords for weapons and soldiers and supplies, allocating troops to patrol the tense borders between the Lands with whom she maintained a fragile truce in the south and, to the northwest, the uncertain threat from the Faith. He kept track of her only by the couriers she sent to Adalon. His heart always lightened when he saw her small, neat writing, but although her tone was always friendly, there was never anything personal in her missives.

She returned from her negotiations with Lord Manauf, exhausted and thin, but looking strangely radiant. She was constantly in the company of Briston, the man never two paces from her side. Kerrick told himself he was pleased with that; the ex-Priest had obviously proven himself to be a worthy shield to safeguard her. He ignored the laughter they shared as much as he dismissed the knowing looks and muted whispers of her armsmen.

Antonya hadn't been back in Laird's Ketch a week when Kerrick sought her out to discuss the delegates expected shortly from Ilona, a small county wedged between Adalon's northern border and the Dark Plains. An armsman directed him toward the small private orchard behind the North Tower, and Kerrick thanked him, disregarding the man's flustered hesitation.

The petals had already started to fall from the apple trees like snowflakes, floating on the late spring breeze into small drifts. He stopped in the archway of the old wall, catching sight of Briston and Antonya alone together.

They sat on the round iron bench circling the trunk of an old tree, shadows dappling their faces under the gnarled branches. Before they could spot him, Kerrick stepped back to remain unseen. Briston held her hands in his as they spoke, low voices too soft to make out. A white petal drifted into Antonya's hair, and Kerrick watched as Briston plucked it gently away. Antonya's back was to him, but he could clearly see the love in Briston's blue eyes. They made a lovely couple, Kerrick had to admit. The blond ex-Priest was a perfect physical complement for Antonya's dark red-gold beauty, the pair as becoming a match as two people in a fairy tale. Briston's finger traced a pattern on her cheek, and Kerrick forced himself to watch as Briston leaned toward her to kiss her.

Antonya's hands slipped under the ex-Priest's arms, holding him against her as she returned his embrace. Afraid he would be spotted, Kerrick slipped back the way he came and walked away calmly.

He walked out through the siege gates between the Towers, and without knowing where his feet were taking him, found himself walking up the stairways onto the ramparts. No one but the watch patrolled these walls, and they left him discreetly to himself.

Staring out over the narrow mountain pass, mists clinging to the red hills, he leaned against the stone. His fingers gripped the edge tightly, until he felt his skin scrape against the rough battlements.

He looked at his bloodied fingers in surprise. Finally, because he thought if he didn't let it out something in his chest would crack, he wept softly. He hung his head as two hot tears trailed a ragged course down his ruined face. When he looked up again, he brushed them away abruptly with the back of his hand, his eyes dry.

47

Tevik Adjer was the Chameleon. A Master Rank Assassin, he killed as he had been trained to do from earliest childhood, efficient, fast and clean. He had murdered men and women, even babies, without mercy. Most of the children had been his own Guild siblings, either emotional weaklings, or hunters gone renegade. He enjoyed killing the wild ones best, a worthy opponent giving the hunt an extra edge. Death always cleansed the latent hunger lingering within him.

At least for a while.

The Guild had sent him to Laird's Ketch to kill the Lady Antonya. Who had hired him, he neither asked nor cared. Paid assassinations were usually for revenge or politics, one indistinguishable from the other. Tevik Adjer cared little about either.

In Laird's Ketch, he was only another of any number of dull, nondescript merchants or cotters. He was not a man of many vanities, and carried few possessions. His only cherished belongings were his battered mandola and a small silver figure of a chameleon he had been given by a boyhood companion after his first kill. His knife he didn't consider a possession; it was as much a part of him as his hands or his heart.

When he arrived in Laird's Ketch, the Lady was away, constantly riding between the network of Lands she had stitched together, relentlessly threatening or cajoling the taciturn Lords into unaccustomed mutual cooperation. She stopped at every village sajada along the way, speaking until her voice gave out, resting it only until she reached the next. Her armies increased with her popularity. While she traveled with them, her troops would often wake to find her gone with only a small escort, leaving them to catch up with her. She never slept, so it was rumored, and horses were said to have dropped dead under her from the speed at which she pushed herself. He admired her energy, although that wouldn't deter him from killing her.

He charmed his way into the household of Judai, one of her women. The laundress oversaw the wash within the Lady's personal household, always grateful for another pair of hands, strong and cheap. He did the backbreaking menial work without complaint, although he was careful to fumble occasionally to allow the woman to patronize him, encouraging her tendency to mother him.

Then he waited. He had stalked prey for far too long to be reckless. He remained patient even when the situation became complicated. Judai had a younger cousin, Yadigar, a childless widow who arrived shortly after Tevik. The older woman obviously hoped Tevik might marry the girl, thus taking the burden of family responsibility off her tired shoulders.

Although Yadigar was neither plain nor stupid, she herself seemed to be content with a match to the bumbling man he presented himself to be. He had to walk a fine line between turning her down and retaining the advantage of his position in their household. If he had to, he would go through the motions of the betrothal and later abandon his would-be bride without a qualm. Meanwhile, he smiled and waffled endearingly while waiting for the opportunity to strike.

He played the mandola and sang love ballads in an unaffected voice, pleasing the women with poetry and earning his evening meal. It was the mandola which was to be the key.

He had been in Laird's Ketch a month when Antonya returned. His arms bare and covered with soapsuds, he was helping Yadigar with her share of the huge wash, exchanging small fusillades of bubbles with the giggling woman. The other attendants watched and chattered among themselves. As he ducked a handful of suds, he realized he was enjoying himself, as happy as the child he'd never been.

Judai burst into the wash-house. "Tevik," she panted excitedly, "you've said you wanted to play for the Lady Antonya. Do you still?"

It took little acting to gape like the simple-hearted man he posed as. Judai laughed and said, "Well, then, get your mandola!"

Hurriedly, he dried his arms and rolled down his sleeves.

Judai fussed over his hair and the wrinkles in his too-snug jerkin as nervously as a hen with her chick. He snatched up his mandola from by the door and trotted obediently behind her.

They crossed the barren grounds toward the high wall separating the laundry and other workshops from the Towers, gray, bleak buildings rising like bookends at either end of the low stone bastions. The inner gates stood open, the self-contained life within the fortress flowing freely between the gardens and smithies, the mill and stables. The newer, rambling brick-and-timber buildings housed resident scholars, decorated with carved columns and rainspouts, while the Guard kept their residences in the ancient stone mansion abutting the North Tower, the Lady's private residence.

As they passed through the private courtyard leading into the North Tower, he carefully noted how many guards stood watch and at which points. The Guard searched him and the woman before they were allowed inside, but were surprisingly negligent. Then again, Judai was known and he himself gave no hint of being a danger to anyone. Now wasn't the time, and he'd prudently left his killing knife behind. But he doubted such a perfunctory search would have uncovered it.

Not that it mattered that much, he knew. He could kill as easily without it, if it became necessary.

As it was, he waited nearly an hour with two armsmen. He passed the time with a few of the more ribald ditties he had picked up in soldiers' taverns to put the men at ease. They guffawed loudly, slapping their knees at the lyrics made even more comical by Tevik's rolling eyes and broad expressions. One of them, Morrel, showed his appreciation by bringing the innocuous singer a tankard of dark beer. Finally, he was allowed into the Lady's private chambers.

Lady Antonya sat behind a screen being attended by her healer, the bone-setter Guyus. Kerrick sat beside her, speaking in low tones as Judai directed Tevik to a seat near the screen. Briston stood visible at the edge of the screen, alert and suspicious. Tevik was suddenly glad he had not met the ex-Priest during the brief time he had been at the Citadel. He did not look like a man who would easily forget faces, even one as bland as Tevik's.

He busied himself with tuning the mandola while listening intently to their hushed voices carrying on a heated debate. He was skilled at playing and singing while able to listen to even barely audible sounds, and it took all his training now.

"The south is nearly secure, madam," Kerrick was saying. "And negotiations are going well with the eastern Lords. You're needed here now, in Adalon."

"But this truce is fragile," Briston argued. "Without you, too many Lords are bickering among themselves again, and what we've already united will fray."

Tevik kept his head bent over the mandola, fingers stroking the strings, adjusting the pegs to the harmonic vibrations.

"She can negotiate just as effectively through delegates, perhaps more so," the Defender countered in an oddly flat voice. "Not only do her people need her here, for you to encourage her in this mad campaign dashing from one county to the next puts her at unnecessary risk."

"I can protect her anywhere, Kerrick. She's not a stone idol to be locked up in a safe temple and worshiped from afar."

Out of the corner of his eye, Tevik watched the woman's silhouette bow its head tiredly. "Gentlemen, please," she said softly. Only the healer Guyus seemed uninterested in the dispute, his hands kneading her shoulder rhythmically. "You are both right. Yes, having finally regained my bloodrights, it would be nice if I could put down the sword and learn to govern my father's Lands. The people of Adalon deserve my fidelity to them."

"Until P'tre Terhune is dead, you will never have a secure hold on Adalon, madam," Briston warned.

"I know that as well. But however much as he hates me, P'tre is no fool. He'll wait until K'ferrin is dead. The Keeper is an old man—who knows how many years he has left? By that time, I must have the south unified into one dependable coalition, else none of us will survive P'tre's vengeance."

To ease the tension, Tevik ran his fingers lightly over the mandola's strings. He sang an old love song in his carefully manufactured country accent, choosing an ancient poem about fools in love. He sang of love and pain, and of friends divided. The archaic words half obscured by time, Tevik wondered if either the ex-Priest or the Defender understood them. His voice clear and sweet, he caught the melody with a counterpoint from his mandola with practiced ease. The restless hunger in him ached underneath the lyrics, a rhythmic power running through the music like a heartbeat.

Reluctantly, Kerrick sat back and the Lady listened quietly, the outline of her head tilted slightly. When the last strain had died away, Tevik's fingers strummed the mandola's strings idly.

The shadow of the lady's hand slid across the screen. She stood, her healer helping her pull the linen robe over her wounded shoulder. Tevik kept his head down like the humble country poetmonger he pretended to be as she stepped from around the screen, tying the robe around her waist.

Tevik was a practical man, with little belief in the Faith, and even less in the Weird. Salt thrown into hearths or thistles nailed over barn doors only amused him. But he wasn't prepared when he looked up into Antonya's pale wolf-yellow eyes. The shock leapt through him, making him feel suddenly naked and exposed, the Weird in her blood calling to him, summoning back its own. He froze, his heart shuddering with an inexplicable fear.

"Who are you?" she asked.

"I am called Tevik of Adarathea, Lady," he said, not having to feign the respect and tremor in his voice.

"Adarathea is quite some distance," she said noncommittally. "To the east, is it not?"

"Aye, Lady. I've traveled a great deal."

Kerrick was now standing behind her, towering over her. The ex-Priest stood to one side, glaring while his hand rested on his knife hilt, the same habit of all Terhune's Elite.

"As have I. Your song was . . . very pretty. Where did you learn to sing Dothinian poetry so well, Tevik of Adarathea?"

Sweat trickled down the inside of his shirt. "I had a master from Roixara, Lady. He taught me lyrics for many of the cantos popular with the southern courts, and I've heard you enjoy them."

She raised an eyebrow. "Have you indeed?" she said blandly. Tevik wondered if he'd been too clever and outsmarted himself.

Kerrick stirred restlessly. Tevik glanced at him. The man's

features had been burned into inscrutable hideousness, a permanent daemon mask. Even for an Assassin as skilled as Tevik, he knew this was still a man to be feared.

Then, to his relief, the Lady smiled and turned away.

"You may go," Kerrick said curtly. Antonya disappeared behind the screen, followed by Guyas and Briston. Tevik stood, knees trembling as he bowed. He managed to find the door, mandola hanging awkwardly in his hand. Judai snatched his arm as he exited the room, pulling him away as the guards snickered behind him.

He didn't care, wondered briefly if he should have, or at least gone through the motions of glaring at them. Judai watched him wipe the sweat from his forehead with a shaking hand, misinterpreting it. "I'm sure you did well," she said sympathetically.

Alone, he paced the tiny corner room above the kitchen barely large enough for his rolled pallet, bare feet padding back and forth with the driven energy of a caged leopard. He dissected every move, every glance, replaying every word over and again, examining them methodically. He could kill the ex-Priest without much difficulty and knew he could probably even take Kerrick, if he struck first and went for the big man before the others. The Lady herself would have been no challenge at all; he could snuff out her life as easily as pinching wet fingers against a lit candlewick. But instead, the incident had left him shaking and uncertain, and he was more frightened of the woman than either of the two men.

When he finally managed to sleep, Tevik dreamed of wolves, pale eyes outlined in black like the kohl-ringed eyes of a courtesan. He saw himself running with them, knife in hand, face drenched in blood. He saw the Guilds destroyed, the Priests fall, the Oracular City in flames, the Citadel itself pulled down into ruins. Freedom, glory, a blazing phoenix of destruction. He saw on a hilltop a regal wolf bitch with shaggy white fur, sharp teeth behind the panting black lips. One leg had become snared in a hunter's trap, a trap not of steel but delicate silken cord, as red as the blood dripping from her paw where she had been worrying it loose. As he approached cautiously with his knife, meaning to free her, she turned, her eyes blazing golden, and with a snarl like wild laughter, she leapt for his throat . . .

He woke with a start, drenched in sweat. He understood the dream, knowing the Weird had spoken to him, knowing what he was meant to do. When he came down in the morning, he put on his humble face, apologizing sweetly for his rude manners. Judai obviously still hoped to hear sajada bells ring out his marriage to Yadigar. But when he glanced up at Yadigar, her round childlike face studied him soberly.

That night she came to his tiny room.

He rolled over as the door creaked open, seeing her outline through her thin gown in the light behind her. When she had come close enough for him to make out her features, she was gazing at him with the calm of a woman hurt before.

"You're leaving," she said.

He was surprised she knew, but kept his irritation to himself. It was impossible for him to feel sorry for her; he had lost that ability too long ago.

"Yes," he said. "I must."

He was grateful she didn't ask for explanations, but annoyed when she lay down on the narrow pallet next to him, her cool hand on his arm, and kissed him. He pulled away from her gently.

"Yadigar, I'm a wanderer, I can't change that. I don't want to hurt you, you deserve someone much better . . ." he said, then stopped as he saw the slow smile on her face, a callous, knowing look.

"If you are leaving," she said, her voice low, "you haven't time enough for all the tiresome stupid lies I've heard before."

His irritation gave way to a grudging respect which, surprisingly, aroused him. Taking her hand, he kissed her palm while watching her face. Behind the mask of innocence, her eyes were as hard as steel. He wondered how he could have missed her strength, and realized he'd never really taken the time to know this woman. He had simply accepted at face value her docile compassion as being weakness.

She pressed him down against the pallet with her sturdy washerwoman's arms, and he yielded, feeling her strong legs entwine with his own. His tongue slid into her mouth, and he whimpered softly when she unexpectedly bit it, holding him

trapped gently with her teeth. His throat constricted as he submitted to the pulse of her desire. The hunger in him leaped,
and he wondered if she, too, had the same fire in her soul.

As her hands slid down to pin him by his wrists, he let
himself relish the sudden vulnerability, letting go of the camouflage he had wrapped around himself so tightly. It fell away
with a sudden rush of freedom. He heard himself making small
animal sounds of sensual torment as she slipped him inside
her, her heat stabbing through his groin with almost intolerable
pleasure. His back arced as she rode him, her eyes dilated with
greed and lust. His heart shuddered against his ribs, his hips
meeting hers spontaneously.

Pleasure and pain had always been two sides of the same
coin for him. It was impossible to spend one while hoarding
the other. He stared into her slitted eyes, and as if she could
read his silent entreaty, she crushed herself against him. He
felt the sharp bite of her nails digging painfully into the flesh
of his buttocks, felt her shudder and cry out against his ear.
The hunger sang as he slammed violently against her, bone
hammering against bone, a long, endlessly deep thrust as he
came forever.

Later, she lay with her head cradled in the curve of his
shoulder, sleeping peacefully. Through the narrow window, he
watched the night sky lighten with the coming dawn. Her
warm, even breath tickled the hairs on his chest. Drawing aim-
less patterns on the smooth skin of her arm, he tried not to
think, and failed.

He couldn't disobey his orders. His Guild would turn
against him and hunt him down with the same ruthlessness
he'd been trained to use in pursuing his own victims. But he
was one of their best; it was possible to elude them.

For a while.

He dressed quickly, his back to her. As he sat on the edge
of the pallet to pull on his boots, he felt her nails softly rake
the bare skin along his spine. He froze, his breath caught in
his throat, and let the shiver travel through him. Then he
slipped his shirt over his head, standing to tuck it into his
breeches as he stared at her.

She was sitting up, knees to her chest, bare arms wrapped
around the woolen blanket. She said nothing as he shrugged

into his jerkin, threw the few personal items he had in the room into his small pack, and picked up his mandola case. She would not weep, no womanly subterfuge to make him stay. But for some inexplicable reason, he felt he owed her more.

"If I could . . ." he started, then stopped.

She angled her head to regard him with something like amusement. "Go," she said simply.

He paused at the door for only a moment before he left.

He picked his way through the predawn grayness, the old corridors of the fortress bone-cold. Wisps of fog that clung to the nearly deserted grounds swirled in his passing footsteps as he headed for the Towers. A light burned yellow in one of the barbicans of the North Tower, the Lady Antonya in the old study with her books and manuscripts. Within the hour, her women would bring her first meal as the rest of the household slowly stirred to life.

Briston would only now be rising from the bed he shared with the Lady Antonya. The guards were surprised to see Tevik up so early, but he was known; Morrel remembered him, even greeting him affably. He was only Tevik the poetmonger, a harmless, timid bard with his battered case and small mandola no threat. The weapons search was casual and almost apologetic. His killing knife, a flat blade nearly as thin as wire, was concealed in the mandola case and the guards missed it completely. He knew after tonight there would never be another search as lax as this.

The guard hailed the ex-Priest in hushed tones fitting the early morning stillness. He came to the door, hair unkempt. He peered at the Assassin with sleep-reddened eyes.

"What do you want, Tevik?" he asked, his voice not yet awake. He was tying his robe with a red silken cord. Tevik stared at it, breathing shallowly to ease his awe before he could go on. He was now convinced the Weird had guided him here, and confirmed his purpose.

"Only a few moments of your time, sir," Tevik said in a tone carefully hinting at an urgency.

Briston scowled, then, ill-natured, waved him inside. The guard shut the door, leaving him alone with the ex-Priest. Tevik tried to see Briston as the Lady herself might: a young man unaware of his own sensuality. Cold blue eyes glared at the musician, a shock of blond hair straying across his forehead. Gold highlights from the unshaven stubble on the man's square jaw, the long neck well set on sturdy shoulders. He felt the vitality of Briston's life with almost tactile awareness, the passion, the joy, the depth of his love for her.

"Well, get on with it, man," Briston snapped.

As Tevik placed his mandola down on a table, he slipped the killing knife out of the case and into his sleeve. "May it please my Lord, I beg leave to ask a few questions . . ."

The ex-Priest was many things, but not a fool. "All right, Tevik. Let's drop the 'by-your-leaves' and 'beg your pardons,' shall we? Ask your questions. Then you'd better have a damned good reason for disturbing me this early in the morning."

Tevik glanced out the window, noting the sun was still below the horizon, and licked dry lips. He began pacing himself like a long-distance runner, feeling the passing time slide by him, heartbeat by heartbeat. "You were once not only one of Terhune's Elite, but part of his inner circle."

Startled, Briston's eyes narrowed. "Aye," he said sharply. "What of it?"

"Only that Terhune recruited his best from his own family."

Briston looked puzzled for a moment before he snorted in disgust. "Have you come to lecture me on the sins of incest, Tevik? Allow me to spare you any conflict you may have with your conscience. I am no blood relation to P'tre Terhune, and thus no kin to the Lady Antonya. Now, unless you have a better excuse, I'm about to pick you up by the seat of your insolent breeches and toss you out of here." Briston stalked toward the door to summon the guard.

"I've come to warn you," Tevik said quickly, "Lady Antonya is in grave danger."

That stopped him, the simplest of ruses, as Tevik knew it would. Briston whirled on him. "From who? Terhune?"

Old habit clicked into place and he let himself ride the hunger licking greedily along his veins. For the first time in his life, Tevik didn't disdain his victim's emotions as mere weaknesses to be exploited. He watched Briston with a strange fascination, just now able to comprehend the lack in his own soul.

He explored the cavity like a tongue rubbing against the empty socket of a missing tooth.

The Assassin allowed himself to back up, as if afraid, toward the balconied window as Briston stalked him, blind to his peril. Tevik could see the effort the man made not to grab him by the throat. "Speak, man! What do you mean? Danger from where?"

The sun broke over the horizon, sending a shower of brilliant light through the open window. Tevik turned and gasped hoarsely. Instantly, Briston was by his side as the Assassin inhaled a single, purifying breath, every fiber poised and ready. The ex-Priest craned his neck to peer down, searching for whatever danger Tevik had seen, his attention no longer on the inoffensive little man beside him.

Time slowed as Tevik's knife floated effortlessly in his hand, a flawless arc seeking its own path. It sliced cleanly through the space between the first cervical vertebra and the foramen magnum, bending slightly as it met resistance. He twisted his wrist and the wire-thin blade slipped up into the brain, destroying the vital life centers. Then in less than a heartbeat he whipped the knife out clean, leaving Briston instantly dead on his feet. Tevik caught the body before it fell and guided it back into a chair. A perfect kill.

"Here, sir," he said quietly to the corpse.

It was done. He had broken the chain that ensnared the wolf bitch. He had done as the Weird had required of him, and sacrificed his Guild and his life to obey. Now he would go . . . where? It didn't matter. His usefulness to the Guild, even to the Weird, was over. His freedom stretched in front of him for as far as he could see, and he was as happy and as frightened as a small child.

Briston's face held no other expression than a last look of inquiry, his death too fast for pain. The wound was tiny; all that leaked from it now were the clear fluids of the spine with a thin trail of capillary blood already thickening into a clot. Tevik tucked the man's robe around his shoulders, hiding the wound, and arranged his hands and feet, leaving the eyes gazing unseeingly into the sunrise.

Tevik methodically cleaned his knife. It was a Guild knife, but he was no longer of the Guild. He allowed himself a twinge of regret as he laid it gently on a small table by the corpse. He fished one finger into the inside pocket of his jerkin and withdrew the small silver chameleon, warmed by the heat of his body. He gazed into its jeweled eyes before he set the talisman down carefully on the table beside his knife.

He looked over the corpse once more, satisfied with his execution, then picked up his mandola and went to the door. The guard peered in at Briston's upright body staring out the window as if lost in thought. Tevik slipped through the barely open door and shut it with exaggerated quiet. "He's asked for a few moments alone," he explained in a stage whisper. "He'll call you when he's ready."

For a few terrified moments as he walked casually away, keeping his back to the guards, Tevik was certain that they would check on the dead man and discover his ruse. But as he turned a corner, he allowed himself a quick glance back, relieved to see that the guards still stood by the closed door.

He walked faster, keeping his pace slow enough not to attract attention, breathing a little easier as he passed through the wide halls of the gallery, out along the walks that bordered the old armories to the inner gates of the fortress. He retrieved his small traveling pack from where he'd hidden it in the crumbling walls behind the fountain just inside the siege walls of the Great Gate. It felt weightless, his mandola case swinging freely, as he walked with light feet nearly skimming the ground. He had never felt more alive and satisfied after a killing.

Love had been the trap. With love murdered, there would be war. The Lady herself might not have understood, but the Weird living within her knew what had to be done. He allowed himself the small conceit that he was the pivot on which the future had turned. The perfect servant of the Weird, he had been the unknown element that would free the wolf bitch and set the Lands on fire in a cleansing blaze from horizon to horizon. He nearly laughed aloud.

Just outside the City Gates, a hand grasped his shoulder lightly. He spun around in alarm. "Yadigar!"

From beneath the heavy shawl covering her head, the woman studied him with a neutral expression. "Briston is dead," she said quietly.

He stared in dread, his whole being shrieking in panic and defeat. How could they have known so quickly? Why hadn't he seen she was his executioner? How foolish he had been to think himself so clever he could defy his Guild. He wanted to weep in frustration, knowing now he would never live to see the results of his work.

"Yes," he said abjectly. His hands hung limp by his sides as he waited submissively for her to kill him.

"Take me with you," she said.

He blinked, the ice in his veins just beginning to thaw. "What?"

"They will be looking for a man alone, not a man with a wife." Her voice was flat. But his brain had started working again.

Of course she was not an Assassin; he should have known better. She was simply a naturally ruthless woman who wanted out of her cramped dull life as badly as he had craved freedom from the harsh servitude in his Guild.

He also realized she was right. Together, it would buy him time, time he desperately needed. He knew they would be good for each other, two people very much alike, and looked at her with new respect and admiration. His heart filled with an unexpected warmth, and a hard lump in his throat made it impossible for him to speak. This was his reward, the Weird thanking him for his sacrifice. He squeezed her hand gently, tears in his eyes as he raised it to his lips and kissed her fingers.

If she became a hindrance, he could always kill her later.

They fled Laird's Ketch, never to be seen again.

48

The frantic knock woke Kerrick, Tobias flinging the door open before he'd walked halfway across the room. Behind him, Daen stood in the dim light of the anteroom, one hand clutching the jamb for support, his face ashen.

"Briston's dead," he said without preamble before either Tobias or Kerrick could speak. "Murdered."

Kerrick let the cold rush of dismay pass before he asked, "Does Antonya know?"

Daen shook his head mutely.

"I'll tell her," Kerrick said, to the obvious relief of the young armsman. He buckled on his sword, and threw his short furred cloak around his shoulders. "How?" he demanded shortly, as the trio strode toward the passageway leading to the North Tower. He took the narrow spiral staircase two steps at a time, Daen and Tobias on his heels.

"The last man to see him was that poetmonger, Tevik," Tobias said, slightly out of breath as he raced to keep up with the big man's pace. "Just before dawn."

"Where the Hell were his guards?"

"Outside. Morrell and S'ashab. They never heard a thing. Tevik came out, said Briston would call when he required them. It got too quiet, and when there was no response to their queries, they went in and found him."

Armsmen swarmed in muted uproar around the doors leading into Antonya's private quarters, plainly waiting for Kerrick. He cursed, his lips pulled back in a grotesque snarl. Daen blanched.

"Where are Morrell and S'ashab now?" Kerrick snapped as he pushed his way through and into Antonya's private chamber.

"Downstairs with the Guard."

Shoving the armsmen aside, he stalked angrily into the room. The morning sun blazed a gold column of light through the window into the chamber. The tapestry around the bed had been pulled back, bedclothes rumpled. Briston sat in a chair, his head now lolling onto his chest, staring sightlessly into his lap. Kerrick examined the tiny wound at the base of his neck, blond hair darkened and still damp from leaking fluid. His body was still warm.

"Has anything been touched?" he asked quietly, staring intently at the dead man.

"Only this," Daen said, and handed him a small silver figure. "It was found with a knife on the table next to his body."

Kerrick held it to the light, almost lifelike in his huge palm. It was a lizard, but unlike his own. Finely detailed, tiny distinct scales rippled on its metal skin. Small green eyes in its flat, horned skull stared at him spitefully, polished cabochon emeralds reflecting the sunlight. As if in sympathetic response, he felt his own lizard stir under his shirt, tiny nails hooked against his skin.

He glanced at the slender knife on the table, the strange small blade whip-thin, its black hilt unadorned.

He frowned. "And the poetmonger?"

"Gone, sir." The answer didn't surprise him. "We've closed the gates and sent out soldiers to search the streets . . ."

"He's long out of the city by now," Kerrick said, and folded his hand around the silver figure. "You won't catch him."

Daen nodded. They both recognized the Chameleon's device. That he had abandoned it for them to find spoke for itself.

The sudden hush of voices outside the room warned Kerrick, and he was out the door within a second. Antonya was looking down from the spiral stairway at the gathering of nervous, silent armsmen. She held a book in one hand, her finger still tucked into the pages to mark her place. Her eyes met Kerrick's, and she suddenly paled, understanding.

In the thin linen night robe, her hair falling in loose waves around her face, she seemed far more fragile than Kerrick knew her to be. Her expression didn't change as she calmly descended the rest of the stairway. Her armsmen made way for her as she stepped in front of Kerrick, looking up at him.

"Briston?" she asked, her voice clear and steady.

"Dead, madam." She stood very still, her gaze sliding to look into the room behind the Defender. After a long moment, she nodded. "An Assassin," Kerrick added, and held up the silver figure.

She stared at it disinterestedly, then walked past him into the bedchamber. Daen looked at the Defender, nervously waiting for instructions.

"Get everyone out of here," Kerrick said in an undertone. "There'll be enough panic and confusion—get your guards out, calm people down. Keep the gates closed, and continue the search, but do it quietly. Understand?"

"Aye, sir."

As Daen began clearing out Antonya's private rooms, Kerrick went back into the bedchamber, closing the door behind him. Antonya stood, not touching the body, simply looking at Briston slouched awkwardly on the chair, one hand hanging limply by his side.

"He looks uncomfortable," she said finally in a deceptively placid voice.

Immediately, Kerrick strode to lift the body from the chair and lay it out on the bed, adjusting the dead man's robes around his legs. Briston's hands were now cold, the nails blue, as Kerrick arranged them across his chest, then gently closed the dead man's eyes. When he straightened, Antonya was gazing out the window, still holding the book with her finger inserted between its pages.

"I thought he'd come for me," she said, her voice still composed.

"You knew?" Kerrick said in surprise.

"Not that he was an Assassin. But I'd heard that song before. P'tre Terhune sang it to me, in the Citadel."

"Why didn't you say something?" Kerrick tried to keep his voice gentle, despite his anger. "We could have killed him on the spot!" He bit back adding that Briston might still be alive.

"I assumed it was merely a taunt, not a threat. But if Tevik was an Assassin, why didn't he kill me?"

Kerrick looked down at the figure in his hand. "The Chameleon is well-known," he said. She turned, the light behind her throwing her face into shadow. He held up the silver lizard. "He would never have left this or his Guild knife behind. He's gone renegade, and wanted you to know it."

She glanced at the silver figure. "Then why kill Briston?"

"I don't know."

She nodded, then glanced down at her book, as if remembering she still held it. Deliberately, she slipped the ribbon between the pages, and closed the book before setting it down on the table, just beside the knife. Kerrick glanced at it, then her, but she appeared not to have noticed the weapon.

"I want someone here from the Assassins Guild within the week to explain it to me, Kerrick."

He looked at her speculatively. "They may not respond," he warned her.

She turned, looking at the body in the bed. "Oh, they'll respond," she said, and the ice in her voice made the hair on his neck prickle. "I'd like to be alone with him now, please."

He gave her a short bow, then turned away. As he closed the door behind him, he heard her first strangled moan. Daen stood at a distance, waiting uneasily, and it took Kerrick several hard swallows against the sudden ache in his throat before he could speak.

"We've got work to do," he said, and clapped the younger man gently on the shoulder.

49

Birds sang, and she wondered how they could be so blindly stupid to go on chirping away while all around them was hatred and despair and death. She knew, of course: Birds had no interest in the affairs of men, no more than she would weep for the sparrow caught by the fox. All the same, she hated the birds for singing.

Standing on the hill in the cold sunshine, it was as if she had never left, even while everything around her was both achingly familiar and horribly deformed. The wind snapped at her linen veil as she stared down at the monastery. The gray stone of the sajada still stood, although the domed roof had caved in. The slender towers were empty, their bronze bells gone. The dry cables of ivy covering the buttressed dorter she had played around as a child were just beginning to send out new shoots to dress the walls in their annual greenery.

There was the kitchen, all the chimneys still standing, but no welcoming smoke carrying the smell of fresh bread. And there was Brother Hasuq's forge, memory supplying the ring of hammer against glowing iron. And there, fallen down and abandoned, were the goat pens. Where were Mee Mee and Yoo Yoo now? Gone wild in the forest to breed without Brother

Alban's loving touch? Or someone's forgotten dinner and discarded bones?

And there. Like the desecrated corpse of an old friend, Father Andrae's library lay in ruins, one wall collapsing in a tumble of stone to expose the interior. The roof had burned, leaving only the lattice of black charred beams. The glazed windows were now square holes like the brow ridge of a staring skull, the face missing. Everything was black inside, black and burnt and empty.

In the center of the claustral garden, three charred piles of ash and wood stood out in stark relief from the spring grass, tiny flowers bobbing their heads in the breeze.

She heard a man's cheerful whistling, hating him as well as the birds for his callousness. His tune broke off as he rounded the small copse. She turned away from the ruins of the monastery to stare at him, unmoving; a fisherman, heavy-bearded with a thick knit cap over his ears, wooden clogs on his feet, oiled padded vest around his barrel chest. He squinted, shielding his eyes from the sunlight.

"Antonya?" he called up hesitantly.

She couldn't respond. She knew the voice, but her eyes told her it was not possible it could be Brother Alban. Standing rigidly in her novice's white habit, she knew she looked more like the ghost she had thought him to be. She watched him grin, then break into a lumbering trot as he hurried toward her.

He stopped an arm's length from her, his smile trembling as his eyes reddened, unsure of what to do. He raised his arms as if to hug her, then let them drop limply by his side when she made no move. She regarded him as dispassionately as if she had been carved out of ice before she turned to stare at the ruins of the monastery below.

"What happened?" she demanded softly.

She heard him sigh. "They found us. It was bound to happen sooner or later."

"Terhune?"

Out of the corner of her eye she saw him shrug. "Not in person. Perhaps he stayed on board his ship. A Purge this inconsequential doesn't require the great man's presence."

He shifted his stance, uncomfortable with her silence.

"Most of us got away. Brother Reule and I are living in Sias. The village hid us after the Purge. When the Priests came *looking, the fisherfolk all vouched for us as villagers, no one to prove them otherwise. A man had drowned and his widow took me in. Swore with her hand on the sajada altar I was her dead husband."* Brother Alban flushed with embarrassment. *"It's hard for a widow with children, no man to feed the family. Worth the risk, I suppose. I took his profession along with his name and wife, grateful to do it, too."*

She simply stared at him silently as he fumbled on, unnerved.

"The hardest part was getting over the seasickness, but I'm not doing too badly at it. Her boys and I made enough from our last catch to buy a new net, and the mainland farmers do good trade with us for vegetables. Brother Reule's set up shop with a lame man, teaching him the trade. With two of them to do the doctoring . . ."

She turned away from him abruptly. He sighed.

"We're still monks, Antonya. We're just waiting for better times before we can return. We will come back, I swear it. Look—" He gestured at the ruins below, his nails cracked and filthy in the fingerless glove. *"Rebuild a couple of walls, put in some roofs, take maybe three months and we'd be back just as before, you'd never know the difference."* He tried to smile.

"Who burned?" Her words came out evenly, clear and hard.

"Brother Sholto," he said reluctantly. She shut her eyes for a moment, the fat cook's face laughing in her memory. Then the image was gone. *"He never could run very quickly,"* Brother Alban said.

She waited in stony silence. *"Who else?"* she demanded finally.

He sniffed, wiping his red nose on the back of his thick knit gloves. *"Brother Migius. Although he didn't feel a thing. He was already dead before they put him to the flame."*

She glanced at him, watching tears run down his red chapped face, wondering why she could not cry as well. *"The leprosy got worse this past winter, and finally he had to take to his bed. He was in good cheer right up to the end, forever making jokes. We'd taken to leaving a tincture of belladonna next to him, in case it got too bad. He claimed he felt no pain, it was only the inconvenience of having bits and pieces of himself fall off that bothered him. When they came for him, all they found was an empty bottle and an empty corpse."*

She felt that if she didn't ask she would fall down on her knees and never get up again. "Father Andrae?" It didn't sound like her own voice, but some creature of the Weird growling through her throat.

He didn't answer for a long moment. "He wouldn't leave his books, Antonya," Brother Alban said gently. "He refused to run, no matter how we begged him. He just sat reading in his study, knowing all the time the boats were coming."

She looked at him numbly as he began to weep, his voice strangled with the effort to get the words out. "Most of us got to the cover of the woods where Terhune's men couldn't catch us. We knew the forest, they didn't. After one of their men broke his leg in a fox trap, they gave it up. But we could see them as they burned Father Andrae with his own books, made a big pyre out of them especially for him."

The monk rubbed the back of his gloved hands across his moist eyes, then blew his nose on his sleeve. He sniffled wetly, looking down at the dead funeral pyres. "He was a brave man, Antonya. He didn't struggle when they tied him to the stake. Even their captain admired his dignity. You should have seen the look on his face when Father Andrae absolved him before they set the fires. And when Father Andrae was calling out for Brother Sholto to breathe in the smoke so as to kill himself more quickly before the flames could burn him, the captain ordered his men to throw green wood and fresh cut branches on the fire to make it smoke even more." Brother Alban's voice was hoarse with hate and derision. "Father Andrae thanked him. He thanked him."

The monk buried his face in his hands, unable to go on.

She listened to him weep, a great pressure rising up within her.

"You never sent word to the Sisters," she said quietly.

His hands dropped away, and he sucked in a ragged breath. "No. I didn't dare. Father Andrae's last words to me were to praise God, he was an old man and could die content knowing you were safe."

Something burst deep within her, pain welling up like water bursting through a small spring. "Did he . . . did Father Andrae ever tell you . . . who I am? Who my parents were?" She watched his face with dread, examining him for any sign that he knew the truth.

If Brother Alban knew, he kept it to himself. "All he ever said was that you were a child of God, blessed by the Holy Mother. What higher lineage could anyone ever wish for?"

She couldn't hold it back any longer, the grief in her throat making horrible grunting noises, like a wounded animal. She shuddered violently, and when Brother Alban wrapped his arms tightly around her, she cried out in pain, tears streaming down her face.

50

Even if the workman had not kept his eyes meekly downcast, no one would have noticed their unusual color, a dark blue almost violet. The high-caste monks strolling the halls of Philoniah's Sector ignored him completely as he bowed diligently to everyone he passed.

The tools in the leather pack slung across his shoulder slapped his back gently in rhythm with his footsteps. He stopped before a doorway, hitching his workbelt up from his narrow hips, and checked a small piece of paper against the address. The guards standing duty by the doorway watched him with disinterest.

"I've been summoned to inspect my Lord's baths," he said respectfully. The guard examined his paper, sneering in contempt at the workman's patched and stained green tunic. It hung shapelessly over well-worn leather breeches, a heavy leather belt also drooping with the weight of tools fastened around his waist.

Finally, the guard knocked on the door. A maid appeared. "You're late," she snapped. "You were expected hours ago."

Although he was a common laborer, as a city-bred free man with enough Ameveth blood to entitle him to wear the clan's green he outranked a mere servant, but not significantly so for the woman to pay any notice. Certainly not the servant of a high official. "Wipe your feet," she admonished before she would allow him in.

He dutifully scraped the soles of his boots against the block of stone before he followed her inside. He looked around with interest. The apartment for an important if midlevel minister, it was elegant without being palatial, stately rather than sumptuous. Rich incense sweetened the air, somewhere a caged songbird trilled. Soft wool carpets muffled footsteps. Ornamental paintings hung on paneled walls, burnished rosewood with gilt trim. The maid caught his look. "We hope you can make repairs without too much damage to the paneling. It is very old and rare, it would be a shame."

He kept any reaction to the servant's proprietary attitude off his face, making only a noncommittal sound as she led him into the Lord's bath. The floor was made of polished marble, with two curving steps around a tub large enough for an entire family. Behind the bath, five slender columns rose into delicate arches, balanced chandeliers overhead. The candles were out, the tub empty, only a chalky white ring of dried scum around the stone, and greenish streaks of corrosion running down from the brass fixtures.

He dropped his tools casually onto the floor, letting the leather pack slide off his shoulder. The maidservant winced as it thudded, but said nothing. He was already on his knees, rump in the air as he pressed an ear to the side of the tub, tapping with his grimy fingernails. He ran one finger against the dark smudge in the corner, rubbing the dirt between thumb and forefinger before he sniffed at it.

"Is that him?" someone barked from the outer room. The workman sat up on his knees as the Lord stomped into the bath. The workman and the servant both made cursory bows. "I'm a very busy man, you. I can ill afford the disturbance, so I assume this will not take too long?"

"I shall do my best, my Lord," the workman murmured. "I beg leave to inspect your hypocaust, if I may."

The servant started to speak before the Lord cut her off impatiently. "Oh, for God's sake, woman, I'm perfectly capable of telling him what needs doing," he said. "Go make yourself useful. Haven't you anything else to do?"

The maidservant glared, not overly intimidated. Dark-haired and plump, pretty despite being past her childbearing years, no doubt her relationship with the monk was more intimate than the usual servant's.

She muttered, "Of *course*, my Lord," with ill grace and

walked away with injured pride. The workman watched her go, his violet eyes crinkling with amusement. He remained kneeling on the floor as the monk settled onto the lip of the tub. They waited until the woman was well out of hearing.

"Master," the monk said to the workman. His surly demeanor vanished, replaced by deference and anxiety. The man in the shabby green tunic barely nodded. "There's been an incident."

"What sort of incident?" the workman asked, his tone mild.

"Your man failed."

The workman exhaled in masked dismay. "Failed? Is he dead?"

"Not that I know, although he will be soon if he isn't already."

The workman absorbed this, the implications distressing. He glanced at the monk, the look inquiry enough.

"The man Briston was murdered."

"Unfortunate." As well as a puzzle.

As a senior Guildmaster, he'd argued strongly against the assassination. He much prefered equilibrium to disorder; the removal of the Terhune woman might have unfavorable repercussions. But once outvoted, he had accepted responsibility for assigning his own agent, completely trusting the man. If Tevik had bungled the job, it would rebound badly on him. *Very* badly. But why would one of their best trained men suddenly go renegade for no apparent reason?

The workman found he was more intrigued than worried, already weighing who would fall and who would profit. He wondered how probable it was he'd be ordered to take his own life as punishment, and saw the same uncertainty mirrored in the monk's eyes. The monk hesitated.

"And?" the workman prompted.

"She's sent word to the Guild. She demands we deliver an explanation within the week."

The workman raised an eyebrow. " 'Demands'?" He nearly laughed. "How interesting." Then again, he speculated, it wasn't unreasonable. She might be owed more than just an explanation.

The monk cleared his throat, plainly reluctant. "It's rumored the Weird is protecting her," he said tentatively. He cut off any further speculation as the workman scowled.

"You should have sense enough not to fall prey to the same superstitious rubbish we use ourselves to spread respect for the Guild among the ignorant. I'll hear no more drivel about the Weird."

The monk nodded, chastened. "But what should we do, Master?"

The workman stood, tugging his breeches up around the narrow bones of his hips. "We should go look at your hypocaust."

The hypocaust under the bath connected to the kitchen ovens. The fires had been damped, although the bricks were still warm from the morning's baking. The workman slithered into the tight space on his back, a candle in one hand. The brickwork seemed solid, no cracks in the masonry, no hidden fractures in the overhead foundation. He pushed himself farther along by his heels, looking for the pipes, his nostrils filled with the smell of dust and mouse droppings and mold.

He found them, as well as a large puddle of water. It soaked instantly into the back of his tunic as he hitched along the damp floor, the candle throwing a wan yellow light barely bright enough to see by. He hummed to himself, a toneless tune, and let his work-roughed hands skim the pipes, feeling what he could not see.

They were old, far older than the bath above, and no matter how well they had been made, nothing lasts forever. Wood rots. Clay breaks. Metal corrodes. Nothing could stand against the infinitely flexible strength of water, the violence of ice and steam, the might of rivers and rain. The workman meditated as his hands explored the damage water had inflicted on a long dead craftsman's best efforts to bend it to his will. He pondered water and time, seeing the solid walls pressing claustrophobically around him as fluid as water.

Buildings sprang up like mushrooms after a spring shower. Constant renovations made them elastic, altered through the centuries as needs changed, to be finally abandoned and driven into ruins and dust by the elements, vanishing into the ground under the onslaught of rain. The man-made structures blotting the face of the earth were as insubstantial as mist; only the brevity of a man's life made his edifices seem solid and eternal.

We are all the creation of water, soft bodies conceived in the water of lust. We are ghosts, believing in the illusion that we are solid. We are individuals, we count, we matter, these specks of fragile temporary life insist. We spend our lives trying to defeat the water constantly trying to escape us, rejoin with itself. Then we die and become only hard, dry bits of leather and bones as our water seeps away. Only water is eternal.

That was what the workman contemplated as he lay on his back in the dank, chill water oozing through his shirt and dripping into his eyes. He crawled the entire length of the hypocaust, examining every segment of pipe before he inched his way back out into the light and air. And he knew what had to be done. He stood up, pulling the filthy wet shirt away from the skin of his back and shook it.

The monk watched him quietly, waiting. The workman knew he would never dare be imprudent enough to question his Guildmaster twice.

"I must confer with my superiors," the workman lied. It was always best to implicate a power above one's head. To muddy the waters. The monk nodded, not at all reassured.

The workman slung his gear over his shoulder, ignoring the water dripping from his hair down his collar. He scratched the stubble on his face idly. "By the way, your water pipes are just about completely shot, the metal's corroded through. They haven't been replaced in decades. Mice have eaten half the plaster between the brick supports and you've got dry rot riddled all through the foundation. Amazing the whole wall hasn't toppled over already."

"Really?" The monk's expression was one of unfeigned worry.

"I'd suggest you not try another hot bath or you'll likely end up with a flood in your nice apartment and your fancy marble tub caving in the floor underneath you."

The monk leaned down to peek into the gloomy depths of the hypocaust, a pointless effort since he couldn't possibly see the damage. "Can it be fixed?" He genuinely seemed more anxious over the fragile state of his plumbing than the fragile state of the Guild.

The workman smiled, dark violet eyes distant. "Oh, yes," he said, speaking more to himself, "I think it can."

51

The arrival of the Assassins Guild emissary was quietly announced to Kerrick. He sent the messenger off to notify Antonya to meet him in her private chambers. When she arrived, he was alarmed to see how pale her face was, her eyes shadowed. She wore only a day robe, her arms bare, the skin white where the sheaths blocked it from the sun. He wondered where her twin throwing knives were.

"Lady," he breathed angrily, whispering for her alone, "it is not well for you to be meeting this man unarmed."

"I'm not," she said, and placed her hand against his arm.

Kerrick snarled, but let it go.

She sat in a large chair by the fireplace, no flames to warm the chilled room, Kerrick standing by her side. Tobias and Nicoli escorted a small, unimposing man accompanied by two other men. An entire flank of Antonya's armsmen surrounded them, weapons at the ready. Kerrick did not feel comfortable having a private meeting with Assassins. Even with only three and stripped of their weapons, his nerves were taut.

Boots clicked across the stone floor in the empty silence. The group stopped well out of range in front of Antonya. Kerrick placed his arm across the back of her chair, leaning with an indifference he didn't feel. The emissary had dressed for the occasion, a sea-green velvet robe with a flash of dark violet undercoat when he moved, a heavy, ornate silver chain draped from shoulder to shoulder across his chest. *Very pretty,* Kerrick thought wryly. His companions were attired in less opulent, black dress. The emissary smiled cheerfully, and bowed in a sweeping courtly gesture bordering on mockery.

"My name is Pajen," he said, his voice pleasant. He gestured toward one of his nondescript companions, who bowed less formally. "My aide, Stephalo." He didn't introduce the third man. He straightened, still smiling benignly. "As you requested, I am here as an official representative of the Assassins Guild."

Antonya produced the small figure of the chameleon from a pocket and tossed it lightly to the emissary. He caught it with a practiced hand, his eyes never leaving her face.

"My man Briston was murdered by your Guild," Antonya said, her voice venomous. "I want to know why."

"An unfortunate accident, Lady Antonya. We offer you our sincere condolences."

"I don't give a damn for your condolences," she said coldly. "I want to know who hired you murdering bastards."

Kerrick had to fight the urge to glance at her, unsure of what she intended. He kept his gaze on the Assassin, and watched as the short man's smile glazed slightly, his back stiff, before the benign façade slipped back into place, folding around him like a beetle's shell.

"As our Guild is a free and sovereign body," Pajen said, managing to look genuinely apologetic, "confidentiality is by necessity absolute. I'm sure you understand."

Antonya leaned back, as if wearied by the necessity of discussing the subject. "Certainly. And since you won't tell me who is to blame for this murder, I must hold your Guild responsible." She glanced at her armsmen meaningfully, her intent not lost on the Assassin.

The emissary exchanged glances with his aide before turning his mild expression back to her. It was a bit odd watching Pajen, Kerrick realized. The man mimicked his emotions with impressive competence, like an actor holding a mask over his face while he recited poetry. The aide, Stephalo, remained aloof, no expression at all.

"I assure you, madam, my Guild deeply regrets your loss." The man's eyes flickered briefly to the figurine in his hand before his fingers closed over it. "But killing us will accomplish nothing."

Stephalo smiled, the faintest tug at the corners of his lips, his body relaxed. Too relaxed. Alarmed, Kerrick dropped his hand to Antonya's shoulder in a casual manner, fingers digging. If either man made the slightest move, she would find herself thrown behind the chair before she could blink. She didn't react, nor even seem to notice his hand.

Stephalo leaned to whisper in Pajen's ear, and Kerrick realized at that instant what he should have seen before. Pajen was this man's subordinate. Stephalo was the true emissary. He glanced at Antonya, seeing her acrid smile and wondered when she had known it as well.

Pajen listened to the whisper in his ear, then nodded before he turned back to Antonya. "However. The Guild recognizes your situation is unusual. We must acknowledge a certain accountability for our lapse as well as an obligation on our part to attempt some form of compensation for your loss."

The emissary snapped his fingers and the third man stepped forward. Moving with deadly feline grace, he wore no distinctive mark on his plain black clothing, none necessary. A slender, wiry man with a sharp-boned face, his black hair was pulled back tightly into a plain braid that hung to his shoulder blades. Sightly tilted dark eyes watched everything.

Kerrick frowned, not liking this unexpected turn in the least.

"We can only offer you our apologies and a replacement for the armsman we admit to killing by mistake, knowing we cannot restore what has been broken."

Stepping instinctively in front of her, Kerrick presented himself as a protective barrier between Antonya and the Assassin. Antonya put her hand on his arm, stopping him. She laughed harshly.

"You must be joking. After one of your poisonous vipers slithered its way across my hearth, you expect me to take another of your fiends into my house?"

If the dark-eyed man felt any insult, he gave no indication, standing passively.

"Was not Briston himself one of Terhune's Elites and once your bitterest enemy? I think you may find that our gift, despite his background, can be also quite useful."

Antonya regarded them both with undisguised bitterness. "Useful. In what way?" she asked.

Kerrick snapped his head around. "Lady, no," he said sharply, and ground his teeth as she silenced him with a curt wave.

"No one but an Assassin would better know the methods

and operations of our Guild," Pajen said. "No one could better identify our Guildsmen than a fellow member. What better way could you protect yourself against us than with another Assassin in your bodyguard?"

Her eyes narrowed, then flicked to the man with the braid. "Do you have a name?" she demanded.

The man tilted his head a fraction in response. "Morgan, my lady." His voice was lighter than Kerrick had expected, as pleasant as water tumbling in a stream. The unnatural contrast raised the hair on the nape of Kerrick's neck.

"Come closer," she said, ignoring both Kerrick's worried glance and the uneasiness of her armsmen. Morgan took three steps toward her. Clearly within killing range, he stood with his arms to his side, relaxed.

She leaned toward him, belligerent. "Why should I accept you?"

"To buy time, Lady," he answered promptly. Her eyes widened in surprise. "We have no wish to become involved in your quarrel with P'tre Terhune. Accept the compromise offered, and you have another day to increase your strength. You will need it, Lady. Reject it and you will force my Guild into a conflict where no one will win."

Neither Pajen nor Stephalo reacted to their Guildsman's words, but their eyes were pitiless as they watched her, waiting.

"And if I accept, who then would you serve?"

"I would serve the Lady of Adalon," he said without hesitation.

"Even against your own Guild?"

"If necessary."

"I don't believe you," she said quietly.

The man lifted his shoulders in a slight shrug, then let them drop, smilingly faintly. "I have only my word."

She glanced at Kerrick, a look of intimacy passing between them, like the breath of a warm autumn breeze brushing the trace of fire against Kerrick's face. He knew, with a sinking sensation in the pit of his stomach, what she had chosen to do. She returned her attention to the man standing far too close to her, then leaned back in her chair, smiling hostilely at Pajen before turning toward Stephalo. "For your sake, as well as mine," she said to him directly, "I accept."

Pajan and Stephalo stepped three paces back. Morgan showed no reaction at all.

"I suggest you leave Laird's Ketch immediately, sirs. My first order to Morgan tomorrow morning will be to hunt down and kill any Assassins left in Laird's Ketch."

The two men bowed politely from the waist, as unconcerned as if she'd spoken of the weather. Kerrick watched them go, exhaling in silent disquiet. No one moved until the doors had shut behind them. Then Antonya stood and crossed the room to gaze moodily out the window, little visible in the small squares of paned glass shut against the cold. Kerrick grasped the Assassin, jerking him by the arm more roughly than necessary to the center of the room. He scowled as the man glanced up at him indifferently.

"You will stay well away from the Lady," Kerrick warned him under his breath. The Assassin stood docilely where he had been placed, but glanced up at Kerrick with an amused smile.

"What was the point to all this, Antonya?" Kerrick spoke to her directly. "You know damned well it was P'tre Terhune who hired the Guild. And now, madam, you've been neatly outmaneuvered." He moved away from the Assassin, leaving the man isolated in the center of the room. "You may or may not have the means to limit further Guild attempts on your life, but *they* have an agent in place to murder you any time they so choose."

She shot him a look of anger. "So what do you suggest I do with him, then, Kerrick? Lock him in a cage and hang him over the City Gates like a parrot? Have him squawk and flap his arms every time he spots one of his brothers in a crowd?"

Kerrick put one foot up on the stone hearth, looking down at her. "That's certainly preferable to letting him run loose. But I strongly suggest you simply kill him."

She turned her attention on the Assassin standing with his hands clasped loosely behind his back, his bearing self-possessed with neither fear nor arrogance. As if taunting the man, she strolled casually toward him, halting a bare six inches away.

"Bastard." The Assassin blinked from her breath. The Defender couldn't be sure the remark wasn't for him. Or, he realized with sudden insight, for Briston. She trembled, and Kerrick tensed for the violence he felt building. "Did you know the man who killed Briston?"

"I did," he said.

Her voice was nearly inaudible. "Was he a friend of yours?"

For a brief moment, Kerrick saw the flicker of something behind the man's eyes as Morgan hesitated. The light died. "He was," the Assassin said finally, unconcerned. Kerrick had the impression the sentence had been left unfinished.

The Defender didn't see the blow coming. She struck the man in the face so hard, Kerrick winced. Morgan's head jolted back as he stumbled slightly, then regained his balance, gazing back at her impersonally. The silence was heavy, Kerrick's stomach in knots.

"You son of a bitch," she whispered, and punched him solidly in the face. Again, the man staggered, blood erupting from his nose, but made no attempt to repel her. With an incoherent animal scream, she flailed at him wildly, striking him again and again. Still, the Assassin made no resistance or sound.

Kerrick started toward her, alarmed, but realized within two steps that her attack was not coordinated, the blows furious and yet inept. An outburst of rage rather than any deliberate intent to do injury, he observed. He knew she was capable of inflicting far more damage than what she was doing, especially on someone who was making no effort to protect himself from the blows. Before he'd reached Antonya, Kerrick stopped, not sure exactly why he didn't try to restrain her.

Antonya beat viciously against the man's face and chest, sobbing, her hair whipping in tangles about her face. "At least you could defend yourself!" she shouted.

Instantly, Morgan gripped her by the wrist, twisting aside as he jerked her around and back, his arm across her throat. She gasped in sudden pain as he wrenched her arm up behind her. Blood dripping from his nose, he held her immobile against his chest, her feet barely touching the floor. Antonya couldn't see the Assassin's face, but his smile turned Kerrick's blood to ice. As gently as a mother tiger licks her cub, Morgan put his cheek against her hair, breathing in her scent while staring at Kerrick with half-slit eyes. The naked lust Kerrick saw in those eyes had nothing to do with sexuality.

The Defender cursed softly for allowing it to have gone this far. It took all his self-control to step between his men and Antonya, halting the appalled armsmen who had rushed forward, daggers drawn.

Antonya was breathing hard, but the madness had gone from her. Her free hand curled around the arm Morgan had clamped across her throat. "I'm not hurt," she said to her armsmen finally, her voice shaking. "You may release me now, Morgan."

The Assassin dropped his arm and stood back compliantly, the vicious animal again hidden. With a low growl, Tobias took a single step toward the man, fury in his face. Kerrick grabbed him, jerking the soldier to a halt and shoving him back toward the door.

"It's over, man," he said firmly, glaring at the younger man. "You can leave." He gave Tobias another push. "*Now*."

Wordlessly, Tobias slammed his dagger back into its sheath, and followed the rest out. Kerrick shut the door softly behind them.

Antonya had a rigid back turned to Morgan, arms crossed tightly against her chest. The Assassin wiped at his nose, regarding the smear of blood on his fingers with mild distaste.

"Have you a knife, Morgan?" she asked suddenly.

Kerrick frowned but said nothing.

"I am unarmed, Lady," Morgan said. He held the cuff of his sleeve against his nostrils, muffling his voice. The blood had slowed to a thickening trickle.

"Hardly true," she chuckled, without levity. She withdrew Briston's Guild dagger in its baldric from her day robe, surprising Kerrick. If the Assassin had known it was there, he made no sign of it. She hesitated, as if she were saying a final farewell, then held it out toward the Assassin. He didn't glance at Kerrick as he stepped forward. She placed the dagger gently into Morgan's outstretched hand.

"If you do intend to murder me," she said to him, eyes hard, "Use that blade, Morgan, and no other."

He bowed slightly and stepped back with a faint smile. He buckled the baldric over his plain jerkin with a practiced ease.

"Now what, Antonya?" Kerrick said quietly.

The passionate anger and grief had vanished, replaced by a coldness Kerrick had never seen in her before.

"Now I'm going to do what I should have done before. I'm going to kill P'tre Terhune."

52

Antonya secretly enjoyed being on the move again. Laird's Ketch was more a soldier's fortress, Terhune's personality firmly stamped on the austere walls and harsh mountain bastions. Even the merchants and artisans of the city catered to the needs of an army rather than dealing in creature comforts for ordinary people; farriers and armorers outnumbered lacemakers and pastry chefs several times over.

Tonight found her in yet another small village in the outlands of Adalon, recruiting anyone wanting to fight in her growing army: farmers, journeymen, even cotters, much to Kerrick's discomfort. He preferred restricting enlistment to Guildsmen like himself, a higher class of warrior, with the help of mercenaries as a necessary evil.

"The Landsfolk have as much say in their future as those who would keep them fastened to their plows and their looms and their ovens, Kerrick," she said firmly. "How will we fight the tyranny of the mighty over the humble if we, too, are seen as only more of the same?"

The village's local magistrate, salt merchant and occasional brewer, had welcomed her as his guest to his modest-sized villa, turning out apprentices and sons to make room for her and her Guard. She and Kerrick stood poring over a map spread out on a large table dominating the small room, one edge of the thick vellum sliced through cleanly where she had cut it from the Great Library of the Citadel. It gave her the strange sensation of hovering above the world, deciding the fate of this Land or that. The impression was marred only by colored stones dotting the parchment, and the vagueness at the borders where the draftsman had sketched in speculative outlines, embellishing them with lovingly drawn fantastical beasts as if to make up for his ignorance.

The stones were divided into three groups, lands controlled by Lords, Priests and the growing number of Antonya's supporters, although the latter still seemed ominously small. Too many of the Lords were attempting to remain neutral, maintaining sovereignty of their own. Some of these Lands were crucial to Antonya, if they were to control the approaches to the Oracular City.

"We'll respect their wishes, up to a point," Antonya was saying, "but we'll not march around them. If they object, well . . ." She shrugged meaningfully.

The sun had set, the darkness outside the window deepening. "It's getting chilly," Antonya said, and looked up at the Assassin standing in a corner, well away from them. Briston's dagger barely made a bulge where it was concealed under Morgan's plain black jerkin. He had quietly asked for the slender knife the Chameleon had left behind, and although Antonya had reacted as if slapped, she'd given it to him without a word. Where he kept that was a mystery. Seemingly unarmed, he watched impassively, limbs loose-jointed, legs braced apart with his hands clasped behind his back. "Morgan, build a fire."

His expression didn't alter as he turned toward the hearth. His back to her, he did pause when she added, "Sweep it out first," but otherwise displayed no reaction. She ignored Kerrick's scowl, his disapproval hypocritical; he might hate the young Assassin, but the chauvinism that resented common laborers fighting in her ranks bristled at her treatment of any warrior, even an enemy, like a lowly drudge.

Tobias entered carrying fresh bread and hot meat. He set the tray down on what little space wasn't taken up by the map, then poured hot spiced ale into plain mugs. He offered Morgan half a loaf of bread before he sat down beside the fireplace to eat his own portion.

"Give me your opinion of Mellas," Antonya said. The little she knew of their newest mercenary chieftain was that the lanky, rawboned soldier-for-hire was often unpredictable, a heavy drinker who sought out fights in taverns whenever he couldn't find a Lord in need of hired men. He fought for the joy of it, addicted to the adrenaline rush of fear and death. Sarnor had already voiced his doubts, warning that in close combat Mellas would fight well, but often "lost his objectivity" in the heat of battle.

Kerrick considered his answer as he chewed. The muscles of his jaw under his scarred face wriggled in an odd movement Antonya found disconcerting, and she looked away. "He'll need a tight rein, and won't like it a bit, I'm afraid. It'll take some doing, keeping his enthusiasm in check."

"Hmmm." Antonya washed the bread down with the ale. "I've heard he has a few other ... enthusiasms ... which might present a problem."

"Ah." She could read more of Kerrick's bemusement from his voice than his ruined face. "His attentions for the moment seem to be limited to one, madam. The boy travels with him, and they keep their business private. If it's not made an issue of, I don't expect it to become a difficulty."

"All tastes are relative," she agreed. "One man's rake is another man's tart."

The door banged open, startling them both. A wizened man the color of dried mud stood in the doorway, as deformed as a troll. Although the man's back was crooked, it wasn't a corruption of birth, but an accident which had contorted his spine into a twisted hump. Close-cropped black hair sprinkled with white curled densely against the man's scalp and he wore a thick gold earring in one lobe.

"I see you haven't given up the habit of collecting strange pets, Antonya," his accented voice called with brash audacity.

Her heart leaped with sudden joy, and she grinned as he walked around the room to inspect its occupants, peering at each in turn. Kerrick drew back as much from surprise as from the ripe odor of a long-unwashed body and dirty velvet green robes that rustled as the little man stepped close to him.

"Mother of God." His dark eyes twinkled as he craned his neck to stare in amazement. "A trained bear with all his fur singed off."

Tobias gasped as Kerrick stood stiffly, glaring down. Unfazed, the troll-like fellow chuckled, not unkindly, and peered myopically at Morgan. The Assassin was on his knees by the hearth where he had been shoveling out ashes, the fire iron still in hand.

"You look as if you should be hunting down something small and helpless and ripping it to shreds with your bare teeth, not playing the demure servant, lad." The Assassin didn't react.

The little man paused for a moment to examine Tobias critically. "Well, you're human enough, at least," he muttered, seemingly disappointed. The armsman stared back with a bewildered mixture of relief and indignation on his face.

The strange little man finished his circuit and stopped in front of Antonya. "So where's that scabrous, stunted, scutellated excuse for a dragon's spawn?"

"The bear has it now," she said lightly.

The little fellow twisted around as far as his broken back would allow to grin at Kerrick. "Careful," he warned. "This girl always did have a penchant for collecting poisonous creatures." He looked thoughtfully again at Morgan. "But you're probably aware of that already," he finished softly.

"How the Hell did you find me here?" Antonya laughed.

"How would you think, my child? I spied you in the liquid depths of my crystal orb and flew on the breath of daemon winds, spouting ancient incantations of vast and unfathomable power at the top of my lungs, weaving such arcane spells of invisibility that would sear the living heart out of mere mortal man, and like any halfway decent sorcerer, *voila!*" He threw his arms out from his sides, making the sleeves of the green robe flap. "Here I am!"

By now, Tobias had regained both his composure and his temper. "If he's a sorcerer, I'm the Queen of Faerie," he grumbled.

"In truth," the hunchback said with a wounded look toward the annoyed armsman, "I've spent the past six weeks either puking over the side of a leaky boat or trying to stay atop a geriatric donkey with a spine like a saw in the company of the sorriest bunch of bellyachers you've ever had the misfortune to bend an ear to. Finally I get here and some sour-faced Amazon in leather breeches gives me a going over more thorough than I've had since I was a horny fifteen-year-old in a whorehouse full of nymphomaniacs." He grinned and winked. "Although I think she likes me. I caught her smiling when she saw my freight."

"Who *is* this man?" Kerrick finally growled.

Antonya came to her feet in one fluid motion, throwing an arm around the little man's shoulders. "Gentlemen, I have the very great pleasure of introducing you to Doctor Tyro of Dothinia, magician, court astrologer and supreme bullshit artist."

The little fellow ducked his head in feigned embarrassment. "Oh, please, you're too kind, too kind. Actually, I much prefer the humble title of Invincible and Exalted Alchemist, if it's not too much trouble."

Antonya grabbed a chair and dragged it toward the hunchback, happier and more relaxed than she'd been since Briston's death.

"Discovered how to turn horse dung into gold yet, you old charlatan?" she needled him.

"Still working on it, getting closer every day, I assure you," Doctor Tyro said cheerfully. "Although I think I've mastered the trick of how to turn gold into beer, unfortunately for my purse."

"Tobias," Antonya said promptly, "get a beer for our guest." The young armsmen moved off, muttering under his breath.

"How much have you brought with you?" Antonya asked him eagerly.

"Fifteen wagons, plus my own workshop," Doctor Tyro said. "It's that cute little thing out there with all the painted doodles and dangly gimmicks all over it. Can't miss it."

Although she could sense Kerrick's confused impatience, Antonya didn't enlighten him. She frowned. "That won't be near enough."

"It's a good start, my impatient lass," Tyro said, patting her hand admonishingly. "You've been quite busy since I saw you last, so many irons in the fire it's hard to tell which one you've got your hand on at the moment. It was difficult enough catching up with you. Tell me where you'd like to set up your dumps, and I'll have the supply lines going in short order. Ah, bless you, you're a lovely buck, you are." Doctor Tyro took the beer from Tobias.

"Speaking of fires," he said after he'd taken a long draught, followed by a belch, "this room is too damned cold for my old bones. Either light one, boy"—this to Morgan—"or go kill something."

The room went still, only Doctor Tyro seemed oblivious to the sudden hush. Antonya realized she was holding her breath. The Assassin stared at the little man, his eyes opaque. Then his gaze flicked to Antonya. Wordlessly, she nodded, and Morgan rose smoothly, heading for the stack of firewood outside. Once he had left the room, she heard Tobias's audible sigh of relief.

Then she caught the cryptic smile on Tyro's dark face; the little man had known exactly what he was doing. She shook her head in disbelief.

Tobias's curiosity finally got the better of his pique. "So you're really an alchemist?" he said, the challenge in his tone tempered by wonder. "Are you an adept, then, of the Weird?"

At the sudden gleam in the hunchback's eyes, Antonya warned, "Don't start."

He subsided, his enthusiasm stillborn, and said, "Actually, I am a very good alchemist, but the Weird has not seen fit to favor me with its sublime and splendid wisdom." He shrugged. "Except now and then for the briefest of glimpses into the netherworld, usually after a bit of miscalculation in mixing morning glory and mandrake," he amended.

"That's still enough in some places to get yourself burned at the stake, sir," Kerrick said matter-of-factly.

"An unfortunate occupational hazard, that is true," Doctor Tyro agreed, unconcerned, and scratched idly at the fleas Antonya was certain infested the wizard's motley robes. "Usually, I try to avoid certain less enlightened locales whenever possible."

"Sorry to drag you out of Dothinia, Tyro. I hope you're not missing any excitement," Antonya said.

The little man grinned, his teeth broad and white behind fleshy dark lips. "Not to worry. The endless court intrigues were getting boring, especially since my invitation to the perpetual round robin of the young ladies' bedrooms always seemed to go astray, for some incomprehensible reason. And this gives me a good opportunity to try out a whole new assortment of wizardly tricks, Antonya. We'll have loads of fun, I assure you."

Antonya finally turned to explain to Kerrick. "What Tyro does best, aside from waste enormous amounts of time looking for the secret elixir of youth and immortality, is make bombs."

"Oil of vitriol, aqua fortis, barrels of wonderful toys to play with," the little man was saying. "You should see what I can do these days with white phosphorus—oh, some beauties I've crafted . . ." Then his ears caught up with his mouth. "*Bombs*," he hissed. "What an awful thing to say!"

"Well, you *do*, Tyro," Antonya said mildly.

"I do not make *bombs*!" He spat the word out as if it had left a bad taste in his mouth. "Bombs are for simpletons and cowards, puny little trinkets of clay and pewter to amuse children with. Any fool can make bombs. *I* create works of art, sublime performances of pyrotechnical power to dazzle the eye and delight the senses, extraordinary exhibitions of incendiary explosives that shake even the most stalwart of souls . . ."

"And bombs," Antonya said cynically, cutting off the little man's oration.

He stopped midsentence, mouth open and one gnarled finger pointed in the air, then settled back in his chair meekly. "A few now and then," he admitted reluctantly, "but only to keep the revenue flowing, you understand. Servants have to be paid, my research doesn't come cheap . . ."

Tobias laughed and even Kerrick was grinning now, in spite of himself. The alchemist turned to him, as if searching for an ally. Antonya wondered if the little man with the broken back felt a sympathetic affinity for the big man with the damaged face.

"Some wizards go into the business in search of arcane knowledge, those fools truly dedicated to science and philosophy. Others for the influence such power brings them in noble courts. Some for the money, some because they're too stupid for honest work. Me?" The little fellow shrugged, a wistful grin on his face that made him look very much like an innocent, bashful child. "I just like blowing things up."

Morgan reentered the room with an armload of wood and began stacking it neatly into the fireplace.

"Doctor Tyro was my sponsor in Roxiara," Antonya said. "He introduced me at the Dothinian court. We got along well."

"She was a fine dance partner," Tyro put in. "Always a

boost for an old man's reputation to be seen at Imperial events on the arm of a lovely nubile lass."

"And he taught me my magic tricks."

"Real magic, or the poppycock you see in any village square?" Tobias scoffed.

"Come here, my charming cheeky chap, aye, that's it," Doctor Tyro said, and scrutinized the young armsman with narrowed eyes. "I do believe you have a mouse in your ear," he said, reaching up to the man's head. Tobias's eyes flew open and he clapped one hand over his ear as Doctor Tyro pulled away, holding a wriggling brown mouse by the tail. "A big one as well," Tyro added, then waved his palm over the squirming animal before unfolding both hands, now empty, mouse vanished. "You should have no more problems with that, I expect."

The armsman sniffed, his blasé affectation a little strained. "Parlor trick."

Tyro shook his head. "Oh, you wound me, lad, deeply you do." He turned toward Morgan. "You finished?" His arm shot out, a flash of green fire erupting from his fingertips bursting against the kindling stacked under the split logs. Kerrick, Tobias and Antonya all jumped in surprise. Morgan turned his head calmly to watch the faggots smolder, then catch, tiny yellow flames licking at the dry twigs.

As if he hadn't been entirely sure it would work, Doctor Tyro gave a sigh of relief and settled back in his chair, pleased with himself.

"Well, he's better at it than you are, Lady," Kerrick admitted.

"He practices more."

The little man raised an eyebrow. "So it's 'Lady,' is it? I'd heard as much on my travels across these fair Lands, didn't quite believe it. Lady of what, may I be so bold as to ask?"

"That remains to be seen," Antonya said, the levity draining out of her voice. "Lady of All or Nothing, depending on the will of God and a little earthly persuasion."

"Ah," the hunchback said with a knowing gleam in his eye that convinced Kerrick he was not nearly the buffoon he pretended to be. He folded his hands together over his round paunch. "You haven't been Lady of Adalon a year, and already you're eager to inflate your borders. I had surmised, what with all this powder, you intended to lay siege to something or other fairly large, ambitious brat. Where exactly did you have in mind?"

"Kaesyn."

"*Oomph*." The hunchback stared at her, dumbfounded. Tobias glanced between her and Kerrick, startled. Only Morgan, sitting back on his heels by the hearth, seemed unconcerned. After a long moment, the alchemist murmured, "My, my." He turned and gazed into the glowing hearth blankly. "I don't need my crystal ball to see the future you have in mind, do I, child?" he said finally. "You're not merely after Terhune's hide to nail to your door, you're aiming for the very belly of the beast, the Oracular City itself."

"Aye," she said softly. Her eyes paled to a tarnished gold.

He nodded, a shrewd smile widening across his face. His eyes, however, had lost their mischievous sparkle, studying Antonya sadly. "I see," he said, but what exactly he did see, she wasn't sure. Behind him, Antonya caught Tobias's superstitious warding against the Weird. Under her glare, the armsman flushed, shoving his hand behind him.

"And exactly how much of your grand scheme did you divulge to my good Lord Vaybern of Dothinia, may he reign in peace and harmony a thousand years, give or take a few hundred?" Tyro asked, his mocking equanimity restored.

"Enough to pique his greed and loosen his coffers, Tyro, but little enough not to scare him off completely."

The dark little man began to chuckle, then threw back his head and guffawed loudly. He wiped at his teary eyes with grimy knuckles.

"Oh, well, what the Hell," he said cheerfully. "No one lives forever."

53

Two hundred miles east of the Oracular City lay the fortress city of Kaesyn. Overlooking the narrow Tarax Valley pass, it was built on the promontory of sheer cliffs cutting straight down into the gorge. All major traffic to the Oracular City, by road or river, had to pass by Kaesyn's watchful eye. At the fortress's back, the jagged peaks of the Hamrya Mountains were nearly impassable even in the height of the summer. The sole route through the pass fed into Kaesyn's gates, easily protected by watchtowers jutting out on the cliffs above. The flashing beacon from the spire of St. Issel's Tower could be seen for miles, a major communication link to the Oracular City.

Over the centuries, a fair-sized city had grown up around the palaces of the Priests' fortified keep. The Xous River flowed out of the high, barren plains in the east, cutting through the Shamris Steppes before it sank underground at the foothills. It flowed through six hundred miles of limestone caverns and hidden grottoes under the Yraz Massif before reappearing in several artesian springs within Kaesyn's walls, supplying the inhabitants with boundless fresh water. Filtered through tons of limestone under the mountains, the water could not be poisoned at its source. Two other untapped springs emptied out through the fissures in the hard bedrock below Kaesyn, blown by the wind into a crystal rainbow of waterfalls.

The terraced hills around the Tarax Valley were fertile, and Antonya knew Kaesyn had stores inside its walls sufficient to feed its population for many months. Proudly impregnable, never in its entire history had the guardian city fallen.

Antonya wanted Kaesyn.

Mellas, Jezral and Sarnor had joined Kerrick, crowding around the map table, while Tyro sprawled in a chair by the hearth, hands laced over his stomach and his head lolling on his chest, snoring gently. Morgan, as ever, remained silent and still, nearly unseen in a corner.

"Kaesyn has three thousand well-armed Elite under the command of one of P'tre's distant maternal cousins, G'untur," Antonya said. "Don't underestimate him, he's competent and fiercely loyal to P'tre. But they're protecting a population of nearly fifty thousand civilians, and won't be expecting an all-out offensive." She traced a pattern on the map with her finger, her bearing self-assured. If she had any doubts or lingering grief, she hid them well.

"Their signaling outposts are well maintained, but the mountains make direct communication with the Citadel more difficult, especially in cloudy weather. I suggest we all pray very hard for rain. On the other hand, she's also connected to secondary outposts, none of which have a direct tie-in to the Citadel, but well-connected indirectly to the signaling network, here and here and here." Antonya pointed them out on the unrolled map spread across the table. Jezral kept her hands on one end and Sarnor held the other to keep the map unfurled. "We'll let Kaesyn keep her direct lines of communication to the Citadel, but I want this one and this one hit and silenced tomorrow." She looked up at Mellas. "You ride tonight. Hit them fast and hard. I would prefer to take them whole, but I want those sajadas silenced if you have to burn the towns to the ground and tear down the towers brick by brick."

Kerrick felt his blood chill, wondering if she realized that what she spoke of was no less than a Purge. But Mellas simply nodded with a callous smile on his long face.

"If we're to besiege Kaesyn, madam," Jezral asked, her lips pursed, "why hit these outposts and not those to blind Kaesyn?"

"Because Terhune will be expecting us to begin massing in the Menhath Valley in the south. No one would be crazy enough to attempt attacking the Citadel by coming through the Tarax."

"No one would be crazy enough to try through the southern route, either," Sarnor said quietly. "Trying to get a heavy army through the marshlands is practically impossible, if not suicidal."

"True," she agreed. "So neither Terhune nor K'ferrin will

be too worried, either way." Her smile faded quickly. "Also, he's already beaten us before. No doubt he's confident he can do it again. We're just a bunch of bothersome rebels, not a real army. So we leave Kaesyn alone, and continue to let him think we're no more than a disorganized band of hit-and-run bandits. Pop up here and there, draw his attention this way and that, vanish into the trees again like the cowards he wants to believe we are."

Sarnor exchanged a shrewd look with Kerrick, one dark eyebrow raised. Antonya's attention was back down on the yellowed map.

"Then we silence this sajada next, and this one after. It looks random, but it's not. I want to blind only the south side of Kaesyn, while leaving Kaesyn in open communication to the Citadel."

"Terhune will soon enough see the pattern," Sarnor drawled.

Antonya looked up at him wryly. "No doubt. We'll have to be quicker than he is, then, won't we?"

"Mmmm," was all the reply that Sarnor gave.

"In the meantime, while our troops are charging up and down the Lands like a bunch of bloodthirsty wild *qazaqs*, we'll be quietly moving people *into* Kaesyn: merchants and crofters, jongleurs and mendicants and harlots. When the Gates close for a siege, we'll have agents in place on the inside."

"Once we do begin the siege against Kaesyn, how many of his Elite do you expect Terhune will send against us?" Sarnor asked.

"None." Antonya smiled.

Her blunt statement met with sudden silence, surprised glances exchanged between her commanders.

"I know Terhune," she said. "We are not a serious threat to Kaesyn. She can't be taken, or so he believes. He'll harry us from behind, distract us where he can, but he'll send none of his troops up the valley to Kaesyn's defense. Once we've breached the city, he'll pull back his troops to protect the Citadel and abandon the civilians to their fate without a single reservation."

Jezral grunted, eyes narrowed as she considered. "Once we've taken Kaesyn, what do you want done with it?" she asked, her raspy voice making the question even colder. Kerrick was gratified that the lanky woman assumed the inevitability of Kaesyn's fall. *I wish I were as confident*, he thought.

"Nothing." Antonya answered promptly. "No undue bloodshed." She looked around at her commanders meaningfully. "Taking Kaesyn will be difficult. But holding it will be even more so. There are fifty thousand civilians in that city, more than a few of them will be ours. We will need the goodwill of the Kaesyn population in the long run. No looting, no pillaging, no raping."

Mellas looked vaguely disappointed, but Sarnor nodded.

"And the Priests?" Kerrick asked.

"Other than Terhune's Elite, they are to be taken prisoner and treated with respect." Sarnor looked at her skeptically. "We are *not* enemies of the Faith, is that clear? There will be many of the Faith inside Kaesyn who are sympathetic to us. We will need them."

"Then are we to take everyone alive?" Mellas asked with sardonic humor. "This may be difficult for my men to understand. They *are* soldiers, after all, not milksops."

Antonya smiled. "You don't have to worry that I'll spoil your fun, Mellas. Anyone stupid enough to wear P'tre Terhune's red you can slaughter to your heart's content."

Mellas grinned, his yellowed teeth feral in his leathery face. "With pleasure, Lady." Kerrick frowned; Mellas would be trouble.

"Any other questions?"

Her commanders shook their heads and saluted her with informal respect before they filed out. The sudden quiet seemed to jolt Tyro out of his nap. He woke with a snort, and blinked rheumy eyes.

"I have one," the old alchemist said sleepily.

"I thought you weren't listening," Antonya said with a teasing chuckle.

The little man drew his green robes closer around himself. "I *am* a wizard, you know," he groused. "I'm quite capable of listening and sleeping at the same time."

Antonya signaled to Morgan and crossed to sit on the hearth, her back to the fire. Kerrick noticed that the Assassin took a circumspect taste of her ale after he poured it, although Antonya seemed not to be aware of it. When Morgan handed

Kerrick his own tankard of ale, the dark-eyed man looked back at him steadily, answering the question on Kerrick's face with an enigmatic smile.

The Assassin poured himself an ale before settling cross-legged at Antonya's feet like a pet leopard. Leaning against the map table, Kerrick drank his ale and watched thoughtfully.

"I'd like to know with everybody running willy-nilly over the countryside, who the Hell's going to help me sew up two thousand cloth sacks?" the alchemist demanded testily.

"Regine has already started organizing the ladies for you, Tyro," Antonya said. "You should be pleased to know you'll shortly be spending large parts of your day with a dozen very young and pretty girls all eager to accommodate your every whim."

"Two thousand cloth sacks?" Kerrick asked, puzzled.

"Aye." Antonya laughed. "One of the agents already inside Kaesyn has been a very busy pigeonnier. A few days before we bring up the siege guns against the city, he and his two thousand pigeons are packing up and leaving town."

"Pigeons," Kerrick said.

"Pigeons," Antonya echoed. "Signaling mirrors are for the Faith's use only. Carrier pigeons are faster and cheaper than a boy on a horse, especially through the mountains. Kaesyn's merchants have paid good money for our pigeonnier to train his birds to return to their favorite nooks and crannies all over the city. In the eaves of houses, in the markets stalls, in the bells of the sajada itself."

Tyro yawned. "We tie two thousand little incendiary devices around the feet of two thousand little pigeons, light the fuses and watch them all fly away. *Ftt, ftt, ftt, ftt,*" he said, flapping his hands like the wings of a bird in flight.

Kerrick's jaw dropped. "That's the most ludicrous thing I've ever heard of," he managed to say, and glared at the alchemist accusingly.

Tyro shrugged with an exaggerated look of worldly-wise cynicism. "Not my idea, I assure you. It's a good thing I *loathe* pigeons. Damned dirty stupid things, crapping all over the place . . ."

Antonya's eyes danced merrily over the tankard as she drank. "No," she said, wiping her mouth with the back of her hand, "I'm afraid I have to take the blame for that one. But it's not near as crazy as what I've done to their wheat crop."

The little wizard suddenly chuckled. "So that's what you were up to," he said to the fire, his eyelids drooping half closed. "I wondered what you intended to use all that ergot thread for. Far more than any good alchemist could ever need. Devil of a time gathering it all, you know—the damned stuff doesn't come cheap . . ."

"Kaesyn obtains most of its wheat from the Tarax Valley," Antonya explained. "The soil is rich and the river provides plenty of irrigation. Kaesyn also holds the mill rights for a dozen villages along the Xous River, and takes fifteen percent of the flour as their multure. The weather was particularly kind this spring when Briston and I scouted the area."

Kerrick observed that she didn't seem to have as much difficulty bringing up her dead lover's name as she once had. He forced himself not to glance at the man sitting by her feet.

"I noticed the terraced fields along the Tarax Valley were bursting with fine tall, sturdy plants all at the peak of their flowering," Antonya went on. "It seemed they'd have a rather bountiful harvest this year. Unfortunately, it's all contaminated with ergot. Acres and acres of it, all the length of the river valley. The wind did a good job carrying the spores a broad distance. Right about now, Kaesyn's stewards should be realizing the entire Tarax Valley crop is infected. Half the crofters aren't even bothering to work their fields anymore. They're too busy putting in a late root crop before winter sets in, hoping to simply survive themselves, never mind stocking up Kaesyn's granaries. It'll be a guess which Kaesyn would rather do: have the wheat harvested anyway and risk mass poisoning, or let it rot in the fields, lock the gates and let the crofters starve."

She laughed cheerfully. The idea of creating a famine in the Tarax Valley didn't seem to disturb her. It disturbed Kerrick, but he said nothing. "Either way, once the siege begins, Kaesyn will be relying on last year's stocks to feed their population. And fifty thousand mouths are a lot to feed."

"How long have you been planning all this, Antonya?" Kerrick asked.

The humor was gone. Suddenly the steel was back in her eyes.

"All my life," she said tonelessly, looking directly at him. "All my life."

54

The siege of Kaesyn was now in its second month. Four of Tyro's iron cannon had been dragged up the Damrogen Ridge and fitted into their cradles. The final, heaviest piece was still en route. While the carpenters sawed and pounded together its artillery cradle with a calm precision and speed that impressed Antonya, Kerrick had gone to oversee the huge cannon barrel's progress up Damrogen Ridge, and like as not would not return before morning. A forge had been set up at a safe distance, smiths repairing swords, harness, armor, and hammering out numerous hollowed hemispheres of iron to be bolted together and filled with Tyro's mix of charcoal, sulfur and saltpeter to make explosive grenades light enough to fling over the walls.

The solid iron cannonballs heavy enough to smash through the city walls would be reserved for the large cannon being brought up. The smiths continued to supply the smaller cannon with grapeshot and melonshot light enough to clear the walls and rain down on the roofs on the other side.

Five cannon were hardly enough for a siege. Two trebuchets supported the artillery while another team of carpenters steadily assembled a huge siege tower to be dragged as close to the walls as possible, the slipway slowly taking shape at its base. Rock, broken lumber and discarded debris of all kinds were dumped into the dry moat to form a crude bridge the tower could be winched across.

Zigzag trenches had been painfully cut out of the rocky ground toward the city walls, and the first of the siege artillery dragged into position. The new parallel struck bedrock, effectively stopping the approach. The zigzag was barely close enough to the ramparts to concentrate its attack, and protected from enfilading fire from the Kaesyn defenders. Sarnor had sent a team of sappers to one end of the trench hoping to drive an underground gallery under the glacis, but the gunpowder had minimal effect against the solid granite foundation under the thin layer of soil. The powder was needed elsewhere, and the mines were given up.

A sturdy palisade had been quickly hammered into the ground on the eastern front of the city walls beside the Great Gate, the stakes cut down from the forest hills and dragged into place by ox and horse. Armed men, messengers and sweating porters scurried along the safety of its base, hunched over as Kaesyn's archers sent arrows whistling over their heads. Antonya had been impressed by Sarnor's and Kerrick's matter-of-fact expertise in organizing the siege, leaving her with both gratitude and a strange envy. It took her a few days to overcome her sense of uselessness and reticence.

With heavy wooden shields covered in watersoaked skins to shield her, she scuttled from siege engine to cannon to sapper camp, up and down the lengths of zigzag trenches, talking to the men, listening to their complaints, gripping hard, calloused hands in her own. The look of adoration on the faces of sweating, dirty soldiers willing to risk their lives for her both awed and frightened Antonya, and left her feeling more alienated than ever.

She opened the flap of her tent to watch the red glare in the darkness as Kaesyn burned. Even at this distance, she could feel the heat on the breeze, an occasional black flake drifting to the ground. Artillery boomed, close in and invisible in the night. Seconds later, the crack of shells burst against the high walls. Hers. She spotted a flash from a bastion tower as Kaesyn answered, almost as regular as clockwork, the sound of shot falling following on its heels.

It would go on all night. The damage done by either side was negligible, more a war of nerves now. The smell of wood smoke, charred meat and burnt powder in the air was deceptively festive, incongruous in the night air. Ephraim and Daen, posted by her tent, glanced at her briefly, close enough to guard her but remaining at a judicious distance.

Regine had already retired, although sleep was problematical in the din. All around, camp noises kept up a steady discord, the metal jangle of harness and weapons, the creak of leather and tent ropes, canvas and banners flapping. Horses neighed, soldiers' voices calling out orders as the guns were reloaded and fired, underscored by faint laughter and curses as card players won or lost, snatches of rude song as men attempted to relax under the pressure and boredom of siege. The sounds enveloped Antonya, swirled around her with a life of their own, leaving her untouched, isolated in the eye of the storm.

She made out the slender shadow of Morgan, his back toward her as he, too, watched the fires in Kaesyn. Seeing him standing alone, a solitary figure shunned by all around him, she felt a rush of affinity for him which surprised even herself. Suddenly very tired, she rubbed her eyes. She'd not be sleeping much that night anyway.

"Drink with me, Morgan," she called out on impulse.

The man turned, no pretense that he had not been aware of her, and walked toward her. As he reached her guards, Ephraim fell in beside him. Antonya stopped him as Morgan slipped past her into the tent. The young guard wavered, troubled.

"Kerrick gave orders . . ." he started to insist, his words trailing off as he realized his error and flushed.

"Did he now?" she said mildly, her tone dangerous.

After a moment's reluctance, Ephraim saluted her and retook his post, exchanging a look of unease with Daen. Kerrick would be most unforgiving if Morgan decided this was the night to murder her. She chuckled but left the flap of the tent open to the night and its sounds.

Morgan waited, hands clasped behind him. Walking past him, she settled into a folding chair next to the table covered with rolled charts. "You know where it is," she said as she swept the table to clear enough space for cups.

He poured the ale into two pewter cups from the chest, then sipped hers before he handed it to her.

"I don't do that," she chided, but took the ale all the same.

"You should, Lady." He drank from his own cup, dark eyes watching her. "You take too many risks."

"Indeed," she said dryly. "Am I at risk now?"

"Aye. But not from me."

She savored the bitter sharp ale, rolling the chilled pewter between her hands, then gestured with her chin to the vacant chair opposite. "Sit." The man eased gracefully into his seat, his attitude suggesting the same indolent vigor of a mountain cat.

At a loss for anything to say, Antonya wasn't even sure now why she had made the impulsive offer. She listened to the artillery as she stared down at the dark liquid in her cup.

"It appears Kaesyn nearly has its arson problem under control," she said lamely.

"So it seems. Fire usually looks worse in the dark than it actually is. And they have plenty of water to fight it with."

She smiled. "Well, the birds were a dubious one-time trick, anyway. Let's hope the rumor they carried Fever as well does more damage than the powder bombs."

As he stared back, expressionless, the laughter died in her throat. This wasn't Kerrick, nor even Briston, not another fun-loving armsman bantering over ale, fighting the tension with boisterous laughter and song, the greater the strain, the louder the noise.

He was as different, as *alien* a being she had ever met. She wondered if he had ever laughed in his life. Some said the Assassins had covenants with creatures of the Weird, strange children born from their unnatural sexual unions. She had never given much credence to diablerie, although she was not loath to use superstition to her own advantage when it suited her. Now, studying the man across from her, she was not so certain that the line between what was human and what was the Weird was that distinct.

"Why you?" she asked him, the question unpremeditated.

He didn't affect not to understand. "I'm a Second Rank Master in the Guild," he said evenly. "My skills are excellent. In a few more years, I likely would have been made Guild-master." There was no vanity in his tone; it was a simple recitation of facts. "It seemed a good choice."

"But was it your own?"

"Personal desire has no place in the Guild. The only ambition an Assassin should ever have is to be the perfect weapon. It was the will of my Guild that I be yours."

She snorted. "And you're mine?" she asked sarcastically.

"Completely."

His flat look quashed any mockery. She stared hard at him, taking in the lean, hard body, his empty eyes, the air of menace he wore as close and as indelibly as his skin. "You're flawed," she said suddenly, realizing. His subtle smile was back, mirthless. "You *look* like an Assassin."

"Aye," he said softly. Something flickered in his eyes. "But if all the world knows I'm your Assassin, what does that matter?"

She shivered, looking away, and pulled her robe closer to her neck although it was not cold. "Does it matter to you?"

When he didn't answer promptly, she glanced back at him. He appeared to be studying a point just above her head. "No," he said finally.

A strange tingle of fear crept along her cheeks. "How many people have you killed, Morgan?"

"Eighteen," he said as indifferently as if they were discussing the quality of the ale, then added unexpectedly, "How many people have you killed, madam?"

As if to underscore his words, three siege cannon were fired in quick succession, followed by the tinny whistle of melonshot falling with a muffled boom inside Kaesyn. A distant cheer from her gunners reflected a deadly success.

"It's hardly the same thing," she snapped acidly.

"Isn't it?" His dark eyes were guileless.

"There's a vast difference between war and murdering someone in cold blood."

"I've never killed anyone in cold blood," he said mildly.

She drank deeply before she dared to speak again. "How old—" She cleared her throat. "How old were you the first time?"

Morgan's expression was infinitely polite. "Why are you asking me these things, Lady Antonya?"

"How old?" she insisted.

"Nine. Nearly ten. I garroted her from behind with a silk scarf. It wasn't easy. She was fat with a short neck and my arms were not as strong at that age."

Antonya found her hands were shaking, and she set the ale down on the table before she spilled it. "Why was she killed?"

She heard him exhale and wondered if it was exasperation.

"I don't know, I didn't ask. Is there anything else you'd like to know?"

"How did you feel?" The words felt as if they'd been torn out of her, leaving behind an aching hole.

The Assassin smiled enigmatically. "This isn't wise, lady."

"Probably not," she agreed, and waited.

He hesitated, eyes suddenly bright. "I enjoyed it," he said simply. "Very much."

She stared at him for a long moment, then looked away. "You are a monster," she breathed quietly, almost to herself. She looked down at her hands clenched together in her lap, as if each were holding the other back. "Yet Tevik looked like just another traveling poetmonger." She swallowed against the pain. "You knew him. Tell me about him. Was that even his real name?"

He shrugged. "As far as I know, it was. We grew up together." Morgan's gaze became distant. "He was brilliant, by nature graceful, gifted with a superb mind. We all knew, even as children, he would eventually become High Guildmaster over us all. While we others had to work hard, it was always a game for him. A game he never lost."

"Were you jealous?"

That broke his reflection. "No, madam, I was not. I learned early the world is not fair, and I respected his talent, even loved him for it."

Her cup was empty. She stood to refill it. When she lifted the flagon toward him inquiringly, he shook his head.

"*Love* . . ." She corked the flagon and replaced it before she turned to face him. "I've been given to believe Assassins were the spawn of stonenymphs raped by vampires. Love is a human sentiment I thought you would be free of."

He regarded her thoughtfully. "I am human," he said simply, and she wasn't sure from his tone how he meant it.

The silence stretched until the boom of heavy cannon fired at close range made her jump. Ale sloshed onto her hand. She laughed at herself deprecatingly, shaking the liquid from her fingers. "My apologies, Morgan," she said with more bitter contempt than she intended. "You were right, this wasn't wise."

His face betrayed nothing. "Will that be all then, madam?" he asked softly.

All the anger suddenly fled, leaving her feeling strangely barren and weary. "Forgive me," she said, sincerely this time. "I was lonely and curious, and we haven't had much to say before, you and I."

When he didn't answer, she waved her hand wearily, dismissing him. He set his cup down and stood, her voice stopping him before he got to the flap of the tent.

"Morgan," she called out softly, trying to mitigate her guilt, "If you are not my enemy, I would wish to call you a friend."

His back to her, he put one hand out to steady himself on one of the thick pine poles supporting the tent. She was stunned to see him trembling, but when he turned to face her, his face was unreadable.

"You have never to fear from me, madam, I swear it," he said, his voice lifeless, "I serve you without question. Use me in any way you wish." His words dropped to a near whisper. In anger or fear, she couldn't tell. "Ask *anything* of me . . . anything but that."

She stared at him silently before he turned and vanished into the warm night.

"Well, then," she remarked conversationally to the emptiness around her. "I guess I'll just get drunk tonight all by myself, shall I?"

In the end, she didn't. She lay sleeplessly on the narrow cot in the dark, listening to the artillery barrage through the night.

55

The couple who had taken the rooms next to the workman's were quarreling again. Their argument filtered into the narrow corridors, echoing off damp stone walls. He struggled with an oversized key to his own door, his workbelt draped heavily over his shoulder. He was tired, his back ached, the middle finger of his left hand throbbed where his nitwit assistant had mashed it with a hammer as they ripped out the corroded pipes under the monk's hypocaust.

He sighed, wincing, as the woman's voice spiraled higher, like a badly tuned instrument. The man she claimed as husband rumbled a sullen contrabass in the nightly opera of jealousy and anger. Only once after one of these melodramatic acts had she come knocking, weeping and bruised, looking for solace and possibly sex from anyone more interesting than her husband. He'd quickly kicked her out, uninterested in becoming a player in their tragicomedy.

"Drinking *again* . . . how *could* you . . . *my* mother . . . a *real* man would . . . miserable *bitch* . . . one more *word* out of you and I'll . . ." The music rumbled through the walls, the shrill chorus occasionally rising in pitch loud enough to make out the libretto.

He locked his door firmly behind him, and in pitch dark, dropped his work tools into a lidless trunk. As he lit a candle to illuminate the windowless room, the woman shrieked in a sustained crescendo. The workman cocked one ear expectantly, then snorted at the dull thud of blows interspersed with sharper openhanded slaps.

He sank onto his narrow swaybacked bed, leaning on his elbows propped on his knees. Usually, the brawls never lasted long, but this evening was a special performance, it seemed, backed up with an orchestra of breaking crockery and the hollow sound of, he guessed, a head banged rhythmically against the wall. Finally, it died away to the woman's weeping and her husband's murmured apologies, as monotonic as a stream bubbling in a brook, oddly pleasant.

He might have dozed, problems sorting themselves out into neat categories even in his dreams. He yawned, stretched, aware time had passed and of the silence next door. He sat up. The candle had burnt to half its length. In the quiet, he heard a rustle and tiny squeak, and grinned, leaning over to look under his bed.

"Gotcha, you little son of a bitch," he said affably to it.

His homemade trap had indeed snared the damned little rodent who had been getting into his meager stock of food, leaving behind dainty footprints and neat brown turds. He dragged out the rough box of woven wire and wood. The mouse sat on brown haunches, humanlike hands with tiny nails gripping the wire of its cage. Black eyes glittered, its whiskers quivering. Then it circled the cage in frustration, naked tail whipping behind it, desperate for escape before it again gripped the wire, gnawing it angrily between its front paws.

He set it down on the crude table, and brought out a half loaf of dry black bread, hard cheese, an onion just beginning to go soft, and an earthen jug of sour wine, his staple diet for nearly twenty years. As he ate, he watched his doomed little captive pensively.

He thought he'd handled it well enough. He'd managed to convince the Guildmasters another attempt would not be in their best interest. Payment for the botched job had been returned to the client, and a use had been found for Morgan, cheap enough redress for the Guild's mistake. With the Lady's safety thus assured, he had hoped she would be satisfied to attend to the business of ruling Adalon, while K'ferrin kept P'tre Terhune at bay. In a reasonable world, the status quo should have settled back down to an acceptable balance.

That was before the Lady of Adalon decided to attack Kaesyn, another unexpected setback. Now Antonya Terhune was holding all of Kaesyn captive, locked within its comfortable trap, nibbling away at its stores in arrogant disdain at the rabble gathered outside the bars of its cage. And the Guild was most definitely displeased with *him*.

He sighed. The mouse had calmed down and squeaked, more in outrage than fear. He poked a morsel of dark bread between the mesh. It sniffed the offering, and nibbled at it between splay-fingered paws with as much elegant decorum as a countess.

"Ah, my noble mouse," he murmured to it. It haughtily ignored him, mere rabble that he was.

Then there was the problem of D'nyel's peculiar behavior of late. He'd known since the beginning Terhune had supplied the healer with doomed men for her research. It didn't interfere with the Guild's interests, and she was becoming a damned good physician in the bargain. But this time it was different. Her methods were hardly refined and the material not of ideal quality, but he recognized the signs. She was fashioning a weapon, and he wondered uneasily what she intended once it had been ground down to a killing edge.

He finished his meal, washing down the last dry crumbs with the wine and watched idly as his unwilling guest groomed itself, quick paws rubbed over ears so delicate they were transparent, the tiny blood vessels stark against the candlelight. It turned, ruffling brown fur as it licked its plump sides, unconcerned with its fate.

Do I kill you now? he thought. *Do I keep you? Do I let you go?* It was peaceful, even pleasant standing on the edge of possibilities. Of course he'd kill it. It was vermin, he was an Assassin, the little thief had been apprehended, convicted and sentenced for its crimes. The guilty felon washed the hairs along its tail with a pink tongue as dainty as a flower petal.

The couple next door started the last act of their inevitable libretto. He started, amused as his little guest hunched on stiff legs on the floor of its cage, as alert and wary as himself, as if it had somewhere to bolt. The thumping came in an urgent cadence, their lovemaking as violent as their quarreling.

He laughed, a low rumble of good humor as the woman shrieked again, this time in a burlesque of orgasmic ecstasy as if to announce her victory to as many of the audience as her voice could reach. Under the shrill sound, he could just make out the harmony of her husband's groans, somehow sad and desperate.

He picked up the cage, intending to kill the little rodent and toss the corpse out into the gutter. It gazed back at him, beady black eyes confident, unafraid. Setting it back down, he shook his head in wonder at his strange emotions. "What is happening to us, my little noble mouse?" he whispered to himself. "What are we becoming?"

A faint snore, roughened by too much drink, snarled softly from next door. He sighed. "Oh, well. Perhaps I'll kill you tomorrow."

He blew out the candle and went to sleep.

56

Doctor Tyro leaned over the map, one hand cupping his chin while his gnarled finger lovingly traced patterns on the unrolled charts. "I don't want to discourage you, dearheart," he said in his mellifluous accent, "but these drafts are based half on exploration and half on overactive imaginations. According to this line here"—he pointed to an ink line snaking across the vellum—"the fissure goes back only a few hundred yards, not even close to the walls, but here"—there was a rustling as another map was unrolled—"it seems to branch out into a series of caves stretching well under the city proper."

"Big enough to get a man through?" she asked.

He glanced up at Kerrick skeptically. "Possibly, depending on how big a man you intend."

"That rock is nearly all granite," Sarnor said. "And the cleft is too far down the cliff. You're not likely to be able to get sappers digging up through that, not in my lifetime anyway."

"I don't intend on trying, sir," Antonya said distractedly. She tapped the diagram and glanced up at Tyro. "The falls. They come out through fissures much like this one?"

"Aye," the little man said cheerfully, "but this'un's dry as my grandmother's"—he hesitated, smiling guilelessly at Jezral's raised eyebrow— "ah . . . bones. No connection, apparently."

"What would happen," Antonya said slowly, "if you made one?"

The Dothinian alchemist looked up, his perplexity giving way to a bright grin. "You'd have yourself another waterfall," he said.

"Would we indeed?" she said softly.

"*If,*" Tyro emphasized, "these charts bear any resemblance at all to reality, *if* the connection could be made between this fissure to those above it, *if* it were blown wide enough. It's all guesswork, my girl. Guess wrong"—he shrugged—"and all you'll end up with is a bigger hole."

"*If* it could be done," Kerrick breathed, realizing, "what happens to the springs inside Kaesyn?"

The Dothinian winced as he straightened, one hand against his crooked back. "Water, like shit, flows downhill. Springs only flow uphill because they don't have enough drainage *out* to balance against the pressure flowing *in* from behind. These falls share the same source as the springs, that much the charts seem sure of. Give the water a big enough outlet"—he beamed at the comprehension on the faces around the table—"the Kaesyn springs will dry up."

"How much powder would you need?" Antonya asked, feeling a surge of excitement in her blood.

The Dothinian scratched his curly beard, thick lips pursed as he calculated. "Can't do it with what we've been using for cannon, have to have a higher brisance grade than that," he mused. "We'd also need to get in first to drill out a few holes to direct the main blast, get a crew to dig out whatever available space we can; it'll still be a bitch to pack it in and keep it dry . . ."

"Just a conservative estimate?" she prompted.

"In round numbers . . . roughly speaking"—he grinned at her—"I'd say one Hell of a shitload, madam."

"One other minor detail, Tyro," Antonya said. "You'll have to work at night. Without light."

"Oh, fine," the man said easily, a wicked gleam in his eye, "What would life be without a little challenge now and then, eh?"

"How quickly can it be done?" Kerrick asked.

Doctor Tyro sucked air between his front teeth as he considered. "Hard to say. Drillers will have to go in first, there's a lot of tedious preparation work to be done with a pick and shovel. We can sneak workmen in before dawn and move them out after sunset, but working only at night to move the powder, I'll need at least a week."

"You have your choice of my men, Tyro," Antonya said briskly.

"Meaning no insult to your armsmen," the Dothinian said, "but I'd prefer boys and young women, the younger the better."

Mellas snickered quietly to himself. Antonya shot him an acid glance, and the man looked away. Tyro ignored him.

"Why?"

Tyro tapped the vellum maps. "The only way you're going to get the powder into those caves is by hauling them down the cliff on your back. These paths aren't much more than goat trails; they're narrow and dangerous even in broad daylight. Boys and women are smaller and more agile." He looked up at Antonya, his dark face smiling, but his eyes hard. "And they're still young enough to consider all this a lot of fun and excitement instead of just another damned stupid way to die."

Antonya was aware of the silence stretching. Then she nodded.

"How many will you need?" Sarnor asked.

"All you can spare," Tyro answered promptly.

"You'll have them," Antonya said. "Regine will round up every available cook, laundress and serving woman, groom, lackey and scullery boy she can lay her hands on. There are a few whores loitering about as well, perhaps they'd enjoy a change of pace. Jezral, will you see that the good doctor's needs are taken care of?"

Doctor Tyro bowed shallowly, unable to manage a smooth gesture with his back fused into an awkward hunch, then followed Antonya's commander out of the tent, clearly fascinated by the way the tall woman's buttock muscles rippled under her taut leather breeches.

"Well, gentlemen, you're all about to have a taste of how the gentler half live," Antonya said wryly. "I suggest you work out among yourselves who will do the cooking and who will do the laundry."

"I can't see my men being overjoyed at the prospect of scrubbing kitchen pots at night after manning artillery guns all day," Sarnor said placidly. It wasn't an objection, Antonya decided, but an observation of possible trouble.

"That's why I'll expect officers to set a good example and

take on their fair share of the load. All the same, additional duty deserves additional ale rations"—she glanced at Mellas meaningfully—"within reason."

Mellas kept any protests to himself.

"In the meantime, we've got two weeks to further annoy the Kaesyns. Any ideas?" she asked, looking around. The others shifted uncomfortably. Sarnor studiously began to clean his fingernails with the point of his knife as Antonya leaned over the table again to study the maps. Kerrick rubbed his chin thoughtfully but said nothing.

"We still have a few of Doctor Tyro's incendiary bird bombs left, madam," Mellas suggested, his voice light. "Might be able to stir up a bit of trouble with those."

"We can't shoot them far enough into the city to do any more real damage, and we're a bit short on birds," Antonya said, still absorbed in the maps. "Unless you've thought of some other way of flying them over the walls."

She didn't see Kerrick and Mellas exchange glances before they both shot a look at Morgan, isolated in the corner and as inert as a statue. Although always discreet, Morgan never left Antonya's side, as close as her own shadow. Only the Assassin's eyes moved, glinting in the shadows. Then he smiled, the effect even more uncanny.

"I suppose not," Mellas murmured.

Kerrick cleared his throat. "What's needed now is to drive as big a wedge as we can between the citizens and the Priests," he said.

Antonya unrolled another chart, holding it open against the table with her palms. "I'm listening," she said, although preoccupied as she was with deciphering the ancient squiggles and diagrams.

"First," Kerrick went on, "convince the population your attack is not directed at them, and that you hold only the most benevolent and merciful of intentions once Kaesyn falls."

"That's what agents and sympathizers are for," Antonya broke in. "I assume they're busily sowing just such propaganda even as we speak."

"Second," he persisted, "menace the Priesthood, show the townspeople they are not invulnerable. Play on all of their worst fears. How do you think the good denizens of Kaesyn would react if a few higher Warrior-Priests like G'untur were to be found very publicly dead under the strangest of circumstances?"

That got Antonya's attention. She looked up. "How strange?"

"A bit of timely Weird theurgy, for example."

She chuckled. "I didn't know you dabbled, Kerrick. Whatever his other talents may be, Doctor Tyro honestly isn't an adept of the Weird. Sulfur has an ungodly stink, but it doesn't raise the Devil."

"Why raise one when we already have one?" Sarnor said quietly, still concentrating on his nails.

She looked at him sharply before she stared at Morgan. "I do believe that will be all, gentlemen," she said softly. Mellas frowned while Sarnor simply sheathed his knife and left. Kerrick waited until they were gone.

"*Use* him, Antonya," he said in a low, urgent voice. "What good is a hawk if you never fly him?"

The muscles in her jaw clenched stubbornly as she refused to answer.

"Put your best arrow in the bow and shoot it, for God's sake." When she still said nothing, he stalked out angrily.

She turned her back to Morgan, moving away from the map-strewn table to pour herself an ale. "Well, my pet Assassin," she said, watching the dark liquid froth into the cup, "have you anything to say about this?"

"Nothing, madam," he replied in his clear voice. Standing at the flap of her tent, she gazed over the horizon of her camp to the high gray walls of Kaesyn, standing in sharp relief against the blue of high mountain sky. The stone façade was pocked by cannonshot, and even as she watched, one of her guns boomed with earth-rumbling resonance. A plume of opaque smoke drifted away on the breeze as the shot burst against Kaesyn's wall, near enough to the top of the battlements to send their soldiers scattering for cover from the hail of splintered stone.

"No, I didn't suppose you would." She deliberated for a long moment, struggling with her conscience. Murder was still murder. "Have you enough of the Weird coursing through your veins to dematerialize and rematerialize inside Kaesyn unseen?" She tried to keep the derision out of her voice, and failed.

"I have no more of the Weird in my blood than anyone else," he said quietly.

She smiled, and when she turned to face him, she had drained her irises to a chalky yellow. "Indeed," she said dryly.

"Indeed," he returned, unfazed. "Nor do I need it."

She made her decision, slightly shocked by how easily it came.

"Kaesyn has a goldsmith's Guildmaster, what the Hellzisname . . ." Shoving aside the rolls of maps and charts, she found an unmarked sheet of parchment, opened a pot and dipped a quill into the ink.

"Achbith," Morgan said.

She glanced up, surprised. "Right, Ach . . ." she muttered, scratching the quill across the paper rapidly, ". . . bith. He's probably the most influential of the Guildmasters, considering he's got the most to lose if Kaesyn falls." She stopped herself. "*When* Kaesyn falls," she amended.

For a few minutes, the only sound in the tent was the scrawl of her quill against paper. Still scribbling, she said without looking up, "Light a candle, will you?"

Morgan placed a cord-match in the small pewter pan, and struck the flint with steel until sparks ignited the sulfur-impregnated string. Catching the flame with a sliver of wood, he lit the candle beside her narrow bed, bringing both it and the box of sealing wax to her.

She had finished, the parchment already blotted and folded. Four drops of red wax dribbled onto a string held to the creased edge. She pressed the seal of her ring into it, lifting it up to reveal the embossed lizard curling around its own tail, and repeated the process, pulling the sealing string taut across the parchment. She handed the sealed letter to Morgan as he blew out the candle.

"Pick three Warrior-Priests—be sure they're officers high enough to be impressive. If you get G'untur, all well and good. Kill them one at a time and be sure the bodies are found in public. Pretty it up to make it look like a rash of demonic slayings, however you want. Be creative . . . you can do that?"

She peered at him uncertainly, reluctant to sound as if she intended to insult him.

He smiled cryptically. "Aye."

"Good. On the last night, give this to our esteemed Guild-master and please try to make sure he doesn't perish of fright. I want him alive. Pissless, but alive."

"When?" Morgan said simply, a touch of eagerness in his voice. He seemed more animated, more *human* than she'd seen him before.

"Tonight. You have a week."

He nodded, tucking the letter into his jerkin as he turned to leave.

"Morgan," she called out, strangely reluctant to see him go. He paused, looking at her inquiringly over his shoulder. "Be careful. I expect to see you back here alive and whole."

The expression on his face didn't change, but she had the distinct impression something had hardened within him, a door to his soul slammed shut.

"It's nothing personal," she added. "You're just too valuable a hawk to lose."

A slow, remote smile touched the edges of his mouth, and she thought she saw understanding in his dark sloe-eyes.

"Perhaps, madam," he said, and was gone.

57

The moonlight was a faint blur behind the clouds as he reached the bastion wall. Above him, he heard the groan of chain and tackle as the defending artillery engines were moved. He started up the wall barefoot, using the corner edge of the narrow barbican for bracing. The stones had been constructed to withstand both artillery and scaled assault, steep and smooth enough to deter most climbers. His mind clear, breathing deeply and evenly, Morgan concentrated on finding the tiny cracks in the stone for support, holding on only by fingertips and toes jammed into the narrow splits in the rock.

He had ascended the wall nearly halfway when the cannon above fired. The vibration rumbled through the stone as he closed his eyes and hugged the wall, keeping his mind empty as he waited for the rock and his muscles to stop shivering. Despite his expertise, he was no cat. A fall from this height would kill even an Assassin.

He was not aware of how much time had passed before he reached the lip of the crenated wall. The ledge of the hoarding projected out several feet over his head, and he groped for purchase, jammed against the rough face of a corbel. Then he found an edge on the face of the hoarding wall and let go, hanging by his fingertips, legs swaying gently over the sheer drop below.

It didn't occur to him to pray for the guns to stay silent a few more minutes. He swung his legs up against the stone gallery wall and within seconds he had slipped between two merlons and vanished down the dark gallery.

The *quartiers* of the town were arranged circularly around the sajada, elegant tiled houses jammed together in narrow streets and crooked avenues spiraling like a pilgrim's labyrinth. The decaying buildings closest to the fortress's ramparts, poorer areas of the town, had been the hardest hit, the powder melonshot clearing the walls falling onto the roofs. Blackened timbers and broken masonry littered empty streets, the buildings abandoned as the citizenry huddled closer to the far side of the town, as far out of the reach of artillery as they could get.

The bomb-laden pigeons had had an effect throughout the town, Morgan could see as he slipped like a cockroach through the darkness. Several houses had burnt to the ground, neighboring buildings scorched, and everywhere the litter of bloody and burned feathers clumped in gutters and alleyways like dead leaves.

A broad boulevard connected the sajada square to the Palaces at the far end of the town. Held by the Priests, this fortress within a fortress was a roughly rectangular complex of galleries and chambers riddled with passages. Built on a raised crown of rock near the promontory, the stronghold dominated the walled city spread at its feet, its back to the sheer cliffs of the valley gorge.

Morgan prowled the perimeter of the Palaces—the old one and the new—adjusting his mental picture from Antonya's maps to the reality. A low rampart bristling with guard towers had been built to reinforce the walls around the two Palaces, the rough stonework of the outer walls newer than the neat block of chiseled stone. Troops regularly patrolled the lists between. Morgan counted off the time and number of men, calculating his windows of opportunity. He climbed the outer walls easily, slipping across the open ground to the walls of the Old Palace.

Troops billeted in the smaller, Old Palace were crammed together in the small chambers of the cloisters bordering a small courtyard. Their officers occupied the Great Consistory dividing the Old Palace from the New Palace. On the other side of the massive consistory, nonmilitary dignitaries and scholars with their households resided in the spacious galleries of the New Palace.

The first kill was easy. The prison, Morgan knew, would be in the ancient crumbling donjon of the Old Palace. He scaled the tower with far more ease than the fortress walls. The prison's Master Jailer, although feared, was a small, almost delicate man who had his private rooms under the high, peaked roof of the donjon. Few guards walked the courtyard grounds; it was late, and the Palace secure. Those who did walk by as he climbed didn't look up, not expecting to see a man in black clinging to bare walls.

The glazed windows had been left open to the night air, but were nearly too small for a man to enter. Morgan had to exhale the air in his lungs before he could slide his body through the narrow opening.

The jailer maintained an austere life, spurning any decoration that might have softened the Spartan room. Leather and chain armor were laid neatly over a rough-hewn chest. A peg holding his clothing and a plain washbasin and chamber pot against one wall were the only furnishings other than the bed. The jailer slept naked, belly-down in tangled bedclothes. One hand hung over the edge of the bed as he snored peacefully.

Morgan let his thin Guild killing knife slide into his hand as he padded silently to the sleeping figure, then stopped as he realized the jailer was not alone. A young woman, barely more than a girl, lay on her back beside the jailer, staring mutely at the Assassin. Her arms were stretched above her head, wrists tied to the bed, blood and burn marks on her body. She might have been one of the Palace's chambermaids, a low-caste servant freely available to any who wanted her. Or, more likely, one of the many prisoners kept in the dank chambers under the tower brought up to amuse her captors. The girl's eyes glittered in the dim light, watching the Assassin approach with a numbed expression.

When he was sure the girl wasn't going to scream, Morgan tapped the jailer gently on the shoulder. The man's brow creased with sleepy irritation as he groaned, rolling onto his back before he opened drowsy eyes. Morgan balanced the wire-thin killing knife on the edge of the jailer's wispy mustache, the tip just inside one nostril, and allowed the man enough time to react. As the jailer's eyes widened in alarm, Morgan jammed the blade up into his nasal cavity, cracking through the fragile ethmoid bones in the skull. With surgical precision, the blade pierced up into the brain, and Morgan twisted the knife sharply before whipping it out.

The man was dead before he could blink, a living corpse as the lungs continued to breathe, the heart to beat. Before too much blood could pour from the dead man's nose, Morgan shoved a thin linen strip into the cavity, packing off the wound. He used his sleeve to wipe the small trickle of blood left on the man's face. As long as no one inspected the corpse too closely, the jailer would appear to have died without a trace on him.

The girl watched without a sound as Morgan spread the jailer's cloak on the floor, then dragged the living corpse onto it, wrapping the body quickly and efficiently. Then he turned his attention to the prisoner in the dead man's bed, eying her thoughtfully.

He'd only been given leave to kill three men, and the girl might be more useful as a witness. Although she didn't flinch, the girl trembled as Morgan gently tucked the bedclothes around her abused body. He left her arms still tethered.

"If they ask why you live," Morgan whispered, "you may tell them that the King of Hell did not want your soul." The girl gazed at him fixedly, and Morgan wondered if she had any wits left.

He set the small leather-wrapped grappling hook over the

ledge of the window and let the rope snake down into the darkness below. It was a bit tricky getting the jailer's body out of the window and carrying it down, but the adrenaline surging through Morgan's blood gave him the extra energy.

As he reached the ground, he flicked the rope, the rippling movement lifting the grappling hook from the window to fall silently into Morgan's outstretched hand. He had the hook unfolded and the rope looped around his waist in seconds, slung the jailer's body over his shoulder and slipped away in the shadows.

The next morning, those merchants still trying to pretend all was normal as they set up their dwindling goods for the day's market found the naked living corpse of the Master Jailer on the sajada's porch, propped standing against the great bronze doors. A neat, thin pentacle Morgan had traced with black powder had been burned on the man's chest. His hair and mustache were liberally festooned with pigeon feathers, stuck to him by the shreds of meat still clinging to their roots. They fluttered as his slowly dying lungs wheezed fitfully.

From his shelter in a burned-out warehouse along the edge of the ramparts, Morgan woke, opening his eyes a crack as he heard the first cries of alarm. Smiling sleepily, he rolled over as the sajada's bells began to ring and the barrage of artillery fired melonshot overhead in the early morning sunrise.

Two nights after the jailer's murder, Morgan prowled the edges of the New Palace, listening to the darkness. He could almost feel the heightened tension in the air, a low hum of anxious inhabitants wandering the passageways, too nervous to sleep. His quarry was the Priests' chief signaling officer.

The old scholar was Citadel-bred, keeping the keys and codes to the elaborate deciphering systems in his head, his subordinates allowed fragments of the old man's knowledge. The Master Signaler would be replaced by another only upon his death or retirement, sent out by the Citadel. But Kaesyn's gates were locked, both in and out. Without a Master, any messages the underlings could cobble together would be garbled and more than likely disregarded.

From the pinnacle of St. Issel's Tower, the Priest jealously guarded the mirror and flame connecting Kaesyn to the rest of the Lands, calling out the sequences of flashes traveling over the hills with gruff irritation to the sweating signalmen. The old Priest was arrogant and quick-tempered, terrorizing his younger assistants. A recluse who suffered from arthritic hips and bad teeth, he spent much of his time memorizing new codes and decoding incoming messages to be sent along appropriate routes to their recipients. He cared little about the contents in the messages he transferred, by nature as well as necessity incorruptible. Bribes and threats were ineffective methods of prying information out of him.

His chief pleasure in life seemed to consist of locking himself into the high signaling tower alone each night and polishing the huge bronze mirror with infinite care. He had little to fear; the tower was well-guarded and virtually impregnable.

The next morning, the signaling room at the top of St. Issel's Tower was still locked, but the old man had vanished and the flame doused. A large pentacle had been scorched into the immaculate surface of the bronze mirror. When the Priest was found, sitting inert but still breathing in the fountain of the main market square, he too had pigeon feathers sticking in his hair, but his sodden robes were weighted with hundreds of shards of broken glass mirrors.

From the derelict attic in a merchant's house, Morgan sat between beams quietly shooing away curious rats with his foot as he ate the bread and onions he had stolen from the kitchen. He smiled as he listened to the apprehensive family and servants in the floors below discuss the bizarre slayings.

Morgan struck the next night, knowing this would be the most difficult, and the most likely to get him killed if he failed. G'untur had his private quarters in the heavy bastion by the Great Consistory. Patrols prowled the lists and Palace grounds with their arms at ready. By now, the Priests were going in pairs, if not whole groups, unwilling to be left alone for a single minute.

It took hours to work his way carefully through the weave of shadows, following a tedious network of doorways and corners before he stood outside the outer rampart walls dividing the Old Palace from the rest of the city near the edge of the promontory. A thick brake of brambles overgrew the crumbling stone wall of a garden behind the Old Palace jutting over the river gorge. Neglected for years, the garden had gone wild, overgrown with thorny brambles and weeds. His delicate killing knife was no match for the stout trunks and branches, and even that absurd dagger Antonya insisted he carry had difficulty hacking through the brambles. His gloves and clothes took the worst of the sharp thorns, face bleeding from scratches before he managed the climb over the thick briar.

Clouds had rolled in during the evening; moonlight glittered faintly in the water of the canal running behind the Old Palace. The night was cold, the only sounds the murmuring of the canal and the rustle of neglected trees. Behind him, on the other side of the wall, a faint yellow glow in a few windows was the only light in the shadowed streets, silhouettes of tiled roofs and overhanging porticoes stark against the night sky.

He removed his gloves, tucking them inside his jerkin, as he studied the plain walls. Hazy figures passed by lighted windows in the bastion towering above him.

The closest gate into the bastion was on the opposite side of the Old Palace. Beside the Great Consistory a tall, plain latrine tower had been built, each floor holding a common toilet for the ordinary troops. While soldiers' toilets consisted of a series of bare open holes occasionally flushed with buckets of used kitchen water, G'untur and other higher officers had their own personal latrines connected to the Consistory itself, private rooms with fresh rushes strewn over the floor to warm bare feet, the toilet furnished with a handy ledge over which to rest one's rear, a supply of soft clean moss and a bucket of rainwater to flush the waste.

Morgan knew he would not be able to scale the outside of the building this time without being spotted, nervous guards now watching the walls above them for leather-winged daemons as well as human intruders. A main drainpipe connected the private latrines with the soldiers' common toilets. The drainpipe itself was narrow, but large enough for a luckless servant boy tied on a rope to be shoved inside once every few years to unblock congealed waste that occasionally clogged the shafts.

The shaft ran down four stories to empty into the canal cutting through the garden, the waste carried away and dumped over the edge of the cliff by the waterfalls. It took

Morgan the better part of an hour to remove the rusting grate from the entrance to the drain, prying at the corroded bolts with Antonya's knife. The work was not made easier by the frigid canal water and thick clumps of algae waving like green mermaid's hair from the metal bars.

Inside, the drainpipe was lightless and cramped. The accretion of decades-worth of reeking filth along the walls made grasping what few handholds Morgan could find difficult, but at least made it easier to slither up the thick muck, much like an earthworm sliding through its burrow. He was by nature a clean man, but he had no aversion to the smell and sludge.

He kept his eyes closed as he worked his way into the drainpipe, visualizing where he was in the system, his ears picking up hollow echoes as troops murmured and walked the corridors behind the stone wall. The pipe branched, one branch to the left to the common latrines, the other to the private quarters. G'untur would have his quarters at the top, and Morgan crawled past two other toilet ducts accessing the main pipe before he reached the upper floor.

The hole was almost too small to allow him access. Only by keeping his arms at his sides and pushing his shoulders upward could he wrench past the narrow opening. The door was closed, and he put an ear against it cautiously before he used the bucket of rainwater beside the ledge to wash his hands and face. A tiny slot window in the wall, far too small for a man to get through, allowed a breeze to alleviate some of the stench.

Then he waited. Keeping his mind blank, his nerves alert and relaxed, he let the minutes tick by evenly without worry. It was close to morning, most of the fortress nervously attempting to sleep if it could. If G'untur didn't come soon, he would have to leave before it was too light and try again the next evening.

Then he heard voices approaching, two men speaking in night-hushed tones. Not even G'untur felt safe walking alone to the toilet tonight. Morgan crouched behind the door as it opened, his knife waiting in his steady hand.

G'untur was a big man, a stout, muscled Warrior-Priest and army commander of several decades. Unlike the jailer or the old scholar, his reflexes had been honed by years of fighting. He saw Morgan's out-of-place shadow before he fully saw the man, but his reaction was instantaneous. He lashed out with one foot, his bare, callused heel smashing Morgan back before he could strike. The Assassin hit the wall hard, his thin killing knife spinning away out of his grip. It clattered against the wall, wobbling for a second on the lip of the toilet ledge before it toppled and vanished down the pipe.

The Warrior-Priest wore a heavy robe against the night chill, and it slowed him down, just long enough for Morgan to spring the short distance between the man and the door, slam it shut and throw down the wooden bolt before G'untur's companion would recover his wits. G'untur carried a dagger, and as he shouted for help, he slashed out, tearing through Morgan's jerkin. The Assassin felt the steel blade bite into his ribs with a distant awareness.

Morgan kicked him once. The impact was lessened by the confined space, but his aim went true—dead center of the man's chest. A thick crack cut off the Warrior-Priest's bellowing as his sternum broke. His own knife clattered to the floor as he staggered back, sitting down heavily on the toilet ledge. Morgan hit him again, this time slamming his knuckles like a hammer into the Priest's throat. The big man went down, grasping at his shattered windpipe but still alive.

Shouts and fists banging anxiously on the door were quickly replaced by the more serious methodical thud of an ax. G'untur, still conscious, groped for his fallen knife. Crouching over the man's squirming body, Morgan unsnapped a metal bracelet from his wrist, uncoiling a thin wire spiraled inside. Working quickly, he slipped the garrote around the dying man's throat and jerked, slicing almost instantly through his neck. The wire stuck at the man's spine.

Morgan was breathing fast and hard, his nerves singing as the first glint of the axhead smashed through the door. He ignored it as it was wrenched out again. He sawed frantically through the vertebrae, his hands slippery with blood pumping out of the man's severed neck. The ax thudded again, a few wood slivers spraying the room. A heavy body slammed against the door, the wood of the bolt cracking under the strain.

With a snap, the wire decapitated the dead Priest. Morgan instantly threw the garrote over the ledge and down the drainpipe. The wooden door bucked again, straining against the splitting plank bolt. He grasped G'untur's head, fingers clenching the hair, and climbed over the ledge, wriggling back down the narrow shaft.

He knew he had only a few desperate minutes to get down the drainpipe and into the canal before the soldiers flooded out of the Old Palace. Shouts echoed overhead as the door finally caved in, the crash echoing in the pipe. A few splinters drifted down. He let himself slide freely along the damp sediment, his raised arms and shoulders squeezed against his face, gripping the bloody head above him. Dim shouting resonated through the stone as he passed the connecting floors. Seconds later, he slid feet first out the open grate into the frigid canal water, bruised, scraped and bleeding.

Upstream was the small mill; downstream the water emptied through a narrow channel in the wall and out over the sheer cliff into the chasm below. He rode the current toward the outlet, washing as much of the blood and dirt from himself as he could, then climbed out of the steep, algae-slicked canal.

He stood panting in the darkness, drenched and shivering, the dead man's head dangling by its hair from one hand as he watched the soldiers with torches scurrying around the perimeter of the Palace. He had lost both his garrote and his killing knife, but he had taken his prize. It had been a fine, gratifying kill, his nerves still singing. He grinned with sheer delight, careful to keep his lips shut over his teeth. The head now dripped more water than blood. Pressing a hand against his side, he felt his own blood trickling sluggishly from the shallow incision. G'untur's dagger had slid over a rib, not able to cut too deeply. His ripped jerkin had taken most of the damage. He would sew both jerkin and wound later.

It would take several minutes before the chaos resolved into an organized search, half the troops on the ground not even sure what had just happened, and others reluctant to start out too eagerly after what might well be a Weird daemon. Morgan used that small amount of time to work his way through the brambles and over the wall of the Palace gardens, then metic-

ulously followed the shadows and disappeared down the first
dark street he came to.

By morning, G'untur's head, elaborately decorated with pigeon feathers, was displayed hanging by its knotted hair from
the wrought-iron sign over a local fishmonger's.

58

Two wiry country lads had risked their lives climbing along
the cliff's rock face in the dead of night, pounding stakes into
the compact soil to string guide ropes along. Above them,
sentries patrolled the watchtowers and ramparts, but they were
more interested in the traffic along the river below. Also, the
watch along this side of the fortress was not as substantial,
having little reason to fear attack from the sheer cliffs.

The sentinels made no attempt to conceal their presence,
and the sound of their boots stamping along the walls was a
clear enough signal for the boys to freeze, waiting under the
cover of darkness for the danger to pass. It took two nights to
get the guide ropes in place before the drillers could begin
their work.

Once the drillers had groped their way to the caves, a line
of a dozen boys and young women crept along the path, passing equipment down from hand to hand like a water bucket
brigade. At the first sign of dawn, the brigade line withdrew,
leaving the drillers behind in the caves to work during the day.
Sand and brush covered the guide rope to disguise it from the
watchtower above. Tyro wasn't concerned with any noise; the
tons of rock between the caves and the fortress above would
muffle most of the hammering and drilling, even if the siege
engines weren't doing enough to cover their racket.

The fissure was larger than Tyro had hoped, and quite dry.
He fretted over the reports from his drillers, relying on secondhand information as his crooked back would never allow
him to make the excursion into the caves himself. But by all
accounts everything was progressing as well as could be expected.

As soon as it was dark enough, a continuous stream of boys

and woman began hauling small packs of explosive powder on their backs, moving as silently as possible in the near total blackness. Candles were too dangerous to use around the powder, and the drillers and sappers worked in the caves without light, packing the charges by feel and memory.

They worked without a single mishap for two nights. On the third, their luck had made the boys careless. Two were killed, losing their footing in the dark, their small bodies lost as they tumbled down to the raging river below. After that, as Tyro predicted, the boys and women were more mindful of the danger, realizing it wasn't just a game. While there were no more accidents, their wariness slowed the work down considerably.

Morgan had yet to return by the time the fissure was ready to blow. The last charge had been set, the fuse wire primed, a candle left to burn down to light it, giving the last of the workers time to retreat. Daylight was just breaking over the valley, mists clinging to the trees.

Antonya worried at a broken bit of thumbnail with her teeth. "Perhaps the candle has blown out?" she asked.

"Patience." Tyro lay on the ground, his back propped against a pile of now abandoned packs, hands laced over his stomach as if he were about to nod off.

The minutes ticked by.

"The fuse must be . . ."

"Hush, child."

She spat out the morsel of nail she'd chewed off. "If this doesn't work, I suggest we all make our peace with God, go home and wait for the Purge."

Tyro didn't answer, his eyes closed. Several minutes later, she jumped when he murmured, "Right . . . about . . . now."

She glanced at him. Nothing happened. He frowned and opened his eyes. The earth suddenly shivered under them in a muffled boom echoing through the mountain peaks.

"Give or take a few seconds," Tyro amended.

Antonya joined the small crowd racing to the edge of the cliff, crawling the last few feet on her belly to peer into the chasm. Loose rock tumbled out of the mouth of the fissure, bouncing down the rock to the misty river below. Above, enemy sentinels leaned out along the ramparts to survey the commotion below, obviously confused. As the last bit of gravel and sand trickled away, the cliff looked pretty much the same.

She held her breath until it hurt, until the doubt became a certainty. Several minutes passed. It hadn't worked. She struggled against the disappointment welling in her throat, biting her lower lip. The stiff wind in the chasm made her blink, and blink again, staring down. A small dribble of water snaked out of the mouth of the fissure, no larger than a finger's width. The wind blew it into a fine mist, like cold steam. More rocks rolled out of the fissure, as if the mountain were clearing its throat, and the trickle became a stream. Another clump of rock disgorged, propelled out of the fissure by the flood of water behind it.

A new waterfall spilled over the cliffs, a rainbow appearing in the mist above it. As the cheer spread, Antonya smiled, then began to laugh.

"Oh, ye of little faith," Tyro retorted.

59

The room was well-lit with burning candles, although the occupants of the bed were asleep, huddled like children afraid of the dark. From his perch on the windowsill, Morgan inhaled the scent in the room and grinned to himself. The candles were more than for light, they had been perfumed with acrid spices to fend off creatures of the Weird. The door had been embellished with various magical talismans, dried blood smeared over the lintel. He dropped soundlessly to the floor, and padded to the bed.

Gold thread winked candlelight from the burgundy tapestry around the canopied bed. The larger occupant snored in a deep bass, one fleshy arm dimpled like a baby's draped over a tumble of feminine dark hair. Swirls and spirals quilted into the watered silk coverlet resembled eddies in a river current, soft and plush under Morgan's bare feet as he crouched at the foot of the bed.

The mass of hair moved, and a woman's sleepy eyes blinked blearily at him before they shot open wide. She sat upright in bed, her mouth open as her lungs sucked in a formidable amount of air.

"Scream, and you die, madam," he said reasonably as he drew Antonya's dagger with a sinister rasp. Although Morgan held such heavy weapons in contempt, he had to admit the sheer size of the blade was a far more intimidating sight than his slender killing knife.

The woman stared, immobile; then the breath whooshed out of her. Now her companion was awake, staring in pop-eyed horror at the apparition which had materialized in his bed. A garland of garlic cloves hung around his pudgy neck, and he jerked the coverlet and lace sheets up under his chin reflexively.

"Who are you? What do you want?" the fat man choked out, his throat constricted with fear.

"I have no intention of harming you, Achbith of Kaesyn," Morgan said smoothly, "if you don't make it a necessity. I've come to deliver a message for you from the Lady Antonya Terhune."

The woman wore nothing beneath the bedclothes and as her companion had jerked the bulk of the bedding toward himself, more than her shoulders were bared. She crossed her arms over her generous breasts, trembling with cold and terror.

"Madam, you shiver," Morgan said lightly. Keeping his eye on the pair, he got up from the bed and retrieved a robe hanging from a hook against the armoire. He held it out to her balanced on the tip of his knife. After a stunned hesitation, she reached out tentatively and snatched it, clutching it to herself.

When Morgan looked back at the fat man, he paused, eyes narrowing. The man's expression was one of nervous victory, his clenched hand holding something too small to be a weapon.

"Begone, foul daemon," Achbith said, voice shaking, and tossed a handful of bright particles at the Assassin. "Back to the flames of Hell where you belong!"

Instinctively, Morgan drew back. A few of the glittering flakes spattered against his jerkin, but the majority fell short, sprinkled across the coverlet. Puzzled, he fingered the sparkle of pale metal, then grinned as the man's triumph gave way to dismay.

He picked up a few of the shreds of metal and let them

flutter between his fingers down onto the bed. "Were I truly a creature of the Weird it might be effective," he said dryly. "As it is, it's only a waste of perfectly good silver."

Then he perched on the bed again, moving with uncanny grace as he leaned over and gently lifted the man's necklace of garlic from his throat with the knife blade. Morgan knew he looked even more frightening under the layer of sweat-streaked dirt and dried blood caked on his face and hands. "Shall we have done with this foolishness now?" he said quietly, his voice malignant.

The man nodded mutely, as docile as a penitent child. Morgan slid the edge of the blade through the garland and pulled the strand away, tossing it onto the floor carelessly. Then he sat back on his heels and withdrew the sealed letter from inside his jerkin. A few spots of blood marred the outside, but he thought it hardly mattered.

The fat man took it from him with badly shaking hands. He stared at it uncomprehendingly, then up at Morgan with testy petulance. "I can't read it without my spectacles," he said peevishly, then started as if astonished by his own boldness.

Gesturing courteously with his knife, Morgan watched the man fumble with the clutter of objects on the bedside chest. In his nervousness, he nearly knocked over one of the candles.

Morgan's free hand snapped out, catching it before it toppled, and set it gently upright, still lit, the flame barely wavering. He smiled sweetly as the jeweler's protruding eyes went slowly from the candle to Morgan's face, now completely cowed by the lightning speed with which the Assassin could move.

He took several moments to adjust the spectacles over his nose and ears before he fumbled with the seals on the letter, his hands quaking so badly as to be almost useless. He looked up helplessly at Morgan, eyes beginning to water behind the thick lenses.

"Try the knife under your pillow, sir," Morgan suggested.

The man swallowed, then retrieved the small, ornate blade more suited for manicures than for defense. He cut the string sealing the letter, unfolded it and began to read. As his eyes jerked across the parchment, his fear subsided. He grunted, wriggled closer to the flame to read by better light, momentarily forgetting the man in black perched between his knees. Finally, he eyed Morgan thoughtfully.

"Do you know what is written here?" he said.

"Nay," the Assassin answered lightly. "I am merely the Lady Antonya's messenger boy." He grinned his best ruthless smile. "Have you a message for her in return?"

The fat man pursed his lips, then shook his head slowly. "It's beyond my authority," he said. "I'll have to talk this over with the other Guildmasters." He glanced up as if suddenly worried his refusal might have unfortunate repercussions.

"Do so, then," Morgan said and ignored his look of relief. "I'll bid you good night."

He studied the woman for a moment, then held out his free hand. Reflexively she lifted her own hand up to him, startled as he clasped her fingertips gently. He brushed his lips against the joints of her fingers in a gracious kiss, keeping his eyes on her face, and smiled.

"You have a very lovely wife, sir," he said, and out of the corner of his eye watched the fat man scowl. As the woman blushed, he realized that the woman in Achbith's bed was not his wife.

He sheathed the knife in the same smooth motion that brought him back to the window ledge. His back to the outside, he crouched on the sill and grinned at the couple.

Then he stepped backward and dropped from the ledge.

He heard the woman gasp, wondering briefly if she would decide to scream after all as the rope caught, breaking his fall. Skimming down the building, he landed soft-footed on the street three stories below. With a quick flick, the grappling hook and rope fell toward him. He caught the hook in one hand, already coiling the rope with his other. In seconds, he had retrieved his equipment and vanished before the fat man could reach the window and lean out over the empty street.

He worked his way through the shadows and sentries toward Kaesyn's outer curtain wall with amused effortlessness. His ascent to the top of the ramparts was almost disappointingly easy. He paused to rest before he began his climb down, crouching in the sanctuary of darkness.

Raising his face to the cold stars overhead, he closed his eyes and listened to the night sounds of the city under siege.

Cannon boomed, men and their arms clattering in the ramparts around him. He breathed in the smells in the air, burnt powder and horse manure, cooking odors and wood smoke. The night breeze cooled the sweat on the back of his neck, stray hairs escaping from the tight braid tickling his cheek.

Freedom.

The thought came unbidden, startling him. For a moment, a delicious fear stabbed through him, nearly sexual in its intensity. Then he sighed, opened his eyes reluctantly, and began the long descent back down.

Halfway down, the middle finger of his left hand began to throb. He had to stop, perplexed, resenting the time necessary to push even the awareness of the pain from his mind. All his concentration had to go into the climb. After several minutes clinging to the rock face, he resumed his descent.

When he reached the ground, he leaned against the fortress wall and inspected his hand. Picking at the hard lump under the skin, he extracted a sliver of metal from the ball of his finger. He frowned, flicking the shard of silver away and sucked the ooze of blood from the tiny wound. Then he forgot about it as he worked his way slowly across the deadly zone of fire between Kaesyn's defensive artillery and Antonya's battery of cannon.

The sky had begun to lighten by the time he made it back to the camp. When Regine entered Antonya's tent with her early morning meal, she stifled a shriek, waking the Lady. Antonya sat bolt upright from her narrow camp bed, startled, to find the Assassin curled up in one corner like a cat, bare knife tucked under his filthy, scratched cheek, fast asleep.

60

The bombardment had stopped, both hers and theirs, the city ghostly still. Kerrick waited with Sarnor, watching as Antonya surveyed the field and glacis under the high walls of Kaesyn. A breeze rolled through the grass, the ground liberally pocked with huge muddy craters where artillery from both sides had fallen short. The only sound other than the wind and the distant roar of the gorge river was the sharp, clear call of a kestrel wheeling high above them.

Kerrick glanced up at the falcon above trailing jesses, some nobleman's hawking bird escaped and gone wild, hunting now only for itself. He wondered if it was an omen, then frowned. If it was, it would probably be unfavorable anyway.

Sarnor stood characteristically with his feet braced apart, hands clasped calmly at his back. Antonya exhaled, a barely audible sound of frustration as she watched the dormant city. Sarnor caught Kerrick's eye, smiled ruefully as he scratched at the growth of gray-peppered dark beard on his face. Kerrick appreciated the old soldier's quiet, gritting his teeth when they heard the apologetic cough from behind. Sarnor twisted to look behind them inquiringly, his hands again clasped behind his back. "Yes?"

"Lord Jonan begs a few moments of the Lady's time to speak with her," Ephraim's voice said quietly. "He's ridden from Ilona, all the way without stopping."

Sarnor raised his eyebrows and glanced at Kerrick before he looked at Antonya. Wordlessly, she nodded and turned away from Kaesyn. Kerrick and Sarnor followed behind.

The young Lord wavered as if his legs hadn't quite adjusted to being on the ground; he and his armsmen were filthy and exhausted. When he spotted Antonya walking toward him, his expression became even grimmer, deep lines in his face caked with dirt and fear.

"Lady, the Faith has struck against Ilona, the fields are burnt, outlying villages already in ruins. What inhabitants haven't fled are inside the city walls, but there is little food, even less ammunition. They can't hold out much longer."

Antonya had stopped, listening impassively. He gestured almost desperately at the lifeless city behind her, including both Kerrick and Sarnor in his sweeping motion. "Most of your men are idle now, we have pressing need of them, Lady."

"I have no doubt you do, Lord Jonan," she said, her voice unmoved. "Unfortunately, I cannot send any." She turned to Ephraim. "Please see that Lord Jonan and his men are given food and lodging. They must be very tired after such a hard journey."

Jonan stared in appalled disbelief as she turned away, his men exchanging troubled looks. Taking a long stride, the young Lord grabbed her by the arm.

"Lady Antonya, there are four thousand innocent people inside those walls," Jonan pleaded. "Ilona isn't a fortress, we haven't a chance against siege guns. If the city falls, you know Terhune will Purge *everyone*. Madam, you must send help . . ."

She didn't shrug off his hand on her arm holding her back, but she refused to look at him. She seemed unaware as Sarnor signaled her own armsmen. Kerrick motioned them into position with eyes and nods as they nervously surrounded her and the Ilonian men, but made no attempt to separate Jonan from the Lady.

"I cannot, Lord Jonan," Antonya said, her voice dead. "I hope and pray with you Ilona can resist, but there's nothing I can do for you. I cannot spare one single man."

Jonan stared at Kerrick and Sarnor wildly. "Have pity on us, lady . . ." the young Lord's voice broke in anguish, "my wife and children are inside Ilona . . ."

She inhaled through clenched teeth before she turned, Kerrick certain she could barely refrain from screaming at the man. "Lord Jonan, don't you think I *want* to help you? But I *cannot*."

"For God's love, why not?" he begged her.

Jonan's men were aware of her armsmen standing discreetly close by, arms ready in case the quarrel turned ugly.

She faced the young Lord's distress steadily. "When a wolf pack hunts, the leader stays close to the prey, just out of range, running alongside and doing nothing, to conserve his strength," she said quietly. Jonan stared incredulously. "The rest of the pack split up and run behind the doe. They take turns biting at their victim's heels, worrying her flanks, herding her in one direction, then the other, bleeding her. Until she's wearied and slows to fight, lashing out with her hooves. Until she turns to look back. Exposes her neck. Then the lead wolf seizes her by the throat and takes her down."

Kerrick watched her carefully, as Mellas and Jezral joined them. She turned her eyes away from Jonan, looking steadily at each of his men and then her own in turn.

"I will not turn my head, gentlemen," she said quietly. "We will take Kaesyn or we will all die. There *is* no other way."

She gestured curtly, and Ephraim stepped in to separate her from Jonan and his men, armsmen leading the reluctant Lord's men away.

As Jezral gently took his arm, Lord Jonan said almost too softly to be heard, "You've murdered my family."

She kept her eyes on the Lord as she said to Kerrick, "Draw up a roster of two hundred men, have them ready to leave on a moment's notice. The moment Kaesyn falls, they will ride for Ilona."

"Aye, madam," Kerrick said quietly, knowing as well as she it was a futile gesture.

Lord Jonan's face twisted in bitterness. "It will be too little and far too late," he said. "My wife and boys will already be dead." A tear ran down his dirty cheek.

"Probably," Antonya agreed noncommittally. "You are free to curse me at your leisure, sir."

Jezral led the young man firmly away.

Kerrick put his hand on her shoulder as she walked toward her own tent, away from prying eyes and the ominous silence of Kaesyn. Tobias held the flap open for them to enter. As usual, Morgan stood in one corner, wrapped in the shadows. Once inside, Antonya sank down into a canvas chair, her head in her hands. Nicoli brought her a tankard of ale, which she took from him but set down untouched.

"Terhune hasn't struck directly at me from behind because I still have sufficient force to repel him," she said, more to herself. "He can't strike at me from the valley, because it's too narrow in the pass. As long as Vodos keeps his troops on the other side of the marshes and waits for us, Terhune isn't going to march his own men out to fight while being sucked into the swamps. The only thing he *can* do is harry me town by town, hoping to draw my attention and enough of my army away to weaken me."

Sarnor stood at the map table silently studying charts. Kerrick swirled the ale in his tankard, watching the foam along the pewter sides. Tobias and Nicoli sat quietly together in one corner mending leather hawking gear. They had all heard this before.

"When Kaesyn falls, they'll abandon Ilona," she said. "They'll pull back everything they've got to the Oracular City. The only hope Ilona has is for us to take Kaesyn."

"At least we can cut off their retreat and rescue any children they might have in their company," Kerrick suggested. He refused to speculate about what would happen if Kaesyn continued to hold out.

She didn't. "Much longer, and there won't be anything left in the Lands worth saving. All I will have done is leave a trail of burned and wasted cities behind me, no better than P'tre. *Why doesn't it fall?*" she said through clenched teeth, not looking at anyone. Then she glared up at Kerrick, her eyes hollow. "If we didn't manage to put out their springs, then Ilona will be destroyed for nothing."

Tobias glanced at Kerrick, worried.

"Madam, even if you knew Kaesyn would not fall and sent troops to their aid, it would not help the Ilonians in the long run anyway," Kerrick said calmly. "Or anyone else."

She smiled bitterly. "I know. Once on this path, I can't very well turn from it, now can I?"

"No," Kerrick answered softly. *What else could go wrong?* Kerrick wondered. God could not have timed the answer any better, or any worse; Morgan stepped from his customary place in the corner and banged solidly into one of the sturdy pine poles supporting the tent. The Assassin held on to the pole with both hands, vaguely puzzled.

"Madam," he said shakily. Kerrick and Antonya stared at him. The Assassin rarely spoke unless first spoken to. Alarmed, Kerrick noted Morgan's labored breathing, his pasty, damp face. "I believe I'm feeling rather unwell."

Kerrick reached the man before she did, shoving him

roughly to one side as he stopped Antonya with his free hand. "Don't touch him, Lady," he said sharply. Tobias and Nicoli rose to their feet, Sarnor looking up curiously from the map table.

The Assassin's skin was hot, and he stared blankly at Kerrick.

"Is it the Fever?" Antonya asked, hushed. When Kerrick didn't reply, she said, "Everyone out. Nicoli, get Doctor Tyro. Quickly."

"You should leave, too, Lady," Kerrick said as he steered the ailing man toward a chair. Morgan's limbs were shaking as he lowered himself cautiously into the seat.

"Kerrick..." She stepped toward them, stricken, then stopped as the big man whirled around angrily.

"Get out!" he snapped. "Damn you, Antonya, I'll not have you risk your life for one man. Get it through your thick skull, he is not important enough."

"I wasn't thinking of him," she said gently.

Startled, his tone softened. "We need you, alive. Now get the Hell out before I throw you out bodily."

She nodded mutely, and hurriedly gathered up the maps.

"It was the silver," Morgan said, his voice oddly clear.

Pausing in the doorway with her arms full, she glanced back at him. His eyes were feverishly bright. Although he was pale and sweating, he was composed.

"What?"

"I cut my finger with a splinter of silver."

Kerrick met her eyes for a long moment. They both understood the implication. Then he jerked his head toward the door, silently ordering her out.

Kerrick stooped over Morgan, loosening the man's shirt and jerkin from his neck. The Assassin leaned his head back and closed his eyes, passively yielding to Kerrick's ministration.

"I'll want to lay you down. Can you stand at least as far as the bed?" Kerrick asked.

"Aye." Morgan braced his hands against the arms of the chair, then paused before he glanced up. "With a little help," he admitted.

Kerrick grasped him by the elbows, pulling the man up easily. Supporting him by the arms to allow Morgan to gain his feet, Kerrick bit his lip for a moment, then said reluctantly, "I could carry you, if it is easier."

The man smiled sickly, head lolling back as he looked up. "Sir, I have no pride you could injure," he said, his breathing coming in painful gasps now.

He was lighter than Kerrick expected as he picked him up like a child. Morgan's head rested against his shoulder, legs swinging disjointedly, and he could feel the shudders wracking the man's body. Kerrick stretched him out on Antonya's bed and began unbuckling his boots. "How long have you been feeling ill?" he asked, concentrating on pulling off Morgan's boots and wool leggings.

"Two days, little more," Morgan said calmly, although his breath rasped in his throat.

Kerrick refrained from asking why he hadn't said something earlier. What would it have mattered? Morgan must have known it was the Fever. *Where is that damned charlatan?* he cursed to himself, his fingers busy working to unlace Morgan's breeches. God seemed unusually attuned to his thoughts this day. As if the alchemist had been conjured, he heard Doctor Tyro bustling outside the tent.

He'd loosened Morgan's breeches, exposing the man's groin as Tyro entered the tent. The alchemist carried his bag, into which, Kerrick surmised, he had hurriedly thrown his palliatives and elixirs to judge by the way jars and bottles rattled around inside. He wore gloves and a crumpled cone-shaped mask tied firmly over his mouth and nose, looking oddly like a misshapen shore bird. But his brown eyes were warm and concerned.

Kerrick stood up wordlessly as Tyro came up beside him, both men staring down. Large swollen lumps had formed under the skin around Morgan's groin and thighs.

Silently, Tyro set the bag onto the floor before he pushed Morgan's shirt up, reaching underneath to probe the man's armpits. Kerrick knew without a word what the alchemist would find.

"I assume you know what it is you're looking at," the alchemist said dryly, voice muffled behind the beaked mask.

"Aye," Kerrick said dully. "All too well."

"I'd heard the rumors," Tyro replied and began to rummage

around inside his bag. "If you didn't catch it before, you'll not likely catch it now. But it also means that you've been appointed his nursemaid by default."

Kerrick nodded as Tyro pushed aside rolled parchments and set out various bottles of potions and chemicals on the table. Working briskly, the alchemist ground powders in his mortar, mixing them with a dark, sticky liquid.

"Undress him, but keep him wrapped warm, draw out the sweat," he said, his attention on his task. "Bathe him occasionally with a damp cloth—that will extract the poison and prevent it from festering into sores as well as reducing the fever. Be sure you save the used water, I'll have to detoxify it before it can be thrown away." The little man seemed confident as he poured the tarry syrup into a cup, and placed a spoon in it. He handed it to Kerrick. "Give him as much of this as he can tolerate, a little at a time, but make sure he drinks a lot of water, as the medicine takes a toll on the kidneys. If he throws it up, as he probably will, keep trying."

Kerrick took the cup, then watched as Tyro laid out a selection of small knives, their handles carved in ivory with mystical designs. Morgan watched with remote interest, as if he had already resigned himself to dying.

"I'll have to prick the buboes in his groin to drain off the corrupt humors," Tyro said conversationally.

"I know," Kerrick said, watching him work and feeling suddenly helpless. The alchemist spread a cloth across Morgan's thighs.

"Will it be necessary to restrain you?" the little man asked Morgan. The Assassin shook his head. "Hold his knees down all the same," Dr. Tyro said to Kerrick. Morgan didn't protest.

The skin of Morgan's groin was stretched tight over the swellings. Tyro held the small knife in one gloved hand while he probed a bubo. His forehead gleamed with sweat, and his hand trembled slightly, but he muttered inaudibly to himself and slid the knife into Morgan's flesh, making a deep incision. The Assassin didn't flinch.

When Tyro removed the blade, thick, yellow pus streaked with threads of blood oozed from the wound. The little man's eyes crinkled as he smiled with relief under the mask, then pressed against the wound, milking out the infected fluids. He repeated the procedure on the opposite side of Morgan's groin, then placed a crushed leaf against each puncture wound, and wrapped Morgan's thighs with bandages to hold the leaves in place.

Then he tossed the cloth he had used to collect the infection into the steel basin, stripped off his gloves and threw them in as well. As he took the basin to the table, he mumbled, "Stand out of my way, please," to Kerrick.

Kerrick watched as the alchemist poured an odorous liquid over the discarded cloth, muttering under his breath. "*Lavabo inter innocentes corpus . . .*" he intoned, and made several passes with his hands before sprinkling red powder on the wet cloth. "*Omnia occultus saecula saeculorum . . .*"

Then he set the basin on fire. An oily black smoke roiled from the basin as the alchemist lifted it in his hands and walked slowly three times around the supine man. "*Visibilium omnium et invisibilium . . .*"

Morgan smiled up at him, unimpressed by this display. The flames in the basin guttered out. "Well, that's that," Tyro said calmly, setting the smoldering basin back onto the table and coughing as he waved the smoke out of his eyes. "I suppose it would be better done by a man of the Faith, but it's the best *I* can do."

Kerrick watched bleakly as the little man repacked his apothecary bag. "Now we'll see if he lives through the night," he said. "You have to stay quarantined with him, I'm afraid. You may be immune to the Fever, but its pestilent vapors can cling to you all the same. We can't let it spread to the camp."

"I'm surprised the entire camp hasn't taken to its heels and scattered to the four winds already," Kerrick said sardonically.

The alchemist eyed him somberly. "You should give the loyalty of your friends more credit, sir," he said. "In the meantime, I will proceed with protective incantations around the outside of this tent, which will hopefully screen the worst of the banes."

Which way? Kerrick wondered silently. *To keep them in, or keep them out*? He followed the Dothinian to the door, lowering his voice so as Morgan wouldn't overhear. "All this babble is for show, isn't it, Tyro? There's no hope, he's going to die."

At that, the little man's eyes flared in anger. "There's always hope, sir," he snapped, but kept his voice down. "I don't know if he'll die or not. If it's too much for you to watch him suffer, then stick a knife in him and be done with it."

Then the man's eyes softened over the absurd beaked mask. "I'm a fine magician and part-time iatrochemist. I can even give a decent haircut and trim you a rakish beard. But that man's fate is in the hands of God, not mine."

Doctor Tyro slipped out of the tent. When Kerrick turned back to Morgan, he found the Assassin watching him. "I'll try not to have my death be too much of an inconvenience for you," the ailing man said, not a hint of mockery in his voice.

Kerrick scowled. "At least your ears haven't been affected."

Morgan exhaled and closed his eyes, and Kerrick wasn't sure if it was meant to have been a laugh.

The incantations seemed to go on for hours. The little alchemist stomped around in an endless circle outside, his toneless chanting interspersed with the spattering of some potion or another against the tent walls. Kerrick fed the Assassin a spoonful of the tarry elixir, sniffing it surreptitiously as the sick man swallowed without a grimace. It stank of burnt coal and sulfur, overpowering the faint bitter smell of medicinal herbs.

Eventually Morgan fell asleep, his eyes jerking under the lids as he dreamed, his hands twitching restlessly. He woke only to vomit, and choke down another spoonful of the noxious liquid before drifting immediately back into a stupor. Kerrick bathed his torso and face, brushing back the damp hair stuck to his hot forehead. Morgan's pale chest rose and fell shallowly, the air bubbling loosely in his lungs.

Kerrick lit a few candles as night fell, the camp eerily quiet, he noticed. Yellow light wavered against the tent walls, throwing up strange shadows. With the siege guns fallen silent, only the rustle of nocturnal animals sifted through the muted sounds of the camp in the stillness. Around midnight, he could even hear the faint bells of the Kaesyn sajada tolling mournfully in the dark.

He was standing with his back to Morgan, tiredly wringing out the used water out of the sodden cloths into a basin to save for Doctor Tyro.

"You bastard," a voice said, and Kerrick looked up in surprise. The words had been uttered with such hatred and contempt, it took him a moment to realize they had been spoken by Morgan.

The Assassin had propped himself up weakly on one elbow, glaring at him intently. Kerrick had never seen such hostility from Morgan before, nor much of any emotion to speak of.

"How could you do it?" Morgan snarled.

Kerrick snapped out of his astonishment. "I humbly beg your pardon, sir," he said stiffly. "Believe me, attending you was not my idea." He started toward him before he noticed that the Assassin's eyes were not focused properly on him at all.

"You betrayed us," Morgan said to the phantom only he could see in his delirium. He sat up farther on the bed, trembling violently, the corded muscles of his arms standing out in sharp relief. "You betrayed *me*." His voice was thick with anguish. "I loved you, *worshiped* you, why did you abandon me, just tell me, *why?*" He reached out to struggle with a ghost, half falling off the cot.

As Kerrick went to hold him down, Morgan launched himself at the big man, grabbing him by the throat. He dragged Kerrick down, and as they struggled, Kerrick was glad the younger man's legs were tangled in the bedclothes. Even weak with sickness, the Assassin was quick and deadly, delivering several bruising blows to Kerrick's head and chest. Fortunately, his aim was spoiled by the contradiction between reality and what he thought he saw.

With Morgan's hands clamped around his throat with deadly force, Kerrick felt his windpipe crimped, the air cut off. His lungs began to burn, blue and red flecks spinning through his vision. Struggling futilely, Kerrick finally threw himself onto the Assassin, letting his sheer bulk and weight crush down. The bed collapsed beneath the two of them, knocking the breath out of Morgan, who let out a pained grunt and lost his grip. Kerrick gasped for air, struggling to keep the lighter man pinned to the floor, cursing as they wrestled.

Morgan abruptly went limp, but when Kerrick cautiously raised his head up far enough to peer at the Assassin's face,

Morgan was still conscious, staring wide-eyed over his captor's shoulder. His eyes filled with tears as he began to keen, a tormented animal wail of grief and fear. Kerrick could only guess at what the man was seeing in the depths of his private Hell.

He raised himself off Morgan, sitting on the floor wearily. Aching where Morgan had struck him as well as from the bruises he'd got when he fell, Kerrick kept one hand on the man's chest as a precaution. Morgan jerked spasmodically, but the energy seemed to have drained out of him. The soft weeping continued unbroken, however.

Kerrick tied the Assassin down to the broken frame of the bed to forestall any further outburst before he finally fell asleep himself, back propped against a large wooden chest. Cloak wrapped around his shoulders, he rested his head on forearms crossed on his knees. He woke once. After noticing that Morgan was now silent and one candle had burnt out, he shifted his numb buttocks and dozed off again.

When he woke, the morning light was pale gray. He raised his head, wincing at the crick in his neck and shoulders, and found Morgan watching him. Stretching his legs out in front of him and groaning at the soreness, Kerrick got to his feet slowly. Rubbing his palms against his eyes, he scoured the throbbing ache in his head, pressing jittery spots of red against his eyelids.

He dropped his hands to peer blearily at the man on the floor. Morgan lifted his head to examine the rope restraints tying his wrists and ankles to the damaged bedframe.

"Did I injure you?" he asked softly, letting his head fall back.

Kerrick put a hand against his throat, grimacing. "No permanent damage, I think."

"How much did I say?"

Kerrick started to ask, *when?*—but stopped; the dangerous expression in Morgan's eyes would not endure any patronizing. "Enough," he said instead.

The Assassin stared at him dully, then turned his face to the wall and did not speak again for hours.

61

Antonya pushed the stray hair back from her forehead, bent over the map spread out on a small table. She still wore a light day robe, not yet dressed. The remains of her breakfast lay on a pewter dish weighting one end of the map, the food barely touched. She traced the lines of the Kaesyn springs with one finger, although she knew them well enough to see the sketches with her eyes closed.

As if she couldn't bear the sight, only one side of the tent had been rolled up, facing away from Kaesyn. She ignored the men standing idle, Daen quietly outside the tent behind Sarnor. Sarnor, she knew, would remain with his legs braced apart, hands behind his back, and watch the damned silent walls of the city all day long without a word. He, like most of the camp, waited in hushed anxiety, the entire camp ominously inactive.

Sarnor turned as Tyro came down the steps of his small wagon, the beak mask discarded. The alchemist crossed the small makeshift square toward Antonya's tent. The dust of the packed dirt swirled in grayish eddies around his feet, the mountain air dry and cold. Ducking under the canvas tenting, he squinted at the unrolled map.

"The configurations of the stars don't say one damned thing or the other," he told Antonya, a scrap of paper in his hand covered with diagrams and mathematical computations. "Not that they ever reveal all that much, anyway, to tell you the truth. Wasted night."

She wasn't sure if he meant Morgan or Kaesyn, and didn't ask.

"Antonya, either it worked or it didn't. There's nothing further can be done about it. We simply have to wait."

She glared. "I didn't ask for your opinion."

"Well," the Dothinian said, unoffended but his eyebrow raised slightly, "you've got it for free, then."

She frowned, regretting her sharpness. "How is Morgan?"

Tyro shrugged eloquently. "Your man Guyus and I have

shoved every concoction we can think of down that poor bastard's throat, and half as many up his backside. I've cooked up a horrid brew of wood sorrel roots and elder bark and Guyus has practically buried him under althea and soapwort-root plasters. But Guyus is a bone-cracker, madam, and I'm just a dabbler in colorful fireworks."

She shook her head. "All because of a bit of silver."

"Or the fact that he went crawling around in a sewage duct with any number of nicks and cuts all over him," Tyro countered. "Evil banes have infinite ways to infest the body. But we aren't discounting the Weird. We've even listened to that disgusting *dombah* crone living with the whores who claims she has mystic healing powers. She had the boy choke down the vilest smelling pottage of garlic and mustard seed boiled in rose vinegar and fermented ass's milk. If we don't cure him, we'll kill him for sure." Tyro patted her hand assuagingly.

"M'Lady," Sarnor said quietly, his eyes still on the city behind her. Heads all around snapped up, a murmur buzzing through as men stood up, attention riveted on the city.

Antonya stepped quickly out of the tent, blinking in the sunlight. A white cloth was being waved from the battlements over the City Gates, and a few minutes later she made out the figure of a man precariously being lowered on a rope, waving his white flag hysterically.

She smiled, then turned to scowl as a few of her armsmen began a low cheer. They could celebrate when they were inside the walls, not before. But she spotted a soldier with a bucket of water in his hand, pausing on his way to water his horse.

"Sir," Antonya called out, and waved him over. Quickly, she unplaited her hair and ran her fingers through it. Shaking it loose, she astonished the soldier as well as the other armsmen looking on by leaning over and dunking her head solidly into the bucket. She whipped her head back, water spraying in an arc, and grinned as the water dribbled down her face.

Sarnor regarded her with an amused twinkle; Daen simply gaped.

"I am *most* displeased," she said in a parody of regal disdain while tugging her day robe haughtily around her neck, "at having my bath disturbed."

Realizing, the soldier holding the bucket suddenly laughed.

If the Kaesyn springs had indeed gone dry and the citizens thirsty, it would be very discouraging indeed for the approaching envoy to find precious water being wasted on mere bathing.

By the time the man arrived, Antonya was slouched arrogantly in a field chair inside the tent, a towel around her wet shoulders. Sarnor escorted the envoy inside, and she was satisfied to see the man's eyes widen with resentful surprise. He covered it as best he could with a quick bow.

"Lady Antonya," he said, "my name is T'ross, Alderman in the Weavers Guild. I have been elected to represent the collective Guilds." He was thin, the skin around his eyes sallow, and she could tell he was in need of a decent bath himself. A very good sign.

She left him standing, and gestured toward Daen without taking her eyes off the envoy twisting his hat in his hands. Barely able to conceal his smile, the armsman poured out a large tankard of ale and handed it to her. T'ross watched unblinkingly as she drank deeply, smacking her lips as she set the tankard down. He swallowed, forcing himself to look away.

"I've come to negotiate the terms of surrender," he said, his voice rasping.

"I've already sent my terms to Achbith, the goldsmiths' Guildmaster."

"Aye, and quite acceptable to us they were indeed. But as you might expect, we haven't managed to achieve an accord with the Faith."

"Not my problem," she said shortly.

He sighed, a bit desperately. "G'untur is dead, as you probably know—killed by a daemon you conjured from the Weird, it's being said. His second is a man called Breme, and I have been directed to speak on the new commander's behalf as well."

"Isn't this Breme one of Terhune's Elite?"

The man's mouth thinned. "Aye, he is, but . . ."

"No." She stood and turned away as if to dismiss him.

T'ross's knuckles were white where he clenched his hat. The velvet may once have been fine but was now worn thin in spots, having apparently seen a good deal of handwringing recently.

"Madam, *please*," he said fiercely, "What harm is there in hearing me out?"

She looked back at him, and waited.

T'ross inhaled to calm himself. "Our wells are completely dry, people are perishing of thirst. Were it up to the Guilds, we'd have opened the gates days ago," he said, his frown drawing two deep lines in his face from nose to chin. Antonya fought down the urge to cheer, hiding her exultation behind a fierce scowl. The man blanched. "But Kaesyn is controlled by the Faith, and we are only merchants, not soldiers. We can't open the gates to you without the consent of the Faith. They have the point of their swords closer to our throats than you, and will kill us just as quickly."

"And this Breme?"

"He will not give up the fortress, but he's willing to exchange the entire civilian population for Kaesyn. Let us go in peace." T'ross pressed on desperately as she began to shake her head. "He's sent word to the Oracular City for help—by now Terhune must know how close Kaesyn is to falling . . ."

She laughed. "My daemon also killed Kaesyn's chief signaling officer, sir. I doubt any such message was sent, or if it was, that it would be trusted. Even if a message was sent and Terhune believed it, he would not send any troops down the valley to rescue you. It is just as difficult for him to strike at us through this terrain as it is for us. His only concern now is the safety of the Citadel. No, if Terhune knows Kaesyn will capitulate, he'll be pulling back his forces as quickly as he can to repel us at the Oracular City."

T'ross said nothing, nibbling on his chapped lips.

"Surely Breme realizes further resistance will only lead to unnecessary loss of life. It is no disgrace to surrender, and holding the citizens of Kaesyn hostage is futile if you all die of thirst."

"You don't *need* Kaesyn now, madam, he's bottled up as tight as if you took it. The Tarax is open to you, he can't stop you . . ."

"No, he rids himself of fifty thousand mouths to feed and loads me down with fifty thousand refugees. Then he's free to strike at my back once it's turned. He must think me a fool."

T'ross looked miserable. "You have been celebrated for

your mercy and compassion, Lady. Have you none for us?"

She was silent for a moment. "Yes, T'ross, I do. You have my complete sympathy." Her tone was ruthless.

T'ross understood. "We want to surrender, Lady Antonya," he said bleakly. "What do you expect us to do?"

"Open the gates."

T'ross sighed. "Breme is prepared to kill every person inside the city before he and his own men commit suicide."

She stared at him a long time. "Open the gates," she repeated finally, very softly. "I give you my word, I intend no harm to any civilian. I will treat with leniency any of the Faith taken prisoner who are not military. But no one in Terhune's Elite will be permitted to flee. They must surrender unconditionally."

The man regarded the crushed hat in his hands. "Are you willing to let thousands of innocent people die for a handful of Priests?" he asked bitterly.

She was aware of Sarnor watching her phlegmatically. "Yes." She turned to Daen. "Please get the gentleman an ale, and all the water he wants to drink." Her armsman nodded as she watched T'ross struggle, knowing he wanted to refuse and hating himself for not being able to. "Open the gates, sir," she said a last time, and left with Sarnor at her side.

"There are more civilians in Kaesyn than in Ilona, madam," he said quietly.

She nodded. "Are you questioning me?"

Sarnor smiled dryly. "No, Lady, not I."

She stopped at the rise of the hill, staring at the towering walls in the distance. "I lied, Sarnor," she said, not taking her eyes off the city. "I wish I could say it hurts. I wish I could say my heart is heavy, that I'll grieve and suffer for those who die." She paused for a long moment, as Sarnor waited patiently.

"But I can't," she finished eventually, thinking of B'nach. "I've learned how to sleep at night with the guilt. It doesn't work anymore, I've become inured to the pain caused in my name."

"Mmm." Sarnor folded his arms across his chest. "Questions of guilt or sorrow aside," he said, no disapproval in his voice, "it does place the Kaesyn Guilds in an interesting strategic quandary. Either way they choose, they risk being slaughtered by the Priests. It's a question of which they think will cost them the least."

"And you?" She studied his wry expression. "Which do you think they'll do?"

He chuckled. "They'll open the gates."

62

Doctor Tyro held the bit of smoldering straw close to the swollen worm, its segmented body distended with blood. With a small popping noise, the last leech let go of Morgan's skin, leaving a tiny oozing wound. Its blind face jerked away irritably from the glow before Tyro snatched it up with tweezers and dropped it into a jar.

The alchemist seemed pleased with how much the swellings around Morgan's groin had lessened, examining the stab wounds briefly before replacing the bandages with fresh leaves and cloth. Kerrick was thankful he didn't repeat his previous fiery performance.

"You may just live," Tyro said to Morgan, his voice suggesting both astonishment and pride. "Either I'm getting better at leeching, or there's more of the Weird in you than you think, dear boy."

Morgan stared back inscrutably, his face drawn and hollow.

The little man had to stand on a chair to sprinkle a musty orange dust over Kerrick. "This'll give you some protection," he assured him. The orange dust already coated everything in the tent, now that the rest of the precious maps had been removed and carefully purified. Once the patient and his nurse were allowed to leave, there would be more purification to suffer through. The tent itself would be lucky; it would simply be burnt to the ground with everything left inside.

Kerrick stoically closed his eyes as the acrid dust sifted over his head and shoulders, wondering briefly if the protection might extend to lunatic alchemists and their sorcerous cures. But he had to grudgingly admit that the hunchback's treatment had worked.

"I'll be back later on," Tyro said, packing up his apothecary briskly, and left with a buoyant spring in his step.

Kerrick dragged a chair to sit beside Morgan, propped up now on a pallet spread on the floor. "Morgan . . ." he began.

"It isn't necessary, sir," Morgan cut him off.

The Assassin lay half-sitting with his hands in his lap folded together. Kerrick studied those hands, impressed by how small and almost delicate they were, yet so deadly. He pensively touched his own neck, still dappled with bruises where Morgan had tried to throttle him.

"Morgan," he started again, more firmly, "you were more than his friend, weren't you?"

The Assassin didn't answer, staring at the roof of the tent.

Kerrick pressed gently. "Do you know why he killed Briston? If there is anything you haven't revealed for whatever reason, surely now would be the time to tell us."

Morgan turned eyes toward him that with a bit more warmth might have been angry. "Sir, do not assume because you've seen something you were not meant to that it gives you some special insight. What you heard speaking was the Fever, not me."

"I don't believe you," Kerrick said grimly.

Morgan sighed tiredly, leaning his head back and closing his eyes. "Your prerogative, Defender. I appreciate your attendance during my illness, but I have nothing further to say which could possibly enlighten you."

"And I think your Guild was both cutting its losses as well as buying time. I think, Morgan, you know more than you've told us. I cannot allow you to become a threat to Antonya."

The Assassin rolled his head to look at Kerrick. "What words could I find that might convince you, sir? What do you want to hear me say? Yes, Tevik was my friend. We grew up together. He was also my brother, my idol, and on occasion my lover. And I did love him, unwisely it seems. I don't know why he killed Briston. His desertion not only reflected badly on our teachers, it cast serious doubts on me. There was discussion as to whether or not my continued existence was advisable." Morgan recited the words with little feeling.

"Fortunately for me, Tevik was a man who shared his favors generously, I wasn't alone in their mistrust. The Guild disapproves of waste. They found a use for me which I accepted, quite happily."

"I have misgivings about exactly what that use *is*, Morgan. I don't trust your Guild, nor do I trust you."

Morgan exhaled, a sound more of weariness than exasperation. "I am no danger to the Lady Antonya. Believe me or not, as you please. Is there anything else you would like to know or have I confessed enough sordid little secrets to satisfy your prurient curiosity?"

Kerrick flushed angrily. "I was not attempting to pry into your private life, Morgan—"

Morgan cut him off abruptly. "You can't pry, sir, as I do not have a private life." He coughed, the phlegm rough and deep in his lungs, before he could speak again. "Or is that what you fear?" he asked, his voice hoarse but his eyes bright. "Is that why my private life is of such overwhelming interest to you? Briston was her bodyguard, perhaps you felt he had usurped your office. She loved him. Now he's gone, and I've replaced him. Were she to call me to her bed, I'd as readily replace him in that duty as well. Is it that you fear I will gain the Lady's affections you desire but can't allow yourself to even hope for . . ."

"Shut up," Kerrick snapped. Unable to tolerate being so close to Morgan, he stood and paced to the opposite side of the tent, the confined space pressing around him like an oppressive trap. He kept his back to the Assassin, unwilling to allow Morgan to see his pain.

Amazingly, Morgan laughed, the only time Kerrick had ever heard him do so. The vicious pleasure in it cut through the Defender like a knife. His fists clenched as he squeezed his eyes shut. "God damn you," he breathed, trembling.

"I've done you a favor, Kerrick," Morgan said softly, "to repay you for your kindness. You assumed camaraderie where none existed. I have no feelings of warmth or affection for you. You are not my friend, nor I yours, and I doubt you'll ever make that mistake again. I owe you nothing more."

Kerrick stayed rooted as far away as he could from the sick man, afraid of what he might do if he came too close. He turned slowly and glared at Morgan with hatred. "I should kill you," he said, trying to keep his voice from shaking. "I should rip out your black heart."

The Assassin smiled, teeth sharp, his eyes once again opaque. "Aye," he agreed. "Perhaps you should."

63

Antonya ordered the barrage to recommence, although Tyro's powder for the siege cannons was nearly used up and the cast-iron melonshot gone. Two of her *belfrois* had been destroyed by fire arrows shot into the wooden siege towers, and the remaining *belfroi* inched closer to the walls. Battering rams and borers in its lower story were useless. Even if it could have been brought close enough, the base of the fortress walls were built against solid rock. But the twin ballistas at its crown kept up a steady pounding against the fortified gate.

Armsmen rolled heavy mangonels dangerously closer to the walls. Behind protective stockade shields, soldiers naked to the waist and sweating even in the crisp mountain air heaved on the ropes, the winch clacking gear by gear as the lever was brought to the ground. Its huge maw was filled with heavy boulders and catapulted as high as the engineer could calculate the angle of trajectory. Now even the lighter trebuchets were using any loose rock her men found lying around at the already pockmarked walls, teams of horses dragging wagons full of rubble to fill the insatiable hunger of the catapults. Smashed fragments of stone littered the ground around the glacis.

A chain of men frantically hauled water up from the river, manning the complicated pulleys and ropes under the wary eyes of marksmen guarding their backs. Runners sprinted to dash buckets of water against the raw hide stretched over the *belfroi* and trebuchets, protecting them from fire arrows, and gleefully splashed each other under the eyes of the parched garrison.

Although the defenders seemed to be tearing down buildings wholesale to supply stone for their own catapults, the Kaesyn archers were responding more reluctantly, their artillery cannons almost silent. Kaesyn's supply of fire arrows and gunpowder was not inexhaustible either, it seemed.

Antonya's assault, however, produced little real devastation, but the cheers of her men anticipating the city's fall grew louder as a merlon here and there crumbled, like an aging matron slowly losing her teeth.

Sarnor heard it first, holding his hand up in a signal for the artillery to cease its fire. As a hush settled over the siege camp, Antonya listened. The sound of fighting inside the walls was faint but clear. A slow, ruthless grin spread across Sarnor's face, his eyes gleaming as he turned to look at Antonya.

"Get the men in formation, officers to horse," she said quietly, her heart racing with excitement. "They're going to open the gates."

Mellas whooped, the command spreading with nearly telepathic speed. The troops scrambled around Antonya in noisy confusion, shouts for arms and horse drowning the sound of battle within Kaesyn's walls. Within minutes, a hastily formed phalanx crowded along the isthmus road. Tobias on his high-spirited roan brought up Antonya's mare while balancing her standard overhead. The silk snapped in the breeze, the plain Terhune red shield against pure white.

The white mare skittered under Antonya as she mounted, the excitement infectious. Sarnor had bulled his horse through the infantry, armor plate gleaming over the face, neck and shoulders of the black warhorse. The animal's hooves had been painted bright red, as if the creature had recently stomped in blood. Better trained for battle than either of the two other skittish horses, the black stood with braced legs, drawing in the smell of the battle with wide nostrils.

Although it seemed like hours, it didn't take long. The huge iron-reinforced gates creaked, a sliver of daylight appearing as the portcullis rolled up with ponderous grace. A cheer went up as Antonya's men surged forward, dragging their breaching bridge in their midst. They reached the ruined edge of the glacis, and cut the winch, the drawbridge slamming down onto the pilings across the wide ditch.

The portcullis was nearly fully up as Antonya's army swept into Kaesyn. Behind the main brigade, Antonya and Sarnor pressed through, their horses chafing at their bits. Once clear, it was all too apparent which way the Priests had gone. The townsfolk themselves pointed toward the keep, urging their conquerors on.

The Old Palace had already fallen, the townsfolk in a frenzy of looting and vandalism. Gray-robed Priests surrendered in frightened droves, bleeding and battered, impeding Antonya's men as they frantically begged to be taken prisoner. None were Terhune's military Elite; most were young acolytes or elderly scholars. But the general hysteria gripping the mob made little distinction.

Another Priest screamed, pursued by a gang of civilians. He beat frantically at his head, his hair on fire. The mare shied away in alarm, then reared, front hooves raking the air. Antonya sawed the reins to bring the animal down. Sarnor grabbed the reins, Nicoli hanging his weight on her saddle to keep the horse under control.

A brick hit a thin, elderly Priest in the head, obviously no soldier, sending him reeling, blood pouring down his face. He stumbled to his knees, hands held out beseechingly before the mob fell on him. He disappeared under a hail of stones and fists.

"Goddamn it," Mellas snarled in frustration. "They're killing them all! These wretched bastards aren't going to leave a cursed one of them alive for us to hang!"

Sarnor watched him stoically for a moment, then shot a quick look at Antonya before he disappeared into the milling crowd. She noticed, but quickly forgot about it as Daen elbowed his way to her.

"The siege cannon is through the gates, madam," he panted.

"I don't think it's going to be necessary," she said, watching uneasily as the townsfolk zealousy assisted her armsmen as they wheeled the big cannon through the hall and out into the courtyard between the Old Palace and the New.

She had guessed correctly. The square keep had been abandoned, the great siege doors open and the courtyard littered with abandoned red robes, their owners attempting to escape in the mass confusion.

A lone Priest stumbled out into the daylight, wearing nothing but a linen sleeping shirt, his legs bare. A collective growl issued from the throats of the mob, making the hair on Antonya's neck prickle. Instantly, the man was surrounded and disappeared under the assault. Her armsmen waded hastily into the crowd, knocking aside the more aggressive to grab the Priest. He was finally dragged forward and tossed, bruised and bleeding, at her horse's feet, half-dead. The animal stamped nervously, nearly trampling the man.

Mellas snatched up a red uniform empty of its owner, and shook it furiously under the terrified nose of the injured Priest. "Where are the rest?" he shouted. "Where the Hell are they?"

Any answer the man might have given was lost in a garbled rush of stuttering. Mellas threw the cloth into his face in disgust, then turned, bellowing in no particular direction: "*Cowards! Dogs! Come out and fight like men!*"

Sarnor had returned, escorting Achbith through the press of the mob. The Guildmaster glanced at the battered prisoner. "He's not one of Terhune's Elite," he said conversationally. "But I don't think you'll have any trouble picking out who's who, however they're dressed. We know them all."

"I had no idea how much the Kaesyns hated the Faith," Antonya said as her armsmen pushed back the more unruly bent on attacking their prisoner.

"We don't. We simply objected to them killing us to prevent our surrender." Achbith turned his dour scowl toward her. "As you would have allowed us to die if we didn't."

"There he is, that's him!" a townsman suddenly shouted, and pointed an accusatory finger, shaking with rage and fright. "That's Breme!" It took Antonya a few moments to recognize the speaker as T'ross of the Weavers Guild. The thin man's fine attire was now ripped and blood-spattered, his face transfigured with the frenzy of violence.

The Priest wearing a gray robe slightly too large for his frame froze, his eyes white, then broke and ran as Antonya's men, as well as more than a few of Kaesyn's own citizenry gave chase. Several of them waved thick clubs of lumber and others tossed broken bricks.

The mob's mood was becoming dangerous, and Antonya's own men were nervous, sensing how the mindless bloodlust consuming thousands of the hysterical Kaesyns could all too easily turn against them. In a few more minutes, Antonya could find herself forced to retreat from her newly won city.

"We'd better do something quickly," Sarnor warned, "before it gets out of control. Offer a ransom."

"A gold coin for every Priest brought to me alive!" Antonya shouted, her voice breaking as she struggled to be heard above the bedlam. It was hopeless. "I want them alive!" Her throat was scraped raw, but she could barely even hear herself.

"*A gold piece!*" Achbith's deep baritone boomed out. Several of the mob faltered, looking around. "A gold piece for every living Priest! They're no good dead, catch the villains alive!"

"A gold piece!" the chant was taken up. "Take them alive!"

Antonya looked down at Achbith in surprise, the fat man rubbing sweat from his face with his rich sleeve. Sarnor nodded grimly, and she realized his warning hadn't been directed to her. "Well, a little more than we'd agreed, sir, but worth it," the mercenary said.

"I thank you, but it's coming out of your own purse, you know," Antonya said to the Guildmaster.

Achbith laughed. "Aye, but I'm charging you fifty percent of your ransom for the use of my melodious voice. Better to make a little back than lose it all. *A gold piece for every living Priest!*" he shouted at another pack of frenzied citizens spilling out into the street in pursuit of another bloodied cleric. The sheer volume of Achbith's voice caused both civilians and Priests to stagger before their ears registered his words.

"Get him!" a woman shrilled. "Take him alive!"

The Priest sprinted down a side street, sandals flying, with the crowd in pursuit.

"Good thinking, Lady," Mellas said, rubbing his hands together cheerfully, metal gauntlets rasping. "At least we'll have a few to string up over the wall. Make the sons of bitches dance on air."

64

Doctor Tyro walked into the tent just as Kerrick had begun helping Morgan to dress. The two men had remained in the cleared center of the tent which Tyro had already purified, the tainted furniture pushed to the canvas walls with kindling stacked around it, ready for the pyre.

The Assassin had lost a frightening amount of weight, his already lean body now skeletal. His breeches and boots on, he sat in a chair with his chest bare, ribs in stark relief against his pale, hairless skin. His hair hung loosely around bone-sharp shoulders, still wet and tangled from the bath. Kerrick took up the comb and began raking it over the man's scalp. Dark eyes placid in the hollows of his skull, he accepted Kerrick's abusive ministrations without complaint.

"You look like death warmed over," the alchemist said cheerfully. He pressed an ear to the man's chest. The wound that G'untur's knife had left along his ribs was an angry red scar. "Breathe in. Hold it. Breathe out." Morgan complied, submitting to the doctor's groping fingers in his armpits and groin as passively as a tart being inspected by a potential patron. Behind him, Kerrick finished braiding his hair into a tight plait, tying it off with a leather throng.

Doctor Tyro straightened and nodded with pursed lips. "Lungs still a bit congested, but nothing to worry about. The rest of you is healing nicely. A few days more rest and some hearty food to fill out that tough body of yours again is all you need now."

Morgan looked at him indifferently, then glanced at Kerrick as the large man tossed a linen shirt into his lap.

"Glad to hear you've recovered," Kerrick said bluntly. "Let's see if you can put that on all by yourself, then." He watched dispassionately as Morgan slowly pulled the shirt over his head. By the time he'd managed to shove his arms through the sleeves and tie the laces, he was panting, his face ashen and glistening with sweat. Kerrick smiled, contemptuous. He threw Morgan's baldric and black jerkin hard against the man's chest. "You're doing fine, man. One might never know you'd been ill."

The alchemist frowned, but didn't interfere. Morgan had to use both hands to push himself upright, using the chair as a crutch before he could stand. He braced one hip against the chair and tucked the hem of his shirt into his breeches before laboriously buckling on the baldric and shrugging into his jerkin. It hung loosely on his frame.

"Excellent, sir," Kerrick said, smiling tightly. "But let's not forget your knife." He tossed Briston's heavy dagger toward him, and watched with grudging respect as the Assassin deftly plucked it out of the air, almost stumbling under the weight.

Morgan held the dagger slackly by his side, every muscle quivering, his eyes glassy. Kerrick grinned and impulsively stepped within the Assassin's killing reach, his hands empty. The Assassin's upper lip twitched with scorn before he tucked the heavy blade into the baldric under his jerkin, his fingers fumbling with the knots.

"Have you two finished, then?" Tyro asked. Kerrick ignored the implication in his tone.

"Aye," he said, disgusted. "We're quite finished."

The hunchbacked doctor lifted the flap of the tent as Kerrick stepped out into the daylight, supporting Morgan's shaky weight on one arm. In the distance, Kerrick heard the dying sound of battle, saw smoke, the wheeling of dust churned up by horse and soldier. *Where are you, Antonya?* he thought, wanting more than anything else to have been at her side when Kaesyn fell, not trapped behind the lines playing nursemaid to a fiend. His eyes watered merely from the blinding sunlight, he was certain, not frustration or disappointment.

Those who were not combatants saw them emerge, the harlots and camp followers, cooks and horseboys, the servant women, the injured. A one-eyed soldier, head swathed in bloodied bandages grinned with blackened teeth as he spotted them. "Morgan!" he shouted, his voice hoarse. "Long live Morgan the Assassin!"

Startled, the Assassin stopped warily.

"*Morgan! Morgan! Morgan!*" It was a chant of victory that grew as other voices took it up, tears smearing the faces of painted whores, the casualties waving their crutches or cheering from their litters. Several others yelled *"Kerrick! Kerrick!"*—and one or two even chanted *"Tyro! Tyro!"*, much to the good doctor's embarrassed delight. But their favorite hero was all too obvious. A blond child of no more than five, dressed in the colorful rags of the *dombah*, ran up to them on bare feet to offer the Assassin a handful of hastily plucked wildflowers. Morgan stared at them without moving, then glanced up as Kerrick gripped his arm tightly.

"Take them," Kerrick said in a low, dangerous voice, the smile on his face stark.

Morgan took the flowers, holding them stiffly in one hand as the child ran back to her mother coaching her from the cheering crowd.

"Now smile sweetly," Kerrick said, yanking the Assassin into a slow walk beside him. "And wave to the good people." He himself raised a hand, acknowledging the cheers. He turned, still grinning savagely, to look down at Morgan's lifeless face. "Do it before I twist your head from your shoulders and shove it up your foul arse."

Kerrick watched a flicker of amusement in the Assassin's eyes before Morgan forced his facial muscles into the semblance of a smile. He lifted one hand to wave as they walked together, a companionable pair. Another child, this one better dressed, offered a ragged bunch of flowers to both. Kerrick took his offering and patted her on the head and watched as Morgan accepted his solemnly. A wounded man grabbed Morgan's free hand, shaking it briefly with tears in his eyes. Then, to Kerrick's astonishment, a harlot dashed up to the Assassin, grabbed his shoulder and planted a kiss on his mouth before running away. Morgan had gone rigid, still braced on Kerrick's arm. The next bold whore who tried was gently stopped by Kerrick, the big man's hand coming down as a barrier between the Assassin and her. "Mercy, madam," Kerrick said, half-laughing, "would you kill him with kindness now that he's survived?"

"I'll be kissin' you, then!" she giggled shrilly, and mashed her painted lips against his ruined ones. Her wet tongue licked him like a cat before she danced away, leaving behind the smell of her perfume masking rank sweat.

He felt the Assassin's body shivering with fatigue through

the arm encircling his own, and stopped, turning to watch as Doctor Tyro ritualistically set the sick tent on fire. It went up with a whoosh of flame and sparkling colors, which Kerrick suspected the doctor had added more for the spectacle than for any medical reason. The crowd cheered louder, celebrating the fire. The two men stood watching it burn.

"So, how does it feel to be a hero, Morgan?" Kerrick asked.

Morgan didn't look up at him. "I wouldn't know, sir, since I'm not a hero."

"Ah, but the good people here believe you one."

This time the Assassin glanced at Kerrick, his dark eyes empty. "Belief does not make it so," he said quietly. "Were truth created by belief, I could sprout daemon wings and fly away."

Kerrick smiled at him, this time with some honest feeling behind it. "God's holy blood, Morgan, you may yet. But you tremble, man. Can it be that you are actually *afraid* to be praised and respected?"

The Assassin blinked, expressionless, and looked back at the camp crowd swarming around them, congratulating him, applauding him. He regarded them as warily as a trapped animal watching the hunter approach. For a moment, Kerrick almost felt sorry for him, then remembered the vicious nature of the creature he supported on one arm, weakened but still lethal.

"Come," Kerrick said quietly. "Let us watch our good Lady as she thrusts the knife into Kaesyn's belly. You will enjoy that, won't you?"

65

The dungeons under the keep of the Old Palace had been painstakingly dug out of the rock, massive pillars supporting the low arches. The smaller cells had been emptied of prisoners, innocent Kaesyn citizens released into the bosom of their families, or at least petty thieves again free to prowl the streets.

Ephraim walked in front of Kerrick down the spiraling stairs holding the single rush-torch, all the light there was in the cold underground prison. Grotesque daemons had been carved into the capitals, crouched under the vaulted ceiling. Hideous grins stared down at the prisoners as the figures tortured their stone victims. A bloated daemon with leathery wings gripped a naked, chained man, talons buried into his chest as it pulled the man's damned soul from his mouth and devoured it. Another with a serpent's body crushed a woman in its coils, her silent stone scream a prophecy to those living prisoners. Nicoli led a half dozen armed men following behind, Ephraim's torch making the shadows of the carved daemons dance along the walls.

Voices echoed off the vaulted walls in the dark as the prisoners whispered to each other, but hushed as they heard the clang of metal and the sound of heavy footsteps descending the stone stairway. The surviving Priests and Elite huddled together in a single cell, only sixty men left of more than two hundred, restless and cramped in the restricted cell suited for twenty. Most were frightened scholars and clerics. But among them were the hardened faces of soldiers, conspicuous even without uniforms. The Priests held their hands up to shield their light-starved eyes from the sudden brightness.

Kerrick stopped in front of the cell, slightly hunched over under the low ceiling. Behind him, the armsmen stood ready, crossbows primed and aimed at the prisoners.

"Commander Breme," he called out.

The Priests exchanged looks, then one of them stood up tiredly. "I am Breme," he said, and carefully stepped through the knot of arms and legs to stand facing Kerrick through bolted iron bars.

The Priest looked older, fear having given his legs a temporary youthful strength. Now he looked haggard and resigned. His overlarge gray robe was torn and spattered with blood, most of it his own. Breme grasped one bar of the grille, leaning against it for support as he watched Ephraim jiggle the heavy key into the lock. He ignored the arrows leveled at his head less than an arm's length away. The Priests' late jailer had kept his cell doors in good working order, the key turning easily in the well-oiled mechanism, the stout bolt opening smoothly.

"Stand back from the door," Kerrick ordered.

Breme did as he was told. The tension in the remaining Warrior-Priests was palpable as the cell door opened, a few balancing on their haunches expectantly. They subsided as crossbows were raised to shoulders and arrows aimed at their chests. Kerrick motioned the commander through the narrow cell door. His arms down by his side, Breme stepped through. He made no resistance as Kerrick jerked him roughly to one side. The iron door slammed shut, bolts snapping into place.

The Priest watched indifferently as Nicoli began clamping manacles around his wrists, the sleeves of his borrowed gray robe nearly reaching past his fingertips.

"You've abandoned your lofty Elite uniform, sir," Kerrick said with the hint of a smile.

Breme raised his chin as compliantly as he would for a barber's razor as Nicoli fastened the iron collar around his throat and ran the chain through the bolt to the manacles. "It's only cloth. Since your men had orders to slaughter anyone wearing it, that seemed to be the intelligent thing to do at the time," Breme commented dryly.

There was no further conversation, the only sound the clank of chains looped around the man's waist and shackled to the iron bar clamped at either end to his ankles. Nicoli stood, nodding at Kerrick, and the armsmen led their prisoner up the stairway. Breme kept his attention focused on negotiating the steps, awkward and slow, but made no objection. Once, as he stumbled, Kerrick caught him by the elbow and steadied him.

The Priest glanced at him with a faint, mocking smile, and said nothing.

The massive door leading into the dungeon cells swung open to let in the light of day, Breme squinting as they reached the top of the stairs. In the light, the Priest's injuries were more apparent. His sparse, graying hair stuck to his scalp in matted clumps of dried blood from a jagged cut across his temple, both eyes bruised and swollen. Despite his age, the Warrior-Priest was still a tough old bird.

Breme looked around the wide hall expectantly. Two armsmen stood guard on either side of another wide staircase leading to the upper floors of the tower. As Kerrick motioned him toward it with a parody of courtesy, the Priest sighed and shuffled forward.

He was out of breath by the time he'd managed to climb the three floors to the top, weighted down by his fetters. The armsmen opened the double doors and pulled back the tapestry to allow the prisoner and his guards inside.

The chamber had belonged to G'untur, and no doubt for a brief period of time to Breme after his superior's murder. Shutters had been pulled back from large windows to allow in the daylight, thick bubbled glass keeping out the chill mountain air. Logs blazed in the massive fireplace, a dozen birds roasting on iron spits. Regine had set several pots of cheese pies to bake along one side, and Kerrick's mouth watered at the savory aroma filling the room. Although he knew the man had eaten nothing but watery gruel, and not even that in over a day, Breme gave no indication of his own hunger.

Daen lounged on the long bench at the foot of the canopied bed with one knee drawn up. Leaning against an embroidered pillow cushioning the planks of carved wood, he plucked a tune idly from the strings of a lute. He looked up as Kerrick escorted Breme into the room, the music falling silent.

Antonya sat at the table by the fireplace in the ornate carved throne, playing chess with Tobias. The armsman ignored Kerrick and his prisoner as they approached, leaning his chin against his fist to intently study the chess pieces laid out in front of him. Opposite the armsman, a gray-robed scribe sat hunched over his writing box, jittery and uneasy as the chained man approached, his quill held over blank paper with a shaking hand. Half-hidden in the shadow cast by the firelight, Morgan leaned against a wall.

Antonya watched them with pale yellow eyes as they crossed the huge room, Breme's chains jangling. She wore the tabard with the plain red Terhune crest over her riding clothes. Tobias moved a chess piece on the board and then sat back on his stool, looking up at the prisoner in vague surprise as if the man had materialized from thin air while he wasn't looking.

As Kerrick pulled Breme to a halt before Antonya, the man's eyes flicked to the crest, then to her face, with no apparent emotion.

"I am Antonya Terhune of Adalon and Ashmael," Antonya said. The scribe bent his head over the paper, his quill scratching diligently.

The Priest said nothing for a long moment. When he spoke, his tone was conversational. "I knew your father."

Antonya gaped at him, shaken. Even the scribe looked up, the scratching of his quill momentarily silenced. Kerrick was alarmed to see how badly her poise had slipped. "My father," she repeated finally, unable to hide the longing in her voice. "Were you friends?"

The Priest smiled wryly, obviously satisfied with the effect of his words. "R'bert? I didn't much like him, to be honest."

Antonya recovered her composure. "Well, now you have reason not to care much for his daughter, either."

Breme conceded the point with a gracious bow of his head, keeping his eyes on her face. "What do you want of me?"

"Your formal surrender." Antonya glanced at the chessboard, examining the patterns with impatience.

"Why?" He held up his chained wrists as evidence. "My submission now seems a rather pointless exercise."

"To make things legal," she said reasonably, and moved a chess piece of her own. Tobias again bent over the board, lost in concentration.

Breme chuckled. "You won, we lost. Kaesyn is yours. You *have* us, madam—do as you like. What more can you want?"

"War has rules, sir, which all civilized peoples must respect. One of which is the necessity to keep written records of official treaties of surrender. It makes the legitimacy of terms agreed to much easier to prove should any objections arise at a later date." She took a sheet of paper covered with the scribe's neat writing and pushed it across the table toward Breme. He glanced at it with distracted interest, then at Antonya questioningly.

"Sign it."

Breme shuffled forward, leaning clumsily over the table to pick up the paper. He brought it as far up to his eyes as his manacled hands would allow and read the document. He rapidly scanned the text, and *tsk*ed like a disapproving schoolmaster. "You've misspelled 'unconditional,' Drizet," he said lightly without looking at the scribe.

Drizet flushed in embarrassment, glancing at Antonya out of the corner of his eye, his ink-stained fist clenching the feather quill tight enough to break it. Tobias made another move, capturing a rook.

Breme lowered the paper. "These aren't the terms you offered Achbith."

"No, indeed," Antonya agreed. She spoke without looking at him, studying the game in front of her. "But you're not Achbith. You rejected those terms, and threatened to massacre the very populace you were entrusted to protect. We were then compelled to take Kaesyn by force. This merely reflects the current circumstances, which you so eloquently described. We won, you lost. Kaesyn is mine and I shall do as I please with her. And with you."

A slow smile widened across Breme's face. He shook his head, and let the paper slip from his hand back to the table. "These conditions are unacceptable. I will not sign."

Deliberately, she moved a chess piece before she spoke. "Check," she said to Tobias, then looked up at Breme. "As you've already pointed out, you're in no position to negotiate anything. I had hoped you would have the courtesy to treat me as an honorable enemy, instead of forcing me to behave like a barbarian."

Breme shrugged. "A piece of paper changes nothing."

Antonya only smiled at the thinly veiled insult. "Then by the same logic, your signature is equally of little value. But perhaps I may be able to increase its worth?"

Breme snorted. "My life in exchange for my signature giving you legal possession of Kaesyn?"

"Oh, not at all, sir," she said. "Unfortunately, I do have to execute you. You've given me no other option. No, your only choice will be between slow strangulation hanging like a common thief or a quick and noble death by decapitation."

If Antonya had expected the Priest to be frightened, Kerrick was not surprised by Breme's disdain. The man obviously had held out no hope for clemency. He knew as well as she that the good citizens of Kaesyn were thirsting for vengeance against the Elite Priests. If at least one suitably dead body wasn't dangled over the ramparts soon, then they might be equally satisfied with her own.

Having already resigned himself to his fate gave Breme a certain freedom to face his enemy with defiant courage. "I have no preference either way. Death is death, madam. No one can ultimately avoid their own end, however it comes. But dishonor is something else again. Defeat and surrender is not treason." He glanced at Drizet, who avoided his eyes. "Do not insult me by expecting me to so easily betray my sworn oath to protect the Faith and the Citadel."

"The Citadel? Or P'tre Terhune?"

"The *Citadel*, madam," Breme insisted, his face suddenly hard. "I swore my most holy oath to the Faith to preserve and protect the interests of the Citadel from all her enemies, from within and without. My loyalty to P'tre Terhune comes second. Further, whatever allegiance I owe the Terhune family does not extend to a bastard's half-breed girl-child," Breme snorted harshly. "You're no Terhune, no matter who your father was. Your blood is plainly tainted, touched by the Weird you no doubt inherited from R'bert's unclean mother. You are neither Citadel bred, nor of any noble lineage of the Lords. You're merely another baseborn peasant, *Lady* Antonya."

Breme smiled like a death's head in the sudden silence, not hiding the triumph in his voice. Drizet seemed to have forgotten his function, his frightened bloodshot eyes darting back and forth between Antonya and Breme, as if waiting to see from which direction the ax would fall. Tobias had forgotten the chess game, staring at the chained Priest with open hostility. His hand settled onto his *poignard*. He subsided under

Kerrick's glance, but his hand remained tightened around the hilt, the knuckles of his fist white.

"Am I expected to feel offended, sir?" Antonya said finally, her tone perplexed. "I have never made a secret of the Landsblood in my veins. Why should I? I am proud of it. I am the embodiment of all the Lands' bloods, equally a daughter of the Faith as I am a daughter of the Landsfolk, both noble and common. Even the Weird has found its voice within me. Who better to join the Lands together as one than a child made greater by the sum of all its separate parts?"

"The Lands will only be joined by the One who is reborn through the Womb of God, as it has been prophesied for a thousand years. *You* could never Walk the Fire; you wouldn't survive."

"I don't intend to," Antonya said quietly. Kerrick glanced at her sharply, not sure if she meant the Walk or surviving. She sat back in the huge chair, relaxing. "Well, if we're quite finished with this theological debate, stimulating and amusing as it is, perhaps we might return to our discussion of your valuable signature on a worthless piece of paper, shall we?"

Tobias had reluctantly turned back to the game, studying it with visible effort. Breme remained silent.

"Give me what I want, Breme, and while I am unable to spare your own life, I'll give you what I first offered. You will buy the lives of the rest of your men. *All* of them."

The Priest slowly shook his head. "Their lives are not mine to traffic in. We were all consecrated to the Faith, madam. If God wills us to die for it, we will."

She sighed ruefully. "You're a hard man, sir. I really would much prefer not having to torture it out of you."

Breme looked surprised. "That would certainly be contrary to your reputation, madam."

She nodded, all the veneer of humor gone. "True. But at the moment, I simply haven't the time for such civilized compassion." She raised her hand, signaling to Morgan. The Assassin stepped out of the shadows and stood next to her, his arm resting loosely on the back of her chair as he watched the Priest with dark, mocking eyes. He had recovered most of his strength if not his weight in the past two days.

Breme glanced at him and swallowed. "I will not sign," he

said doggedly. Morgan smiled, his exposed teeth sharp in his thin face.

"You know my Assassin. And you know he can do it."

"Most likely." The man had paled, the muscles in his jaw twitching. "But it will take time, and I swear I'll cost you as much of that precious commodity as I can humanly bear." The chain links of his irons chattered like tiny bells and he clasped his hands together to stop their trembling.

The fire crackled pleasantly, but Kerrick's blood had gone cold, the smell of roasting fowl no longer appetizing. The scribe Drizet huddled away from them all, slumped down in his seat as if trying to vanish by sheer act of will.

"The line between tyrant and hero is very thin," Antonya said softly. "I'll have what I want from you no matter what it takes."

Breme stared at her. "I was wrong, Lady," he said, hoarsely. "Now I can see the Terhune blood in you quite clearly. How much like P'tre you are, after all."

Antonya reacted as if the man had struck her across the face. Her face drained as white as her prisoner's, her hands clenched the arms of her chair.

"The difference being I get no joy from it, sir," she said, her voice thick.

Breme laughed, the effort forced. "Do you think that really matters to the man being broken on the rack?"

He kept his gaze level as she glared at him in the strained hush. Finally, she reached for the paper lying on the table. Her palm settled into its center, the scribe's neat black letters stark between the spider of her spread fingers. The silence lengthened as Breme stared at her motionless hand, mesmerized by it.

Slowly, her fingers curled, her nails gouging into the delicate parchment. She deliberately crumpled the torn document, her fist squeezing it harder and harder into a small crushed ball. Breme didn't flinch as she threw the ruined wad of paper at him. It bounced off his chest onto the floor, rolling under the table.

"Hang him," she ordered, her voice dead.

Breme closed his eyes and exhaled, his head bowed, shivering in relief. His strength now exhausted, he looked depressed and subdued, only a tired old man. He didn't struggle as Kerrick took his arm and turned him toward the door, shuffling his chained feet awkwardly.

"Wait . . ."

It was Kerrick who turned in anger, ready to upbraid her. *No more!* Breme paused without looking back, indifferent.

"Weight his feet," she said.

Breme's mouth had twisted in a contorted, hollow smile when he turned and bowed. "Thank you, my Lady. You're most gracious."

With the proper weight, the noose would snap his neck, and he'd be killed instantly rather than suffering the agony of strangling at the end of the rope.

"I'm not P'tre," she insisted. "You're an honorable man, sir. I wish you had been mine. God curse you for being on the wrong side."

"Then perhaps you will grant me the kindness of a condemned man's last request?"

Kerrick heard the distinct sound of a trap snapping. He glanced at Antonya, and saw the realization in her eyes. "Aye."

"I would ask you to find my widow. Tell her my last thoughts were for her and my love for our three children and little granddaughter."

Breme knew he would have his revenge. He smiled mirthlessly as she nodded, unable to speak.

Kerrick pulled him away quickly, hustling him out the door. Ephraim and Nicoli shut it behind them, the sound of chains and footsteps fading. Antonya stared sightlessly at the door.

"Monsters," she whispered to herself.

"Lady?" Morgan asked behind her, still leaning casually.

"We are all monsters, every one of us."

She stood, and walked unsteadily toward the window. Daen laid the lute down on the bench, careful it made not the slightest sound, and exchanged a wary look with Regine. She turned to the hearth, poked at the fire and turned a pie, tapping the surface, ignoring him. Drizet kept his attention fixed on his shaking hands, fiddling endlessly with his quills and pots of ink, packing and repacking the contents of his scribe's box.

Tobias stared down at the chessboard and moved a piece, trapping Antonya's king. "Checkmate," he said very quietly to no one in particular and looked up into Morgan's sly smile.

66

Kerrick stood on the watchpath, the overhead timbers charred and open to the sky. The light breeze wafting across his brow felt good. He leaned his elbows against the granite merlon, watching the men below. Breme's lone corpse had been taken down from the wall over the gate once the cheering had ceased, and quickly buried in the sajada. No one seemed too interested in further executions, the blood frenzy withering away.

Kaesyn still smoldered as a good many of its citizens began to desert their city. Although Antonya had promised the Kaesyns their security, more than half chose to leave, horses and oxen straining at their harness as they carried away their owners and their possessions to hopefully safer regions. The citizens who chose to remain behind were mostly those too poor to leave or those too rich to bear abandoning their property and assets.

The line of refugees snaked around the tents of Antonya's army, but were allowed to escape without further assault. Indeed, a number of wagons appeared to have halted on their flight, an impromptu market materializing along their way. Money was lighter and more practical for refugees, and former foes dickered briskly under the clear skies.

Sunlight gleamed along the cannons and sparkled from the armor and lances of armsmen milling through the camp and the streets, too busy singing and laughing among themselves to bother with military precision. They'd earned it, Kerrick thought bitterly, they could enjoy it, at least for the moment.

"Defender." The voice startled him, and he spun with one hand on his dagger. Morgan stood at the arch of the watchtower a few paces away. Kerrick had not heard him approach, and wondered, not for the first time, how the man could move so damned silently.

"Morgan."

He watched warily as the Assassin walked past him and stopped at a crenelation between them. "Terhune will be gathering his army together to meet them," Morgan said, looking down at the moving column of troops and equipment in the narrow valley. "We will not have long to celebrate."

"True," Kerrick agreed. "But they have a day." Somehow, he knew the Assassin hadn't sought him out to discuss the fighting.

"You've said nothing to the Lady Antonya," Morgan said.

Kerrick knew what he meant. "No."

If he was expecting a measure of thanks, the Assassin's next words surprised him. "Why not? Do you hope to use it to destroy me at some future moment? Or as blackmail to give you a hold over me?" Morgan looked up at him, the question asked out of curiosity, Kerrick realized, not hostility.

"Please, sir," Kerrick said contemptuously, "your gratitude is quite overwhelming. You really must learn to restrain yourself."

Morgan studied him for a long moment. "I see," he said, as if figuring out a piece of a puzzle. He looked bored, and rather disappointed, Kerrick thought.

"I profess my loathing for you, Morgan, and destroying you would no doubt give me a great deal of satisfaction. But isn't honor enough of a reason for you?" Kerrick said angrily. "Or is honor only another of our *human* sentiments you disdain, like mercy or love?"

Morgan surveyed the army below, standing so still at the watchpath he might have been another stone gargoyle. "We are not so different, you and I," he said, his voice almost too soft to make out. "There's plenty of the fiend in every man; you need not look to the Weird for evil. But I have no need to justify the violence of my actions with distorted illusions of righteousness or honor. Honor is too brittle a thing for a killer."

"Is your bloodlust never satiated, then?" Kerrick asked scornfully.

When the Assassin turned, Kerrick was stunned by the naked hunger in his face. It flickered and was gone. "Never," Morgan said simply.

Sickened, Kerrick looked away, back down over the cliff to the line of soldiers moving slowly along the pass. "It is up to God, then, to judge you. You'll burn soon enough."

Morgan smiled blandly. "Whose god, sir? Yours or mine?"

Kerrick had lived with soldiers too long to be shocked by heresy. "Any god you like," he snapped, irritated.

"I doubt God has much interest in me. The flea may worship the dog, but the dog still scratches."

Kerrick expected the man, now that his question had been answered, to take his leave and go. But to his surprise, Morgan lifted himself up to sit on the narrow watchpath ledge, drawing his feet under him cross-legged. Any lingering weakness had vanished, his movements again graceful, controlled. The Assassin regarded the Defender with an uncertain expression, as if struggling with an internal debate of his own.

"I'm a predator, Kerrick," Morgan said, almost chattily. "I was raised very deliberately to be one. The raw nature is there in any child. Young children are innately selfish, both innocent and cruel. They delight in pulling wings off insects and tormenting small animals, naively unaware of the pain of others."

He smiled, as if remembering his own childhood cruelties with nostalgic fondness. Kerrick repressed a shudder, wishing he could simply shut his ears and walk away from Morgan, but oddly too fascinated to leave.

"Empathy is a learned trait, not inbred. My Guildmasters know exactly what they create when children are twisted from birth into unnatural beings."

The stiff breeze this high over the gorge ruffled the sleeves of the Assassin's shirt and played with the black braid down his back. He seemed completely indifferent to the sheer drop behind him.

"First I learned to love hunting; I was trained how to do it well. Then I was taught it is an animal thing to want, and human to control these wants. Discipline is what makes the difference between being an animal and being human. Those who cannot learn to control their desires are destroyed like the animals they are."

Kerrick wondered why he wasn't as alarmed as he knew he

should have been. But it gave him an idea. "If Antonya were to release you, give you your freedom . . ." He wasn't prepared for how white Morgan's face suddenly became, his dread visible as he stared at Kerrick.

"Have you suggested this to her?" he asked softly.

"No."

"With all due respect, sir, I think it would be unwise."

Kerrick pushed away from the merlon, pacing the wide gallery in a semicircle around Morgan, keeping the Assassin between himself and the high drop over the edge of the wall.

"Why? Would you kill her, then?" Kerrick asked, more out of interest than concern. It pleased him that he was able to hurt the man, as he had been hurt. And despised himself for it.

If he rushed the Assassin, he could push him over the edge. Morgan watched him, as if aware of his thoughts, but made no motion to protect himself. The color was coming back into his face and he regarded Kerrick with a languid animation in his narrowed eyes that held the same lazy malice as a cat supervising her kittens playing with a crippled mouse.

"No. The Lady Antonya has nothing to fear from me, now or ever." Morgan smiled thinly. "But I'd kill you."

"You could try," Kerrick said, contemptuously. "Why are you here? What do you want from me? I've as much as said you have a right to your privacy. You may scorn my honor, sir, but rest assured, whatever devils live in your conscience are your own concern. Dead or alive, I'll say nothing."

"You misunderstand. I don't scorn your honor, Defender," Morgan said quietly. "I shall depend on it." Kerrick met the man's eyes evenly. For a moment, Kerrick knew . . . *knew* . . . Morgan was allowing him to see the Assassin as he truly was, at his core, his soul laid bare before him. Morgan's desperate hunger hit Kerrick with more force than he would have admitted.

"Within a very short time, we will reach the Oracular City," the Assassin said. "P'tre Terhune will be waiting for her. She could be killed then, Kerrick. Quite easily."

"Aye," Kerrick said impassively, watching the Assassin closely.

"She is not sleeping more than a few hours at night."

"She never has."

Morgan exhaled, as if reluctant to be more direct. "The Lady has become increasingly . . . how can I put this respectfully? . . . reckless in the pursuit of her ambitions."

Kerrick stared at him, then laughed angrily. "She is not mad, if that's what you're insinuating."

"I am not presuming to judge either her motives or her sanity, sir, only her actions. And her intentions. If she does take the Citadel, you know as well as I she will not hold it. No one can take God hostage for long."

Kerrick listened to the man's impassive voice calmly uttering his own private fears. "Are you suggesting we try to stop her?"

"Indeed not, sir," Morgan said easily. "My purpose is to obey her, not to interfere with her wishes."

"And to keep her alive." Kerrick insisted.

Morgan smiled with the eerie ruthlessness Kerrick had seen before. A prickle ran along the back of his neck as he remembered the Assassin brushing his face lightly against Antonya's hair, almost erotically as he held her tightly against his chest. "I have my own reasons to keep her alive as long as I can. But I cannot stop her from risking her own life if she so chooses. I no longer belong to the Guild," the Assassin said as if the words were physically difficult to utter. "They have forsaken me and I will never be allowed to return."

Kerrick eyed him warily, understanding finally blossoming. Morgan nodded, as if he could read the abrupt insight in the big man's face. "But you are far too dangerous to be let loose in the world," Kerrick said slowly.

"Aye." The Assassin's eyes were too bright. "Once Antonya is dead, there will be no place for me, and nothing to restrain me. Men like me cannot be redeemed. It is a waste of your time, and mine, to even try. I don't want to be. I enjoy what I do, and I will keep on doing it until I am stopped."

His eyes flicked to Kerrick's hand tightening around the hilt of his dagger, and he smiled brittlely. "I can think of no one I could respect more than you, Kerrick. Swear to me: On the day she dies, you must hunt me down."

Morgan would be a difficult and lethal quarry, Kerrick fully realized. But he nodded amiably. "It would be my very great pleasure, sir."

"And mine, Defender."

67

Kerrick knew much of what the Assassin had said was true. Antonya slept no more than one or two hours a night, and even those were restless hours. The fare had improved since Kaesyn's stores had been plundered, but she ate little of it. Her face became increasingly gaunt, the skin around her eyes bruised with fatigue. She spent most of her time riding along the length of the column slowly filing down the narrow valley, talking with the men-at-arms, examining the cannon wagons. At night she stood at the perimeters of the camp, staring silently into the darkness to the west. With the watch fires at her back, she either ignored or was unaware of the whispers of her nervous armsmen, now as afraid of her as they were of her silent, sinister Assassin shadowing her every move.

The celebratory mood of the army after the fall of Kaesyn was short-lived. The sunshine they had been favored with during most of the siege of Kaesyn vanished. Gray clouds filled the valley in low-hung mists, the rain turning the mountain road to sludge. The column of troops and equipment slowed, the heavy carriage wheels fighting the sucking mud, hooves slipping, men cursing the cold and stinging wet.

Of the sixty captive Priests, only twenty-three had been members of Terhune's Elite Guard. The Elite remained with the main army headed for the Oracular City, chained as beasts of burden alongside the cannon wagons. The rest, cowed scholars and frail clerics, had been sent as prisoners with those troops riding to Ilona's relief. As the rain continued to fall incessantly, whips once used only on the backs of stubborn oxen and cart horse were now being liberally applied to the Elite as well, more out of frustration, Kerrick knew, than for any defiance from the captive Priests. They ignored the lash and pushed their shoulders against the wagons, muscles in stark relief as they slipped and labored and fought the mire behind the straining oxen. When they stopped at nightfall, the Priests dropped where they stood. Exhausted, they huddled for shelter as best they could under the wagons, shivering in the damp cold. Even had their guards allowed it, they were too fatigued to talk among themselves.

Unsurprisingly, several fell ill. One of the injured finally died, his body dragged along for several miles before his captors noticed and unchained him from the rest. His former companions watched with dulled eyes as the body was dumped unceremoniously over the edge of the cliff road, tumbling down the rocks toward the seething river below.

Morale continued to deteriorate while Kerrck did his best to minimize the damage. Still the army made less than ten miles a day through the slippery, treacherous valley.

A break in the rain did more to lift the men's spirits than anything Kerrick could have done, and there was actually some scattered laughter and halfhearted attempt at song that evening, a praise for the stars and the moons shining overhead. The mood was shattered all too quickly as clouds masked the stars and another scuffle broke out in Mellas's camp. Having expected trouble and prepared for it, Kerrick signaled his own men and they waded into the fight, breaking it up within minutes. Three men, all drunk, roared insults and swung wildly, easy enough to seize and subdue. Two of them were Mellas's men, the third a mercenary from the flatlands, arguing over their share of ale from a single wineskin. A campfire had been knocked over, the evening stew sputtering in the coals. The trio now crouched or sat on the muddy ground, sullen, one nursing a scalded hand.

It might have resolved itself if Antonya hadn't arrived as well. As she walked into the gathering, armsmen drew back from her path; the silence that followed her was as palpable as a cloak. She stood observing the scene, then glanced at Kerrick.

"It's over, Lady," he said calmly. "It's taken care of."

One of the men on the ground sniggered. "Like she'll be

taken care of, soon enough the way we're goin'," he muttered, his voice slurred. He giggled drunkenly.

Kerrick swiftly lashed out, kicking his boot solidly into the man's ribs. "Silence, you!" The man groaned, doubling over and clutching his side.

"Nay," Antonya said, her voice soft. "Let him speak."

Inwardly, Kerrick groaned. But he forced a look of contempt onto his face and said, "The man is drunk, his mind too pickled in ale to know what he's saying . . ."

"I said, let him speak." Her voice was mild, but Kerrick knew her well enough to hear the tension behind it. He glanced around, aware that the crowd had suddenly grown, watching.

The drunken man glared up with reddened eyes. "Wha' kinda army is this, an'way?" he demanded. "We're soldiers, we are, eh, lads?" He smacked one palm against his companion's shoulder, near knocking him facedown into the wet ground. The third man, less inebriated than the others, watched Antonya warily, his scowl scornful but still cautious. "We spend months to take down Kaesyn, *months*, riskin' our lives, eating rat turds for supper, sleepin' on rocks, but we don' complain, no, ne'er complain, 'cause we're soldiers." He nodded vehemently, "But when we fin'lly bring the bitch to her knees, wha' happens? D'we get what soldiers earn? Wha' we *deserve*?"

Kerrick studied Antonya as she watched the man work himself into a tirade. He listened to the murmurings in the crowd, some disapproving, but too many agreeing with the rebellious soldier.

"No! We hang one lousy Priest and gotta be polite t'the same buncha miserable fat townsfolk busy tryin' to kill us the day afore! No lootin', no pill . . .'illgerin' "—he hiccuped, but plowed on—"no women, e'en. No *women*!" His outrage at being denied a victorious soldier's usual benefits at the expense of the conquered female population after a battle was one of nearly childlike resentment.

Kerrick glanced warily at Antonya, but she didn't so much as blink as the murmurs grew, the resentment rising.

"Y'need a *man* to lead an army of men, so you do, meaning no offense t'you personally, Lady. But look *around*!" He waved an arm in no particular direction. "Tha's the problem, it's the weakness a' women. Beggin' yer pardon, but 'struth, yer too softhearted to be leadin' hardened soldiers. Mercy has no place on the battlefield, Lady. It'll kill you, for true. You forgive this one and that, they're not grateful, they'll just wait till yer back is turned."

She stared at the man, listening silently, her yellow eyes as nearly as pale as her face. Kerrick wondered if she was even aware of it anymore when the color drained from her eyes.

"Now we got Terhune's bastards in our midst, y'won't cut their throats like the vile dogs they are! Y'should make examples outta them!" He was warming to his vision, eager to advise her. "Nail their worthless hides to the trees and run their guts out on the ground. Leave 'em to show the emen . . . emeny what they have to fear from you!" A scattering of laughter and approval from the crowd encouraged him. "But we're becoming milksoft, Lady!" he whined. "Terhune'll be laughing up his sleeve. Even God Hisself is pissin' on us!"

Antonya seemed deaf to the muttering and halfhearted cheers, even if the soldier was not. "Wha' you should do"—the fellow nodded amiably—"is appoint a champ'on, a strong general to lead us into battle, an' you stay b'hind, see? We'll do the work, you take the credit. But we can't afford a woman's weakness draggin' us down now, not now! Right, lads?"

The two with him mumbled varying degrees of accord. The mood of the crowd changed; growls of anger clashing with snarls of agreement. Morgan materialized from the darkness like a spirit, black eyes alert.

"I see. And exactly who did you have in mind, sir?"

Kerrick glared at her.

The soldier waved in the Defender's direction. "Well enough Kerrick 'ere would make a fine general, what say you, eh? We'll follow you, sir. Kerrick! Kerrick! Kerr . . . hick!"

"Shut up, man!" Kerrick said sharply. "You're speaking treason!" The armsmen crowding into the firelight had not picked up the man's chant, Kerrick was relieved to notice. Killing Priests was one thing, but to countenance usurping the Lady's office was quite another.

The drunken soldier peered up with an offended expression. "Treason?" he sneered. "Issit treason to speak the truth? Issit treason to want to *win* this war?"

"Are you saying you fear my womanly nature will cause us to lose this war, sir?" Antonya's voice was dangerously soft. "That I am too weak, too gentle, to lead men like you?" Her eyes were nearly drained white, but in the firelight, her pupils were dilated, black as the night surrounding them. Suddenly Kerrick understood, and felt ill. And knew he could do nothing to stop it. He glanced at the Assassin. The man was watching the spectacle avidly, his mouth slightly open like a leopard panting in the summer sun. He understood as well.

"Aye, Lady," the self-appointed spokesman said brashly. No doubt he was trying to make his expression charitable, but the insolence in the ale was too obvious. "Go on back to Laird's Ketch, tha's the place for you. We'll protect you, we'll raise y'r banner an' fight in your name, but there's no place here for softhearted mercy. Y'canno' be expected to do a man's work. Go home and let us do the job the way it should be done afore it's too late."

Antonya turned a questioning look on the two men on either side of him. "Aye," they both muttered, but with less conviction.

As if aware for the first time of the gathering around her, she looked up, slowly turning around to face the armsmen in turn, as if confronting the eyes of animals gleaming in the forest cover. When she had made a full circle, she eyed the three drunks. "Stand up."

The other men were able to rise without aid, but Kerrick had to help the loudmouthed one to his feet where he wobbled.

She stood motionless for several moments. Then her hand flashed to the shortsword at her side, the steel rasping out. Taking a single step forward, she gripped the hilt with both hands and before the drunken soldier could do more than gasp and stumble back, she drove the blade into his chest, the point emerging from his back. He opened his mouth as if to protest, but only a trickle of blood emerged before he slid backward off the blade. It grated through bone and sinew as she jerked it from the man's chest. His companions had scrambled away from him, watching in horror as the body fell to its knees and thudded facedown to the ground. His legs kicked once as he died.

Blood speckled her face as she turned and held the blade before her. She strode the short distance to where the second man crouched, white-eyed and gasping. As she raised the blade, he snarled in hopeless anger, reaching for his own dagger. It was out of the scabbard and his head was off his shoulders a second later. When she turned toward the last man, her teeth were bared in a bizarre grin. He stumbled away from her, scrabbling frantically across the sodden ground as she stalked him. The spectators moved away, leaving a fluid ring around them both.

Trapped, the last man drew his own shortsword, but threw it down at her feet, kneeling in the mud to raise empty hands imploringly. "Mercy, Lady, for the love of God!"

Her tunic was splashed with blood, the blade in her hands dripping. She stopped, pressing the tip of her sword against the man's heaving chest. Her eyes were as blank as stone as she stared back at him, indifferent.

"Mercy?" she said, her voice hoarse. "I thought that was exactly what you did *not* want in this army." But her manic energy had subsided. She blinked, as if awakening from a dream; the point of the blade lowered. The man on the ground quaked in relief as she turned to stare at the sprawling corpses with vague surprise. When she looked up at the men around her, the silence was complete. Kerrick scanned the crowd, nervously gauging the mood of the armsmen.

From the rear, he caught sight of Mellas shouldering his way to the front. The mercenary chieftain gazed down on the dead men, his florid face and bloodshot eyes more than enough evidence that his state of intoxication was not that far from those who had died.

"Are there any further protests?" Kerrick demanded.

Mellas looked up at Antonya, unsmiling. "None." He gestured curtly to his armsmen in the crowd, and watched as the bodies were taken away. The surviving man had to be lifted to his feet and hurried off. Pools of blood stained the ground.

Antonya's face twitched, and she turned her back to Kerrick to walk away, bloody sword held loosely by her side. She paused as she passed Morgan. "Come snuffling along when you scented blood, did you?" Morgan answered her with a sharp smile. "Keep away from me tonight, fiend." The Assassin bowed slightly, wordless.

Kerrick followed her back to her own tent, stopping halfway there to retrieve the bloody sword she had let fall from her hand. She pulled down the flap of the tent behind her, cutting him off. Tobias and Daen stood guard outside, watching Kerrick uncertainly as he considered. He heard her moan, and neither guard spoke as he shoved his way past them into the tent.

She had fallen on hands and knees, vomiting onto the ground. Quickly, he knelt beside her and held her tightly as she convulsed, her body rigid as she threw up again and again, until nothing but a thin line of green drool emerged from her mouth. She was panting, her skin moist with sweat. Turning away from the pool of vomit, she sat on the ground, trembling violently. She grabbed Kerrick's arm as he tried to stand, her eyes glassy.

"I can't be seen like this," she whispered, unseeing.

He nodded, stepped to the tent flap and lifted it carefully to screen her. "Call Regine," he said quietly to Daen. "The Lady wishes to bathe before retiring."

The two armsmen exchanged a knowing look, but said nothing.

Nor did Regine react to Antonya's disheveled appearance. As she stripped off the Lady's clothing behind the screen to wash the dirt and blood from her, Kerrick cleared away the vomit-spattered rushes with a shovel and bucket and spread fresh straw over the spot. Regine appeared around the side of the screen, handing him the bundle of bloody clothing. "Burn it," she said softly. "Send for Doctor Tryo to give her a draught. I'll stay with her tonight."

But not even Tryo's poppy sedatives could keep the restlessness out of Antonya's blood. She was up before dawn, overseeing the men breaking camp as horses and wagons were readied for the day's laborious journey. Rain drizzled from steel-gray clouds so low in the valley Kerrick imagined his head brushed the ceiling of the sky. Although the treasonous spirit had been broken, there was little talk and even less laughter as the army trudged along the mountain's twisting road.

And the rain came down.

68

B'nach hurried toward D'nyel's rooms, out of breath when he knocked rapidly and entered before she could answer. Then he stopped, staring in confusion.

She sat on the floor next to a naked young man, the two of them bent over his arm intently, like coconspirators. Their heads jerked up as B'nach barged into the room, her expression angry, the man startled. They stood, and the man furtively backed out of the room, quickly disappearing into her bedchamber.

B'nach took two steps toward the bedchamber, his legs seeming to move of their own volition as a jealous rage swept through him, before D'nyel pushed in front of him. Her hand slapped against his chest as she glared at him. He stopped, hesitating, his jealousy subsiding.

"I wasn't . . ." he started.

"No," she said firmly. "You weren't."

Then the details crowded into his head. The look in the young man's eyes hadn't been that of an ardent lover, but one of terrified suffering. His chest and arms had been strangely scarred, his face haggard. Not a lover. A patient. A candle guttered on the low table, white linen cloth dotted with blood, a small stained knife.

Whatever clandestine healing she was performing now, for whatever reason, there were certain things about D'nyel he preferred not to know.

"What are you doing here, B'nach?" D'nyel demanded. He had to struggle to remember, staring down into her lovely eyes, now curious rather than angry. "What has happened?"

Eyes that once he would have died for. Eyes empty of anything other than vicious greed and ambition. She didn't love him, had never loved him, would never love him.

"Kaesyn has fallen. Lady Antonya is marching against the Oracular City."

He got no pleasure from seeing her gasp in shock, genuinely surprised. For once, he knew something before she did. "Sweet Mother. What are we going to do?"

He laughed, feeling no mirth. He jerked his head toward her eerily silent bedchamber. " 'We'? *We* aren't going to do anything."

"B'nach . . ." The hand with which she had slapped his chest now clutched at his robes, drawing her nearer to him. He shuddered, wanting to crush her to him, kiss her hard until she moaned against his mouth. "It isn't what you think . . ."

"I don't want to think anything, D'nyel," he said, his voice hoarse. He gripped her slender wrists to push her away from him. "Keep your secrets, I want no part of them anymore."

69

By midday, Kerrick rode past Tyro's brightly painted wagon, rows of brass bells chiming in incongruous cheer to the hunchback's sour expression. He pulled in the bay to a slow walk beside the wagon. They both watched Antonya ahead, a thin, erect figure over the white rump of her mare as she rode in the pouring rain alongside the column.

"She can't keep this pace too much longer," Tyro said, his raspy voice pitched low. "She's killing herself, and us along with her."

They stopped as the column ground to a halt with the shouts of armsmen and the thin crack of a whip as one of the cannon was manipulated around the narrow curve of road. Even the usually placid Shire was irritable, tossing its head in the stinging cold rain and gnawing at the steel bit in its mouth. Kerrick leaned over to pat the beast's neck consolingly. "I'll go see what's holding us up," he said, not commenting on Tyro's remark.

The road around the mountainside had once been wide, easily passable by three men side by side on horseback. Now the rain and a mudslide had carved away the roadbed on a tricky curve, leaving barely enough room for the wheels of the cannon wagon on either side. The oxen had their heads lowered, hooves digging into the muck as they pulled their burden, while the captive Priests chained to the sides strained to push the heavy cannon. Those on the mountainside scrabbled up the rock as far as their chains would allow, the space between the mountainside and the wagon crushingly small. Those on the other side hugged the cannon with barely enough room left for precious toeholds on the crumbling edge.

On the wide arc of road behind them, armsmen gathered to watch, shouting advice to others at the other end of the bottleneck. Four men held the oxen's muzzles, pulling at their harness as a fifth snapped a whip expertly over their heads to flick at their struggling rumps. The armsman on this side, Kerrick was somehow satisfied to see, had his own whip coiled in one hand, waiting with his fists resting on his hips. Nothing was to be gained by lashing the prisoners. They were doing their best to get the heavy cannon past the washout, the sheer drop down the cliff to the churning river below all the incentive they needed.

"Ho!" the armsman on the far side shouted, and the oxen jerked the wagon around the narrow bend a few more inches. "Ho!" A Priest screamed as the heavy ironshod wheel rolled over his foot, crushing the bones. He clung desperately to the wagonside, his eyes shut tight in his ashen face. His companions murmured encouragement to him as they shoved and slipped and struggled to move the cannon a few more inches. "*Ho!*" They nearly had the cannon across.

This time when the wagon moved, the roadside crumbled. To Kerrick's horror, the remaining road disintegrated between the rear of the wagon and the rest of the army, a slab of earth sliding down the rock face to the river below. It carved a wide-angled slice of ground from under the riverside wheel, leaving nothing for the prisoners to stand on. The belly of the wagon slammed into the ground, the wheel spinning freely in the void. Slowly, majestically, the muzzle of the heavy cannon began to tilt backward. The prisoners hung on desperately to their chains, fingers clawing through iron links before they realized they were being dragged inexorably along with the snout of the cannon. Wood cracked, the brace of the cradle snapping under the weight. The oxen fought the weight, reluctantly stepping backwards.

Men shouted in the confusion, the oxen bellowing in frustration. Within a few seconds, Kerrick knew, the cradle bracing would snap and the huge cannon would topple down the valley cliff taking the chained men with it. Vaulting from his horse, he ran up the short distance to where the road narrowed and shoved his way through. He jumped the space between the road and the wagon, scrambling across the curved barrel of the cannon. At the rounded end, the prisoner's chains had been secured through the same iron ring bolting the cannon to the wagon's cradle. For a moment, his weight on the barrel was enough to balance the cannon's tilt, and he held his breath, hoping. He looked down into the wide eyes of one of the chained Priests no more than a foot away, both of them praying. Then he felt the sluggish skid through his feet and knew it was lost.

He howled in frustration as he drew his longsword. Standing on the cannon's back he brought the heavy blade down with all his strength on the chain. Sparks flew. The blow had numbed his arms as he lifted the sword again and pounded against the chain.

On the fourth strike, the blade broke, sharp steel whirling out into the valley below. He lost his footing as the cannon lurched, dragging him along with the captives to teeter over the edge. Someone cried out in pain. Sprawling along its length, he hammered the hilt against the chain, bright gouges of metal in the corrosion. One link slowly pulled apart, then snapped. As the chain whistled out of the ring, the end whipped Kerrick across one cheek as it snaked by.

He let go the broken hilt, grabbed the edge of the carriage with one hand and the wrist of the Priest with the other. The cannon slanted underneath him, sliding out of the cradle to launch itself into the valley. With the weight gone, the oxen easily jerked the empty carriage over the edge of the missing road, trotting several yards before the men at their muzzles could drag them to a halt.

With their manacles no longer chained together and their hands free, the Priests clung to the wagon or went down on hands and knees, scattering as they scrambled away from the crumbling road. One lay on his stomach, legs splayed, with his arms stretching to grip another Priest dangling over the edge. He slid closer to the edge, his feet leaving tracks, as the weight of the man began to pull him down. Before Kerrick could react, Nicoli had thrown himself onto the ground behind him, sprawled as he grabbed the Priest's legs. Together, they wriggled backward, drawing the third man up over the side to safety.

Kerrick stood, his mind blank, staring across the chasm cutting the army column in two. Sweat trickled down his forehead, but when he wiped it away, blood smeared his palm. Gingerly, he explored the cut on his face, realizing with a sudden twist in his gut how close he'd come to losing an eye. Although he felt oddly lightheaded and not the least fearful, he was shaking. On the other side of the divide, Kerrick spotted Doctor Tyro gazing across, standing in the rain and holding the bay's reins, dwarfed by the massive animal.

"Hands on your head, sir," said a gentle voice behind him, and he turned in surprise. One of Sarnor's mercenaries held a crossbow, arrow at the ready, aimed at the Priest Kerrick had rescued. The man glanced once at Kerrick, smiled cynically and complied. The two other Priests joined him as they were escorted to the oxen wagon, where the rest of the prisoners had been rounded up. All but one squatted in the road with hands laced together on their heads. The last man lay on his back, the same man whose foot had been crushed under the wheel. Now, his head in a companion's lap, he whimpered through clenched teeth. His foot was swollen and purple, but his leg jutted out at an unnatural angle. Blood leaked from the wound where the sharp edge of a broken bone had speared through the skin of his ankle, dark meat and white fat exposed in the gaping hole.

Kerrick glimpsed the flash of white before he saw her. Antonya nudged the mare past the empty cart in the sudden hush, her men making way as she rode to the very edge of the washout. The nervous horse's hooves sent small stones spinning over the brink. Its eyes rolled white, the beast sensibly terrified, Kerrick thought heatedly as he quickly strode toward her to grab the bridle and drag it back.

"Careful, Lady, it's a long drop down."

She laughed, the sound humorless. "God might enjoy making my life difficult, Kerrick, but He'll dare not take it from me until I've reached the Oracular City." Her words carried clearly across the chasm, the armsmen on the opposite side listening. If any of them heard the madness behind her voice, they gave no sign of it.

She stared down at the cannon lying on the rocks below. Split trees and torn branches showed its path down the cliff. From this height, it looked as small as a toy, smashed in two. The river gushed through the fractured mouth, the muzzle of the cannon now spitting only an angry froth of water.

"It's broken," she said petulantly.

"That it is." She looked back at the Priests huddled by the oxen before she stared at Kerrick. The question in her eyes kindled his anger, knowing once she would not have mistrusted his judgment. He had not tried to save the cannon. "There was no way it could have been prevented, Antonya. It was a miracle that lives were saved at all."

"Lives?" she repeated wonderingly.

He let her horse go as she twitched the reins to one side, wheeling it around. She drew it in to a halt before the prisoners crouched on the ground, blinking away the rain in their eyes as they peered up at her. Nicoli and Gesham stood on either side, waiting. Nicoli's entire front was crusted with mud, the rain cutting channels through it on his clothing and face. The man with the broken leg held it clamped with both hands, blood and rain leaking around his fingers. No one spoke. The mare danced under its rider nervously. Kerrick murmured soothingly, stroking its neck and shoulder as Antonya sat stiffly in the saddle.

She glanced back over her shoulder at the fissure separating the column. "We'll have to build a bridge," she said tonelessly, "and lose the rest of the day. Every day I lose, P'tre gains. I can't afford any more lost days, Kerrick, not in this weather." He studied her, unable to recognize under this mad façade the woman he had known. She was as white as stone, skin slicked with rain, her pale eyes inhuman. His chest ached as she nodded at Gesham.

The young armsman grimaced, unhappy, but drew his dagger. The injured man inhaled sharply with sudden understanding. His companion shielded him protectively. "I can carry him, Lady," he cried out. "Give me a rope to tie him on my back, and we'll not slow you down."

As she started in surprise, the Priest realized she had meant to kill them all. As a younger man beside him tried to struggle defensively to his feet, he shoved him back. "Peace, lad," he said quietly, his eyes still on Antonya. The group of captives were pale, but calm as they faced the knife.

Standing by the mare's head, Kerrick gazed up at Antonya, watching the glassy expression crack. Her mouth opened, she licked her lips, her face contorting as she struggled with her emotions. When she looked down again, she had herself under control.

"Call Guyus until we can bring Doctor Tyro's wagon across," she said to Gesham, to his obvious surprise. She gazed up the mountainside ravines and fern-filled gorges to a stand of trees. "As for the rest of these men, give them axes and saws. They'll need something to do now that their hands are idle."

Armsmen and prisoners alike watched her kick the mare into a trot, heading for the front of the column. The injured man cried out only once as he was gently lifted and carried off, arms over the shoulders of Antonya's men. Kerrick watched the Priest who had spoken close his eyes, his lips moving in a silent prayer of thanks.

The reprieved captives stood slowly, waiting for the carpenters to arrive with the equipment, already studying the trees above them. They pointed as they discussed among themselves which to fell first, how best to bring the logs down the near-vertical slope thick with bushes and ferns without losing them to the canyon below. As the carpenters arrived, they took up the axes and saws without complaint, tying ropes around their waists to begin the steep climb. The man Kerrick had rescued lingered until he caught the Defender's attention.

"We owe you our gratitude, sir," the man said quietly.

"It wasn't intentional, man," Kerrick retorted gruffly. "and was entirely foolhardy."

The Priest grinned. "Aye, perhaps." He hesitated, and Kerrick realized the man had almost extended his hand. Despite his emaciated body, ribs stark on his naked chest from too little food, the dirt encrusting his rags and skin, the Priest held himself with an air of dignity. "My name is Cyler." The sharp crack of an ax biting into a tree echoed above them. "We'll build your bridge to repay our debt. Then our accounts will be even again."

The rain let up, although the clouds still clung to the valley. The Priests felled a dozen trees, stripping the branches from the trunks. They lost only one when a rope broke as they lowered the log down the slippery hillside toward the road. Kerrick watched the struggle, captives and armsmen alike, shouting and straining, desperately trying to keep the denuded tree from rolling off the edge of the road. When they were forced to give up the effort, they watched it tumble down the long slope to the river, crashing into the water scant feet away from the broken cannon below.

"*Shit!*" Kerrick heard one man curse, his frustration heartfelt, and was surprised to see it was one of the prisoners. From the armsmen's expressions, no one presumed the loss was intentional, a ploy to slow their adversaries. It was Priests who climbed the sheer rock face above the chasm for the dangerous job of setting the tackle, anchoring it to trees farther up the mountainside. One by one, the stripped logs were lowered across the divide and lashed together. When it was finished, the carpenters diligently inspected the Priests' work, searching for any hint of sabotage. The weary captives watched expectantly, scratched and bruised, and grinned when none was found.

The sun had not yet set, several hours of rain-darkened daylight left as the column began to move once more. Gingerly, horses and oxen were led over the makeshift bridge, wagons painstakingly pulled one by one across, breaths held as the wood groaned, iron-shod hooves and wheels churning up chips of bark and the smell of pine. When the last horse, man and wagon had crossed, camp was already being set up for the night a mile farther along the road where it widened out into a long, flat valley meadowland.

The smithy had started up his fire, promising Kerrick a new sword of his finest thin-hammered Sidon steel before daybreak, and began dismantling the ornate hilt from the broken blade. Kerrick suspected it would take more than a day before they both were satisfied with the work. Until then, he accepted a longsword from one of Sarnor's mercenaries, the heft lighter in his hand than he liked, the balance unfamiliar. He would have little time to get used to it, either way.

Still enemy prisoners, the Priests were once again chained together and under guard, but a length of canvas had been draped over three crooked pine poles to shelter them from the rain, and a small campfire lit to warm their food and stave off the mountain's sharp cold. They huddled two and three together for warmth under rough woolen blankets, most already asleep, the rest talking among themselves in subdued voices, this infraction disregarded by their guards. As Kerrick strode by, they fell silent, watching him pass with firelight glittering in their eyes. Cyler nodded to him with the barest hint of recognition. Kerrick did not respond.

The Defender strolled through the camp, listening. The tone had changed, an air of zealous urgency. Antonya's name was spoken now not with the affection or respect of soldiers for a popular commander, but with nearly breathless reverence for a heroine no longer quite human. The crisis had passed, but Kerrick was afraid what had replaced it might be far more precarious.

Guyus was with Tyro in the wizard's gaudy wagon, the injured captive on a pallet balanced between boards. A candle burning in a glass lantern hung overhead threw out a steady light. The wagon creaked as Kerrick planted a foot on the step, leaning in the back. "How is the boy?" he asked. The prisoner lay still, eyes closed, the blanket pulled up to his chest not hiding the irons on his wrists chained to the pallet. His fingers twitched spasmodically at the cloth. His eyes moved under his lids fitfully.

"Asleep," Tyro said in a hushed voice.

"Tyro had to sedate him well before we could set the bone," Guyus added. "It's a clean break, if it doesn't become infected. We'll know in a day or two if it has to come off. God's will now." The bone-cracker didn't seem too concerned about his patient either way. He stretched his arms idly. "I'm done here, I'm going to bed." He rose and brushed by Kerrick, vanishing in the night.

Kerrick regarded the sleeping man pensively before looking

up at Tyro. "Tell me," the doctor said lightly, "my determined, devoted, and dependable Defender, do you doubt our dear Lady is demented?"

"That isn't the word I would have chosen," Kerrick said slowly.

"No? What word describes it, then? Disturbed, delirious, deranged?" The hunchback grinned at Kerrick's warning look, thick lips tight over his crooked teeth. Despite his witticism, Tyro was deadly serious. "It isn't about revenge any longer, Kerrick. This has nothing to do with repaying P'tre Terhune for Briston's murder, nor reclaiming her bloodrights, nor even fighting for the rights of the Landsfolk. She's like a stone rolling downhill, ever faster, unable to stop. This war is beyond her control now. This *is* insanity."

"I don't want to hear this . . ."

"But I do," Antonya's voice said from the darkness behind him.

Both men started, and stared as she stepped into the wan light leaking from the wagon's open doorway. She was smiling, her eyes deep brown. Kerrick noted the Assassin's inert silhouette in the distance, a blot of darkness against the night.

She looked from Kerrick to Tyro and back again speculatively. "Perhaps you're right, and I'm mad. Perhaps I'm only leading us all to certain death."

"Then why, Antonya?" Tyro said calmly.

"Have you ever seen the Oracle, either of you?" They both shook their heads. "I have." Tyro sat up straighter, listening now with obvious interest, but Kerrick wasn't sure he wanted to hear any more. "Somehow, the Ancients preserved an element of God's own Holy Body long ago within the Light, for reasons we can't fathom. God *lives* within the Oracle. The Light *is* God. And I know why all the Saints have failed, and will always fail, no matter how pure the Faith tries to make them. They're alive. They're *human*. Nothing of flesh can survive in the very Hand of God."

"And you intend to Walk the Fire," Tyro said calmly. Stunned, Kerrick stared at the wizard, then at her.

"Yes," she said, to Kerrick's horror.

"Madness, my dear. Pure madness." Tyro was inexplicably unruffled, until Kerrick understood he was doing his best to deal with a dangerous lunatic. "Do you really expect to succeed where all others have failed?"

"No," she said serenely. "Of course not. The Faith has been trying to create the One who can survive the Fire and transform the Light into Flesh. Transform themselves into God. Control God. They can't hear Him scream in anger. They refuse to accept the message He gives every time another would-be usurper is crushed in His fist."

She was no longer looking at them, her awareness lost somewhere in the distance of her memory. "But I've heard it," she said, almost inaudibly. "I heard God's voice in the call of dying birds, heard Him pleading in the beating of their bloodied wings. I've seen His face smile at me in the light of the moons, I've felt His gentle touch in my dreams when I sleep. He wants no more innocent blood."

Although he was not a superstitious man, Kerrick shivered, unsettled. She refocused sharply and grinned, wolfish. "Kerrick, those men were right. I'm *useless*." Her voice was light, once again that of the energetic, spirited woman he had known long ago. She laughed at his startled expression. "I'm a woman in a world with not much tolerance for women. I'm no warrior, no military genius. I'm no good for anything other than as a figurehead for other men to follow, a bloodless ghost on which to focus their strength, a limp and rather tattered flag of feeble cloth for men to cheer and march behind."

"You sell yourself short, Lady," Kerrick retorted.

"Oh, no." She smiled. "I've sold myself quite dearly. I've lost all I thought I wanted in order to learn that. My heritage, my Lands, my integrity, my freedom. Those I've loved and those who loved me. My life is worthless, but with my death, I can buy freedom for these Lands. The Faith has used the Oracle in a corrupt perversion of God's true will. I must stop it."

It was several seconds before Kerrick could speak. "How?" His voice was thick, not even sounding like his own. "How is dying in the Fire going to stop it?"

"B'nach provided me with more information than I think even he suspected when he gave me his *Praenuntairium Caelestis*. Whosoever Walks the Fire becomes more than a Saint. Their last words are given to them by God, and become Sacred

Law which *must* be obeyed. I trust God will grant me enough
time to tell the world exactly what I've told you before I'm
ripped into shreds and translated straight up into the heavens"—she shrugged—"or thrown down into Hell. I must fulfill
the prophecy, be crowned with the Light, be the Last of those
who Walk the Fire. And I will give the Land back to the
people to whom it belongs, unmask the Faith and give God's
clearest command: Never shall living flesh again be sacrificed
into the Fire."

"You've no doubt already worked out exactly what it is God
plans to say through you?" Tyro asked, ironic. "Practiced your
pretty proclamation to perfection, have you?"

"Oh, aye," she said, almost laughing. "I could say it in my
sleep, Tyro."

"It isn't like you'll be around afterwards to make certain the
Faith obeys your holy word, Antonya," Kerrick said dryly,
"however well you've rehearsed it."

"I know. But when I Walk the Fire, it will be because we
will have possession of the Oracular City. *You* will, Kerrick,
because you will inherit my last wish. You have walked a fire
of a different sort. You will be my heir and rule these Lands
in my name. *You* will be the One. God Himself will choose
you through me."

Kerrick said nothing as the hunchback shook his head with
disbelief. Antonya wasn't looking at Tyro, however, but at
him, and her eyes were a steady, dark brown.

"No," he said finally.

At least he had the satisfaction of seeing her shaken.
"What?"

"No," he repeated, this time more firmly. "I will not be an
accomplice in this sham."

"You must," she protested. "Kerrick, you're my Defender,
you've sworn your life to me . . ."

"And I will serve as you wish, on my oath, until one of us
is dead. But I will *not* serve you from the grave."

"It is God's will!"

It took all his will to keep his anger from exploding. "Now
you will listen to me, you arrogant, selfish, sanctimonious
bitch," he said quietly. "God has never spoken to me, Antonya,
and I am only your Defender. Kill yourself if that's what you

want to do. If it is truly God's will, then you will not need me, and if it is not, I will not be a party to this scheme. I will never tremble before Priests nor *you* invoking God's will to keep me chained. Die however you wish, but if you so much as mention my name from the Fire, I shall follow you into it and expose your last words as the hollow lies they are."

She stared at him, stunned and pale. Tyro watched them both with one hand thoughtfully stroking his beard.

"Antonya—" Kerrick's voice cracked, the sound more a hopeless protest than anger, "you don't have to die to win."

"But the Prophecy . . ."

"To Hell with the Prophecy!" he shouted. "Create your own prophecy, cut the Phrygian knot in half if it refuses to loosen for you." She had bowed her head like a repentant child, her eyes lowered, and he softened his tone. "Make your own legends, Antonya. You've done quite well at that so far."

For a moment, he thought he might have persuaded her, might have found the chink in the armor of her madness. Then his heart sank as she looked up at him, her eyes paled nearly to white.

"I must take the Lands back through the Fire," she said tonelessly. "I *must* be Crowned in the Oracle."

He wanted to weep, and took a shuddering breath. "Then do it, if you must. For as long as you live, I will follow you, and serve you as your Defender however you wish. But you will never be able to make me love you for it."

He brushed past her, unable to say more, and strode quickly away into the cover of night to hide his tears.

70

B'nach stood on the far ramparts of the Citadel, surveying the movements of the troops in the distance, the chill wind off the sea rustling his robes. He held his spectacles in his hands, the damp fogging the lenses. He squinted, sight blurred without his spectacles, Antonya's distant armies on the other side of the marsh no more than a movement of colors blending one into the other.

He didn't feel the cold. The clatter of footsteps drew him out of his meditation, but he remained where he was, staring out into the gray distance. Above, a hawk called, wheeling in the wintry sky.

"Here you are," K'ferrin said testily. "*Brrr*. What are you doing up here alone?"

"Watching them," B'nach said, unconcerned with the old man's anxiety. "What could you possibly want of me, Grandfather, that could drive you up here into such vile weather?" He found he was mildly irritated at the old man's intrusion, amazed he could feel free enough to allow himself the luxury of openly disliking K'ferrin.

"Mind your tongue, boy," the old man snapped. He glared acidly, tugging his robes around his thin frame. "You would do well to show a bit more respect. Arrogance ill becomes you."

B'nach smiled, and turned to his grandfather. At a deferential distance behind the old man, but not out of earshot, K'ferrin's retinue of bodyguards waited impassively. He bowed slightly. "Forgive me, Grandfather," he said, his ironic smile still intact.

He straightened and waited as the frail old Priest huddled in his robes.

"I want what you've always given me, B'nach," he said finally. "Your opinion, barren as it is of deceit and avarice. Give me your objective evaluation of the situation."

Fear clouded K'ferrin's voice as well as haughtiness, and

B'nach realized that the old man was losing ground, battling against quicksand to maintain his power. B'nach allowed himself to lift his chin slightly to the chill breeze, suddenly understanding the power he possessed to destroy his grandfather, a salutation to the change.

He slipped his hands inside his sleeves, his fingers hurting from the cold. The stiff breeze made his eyes water, and the moving figures in the distance were even more blurry in his myopic eyesight. It didn't matter. B'nach felt the tension in the air, the way the Citadel's guards stood, nerves raw, the stillness in the passages and the streets. The sajadas outside the Oracular City had been silenced, the Great Gates of the city itself closed against the Landsfolk waiting outside. Those of Terhune's Elite still loyal prowled the Citadel, restless and impotent, while soldiers patrolled the streets of the city, ready to quash any sign of insurrection.

"We've lost," B'nach said simply.

The baldness of his reply startled the old man, and the guard behind him shifted uneasily.

"That's absurd," K'ferrin protested. "What do you mean?"

"Which word didn't you understand? It's quite simple; we've lost, Lady Antonya has won."

"Just like that?"

B'nach had trouble keeping himself from laughing. "Aye, Grandfather. Just like that."

"That's ridiculous. There are always alternatives . . ."

"The Lady Antonya has already won, dead or alive. She's won the will and the hearts of the people you despised for too long, and brought them together in a common cause. We have been cut off from the Lands, where the true power of our strength always lay. We've squandered it, and while we were too busy bickering among ourselves and murdering each other, Lord Vodos has united the entire South against us, Antonya the eastern counties. Even our faithful Lord Creskar knows when to cut his losses and switch to the side that's winning; there's the North gone as well. I've heard the same rumor as you that D'arim himself is leading the Steppes and the Dark Plains people against us. Face it, Grandfather. We have become the dirt and she the blessed."

"We still hold the Oracle," the old man grated out.

"It won't be enough," B'nach said, still smiling as he watched the hazy figures in his bad vision like angels swirling behind gauze. He slipped his useless spectacles into the pocket of his sleeve.

"No one would dare violate the sanctity of the Oracle . . ."

This time, B'nach was unable to stop the laughter that suddenly rose in his throat, the harsh sound stopping K'ferrin cold. His grandfather gazed at him, appalled.

"You old fool, there *is* no sanctity of the Oracle," B'nach said firmly, once his bitter laughter had died. "You and all the rest of your kind sold it long ago." He gestured angrily toward the army built up around the city walls. "*You* caused this, Grandfather. You and P'tre Terhune couldn't have managed it better had you conspired together."

K'ferrin opened his mouth, and B'nach cut him off sharply. He stared down into the old man's stricken face, speaking calmly although he felt his anger heating his face. "You wouldn't allow Terhune to use the Army of the Faith against her when she was vulnerable because of your quarrel with him. You weakened the one man who might have been your strongest ally, the two of you squabbling like brats over a pet dog. You tried to murder her with hired Assassins and shift the blame onto Terhune to destroy them both, but each time you failed she grew stronger. You dismissed the possibility a humble woman could be capable of a man's boldness, until now she is no longer vulnerable and it is far too late. It's over. You've backed us all into a corner and now there's no way out. Today, tomorrow, the next day, but soon, she'll come for you, for us all. She will squash us like the witless insects we are, Grandfather, and *nothing* can stop her."

He was speaking not only for his grandfather's benefit, but for those armsmen listening intently behind him.

"The Oracular City will stand against her . . ." K'ferrin started to protest.

"The city is hers already," B'nach snorted, disgusted. "For God's sake, open your eyes! The city is in mutiny; half our citizens are struggling to keep the other half from throwing open the gates. How safe do you really think you are now from your own servants, the slaves living in the darkness of their grottoes under your feet? The ones who feed you and clothe you and wipe your ass for you? The ones to whom you preach suffering as a pious virtue while you fatten yourself on their meat, warm your beds by stealing the heat of their bodies, dress yourselves in velvet and furs while they shiver naked in the cold. The ones you've abused and spit on all their lives. Your servants look over the strong walls of your precious city, and they are no longer listening to your pretty lies. They see freedom gathering on that horizon, and not even the fear of God will keep them down any longer. The city was lost the day Kaesyn fell."

"*No*," the old man gasped out hoarsely, starting toward B'nach as if to strike him, his bony hand lifted in wrath. B'nach lifted his face to the blow without fear, almost in welcome. K'ferrin stopped, and his hand fell dispiritedly to his side. The wind gusted around them, the scent of ice in the clouds.

"No," K'ferrin said again, this time in despair. He had paled, staring out at the army. Over his grandfather's shoulder, B'nach caught the expression on the faces of his guard, startled by the unaccustomed respect they regarded him with.

"What can be salvaged, then," K'ferrin asked finally, his voice bleak, "before it is too late?"

B'nach smiled thinly, knowing he was shivering in the cold wind, but feeling an oddly warm sensation in his blood. "Whatever do you mean, Grandfather? Surely you aren't suggesting betraying the Faith?"

"Of course not," the old man snapped, but his frightened eyes said otherwise. "It is our duty to save the Oracle at all costs, B'nach. You knew the woman best, surely we can negotiate with her . . ."

It had honestly never occurred to B'nach until that moment that it was possible to ever be more than his grandfather's drudge, allowed to live only under the protection of the old man's power, existing only by remaining meek and submissive. For a moment, the electric sense of release made him lightheaded.

"Yes," he said slowly, still staring out across the fields but no longer even seeing the swirl of colors. "I knew the Lady well. She might listen to me . . ."

"Then I shall authorize you as our envoy," K'ferrin said with renewed energy, although he couldn't keep the desperation out of his voice. "I'll call a meeting of the Council . . ."

"No," B'nach said, amazed at himself. He turned to look at his grandfather, hearing his own words as if he had suddenly become two people, one speaking, one listening. "Not as an envoy, not as a messenger, not as your servant."

K'ferrin stared at him, baffled, uncomprehending. B'nach smiled. "I know your price for selling out your brothers, Grandfather, I know it all too well. Now hear mine: It is time for you to retire. I am your heir. You will publicly pass on your complete authority to me as Keeper of the Holy Oracle *before* I speak with the Lady Antonya."

K'ferrin's look of bewilderment turned to open-mouthed outrage. "Never!" he finally sputtered.

B'nach shrugged, unconcerned and turned back to the wave on wave of tents and horses, soldiers and siege engines, covering the hills outside the Oracular City, nearly as far as the eye, even eyes as blurred as his own, could see. "Then die," he said calmly.

K'ferrin stood a few more moments in speechless rage before he whirled around and stormed away. B'nach heard rather than saw the apprehension in his retinue of guards as they clattered behind the old man, and grinned. For the first time in his life, he felt an odd sense of joy mingled with the hopelessness.

Whether or not he became Keeper of the Oracle was irrelevant. He was in control of his own life. However briefly. The weight of responsibility felt good around his shoulders.

71

When her army poured out of the mouth of the Tarax Valley into the wide plain facing the marshlands of the Oracular City, even Antonya had been surprised that they met with not even the slightest resistance. The autumn weather had given way to the early signs of a bitter cold winter, leaves turning color overnight and tumbling from the trees like red snowflakes to coat the ground.

Vodos had already set up his camp along the southern border of the swamps, and in the distance, she could just make out several tiny specks detached from the speckled horizon, riders coming to meet her.

The moon-driven tides pushed the sea around the towering bedrock under the city, flooding the marshes, thin breakers rolling across the expanse of sandy plains. The wooden bridges connecting the narrow strips of road to the city Gates were nothing more now than charred posts, still smoking as they jutted up from the mud like broken teeth. The Great Gates were sealed shut, and the top of the high stone walls bristled with soldiers, archers and artillery facing out over the marshlands.

Tyro sat huddled against the cold on the steps of his motionless wagon, his horses' heads lowered. Antonya reined in her own mare parallel to him, staring out at the Citadel in the distance, roiling sea mist obscuring its foundations.

"Unless you've got any more bright ideas, child," Tyro said conversationally while picking at one wide nostril with the nail of his little finger, "it looks like you're in for one Hell of another long siege." He pulled out his finger to examine his gleanings, then flicked it off into the sand.

"Does have that look about it, doesn't it?" she said, watching the distant movement of men along the walls.

"Mm-hm." Tyro shivered, drawing his green cape up around his neck. "Your army is tired, and this is only the beginning of winter. Wait until the sea foam freezes into ice and snow whitens the sands even further, and I wonder how fervently your men will want to stay while doing nothing."

"Probably not that long." She looked around over her shoulder at the steady stream of men, horse and equipment swelling out onto the hostile plains. "This place *is* quite unpleasant, isn't it? Large armies on a siege do tend to get bored and restless."

She turned to find Tyro watching her shrewdly. "My wizardly expertise isn't likely to be of much use here, Antonya. In a way, it was a good thing we lost the main cannon, lovely piece of work that it was, shame, really. But it would probably have been sucked straight down in the mud before we could get it two feet out into the flats."

"Very true," she agreed amiably.

"Other than agreeing with everything I say, dear heart, are you planning on doing anything else particularly useful?"

She smiled. "Not at the moment, no." She watched him

shake his head ruefully before she kicked her mare into a canter, heading toward where Kerrick directed the various companies of men into groups, organizing the camp. Even with her astride a horse, he stood tall enough that she could look at him nearly face-to-face as she reined in. A fine mist threatened to solidify into credible rain, condensation streaking Kerrick's leather armor like sweat. She stared at his ruined noseless face, only his green eyes unchanged in the webbed skin.

"Well, here we are at last," he said. She heard the caution in his voice, and looked away, across the marsh flats to the Citadel reflected in the shallow tidewater.

"Aye."

He smiled bitterly. "They have warships to sail supplies and men in and out along the sea access where we have only fat, slow fishing vessels jury-rigged with cannon and shot. They have provisions enough for years, and soon those innocents they don't massacre will be turned out for us to feed, conserving their stocks while straining ours."

"All true," she agreed dryly. "You and Tyro have convinced me. Let's surrender now."

"What, my Lady?" Kerrick pressed. "No more tricks up your sleeve? No more incendiary pigeons? Secret waterworks? Shall we send Morgan creeping over the walls? We won't be able to take the city by force."

"We won't have to," she said quietly.

He seemed unsurprised, although the scarred damage could hide many thoughts. "You may think me a wicked deceitful hoaxer, Kerrick, but my belief is sincere. Either we've already won, or there is nothing we can do further. We truly are in God's hands now."

72

B'nach and his small retinue left the Citadel the next morning, riding the shallow tide in flat-bottomed skiffs, each boat poled slowly across the marsh by a grizzled fisherman. He sat huddled against the cold in new robes, the heavy chain of his new office draped and fastened around his shoulders. One hand gripped the gold staff while the other occasionally reached to steady the top-heavy miter settled uneasily around his brow. The half-naked fisherman stood behind him at the stern, indifferently thrusting his own wooden staff into the water to propel the boat around sandbanks. As the boats approached, Antonya's warriors began filling the horizon, more in curiosity than belligerence, their buzz of conversation floating across the open water like a cloud of mosquitoes.

B'nach kept himself erect as he watched armed men trot through the scrubby sand dunes on the marsh's edge, trying to look more confident than he felt. As the fisherman drove his craft up onto the bank, B'nach stood, and almost lost his balance, arms wheeling as the boat rocked from side to side against his lumbering gait. An enemy armsman waded out to grasp him by the arm before he could pitch headlong into the shallow surf. Behind him, his silent Elite guard plunged into the water up to their thighs and waded to the shore.

It was not an auspicious entrance, he realized, the hem of his robes soaked to the knees and speckled with sand. But he did his best to maintain some semblance of dignity, ignoring the faint sniggers. His Elite guard formed an escort around him.

"I am the Reverence B'nach, High Lord Keeper of the Holy Oracle," he intoned, pitching his voice not only to make it carry but to keep it from shaking, "who the Lady Antonya knew as Chief Librarian . . ."

"We know who you are, Priest," the armsman said casually. "The Lady Antonya has been expecting you."

Surrounded by his own armed men, B'nach followed Antonya's armsman up the worn path through the wind-twisted shrubbery to the border of the tent city which had sprung up like mushrooms after a rain. He ignored the jeers and taunts of both men and women watching his progress, hoping his ceremonial trappings hid his shaking knees. Only once did he lose his restraint, stopping at the sight of captive Elite chained together huddling under a crude shelter with shabby blankets draped over their bony shoulders.

He gulped, scanning them for a familiar face and spotted Cyler, nearly unrecognizable under the dirt and beard covering a gaunt face. As he stared, the prisoner slowly stood, the other captive Elite following his example, and silently bowed their heads in cautious respect. That recognition somehow impressed B'nach more than all the ritualistic formality he had received from the Reverences in the Great Sajada. The ridicule of enemy armsmen diminished markedly.

"Come, honored sir," a deep voice said at his elbow. B'nach turned to face a monster, stumbling back involuntarily, aghast at the hideous mask of ruined flesh on the face of the huge man before him. The man smiled, unoffended. "I am Kerrick, First Defender of the Lady Antonya." He gestured to the young armsmen with him. "These men will show your Guard every hospitality while you meet with her."

B'nach nodded in answer to his own Elite captain's questioning look, before Kerrick gripped him firmly by one elbow to steer him in the direction of the tent in the center of the camp.

Two armsmen stood guard, allowing him and Kerrick to pass inside, then pulled the flap closed. Antonya sat in a folding camp chair, clad in men's clothing, one leg thrown across the arm of the chair. Behind her stood her Assassin, as still as stone, and as cold.

Antonya smiled. "Be welcome, B'nach. You have nothing to fear from me."

He bowed, a court gesture, but said nothing when he straightened. Her eyes examined his clothing with unconcealed amusement. "Tell me, how is your venerable grandfather?"

"In a foul mood as he digests an early retirement."

"Mmmm. This is official, I take it?"

"Confirmed in a rather hasty, but all the same binding ceremony of confirmation late last night. I am now the new Keeper of the Oracle, and carry full authority of the Citadel in that capacity."

"And my dearest uncle?" Her voice was too detached.

"Even more annoyed than my grandfather."

She smiled brightly, her brown eyes warm. "Terhune blood always did tend to run a bit hot." She motioned him to another camp chair. "Will you drink with me?" she said as he settled himself carefully into the wobbly seat.

"Aye, with pleasure."

To his surprise, she stood up and poured the ale herself, then astonished him even further when she strolled to him, sipped from the tankard and held it out to him.

"You need not taste for me, Lady," he said, taking the ale. "I place myself willingly into your hands." He drained it to the bottom.

"Careful, B'nach. We may be setting a precedent." She drank from her own cup before adding, "And how will your conscience bear the deaths of thousands inconsiderately poisoned by following our courteous example?"

"I hope to save those same thousands from being slaughtered, should your armies meet ours."

"We're out here shivering in the mud, B'nach. You're in there, toasty warm and dry and well-armed. What likelihood is there your armies will politely invite us in for a fight, or join us out here in the miserable cold and wet?"

B'nach smiled wryly. "Antonya, let's not spar like this. You've won, we both understand that much. You've taken the city without a blow; there's not a single citizen who would not welcome you inside the walls. But not the Citadel." He waited as she signaled the wiry Assassin, and tried to keep his hand from shaking as he held out his tankard for the fiend to refill. "It's only a matter of time, a week, two, before you're inside the city where you can besiege the Citadel and can starve us out in every comfort."

Her eyes had paled, not quite the ashen gold that had so unnerved him, but enough to make her expression flat and unreadable.

"On the other hand, our citizens may support you now, but you would still be, after all, attacking the holiest site in civilization. They may hate us, but they still fear God. And a siege of the Citadel will take time. How long before they tire of having to feed and billet your soldiers? Once the Citadel did fall, how long do you think you could keep it? You know what it's like, all the plots and schemes and intrigues. The Faith thrives on conspiracies. You'd have to massacre most of the Priests to root it out."

"Or join in the fun," she said bluntly.

He frowned, conceding the point. "You are not P'tre Terhune," he observed, adding as she burst into laughter, "and his Elite will not support you should you attempt to become his replacement."

"No," she said, smiling. "I don't suppose they would."

"But they will follow D'arim." He was rewarded by her start of surprise.

"D'arim?"

"I've heard he's your man now."

"Then you've heard wrongly. He's his own man, not mine."

"I see. Our communications have been badly damaged by your energetic activities, I'll admit. But I don't believe his armada is on its way down the coast to rescue the Citadel."

At that she glanced at the Assassin, her eyes bright. He nodded, and left at her silent command.

"How many ships?" she demanded eagerly.

"Enough. The word came late last night. We were all astonished, frankly, as we had expected him to come overland. There is a huge army approaching from the Steppes through the Dark Plains, but P'tre now has reason to regret having educated his *qazaq* servant in the maritime arts. D'arim is expected to arrive within two days to set up a blockade of the city from the sea." B'nach drank the last of his ale and set the tankard on the ground. Lacing his hands over his stomach, he eased himself lower in his seat. "I wasn't to have told you about D'arim's armada, Antonya."

"So why did you?"

"My grandfather expects me to barter with you now, before D'arim arrives. But I'm actually part of a conspiracy. You get the city without a fight while the Faith keeps the Citadel." He smiled. "We even have plans to give you P'tre's head on a plate, apple in his mouth and all. By the time D'arim arrives, my grandfather and his cronies will have lured you into the city and had you assassinated."

"I see."

His smile evaporated. "Once you are safely dead, so am I, and my grandfather once again becomes Keeper of the Oracle with both you and P'tre Terhune out of his way."

"Naturally. So what do you intend to do?"

"Surrender."

"Even the Citadel? All of it?"

He nodded. "Surprisingly enough, I've found I have supporters of my own inside the Citadel. I can have the coastal defenses lowered, allow D'arim to enter the city from the sea, at the same time as the City Gates are opened to your armies. But instead of occupying the city, your men will be allowed to enter the Citadel from key points all along the inner walls; the Oracle itself can be surrounded within minutes. Terhune's Elite, those who haven't defected by then, will be cut off. With the Oracle in your possession, no one can defeat you."

Her eyes narrowed, incredulous. "Why, B'nach? You would betray the Citadel and the Faith? The Oracle itself? You'd make yourself a traitor of such magnitude your name would be reviled for the next thousand years!"

At that, B'nach burst out laughing. "Antonya, my name is already so reviled! Why should I care?"

She didn't return his mirth. "I know you, B'nach. You care."

His own laughter quieted. "Yes," he admitted. "I care. I care about the Faith, the *real* Faith, the way it once was. The way it could be again. I want an end to the corruption in the Citadel, the evil that has made a mockery of everything I once believed in. If that means my name is reviled as a traitor for a thousand years, then it is a small enough price to pay. I'm not offering you unconditional surrender, Antonya. I have my own price."

"I get the city, *you* get the Citadel?"

"Yes. And no one ever has to Walk the Fire again."

He was startled by the ferocity of her smile, all sharp teeth and no mirth. And even more startled as she said, "One more, I think, B'nach. One last Walk."

73

Things hadn't quite gone accordingly to plan. Then again, nothing ever did, the workman anonymous in the crowded balcony thought. He smiled, dark violet eyes taking in the scene below. That was what made life interesting, all the unforeseen snags in the most carefully plotted strategies.

He had been one of those allies B'nach counted on. While the Great Gates of the city had been opened to Antonya and her troops, the sea gates were lowered, the chains and gears of the huge portcullis sabotaged, exposing the Citadel's fleet to D'arim's ships now busily bombarding the harbor. And, true to plan, once Antonya's forces had entered the city, they had immediately rushed the Citadel, penetrating it rapidly.

But they hadn't quite reached the Oracle when Terhune's Elite had poured into the magnificent hallway leading to the Great Sajada, heavy boots ringing against the inlaid marble. They charged the rear of Lady Antonya's battalion already fighting a third company protecting the Oracle from within.

"P'tre, this way!"

The workman glanced down at a woman's voice, saw D'nyel gesturing wildly at Terhune at the head of a band of his Elite slicing their way toward the Sajada. At their core, G'walch shuffled as best he could tightly defended by his bodyguards. P'tre slashed around him with indiscriminate fury, intent on getting his nephew through the fray and into the Sajada regardless of friend or foe.

At a slight movement from above, the workman looked up to see D'nyel's pathetic creature creeping along the catwalk ledge above the gallery, and realized what the beautiful healer intended. He had to admire the poor man's endurance, clinging obviously terrified on a foothold barely six inches wide over the sheer drop below.

He scanned the walkway, deducing Catrus must have entered from the outside, through one of the high windows, and, sure enough, he soon spotted where one of the precious glass panels had been smashed. Grunting to himself as he weighed his alternatives, the workman knew he'd waste valuable minutes if he followed by the same route, fighting his way outside through the pack of milling, frightened civilians. Or he could risk detection by unlocking the door to the narrow service stairs, and take the long way around the catwalk ledge. Heights meant little to him, he'd had to feign nervousness whenever he'd made the climb to clean the windows. But detection at this point was not one of his main worries.

As the battle raged around him, he pushed his way through to the service door, picking the lock with casual speed, and raced up the stone staircase three steps at a time.

By the time he'd reached Catrus, the boy had wedged himself on the ledge firmly behind a pillar, trembling violently as he braced the small riflebow across his knees, his back to the workman. The battle raging below echoed strangely from this height. As P'tre Terhune and his men rounded the arch, fighting in the open, the boy, with a clear shot from above, brought up his riflebow, aiming for the heart. The workman knew he had very little time.

"Catrus . . ."

The boy nearly fell off the ledge in surprise, twisting around to find a poorly dressed workman hunched over him. He gaped, stunned, as the man deftly grasped his head and snapped his neck. A dull crack, a shudder, and the body went limp, still wedged behind the pillar.

The workman risked a quick look down, to find his only witness was the beautiful healer. Her mouth fell open in confusion, then twisted in alarm as he smiled, and pointed a finger directly at her. His meaning wasn't lost on her. Panicking, she glanced around for escape, and with one last look of horror, vanished in the crowd.

74

The battle inside the Great Sajada had an odd air of madness, the presence of so much metal stirring the Oracle to virulent life, its unearthly heat pressing enemies back to the portals of the Sajada as more troops strained to get in.

Terhune's Guard hammered their way into the Sajada, G'walch at their center. The boy ignored the fighting around him, pushing his way down the aisle to the *pulpitum*. Terhune himself helped the boy up onto the steps, ignoring the scorching heat of the Oracle behind them.

"Hold!" Terhune shouted, his voice hoarse. "For the love of God, stop your hostilities!"

Serene, dressed in a plain white robe, G'walch held up one hand, waiting patiently as fighting men caught sight of him, one by one, and the battle slowly abated, swords still at the ready in suspension. Antonya's armsmen looked at her questioningly.

"Cease fighting."

G'walch gazed around, eyes brimming with tears. "My brothers," he said quietly, yet his clear voice carried to the far ends of the Great Sajada. He looked at Antonya, adding in a wry tone, "and sisters, will you not have peace? Will you not be as one people?"

Although he had made no move toward it, the Oracle's feverish light brightened, as if it knew it would shortly be fed another human body. A murmur rippled through the warring soldiers.

"G'walch," Antonya said softly, "goddamn you, no . . ."

"There is but one way," the boy continued, ignoring her. "The Lands are being ripped apart with war, the madness of brother murdering brother, good men turned to evil. The rot has spread everywhere, even to the core of what was once too holy to think of desecrating."

His voice quavered, breaking with emotion. "The Mother of

God cannot allow Her children to perish in this manner! The promise was made Light and set among us to lead us on the path of righteousness. We have pushed ourselves to the edge of destruction, to look into the depths of the abyss we have risked by the evil in our nature."

Antonya gazed up at him, speechless. G'walch smiled at her.

"This bloodshed must stop," he said gently. "I am the Hope and the Light. Only I can Walk the Fire of Prophecy to transcend human evil, give myself willingly to God as His Mouth and so to give the world peace again."

Antonya took a step toward him before she felt arms restraining her. Kerrick held her by one arm, and, to her surprise, B'nach held the other. She struggled for a moment, then allowed herself to be pinned, staring at G'walch.

"He *is* the One," K'ferrin's voice said from behind her, his voice quavering on the edge of hysteria. Those Priests around him stared at him in astonishment. "Put down your arms! Obey him!" Slowly, a few of them, unsure, did as the old man commanded.

She didn't turn her head as K'ferrin shuffled unsteadily down into the sajada. P'tre Terhune smiled maliciously as K'ferrin crossed the hall to stand beside him.

"He is the Crown and the Pinnacle," Terhune breathed, reverently. "All my life, I have waited for this moment."

"I have come to Walk the Fire," the boy said calmly.

K'ferrin gaped at the boy, then whirled on Terhune, white-faced and shaking with rage. "No! This is not what we agreed!"

Terhune laughed and backhanded the old man without even looking at him, as casually as swatting a fly. K'ferrin crumpled to the floor, and sat holding his bony hand against his terrified face.

The Great Sajada was silent as the boy turned to face the Oracle. The Fire suddenly blazed, pulsing into a radiant pearl of light suspended on the Oracle. He stood on the lip of the Chalice, and bowed his head respectfully as the light washed out his features. The Fire shone through his gown, a ghostly trace of his skeleton beneath the translucent red shell of skin and blood.

Antonya shook off the hands holding her forearms, but made no move to stop G'walch. When G'walch looked up, he stared into the light of the Oracle, but spoke to her.

"Cousin," he said quietly. "You would be a leader of men. You would have given your life in the Fire to unify these Lands, to stop the killing by your own death. Your sacrifice is admirable, but you would achieve nothing. You are corrupt. You have not been able to fight the evil of the world without being tainted by it yourself. You've allowed all its hatred and violence and wickedness to hollow you, as it has hollowed me. But you've let yourself be filled again with the poison of human corruption and misery instead of God's love."

He smiled gently into the Light. "You would speak from the Fire and lie, cousin. I can see deceit in you like darkness shadowing your soul." She flinched, but did not look away from him. "How could you hope to stand before the throne of truth?" He closed his eyes, basking in the lethal glare of the Fire, his arms raised as if to embrace it. "Now you dare seize the holiest of places by force, and steal the rightful authority of the Faith. You would play the sacrificial lamb to throw down the altar of God. But your death would only serve to shatter the world, not join it."

The Fire pulsed, the electric tingle of the Light scraping against Antonya's face as she watched him. His hands slowly lowered, palms inward against the deadly heat of the Oracle. "The Light calls me, it is the very thoughts in my head, the beating of my own heart. It does not speak to you, you cannot bend it to do your will. It owns me, I have no will but the Light's, I have no existence but through the Faith. I am the last, and you could never Walk the Fire."

Eyes turned toward her expectantly. She ignored them, her attention riveted on G'walch. "No," she said. "Nothing human can."

At that, he turned, smiling at her. In the wash of light, she could not make out his expression, seeing only the dance of the Oracle's light in his eyes. "No," he affirmed gently. "Nothing *human* can."

He lifted his arms, shrugging as the white robe fell from his shoulders. He was naked, his body as hairless as a baby's. He was as beautiful as an angel, and as unearthly. One of his aides retrieved the robe from the floor as the other knelt at his feet, his quill hovering above parchment as he gazed at the boy worshipfully, ready to preserve the Divine moment for all time and history. Terhune stood to one side, one leather-gloved hand on the hilt of his sword, the other bunched into an impatient fist at his side in anticipation.

"The time has come," G'walch said, his voice tranquil in the hush. "Surrender your violence before the Chalice of God as I surrender my body and my soul. I will be crowned God's Servant in the Fire, His Voice will speak through His instrument. He will step reborn into the Lands to lead you to a millennium of peace."

Beside Antonya, B'nach slowly knelt, his face desperate with hope. Kerrick was muttering Our Mother under his breath, almost resentfully. Throughout the sajada, there were faces streaked with tears; others displayed fear and longing. Several had gone to their knees, praying with their weapons held slack in their hands.

G'walch turned slowly toward the Fire, his head held up with immense dignity and confidence as he stepped into the ring of the Oracle. The light, already painfully bright, ignited in a cold brilliance. G'walch stepped determinedly into the center of the Fire. He spread his arms out from his sides, bathed in flame as he turned to face the witnesses around him. The Light shimmered against his naked flesh. He laughed, a sound of pure, innocent joy.

"*I am the Prophecy made Flesh! I am the living Voice of God,*" G'walch cried out, the exultation in his voice echoing eerily from the Fire. "*Born of the Blood of Light! I am the Love through which Mankind shall be reborn!*"

He stood transfixed, his head thrown back with a radiant smile as he gazed upward. Slowly, his eyes lowered until they stared directly into Antonya's. They glowed with an uncanny red. "*My beloved child, the boy G'walch is dead. I am the One Lord born anew. Will you not bend your proud neck before your God, even now?*"

She said nothing, impassive as he gazed at her sadly. Then he lowered his arms and stepped toward her . . .

   . . . or tried to.

He blinked. A tear of blood ran down his cheek. His expression of confusion giving way to surprise, then horror as he realized he was trapped in the Fire. His limbs moved jerkily as he struggled, his dignified manner vanished. "*No,*" he breathed, unbelievingly. "*Not possible . . . this cannot be possible . . .*"

A murmur of dismay brushed through the crowded sajada as G'walch struggled futilely. Then he stopped, hands dropping to his sides as he stared through the prison of Fire, desperately searching through the crowd, his eyes now entirely too human. "*P'tre?*" he said, bewildered, childlike. "*P'tre? I don't understand . . .*"

She heard B'nach choking softly beside her, his face buried in his hands as he wept. Then that small sound was muffled in G'walch's sudden scream of pain. The Fire had begun to consume him.

Numbly, the aide bent his head over his parchment, fingers jerking his quill as he tried to preserve what Prophecy the Oracle would deliver from the tortured lips of yet another failed Saint. The Light held G'walch impaled like an insect on a child's stick, writhing in agony as his body was ripped into oblivion, molecule by molecule. His skin turned an unnatural white, then red as blood oozed from his stripped pores. But as the boy shrieked, his eyes rolling white into his head, his words were gibberish through the pain. She knew there would never be any Prophecy from his mouth. His or anyone else's.

God would never speak from the Fire. He was not there.

Her arm twitched as she shook her throwing knife down into her hand. Her fingers curled around the cold blade, feeling the razor edge bite into her palm. It quivered like a living thing in her fingers. She prayed her arm was strong enough—let her aim be true.

"Forgive me, my friend," she whispered to the knife.

Kerrick's head jerked around at the words, but he was too late. In one smooth movement, she threw the knife straight at the doomed child locked in the globe of Light.

In a split second, she saw the knife pierce through the sphere, heard the dull crack as it buried itself to the hilt in the boy's chest, killing him instantly. His anguished screams were cut off in a moment of silence before the knife suddenly glowed, the gold band worked in the black hilt becoming impossibly bright. She thought she saw the steel blade melt as her hair stood up on end in the sudden rush of electricity through the static air. She stood paralyzed in the Light, her skin itchingly alive.

The Oracle exploded.

"No!" B'nach shouted, and flung his arms across his face as he was thrown backward.

Reflexively, she squeezed her eyes shut and turned away from the blinding light before Kerrick knocked her down, landing heavily on top of her. The image stamped its impression on her aching retinas.

Cold, dazzling Light burst out of the sphere, a thousand years of captured starlight suddenly set free in a blaze of glory. It shot straight up from the floor of the Oracle, a solid column of fire smashing through the Crystal Dome of the sajada. Shards of colored glass showered down on the writhing mass of men cowering on the floor of the sajada. A blast of wind left in the wake of fleeing Light howled as it poured upward into the sky.

The storm clouds above the ruptured dome shredded in the path of the column. Splinters of lightning erupted wildly on all sides of the rush of Light, bleeding out of the clouds into brilliant electric energy.

For a sickening moment, Antonya felt the floor underneath her heave, the stones of the sajada's floor cracking. The center of the earth seemed to groan in agony as the Light wrenched itself free. A pillar of stone toppled majestically, smashing a few feet from her head. Another swayed, sections of the carved column falling like a child's construction around them. Heavy pieces of stone danced over the buckling floor, crushing the bodies trapped beneath them.

She heard Kerrick cry out her name before she was ripped away from him by the force in the air. She slammed hard against a stone wall, the breath knocked from her. Squeezed against the marble, her feet several meters off the ground, wind thundered in her face. The power of the Light tossed the helpless figures in the sajada bonelessly about like broken dolls in a tempest. She gasped for breath, her lungs burning as the very air was sucked out of the sajada in the wake of the Light, and she knew they were all about to die.

Then it was gone.

The sajada was plunged into blackness as the Light vanished, its power abated. She slid down the face of the wall and crumpled, her back scraped raw. For a moment, she'd thought the silence in the darkened sajada absolute, then realized she'd been deafened as her hearing slowly returned. The only sounds now, however, were moans of pain and soft weeping and the tinkling of glass still raining down from the shattered Crystal Dome. The indistinct forms of bodies moved sluggishly around her, illuminated only by the occasional bursts of lightning still flickering through the clouds overhead.

She got to her feet shakily, the mounds of broken glass shifting under her feet. Tiny cuts slashed by flying glass in her arms and face bled freely. "Kerrick?" she called out softly, squinting in the dim light.

"Here, Antonya." She heard his voice. A man stood some yards distant, only the size of the body's outline giving any indication it was Kerrick's. She felt a wash of relief, and with it a surge of confidence.

"Morgan!" she called out in a stronger voice.

"Here, Lady," she heard him call out, closer to her than she expected. In a sudden crack of lightning, she saw him standing a few feet away, legs wide as he balanced on the piles of splintered glass and broken bodies. The light flashed on the naked blade of his knife, and blood oozed from a deep gash in his forehead, dripping across his face in black starkness. But he smiled fiercely at her, a strange look of triumph and rage in his dark eyes.

"Daen! Gesham! Nicoli!" she called out, rewarded with the answers from her armsmen. She slogged through the thick drifts of broken glass toward the Oracle, the floor uneven with jutting slabs of stone pushed up at odd angles. Her sight had almost completely readjusted to the dim light. Around her, the dazed survivors began to stand, checking those bodies littering the floor for life, helping their neighbors, ally or enemy, to rise to their feet, hostilities forgotten. Several milled about aimlessly, confused, broken glass crunching underfoot.

Recognizing a shadowed lump sprawled on the floor she knew was B'nach, she reached down apprehensively.

"B'nach?"

To her relief, the man looked up, his face pinched and white. "I think my arm is broken," he said in a voice calm with shock, then whimpered as he tried to move. "Yes, I'm certain of it."

She touched him gently on the shoulder. "Don't move, stay still, there'll be help soon."

She turned and continued walking toward the Oracle, not seeing the men who moved out of her way. She stopped when she reached the lip. The black stone circle was cold and dark, its base cracked in two. A thin wisp of smoke and dust trailed from the fissure. The Oracle was dead.

She brushed fragments of glass away before she lifted herself onto the Chalice. The black stone was littered with broken glass as she stood in the center where G'walch had been only minutes before. The wondrous moving figures of the Crystal Dome had been reduced to splintered rubble, a few clawed fingers from a daemon's hand recognizable among the debris, a bit of ornate border from a cloak, the single blind eye of a sibyl glaring up at her from the pile of colored fragments. A flash of lightning picked out a glint at her feet, and she kicked aside the glass debris with one booted foot.

Gold. A bent and twisted band of gold. She smiled. All that remained of her knife.

She stooped to pick it up. It was cold in her hand, a stab of bitter, uncanny cold that made her hiss in sudden pain. It hurt only for a moment before it warmed to the touch of flesh. *Human* flesh.

She turned to regard the faces turned toward her. No one spoke. Every muscle in her body quivered, aching. She was suddenly very tired. "No one will give us peace but ourselves," she said. "God has been freed from the unholy prison in which we trapped His Light for too long. The divided born of darkness has been made whole again. He has regained His freedom. Now He has given us back ours."

She examined the gold band in her hand, then twisted the ends together in a crude circle. Lifting it over her head so that all could see, she held it aloft for a moment before she settled the crooked crown onto her own head.

"As it was Prophesied," she said. "Crowned in the heart of the Oracle." Her voice was calm. "I am the one True Heir of the Lands. Are there now any left among you who do not believe?"

She gazed down at a man directly in front of her, a common workman staring unblinkingly at her with blue eyes so dark they were nearly purple. Slowly, he knelt before her. Behind him, a few more men knelt, then more, until it became a wave undulating across the ruined sajada in silence. She saw K'ferrin, miraculously unscathed, gaping up at her in sick fear before he, too, gingerly went to one arthritic knee and lowered his head.

It began to rain, large drops of water spilling down from the black sky like crystal tears. The thunder rolled above them, and the scatter of raindrops grew to a downpour, drenching the figures held in the broken bowl of the sajada.

She turned around, unhurried, head held high in the rain, gazing down at the sea of bowed heads. She stopped as she came to the solitary figure still standing, staring at her. P'tre Terhune.

"Still?" she said to him softly.

The Warrior-Priest stood swaying slightly, his face scratched from the flying glass, water and blood dripping from his head. His scabbard was empty, sword torn from his grasp by the wind. He stared at her, pale gray eyes wide in stunned incredulity. "G'walch?" he whispered hoarsely.

The man kneeling next to him pulled anxiously at his sodden clothes, and as he staggered, she realized.

P'tre Terhune was blind.

75

"B'nach..."

The whispered voice woke him abruptly, startling him. His heart raced as he stared into the darkness. He heard his guard stir, the rasp of metal as a dagger was drawn. When it came again, he knew who it was.

"B'nach, please, let me in," D'nyel pleaded urgently.

B'nach grunted his assurances to the guard, and fumbled with his robe, using his one good arm, as the man padded silently to the door. D'nyel's eyes were wide, glittering with alarm as she staggered into the room. B'nach lit a cord-match with an ember still glowing in the hearth, the yellow flame throwing their wavering shadows against the room, large and ominous. He lit a candle with the burning string before he turned to D'nyel.

She stood compliantly, hands held away from her body, as his guard briskly searched her. Her hair was disheveled, she looked stunned and frightened. The man took her small knife, handing it to B'nach and looked at him inquiringly. Keeping his eyes on D'nyel, B'nach nodded his head toward the door, dismissing the guard.

When they were alone, D'nyel stumbled toward him, as if her legs were too numb with fear to work properly. Still holding her knife, he took a cautious step back from her.

She reacted as if he'd struck her, eyes wild as she fell to her knees, arms reaching out to him. "Oh, B'nach, please, you must help me, don't let them take me, I don't know who else to turn to . . ." She began to weep, tears running down her face. "If you ever loved me, I'm begging you, help me!"

"Who will take you?" he asked, hating the instant concern in his voice that he couldn't control.

She stared at him imploringly. "P'tre Terhune is blind," she said simply, as if afraid to name her enemies. "K'ferrin is disgraced. D'arim has returned, and he holds no love for me.

You're the only one who can protect me now, B'nach."

He put down the knife, out of her reach, before he crouched beside her to hold her gently, stroking her hair. She clung to him frantically, pulling him down to the floor as she sobbed in relief. He winced with pain, his broken arm throbbing.

"They know. Everyone knows now. They'll cut me to pieces if they catch me," she wept. "I'll be torn limb from limb, B'nach. You can talk to the Lady Antonya. If she gave her word, they couldn't touch me then—*please*, she'll listen to you . . ."

Sitting on the floor with her head pressed against his chest, B'nach felt sick, closing his eyes as he suddenly understood. And realized he had always known—known and denied it. Carefully, he wrapped his arms around her to pull her against his chest. He felt the wild pulse of her heart as he rubbed his cheek against her soft hair, inhaling her warm, sweet scent.

He shushed her gently, drawing her up to lead her to the floor cushions still warm from his bed. "No one will hurt you here, D'nyel," he said gently, holding her face close to his, her chin cupped tenderly in his hand.

She stared at him for a long moment before she grasped his hand in hers, kissing his palm in gratitude and relief. Her warm salt tears stung the cuts on his hand.

"I'm not evil, B'nach, you know me well enough," she said, her voice low and shaking. She looked up at him, her beautiful eyes sending an instant shiver of need into his gut. "I'm no worse than anyone else. I did what I did for knowledge, like you, B'nach." The moment of defiance passed, and her voice pleaded with him again, "I've saved lives with what I learned."

"Yes, I know," he assured her gently.

"Please, make her understand . . ." She trembled violently in his arms. "Tell her I could help her, I've learned ways to treat her First Sworn's scars, I know how to repair his face, make him appear whole again. She would find me useful—talk to her, B'nach, please don't let them take me . . ."

"I will, D'nyel, hush, my jewel, no one will touch you here," he comforted her. She babbled on, still terrified, as he rocked her and made soothing noises. Slowly she calmed, her shivering subsiding.

He pulled away gently, gazing down into her still lovely face, distorted as it was with tears and dread. He smiled, kissing her forehead before he stood. "I'll pour us some wine," he said. "It'll calm your nerves, beloved."

It was awkward with only one hand, but he managed. He held out two glasses to her, grasped in one hand, allowing her to choose which she preferred. Hers were still shaking badly as she took the glass, nearly spilling it as she brought it to her lips. Then stopped, staring at him suspiciously without drinking as he clumsily settled on the cushion beside her.

He smiled, sipped his own, and set it on the floor. Her skin flushed slightly, ashamed at doubting him, and drank deeply.

She took a deep shuddering breath as the wine settled her, then smiled weakly at him. "I knew I could trust you, B'nach," she said, and ran slender fingers through the tangled mass of her black hair. "You're the only good man left in the Citadel."

"Am I?" he said dryly.

Now that her terror had subsided, a hint of the old look crept back into her face, the calculating, wary intelligence. "I'm sorry I was ever cruel to you, B'nach. I've been very foolish, my love. Please, forgive me . . ."

He said nothing, watching the flicker of candlelight sparkle in her eyes, feeling an overwhelming adoration for the curve of her full lips, measuring his own heart by the pulse of life beating against the smooth skin of her throat.

She slid closer to him, her fingers trailing lightly over his good arm as she pressed the curves of her body against his. "There's no one else, B'nach. You hold my life in your hands, I am yours if you still want me."

He touched her face gently, kissing her mouth and tasting the spice of wine on her lips. "From the moment I first saw you," he murmured against her cheek, "I wanted you. I've never wanted anyone as badly as I've wanted you, D'nyel." She pulled away from him, just far enough to study his face.

He smiled, his free hand caressing the satiny dark skin of her throat. "Every time I knew that you lay with someone else, I thought I would go mad. But I needed you so much, I never tried to stop you for fear I'd lose even the smallest part you gave to me. I never allowed myself to hope you could ever be mine alone."

She smiled at him, as beautiful as the first day he saw

her, and he felt the old heat of desire surging through his limbs.

"Then we both can have what we want," she said softly. "Protect me, B'nach, and I will belong to you, yours only." She arched her neck toward him, her body open to him, vulnerable.

"Yes," he breathed. "Mine only."

He pulled her tightly to him to kiss her fiercely, his arm locked around her shoulders. She whimpered, the sound igniting years of frustrated hunger in him. He ripped the delicate cloth from her shoulders, jerking it away from her body and pushed her down ruthlessly, crushing her underneath him.

She responded, her caress mechanical, more fear than passion in her ragged breathing. The sighs she made were false, grating in his ears. He kissed her flesh, her smooth skin cold against his lips, his own rage and lust a burning fever. He wanted to scream, hating himself as he roughly yanked her gown up above her hips. She opened herself to him compliantly, a motion as automatic as a whore's and as impersonal. He froze, unable to enter her. Supporting himself by his one good arm, he drew away from her, suddenly weeping.

"B'nach, my love . . ." Her eyes gazed at him with a parody of desire, her frightened dismay all too obvious. He sat up, smearing the back of his hand across his eyes to clear away the tears blurring his vision as she crept into his embrace, desperately trying to fondle him into excitement. He restrained her touch, unable to bear her fear, but held her against him gently, his lust gone, his love finally dead, lost with all else in his past.

She allowed him to hold her before he heard her suddenly gasp and stiffen. Struggling, she clawed her way back from him, staring at him now in disbelief and horror. He averted his eyes, unable to look at the betrayal he saw reflected in her eyes.

"*No*," she whispered hoarsely, and she shuddered violently.

Laboring to breath, he clutched her desperately against him, embracing her like a violent child as her hands tore at him. She kicked in frenzy as she strove to break his grip on her, body convulsing with panic. Her struggles became uncoordinated, and he held her in his lap, rocking her back and forth as she moved sluggishly, tremors racking her body. She stared unseeing at him, a thin line of saliva rolling from the corner of her mouth.

He smoothed the sweat from her forehead, whispering to her gently, kissing her hair, her cheeks, her eyelids, as the poison slowly leached the life from her. He rocked her in his arms, weeping softly, long after she was dead.

76

The jailer's boy carried the lantern, his hand shaking, making the light tremble as it was thrown against the stone walls of the catacombs deep beneath the Citadel. No one spoke as Antonya walked behind the terrified boy, D'arim and Ephraim beside the jailer. Their footsteps echoed in the vaulted corridor, every sound magnified in the oppressive cold and dankness. Rats squeaked in the dark.

The boy stopped before a fortified door, holding the lantern higher as the jailer fumbled with his keys, huge shadows fluttering caricatures of the silent group. The jailer lit a fat stub of candle shoved into a spiked cup and handed it to D'arim before he pulled the heavy door open, hinges protesting.

The cell was barren and tiny, even smaller than the one Antonya remembered with a shudder. It reeked of mold and piss. P'tre Terhune sat on a ledge carved out of the living rock, his red cloak wrapped tightly around his shoulders against the damp. His hands lay curled in his lap, wrists manacled to a chain around his waist. He looked up as the door opened, his pale eyes darting at the sound, wide and luminous in the dim candlelight.

"Who is it? Who's there?" he called out.

Antonya stopped, regarding him silently for a long moment before she turned to the men behind her. "D'arim, you stay with me. Ephraim . . ." She nodded toward the jailer and his boy. The armsman nodded, and escorted them outside, dragging the door shut behind him.

"Antonya." P'tre drew in a long, shuddering breath before

his head bowed over his chained hands. His shoulders slumped, his unshaven face twitching uncontrollably. She had been told, but was still unprepared for the sight of this beaten man.

"Uncle," she acknowledged.

D'arim stood against the door, holding the candle as she took the few steps into the cell to face Terhune. The man recoiled from the sound. His blind eyes jerked from side to side as he strained vainly to see her. She leaned back against the wall, feeling the cold even through her thick leather jerkin. Her hands, balled into fists, she shoved under her arms.

"Have you come to take your revenge on me?" Terhune asked quietly. "Take it, then—do what you will with me."

"I've dreamed of killing you, P'tre," she said distantly, her voice not matching the deep rage within her. "when I could sleep at all. I've spent so many sleepless nights inventing ways for you to die, as slowly and painfully as possible. I've been looking forward to making you suffer. As you made me suffer."

Terhune flinched. D'arim watched him impassively.

"I've been terrified of you ever since I was a child. You have been the stuff of nightmares all my life. Tell me, P'tre, how well do you sleep at night?"

"You killed G'walch," he accused her, a glimmer of his former arrogance surfacing.

"No," she said sharply. "The Oracle killed G'walch. *You* killed him." The blind man's eyes shifted, desperately seeking her. "You murdered him just as you murdered all those I ever loved. You murdered Briston and Father Andrae and Brother Sholto and all the innocents who ever stood in your way." Her voice was thick with rage.

She took a single step forward and struck him hard in the face. Terhune's head snapped to one side, his mouth gasping open in surprise. D'arim winced, then averted his eyes as she hit P'tre again. His chained hands jerked upward, trying futilely to ward off the blows he couldn't see.

Abruptly, she stepped back, spinning away from him. Her hands clawing against the wall, she shuddered violently. "Bastard," she whispered, her throat constricting painfully.

She turned back at the ragged sound of weeping, Terhune's face buried in his hands. His back hunched as the grief tore from his chest. He had lost everything, and with it his vitality had drained away, leaving him derelict. The candlelight fluttered, and when she glanced at D'arim, she was dully surprised to see his eyes were wet, a tear glistening down his flat cheek.

When P'tre's hands dropped back into his lap, the last remnants of his defiance had crumbled. He sagged against the wall, his will broken. His sightless eyes no longer tried to search for her. "You've won, Antonya. I will not ask your mercy." Nor did he want any, she realized. "Will you execute me now?" It was a hopeful plea.

She was suddenly very tired.

"No." She ignored D'arim's glance of surprise. But there was no longer any point in killing Terhune. The man she had hated was gone, leaving only this broken shell behind. She felt cheated of her vengeance. "No, P'tre, I will not." She took a deep breath, trying to clear her head. "On the Isle of Tembris in the White Seas, there used to be a monastery. There are only ruins there now. You Purged it a decade ago. You murdered the abbot and burned him with two other Brothers." D'arim stared at her, his narrow eyes alert and wary as Terhune lifted his face, listening passively.

"I will have it restored, and the Brothers of Blessed Reason reinstated. I have nothing more to fear from you, P'tre. You will be sent there to live among the Brothers for the rest of your days, as a humble monk in quiet meditation."

Terhune sat still as stone, his face ashen. "I want no charity from you," he said, his voice hoarse. "I will never repent of what I've done, it is too late for that."

"You know as well as I this is no charity on my part. It is only fitting that the Brothers and the world see you as you are now, only a broken, blind man—no longer the invincible tyrant they feared, no threat to anyone." Antonya smiled, the expression forced, although the man could not see it. "I don't care if you atone for your sins or not, P'tre. You must ask God for forgiveness if you want it, as I can never forgive you. Your conscience and penitence is your own affair."

He opened his mouth to speak, closing it again when no sound came out. His face worked painfully as he struggled, his agony plain.

"And if I refuse?" The question was nearly inaudible.

"You'll be sent anyway," Antonya said, relentless.

The silence stretched out between them. Slowly, Terhune nodded, his head bent in defeat. "D'arim?" he called out softly.

"I'm here, P'tre." The *qazaq*'s voice was gentle.

"Stay with me awhile?"

D'arim glanced at Antonya questioningly. She nodded. "Yes," he said. "I'll stay."

The cell was oppressive; she had no desire to spend a minute longer within it. D'arim pushed the door open as she crossed toward it, then slipped out behind her, the huddled figure of P'tre Terhune still visible in the open doorway. D'arim touched her on the arm, stopping her.

"Lady . . ." he said, reluctantly.

Ephraim looked up from where he waited with the jailer and his boy, then halted as she raised her hand, her eyes on D'arim.

"What is it?"

The *qazaq* sighed, rubbing his palm against his chin. His eyes darted uneasily around the shadowed corridor, looking at everything but her. "Terhune wasn't responsible for Briston's death. It was K'ferrin who hired the Assassin."

Antonya felt a muscle in her jaw twitch, unmoved.

"Nor was he ever in the White Seas. P'tre never set foot on Tembris." He licked his lips, and spoke so quietly only she could hear. "Ten years ago, I was sent as the commander of a warship into the northern coasts, under orders to hunt heretics." He looked up at her directly, and stopped.

She felt her skin turn cold. "No," she breathed. "Don't say it. Don't say another word." Her voice shook. "I don't think I could bear it."

He nodded as she gestured abruptly to Ephraim. She turned away, walking almost blindly in the dark before the jailer and his boy caught up to her with the lantern. She didn't see the quizzical look the armsman gave to D'arim as he passed.

D'arim watched her walk away before he reentered the cell. He sat silently with Terhune until daybreak, his arm around the shoulders of his childhood friend, holding him tenderly.

77

"We should have killed her when we had the chance," the younger man said bitterly, his blue robes of the Sacred Sciences Order and gaunt build marking him as one of Philoniah's ascetic Flagellants.

The second man with dark blue, almost violet eyes was dressed as a common laborer, patched green blouse belted around well-worn leather breeches. Beside him, the white meat of a half-eaten apple glistened. The two men sat in the sunshine pouring through the Citadel's windows, scrolled diagrams spread out over their laps. They conversed in low tones, switching to a complicated architectural discourse, of plumbing and plaster and painting, whenever anyone wandered into earshot.

The workman picked up the apple, biting into the fruit. "Peace, brother," he said, chewing his mouthful, his voice soft, nearly a whisper. "What is done is done and cannot be undone."

"Your prodigious wisdom slays me," the first man sneered. He ignored the apple with too-obvious indifference. "But beyond astounding me with your dazzling erudition, there still remains the vexing question of what the Hell do we do now?"

"We do nothing," the second man said firmly. "Like all good hunters, we watch and we wait. I think it wise you remember that, brother." He put down the apple and licked his fingers.

The younger man sighed with frustration. "You need not lecture me like a child," he said, his eyes wary as a group of chattering monks passed them several meters away. "But do not expect me *not* to question my masters' logic, even in the privacy of my own skull."

The second man smiled, his work-stained hands busy rolling up one scroll and unknotting the binding from a second. "I wouldn't dream of lecturing you," he said in a tone that clearly conveyed his contempt. "But consider this: Heroes martyred in their prime have an annoying tendency to take on mythical dimensions. Their sins are forgotten, their slightest virtues transforming them into Saints. Their bones cure lepers, their blood restores the blind and lame. They become legends, immortal."

The younger man said nothing.

"But where murder elevates heroes, the petty slings and arrows of worldly life slowly erodes their enchantment, tarnish the luster. Look above you, brother. What do you see?"

The younger man glanced at his companion questioningly, then gazed up. He shrugged. "The ceiling."

The second man chuckled. "A frescoed ceiling. Artists who have filled every corner of your plastered vaults with young heroes and martyred Saints, all sad eyes and elegant wounds dripping blood like rubies as they're carried to Heaven in the arms of angels. Death by fire, death by flaying, death by lance and arrow. So tell me, brother, how many of these glorious illustrations decorating our fair Citadel have you ever seen portraying a hero dying courageously by shitting his life away with dysentery or his flesh eaten with syphillis or simply tripping headfirst down the stairs while vomiting drunk?"

The acetic grinned slowly, making his face cadaverous as his mouth squirmed trying to control his amusement.

"Time wears away heroes with gout and pox and bad teeth and bleeding ulcers and impacted bowels. They make mistakes, choosing nepotism over justice, levying unpopular taxes to finance monuments to their own glory. And when they die, they are buried, not revered. The world has no love for old, flawed, human heroes."

He picked up the rest of his apple and finished it in two bites, then tossed the stem and a bit of core behind the bench.

"So just how long must we wait for her to expire from old age and indigestion?" The younger man perhaps spoke more sourly than he'd intended, the sight and smell of forbidden food making him irritable.

The second man turned to look at his companion directly, dark blue eyes intense. "However long it takes." The words were spoken mildly, but the younger man recoiled slightly, his eyes widening. He bowed his head, suddenly docile.

"Your Grace," he said, meekly.

The workman rolled up his scrolls and tucked them under one arm before he stood. The monk also stood, holding out his hand. The workman bowed respectfully, leaning over to kiss the hem of his companion's sleeve before the monk walked away.

The man in the patched green tunic thoughtfully watched the thin monk disappear into the swarm of midday pedestrians wandering the halls of the Citadel. The man might have to be killed, were he to become too defiant. The workman stuck a fingernail into his mouth to pick at a morsel of apple skin stuck between his teeth, then sucked the last taste of the fruit from his fingers. Then again, perhaps the monk was exactly what the Guild needed, more rebellious spirits to shake up the old order.

He had been the most powerful First Rank Guildmaster for two decades, yet lived most of his life camouflaged as a lowly laborer within the hierarchy of the Priests. He had enjoyed it, for the most part; there was a certain amount of peace and satisfaction in working with his hands which left his mind free to watch and consider.

Despite all the reasons he gave his subordinate, he knew he could never admit how deeply involved he had been in seeing the Terhune woman on the broken Chalice. The old world was gone, the balances shifting day to day. Some of his Guild brothers would have to be culled, no longer any place for them. Some would dislodge others in the struggle for power within the Guild, their eyes focused only inward on their own selfish interests, locked into an inflexible past.

Others would help shape a new world, adapting to new forces, seeing limitless possibilities moving in from the horizon. And he would continue to do all he could to make sure the Terhune woman survived to see this new world born.

No doubt he'd gone wild, as much a renegade as Tevik,

perhaps more so. It would be hard to shake off centuries of discipline, to yield to the ever-present desire for freedom, to learn to *want*.

The laborer stood, work-roughened hands rubbing one another under his sleeves for warmth. He breathed in, drawing in the smell of the Citadel's humanity through his pinched nose. The apple had been more of a prop to irritate the Flagellant, and now, he realized, he was hungry. From somewhere along the long hall, the odor of roast meat wafted. The smell made his mouth water. He *wanted*, for the first time in years, a decent meal, rich meats and pastry and spiced sweetmeats of all kinds.

He was ravenously hungry, feeling suddenly more alive than he had in years. It was a good feeling.

78

This time Antonya was crowned with considerably more pomp and ceremony, and while B'nach had meant every word he spoke, he was dreadfully tired, only wanting to get through it as quickly as possible before he dropped from sheer exhaustion.

He had ordered the Great Sajada swept clean, every fragment and minute speck of the broken stained glass gathered up and carefully stored in the repositories under the library. He himself had personally overseen the cleansing of debris from the broken cradle of the Oracle, no one allowed to step one foot on the holy stone as they maneuvered their longhandled brooms to painstakingly clear away the shattered glass. The Oracle was to be left as it was, cracked and scarred and sacred, an object of worship in itself. Overhead, the dome of the sajada lay exposed to the open sky. He had already looked over preliminary sketches of plans to rebuild the dome, as the remains of the Holy Oracle would have to be protected from the elements.

Antonya had exchanged her leather breeches and jerkin for women's skirts, richly embroidered and elegant. She was led to the Oracle on Kerrick's arm, then knelt before the lifeless black stone. B'nach stood behind her, the new crown heavy as he held it one-handed above her head. The twisted band of gold had been worked into a solid diadem of engraved silver and encrusted with precious stones. When she stood, he settled it onto her head and stepped back. She turned, her eyes as pale as the crown on her head, and all who had had the good fortune to be invited to the coronation knelt.

B'nach's bound arm throbbed as he also went to his knees before Antonya, bending over cautiously with his weight balanced on his good hand and lowering his head far enough to kiss the hem of her skirt. Barely brushing the fabric with his lips, he grunted as he pushed himself back onto his knees. "The Faithful acknowledges you as Our One Lady of the Lands, and our most gracious sovereign," he said, trying to pitch his thin voice to carry, already missing the perfect acoustics of the old dome.

She held her hand out to him, more from necessity than courtesy, as he hadn't a hope of getting up off the floor on his own. When she smiled, his hand gripping hers tightly, for a moment an intensely personal look jumped between them, as if it were all a private joke they alone shared. "Rise, most reverend Keeper of the Faith."

After a few more hours of this ritualistic flummery, he had escorted her out onto the high walls of the Citadel overlooking the city, Kerrick on her left. As soon as the crowd spotted them, a cheer went up for their new sovereign, flags and banners and bits of colored cloth and what B'nach suspected were even ladies undergarments waved in the air, the atmosphere suddenly one of delirious carnival. The cheering went on long after they had left the draughty, cold wall, the dancing and music and drinking and brawling going on throughout the entire night and well into the the next day.

It hadn't surprised him that his grandfather had not attended the ceremony, nor was the old man in evidence anywhere during the rest of the day. No doubt he was hiding from his grandson, unwilling to face his reward for a lifetime of abuse and humiliation. B'nach hadn't yet decided what he was going to do with the vile old man, but had given some consideration to packing him off with P'tre as another humble monk in the Tembris monastery, smiling at the thought of the two sharing the same cell the rest of their lives. Toward the early hours of the morning, when the horizon appeared as a pale blue line to separate Heaven from earth, B'nach begged to be excused from the festivities, pleading fatigue and soreness.

He hadn't expected to change quarters, content with his little room. K'ferrin's dark and macabre chamber overlooking the interior garden held no appeal for him. He faltered as the Guard at the door of the Sector bowed deeply to him as he approached, their arms at ready, before he remembered; he was no longer the lowly, miserable scribe who once had apologetically scuttled past them, but Keeper of the Faith, second only in power to the Lady herself.

His face burned with embarrassment as he forced himself to walk past with some pretense of dignity into the study. It was a relief to have the doors shut silently behind him, shortlived as he spotted one of the hideous twins waiting for him, the other trembling in the shadow of the doorway leading to his grandfather's chambers.

"Cousin," it said in its husky child's voice.

He stared at the two grotesques with sudden comprehension, then glanced up at the open door at the top of the stairway before he brushed past them without a word. Inside, the vast room was dark and silent. The burnt perfume of incense masked another smell, one darker and far more sinister.

The little freaks followed, padding silently behind him with the adroitness of years of servitude to the old man. Although one of them, he noted distantly, was unable to completely stifle its terrified whimpering.

Fine gauze drapes obscured the figure lying on the huge carved bed, unnaturally still. B'nach's palms sweated with childish nightmare fear, as if afraid that when he pulled back the curtain the monster might sit up, not really dead after all, and laugh at B'nach's horror. He swallowed hard, and drew the filmy curtains to one side with a shaking hand. One eye spasmed in a series of tics before he could focus, staring down at his grandfather's corpse.

K'ferrin lay on his back with his arms crossed over his

chest, fully dressed in his sumptuous robes of office, his gold staff clutched in one dead claw, the tall miter slightly askew on his head. His eyes had rolled up sightlessly in the sockets, slivers of white, and his mouth hung open as if frozen in mid-snore. Vomit crusted his chin and darkened his chest and even from this distance, B'nach could smell where the body had voided itself in his fine velvet clothes. Here lay the final Keeper of the Holy Oracle in all his finery, taking it all spite-fully into death with him.

But faced with the reality of the body, B'nach found his terror subsiding as he studied the empty shell, K'ferrin some-how seeming smaller than he'd been in life, more fragile, more insignificant.

"Did you murder him?" he quietly asked the gargoyles still hovering behind him.

The whimpering intensified and he turned to find one of the twins huddled behind the other in abject alarm, the bone-less Siamesed arm flopping pathetically. Its brother gazed up at him with eyes far too bright in its ashen child's face, trembling but facing him with as much courage as it could muster.

"No," it said. "Although we would have done so gladly. He took poison by his own hand. We found him like this."

The stench of death and corruption roiled in B'nach's stom-ach. He staggered toward the window, grabbing the heavy tap-estries and jerking them open with far more violence than necessary. The fabric ripped as he flung them back, tiny par-ticles of dust showering down, glimmering as they caught the first rays of dawn. He blinked, temporarily blinded, then al-most sobbing with the effort, he pounded the windows to get them opened, wanting more light than the rounded circles of glass could let in. They yielded, swinging open, and he gulped the fresh air gusting in from the garden. He turned to squint back into the interior, suddenly illuminated for the first time in many decades, B'nach was certain. He slumped onto the wide stone window ledge, gasping harshly; it was several minutes before the blood stopped pounding in his ears and he could breathe normally again.

"Cousin . . ." the little freak said softly, and cringed when he glared. "Your Reverence . . . have pity on us; we are your blood kin."

"*No*," B'nach hissed, twisting his face away.

"We *are*." The freak stepped toward him, dragging its reluctant twin with it. "Our mother was your father's sister," it insisted in a shaking voice. "We are not so different than you. Had either of us been born whole-bodied and single-souled, we might have gone into the Fire ourselves. Do you suppose we don't wonder if that might have been better? What crime did we commit that we should have been born like this, B'nach? Do you honestly believe our minds and souls must be as deformed as our bodies?" It was a cry of such despair, B'nach found it compelling, unable to look away.

The little creature's eyes were haggard, the child's face and malformed body a deception.

"Look at us, cousin. We are as much slaves of our birth as you were of yours, but we are still human beings. See us for what we are, as *he* never could."

B'nach stared at the twin until it became intolerable, burying his face in his hands, not to weep, certainly not for K'ferrin, but because he was suddenly overcome with fatigue.

"If you cannot"—he heard the bitterness in the twin's voice—"then try to see us for what value we can be to you, Your Reverence. We know his secrets as if they were our own, every scandal, every grain of corruption of all those who sit on the Council and presume to judge the defects of others. We know where he kept the evidence he used to sway others to his will. It can be yours, B'nach, and you well know you will need it if you hope to survive here."

He dropped his hands from his face, smiling, but there was no humor in the expression, lips drawn back from his teeth in a snarl. "For a price, I assume? What do you want? Your freedom? Money, power?"

The twin hugged its silent brother protectively, still frightened but bravely standing its ground. "Freedom to do what, B'nach? How long do you suppose it would be before someone within the Citadel murdered us were we to suddenly appear at liberty to roam the corridors, whether from fear of what we know or what we are? Leave the city? And do what? Become freaks performing for coins in a sajada square? Money? Without freedom, what good is it? Power? To do what? Treat others as we have been treated?"

It shook its head, wise if sad. "No, there's only one place we can live in any measure of safety or happiness. Here. With you. All we ask is that you use us if you wish and protect us as you can. And allow us to live in what little peace and dignity as is possible."

B'nach looked away from the corpse, away from the twins, closing his eyes to see only the red of the sunlight behind his eyelids. He sighed, deeply tired, more tired than he'd ever been in his life. When he looked back at the twins, they somehow seemed less grotesque, more human, and B'nach could almost imagine he saw a family resemblance in their faces.

"I have never even known your names." It was as close to an apology as he could manage at the moment. Perhaps later there would be time enough for amends.

The little man smiled, tears in his eyes. "My name is Rance, may it please my cousin Lord Reverence," he said quietly. "And this is my brother, Husken."

79

Kerrick hadn't seen much of Antonya since her investiture, both of them busily reorganizing the Citadel's power base. While he and D'arim secured the future of the Oracular Army and her new Elite, she spent much of her time with B'nach and the frightened Council, hammering out deals and culling the worst of the rot. Several weeks went by before he was summoned to her private rooms, well after sundown.

Antonya had bathed, her hair loose over her shoulders. Regine smiled and closed the door behind her, leaving Kerrick alone with Antonya. She sat up in the huge bed, white linen shift making her seem like a young girl rather than the absolute ruler of a world.

"You asked to see me?"

Antonya patted the bedclothes beside her, inviting him to

sit. He did, feeling awkward and suddenly tense.

"These were P'tre's rooms," she said conversationally. He looked around cautiously, taking in the rich but very masculine furnishings. "Thirty generations of Terhunes have occupied these chambers. Some traditions I don't care to break."

"I see," Kerrick murmured vaguely, while wondering why she had asked for him. Surely it wasn't to give his opinions on decoration.

"Why have you never told me you loved me?"

The unexpected suddenness of the question took his breath away. "I . . . of course I love you, Lady."

She laughed, a wry exhalation. "Please, Kerrick. Don't 'lady' me. I'm still Antonya, the same scruffy little thief you met not so long ago in a winter forest."

He regarded her thoughtfully. "No, that you're not," he said gently. Then he smiled and added, "Antonya."

She returned his smile. "I know you love me as your Lady, as your Sworn. But not as a woman?"

He stiffened, uneasy. "Where's Morgan?" he demanded.

Her eyes widened in surprise, eyes he was glad to see were a deep brown. "I don't know. Probably out prowling the grounds like a cat hunting for mice, I would expect." Her smile widened. "The fiend is not my lover, Kerrick. Even I am not that crazy."

His face was hot, and he wondered if the ruined skin would betray his emotions. "And what use do you imagine I would be as your lover, Antonya? I am no beauty, no Briston." His hand gestured vaguely at his face. "How could you possibly feel passion for . . . *this*?"

"Oh, I didn't realize . . ." She reached over, and grabbed his crotch. Startled, he jumped off the bed and away. "But no, I see that I was right. Only your face was burned, not your manhood."

"Goddamn you, girl," he growled, hating her while her touch had inflamed a part of him he had thought relegated to the past. "Don't mock me."

The amusement in her face evaporated, replaced by a solemn honesty he thought would break his heart. "I'm not mocking you, Kerrick. And don't be jealous of the dead. I loved

Briston for more than his beauty. As I love you for more than your loyalty. And if you'll have me, Kerrick, I would do more than take you as a lover. I would make you my husband. Marry me."

He stood immobile, stunned speechless. But he didn't resist as she stood on the end of the bed, like a child, to reach his shoulders and put her arms around his neck. He couldn't respond, unable to do more than tremble as she tenderly stroked his scars, light fingertips curiously exploring the webbed tissue. He closed his eyes as they brushed across his amputated nose, examined his eyelids, the hairless brow. When she caressed his mouth, it took him a moment before realizing lips had replaced fingers. Slowly, his arms went around her slender waist, pulling her gently into his embrace as if terrified of breaking her. Her tender kiss became passionate, then tender again as she kissed away the tears on his face.

Much later, she curled up against him, as small as a sleeping cat in the arms of a child, her head resting on his chest. He lay on his back, eyes staring at nothing in the dark, his hand stroking her hair. He tried to recall Rayme's face, remembering only that his young wife had had dark curling hair that smelled of jasmine blossoms. Even the memory of his son was more sound than form, a baby's laugh, pudgy dimpled hands with astonishingly tiny fingernails waving to clutch at his face. Having pushed the memories of that lost life away for so long, he found now that he could only recall vague fragments.

And that he had been very happy.

"No," he said suddenly.

She stirred sleepily. "No what?"

"No. I won't marry you."

There was a long moment of silence and he felt the round ball of her cheek press against his chest as she smiled. "Why not?"

"You've gotten everything else you've wanted. I don't want to be just another of your conquests."

She rolled her head over to stare at him, but said nothing, watching him with a slightly puzzled expression.

"If you want me, you'll have to earn me," he said, and was a little surprised at the painful knot in his throat making his voice harsh. "And I must warn you, madam, I intend to be the hardest thing you ever win in your life."

Epilogue

(Ten years later…)

B'nach stood up as she entered the Great Hall, keeping his hands inside the sleeves of his traveling cloak to hide their shaking as she approached. It never failed to amaze him, the unruliness her subjects displayed for the most powerful ruler in the world. In B'nach's opinion, the mob of hopefuls abused her tolerance for informality, bordering on disrespect. Courtiers shouted at her as she strode through the hall, waving their papers. An elderly astronomer limped after her, babbling as quickly as he could before he was stopped by one of her guards. Red-faced, the old man had kept on shouting, reaching past the guard's restraining shoulder to wave one finger at her retreating back. Two hopeful mariners trotted beside her, rapidly pleading for funds to finance another sea expedition. She accepted a sweat-stained roll of parchment from one, smiling and nodding while promising nothing. The two mariners were halted, looking pleased, as the great doors leading to her private apartments were opened.

"Welcome back, B'nach!" she said, genuinely pleased to see him, which made him feel all the more troubled. "You were greatly missed."

He noted the lines beginning to etch her face, the silver thread in the red-gold hair. Daen trailed in her wake, the armsman wearing his extra weight with dignity.

She wore the latest fashion, the tight-waisted bodice cut low enough to reveal the string of pearls disappearing in her cleavage, the full skirt drenched with intricate beading. He noticed the elaborate sleeves, artfully sewn with two different silk fabrics winking as she moved her arms, and knew before the month was out, every woman at court would be demanding the same design from their tailors. Antonya's style over the years had become more complex and cumbersome, as if she knew how slavishly her tastes were followed, taking delight in burdening others with the extravagant clothing B'nach knew she privately detested.

She grasped his arm, propelling him with her as she swept through before the doors were shut, cutting off the din of hopefuls behind it. He was suddenly deeply conscious of not having changed from his journey, smelling of sweat and horse and leather, covered with dust and weariness.

She unrolled the mariner's parchment, scanning it quickly with interest. "Another scheme to find the fabled Golden Isles in the Western Seas," she said to Daen. The armsman grunted noncommittally. "Diamonds and rubies and emeralds as big as a man's fist dripping from trees, rivers choked with oysters barfing up strings of pearls, boulders of gold falling off cliffs. Fabulous wealth for the taking, and I'm guaranteed fifty percent of it if only I finance all the boats and the equipment and the sailors and the supplies and sundry other minor expenses." She handed the scroll to the armsman. "Still, it's not as harebrained as most. Give them a quarter of what they ask and tell them I'll take seventy-five percent of whatever they find."

"And if they balk?" Daen asked.

She shrugged. "Tell them to go piss themselves. I don't believe in their fantasies of riches any more than they do, I just want to know what's out there. They'll still get enough to finance their voyage without all the bells and whistles, and seventy-five percent of nothing still makes them a damned good profit. They'll take it."

Daen bowed, scroll in hand, and turned to leave.

"Where is Kerrick?" she asked lightly, although anyone with ears could hear the longing in her voice. After ten years, the bond between the Defender and his Lady had grown even stronger, and although she had tried several times to change his mind, the big man had steadfastly refused to become her Consort.

Daen glanced back over his shoulder to grin, not slowing as he strode away. "Off with Cyler to oversee the Maychell wool fair, madam," he called back, "tired of your grumbling about needing something to keep you warm at night when he's off on your business."

"Cheek." She laughed as she settled into a chair, her heavy skirts like a froth of cake around her. The irony wasn't lost on her, as she surveyed B'nach wryly. "Well, well. How the times have changed, my old friend. It's you off to every corner of the world while I'm stuck in the city, a captive of my own success." Although she was complaining, her voice was pleased. "So where have you been this time, B'nach? What delightful souvenirs have you brought me?"

Morgan moved out of the shadows behind her discreetly, the ever-present Assassin menacing as ever. B'nach had never been comfortable in the presence of the fiend, although Antonya often appeared to forget his very existence, ignoring him as thoroughly as she might a piece of furniture. Morgan was the one man in her retinue who never seemed to age, although his eyes glittered with a fanatical adoration that prickled the hair on B'nach's arms.

"May it please Your Grace . . ." he said nervously, hesitating when she looked at him sharply. He rarely used honorifics to address her.

"Your Reverence?"

He glanced meaningfully at the fiend. "May we speak in private?"

She glanced at Morgan and nodded. The man gave him a cold look before he bowed slightly and retreated, closing the doors quietly behind him. "Well?" she said.

"Lady Antonya . . ." B'nach found it difficult to speak around the constriction in his throat, and looked down, busying himself with stripping the riding gloves from his hands. "Recently I decided to undertake the writing of your official biography, to celebrate the anniversary of the past ten years of your illustrious rule . . ." His voice trailed off as he stared at the gloves in his clenched fist, unable to meet her eyes.

"Ah."

"It had been hard enough drawing from recent events; the Library has become inundated with documents and manuscripts from all over the Lands tracing the events of your life and deeds, some of them quite obviously too exaggerated to be true. I wanted my biography to be complete, as well as accurate."

"No pompous hagiography this, I take it?"

He looked up, not sure if he could detect the trace of a smile. "There was almost nothing in evidence about your childhood, my lady," he said, "although the legend of your father's love for the lady Latticea is apocryphal. All the Lands know the tale by heart."

She leaned her cheek against one hand, elbow propped up on the arm of the chair as she watched B'nach silently.

"I've been . . ." He stopped, clearing his throat. "I went to Ashmael to research your origins, to give my biography more depth and detail. Ashmael is tiny. A horse could cross it in a single day at a walk. The capital is more a village than a city. The people are for the most part simple fisherfolk, the land too meager and cold for much farming. The Lord's palace is little more than a two-room stone cottage on barren salt flats. Goats and chickens live in its undercroft. It had no towers. Lady Latticea was indeed the heir to Ashmael, and it is true she spent most of her short life in her father's rather shabby palace silently gazing out the window."

Now he was trembling in earnest, unable to constrain his fear. "The Lady Latticea of Ashmael never spoke. She was a congenital idiot, a deformed child kept hidden from public view. Even so, there were those who struggled bitterly over who would take her to wife, if only to inherit her father's Lands. When her father died, she was killed in a struggle for succession. Murdered by her own servants."

Antonya hadn't moved, watching him steadily with no expression on her face but mild interest. He found that more unnerving than had she reacted with anger and denial.

"The dispute over Adalon was well known in the Citadel. R'bert Terhune was the older of the two brothers, but his mother was a common Landswoman and R'bert was not even born in the Oracular City. He was not well-liked. He had a mercurial temper, was vain, arrogant, often viciously drunk. He indeed traveled throughout the Lands, but it is unlikely he was ever as far north as Ashmael. He fathered any number of bastards on Landswomen, but none of them were on the Lady Latticea. R'bert may have been the rightful heir of Adalon, but he never had many supporters for his claims, in any case. When he died, he was barely seventeen and had no recognized legitimate heirs. His half brother was sixteen, and in his majority."

B'nach used his gloves to wipe away the sweat gathering on his forehead, fumbling as he mopped his face. He wondered if it had been wise to speak with her alone, without witnesses. She had but to say the word, a shout to the Assassin he knew waited outside, and he could be silenced. Permanently.

"I then traveled to the Isle of Tembris in hopes of finding some documentation of your birth. The monastery has recovered from the ruins, profiting well by its connection with you. They're having to turn away pilgrims and postulates by the boatload. You may also be interested to know P'tre has made quite a reputation for himself as one of the monastery's most devout and loyal brothers. He . . ." B'nach found his throat tightening, and coughed gently to clear it. "He spends his days in mortification for his past sins, voluntarily secluded in his cell to prostrate himself in prayer. Pilgrims come to watch him through the hole in his door. He begged me on his knees to convey to you his most humble devotion and respect."

She smiled fleetingly. "There's none so zealous as a convert," she said without rancor.

B'nach studied his hands again. "The abbot also sends his greetings, remembering you fondly. He was the only one to remember you at all, as the rest of the brotherhood are either novices or transferred there from other monasteries. The old abbot, Father Andrae, had confided in no one. All the records were lost when the monastery burned in the Purge. Those monks who survived have since either died or scattered and disappeared. Father Alban was most apologetic he could not be of more help. He did, however, recommend I visit the Sisters of Beneficence, as you were once a novice there."

He hesitated, waiting for her to speak. When she didn't, he coughed into his fist nervously.

"Mother Charity is now the Mother Superior, Mother Clemence died two years ago. Mother Charity knew you only briefly, you left the convent just about the time she arrived. However, Mother Charity is a most learned and literate woman, and quite proud of the superlative condition of the convent's manuscripts. According to their records, the abbot of Tembris was a kinsman of Mother Clemence, but she was quite certain neither the abbess nor Father Andrae were any blood relation to the Lords of Ashmael. The convent's genealogical registers go back more than ten generations, there is no doubt of it. The accounts also record that the abbot of Tembris paid the Sisters a visit, asking for advice on child care after having found himself unexpectedly in charge of a newborn baby girl. The dates are quite accurate, but there is no mention of the child's parentage. Apparently, Father Andrae never told anyone who you were or where you'd come from."

He stopped, eying her nervously.

"Please do continue, B'nach," she prompted him mildly.

B'nach's shivering and clearing the constriction in his throat made him feel strangely palsied. "It is however true that R'bert was killed by an Assassin. I have the testimony of the man who hired the Guild to kill him. He is terrified you should find it was he who had your father killed, but at the time he contracted the assassination, it was no secret. Few mourned for R'bert. He was killed over an unpaid gambling debt, cut down during a drunken tavern brawl. More than a year before the Brothers at the Tembris monastery took you in as a newborn foundling."

Antonya listened to him with her head slightly tilted to one side, a faint smile on her face.

"You are not the daughter of either R'bert Terhune or Latticea of Ashmael." It was almost a relief to have it spoken. Now he waited for the roof to fall in on his head.

"I'm not," she said. He wasn't sure if it was a question.

He hesitated. She watched him quietly for a very long moment without speaking. "But you knew this, didn't you?" he finally said, his voice low. "You've always known it."

She didn't answer him, but rose from the chair to stand calmly at the window, looking out over the Oracular City. He stared at her back, feeling a hollow ache in his stomach. "Antonya, you've lied all this time. Your people *believed* you were the rightful heir to R'bert Terhune. They fought for your bloodrights . . ."

"B'nach—" She stopped him, sad contempt in her voice. When she turned, the light reflecting from her eyes made them seem as hard as marble. "Nobody fought for my bloodrights. They fought for whatever they believed in. People want flags to rally around, but they're not following bits of cloth into battle, are they? They want simple myths to fuel their imagination, not the sordid tangle of facts. They want their leaders to be brilliant and noble heroes, a little better than themselves." She smiled wryly. "But not too much better."

"R'bert Terhune . . ."

"Was a drunk and a fool and a coward," she snapped. "From everything I ever heard about R'bert Terhune, I'm most likely better off he had no hand, so to speak, in my creation. As for the Lady Latticea, she was a pathetic child who died before she had the chance to live long enough to be despised."

"Then . . . who are you?" he asked softly, his throat dry.

"I am the Lady Antonya Terhune of Adalon and Ashmael, the One Ruler of these Lands. Not only because I say I am, but because I have *made* it so."

He floundered desperately. "Do you know who your real parents were, then, Antonya? Perhaps you may still be of noble blood." It was only a faint hope, and she didn't bother to break it gently.

She laughed and shook her head. "*You*, of all people, should know how worthless the claim of noble blood is. Who cares who my parents were? They were two people who enjoyed each other's bodies for a few minutes of lust decades ago. Has what I've done been made any less by the quality of my parents' blood?" She smiled. "I think not. *I've* lied, B'nach? All blood is red. The entire notion of 'noble blood' is, has been and will always be, a lie and a pretext for unprincipled men to suppress and exploit other men better than themselves."

B'nach swallowed. "But if it became known you have falsely claimed the Lands of Adalon and Ashmael, there would be those who would use it against you." He felt his pulse rushing in his ears. "It could tear the Lands apart again."

"Falsely? Perhaps," she said, unruffled. "There will always be those who wish me harm. Those who hate me because I'm a woman and others because I'm a Terhune. Those who fear the touch of the Weird in me. Those who hate me because they believe I am the Devil who destroyed the Holy Oracle rather than a savior who freed God from the prison of the Ancients. Those who cannot accept the twisted outcome of the Prophecy. Even those who would kill me for no other reason than they are incapable of doing anything else to make a place for their name in history. The Lands are filled with greedy and capricious men, quicker to fight than think, unhappy with the established order and wishing for change just for the sake of novelty." She smiled. "So. You have the knowledge and the power, your Most Holy Reverence. What do you propose to do with it?"

"I have no intention of blackmailing you, if that's what you think," he said hotly, surprised at the anger in himself.

She chuckled softly, her shoulders shaking. "I'd be most disappointed in you if you tried. But I'm not anyone you could blackmail."

He blanched, but was proud he had finally recovered his bearing. "Perhaps you should have me assassinated," he said, still amazed at his own words. "I've told no one else."

"I suppose I could," she said reasonably. "Then I certainly couldn't trust fear to keep the man who paid for R'bert's murder to stay silent. I'd have to track down those of my beloved Brothers who might know my secret. Mother Charity and all her immaculate records would have to disappear. No doubt the rest of the Sisters of Beneficence probably have figured it out as well by now, thanks to your diligent efforts to seek out the truth. Of course I'd have to Purge Ashmael, no sense taking any chances." She raised an eyebrow. "No, B'nach, I will not murder you, or anyone else."

"I could destroy the records, Lady Antonya. Or alter them. No one else need know."

He saw a flicker of anger that died away quickly. "You would have to burn down half the Library to suppress all the knowledge that might ever be harmful to the stability of my rule or the unity of the Lands, B'nach, a crime I consider nearly as evil as murder. I didn't prevail only to become another petty tyrant."

She glanced out the window again, her expression weary.

"The wars have taken a heavy toll on the nobles and ordinary people alike; they hunger for peace. I have given them what they wanted, a chance for freedom and prosperity, fragile as it is. I doubt anyone will care about your revelations, if they even believe you."

She turned to face him. "Look around you, B'nach. A thousand universities are teaching where once there was only one, every town on every road for hundreds of miles is deafened with the clamor of masons and carpenters, new buildings going up, architects designing new sajadas to be more beautiful than ever. Young Lords with nothing better to do fight out their stupid battles in tourneys, and instead of hating them for it, people *pay* to come and watch and cheer them on as they conveniently kill each other off. Farmers are protected against the destruction of their crops; artisans and merchants are getting rich enough to bargain with their noble overlords."

She laughed harshly. "Even *you* should be happy; Priests are debating with heretics instead of slaughtering them, and people come for miles to pack the sajadas and listen to sermons. You've had more novices join the Faith in the last three years than the past thirty. The Citadel is the richest city on earth, and the taxes coming in pay for everything from paved roads to the gilt on the new Sajada's dome to the clothes on your own pious back. We are rich and growing richer, every day. Who is willing to give all this up to squabble about someone else's dubious pedigree?"

B'nach ran the tip of his tongue over dry lips and opened his mouth to speak. She cut him off abruptly.

"I am the most powerful ruler in the history of these Lands, B'nach. My word is law. No one, *no one* objects if I use my armies to stamp out a war in some Land a bit slow to get the message. I lift a finger and an entire village or city or Land is laid to waste. That I do not choose to do so does not mean I am a perfect being, nor am I God. I *am* but mortal dust, and weak, B'nach, plagued with doubt and passions and folly. It would be all too easy to give in to the temptations and pleasures of becoming a tyrant. I am human. Someday I shall die, but I pray that what I have built will survive."

He had bowed his head, his hands folded deferentially as he listened to her outburst. He looked up as she went on. "Write your biography, tell the world whatever you like. Or not, as you choose. It won't matter. What I have accomplished must be strong enough to stand on its own merit. If the mere question of my birth causes the Lands to collapse, then they deserve to be abandoned to their fate, and I shall curse it."

"Does Kerrick know?"

She shrugged. "I'm not sure he ever believed me anyway. I don't think it would surprise him."

"But it will be his heir who will succeed you . . ."

She cut him off sharply. "There will be no heir, B'nach. I have no intention of ever producing or naming an heir to replace me. I will not beget a line of anemic blood ties. I will found no useless dynasties. Once I am dead, the Lands will have to either stand or fall of their own accord, and men will have to lead from their abilities, not from their loins."

Her eyes had paled when they flickered back to him, mischievous humor in the pale depths.

"And, once I am dead, I won't care if all the world knows I was the bastard of an errant monk begat of a whore."

"Were you?" B'nach said with sudden interest.

She laughed. "I have no idea. But that's as good as any other way to start life, don't you think?" She continued to laugh, great, free, open laughter.

Sharon Shinn———————————